2004

FIC   Martin, William,
MARTIN   1950-

           Harvard Yard.

$25.95   01/15/2004

BOOK "MARKS"

If you wish to keep a record that you have read this book, you may use spaces below to mark a private code. Please do not mark the book in any other way.

PLEASE
DO NOT REMOVE
CARD
FROM POCKET

Harvard Yard

Harvard Yard

WILLIAM MARTIN

WARNER BOOKS

An AOL Time Warner Company

This book is a work of historical fiction. In order to give a sense of the times, some names or real people or places have been included in the book. However, the events depicted in this book are imaginary, and the names of nonhistorical persons or events are the product of the author's imagination or are used fictitiously. Any resemblance of such nonhistorical persons or events to actual ones is purely coincidental.

Warner Books, Inc., 1271 Avenue of the Americas, New York, NY 10020

Visit our Web site at www.twbookmark.com.

An AOL Time Warner Company

Printed in the United States of America
First Printing: October 2003
10 9 8 7 6 5 4 3 2 1

Library of Congress Cataloging-in-Publication Data

Martin, William
  Harvard Yard / William Martin.
      p. cm.
  ISBN 0-446-53084-0
  1. Shakespeare, William, 1564–1616—Manuscripts—Fiction. 2. Manuscripts—Collectors and collecting—Fiction. 3. Harvard University—Fiction. 4. Cambridge (Mass.)—Fiction. 5. Boston (Mass.)—Fiction. I. Title.

PS3563.A7297H37 2003
813'.54—dc21

2003012329

*in memory of
my father
1915–2001
The oldest trees give the best shade.*

Acknowledgments

I can remember thinking, in my last semester at Harvard, back in 1972, that just as I was beginning to figure the place out, they were showing me the door.

I returned to Harvard, in more ways than one, to write this book and continue the process of figuring out an institution of modern complexity built upon a foundation of ancient tradition. Many people were willing to help me bring form to the contours of Harvard history, accuracy to the details of Harvard life, and insight into the workings of Harvard itself.

My thanks to Scott Abell, former President of the Harvard Alumni Association; Michelle Blanc, also of the Alumni Association; Lisa Boudreau, Director of Development and Corporate Relations; Beth Brainerd, Director of Communications at the Harvard libraries; Charles Collier, Senior Philanthropic Advisor; Reverend Peter Gomes, Plummer Professor of Christian Morals, whose Religion 1513 explores the breadth of Harvard history; Sandra Grindlay, Curator of the Harvard Portrait Collection; Scott Haywood, Superintendent of Kirkland House; Leslie Morris, Curator of Manuscripts at Houghton Library; Terry Shaller of the Alumni Association; Stephen Shoemaker, instructor in Religion 1513; Deborah Smullyan of *Harvard* magazine; and my son Dan and his friends in the Class of 2004, who gave me a few glimpses of undergraduate life.

Thanks also to Linda Ayres, James Banfield, David Case, Gary Goshgarian, Christopher Keane, Lois Kessin, William Kuntz, and John Spooner.

Special thanks to Peter Drummey, Librarian of the Massachusetts Historical Society, for his enthusiastic assistance with every question and research problem; to Conrad Wright, classmate and Director of Publications at the Massachusetts Historical Society, who first suggested that I explore the relationship between Shakespeare and the Harvard family; and to antiquarian Martin Weinkle, for his willingness to share his insights into the world of rare books.

Thanks to my editors, Jamie Raab and John Aherne; and to all my friends at Warner Books, who have been publishing me for fifteen years, including Larry Kirshbaum, Maureen Egen, and Harvey-Jane Kowal; to Wendell Minor, whose cover art has graced so many of my books; and to my agent, Robert Gottlieb.

And as always, thanks to my wife and all my children, who continue to serve as research assistants, proofreaders, opinion-givers, and general inspirations.

WILLIAM MARTIN
June 2003

Harvard
Yard

Wedge Family Tree

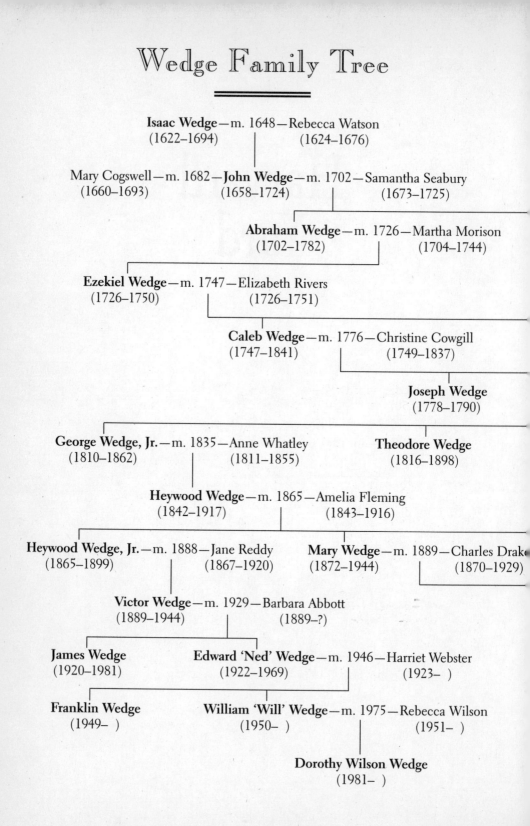

Isaac Wedge—m. 1648—Rebecca Watson
(1622–1694)   (1624–1676)

Mary Cogswell—m. 1682—**John Wedge**—m. 1702—Samantha Seabury
(1660–1693)   (1658–1724)   (1673–1725)

Abraham Wedge—m. 1726—Martha Morison
(1702–1782)   (1704–1744)

Ezekiel Wedge—m. 1747—Elizabeth Rivers
(1726–1750)   (1726–1751)

Caleb Wedge—m. 1776—Christine Cowgill
(1747–1841)   (1749–1837)

Joseph Wedge
(1778–1790)

George Wedge, Jr.—m. 1835—Anne Whatley   **Theodore Wedge**
(1810–1862)   (1811–1855)   (1816–1898)

Heywood Wedge—m. 1865—Amelia Fleming
(1842–1917)   (1843–1916)

Heywood Wedge, Jr.—m. 1888—Jane Reddy   **Mary Wedge**—m. 1889—Charles Drake
(1865–1899)   (1867–1920)   (1872–1944)   (1870–1929)

Victor Wedge—m. 1929—Barbara Abbott
(1889–1944)   (1889–?)

James Wedge   **Edward 'Ned' Wedge**—m. 1946—Harriet Webster
(1920–1981)   (1922–1969)   (1923–)

Franklin Wedge   **William 'Will' Wedge**—m. 1975—Rebecca Wilson
(1949–)   (1950–)   (1951–)

Dorothy Wilson Wedge
(1981–)

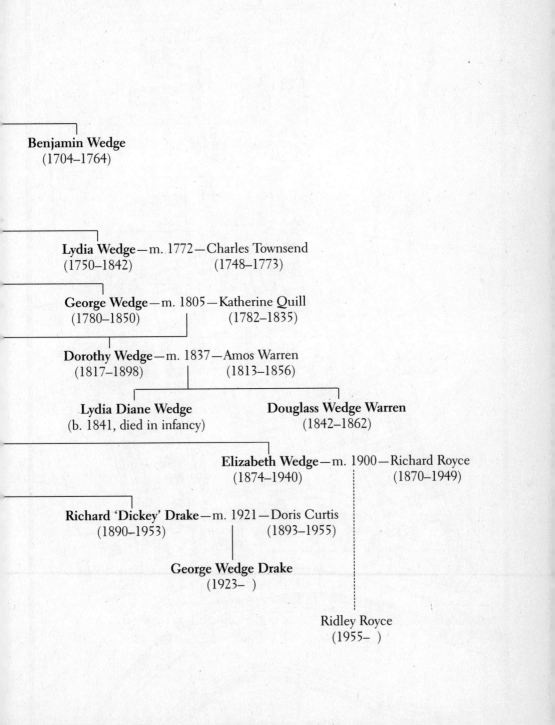

Benjamin Wedge
(1704–1764)

Lydia Wedge—m. 1772—Charles Townsend
(1750–1842)　　　　　　　(1748–1773)

George Wedge—m. 1805—Katherine Quill
(1780–1850)　　　　　　(1782–1835)

Dorothy Wedge—m. 1837—Amos Warren
(1817–1898)　　　　　　(1813–1856)

Lydia Diane Wedge　　　　**Douglass Wedge Warren**
(b. 1841, died in infancy)　　　　(1842–1862)

Elizabeth Wedge—m. 1900—Richard Royce
(1874–1940)　　　　　　(1870–1949)

Richard 'Dickey' Drake—m. 1921—Doris Curtis
(1890–1953)　　　　　　　(1893–1955)

George Wedge Drake
(1923–)

Ridley Royce
(1955–)

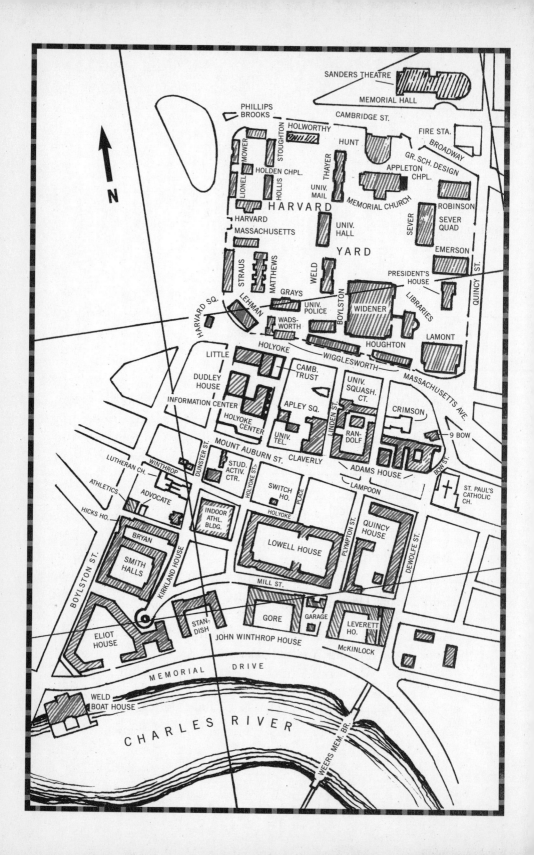

Chapter One

====

1605–1637

ROBERT HARVARD went often to Stratford-on-Avon, but never before had he gone with such trepidation. Never before had the sight of the tower at Guild Chapel turned his stomach to jelly, nor the sound of his horse's hooves upon Clopton Bridge given him such cause to turn and ride the whole eighty miles back to London.

Ordinarily, he went to buy cattle, for he owned a butcher shop, and the farmers of Warwickshire raised the fattest cattle in England, and a butcher without cattle was like a tailor without cloth. But on this August afternoon, Robert Harvard went to seek a wife, for he was also a man, and a man without a wife was like a butcher without cattle, or a tailor without cloth, or a playwright without a stage. . . .

And that, he thought, was a string of metaphors to charm the birds from the trees. . . . Or were they similes?

No matter. Will would know. Will would calm him, too, and give him the confidence to court a young woman as beautiful as Katherine Rogers. Of that he was certain. So, once across the river, Robert Harvard made for the rambling big house known as New Place. Will would tell him which of his words would work best. Will would also tell him the difference 'twixt a metaphor and a simile.

* * *

"'A butcher without cattle'?" cried Will Shakespeare. "You call that an image of love? You call that poetry? Or 'a tailor without cloth'?"

"Well . . . what of 'a playwright without a stage'?" asked Harvard in his strong Southwark accent.

"You court a wife, man, not a cutler. Sharpen your wit with soft words."

"Soft words? Words like . . . like *featherbed?*"

"Aye, *featherbed,*" said Will. "Featherbeds *are* soft. Pudding is soft. The dung that manures my roses is soft. But we speak here of a woman's heart."

Shakespeare was forty-one and far heavier than when first he appeared in Harvard's butcher shop some fifteen years before, a young man come to London hungry for fame but hungrier still for sausage or beef suet or even a marrow bone to fill his belly. Now, his face had filled and his belly had settled, as happened with most men whose purses had filled and whose lives had settled. But when he moved, Will Shakespeare was ever the actor, shaping each gesture and step to the role he played. And the role of the moment was poet.

He pushed open the windows of the great room and gazed out at his roses. He did not ruminate or pace upon the polished stone floor. His poetry came quickly. He gazed, he thought, and he said, "'Tis a beautiful day, Rob."

"Aye." Rob clasped his hands behind his back, then folded them in front of himself, then rested one on the hilt of his dagger and the other on his belt. Though he owned property in London, served as a warden in his church, and could afford to dress for courtship in a fine crimson doublet of crushed velvet, he still had the hands of a tradesman—big and coarse and never at ease unless holding a tool.

"'Tis a beautiful *summer's* day," said Shakespeare.

"Aye."

"Were I in your place, I'd say to her, 'Shall I compare thee to a summer's day?'"

"A summer's day, Will. Yes . . . 'Tis warm . . . *and* soft."

"Indeed. 'Thou art more lovely and more . . . more—'"

"Temperate?" Robert Harvard offered a word that sounded eloquent.

"Temperate"—Shakespeare counted the syllables on his fingers—"'Thou art more lovely and more tem-per-ate.' Not a word to describe the passion of love, but as a word for Katherine Rogers, I suppose 'tis aptly chosen, *and* it fits the meter."

And on he went, composing a sonnet to the fleeting beauty of summer and the solid nature of Robert Harvard's love.

"'So long as men can breathe or eyes can see, / So long lives this'—the sonnet, I mean—'so long lives this, and this . . . this gives life to thee.'" With a flip of his hand and a little bow, Will was done. "Soft words for Katherine Rogers."

Too many words, thought Robert Harvard, and too many metaphors . . . or were they similes? But who was he to question a man whose poetry had earned him that handsome house and beautiful garden?

"Many thanks, Will. Courtship never come easy, even to a man of thirty-five."

"She's an angel, Rob . . . reed slender, to be sure, but still an angel."

"And I be a mere mortal, widowed once and wantin' a new wife."

"You've been an angel to many a hungry actor."

"'Twas only what a Christian should do."

"There were Christians aplenty who denied victuals to this glover's son. But you gave him to eat. So"—Will gripped Robert's shoulders—"screw your courage to the sticking place, as we say. Speak to her father, then go to Katherine and tell her of a love as warm as a summer's day."

"Would that you'd stand aside me, Will, and whisper these words in me ear."

"'Tis for you to do yourself, Rob. And you'd not want me whispering in your ear on a day when malevolence whispers in mine."

"Malevolence?"

"By the name Iago, servant to the blackamoor Othello. He has deranged Othello with his lies." The excitement danced on Will's face, and malevolence crept into his voice. "Othello is about to strangle his flaxen-haired wife in a fit of jealous rage. He wraps his hands round her neck and—" Will calmed himself, as if his imagination were a pitcher full to the brim, from which he could afford to spill only a little. "So, then . . . you to your muse, and I to mine."

"'Shall I compare thee to a summer's day?'" Robert Harvard repeated the words as he walked from New Place to the Rogers home in High Street.

A *temperate* summer's day. On such a day, how could a man see deranged Moors strangling flaxen-haired women? Playwrights were foreign creatures altogether, he thought, that they could imagine such things and not themselves be deranged. He tried to banish these dark visions, but he feared to lose the better images Will had put into his head, as when we seek to banish the thorn, we lose also the petal. So he turned his mind to the bouquet of roses he had cut in Will's garden and to the thorn pricking his finger.

The house of Thomas Rogers was one of the finest in Stratford, rising in three half-timbered stories, with great windows flung open on every floor. Rich man's windows they were, overlooking a street wider and more welcoming than any in London. And there was no man in London or Stratford more welcoming than Thomas Rogers, alderman and cattle broker.

Next to cattle, good cheer was his stock-in-trade, but what man would lack for good cheer who profited from Warwickshire beef and ate it, too? His good cheer grew even greater when he learned the purpose of Harvard's visit, for Rogers had seven daughters, and the girl in question had reached the ripe old age of twenty-one without a husband.

It did not surprise Robert, then, that they settled on a dowry more quickly than ever they had settled on a price for cattle. It did surprise him, however, that Rogers would honor the bargain only if the girl went willingly to marriage.

"Willingly . . . aye," said Robert, "or not at all."

He found Katherine in the garden, in a shaft of golden sunlight, and the shimmer of her flaxen hair caused him to forget all the words Will Shakespeare had given him. He nearly forgot his own name.

"Why, Master Harvard," she said, "'tis pleasure to see you."

Rob reached for Will's words, but the first image he found was of a deranged Moor, fingers twined round the neck of his flaxen-haired wife, an image to be banished yet again. And just as he feared, Will's soft words went with it, so that he could only stammer, "I . . . I . . ."

"Roses?" said Katherine. "Roses are a joy."

"Yes." And now he found a few of Will's words, hiding in his memory . . . old words, but good ones, and soft, spoken by the character of Romeo. "Roses they are, miss, but . . . that which we call a rose, by any other name would . . . would . . ."

"Smell as sweet?"

"Yes . . . though not so sweet as you, miss." And that, he thought, was well said.

In taking the roses, she noticed the blood on his fingertip. "Why, good sir, you bleed for me? How noble." And gently she touched him.

His hand trembled at her touch, and yet did her touch itself tremble, which he found strangely calming, for it meant that she was as nervous as he . . . and perhaps as willing. And a small measure of his wit returned. He said, "I bleed for love, miss."

And she said, "I yearn for it."

And Rob found a few of Will's softer words to speak. "I bleed willingly for love, on a . . . a summer's day."

"'Tis a fine summer's day that Robert Harvard brings me roses."

"A *temperate* summer's day." And then did his wit return in full. "I promise many more, even when the cold December of our lives has been lived to the solstice, even then shall I find a final summer's day with thee, miss, should you say yes to marriage."

And her smile spoke more eloquently than all the words that Will Shakespeare had ever written.

Two years later, if one were to ask Robert Harvard the season, he would say "summer," no matter the angle of the sun, for no northern blast could cool the summer he knew in the bed of Katherine Harvard, a rose even sweeter now that she bore his name.

And no day was more June-glorious to him than the damp November afternoon when he and Katherine brought their firstborn son to St. Saviour's in Southwark. Robert Harvard would never know with greater certainty of God's love or his own immortality than at the moment when the tiny head was held over the font and the spirit-cleansing water poured down. Nor would he ever know better that the love of his fellow man reflected God's love than on that night, when friends and neighbors went to the Queen's Head Inn to celebrate the birth of the baby named John.

As Robert Harvard was a part owner of the inn, the presence of the babe brought no scandal to the taproom. In truth, there was little that happened on that side of the Thames that could cause Southwark to appear more scandalous than it already was.

City fathers reigned on the north bank, but their power did not cross the twenty-arch bridge. So here would be found prostitutes in their stews, selling favors to pay rents to the corrupt bishop of Winchester. Here cutpurses thrived in alleys, and convicts served in Clink. Here animal baiters brought beasts to fight in the pits, and when the beasts were killed, the baiters learned new skills from convicts and cutpurses, too. And here, performing by day in the theaters, carousing by night in the taprooms, were the actors.

But here also the bell tower of St. Saviour's rose like a father confessor above his sinners. And here men like Robert Harvard, men of business and sometimes of property, saw sin for what it was and rose above it, too, though Robert believed in the Lord's admonition that "what you do for the least of my brethren, you do for me." So on that night of celebration, he opened the tap for all and asked payment of none.

Most brought good wishes. A few brought gifts of silver coin. Others brought no more than their thirst. But one, who came in from the cold wearing a cape trimmed in rabbit fur, brought a gift of paper and leather that would prove more valuable than gold.

Will Shakespeare elbowed through the crowd, neither expecting nor offering ceremony to those who greeted him with shouts and handshakes and resounding slaps upon the back.

Rob called for Will's tankard to be taken from the shelf and filled.

Katherine, no longer reed-slender, but a young mother in all the fullness of life, proclaimed, "Master Shakespeare, you do the Harvards a great honor."

"I honor the child, ma'am." Shakespeare bowed. "And his beautiful mother."

"Many thanks, Will," said Robert.

"Many thanks for all your favors," added Katherine. "My husband has oft spake of your help one *temperate* summer's day. Do you know what now he calls our son?"

"Aye," said Will with a laugh. "'Love's Labours Won.' 'Tis a description to flatter a playwright. But the babe surely tells of love's victory."

"Aye!" cried Robert a little drunkenly. "To my own Love's Labours Won!"

And the crowd roared.

Then Shakespeare reached under his cape and withdrew a volume of quarto size, bound in red leather, held with a blue ribbon. "The very play, *Love's Labours Won*. In a prompt book, transcribed by my own hand from my foul papers."

"'Tis a thing of beauty, good sir." Katherine held the book in front of her child. "Look you, John, see what Master Shakespeare gives you."

The babe was more interested in the taste of his own thumb, but Robert Harvard received the book with all the awe he might muster had the rector of St. Saviour's given him a relic of the true cross. He caressed the leather binding, thumbed the pages, and asked, "But, Will, would you not stage this play again?"

Shakespeare waved a hand. "The King's Men have another prompt book, though the play be all out of date, and a trifle as 'tis."

"Would you not print it, at the very least?"

"Once a play sees print, any man may stage it, which be money from my pocket," said Shakespeare. "'Tis the reason I seldom give such gifts as this. But for the Harvards, *Love's Labours Won* be a talisman of good fortune. Should you sell this to a printer—"

"Oh, never, Will."

"—'twill fetch ten pounds. As companion to *Love's Labours Lost*, which they say sold well, perhaps more. A good start for the child's future."

"I'll never sell, Will. This takes a place of honor with me Bible, a reminder of this night and that summer's day in Stratford."

"Good." Shakespeare touched the child's head. "Let its title remind him that a happy man enjoys his summer days and knows the miracle of love's labors."

At that, Rob raised his mug again, "To Love's Labours Won!"

ii

God gave the Harvards eighteen summers more to labor in their love, and they produced a family of seven children. Then God sent the coldest of winds.

It was in the third week of August, anno Domini 1625, that the first blast struck their son Willie, who went stumbling to his bed, chilled and feverish. Within an hour, he was vomiting. He brought up the gruel he had eaten in the morning, then remnants of stew from the night before, then streams of bile so green and viscous, it seemed that his very insides were shredding.

Then young Robbie came home freezing despite the damp heat that lay like a quilt upon London. He threw an extra log onto the great-room fire, wrapped himself in a blanket, and began to sweat and shiver all at once.

Then Kate, a gentle child of thirteen, looked up from her knitting, cried out in shock as her bowels suddenly let go, and collapsed into a puddle of her own stool.

That was when Katherine Harvard shouted up the stairs to John that he put by his books and hurry to fetch his father.

John was sitting in his favorite spot, by a window on the top floor, oblivious in the sunlight to all save his study of a Latin text on the epistles of Paul. But from the sound of terror in his mother's voice, he knew what was upon them. Stumbling down to the great room, he was struck first by the stench, then by the heat of a roaring fire in August, then by the sight of his brothers and sister.

"Hurry, John," cried his mother. "Hurry and tell Father. He'll know what to do. Hurry . . . but don't forget your rosemary."

John plucked a few leaves from the sprigs hanging by the door, rolled them, and stuffed them into his nostrils and ears for protection. Then he went out.

He ran down an alley to the galleried courtyard of the Queen's Head Inn, which was much like the courtyards of the George or the Boar's Head or a hundred other London inns where a man could find food and lodging. But curtains of fear hung from every railed balcony, and the drain that carried chamber wastes to Borough High Street was all but empty, for the Queen's Head itself was all but empty, for the bubonic plague had descended, not only on the Harvard house but on all of Southwark.

John took another alley that led to the street. He moved quickly, being the long-legged and lanky sort, heir to his mother's slender height and ready smile. People called him too bookish by half and said that he had inherited little from his father but a square jaw and a good heart. In John's mind, that was gift enough, for he had no interest in his father's trade. Let other men cut meat. John Harvard would study God's word and nourish souls.

A young man of such faith should not have feared the sight of the death carts and their corpses, for it meant that souls were now rising to their reward. But the cry of "Bring out the dead," followed by the clanging of the gravedigger's bell, caused him to stop a moment in the shadows. Even one as strong in spirit as John Harvard needed the strengthening of a small prayer before he could step into the street in that season of death.

And the sight that greeted him was more fearful than any death cart. It was his father, staggering toward him, eyes wide and glassy, body hunched in pain.

"John!" cried Robert Harvard. "Help me. Help me. I burn."

"Aye, John. Help him," growled the gravedigger. "But come not into the street again, 'cept to bring out your dead. Once the pestilence be on your house, you must stay till it leave. 'Tis the law."

John turned quickly from the black-shrouded figure and led his father up the alley.

"Oh, Rob," cried Katherine as they came in the door, "we are . . . Good God!"

Robert reached toward her, and a stream of vomit shot from his mouth.

* * *

John Harvard did what he could to comfort his family, then stuffed more rosemary into his nose, said a prayer for strength, and went out again. If the plague was soon to take him, he would see St. Saviour's and the face of Rector Morton once more, no matter the laws, for no man-made law would stop what God wished otherwise.

He moved quickly through death-gripped Southwark. The ringing of the bells and the cries of the gravediggers could be heard on every corner, as if this were some black festival. Guards with fearsome pikes and frightened faces stood outside the Globe Theater and the Bear Gardens, both closed to keep people from congregating. Men lay dead in the gutters, their plaguey sores a feast for the rats. In Clink Street, the corpses were piled before the gates of the prison like kitchen slops. But the Winchester geese, the Southwark whores, had all flown, rents to the bishop be damned.

Soon enough, John Harvard arrived at St. Saviour's. He took a pew in the same small chapel where he had been baptized, and he began to pray.

"Why, John!" cried Rector Nicholas Morton at the sight of him. "The plague be on your house. You must go home. 'Tis the law."

"I come to pray, sir, to understand God's purpose in sendin' a plague."

"You have only to read your Holy Scripture to know." Morton peered from across the room, as if to make sure that no signs of the infection were yet upon John Harvard. "Why should God treat sinful London different than he treat the Egyptians?"

"But we have not enslaved the Israelites."

"We have enslaved ourselves, John, to vain amusement, to Whitsuntide revel, to pomp and arrogance that mask corruption. Reason enough to incur God's displeasure."

"But my parents? They be good Christians. Why does this happen to them?"

"I know not. Though there be some in the church who would say that your father's friendship with actors and the like was . . . was too frivolous."

"Will Shakespeare worshiped in these very pews, sir. He was a faithful friend."

"I said *some* in the church, John. Not all."

John looked up at the stained-glass windows of the chapel. "There are *some* in the church who would say that even the colors in that glass be too frivolous for worship."

Rector Morton now slipped into the pew, pulled a few sprigs of rosemary from his pocket, and waved them as if to ward off a bad smell. "You aspire to Emmanuel College at Cambridge, do you not, John?"

"Yes, sir." John took comfort, as always, in the round, solid presence of the rector, despite the waving herbs.

"'Tis high ambition for a tradesman's son to attend any college," said Morton, "and for certain a college given to producing men who would purify our ritual and bring preciseness to the manners of this world."

"I'm aware of it, sir, and if this plague pass over me, I'll shoulder it."

"And I'll speak for you." Morton clasped the boy's forearm. "But remember . . . at Emmanuel, men of wisdom see the works of Shakespeare and his ilk as tools of the devil, glorifications of man's vanity, his passions, his appetites, all the things that lead us toward sin. Do you understand?"

"I believe so, sir."

"Then turn your mind to higher things. In them will you find the answer to your hardest questions. . . . Now, a prayer for all the Harvards."

Whatever the prayer, it was not answered.

Just after sundown, a delegation of bishop's men did as the law prescribed. They boarded up the windows and painted a red cross on the door of the Harvard house, now one of hundreds of plague houses in Southwark.

The first to die was Kate, whose fever rose so high that she all but burned to death, which was merciful, for it saved her from far worse.

Robbie lay moaning until the third day, when the buboes erupted on his neck and under his arms. They began as small black blisters, swelled quickly to the size of hazelnuts, and within a few hours were as big as hen's eggs. Then they split and began to ooze black blood, and this boy with his whole life before him cried out for death.

Peter, the youngest, went feverish, erupted, and died—all in a single afternoon.

John and his mother rushed from misery to misery, from the third floor to the master bed to the great room, giving such care as they could—a wet cloth to cool a burning forehead, a clean shirt to cover a suppurating body, a prayer to calm a terrified spirit—and all the while, they watched one another to see which of them would fall next.

By the third day, Katherine Rogers Harvard had lost three sons and a daughter, all of them now laid out on the table in the great room. She herself had fallen into a pit of grief that left her wordless and motionless on a chair in the midst of her dead children. And neither urging nor prayer nor imprecation from John could induce her to mount the stairs and speak a final time to the man she loved.

So it was left for John to comfort his father, to pray with him, to read Scripture to him, to give him drafts of ale to cool his fever, and finally to watch the buboes erupt and grow, bringing with them their unconquerable agony.

By the morning of the fourth day, Robert Harvard was a living corpse, putrefying through the open black sores at his neck and groin. Yet he raised his head from the pillow, looked about the room with eyes suddenly clear, and called for Katherine as calmly as if he were calling for a cup of broth.

"Father," said John, who had spent the night at the bedside, "she cannot come."

"Is she . . . is she dead, too?"

"No . . . but—"

"She must come then. I must tell her that it still be summer."

"Yes, Father. 'Tis August. 'Tis still summer."

"No . . . *summer* . . . soft summer . . . *temperate* summer . . . 'tis a metaphor . . . or simile . . . 'tis . . ." He knitted his brow, as if a new idea had come to him, something to which he must give breath. "Johnny—"

"Aye."

"Me books." He looked toward the volumes on a shelf by the window.

"Yes, Father . . . your Bible, your Homer . . . a man will be known by his books. 'Tis what you've always said."

"*All* me books," said Robert with a sudden vehemence that made him seem to rise from the pillow like a demon in bloody bedclothes. "I want you to keep 'em all."

"Yes, Father."

"Even . . . even Will Shakespeare's book."

"*Love's Labours Won?*"

And Robert Harvard was wracked by a spasm of pain that caused his whole body to shake. When it passed he said, "I . . . I know your heart. That you would go to the college at Emmanuel, that you hold with them who would purify the church. . . ."

"Yes, Father."

"Rector Morton be a good friend, a good man, a learned man . . . I be a simple butcher. But I tell you . . . you must cherish what Will give us."

"Yes, Father."

"Cherish joy. Know . . . know love's labors . . . in book and life." The father grabbed for the son's collar, pulled him close, and whispered, "Give . . . me . . . your . . . word."

The stench of his breath was like rotting meat, but John did not pull away.

He grasped his father's hand in both of his and said, "My word."

And Robert Harvard sank back onto the pillow, back into himself, back toward some inner peace. Then he lay silent. . . .

John sat for some time contemplating the body. Then he covered his father with the bloody sheet and spent several minutes more contemplating the shelf of books.

A man, he knew, would be known by his books.

iii

Twelve years later, a small ship called the *Hector* pounded west into the Atlantic.

John Harvard, master of arts, Emmanuel College, the last of his family line, heir to the Queen's Head Inn and other London properties, clerk, cattle breeder, putative minister, and husband to Ann Sadler, was going to America. The Harvards were part of the great Puritan migration. Men and women of conscience, who did not hold with the rituals of the church and despaired of the corruption in the state, had obtained a charter to build a new England some three thousand miles from the old, well beyond the reach of robed bishops and royal authority.

They were a week into the journey, and Ann Sadler Harvard was seasick. With skies darkening and seas rising, it was likely that she would be seasick some time more.

So John put his body between his wife and the sea-foam spraying over the bow, in hope that she could vomit in peace.

"Good Lord, but what a stream," cried Nathaniel Eaton, a young man of such surpassing strong stomach and lack of compassion that he went about the seasick deck chewing on a piece of smoked herring. Black-bearded and burly, he might have been taken for a sailor, though he was the son of a leading churchman, brother to a member of the Massachusetts Bay Company, which backed the voyage, and author of a respected treatise on the meaning of the Sabbath. All of this had put him in line to be first master of the colony's new college. None of this, however, meant that he had received the gift of tact.

"John," he said, "she pukes like a grass-fed dog, but no man on the ship show better devotion to his wife."

Ann Harvard looked up, her delicate features sharpened by sickness and fear, her skin the color of the sea. "'Tis the same devotion my husband will show to a flock, once we reach America, sir."

"A fine place for man to become a preacher," answered Eaton, "though the company shows true foresight in bringin' aboard a dozen Warwickshire breeders. Such beasts will give birth to a mighty herd, should they survive. Though they do stink, do they not, ma'am?" Eaton grinned, as if he enjoyed turning a lady's stomach by mere suggestion. "Ship smells like a floatin' barnyard."

And the face of Ann Harvard grew a little grayer.

"'Tis as if we travel on the ark," said John Harvard, who himself looked more gray than pink, "on our way to make a new world of righteousness."

"My husband will nourish men's minds," said Ann Harvard, "with books."

"Books shall nourish, especially in the college, where we shall raise up new Puritan ministers and magistrates." Eaton popped the last of the herring into his mouth. "But if your belly be empty, food matter more than books."

"I carry four hundred books." John Harvard shivered off the cold, then sought to cough it away, then spat a phlegmy splatter over the side. "Books to enrich our souls and lighten our lives. A man will be known by his books, Nathaniel."

"Had I such a cough as that, I'd see to my health, John, before my books."

"I've survived worse, Nathaniel. The plague carried away all but my mother and one brother. Now they, too, be gone. The Lord spares me for a purpose. That I know."

Suddenly, a great wave struck the bow and sent a shudder down the length of the keel. A fountain of water burst over the rail, knocking the Harvards to the deck and knocking the bulk of Nathaniel Eaton on top of them.

The ship rode down into the trough behind the wave, then up the side of the next, and from belowdecks came cries of fear as the green sea poured down the gangways.

Ann said, "The books, John!"

"Fear not for the books!" cried Eaton. "Worry for the cattle."

John Harvard prayed for his books but imagined the water doing its damage, spilling down into the hold full of trunks, trickling down into one of his trunks of books, seeping down through the oil-cloth lining, swelling the bindings on his Latin texts, staining the covers of his Calvin, and causing the ink to run on the pages of one book that should never have been in the trunk of a good Puritan— a play by William Shakespeare, a play that he kept to keep a deathbed promise, a covenant with his father as sacred as that he had made with his God.

Chapter Two

════════

PETER FALLON stared into the eyes of William Shakespeare.

William Shakespeare stared back.

Peter Fallon blinked.

William Shakespeare didn't. But, then, Shakespeare hadn't blinked in almost four centuries.

They met in what Peter Fallon considered a perfect environment: constant temperature of sixty-eight degrees, constant humidity of 50 percent, u.v.-filtered glass on the windows—the Harry Elkins Widener Room, sanctum sanctorum of Harvard's Widener Library.

Peter was looking at a First Folio, the first complete collection of Shakespeare's plays, published in 1623. It was displayed next to a Gutenberg Bible, in a case that defined the term "embarrassment of riches."

In the frontispiece portrait, Shakespeare was staring across the centuries. The eyes were piercing, smart, and just a little puffy, as if he'd stayed up all night to finish a scene. The nose was sharp and straight, the nostrils slightly flared, suggesting his impatience to get back to work. The mouth didn't tell much, though it could probably tell everything. And that high forehead? Well . . . it looked as monumental as the dome on St. Paul's.

What a face. What a book. All man's best thoughts and basest emotions, all his joys and tragedies, all the vast parade of humanity, all in a single volume worth . . . *what?* There were some two hundred First Folios, though only seventeen in what the rare-book dealers called "very fine" condition. And one of them had recently fetched close to $6 million. *Six million.*

Peter Fallon dreamed of selling a First Folio. He dreamed of just holding one, of touching the leather binding and fine rag paper and feeling the words imprinted on every page . . . those ageless, wondrous words and wisdoms and cadences and characters. And if not a folio, then a quarto, a single play published in Shakespeare's lifetime. Very rare. A quarto of *Hamlet* could be worth a million or more.

Peter Fallon knew all this because it was his business to know. He was a dealer in rare books and documents. And he visited the Widener Room every few months because for someone in his business, this was a shrine.

The portrait of Harry Elkins Widener, Class of 1907, hung above his treasures, looking as ethereally handsome as an angel . . . a book-loving angel who went down on the *Titanic* because he left his lifeboat to retrieve a rare volume from his stateroom. That was the legend, anyway. Another legend was that every Harvard freshman had to pass a swimming test because Harry hadn't been able to swim a stroke, and when his mother honored him by giving Harvard a library, it was swimming tests for everyone . . . even though Harry probably froze to death before he had time to drown.

But no tradition in America was older than giving to Harvard. They'd named the place after a Puritan who gave books and money in 1638. And they'd been naming things after big donors ever since. And sometimes, big donors made strange requests.

Peter Fallon was a small donor. He gave five hundred dollars a year to augment Harvard's $19 billion endowment, which was like pissing in the water to raise the level of Cape Cod Bay. But he'd gone to Harvard on a scholarship, and he believed in giving something back. That was one of the reasons he was at Harvard that evening.

Outside, the October dusk was coming down.

The students hurrying to the dining halls, the workers making for the subway, the chill wind blowing leaves through the air—it was all like a thousand October evenings before. You could come back after decades and still feel as if you were part of the place, because the lay of the light never changed from one year to the next, and the buildings in Harvard Yard seemed as solid and resolute as New England's old mountains. They always reminded you of your youth, no matter how far your belly had sagged.

But Peter Fallon didn't have a belly. He weighed just five pounds more than when he had rowed for the Harvard crew, his hair was still black, and he could run five miles without breathing hard. Not bad for a guy in his late forties.

He glanced at the statue of John Harvard in front of University Hall. Two tourists were rubbing the toe for luck, an old tradition, even though nobody had any idea of what John Harvard really looked like. The bronze Puritan staring quizzically at his shiny left shoe was just a figment of the sculptor's imagination.

But good luck was good luck.

So Fallon went over and gave the toe a rub. He didn't get nostalgic about Harvard. He wasn't one of those "best years of your life" types. But he was thankful for all that he'd learned there, for the friends that he'd made there, for the doors that had opened to him . . . so thankful that he wanted his son to go there, too. That was why he rubbed the toe, and that was the real reason he was at Harvard that evening.

A short walk across the Yard and through the Square brought him to the offices of the Harvard College Fund.

As Peter knew from experience, it didn't matter whether your parents could pay the whole $35,197 annual tuition or whether they lived in a cardboard box under a freeway. If you were smart enough, creative enough, athletic enough, or had whatever other *enough* the admissions department was looking for, you, too, could go to Harvard, because if you got in and couldn't pay, Harvard would give you the money. It was called "need-blind admission," and it guaranteed that Harvard always got its pick of the best students. Even the ones from under the freeways. *Especially* them.

Most need-blind money was raised by the Harvard College
Fund. Every alumnus heard from the Fund every year, and usually
more than once. If you hadn't given, you were urged to give. If you
had, you were urged to give more. And every five years, you were
deluged with letters and phone calls urging you to give even more
than before, because it was a reunion year and you wouldn't want
to embarrass your class, now, would you?

Harvard fund-raising was polite, efficient, professional, and enor-
mously successful. It could also be relentless and shameless. Since
Peter Fallon could be all of the above, he knew he'd fit right in at a
Fund phone-a-thon. If he raised a few bucks, he might score a few
points for his son's Harvard application. And a divorced dad liked to
score all the points he could for a son he saw only on weekends.

At the Fund office, Peter put on a name tag, picked up a pile of
solicitation cards, and was directed to a large room of office cubi-
cles where Fund functionaries labored by day and alumni called
classmates by night.

As he slipped into a cubicle, a balding head popped up on the
other side of the partition: "I expect you to raise ten thousand
tonight, Peter." It was Tom Benedict, one of Peter's old classmates,
now a professor of English who had ridden the fast train to tenure
and straight through to middle age. His stomach looked like a soup
bowl under his sport coat, no matter how hard he tried to hold it in.
And wise-ass students referred to his course, the Literature of the
American West, as "Cowboys with the Combover."

But Peter knew that Benedict still liked a little competition, so he
said, "One bottle of 'ninety-six Burgundy, premier cru, to the one
who raises the most money tonight."

"You're on."

Then Peter looked at his cards. He had been given the R's. First
call: someone named Raab. The printout next to the name said that
he was an attorney in Chicago who gave five hundred dollars every
year.

"Bingo!" said Peter as soon as he hung up.

"How much?" asked Benedict.

"Five hundred."

Second call: John Ripley. Peter remembered him from crew and remembered him as notoriously tight. He remembered right. *Twenty dollars.* Peter thanked him, since any contribution moved the class closer to its participation goal, but no bingo.

Third call: a Boston doctor named Ramsey: Five hundred and bingo!

"Peter"—Benedict looked over the partition—"this is the Harvard College Fund, not some sweaty boiler room selling aluminum siding to old widows. Stop with the 'bingo.'"

Fallon just laughed and delivered another bingo.

That was when Benedict slipped him a name and address. "They gave me the D's, Peter, but I think that you might want to call this one yourself."

Fallon looked at the name: John Dalton. Spouse: *Evangeline Carrington.*

"Of course, if you're not up to it," said Benedict, "I'll call. I'll tell her that her old boyfriend is sitting right here, but he doesn't want to talk to her."

"You're playing dirty, Tom," said Peter.

"Bingo."

Of course Peter wanted to call her. There had been weeks since his divorce when he'd wanted to call her every night. And never a week went by that he didn't wonder what his life would have been like if he'd married her.

They had met in their late twenties, when Peter Fallon, Harvard graduate student, was writing his dissertation on her famous old family. They had fallen in love as they unearthed the family scandals and a Revere tea set, then faced the legal mess they made in the process. She had moved in with him while he finished his dissertation. Then they had gone together to Iowa, where he spent two years teaching history at Southeast Iowa State. It was hard to say if he was unhappier with teaching than she was with Iowa, but she left him one cold January. She said she was going to Columbia to study journalism. Six months later, he left Iowa—and teaching—and started selling rare books.

They had kept in touch sporadically since then. They had followed each other's careers and marriages. He subscribed to *Travel Life* magazine so that he could read her articles. She put her name on the mailing list of Fallon Antiquaria so that she could see what rare books he had for sale.

But talking to her now, especially when her husband answered the phone, was always more work than it was worth.

So he made a few other calls: two R's who weren't home, and a third who said, "Harvard has more money than God. I have less than a day laborer. Why should I give them anything?" *Fair question.*

Then Benedict popped up again. "An investment banker just gave me five thousand, Peter. Make that wine a Corton-Charlemagne."

"It's not over yet."

Benedict's eyes shifted to Evangeline's phone number. "Dalton's a New York plastic surgeon. Big money in East Side eyelifts."

That did it. Fallon dialed her number.

"Hi. This is Evangeline." It was a recording. Her voice had awakened Peter every day for four years, and it still hurt him to admit that even on a cheap answering machine, she sounded happier now than she had at the end of their time together.

"I'm on an assignment," she said. "Leave me a message. I'll get back. If the message is for Dr. Dalton, you can reach him at his office."

Probably running around the south of France, checking out the *gîtes* for an article in some travel magazine, thought Peter. But he couldn't just hang up, so he said, "Evangeline, this is Peter . . . Peter Fallon. We haven't talked in what? Two years? Anyway . . . I'm calling from the Harvard College Fund. Looking for money. If you or that alumni husband of yours have any, I hope you'll give some to Harvard. . . . And give me a call sometime. Bye."

He was glad that was over. Worse than calling for a date.

Next on the list: his old pal Ridley Wedge Royce.

Harvard graduates often said they learned more in the dining halls than they ever did in the classrooms. And Peter had learned plenty whenever he and Ridley had eaten together in Eliot House. He suspected that Ridley would say the same thing.

One descended from an old Massachusetts family, the other was a South Boston boy whose father had been a bricklayer. But over three years of meals, Ridley had taught Peter about sailing, Peter had taught Ridley about rowing; Ridley had taught wine, and Peter, beer; Ridley had taught theater, and Peter, movies. And even if they hadn't spoken in years, whenever they talked, it was as if they had just seen each other at lunch.

"Peter?" said Ridley. "How's the rare-book business?"

"Just fine, Ridley. How's the life of a Broadway producer?"

"Would you be calling me in Massachusetts if I'd had a hit in the past five years?"

"I don't suppose. . . . Listen, Ridley, I'm calling from the Harvard College Fund—"

"Peter, I'm broke."

"Broke? I'm . . . I'm sorry, Ridley."

"Don't let it bother you, because this phone call is kismet."

"What's kismet?"

"Well . . . a wonderful show starring Alfred Drake. Songs like 'Stranger in Paradise,' 'Baubles, Bangles, and Beads.'"

"C'mon, Ridley . . ."

"It also means good fortune, Peter, happy coincidence. And that's what your call is because *I* was planning to call *you.*"

"What about?"

"I've come across something that might interest the only rare-book dealer in the Class Report, something from the antiquity of the famous old Wedge family."

"The Wedges? What is it?"

"Can't say, Peter. Not over the phone. But worth a mountain of money."

Peter understood. Discretion was part of his business. But if it was discretion Ridley was after, why did he want to meet on Saturday afternoon, in the sea of tailgaters collecting for the Harvard-Dartmouth football game?

Ridley sure hadn't changed. In college, someone had coined a term for his little fits of obtuseness and obfuscation: Ridley Riddles. Here was another one.

"Look for a Class of 'Seventy-two banner," said Ridley, "and the ancient Ford beach wagon. You remember . . . the one they call the Wedge Woody."

"I remember. I'll be there."

* * *

Peter made another ten calls—eight hang-ups, no-thanks, and not-homes balanced against a thousand dollars in pledges. But when the night was over, he owed Tom Benedict one bottle of very expensive wine.

"It'll be worth it," said Benedict as they walked through the Square, "if you get to have lunch with Evangeline. God . . . she was gorgeous."

"It'll be worth it," said Peter, "if this 'something from the antiquity of the famous old Wedge family' has any value."

"What do you think it could be?" asked Tom.

"Who knows? There've been Wedges at Harvard since the beginning. Maybe it's the Freeman's Oath, the first document printed in America, printed in Cambridge in 1636. . . . American Antiquarian Society bid a million bucks for one about fifteen years ago. Turned out to be a forgery."

"A million?" said Benedict. "You can't put a price on something priceless."

"Spoken like a professor. You put a price on something because it's how the world works."

"Spoken like a man who makes his living plundering the past," said Benedict.

Peter had heard that "plunderer" business before, from people who *weren't* joking. But he knew that he served the past by bringing it into the present. And when he sold a piece of it for big bucks, he brought it to life, because in America, big bucks didn't just talk, they breathed . . . and snorted . . . and walked upright on their hind legs. Big bucks meant visits from CNN, interviews on *Nightline*, articles in newsmagazines. Big bucks made the past more valuable, which made it more respectable. And if people respected it, they might learn from it, or at least try to understand it. That's what he told himself, anyway.

Besides, was there another Harvard history major who'd had as much fun? Another Ph.D. who had handled the sale of an original Declaration of Independence? Or ridden the night train from Rome to Florence with a million-dollar incunable on his lap and a book thief prowling the cars? Or blown a hole in a subway wall, stuck his arm into the mud beyond, and pulled out a priceless Revere tea set?

Sure, he had a nice office in the Back Bay, his clients seldom bounced checks, and most of his research was as dull as scraping old paint from a fluted column. But when Peter Fallon went after something—at the Harvard-Dartmouth football game or on the other side of the world—he became, as his ex-wife once said, "Indiana Jones in a monogrammed shirt," a bonus-miles adventurer traveling through time, chasing down books and manuscripts, buying them when he could, brokering them when he couldn't, investigating, negotiating, mediating, and once in a while, running for his life.

The pedestrian light in front of Holyoke Center flashed WALK. Peter and Tom Benedict started across Mass. Ave. But right in the middle, Peter stopped.

"Come on." Benedict pointed to the digital clock beside the little animated pedestrian on the traffic light. *Fifteen seconds to cross . . . fourteen . . . thirteen . . .*

Peter was looking at a pair of brass plates embedded in the street and worn smooth by decades of traffic. "Do you know what those are, Tom?"

"What?" *Ten . . . nine . . . eight . . .*

"Corner bounds. They mark the foundation of Peyntree House, the first building at Harvard. It was discovered when they excavated the subway about 1910."

Peter looked around . . . at the ten-story glass cube of Holyoke Center, glowing in the night . . . at Wadsworth House and the other old buildings . . . at the cars on Mass. Ave., all ready to run him over in just *six . . . five . . . four . . .* "Imagine what all this looked like, Tom. Imagine it on a summer's day in 1638. That's when the first of the Wedges would have seen it."

Chapter Three

===

1638–1639

ISAAC WEDGE first saw Cambridge on a glorious June morning from the back of a borrowed horse. He had said little on the journey, because the man with whom he rode had said even less.

That man was John Harvard, and he was dying. One needed only to look upon his consumed body to know his fate. But such knowledge was unspoken between the teaching elder of the Charlestown church and his best student, between a man with no children and a fatherless boy of sixteen.

It was not until they came to the gate at the end of the Charlestown Path that Harvard peered from under the brim of his hat and said, "You'll not regret this, Isaac."

"Thank you, master." Isaac jumped down and opened the gate that led into the Cambridge Cow Commons. "I fear, however, that my Latin and Greek are—"

"More than adequate." Harvard stifled a cough, but to those who spent time in his company, his coughing had become as common as his breathing, and the familiarity of it made it all but unnoticed. The bloody flecks that splattered his neckcloth, however, could not be ignored.

"I fear the opinion of Master Eaton," said Isaac.

"Fear not," answered Harvard. "His writings, his family background, his work with Reverend Ames at Leyden—these have given the Great and General Court good cause to name him master of this new college. But for all his learning, you'll find him a simple man in many ways, direct, blunt, and the better for it."

They rode south across the Common, followed by the curious cows. They went through another gate and passed the watchhouse, which overlooked the place where the roads of the village converged. There were fifty solid dwellings between there and the river, all roofed in slate or shake, not a bit of thatch to be seen. Only recently had the name of the settlement been changed from Newtowne, to honor the place where most of the learned men in the colony had studied, and to bestow upon this new Cambridge an air of importance commensurate with that of the old.

As for Isaac Wedge, he would have been happier to keep riding . . . right down to the river . . . and spend the day fishing. He could see the brown curl of water on the marshland to the south, and he was sorely tempted.

But Harvard was leading him up to the gate of a spacious two-story dwelling, one of a trio of houses on the south edge of the cow yards. This was the former home of a man named Peyntree and the new home of the college.

The morning sun raised wisps of steam on the wet roof. Diamond-shaped panes of glass shimmered in the window casements. And a small cloud of dust puffed out the front door as a servant swept the foyer.

A clean house, thought Isaac, which meant it would be a godly house, which gave him hope for his prospects there.

But the morning peace was shattered by the cry of a woman. "Damn your eyes!"

"No, ma'am!" came a male voice.

"You'll not dig a finger in me stew again!"

"No, ma'am!" A blackamoor came tumbling out. "Put up the knife, ma'am."

"I'll put up the knife . . . up your poxy nose, you little black squint!" And out of the house burst a great barrel of a woman whose voice proclaimed her a fishwife but whose bonnet, fine dress, and starched ruff suggested she was better born.

"What's all this, then?" A burly man with a black beard emerged after her, and the faces of several young men appeared in the windows of the upper chambers.

"Stealin' food he is, Nathaniel," said the woman.

"Well, we'll put a stop to that." The man slipped a bulrush rod from his belt.

And John Harvard said softly, "Good day, Master Eaton."

It was plain that in their anger, the Eatons had not noticed the arrival of visitors. Mrs. Eaton slipped the knife back into her skirt. And a grin opened in the hairy nest of Nathaniel Eaton's beard. "John Harvard. How fare thee?"

"Well, but for a small cough."

Eaton turned his eyes to Isaac. "And who be this fine lad?"

Isaac was still staring at the rod in Eaton's hand.

Eaton lowered it and said, "My rod and my staff, they'll comfort thee, son. There be need for both in this life. But how often you see one or the other be up to you."

"Isaac Wedge will need no rod," said John Harvard. "He's a fine lad. I've come to vouchsafe him to you and pay for his schooling." Harvard swung his leg carefully from the stirrup, as though he feared breaking were he to move too quickly.

"John, you've lost weight," said Eaton. "How bad is your cough?"

"You'll see before our business be done." Harvard looked at the woman. "Now, then, Mary Eaton, might a thirsty traveler find a draft of beer in your home?"

Eaton's chamber was in the back of the house—a desk, two hard chairs, three bookshelves, and a bucket in which three more bulrush rods soaked and seasoned.

"We only just moved in," said Eaton. "'Tisn't a great house, and the stink of the cattle be somethin' fierce, but it must do till we build us a true college." Eaton pointed out the window. "Do you see those lads swingin' shovels in the middle of the cow yard?"

The land behind Peyntree House and its neighbors, the Goffe and Shepard Houses, was divided into eight enclosures by long runs of split-rail fencing that reached a hundred yards north to the common pales, which in turn ran east a mile or more, from the Cambridge Common to the Charlestown line. Each night the cattle were driven into the yards to protect them from wolves; each morning they were let out to graze.

"The ground is being cleared," Eaton went on. "The governor and the General Court have approved four hundred pounds for the building of the hall."

"A great sum," said Harvard.

"Great, indeed. A quarter of the colony's tax levy from last year, fully half from the year before." Eaton looked at the boy. "You see how serious they do take to the task of educating you, young Isaac Wedge?"

"Yes, master."

" 'Tis only half as serious as I take the task they have laid upon me. None shall ever say this colony wants for learned ministers or educated freemen whilst I be master here." Eaton leaned his hands on his desk. "Now, should I determine that you be worthy to study here, what calling would you answer?"

Isaac looked at Harvard, who nodded, as if encouraging the boy to speak. "I . . . my late father, Reverend John Wedge—"

"A man of goodness," said Eaton.

"A man called too soon by God," said Harvard. "Drowned on the crossing."

"He wished the ministry for me, sir," said Isaac.

"Done, then"—Eaton cocked his brow toward Harvard—"so long as he can read Latin *ex tempore* and decline his Greek paradigms."

"So he can. And his exegesis will make for lively conversation."

"Good. *Lively* is welcome." Then Eaton snapped a rod from the bucket and pointed it at Isaac. "But remember you, boy, *lively* must not mean *heretical*. There'll be no Arminian controversy, no Hutchinsonian heresy, and no devil-worshiping Romanism at my school. Our covenant with the Lord is firm and our calling is clear. Do you understand?"

John Harvard cleared his throat, as if to suggest disapproval of such display, but a cough erupted instead and went on for so long that it seemed his lungs might be shredding inside him. When finally it passed, he looked as gray as his doublet.

And Eaton said, without a bit of tact, "John, were I you, I'd see to my affairs."

"My affair"—Harvard composed himself with a bit of beer and a bloody expectoration into the fireplace—"is to see Isaac Wedge matriculate at the new college. I bring sixteen pounds to cover his tuition and board, and a letter of permission, written by his mother at Charlestown."

Eaton barely glanced at the letter but took great care with the coins that Harvard dropped on the table, counted them, and placed them in his purse.

And thus did Isaac Wedge become one of the first students at the first college in English America, founded on the edge of a wilderness, just six years after the settlement of the colony itself. Such business might have waited. But those who had made this beginning, those who had hired Nathaniel Eaton, did not believe that they could wait, for they knew how fleeting was man's time on earth, and as one of them wrote, they "dreaded to leave an illiterate ministry to the churches when the present ministers shall lay in the dust." They dreaded also to leave magistrates who lacked the wisdom that flowed from Christian knowledge, or a populace too unlettered to appreciate God's word. Their ideals were high and well placed, but their judgment in choosing a master was not.

ii

"Take down your breeches," said Nathaniel Eaton.

"But, sir . . ." Isaac was trembling. Of the ten students at Peyntree House, only he had avoided a caning, until now. "I studied the wrong lesson, sir. But I *did* study."

"I say you studied not at all. I say you are lying."

"Please, sir, allow me to read to you from Cicero. Allow me to prove—"

"Take 'em down and stretch across the desk, or ten stripes become fifteen."

Isaac did as he was told, and an instant later, he heard the rod whistle, felt the sting, and twisted away.

"Stay still!" cried Eaton. "The sentence is fifteen. Squirm and take twenty!"

Isaac ground his teeth and endured. By the tenth whistling whip, he was no longer trembling in fear but anger, for each time Eaton struck, he demanded that Isaac admit he had not studied.

"But I did, master." A whistle, a whip, and a demand for confession. "But I studied, master." Whistle and whip, and "You did not." "But I did." Whistle and whip, and "You lie. Say you lied, or this shall go on all night!" And finally, furiously, Isaac said that he had been lying, that he had not studied; and that in itself was a lie.

Only then did Eaton put up his rod. "Now, then, you may give me your thanks."

"My thanks?" Isaac lowered his shirttail over the bloody flesh and straightened himself.

Eaton's voice was soft, as if the beating had drained him of rage and filled him with satisfaction. "You may thank me for showing you the error of your ways."

Being a young man of intelligence, Isaac did as he was told. Being a young man of spirit, he resolved that he would never let Nathaniel Eaton cane him again.

Such resolutions were hard to keep, however, in the college that students soon came to call the School of Tyrannus. Lessons were taught in fear, learned in terror.

Ten young men, "the sons of gentlemen and others of the best note in the country," began each day at the meetinghouse, where they prayed with Reverend Shepard. Then they would return to Peyntree House for morning bever—a cup of beer, a bit of sour bread, some watery gruel to break their fast. After that they would repair to the front room, where Eaton and his impatient rod awaited their recitations from Cicero and Aristotle, from Greek grammar, from mathematics and reasoning.

Eaton proclaimed that he had taken this course of study from that which freshmen at Emmanuel College, Cambridge, pursued. No student was so bold as to point out that while Eaton may have gone to Cambridge, he held no degree. And no student, no matter how assiduous in study or prayer, was able to avoid punishment for more than a fortnight.

When Isaac was summoned to the master's chambers one September evening, he thought to bid his fellows farewell, as he expected a beating for some unknown infraction, a beating that this time he would resist.

He found Eaton before a guttering candle, a letter on the desk, a mug of beer beside it, and the blackamoor servant hunkered in the shadows.

Eaton gestured to the letter. The seal had been broken, the letter read. "You may wish to answer it. The slave stands ready."

Isaac made certain that this was no trick, that Eaton had no rod hidden under the desk, then he slid the letter toward himself as carefully as he would slide a bone from under the nose of a drowsing dog.

It was written in the hand of Ann Harvard, and it urged Isaac to come to Charlestown as soon as possible. "My husband has taken to a bed from which I fear he may not rise. His strength ebbs. He asks for his friends. 'Tis my hope that Master Eaton will release you, that you may visit him before he goes to his reward."

Isaac read with sadness but little surprise. He did not look up, however, until he had gathered his resolve, for if Eaton would deny a man's dying request, Isaac would defy him. And if Eaton raised his rod, Isaac would fight back, even though he was a skinny lad, sapped of strength after two months of beatings and Mary Eaton's bad food. He set his chin and said, "I must go, sir. Don't try to stop me."

And Eaton shocked Isaac by offering to accompany him. "For no one—boy or man—should look upon the face of the consumption alone."

Perhaps, thought Isaac, there was charity in Nathaniel Eaton after all.

The following day, after recitations, they set out. They went by the Charlestown Path through the green world of late summer. To the south, green meadows of marsh grass rimmed the river and the wide estuary called the Back Bay. Deeper green pasturelands and cornfields expanded around them. And stands of hardwood, their dark green leaves dancing in the breeze, retreated to the north.

Charlestown occupied a peninsula a short ferry ride from Boston, and already there were 150 dwellings clustered near the water or, like Harvard's house, perched on the side of Windmill Hill. Isaac had hoped to work in the windmill as an apprentice. Then Master Harvard had urged him to the college. Many times since, Isaac had wished he were grinding corn in Charlestown rather than studying Cicero under the rod of Master Eaton.

The two visitors were admitted to Harvard's house by Elder Nowell of the Charlestown church.

Against doctor's advice, the windows of John Harvard's bedchamber were thrown open to the September breeze, giving his room of sickness a strange air of hope. He lay propped on several pillows so that he could gaze out on the harbor and town and hills beyond, but his eyes were closed, his face as white as the pillows.

Upon a whisper from his wife, his eyes opened, focused, sought about the room until they found Isaac. Then a hand rose from the bed.

Isaac took it. "Master Harvard."

"How fares your study?" Harvard's voice was all but inaudible.

And Eaton's face appeared over Isaac's shoulder. "He'll make a fine minister, John. You know quality."

" 'Twas a simple matter," said Harvard, stifling a cough. "My father always said a man could be known by his books, and Isaac's Bible be well thumbed."

Isaac felt sudden and powerful emotions rise in his throat. He stepped back and brought a hand to his mouth, as if to keep them from escaping.

"Don't cry for me," said John Harvard. "I look to a better world. But my books—"

"Yes, John," said Eaton, taking Harvard's hand in both of his. "What of them?"

"My books remain in this world." Harvard looked past Eaton to Isaac. "Can the students be trusted to respect them?"

Eaton said, "They're students, John. They live for books."

Harvard did not even look at Eaton. "Isaac?"

"I would trust them, sir," said Isaac.

"Good." Only then did Harvard turn to Eaton. "May I trust that at the college, my library will be respected? Not scattered about?"

"Of course," said Eaton.

"Good. If a man is known by his books, I would keep mine together."

"Your books will have their place in our library," said Eaton, "when it's built."

"Good." Harvard shifted his eyes to his wife and then to Elder Nowell, as if it was too great an effort to move his head. "I bequeath all my books to our new college, in the knowledge that students like Isaac will respect them . . . protect them . . . and benefit from them, and that they will be kept together as the seedbed for a greater library."

"So shall it be attested," said Elder Nowell.

"And, Isaac"—Harvard coughed and a foam of blood appeared at the corners of his mouth—"you will find in my library books on many topics. Some may surprise you. But you must respect every volume."

"I will," said Isaac. "I promise."

"Of course he will, John," said Eaton. "We all will, for there can be nothing in your library to make a man anything but enriched . . . in spirit, at least."

Harvard kept his eyes on Isaac. "There may come times in your life when the words you read and the ideas you meet do not glorify God but man, his vanities . . . his passions . . . his appetites . . . all things that lead us toward sin."

"Not at my college," said Eaton.

"Quiet, Nathaniel," said Harvard. "You have many years yet to speak your mind. Let me say my piece now."

But another fit of coughing took Harvard, cracking in his chest and bringing up bloody shards of lung, which he left in his spittoon. Then he sank deeper into his pillow, gasped for breath, and said, "So . . . Isaac, when your reading challenges your beliefs, remember the words of Rector Morton, who saw St. Saviour's through the plague: Turn your mind to higher things. In them will you find the answers. . . . Now, friends, a prayer."

The prayer by Elder Nowell was a good one, thought Isaac. It did not request John Harvard's return to health, for that was plainly not in God's plan. It did not request the repose of his soul, for that time had not yet come. It simply expressed a faith in God's goodwill, and that was something in which all, even a dying man, could take comfort.

Then John Harvard closed his eyes and seemed to settle into sleep.

Elder Nowell gestured for Isaac and Eaton to leave, but Ann Harvard said to her husband, "John, is there not one thing more?"

Harvard's eyes opened. "Oh, yes. Nathaniel—"

Eaton again took Harvard's hand. "Yes, John."

"Half of all my earthly possessions go to Ann, to see to her future."

"Yes, John."

Harvard coughed again. "But I have no children."

"No, John. No, you don't."

It seemed to Isaac that Nathaniel Eaton was all but salivating as the direction of Harvard's words came clear.

"So the other half," said Harvard, "some eight hundred pounds' worth, I give to the college."

"Eight hundred," whispered Eaton with awe. "Why . . . that's twice what the Great and General Court give to start the school. You'll never be forgot for this, John."

"Let Isaac and all his brethren and all their descendants remember me. Let them be my heirs." John Harvard shifted his eyes to Elder Nowell.

"I shall be the witness," said Nowell.

Eaton and Isaac restrained themselves, though for different reasons, until they had left Harvard's home and gone halfway down Windmill Hill.

Isaac fought the impulse to run off and seek comfort at his mother's house. But he could not fight the sob that burst from his chest or the tears that finally came.

Eaton, on the other hand, seemed unable to stop a pleased expression from becoming a smile, which grew into a grin. "Come, lad. You've known for months that he was dyin'. 'Tis a mercy."

" 'Tis hard, still, sir."

"You lose a friend, Isaac, but our lives as scholars are assured. I planted this seed in Harvard's mind when I saw how sick he was." Eaton mounted his horse. "Books be a rare flower in this land, but money be the blossom that bears fruit we can eat."

Isaac realized that Eaton had not hurried to Harvard's bedside out of anything but self-interest. And he had gotten there in good time, for two days later, on September 14, John Harvard died of the consumption. He was thirty years old.

iii

All through that glorious autumn and bitterly cold winter, Nathaniel Eaton continued to teach his students, and to beat them, and to beat his servants and his children, and perhaps his wife, too, all in the name of Christian knowledge and obedience.

Isaac Wedge grew inured to the beatings and learned to remove the pain from his mind. Whether receiving a rap on his knuckles for an incorrect response, or a caning across his back for some greater transgression, he would think on higher things, on the Passion of Christ, on the gifts of Master Harvard, and on the beauty of a girl named Katharine Nicholson, who appeared to him as out of a vision one brilliant January day.

Isaac was returning from Reverend Shepard's when the Nicholson sleigh stopped in front of Peyntree House, and Isaac was smitten straightaway by a bright smile, milk-white skin, delft-blue eyes, and strong black brow. The whiteness of the day served only to complement her coloring, and if winter could enhance her so, he wondered, what would summer do?

"Good afternoon," said her father. "Be this the home of the new college?"

"Yes, sir. I'm a student. My name is Isaac Wedge."

"And we be the Nicholsons," said the father.

"The family of James?" asked Isaac. "James Nicholson of Boston?"

"Do you know him?" she asked.

And Isaac found that months of recitation under the threat of Eaton's rod made it easy to find words before a beautiful girl. "Miss, there be only ten of us. We are all acquaintances, and I'm pleased to say we are all friends."

He wished for more talk, but Eaton appeared now in the doorway, and Isaac, knowing his place, excused himself with a polite bow.

The Nicholsons bore gifts of food—ten packages for ten young men who had eaten too little beef and too much spoiled fish at the School of Tyrannus. Each package contained molasses cakes, hardtack, a small round of cheese, and a jar of pickled oysters.

Eaton did not object to their distribution, since the Nicholsons brought a larger basket of food for the master and his wife. He did, however, object to the attention that several of the boys paid to Master Nicholson's daughter.

"This be a godly school," he shouted after the Nicholsons had left. "I will not have any of you slobbering over a young lady of such quality as Jamie Nicholson's sister. Any further slobbering will be met with punishment."

But for the next month, Isaac Wedge could not erase her image from his mind. To his disappointment, when she and her father returned in February, Isaac was cutting firewood at Reverend Shepard's, so he missed seeing her. When they came in March, he managed to speak with her briefly before Eaton appeared and scowled at him.

That night in commons, James Nicholson told Isaac that Katharine wished to be remembered to him and that she would look forward to meeting him on their visit in April. Nothing in his life had ever made Isaac Wedge happier.

There was an assistant at the college named Nathaniel Briscoe, who slept in the upper chamber with the students. Most nights, after the candles were snuffed, he would call out, "Remember Onan, boys. Remember that his sin be a hangin' offense, so banish temptation from your mind." But most nights, there would be furtive movements and sounds that suggested someone was ignoring Briscoe's words. And most nights, Briscoe would ignore the sounds.

But one March night, Briscoe was in Boston. So Master Eaton paid a visit to the upper chamber. He came on stockinged feet and masked his lamp, so it gave off no telltale shadows. He silently climbed the ladder from below and stopped when only his eyes and ears had risen through the attic hatchway.

Isaac did not see him, for Isaac was busy. The only person Isaac saw at that moment was a certain young lady. And she was only in his mind's eye. And it was her image that made him busy, and he rose toward a release that—

"Isaac Wedge! Stand up! Now!"

At the explosion of sound, Isaac leapt to his feet, even as his body leapt in a series of spasms that were suddenly no more than wet embarrassment beneath his nightshirt.

"We are here to root out sin," cried Eaton to all the boys, "no matter where it be found. Strangle the eel in my house and feel the sting of my rod!"

Why was Eaton the man that he was? And why had they made such a man the head of the college? Those were questions that Isaac asked himself as he was led, barefoot, to the master's chamber to receive twenty snaps of the rod. But there was no answer, except that some men were cruel and some men were kind.

And some cruel men considered cruelty a strange kindness, usually voiced as Eaton put it to Isaac: "I do this for your own good," the words followed by whistle and whip. "I have the authority, and I will exercise it!" Whistle and whip. "It is my right and it is my duty." Whistle and whip. "What you've been up to is a hanging offense." And whistle and whip once again, all the way to the count of twenty.

Then Eaton stepped back, breathed deep, and spoke in a voice as soft and gentle as always after a beating. "Now, then, Isaac Wedge . . . 'tis said that an idle mind is the devil's playground. Be your mind idle?"

"No, sir. I have my studies."

"Then it must be your hands that are idle. We'll give them something to do and save you from hanging." Eaton pointed to the two trunks in a corner. "Master Harvard's books. They be yours to catalog . . . in your idle time. Do a good job."

"I'd do nothing less, sir. I promised Master Harvard on his deathbed."

"They be the physical legacy of our first benefaction, which has inspired the Great and General Court to give our little school a name: Harvard College."

All the more reason, thought Isaac, to do the job well.

But Eaton was a fickle man. What seemed a fine idea at night, after the pleasure of a good beating, might look less palatable in the morning, especially as March brought earlier dawns and warmer days, during which he hatched grander plans.

The fence directly behind Peyntree House had been taken down, the cows squeezed into adjacent yards, and the posts and beams of the new college hall had risen. So Eaton proclaimed that he would plant an apple orchard to frame the grand structure.

His account books would show that he paid local workers to do the planting, when in fact he pocketed the money and put students to work digging wild apple trees and going to Boston to fetch trees brought from England. When the ground thawed, the few hours of free time he had given the students each day he gave over to planting. By May, thirty trees were in the ground. Some died before they took up water. Some leafed out. And a few made pink blossoms that promised fruit and fresh cider by fall.

And one evening, Isaac Wedge walked boldly beneath the blossoms with Katharine Nicholson.

"What if the master see us?" she asked.

"You say that your father has come to discuss a contribution?"

"Aye. He offers to build a lean-to on the side of Peyntree House, as a library for Master Harvard's books . . . at least till the college hall is completed."

"Then Master Eaton will pay no mind to anything else."

"But what if he glance out and see us?"

"The beating will be worth it."

"You're a brave one, Isaac Wedge," she said. Then, with a conspiratorial little smile and a furtive glance toward the house, she brought her lips to his.

It was the gentlest of touches, but Isaac's legs went weak. He thought he might fall over. And later he thought it might have been a good idea . . . to fall over and feign sickness, for at that moment, Mrs. Eaton emerged from the outhouse, straightening her skirt. At the sight of a student kissing a girl in the orchard, she gave out with a shriek, almost as if the student had tried to kiss her.

The beating was painful, but the greater pain came with the threat of expulsion that Eaton now laid upon Isaac, should he be so bold as to see Katharine again.

"And what would John Harvard say, were such a thing to happen?" asked Eaton.

Isaac could not imagine. But how terrible would it be to avoid Katharine until he graduated? And why? Because Master Eaton would control nature as he controlled everything else at that school? He seemed a man well disposed to satisfying his own natural appetites—for food, for drink, for lust, too, considering his four children and the nightly sounds that rose from the chamber below Isaac's bed. But Eaton's greatest appetite was for money, and therein lay the answer to Isaac's predicament: Eaton feared to anger Master Nicholson before the latter had opened his purse for the college.

To inspire Nicholson's charity, Eaton set Isaac at last to an accounting of the books that would be housed in the library. This would show Nicholson the profundity of Harvard's collection, and it would keep Isaac away from Nicholson's daughter.

One June evening, while the other students spent a few hours out of doors, Isaac and the blackamoor dragged the two trunks of books to the recitation room. When Isaac opened the first trunk, he felt as if he were looking into the mind of John Harvard himself. For the rest of his life, whenever he smelled leather—a new boot, an old saddle—Isaac would think of the bindings of Harvard's books. And he would remember the words that Harvard had said so often: "A man will be known by his books."

As Latin was the language of learned discourse, there were books with titles such as *Anglorum Praelia* and *De Habitu et Constitutione Corporis*. Also in Latin was a seventeen-volume edition of *Summa Theologica* by the Roman Catholic Thomas Aquinas. Isaac read a few pages and found no "devil-worshiping Romanism," as Eaton had phrased it, but a mind that was serious and supple and filled with the love of God. Aquinas, however, was flanked in the trunk by those plain thinkers of Protestantism, Martin Luther and John Calvin.

There was a Latin grammar and dictionary, likewise for Hebrew and Greek, the other languages an educated man should know. However, Plutarch, Pliny, and Homer had arrived in English translations, and what wondrous worlds they must have shown John Harvard in any language.

The next evening, Isaac worked on the second trunk, and before he had dug far, he came across several items that surprised him even more than the Aquinas had. They were plays. Two were in Latin, comedies by the Roman playwrights Plautus and Terence. Another was *Roxana*, by the English author William Alabaster.

But none of these was as shocking to find as the play in the red leather binding, about six inches by nine, ink-written on heavy paper about a hundred pages in length. The first page was blank but for the words " 'Love's Labours Won' by Will. Shakespeare."

Isaac almost threw down the book. His father had oft railed against theater, and against no one more loudly than this Shakespeare, who had written of regicides bedding their brothers' wives, of blackamoors wedding flaxen-haired women, of fairies running naked through summer nights, of men dressed as women and women as men, of blind love and magic potions and murder, of man's—here were John Harvard's words on his deathbed—man's vanities, his passions, his appetites, all the things that lead us toward sin.

It was plain to Isaac that Master Harvard had been warning him that one day he would find this book and that he must respect it as he did the works of Martin Luther or John Calvin.

But why? Had they not planted this colony as a place where such sins as would be found in London could not survive? What greater public sin was there than the theater?

Still, Isaac could not deny his curiosity. How could reading a few pages damage his mind or his soul or his personal connection with God? And how much more would it teach him about John Harvard?

A friend in London had once shown him a handmade book—drawings of men with erect members penetrating women in every angle of copulation. And though he knew it was wrong, he had not been able to take his eyes from the images or control his physical response as he turned the pages. Opening this book, he felt a similar excitement, a tingling in the mind and, strangely, in the loins, at entering a forbidden world.

The second page contained the words *dramatis personae* and a list of characters. Then the play began: "Enter Ferdinand, King of Navarre, Berowne, and Costard, a clown." And then came the words. Flowing, flying, all but leaping from the page. Furtively, Isaac read, and quickly, as quickly as ever he had. At times, he found himself laughing out loud. At other times, he gasped in surprise at the scenes playing, not on the page, but in his mind's eye. And he was absorbed so completely, he did not notice the gathering darkness until he heard doors opening, students returning. . . .

But there was one act of the play yet to read. And he had to see how it all ended, so he lit a candle. He should have known that while all lit candles attracted insects, lit candles in Peyntree House also attracted Eatons.

First came Mary, who could skulk like a cat despite her girth. Drawn by the light, she peered into the recitation room, then went slipping away.

Moments later, the master appeared. "Who is wasting money on—"

Isaac came to his senses. He closed the book and stood, as embarrassed and frightened as he had been on the night that Eaton had found him strangling the eel.

"What is that?" Eaton stepped close to Isaac, as if to intimidate him with his bulk.

"A . . . a book, sir." And for the first time, Isaac realized how much he had grown in a year, despite the bad diet, because he was now on eye level with the master.

"Most boys don't light candles to keep reading. They quit at the comin' of dark."

"I do my job, sir. Sometimes I must read a bit to know the—"

"You need only to read the title and author." Eaton snatched the book and glanced at it, and his eyes bulged. "A play? Shakespeare! This be filth."

"'Twas one of Master Harvard's books, sir. It can't be filth."

"Most certainly it can." Eaton flipped to the back and read the words "'Transcribed by the author.' The very devil himself. How much have you read?"

"A . . . a few pages."

Eaton whipped his rod across Isaac's face. "Don't play sly with me, boy. You've been sitting here reading this play. How many murders have you read of? How many women have been ravished? How many bellowing oaths have you heard from besotted clowns like John Falstaff?"

"Who, sir?"

Eaton struck again, on the other cheek. "There will be no wooden theaters in New England. Glorified bear pits filthy with cutpurses and fops and courtiers in codpieces. And there will be no plays in this library, as long as I have breath."

"But, sir, Master Harvard wanted his books kept together."

Eaton raised the rod again. "Do you dare to question me?"

"No, sir. I merely remind you."

Then Eaton seemed to give more thought to all of this. He opened the book and flipped through it. "His own handwriting. The handwriting of the devil. There be some—misguided sinners—who would pay handsomely for such evil."

Isaac picked up the other plays, thinking there might be safety for Shakespeare in numbers. "Here are Plautus and Terence, sir, and the English playwright Alabaster."

Eaton snatched at the Alabaster. "*Roxana*. 'Twas performed at Trinity College. Trinity men were less worried about such sin than the Puritan scholars of Emmanuel."

"And what of these?" Isaac offered the other two books.

"They're classical plays. Reading them will enhance a man's spo-

ken Latin. But this"—he weighted the Shakespeare in his hand—
"this must be destroyed."

"No!" Without thinking, Isaac grabbed Eaton's arm and tried to
get at the book.

Eaton must have been expecting an assault by some one of his
students. For he was ready and responded with a closed fist.

Isaac heard his own nose crunching, and he thought, for just an
instant, that he saw the Big Dipper, all as he flew backward, banged
against the wall, then bounced into Eaton's fist again. He had been
in plenty of scuffles and once had been struck by a falling roof slate
on a London street, but never had he experienced the kind of ear-
ringing senselessness that now staggered him.

"You do not strike your master! And you do not question him!"
Eaton raised his fist to strike again but stopped in midair, as though
a better idea had entered his head. Then he turned and hurried out
of the room.

Isaac was too groggy to notice if Eaton had the book with him,
but in an instant, Eaton was back with a cudgel, raised for action.

Fortunately for Isaac, the front door opened at that moment,
and Nathaniel Briscoe appeared in the foyer. "What goes on here,
master?"

"A student is chastised for laying hands upon me. See that the
others are in their beds, and lock the trapdoor to their chamber."

"But that boy is bleedin'."

Only now did Isaac realize that the red droplets striking the floor
were falling from his broken nose.

"Do as you're told," commanded Eaton.

"No. You've beat your last student." And Briscoe threw himself
into the room.

But Eaton was as practiced with the cudgel as he was with the
rod, and he delivered a single short stroke that sent Briscoe stumbling back into the foyer. Then he drove his boot into Briscoe's
belly and sent him flying out the front door.

Through the window, Isaac watched Briscoe land in the dirt,
then stagger to his feet and pull out his knife. Isaac should have
been watching Eaton, who rounded on him with the cudgel
swinging. . . .

Isaac awoke sometime later. He inhaled and breathed his own blood back into his throat. *Where was he?* On the floor. *On the floor where?* He saw shadows dancing on the wall. He heard the shuffling of feet, the groaning of a man . . . Master Briscoe.

Then he heard Eaton's voice, "Did you not pull a knife on me? Admit it!" This was followed by the hollow thunk of a walnut cudgel against a man's head.

"Sir . . . sir . . ." It was the voice of the blackamoor. "He can't take no more."

"Be quiet and hold him up, or I'll beat you, too," said Eaton.

Isaac scuttled from the room on all fours. As soon as he was outside in the starlight, he ran, half stumbling, to the house next door.

There lived Thomas Shepard, minister to Cambridge, overseer of the college. He was considered a man of great probity in private counsel and great power in the pulpit, despite a body that was slender to the point of weakness and a complexion as pale and diaphanous as a cloud. He gasped at the bloody sight that greeted him when he opened his door, and gasped again when it said, "You must come, sir. You must stop a murder."

iv

The General Court convened at the Boston Meeting House to hear testimony in charges brought, amazingly, by Nathaniel Eaton, who claimed that Briscoe had pulled a knife on him and had also— even more grievous—uttered an oath to God.

Briscoe himself stood first at the bar, before the magistrates, learned men elected by the freemen of the colony to govern and to render judgments in criminal matters and disputes.

"For what reason did you pull a knife?" asked one of them.

"I feared that Master Eaton would kill a student that he was chastising," said Briscoe. "The oath I uttered was a prayer. I cried out to God to save me from death when Eaton turned his cudgel onto me."

"Cudgel?" Governor Winthrop leaned forward. "He beat students with a cudgel?"

"Usually 'twas a rush rod. But that night, sir, a walnut tree cudgel, big enough to kill a horse, a yard in length."

John Winthrop turned his gaze to Eaton, who sat with an expression of complete disdain upon his face.

After Briscoe, the students were called in alphabetical order. And thus began the chronicle of beatings and bad food meted out by a brutal master and his miserly wife. And with each testimony, the magistrates shot ever more glaring looks in the direction of the Eatons.

In an attitude of supreme disdain, Nathaniel Eaton folded his arms and turned his attention to the rafter beams above him. But his wife began to fidget when a student charged her with serving ungutted mackerel, and by the time Jamie Nicholson testified to goat's dung in the hasty pudding, Mrs. Eaton had twisted her apron into a single giant knot.

Their appetites apparently whetted by talk of food, the magistrates recessed for dinner. They had heard the testimony of eight students. The ninth would be Isaac Wedge.

But he had no fear. So confident was he of his testimony, and of the fate awaiting Eaton, that he sat boldly under a tree with Katharine Nicholson, shared a wedge of cheese and a loaf of bread, and talked of the morning's proceedings.

As he returned to the meetinghouse, however, his way was blocked by Eaton's bulk, and though men were flowing past them and filing back to their seats, Isaac felt suddenly alone, fixed by Eaton's false smile and frozen glare.

"Be as bold as you want with the girl today," said Eaton in a low voice, "and be as honest as you must in your testimony. But if you speak about a Shakespeare play, these magistrates will root it out and burn it themselves. Then will your mentor's library be broken forever . . . his reputation, too. Be more circumspect, however, and I'll be your ally in protecting the Harvard legacy." Then he turned on his heel and went inside.

Though he saw little wrong in the play, Isaac knew that Eaton was right about the magistrates, good Puritans every one. So all the while that he waited, that he walked to the bar, that he swore his oath, he was wondering how he could phrase himself truthfully and yet reveal nothing of that play.

"Why were you under the lash . . . er . . . cudgel that night?" asked Winthrop.

"Master Eaton objected," answered Isaac, "because, when I should have been cataloging Master Harvard's books, I was reading one instead."

"You were shirking your duties, then?" asked another magistrate.

"I fear that I was, sir. And when Master Eaton snatched the book, I struck at him and tried to snatch it back."

"You dared lay hands on your master?" said Winthrop solemnly.

The ploy had worked. By turning the court's attention to his own transgression, Isaac had distracted them from the book. After chiding him for what he had done, they moved on to the beating, the earlier beatings, and never once did they ask for the title of the work that inspired Eaton's anger. Isaac's conscience was safe for the moment.

"As the young man who started all this"—Governor Winthrop pointed his chin whiskers at Isaac—"what would you say of Master Eaton?"

Isaac could not see Eaton behind him, but he knew that he should choose his words carefully, for Eaton could be a vengeful man. Then he breathed deep and remembered breathing his own blood through his broken nose, and he decided that no man would ever frighten him again, vengeful or not. "I would say, Your Honors, that a man given such charge should know of Christ's mercy as well as God's wrath. What I have learned at the college has been in spite of him, not because of him. Were it up to me or my classmates, we would banish him tomorrow . . . good sirs."

As Isaac stepped down, someone began to clap his hands. An instant later, every student was applauding and the governor was pounding his gavel.

Not a one of the students left before the testimony of Eaton and his wife.

First, Mary Eaton stood, her hands still twisting her apron. She admitted to denying cheese to the students, for which she humbly begged pardon. But she claimed never to have served mackerel with their guts in them. "And as for goat's dung in the hasty pudding, 'tis utterly unknown to me."

"And beef?" asked a magistrate. "And beer? 'Tis stated they had little of either."

"I . . . I confess that we live on a cow yard, but I cannot remember that ever they had beef. As for their wanting beer, betwixt brewings, a week or half a week, I am sorry that it were so, and should tremble, good masters, were it to happen again."

But the magistrates were more interested in the husband, who came next to the bar and stood rocking on the balls of his feet, in an attitude of utter defiance.

For every beating, he gave a reason and finally, when he tired of the questions, he said, "Gentlemen, I had this rule—and a good one—that I would not give over correcting until I had subdued a student to my will. Students are recalcitrant beings, as you know."

"So are some schoolmasters," said Governor Winthrop.

"And so must they be," answered Eaton. "For they seek to restrain beings whose minds are yet weak and whose morality is unformed. 'Tis a hard job."

Two days later, Eaton and his wife stood before the bar to hear Governor Winthrop read the court's decision: "For the cruel and barbarous beating of Mr. Nathaniel Briscoe, and for other neglecting and misusing of your scholars, you are to be discharged from keeping school, with or without a license, and fined sixty-six pounds."

Then Winthrop lowered the paper and looked at Eaton. "One of your students put it best, sir, who said that a man given such charge should know of Christ's mercy as well as God's wrath. Now, what have you to say in response to our justice and clemency?"

And to the amazement of all, Nathaniel Eaton turned his back on the magistrates, saying, "If sentence be passed, then it is to no end to speak."

Within a week, the college was closed. The students were sent home, having been charged to continue their study with the ministers in their respective communities. And Peyntree House was left empty but for the Eatons, who awaited a second trial before the members of their own Cambridge congregation.

Isaac Wedge, however, had been engaged by Reverend Shepard to whitewash the meetinghouse. He also hoped to finish work on Harvard's library, once the Eatons had departed. And most important, the Nicholson family, drawn to Cambridge by the eloquence of Reverend Shepard, had settled in a fine house overlooking the new wharf.

Most days, before morning prayer, Isaac would walk down Water Street, past the wharf, around the sweeping curve of the town creek, through the town square, and back to the home of Reverend Shepard, where he lived in the attic.

On fine mornings, Katharine would rise to offer a greeting, a bit of conversation, perhaps a cup of beer. But if the clouds lowered, she would stay abed and Isaac would simply walk, ruminating on the closing of the college and on the fate of the Shakespeare play. Sometimes he even wondered about the fate of the characters in the play.

It happened to rain on the last day of September, the day that Eaton's church trial was to begin. So Katharine was abed and the morning dark.

But as Isaac came round the corner of Water Street and looked toward the wharf, he saw a vessel he recognized as *Nell's Bark*, out of Piscataqua. He went closer to see what the men would be loading in the gray dawn. And there on the wharf, flinging sacks of belongings aboard, was Nathaniel Eaton.

At first, Isaac thought to run for Reverend Shepard or the constable, but Eaton saw him and growled, "Stay there, boy, or this time I'll finish you, so help me God."

"But you are to appear before the congregation this morning."

"And so I will, boy. So I will. You have my word."

Isaac might still have run, but this was the first time he had seen Eaton since the trial, and there was something he had to know. So he drew closer. "I also have your word that you will be my ally in protecting the Shakespeare book."

"Never trust a man better versed in God's wrath than in Christ's mercy, as you say. I could sustain no further censure from the

colony, which surely would follow if they found a play in my possession. So I burned it."

"Burned it?" Isaac felt as if he had been struck.

Just then, the captain of the sloop said, "Hurry up about it,
Eaton. The tide turns."

On impulse, Isaac grabbed for Eaton's bag. Eaton pulled back,
and as he did, the bag tore open, spilling onto the wharf a jumble
of clothes, a box of iron nails, glass trinkets such as white men might
use in trading with the Indians, and—yes—several books.

In the dim morning light, Isaac could not tell if one of the books
was the play, nor did he see the walnut cudgel appear in Eaton's
hand. But he felt it strike the side of his head, and his world went
black. By the time he awoke, *Nell's Bark* had slipped down the
creek and turned for Boston.

Isaac rubbed the lump rising under his hat.

Then he heard the gentle voice of Reverend Shepard in his ear.
"Let him go."

"But the trial?"

"We know enough about him. It took me far too long to see his
sin. My own ignorance is a sin I repent of, and my lack of watch-
fulness over him—over all of you—is a sin I shall mourn."

Some men were cruel and some were kind, thought Isaac. And
as there were few as cruel as Nathaniel Eaton, there were few as
kind as Thomas Shepard.

Isaac resolved to know better such as Shepard. He also resolved
that someday he would track down Eaton and find the truth about
Love's Labours Won. And if the book had not been destroyed, he
would restore it to John Harvard's library, for he had made John
Harvard a deathbed promise. No man had ever been as kind to
Isaac, and the kindness of John Harvard had to be known by future
generations, and a man would best be known by his books.

Chapter Four

=====

GAME DAY *in Cambridge.*

No one would ever mistake it for game day in South Bend or Ann Arbor, not for the quality of the football or the intensity of the fans. But Peter Fallon loved it. He loved to hear the band play "Harvardiana" on a crisp October afternoon, to meet old friends at tailgates, to sit in the stadium and pass a flask as the shadows lengthened and the air went from crisp to cold. And he loved bringing his son.

They were part of the crowd flowing down JFK Street, and Peter was saying, "Did you know that there was a wharf near here in the seventeenth century?"

"Cool," said Jimmy Fallon.

"It was on a creek that bubbled up in the Yard, took a right in the Square and came around in a big semicircle. Eliot Street follows it exactly."

"Cool."

They were passing Hicks House, a little white Dutch Colonial that served as the Kirkland House library, one of the last relics of eighteenth-century Cambridge.

"Near here, the creek turned for the river," Peter went on.

"Cool."

"Imagine a sloop sailing down this street, instead of all these cars and people." Peter pointed ahead, through the shallow brick canyon created by the Kennedy School on one side, Kirkland and Eliot Houses on the other.

"Yeah . . . Cool."

"Is that all you can say? Cool . . . cool . . . cool?"

Jimmy shrugged. He was taller than his father, but he had the same black hair and dark brow, the same scowling first impression that faded as soon as he smiled. "I'm more interested in Harvard's future than its past, Dad."

Peter knew why. The kid's head was still spinning. They'd started the day at an alumni seminar: "Who Gets Into Harvard?" Peter had wanted Jimmy to hear about his chances, which Peter thought were pretty good. Jimmy, however, had only heard about the competition, which was also pretty good.

So Peter started pep-talking. "Harvard has its pick of the smartest kids in America. You're one of them. That means you have as good a chance as anybody. Your SATs are—"

"Harvard rejects people with sixteen hundreds all the time, Dad."

"Your grades are all A's."

"They turn down four-point-ohs all the time."

"Not from high school track stars."

"They have four-point-oh stars in everything. And I go to Boston Latin. I'm also a white male from Boston, and no matter what they say, they have quotas—"

"Because eighty years ago, most students were white males from New England and New York. Pretty boring."

"No more history, Dad."

They kept talking across Memorial Drive and onto the Larz Anderson Bridge, a graceful span choked most of the time—not just on game days—with cars, cyclists, and pedestrians. The Charles River sparkled below, and up ahead two flags fluttered atop the stadium. One was crimson with a white *H*, the other green with a white *D*. Harvard vs. Dartmouth, fourth Saturday in October, as always.

"Listen, Jimmy, you've got the goods. If they don't let you in, it's their fault."

"They get nineteen thousand applications. They admit eighteen hundred."

"So at some point, it's a coin toss. Just stop worrying and apply." Peter clapped his son on the shoulder. "Now let's go find the Wedge Woody."

"The Wedge *what?*"

You couldn't miss it: a 1934 Ford beach wagon floating in that sea of SUVs, minivans, and BMWs around Harvard Stadium.

In his student days, if Peter didn't have an invitation to a tailgate, he'd just cruise. He could walk down a row of cars, past picnic tables and charcoal grills, and before game time, he'd have sampled steak sandwiches, lobster, shrimp as big as his fist, along with all the hot spiked drinks he could hold. And if he'd kept his ears open among the alums, he'd have picked up hot rumors from politics, business, and publishing, too.

Back then, the Wedge Woody had been presided over by Harriet Webster Wedge, who played her role like Bette Davis—the accent all broad *a*'s, the bourbon straight up, the Camels as unfiltered as the opinions.

And she was there now, standing by the old station wagon, puffing away, giving orders, acting as if she were still in charge, even though it was her son who was now master of the pregame revels.

That was Will Wedge, the guy in the crimson-colored pants, greeting, pouring, laughing out loud at the lamest jokes—a man for whom life was good, or who wanted it to seem that way. He had sandy blond hair graying at the temples and the same kind of long face and toothy smile his mother had, a physiognomy so familiar in New England that it might have been sculpted by the last glacier. He was also six-four and seemed to know the first lesson of good height: make them look up to you.

A mug of bourbon and hot cider appeared under Peter's nose, in the hand of Ridley Royce, who didn't even say hello. He just whispered, "The story of the Wedges . . . eleven generations from noble Isaac to a guy wearing pants the color of cranberry sauce."

"Hello, Ridley." Peter took the mug. "Meet my son."

Ridley gave Jimmy the once-over. "Apple didn't fall far from the tree. Can he have a beer?"

"No, thank you," said Jimmy. "Against track team rules."

"A Fallon turns down a beer? I take back what I said about the apple."

Ridley's great-grandfather had bred a few short genes to the Wedge strain, so Ridley didn't resemble any of the Wedges around him. Bald had also been part of his legacy, but discreet little plugs of hair defied that bit of Wedge DNA. And after four generations, there really wasn't much Wedge in him. But Ridley was still family. "Drink up, Peter," he said. "You're about to get what I call 'the Full Wedge.' Here comes Will."

"What does he do these days?"

"Venture capitalist, former president of a bought-out bank, tireless Harvard fund-raiser. Nicknamed Williwaw at prep school because he reminded friends of a whirlwind . . . always spinning from one thing to the next."

"And he really *does* look good in crimson pants," said Peter. "As long as he wears a blue blazer to tone them down."

Will was within earshot now, hand extended. "Mr. Fallon, I presume."

Peter introduced his son, who was shoving his hands into his pockets and pulling them out and shoving them back, miming the nervous boredom that came upon most kids caught in the midst of grown-up greetings.

Will Wedge looked Jimmy over. "Do we have a legacy here?"

"It's up to him," said Peter.

"Can't go wrong at Harvard," said Wedge to the boy. "Now go get yourself some food, and say hello to some of my nieces around the grill."

"And be polite," said Peter.

"So"—Wedge turned to Peter—"what brings you to the Wedge Woody?"

And Ridley intervened. "He's an old friend, Will."

"Who also happens"—Wedge's voice lost some of its good cheer—"to be one of the best-known antiquarians in Boston."

"Documents *and* books," said Fallon.

"Yes," said Wedge, all the good cheer gone, "it's good to bring the past to light."

Peter saw a nasty look pass between Wedge and Ridley, but an old classmate was calling to him, so Will plastered his grin back on his face, gave out with a loud greeting, and went off through the char-coal smoke.

"What's his problem?" said Peter, not taking his eyes from Will Wedge.

"I'll tell you later. First, let me introduce you to—"

Harriet Webster Wedge, carrying a plate of shrimp. "These are what a treasure hunter would enjoy," she said.

"Thanks." Peter dipped a shrimp. "I haven't been called a trea-sure hunter in a long time."

"Oh, but you are. And I've always wondered . . . That Revere tea set that you found years ago. Didn't you save a piece?"

"The sugar urn. By accident. Sold it to pay for the damage I did finding it."

"You blew a hole in the subway at Copley Square, didn't you?"

"Yes, ma'am." Peter no longer reddened with embarrassment at the old story.

"Amazing the things we'll do for money," she said.

"I did it for history," he said.

"Oh, bullshit on that. Say you did it for the money and we'll get along. But I'm too old for stories." And off she went with her ciga-rette dropping ashes in the cocktail sauce.

"I didn't call it 'the Full Wedge' for nothing," said Ridley.

"I could be having lunch with my son, *alone*. Tell me again why you invited me."

"At the game. First, come and meet the famous Pacifist Physi-cist."

That was tweedy old George Wedge Drake, Harvard professor of physics (emeritus), eighty years old and known to everyone as Prof. G. He was with Olga Bassett, retired journalist, in her late seventies, still looking good in slacks and camel-hair blazer.

They had done business with Fallon and seemed genuinely glad to see him.

"We read the Fallon Antiquaria catalog all the time," said Olga.

"Yes," said Prof. G. "Right now we're looking for a book called *Anglorum Praelia*—"

"By Christopher Ocland," said Olga, "printed in 1582."

"Sounds rare," said Peter. "Could be expensive."

"We're very interested," said Prof. G. "And what brings you here, Mr. Fallon? Rare books or football?"

Fallon shifted his eyes to Ridley.

And Ridley said, "Peter's mixing business with pleasure right now. He's networking with you." Ridley guided Peter away from the professor. "Now, let me introduce you to the most important Wedge of all."

As they moved through the crowd, Peter felt the eyes of Will Wedge tracking him . . . like a trout, or a golf ball, or maybe a duck, depending on Wedge's hobbies. Fallon expected to be hooked, clubbed, or shot any second, because Ridley was introducing him to a girl with good Wedge height and firm Wedge features and loud Wedge laugh: Will's daughter, Dorothy.

"Dorothy's a senior," said Ridley. "Her boyfriend is playing today. Halfback."

"He ran rings around Dartmouth last year," she said.

"Dorothy just started her honors thesis," said Ridley.

"It's game day, Uncle Ridley. Let's not talk about work," she said.

And a woman in her forties came ambling over: Dorothy's mother, thought Peter, given the resemblance. She said, "Dorothy, the teams must be on the field by now. Shouldn't you be getting inside?"

"But we're waiting for the lobster," said one of Dorothy's roommates.

"What will Chad Street say if Dorothy isn't there to cheer him in his last Dartmouth game? If he's worrying over her, Harvard might lose. So, girls, get into the stadium, and I'll see that they save some lobster for you at halftime."

Then, Rebecca Wedge introduced herself to Peter and assured him, as she glided back to her guests, that Cousin Ridley would take care of him.

Ridley whispered: "A nice way to say they don't want you talking to Dorothy."

"What about?"

"A term paper. This all began with a term paper."

Harvard Stadium: the first major structure ever built of steel-reinforced concrete, as modern as the electric light when it opened in 1903, yet designed to resemble a Roman arena, with Colosseum-like arches ringing the exterior and a colonnade around the inside, lending an air of classical dignity to the controlled violence on the field below.

Peter and Ridley sat under the colonnade, while Jimmy sat in another section with one of the pretty nieces he'd met.

Ridley took a sip from his flask and gestured toward Jimmy. "Let me reverse myself again. The apple *doesn't* fall far from the tree."

"He's smarter," said Peter. "I just wish I got to spend more time with him."

"It's all we have . . . time." Ridley looked out at the field. "Do you remember the production of *Oedipus Rex* I directed here one spring? Greek drama the way the Greeks had seen it . . . stage in the south end zone . . . amphitheater seating in the stands . . . masks, buskins, actors declaiming without microphones . . . Professor Alfred loved it."

"*Untrained* actors without microphones . . . you couldn't hear a thing."

"So, once in a while"—Ridley took another sip—"ambition exceeds talent. After all, I was the guy who thought Broadway was ready for *King Lear, the Musical.*"

"With a cast of stars from a Fox sitcom?"

"So Lear was only twenty-nine . . . I was going for a younger audience."

Harvard took the kickoff and moved to the Dartmouth forty in three plays.

"I bet you were after a younger girlfriend, too," said Peter.

"My Cordelia . . . That was temporary. So was my financial backing. And once the bank foreclosed on my co-op, which I mortgaged to keep the show up, so was the roof over my head. Now, I'm living in the old family manse in Rockport . . . alone."

A roar went up as Chad Street, boyfriend of Dorothy Wedge, took a handoff on a draw play and ran forty yards to the end zone.

Ridley toasted with his flask, "Fight fiercely, Harvard!"

The band began to play "Yo Ho!"

Fallon took the flask, swallowed, and said, "What about this term paper, and 'something from the antiquity of the Wedge family'? And why are these Wedges so suspicious?"

Ridley looked around at the fans under the colonnade, then whispered, "Dorothy Wedge is an English major, writing her senior thesis on the Puritans."

"Not exactly a fresh topic."

"She started developing it last spring, in a class in early American literature. She wrote a paper about Thomas Shepard, the first minister of Cambridge and one of Harvard's first overseers. He's pretty obscure today. But—"

"She came across something in his writings?"

Ridley slipped the flask from Peter's hand. "References to one of her ancestors, Isaac Wedge, and 'a play.' So she came to me. She thought the cousin who comped her whenever she wanted to see a Broadway show might know something about Puritan theater. Of course, there was no such *thing* as Puritan theater."

"They hated the theater, didn't they?" said Peter.

"Because they knew how seductive it was . . . For a hundred and forty years, if you tried to put on a play in Massachusetts, you were run out of the colony. And in 1767 the Colonial fathers got around to making a law against theater. There was not a legal public performance of a play in Massachusetts until after the Revolution."

On the field, Dartmouth tied the score, and their fans brought out handkerchiefs and waved them at the Harvard side. Another old tradition. Better, thought Peter, than giving the finger.

"So," he asked Ridley, "were you able to help Dorothy?"

"I need an expert opinion. How about reading her paper? Look at her references to Isaac Wedge and 'a play,' read the Shepard diary, too. I'll e-mail it all to you. We can talk over dinner. Tomorrow night."

"You're a pain in the ass, Ridley."

"Why?"

"Because this is one of those Ridley Riddles. You know more than you're saying, but you won't say what you're thinking."

"That's because I never gave an actor a line reading in my life." Ridley capped his flask. "The performances are truer if they discover the truth of the characters themselves."

"I'm no actor."

"'All the world's a stage. And all the men and women merely players.'" Ridley stood. "'They have their exits and their entrances.' And this is my exit. I'm auditioning a young actress in an hour."

"But you're broke, and you have no show."

"She doesn't know that."

Harvard won the game, 20–17, on a last-minute field goal.

Afterward, Peter and his son had dinner at Grafton Street, Peter's favorite Harvard Square haunt, now that the venerable Wursthaus had been closed to make way for yet another chain-store T-shirt outlet. They talked about the game, about the Boston Latin cross-country team, about the Wedges, too.

It was a good evening.

Then Peter drove Jimmy back to the house on the West Roxbury Parkway where the boy lived with his mother and stepfather.

And as always, the conversation dried up as they pulled into the driveway.

Peter didn't mind that he had paid the mortgage on the Colonial with the big lawn. He didn't even mind that another man now lived there. At least the accountant who'd married his ex-wife was no deadbeat. He paid the bills, he'd freed Peter from alimony, and he treated Jimmy well. It was just that Peter had saved some of the hardest things he'd ever said to his son for that driveway, starting with "Jimmy, I'm not coming in tonight. Your mother and I are separating." The boy had been twelve at the time.

Quick exits were now the best, for father and son both, so Jimmy said, "See ya, Dad," as soon as the car stopped.

"We'll go on a campus tour next week," said Peter. "And Jimmy—"

The boy stuck his head back into the car. "Yeah?"

"Remember . . . some guys never get over the fact that they didn't get into Harvard, and some guys never get over the fact that they *did*. I don't want you to be either kind."

Peter Fallon—trustee at local museums, regular at charity events, featured face in a *Boston* magazine article titled "Most Eligible Divorcés in Town." Such a big deal should have had something better to do on a Saturday night. A late party, maybe, or dinner with a model.

But there he was, cruising the Back Bay, looking for nothing more exotic than a parking spot. On weeknights, he could usually find one in four and a half minutes. But on a Saturday night, it might take fifteen.

He'd been looking now for ten, and there'd been a guy on his tail the whole time, as if he was looking for the same spot, as if this was some kind of game, which it was.

Peter lived on Marlborough Street, in the block between Clarendon and Berkeley, so he usually began the hunt on Marlborough, then moved to Arlington. *No spots.*

He noticed his competition when the guy tried to pass him on a turn. But rule number one of Back Bay cruising: never let anyone behind you jump ahead, because he might get a spot that you didn't see. This wasn't too hard, because the other guy was driving an old brown Toyota, and Peter was in his BMW 325i.

The first block of Commonwealth was resident-only parking, but every spot was taken, all the way to Berkeley Street. So Peter gunned the engine, shot up to the corner, then turned right onto Berkeley. The Toyota came around the corner a moment later.

Berkeley usually carried two lanes of traffic, even though it had been laid out in the era of the horse and buggy. Peter cut from the right lane to the left, but he didn't signal, which would have showed weakness. Horns blared, and fingers rose in the Boston salute, but he made a left onto Beacon just as the light turned red, trapping the Toyota.

And . . . success. Peter found a spot. His BMW was slick enough that he was able to snap right in without pulling forward and backing up: a major tactical advantage in the parking wars of Boston.

As the Toyota cruised past, the driver glanced at him, and Peter noticed the yellow and white of a Boston Bruins cap.

"You lose," muttered Peter. He got out and pushed a button on his key ring. The car whooped. System armed.

He glanced up Beacon Street and noticed that the Toyota had found a spot on the next block. But only the passenger was getting out. The guy in the Bruins cap stayed in the car. *Strange.* But strange things happened on Saturday nights in the Back Bay.

Peter scuffled along through the leaves and turned onto Marlborough. That was when he noticed the passenger from the Toyota turning the corner and coming along Berkeley, too, head down, hands in his pockets.

Peter's condo was halfway up the Marlborough Street block. He quickened his pace, reached the stoop and pretended to fumble for his keys.

A streetlamp threw a pool of light onto the sidewalk, so Peter expected he'd get a look at this guy, but all he could see was gray hair, black raincoat, scally cap. Whoever the guy was, he went right past, didn't even glance at Peter Fallon.

Peter watched him walk up to the corner of Clarendon, then turn back toward Beacon. Back to the Toyota? Was this guy casing the house? Or Peter? Most people might wonder a bit and let it go at that. A coincidence.

But not Peter. He lived in the Back Bay and drove a BMW and sold rare and beautiful objects for a living, but he came from a part of town where you never backed down. It had been bred into him. So he moved quickly off the stoop, went along Marlborough, across Clarendon, and onto Beacon. He looked up the block, but the black raincoat was gone and the Toyota was disappearing in the traffic.

So . . . if people were watching Peter, what were they after? A book that he had? It wouldn't be the first time. Or did this have something to do with Ridley and the Wedges? He had the feeling at the football game that he was sticking his nose into something a lot more complicated than it first seemed. And it wouldn't be the first time for that, either.

In his condo, Peter kicked off his shoes and flipped on the radio. "Strictly Sinatra" on Saturday nights. That should relax him. And he had an open bottle of '63 Fonseca port to finish, so he poured a glass and checked his e-mail: *three messages.*

Two came from Ridley with attachments: the term paper and diary. The other came from . . . EvangCarr. He immediately forgot about brown Toyotas and Back Bay stalkers, took a deep breath, and clicked on the little envelope:

Hi, Peter. Good to hear from you the other day. Sorry I wasn't in. I'm in Italy. Doing a piece on Tuscan villas for *Travel Life* while I forget bad divorce.

Divorce? Peter took a swallow of port. That's what it said. *Divorce.* Evangeline Carrington was divorced. Like him. He realized that they hadn't talked in a couple of years. Just enough time for a divorce to unfold, especially if it was messy.

Peter's divorce hadn't been messy. Just sad. His wife had been a legal secretary until their baby was born, a patient and loyal wife until one night he came home late and she threw a plate of cold spaghetti at him because he had been out with other women. It didn't matter that the women were named Austen, Brontë, and Cather, part of a collection of first editions he was building for a client who focused on female novelists. His wife had simply tired of his obsessions and the danger he seemed to attract . . . like those two in the brown Toyota.

So he sipped his port and went back to the e-mail:

Coming to Boston on Tuesday. See you then. By the way, do you remember a classmate named Ridley Wedge Royce?

Tuesday? To see Ridley? Another Ridley Riddle. At least he wouldn't have to wait too long to solve it.

He took another sip of port and opened Dorothy Wedge's term paper. It had a typical term-paper title: "The Confessions and Diary of Thomas Shepard: The Birth of the New England Puritan Literary Style." And a typical term-paper opening:

One of the most important figures in the early history of Harvard College was a minister named Thomas Shepard, born in England, on November 5, 1605. He came to Massachusetts during the Puritan migration and settled in the First Parish of Cambridge. One of the reasons that Harvard College was established in Cambridge was because of his presence.

Shepard's contemporary, Edward Johnson, in *Wonder Working Providence,* describes him as "a poor, weak, pale-complectioned man . . . of humble birth, timid by nature, no great scholar, sweating out every sermon with moans and groans at his own vileness and inadequacy. His natural parts were weak but spent to the full."

There is no record of his words at Harvard's first commencement, but we know that he was there, leading the young men in prayer. . . .

Chapter Five

═══════

1642–1647

ISAAC WEDGE could see that Thomas Shepard's hands were shaking.

Shepard's hands always shook when he preached, so deep was his humility before God. But he could be forgiven his nervousness on that September day, for he had received the honor of invoking the Lord at the first commencement of Harvard College, the first event in the new college hall.

On a platform behind Shepard, wearing their best white bands and doublets, sat Governor Winthrop, the magistrates, the overseers, and college president Henry Dunster. Before him sat the candidates for *Ars Bacheloris*, "ten young men of good hope," as Winthrop called them, who had completed a course in the liberal arts, the three philosophies, and the learned tongues. At the rear of the hall sat those gentlemen fortunate enough to have secured places for perhaps the most significant event yet to occur in the colony of Massachusetts Bay.

Shepard gave thanks to God for bringing them safe to New England, for allowing them to plant a colony, despite the enmity of nature and the evil of heretics, and for sending them Henry Dunster, a Lancashire schoolmaster who had revived their "School of the Prophets" a year after Nathaniel Eaton fled.

Isaac thanked God for Shepard himself, who had taken up Isaac's care, lodged him, and sponsored him as an apprentice to printer Stephen Day.

"Learn to print the Lord's word," Shepard had told him, "and thou shalt have a greater impact than all the preachers yet arrived. Learn to print it, then to preach it, and God will smile upon you twice."

So, in the year that the college had been closed, a year made worse for Isaac by the death of his mother, he had buried his grief in a printer's apprenticeship. He had inked galleys for the Freeman's Oath. He had set type for the *Bay Psalm Book*. And on that day of commencement, he could take pride in the *Quaestiones in Philosophia*, for he had done the whole printing job himself.

The *Quaestiones* were theses, some as ancient as Aristotle, that served to stimulate disputations—in grammar, logic, rhetoric, ethics, physics, and metaphysics—which formed the final act of commencement. Article III on the sheet distributed to the gentlemen entering the hall: *An Anima partitur a corpore? Negat Respondens: Isaacus Wedgius*. "Is the soul part of the body? Arguing the negative: Isaac Wedge."

The prospect of a Latin disputation should have been enough to cause Isaac's own hands to shake, his mouth to turn dry, his stomach to clench. But there was another reason for all that: the specter of Nathaniel Eaton had returned. . . .

That morning, Isaac had gone to the print shop in Crooked Lane to collect the sheets of *Quaestiones*, which he had hung to dry the night before. As usual, he had found Stephen Day, master printer, bent over a box of type.

"So, Isaac," Day had said, squinting up from his work, "commencement at last."

"Indeed, sir."

"Master Dunster be a fine gentleman. We could have done much worse."

"We did . . . at the beginning," Isaac had answered.

"Eaton?"

"Aye . . . You knew him, did you not?"

"Enough to dislike him, though not so much as the Lord disliked him."

The story of God's retribution upon Eaton was well known: After he fled, it was discovered that he had left enormous debts and a college treasury emptied of hard money. So three constables had pursued him to Piscataqua, but by ruse and bluster, he eluded them and fled to Virginia, where he established himself as rector of a small parish. Then he sent for wife and children, but God sent holy punishment in the form of winds that roiled the sea and sank the vessel carrying Eaton's whole family.

"I hear that he's gone back to London," Stephen Day had said, "gone back to find a new wife. Maybe a printer, too, eh?"

"A printer?"

"A printer, aye." Stephen Day had again turned to his galley. "For a play."

"Play?" The word had caused Isaac Wedge to drop the sheet.

"Aye. Before he fled, he asked if I knew a printer in London who would print a play, and what profit he could expect."

"Did he name this play?"

"He spake only what I needed to know and swore me to speak none of it. But . . . since he's gone, the Lord won't mind if I tell you what I told him: there be half a dozen London printers who'd pay ten pounds for a play. I give him a list of them and wished him luck. . . ."

And now, Isaac sat in the new hall, thinking not of his disputation but of the play that had haunted him so long, part of the library that was the legacy of his greatest friend. The play had not been burned, as Eaton had said, but stolen, as Isaac had long suspected.

Nevertheless, Isaac delivered his disputation, withstood the pro forma arguments from the other candidates and the learned gentlemen, and sat to the approbation of the assemblage.

After all the disputations had been completed, President Dunster rose before the candidates and proclaimed, in Latin, "I admit thee to the First Degree in Arts. . . . And I hand thee this book, together with the power to lecture publicly in any one of the arts which thou hast studied, whenever thou shalt have been called to that office."

They recorded their names in Dunster's book, and it was done. Harvard College had made its first graduates.

And whither now, Isaac Wedge? He had been asking himself this question for weeks. Knowledge of the play would make an answer even more difficult to come by.

ii

"And whither *us*, Isaac Wedge?" Katharine Nicholson had been asking this question for months, and still Isaac could not answer to satisfy her. She asked again that night as they strolled Fort Hill, within the grass-covered redoubt that overlooked marsh and river and afforded them a most delicious privacy.

"Had I the money," said Isaac, "I would go to England to study for a master's, as Woodridge intends, or perhaps to Padua, like Harry Saltonstall, to study medicine."

"But you have *not* the money," she said. "So you must stay here. Ask my father for permission to court. Then may we go about more open. And my father will offer you work in the mercantile trade, or perhaps support you as a printer."

"You know that my mind is bent to the ministry, Katharine."

"An honorable life," she said, "but a poor one."

" 'Tis one of the promises I made to Master Harvard."

"There were others?"

"Aye . . . that I would see to his library . . . keep his books together for the future . . ."

She gave him a look that suggested he was mad.

He realized how strange his words must have sounded. So he said, "A man will be known by his books."

"When we marry, we'll keep a room for your books, though I'll need no books to know you." And she stood so close to him that he could smell the sweetness of her skin, so close that, were he not a young man of strong will, he might have reached out and touched the tops of her breasts, offered up by a tight bodice. As it was, he could not keep from kissing her. And she kissed back, but never before had she opened her mouth against his and touched her tongue enticingly to his lips, as if inviting him into her.

But Cambridge was a town founded to deny the darkness, whether it was the darkness of spirit confronted at the meeting-house; or of ignorance confronted at the college; or of night itself, confronted by Diggory Venn, village lamplighter. Each evening, he moved through the town with a cartload of rushes, which he would pile into cressets—tall wrought-iron stands—which then he would light. The tallow-soaked rushes would burn two or three hours, just long enough, as he said, "to light honest men to their homes." And his last stop was atop Fort Hill.

"A pleasant evenin' to you, young'ns," said Diggory. "Hardly noticed you in the shadows, me torch be so bright. Hope you be doin' the Lord's work." He gave them a grin, lit the cresset, and said, "Let me lead thee home."

Isaac looked at Katharine, and she shook her head, as if to say that they had business yet to finish.

But it was incumbent upon all members of a Puritan community to see that sin did not break forth, for any sin—public or private—might bring God's displeasure upon all. So Master Venn went a few paces, then turned and said, "Come along. Evil vapors be risin' off the marsh. 'Tis no night to be abroad."

And they followed, like chastened children, with Venn's torch bobbing and sputtering ahead of them. And Isaac felt a deep coldness radiating from Katharine, as though she expected a profession of love that he could not yet give.

At her garden gate, she turned and looked into his eyes. Her black brows, which by day offered such fine contrast to her pale skin, served only to heighten her anger in the moonlight. "We have known each other near four years, Isaac. 'Tis time to look to a future together."

"And so we shall," he said. But in truth he was not looking further than the next morning and a meeting with President Dunster.

No man who gazed upon the new college hall would ever doubt that the School of the Prophets had a future.

It was the largest structure yet erected in New England, presenting an expanse of clapboard a hundred feet in width and two full stories in height, with a steep sloping roof and a cupola from which one might see the hills of Boston. The back, however, by which door Isaac entered, reflected less austere majesty and far more utility. There were dormered wings at each end and a tower in the middle supporting the cupola. There were privies, woodshed, well, brewhouse, barn, and cow yards on either side. This was to be a college in the best English style, a place for students to live, eat, and learn together, immersed in their studies and in the company of other scholars.

President Dunster met Isaac in the library, directly above the Great Hall, where they had commenced the day before. Dressed in a simple collar and brown doublet, Dunster was a man of no great presence in public or private, yet his eyes did not stray when one spoke to him, and most students understood the message in his gaze: here was a man who listened and cared.

"How do you feel on your first day as *Ars Bacheloris?*" he asked, inviting Isaac to sit at the library table, the finest piece of furniture in the building.

"Inadequate, sir." Isaac looked at the books around him. "I once made it my task to read all four hundred volumes in John Harvard's bequest. I have barely begun."

"The wise man knows that the more knowledge he gains, the more there is to get. So . . . you would now take a master of arts?"

"Under your direction, sir."

"And how would you pay for it?"

"It has been my hope to serve as a tutor, sir."

"I can offer a tutor no more than four pounds a year," said Dunster. "And he cannot marry, for you know well that a tutor is expected to live in chambers."

"Yes, sir."

"So"—Dunster ran his hands over the tabletop—"if the temptations of the flesh that bring you to Fort Hill are too great . . ."

Isaac tried to hide his surprise, but his was not a face made for subtlety.

Dunster gave a gentle laugh. "'Tis a small place, this Cambridge, but I have a proposal that will take you far from here, all the way to the largest city on earth."

"London?" This was more than Isaac could have hoped for.

He had lain awake all the night before, tossing right and left. When he lay on his right, his mind had filled with images of Katharine, angry in the moonlight. When he rolled left, he had heard the voice of John Harvard, charging Isaac to keep his books . . . including one stolen by Nathaniel Eaton. And here was Dunster, offering Isaac the chance to consider Katharine and her moods at leisure while voyaging to the city where Eaton had fled.

Dunster slid a copy of the *Quaestiones* across the table. "This is to be delivered to Thomas Weld. He went over last year to raise funds for us. He has written a pamphlet called *New England's First Fruits* to describe our work. He would print the *Quaestiones* with the pamphlet, to prove that we've graduated a class and are holding to our purpose. Would you care to deliver your handiwork?"

"Gladly, sir. But might it not be carried as a dispatch?"

"They've asked that we send over a student, too. A certain Lady Mowlson of London is considering a contribution. 'Twould produce an annual stipend for 'some poor scholar,' as she puts it. Weld believes that seeing a poor scholar—poor in purse, but rich in learning—will inspire her generosity."

Though Isaac believed in the beneficence of Henry Dunster, he was not naive. To make such a journey, there had to be some gain. He sought a polite way to word it, could find none, and so said, "May I count on a position as a tutor here when I return?"

"If Lady Mowlson offers a sum, I shall argue that you deserve the first stipend."

"Then I go gladly."

"But what of Mistress Nicholson? Do you love her?"

"I believe so, sir."

"You believe so? And what do you believe she will say to all this?"

"I believe she will be happy for me."

That evening, Isaac took a copy of the *Quaestiones*, rolled it, tied it with a strip of colored fabric, and went to the home of the Nicholsons. A small gift might smooth the way for his bad news . . . if not with Katharine, at least with her father.

Charles Nicholson answered the door. He was a big man with fleshy features that always brightened at the appearance of Isaac, who had grown into a tall, square-jawed young man of the sort that any father would be proud to call a son-in-law. "Congratulations, my boy. A graduate at last. Would that my Jamie had stayed till Dunster arrived. But he preferred to learn the family business in Boston."

"I brought a remembrance of commencement, sir." Isaac offered him the *Quaestiones*.

Nicholson unrolled the paper, studied it, and announced, "History is writ here, son. A hundred years hence, men will look to this and feel the spirit of their ancestors."

"Printed by my own hand," said Isaac proudly.

"And a fine job you've made of it, too." With great ceremony, Nicholson took the *Quaestiones* to his Bible, a large and magnificent volume in a gilt-edged leather binding, opened it to the back, and slid the sheet into the endpapers. "This will I keep in my safest place, next to the oath I swore when I became a freeman of the colony."

"A sacred place, sir."

"Now, then, what can I do for you?"

"I've come, sir, hoping for permission to court your daughter . . . formally."

The request was met with a shout, a warm embrace, and a promise of employment as soon as the date was set.

The shout brought Mother Nicholson and Katharine rushing from the next room, and a scene of great joy began, only to end abruptly when Isaac extricated himself from Master Nicholson's grasp and said, "Thank you, sir, but it would be premature to set a date, as I've been engaged by President Dunster to go to London—"

"London!" cried Katharine, and she stalked out, with her mother following in her wake.

After a moment, Nicholson said, "Saw that sight myself, once, some twenty-five years ago. My wife wanted marriage and I wanted a business. 'Tis like livin' my own life over to see them go runnin' off like that."

"I'm . . . I'm sorry, sir."

Nicholson pointed a finger at Isaac. "Play not with my daughter's affections, boy, or I'll have you in the stocks. But remember that women are creatures who see only the ground in front of them. We men must keep our eyes on the horizon. Now then, we shall call her back, and you can tell her your reasons for goin' so far."

After some coaxing, Katharine returned. And while her parents took a stroll in the September night, she and Isaac had their talk.

"You cannot love me too well," said Katharine, "that you would prefer to be message carrier for the college than my husband."

"Katharine . . . were it only for the carrying of a message, I would stay and marry you and make a dozen children—"

"A dozen? I'm no brood mare, Isaac."

"Then a half dozen."

"You think me incapable of mothering a large family, then?"

"No, my dear." He thought to tell her that she was incapable only of listening to logic, but he would not venture into such places.

She said, "Simply tell me why you are leaving me to go to London when my father has offered you a position."

"For the stipend. And . . . other reasons."

She furrowed her brow. "What other reasons?"

"To fulfill my promise to John Harvard." He paused, hoping he had said enough.

She looked at him, her brows a single hard line across her forehead.

So he said, "I must bring back a book that Eaton carried off."

"A book? What book? What book could be so important?"

"'Tisn't the book but the promise. The book be mere trifle. But as I told you, a . . . a man will be known by his books."

"A man will be known by his trifles, you mean. You go to London to pursue a trifle. A book of poems? Love sonnets, perhaps? If so, be sure to read them. For you have need of tutoring in the ways of love. . . . Now, what is the book?"

He might have dissembled, but he decided on the truth, in hopes of drawing her into his pursuit. "I'll tell you, if you agree to keep it secret."

"If you do *not* tell me, I shall agree never to speak to you again. And if you go, you'll be gone months, and John Howell makes warm eyes at me every Sabbath."

So Isaac took a deep breath and said, "The book is a play."

"A play!" she cried. "What kind of play? A modern play?"

And he decided that he had told enough truth. Mention of Shakespeare would only bring more anger from a good Puritan girl. So he told her it was by Aeschylus, to serve in teaching students their Greek. "The title," he said, "is not important."

"And by the look of things," she answered, "neither am I."

All summer, Isaac had been preparing for membership in the Cambridge church. Sabbath attendance was required of all, but to join the church as a full member, one had to study Reverend Shepard's Theology of Conversion, learn all the steps from Election to Illumination of the Spirit, appear before the elders, then confess conversion before the congregation. With a long voyage ahead, Isaac wished to take the final step, and Reverend Shepard agreed, despite Isaac's youth.

So, on the Sabbath before his leaving, Isaac walked through a heavy rain, down Water Street to the meetinghouse, all the while rehearsing his confession.

At the appropriate moment, he was summoned to stand before the congregation. With the sound of the rain and the smell of wet wool so strong that they seemed to bear weight, he looked out on the familiar faces of his world—Reverend Shepard, President Dunster, Diggory Venn and Samuel Day, Master Nicholson and his wife, and finally, Katharine, her expression set hard in a gray mortar of disappointment.

"As I go to England," he began, "I will carry the Lord with me. He is my strength and my shield. But I confess that it was not always thus, for the Lord saw fit to cast my father into the deep, and I didst cry out with all the despair of Job, all the anger of one who sees not the Lord's grander designs but only his earthly outcomes."

All were listening closely, and Reverend Shepard was writing furiously, for he copied down the words of every confession.

"My anger remained until my mother and I reached these shores, like the Jews of Exodus. And then, when my soul didst sink to its lowest ebb, the Lord held forth testimony of His love in the person of John Harvard, who showed me that God's ways are not always to be understood but are always to be accepted. Now my chiefest desire is that I may live to honor Him." His speech, which continued in this vein for some time more, brought murmuring approval and nodding heads, and he sat, confident of his acceptance.

"Thank you, Isaac," said Reverend Shepard. "We beseech the Lord's blessing as you sail to serve our School of the Prophets. Now then, my brethren, Isaac Wedge has been propounded to you, desiring to enter church fellowship. If any of you know anything against him, why he may not be admitted, you may speak."

For a few moments, the drumming of the rain on the roof was the only sound. Then, the slender figure of Katharine Nicholson rose. "I would speak, Reverend."

"The daughter of Master Nicholson has not yet confessed herself," said Shepard, "but as her father has been admitted to membership, we shall exempt her."

Isaac sat on his hands so that no one would see them shaking. He could not know what she was about to say, for she had not spoken to him in a week. But the look that she shot at him made plain her intention to skewer him like a leg of lamb.

She began softly, her eyes cast downward in deference to those before her. "I am a servant of the Lord Jesus Christ. He is my strength and my protection. That I would be subject, without Him, to the most wicked of impulses is a truth I freely admit. Indeed, I might have submitted already to the temptations offered by a certain young man."

Isaac felt a change in the room, sidelong glances, eyes shifting in his direction.

"And worst of all," said Katharine, her voice rising, "I might have been inspired to read what this young man promises to bring back from England. A play!"

"A play!" came the cry from the back of the room.

"Blasphemy!" cried someone else. "The work of the devil."

And suddenly, all eyes were boring holes into Isaac, and the sharpest bit of all was in the gaze of Master Nicholson himself.

"Aye," said Katharine, "'tis a play he says belonged to John Harvard."

And Master Nicholson growled, "A modern play, or so my daughter fears."

Samuel Day whispered to Isaac, "Blasphemy be the word for this, lad. Plays be blasphemy for certain. Best explain yourself."

So Isaac leapt to his feet, and if he had not committed blasphemy yet, he committed it now, for he lied to the congregation as he had to Katharine, telling them that he sought to bring back books to enrich the college library, and among them would be a play by the Greek Aeschylus, to help students learn one of the classical languages.

That night, Shepard transcribed Isaac's confession, as he did all of them, because he believed that each person's journey to the Lord might provide instruction for those who came after. He also set down notes on the words of Katharine Nicholson, which Isaac had answered to the reverend's satisfaction but which had led the congregation to defer his acceptance until his return from England.

Shepard then recorded his observations on the parting of Isaac and Katharine outside the meetinghouse: "She spake harshly to him, that he had thrown over her love, and that should he return with all the books ever printed in London, he should not get her back. He pleaded that this journey would firm his future and hers, too, if only she would wait. Her answer was to turn and walk off into the rain. Then did Isaac spy me and say, 'Reverend, should I bring back any book offensive to you, it shall be yours to destroy.'"

iii

Civil war had erupted in England by the time Isaac arrived. Suffice it to say that the Puritans stood on one side, the High Churchmen on the other, and the clash of politics was as significant as the clash of theologies, for Parliament was mostly Puritan and Anglicans supported the king.

London was a Puritan city and Parliamentarian stronghold, and in late October of 1642, a defense force was forming to resist the royal army. The beginning of a war may be a time of great excitement for a young man in search of adventure, but Isaac Wedge was not tempted to join his Puritan brethren. As Thomas Weld, college emissary, reminded him, "You've come here for one purpose—to serve your college by impressing an old woman."

The next day, Weld presented Isaac at the home of Anne Radcliffe, Lady Mowlson, in the parish of St. Christopher's. It was a large house, as befitted the lady's late husband, once lord mayor of London. A large house for a small woman, thought Isaac, a small and slumped woman of sixty-two, toothless and wizened, her face squeezed into a wimple, gray hairs growing at the corners of her mouth, yet a woman who seemed in command of all around her, even the sunlight that fell obediently across the table where she sat.

"So this be one of the poor scholars," she said, looking hard at Isaac Wedge.

"Yes, my lady," said Weld.

"Has the boy a tongue?" she snapped.

"Yes, my lady," said Weld, and he glanced at Isaac.

"A poor scholar," said Isaac, "come across an ocean to meet you, and to bring you this." Isaac handed her a copy of the *Quaestiones*, wrapped in a red silk ribbon. "To show you that our first class has been properly raised up and sent out into the world."

She read a few of the *Quaestiones* and said, "So . . . is the soul part of the body, *Isaacus Wedgius?*"

"I believed that it is, my lady, whilst we live. But the afterlife does not await in the grave. 'Tis in a place that the Lord predestines. Whilst our corporeal being corrupts, our essential soul must seek that other place."

She gave a grunt, as if he had given the right answer and it did not matter a great deal to her. Then she took the *Quaestiones* over to the window. "I did not know there was a printing press in New England. Or any printer who could set type so well."

"You appreciate good printing, my lady?" asked Isaac.

"I am an old woman with failing eyes. When I see a well-printed sheet, one I that may read with ease, I know that God still loves me."

"Then you will be pleased to know," said Weld, "that it was Isaac himself who printed the sheet."

And the rheumy eyes of Lady Mowlson brightened. "Did he? Did he indeed? A printer, then, as well as a scholar. Now I be impressed."

After that, Lady Mowlson received Isaac every day for a week. She questioned him about his world, about his college, about his hopes and his love, which he found growing dimmer the farther he traveled.

And after their talks, which always concluded with a leg of mutton or a piece of beef, Isaac would take to the streets and follow the list of printers given him by Stephen Day. The streets were not unfamiliar, as he had lived in London until the age of fourteen. And while he had tried to forget the crowds, the rats, and the filth, he had not forgotten his way or the swagger he needed when visiting the city's less savory parts. It was in one such, at the shop of G. Snitterfield and Son, that he found his answers.

"Nathaniel Eaton?" said the skinny Mr. Snitterfield. "He come by some six months past. Remembered him, for I knew his father. A fine honest preacher, his father. Begat himself somethin' less of a son, though."

"Did Master Eaton come to you with anything to print?" Isaac spoke over the familiar sounds of creaking presses and shuffling papers.

"Aye. A play," said Snitterfield. "I did say to him, 'What manner of Puritan son are you that you'd wish to print a play? 'Twould please no one but the bishops, who ban decent works and let such filth as plays be spread about.'"

"Do you recollect the title of the play, sir?"

"Aye. *Love's Labours Won.* Nothin' for decent folk, which be what I told him."

Isaac swallowed his excitement. "What did Master Eaton do, sir, after you chided him?"

"He said he'd find another printer." Snitterfield shook his head.

" 'Twas a true disappointment to see how deep the son of Richard Eaton had sunk."

"Did he take the play to another printer, then?"

"Aye," said Snitterfield. "John Barney, who told me he offered ten pounds for it, a fair price. Eaton said he had as lief throw it in the Thames as give it over for so little."

"Why look you so miserable?" asked Lady Mowlson the next morning. "You cloud my goodwill on the day I give your college one hundred pounds."

"Many thanks," said Isaac. "Reverend Weld will be most pleased."

"So"—she sat back and studied him—"a cheery demeanor should be upon you. Yet you look as if you've heard news of another plague."

"I'm sorry, ma'am."

"One of my servants saw you enter Snitterfield's yesterday. I think that you have come to London with more than one purpose, boy."

"Yes, ma'am." And he decided to tell her the truth, for he now felt that he was in the presence of a loving aunt. "I have spake to you about John Harvard and Nathaniel Eaton."

"So you have."

"Well . . . Eaton absconded with one of the books in Harvard's bequest."

"And you come all this way to retrieve it?"

"Yes, ma'am."

She studied him a moment and asked, "And how will you do such a thing?"

"I know not. London be so big." He put his head in his hands. " 'Tis a fool who thinks he can find a needle of flesh and blood in such a haystack. But I made a promise to John Harvard on his deathbed, and—"

She patted his arm. "Worry not, lad. I be widow of a man who was lord mayor of London, daughter of one who was sheriff. I still have my friends and my ways. I shall find the whereabouts of Master Eaton for you." And she did.

iv

A month later, Isaac Wedge arrived in the Italian city of Padua, where the November sun still burnished the red tile roofs and warmed the wide piazzas and sent bright slanting rays under the arches of the majestic palazzos.

Isaac was properly awestruck.

How feeble seemed the efforts of New England's Puritans at their fledgling Harvard College when he saw the grandeur of the University of Padua, which had stood for four centuries. And if the church of Rome was as corrupt as Isaac had been told, how had God allowed it to produce such beauty as could be seen here, in the Duomo, in the Basilica di Sant'Antonio, in the beautiful statues and frescoes? This was a question to lay alongside another that vexed him: If plays were evil, why had God given Shakespeare such talent? But better Protestant minds than Isaac's had found the answers, so he turned to the business of finding Eaton and fulfilling his promise.

Even if his *Ars Bacheloris* came from a tiny school on the edge of the wilderness, it gave Isaac confidence in his resourcefulness. He took a bed in a small inn, purchased a peddler's apron and a hat with a floppy brim, and placed himself outside the gate of the university medical school, one of the most famous in all Christendom.

He did not have to wait long, though at first he did not recognize Eaton, who had shaved his beard and put on the robe of a medical student. Isaac's old tormentor was studying to be a doctor, as if he had not yet inflicted enough pain. But nothing could hide the arrogance of Eaton's barrel-chested swagger, and when Isaac saw it rolling through the gate, he knew that Lady Mowlson's information had been accurate.

So Isaac hunched himself up, let several people and two donkey carts move between himself and Eaton, and followed his old schoolmaster.

After a dozen twists and turns among the narrow streets, Eaton went into a doorway. A moment later, second-story windows swung open and Eaton reappeared, rubbing his belly and surveying the little square below. A beautiful Italian woman appeared in the window and handed him a glass of wine. He said something that caused her to giggle and give him a playful slap, which he answered with a louder slap on her bottom. If he grieved for his lost family, thought Isaac, he hid his pain well.

Isaac found a spot in an entryway across the square, from which he could see more directly into Eaton's front room—the chairs, the tables, the tapestries on the wall, and, yes, the bookcase. For a week or more, he studied the movements of Eaton and his Italian paramour, and he made his plan.

Though he had grown heavier and stronger since last he had been struck by Nathaniel Eaton, Isaac planned to avoid confrontation. Indeed, he planned to avoid exposing himself to Eaton at all. The revenge he sought would be quieter and, in its way, sweeter. If the Lord looked upon revenge as a sin, Isaac would repent of it later.

On a bright Friday morning, after Eaton had bustled off, Isaac presented himself at the door of Eaton's lodging, wearing his brown doublet, his plain collar, and his own simple hat.

The young woman who answered wore no more than a shift, which barely covered the outline of her breasts and other parts, and she conveyed a beauty so sensuous and earthy that he nearly forgot his plan. But he managed to stammer, "*Buongiorno.*"

She pulled a robe around herself and studied him suspiciously.

He said, "*Scusi. No parlo italiano. Parla inglese?*"

"*Si* . . . yes . . . little bit."

"My name is Stephen Day"—Isaac used a name that Eaton might have mentioned in a good light—"I am a friend of Master Eaton's, from America."

"He no here. He back soon." She started to close the door.

"*Scusi* . . . I have nowhere to stay, *signora*, and Master Eaton is a fine friend. I come with a business proposition. May I wait for him?"

She looked him up and down and, with some reluctance, admitted him into the front room. In the morning light, the white

walls were glaring bright, though softened by the tapestries, one depicting Madonna and child, the other Christ's bloody crucifixion.

"You wait." She left him standing alone and went downstairs.

From the window, Isaac watched her give a coin to a boy, who
went running off. Then Isaac turned to the bookcase and his eyes
fell upon the red morocco binding, which stood out between two
anatomy books like a silk scarf in the folds of a brown cape.

Her footfalls were rising again, so Isaac pulled the book from the
case and flipped quickly through it. A glance at the handwriting was
all that he needed. *Love's Labours Won*. In an instant, he exchanged the Shakespeare for another book in a similar binding that
he carried in his satchel, and it was done.

"He back soon," she said, stepping into the room. "You wait
here."

As soon as she went to put on more decent clothing, he would
slip out, leaving a small surprise for Nathaniel Eaton. Of course, in
that she had just gone into the street dressed as she was, she might
consider herself to be as decent as need be.

Indeed, she now grew warmer, showed him to the seat by the
window, and offered him a glass of wine, which he had no choice
but to accept. As he brought the glass to his lips, there came a knock
on the door, a knock preceded by not a single footfall.

Isaac almost gagged on the wine. Before the door had opened, he
was gauging the distance to the street below. Could he leap without
breaking a leg?

But it was not Eaton who entered. It was his English friend from
across the hall, Robert Danby, whose movements Isaac had also
tracked, though not as well.

"Good morning, Francesca, and"—Danby's eyes fell upon Isaac—
"to you, sir."

Isaac gauged that he was a head taller than the slender gentleman with the fine-razored beard. But Mr. Danby carried a rapier at
his belt and looked to be the kind who could use it. Isaac had only
a dagger, never drawn in anger.

Francesca, in her broken English, introduced Stephen Day,
from America.

"Master Eaton speaks no good of anyone in America," said Danby suspiciously.

"Ah . . . but a man as well liked as Nathaniel—"

"Well liked?" Danby laughed. "Do we speak of the same man?"

Then came the sound of heavy footfalls in the stairway. Someone was taking the steps two at a time, and a familiar voice was bellowing, "Stephen Day! In Italy? Stephen Day, the printer . . ."—and the door was swinging open—"Stephen . . . you . . . *You!*"

"This no Stephen Day?" asked Francesca.

"What are you doing here?" demanded Eaton.

"Fulfilling a promise," answered Isaac.

All at once, Danby went for his rapier, Eaton went for Isaac, and Isaac went for a tapestry suspended from a molding. With a snap of his hand, Isaac tore the tapestry loose and brought it down onto Eaton and the others. Then he threw himself into the jumble of bodies, sending Eaton's bulk into the other two, so that all three landed on the floor, tangled in the fabric of tapestry and academic gown.

Then Isaac was out the door, slamming it behind him and jamming a wooden chair under the latch. He flew down the stairs and into the square. He turned down an alley and ran. He came to a street and ran. When he reached the broad Piazza dei Signori, he stopped running. Here, he knew, it would be best to flow through the little rivulets and eddies of humanity that filled the square each day.

Soon enough, he rode a stream of people into the Piazza delle Erbe. He retrieved his peasant hat and apron from behind an archway pediment where he had hidden them. He put on the hat, tied on the apron, and gave a glance over his shoulder as Eaton appeared beneath an archway on the far side and scanned the square. So Isaac turned down another alley and ran. But he knew exactly where he was going . . . to church.

The first time that he entered the Basilica di Sant'Antonio, he had expected his Protestant God to strike him dead. Now, he was bold enough that he dipped his finger in the font of holy water and blessed himself, so as not to attract attention. He moved through the nave, genuflected before the main altar and Donatello's mighty statues of the Crucifixion and the Virgin, then moved into the north transept, and knelt before the tomb of Saint Anthony.

Gifts of food and offerings of money were scattered around the altar in a small demonstration of Romanist superstition. On either side of the transept, priests sat in small wooden boxes, and penitents slipped into the boxes to confess their sins, in what Puritans considered a much larger demonstration of Romanist weakness.

Of all the places that one Puritan might find another, a Catholic church seemed the least likely. But it should not have surprised Isaac that a Puritan as profane as Nathaniel Eaton would have no fear of the Holy Host or graven images. Isaac almost felt the wind as Eaton swept through the great nave and stopped at the place where he could look into both transepts. But fate favored Isaac, for Eaton looked first into the south transept. When he looked to the north, Isaac was gone.

From within one of the wooden boxes, Isaac watched Eaton, safe for the moment, until . . . *in nomine patri, et filii, et spiritu sancti* . . . a little wooden shutter slid open.

Isaac swallowed hard and looked into the eyes of a priest, a benighted servant to the Papist Whore of Rome, or so good Puritans were taught.

"*Si?*" The priest seemed a kindly little man wearing a purple vestment around his neck. "*Si? Tua confessione?*"

"*Scusi, Padre. No parlo italiano.*" Isaac's eyes shifted, and through the space in the confessional curtain, he saw Eaton, red-faced and sweating, standing before Saint Anthony's tomb.

"*Inglese?*" The priest was peering out at Eaton, too.

"*Si,*" said Isaac, and then he said, "*Parla latino?*"

In Latin the priest said, "I am a man of God. All men of God know Latin."

So Isaac said, "I need the protection of your sanctuary."

"From the big one? Who looks like an Inglese?"

Isaac shifted his eyes again. Eaton was peering into the faces of those who were kneeling at the altar rail and bringing gifts. Isaac wondered if he should jump up and run or fly straight at Eaton. But before he could decide, the priest pushed aside his curtain and delivered a torrent of angry Italian, of which Isaac understood only *"Inglese"* and *"Protestant."*

Seldom a man to retreat, Eaton fell back before the priest's anger and, with his academic robe fluttering behind, scurried out.

The priest stepped back into the confessional and chuckled.

"What did you say?" asked Isaac.

"I told him a foul sinner had come to confess, and the sight of an English Protestant was like the sight of the devil. I told him to go, or I would put a curse on him."

"A curse?"

"Is that not what English Protestants believe, that we are witches who curse men rather than priests who free them of the curses they bring upon themselves?"

Isaac had no answer for that.

So the priest said, "Even the English know the Lord's Prayer. Say it with me. And when we are done, it will be safe to go. *Pater noster, qui est in caelis . . .*"

Isaac did not take the road back to Venice, as he had told his innkeeper he would, for it was likely that Eaton would visit every inn in Padua and offer bribes for information. Instead, Isaac pulled his hat over his face and fell in with a group of peasants leaving at dusk through the north gate.

By midnight, he was ten miles into the countryside, following a road toward the North Star. By dawn, he could see the mountains. And it occurred to him that if he kept walking, he could reach them. So he did, for he had decided that a young man should see as much of God's world and meet as many of God's people as he could.

He was warmed, on his way, by the expression that would form on Eaton's face when he opened the book that Isaac had left in Shakespeare's place: *A Chronicle of Beatings, September 1638– August 1639.* Isaac had written the names of every student caned by Eaton, and at the end, "'A man will be known by his books.' — John Harvard."

V

Harvard College was a poor school in a poor place, despite the contributions of benefactors such as Lady Mowlson. There was only one source of steady support: the United Colonies of New England had agreed that every town would be called upon to contribute some measure of grain, which came to be known as the College Corn.

Though the levy was voluntary and contributions at first were generous, some saw the College Corn as a tax, and in time they resented it, especially since so many young men educated at the college would, at the first opportunity, leave New England. In the taverns and around the meetinghouses, men complained that those who should have been ministering in frontier villages were on the far side of the Atlantic, earning degrees, pursuing fortunes, building reputations.

Often they talked of a graduate who had gone abroad at the behest of President Dunster to solicit Lady Mowlson and had then disappeared. They did not know that this graduate had wandered Europe, absorbing as much as he could of the wondrous works of man and God, then returned to England and joined the parliamentary army just before the battle of Naseby.

Nor would they have known that he timed his return to Massachusetts for June 9, 1647, the day of the Great Indian Convocation. He followed a familiar route down the Charlestown Road, and though there were several groups of gentlemen moving along— some mounted, some on foot, some brightly dressed, some in black doublets and white bands—he kept to himself. He felt their gaze but had no fear that they would recognize him, for his size, his trimmed beard, and his sword gave him a presence in no way reminiscent of the "poor scholar" who had left for England years before.

Isaac had chosen that day to come home because the appearance of a stranger in the Yard would not be unusual. What could be more unusual than hundreds of feathered Indians gathering to hear Reverend John Eliot preach to them?

A pulpit stood on the steps of the college hall, the Indians were gathering around it, and hundreds of curious Cambridge ladies and gentlemen had come to observe. For the colony, it was a day to celebrate a victory of Christ over heathen darkness. For Isaac, it was a day to celebrate more quietly the fulfillment of his promise to John Harvard.

As Reverend Eliot stepped to the pulpit, Isaac edged his way around the crowd, then made for one of the privies behind the building. He spent a few minutes there, with the flies buzzing about his head, until he was certain that anyone watching him would have lost interest. Then he slipped out and went into the college.

The building was deserted. So he mounted the stairs to the library, where his adventure had begun with Henry Dunster almost five years before. How much he had seen since then, how wide his world had become, and yet how comforting it was to be home, to move again through those familiar halls. And how easy it was to let himself into the library with the key he had kept from the days when he cataloged books.

In his doublet, he carried a quarto bound now in brown leather. On the flyleaf he had inscribed the words of John Harvard: "A man will be known by his books." This volume he intended to slip into the place where a book on entomology would have been found, had John Harvard ever had such a book. Its title would be *Corporei Insectii,* or *The Bodies of Insects.* He would write it into the catalog, and since he had entered many books there, his careful handwriting would not stand out. It would all take just a few moments.

But a woman's voice echoed from the hallway. "Good afternoon, Isaac."

His hand was in his doublet, the book in his hand. Keeping them there, he turned slowly. "Why . . . Katharine, I did not see you outside. I did not hear you come up."

"And I did not recognize you until my cousin Rebecca did ask me, 'Who is that handsome man with the black beard?'" Katharine took a tentative step into the library. "I did not know that you had come back."

"I arrived only last night." He casually removed his hand from his doublet.

"It's been said that you sent a trunk of books to President Dunster from England. Are you here to see them?"

"It seems they have not been cataloged. I . . . I hear you have a family."

"Yes," she said. "A faithful husband and happy children."

Then there was silence between them, made all the heavier by the echo of Reverend Eliot's voice, proclaiming the gospel in the Algonkian language outside.

Finally, she said, "A year, Isaac, a whole year did I wait. Where did you go?"

"To more places than you could have imagined. I saw the world."

"You could have seen my soul." Katharine spoke with neither bitterness nor regret. Women with faithful husbands and happy children were seldom bitter or regretful. She spoke instead as if to inspire regret, to remind Isaac that her soul and her happy children could have been his, but for his bad judgment.

Isaac had seen French plays and Italian frescoes and fought on English battlefields. He had known women, from the Italian widow who first showed him fleshly pleasure to noble English ladies to skillful Southwark whores. But looking at her now, he could not deny his regret at what he had left behind.

"All for a book," she said, twisting her words like a knife, "a play."

And it was as if her twisting drained his wound rather than deepened it. Regret passed, and he said, "You'll find no plays among my books, but for the Aeschylus I promised."

"I shall be sure to look the books over," she said, "once they are cataloged."

And the distrust in her words made two things clear: There had never been enough between them to regret, and the play should remain hidden until her suspicions faded. So he changed the subject. "I would like to meet your family."

"I hope"—another woman appeared in the doorway—"she would start by introducing her cousin." And into the library stepped Rebecca Watson, as beautiful as Katharine, though with strawberry-colored hair rather than raven.

"Rebecca has come from the village of Natick," explained Katharine, "where her father preaches to the Indians."

"We do the Lord's work," added Rebecca. "It is said that you, too, have done the Lord's work . . . in England. I have always hoped to visit England again."

"I shall tell you about it," said Isaac, warmed by her smile. And with the book secure in his doublet, he led the ladies out and closed the library door.

That night, Thomas Shepard wrote in his diary:

Isaac Wedge has returned, several years after Lady Mowlson's money arrived in our coffers. He revealed himself following the Indian confluence. Word of his presence spread quickly, and men who wished news of England gathered round him. The news was hopeful. Our Puritan brethren are on the rise, the king and his bishopric are brought low, and England is a godly place once more.

There followed a comment from President Dunster that must needs be included here as to end a story that began near five years ago. Dunster thanked Isaac for the trunk of books that had been delivered to the college, a collection showing Isaac's good taste and Puritan spirit. And from Master Nicholson, father of Katharine Howell, came this question: "Were there a play in the trunk?" "Yes," said Dunster. " 'Twas a play in classical Greek, by Aeschylus." And so endeth the old controversy.

I invited Isaac to remain in the parish. But he said that he is drawn to wilder places. He said that he might preach, as he promised his father and Master Harvard. Christianizing the Indians seems a task of importance to him. I warned him that most Indians have the eyes of Satan. He said that he had looked into the eyes of Papists, so he fears no Satan amongst the Indians. Methinks he may also have designs on the daughter of one who preaches to the Indians. Tomorrow, he says he will follow the river inland.

Chapter Six

================

So, DID Isaac Wedge bring back a "modern" play?

Stroke.

And did he have it with him when he followed this river inland, as Reverend Shepard said?

Inhale on the stroke. Exhale on the backstroke.

Shepard also said that the play Isaac Wedge brought back was by Aeschylus.

Stroke. Stroke.

And no seventeenth-century printing of Aeschylus is worth that much.

Pump the legs. The strength is in the legs. The legs are always the first to go.

So why does Ridley Royce think this play is worth a lot of money?

Keep the back straight and stroke. Keep the oars straight and stroke.

Ridley knows more. He has to know more.

Think about the stroke and not about Ridley. When you think about the stroke, everything else straightens itself out, if not in your life, at least in your mind . . . like the guy in the black raincoat . . . or Evangeline Carrington . . . or the Wedges, past and present . . .

Including the Wedge driving a Boston Whaler upriver and shouting, "Ahoy, there!"

"Nobody's said 'Ahoy, there' to me since I was a little boy in a sailor suit." Peter Fallon pulled his scull under the north arch of the Weeks footbridge, which crossed the Charles between Dunster House and the Harvard Business School.

"I keep a boat down at the . . ." Wedge drove under the south arch and was still talking when he came out the other side, his voice all but lost in the echo of the engine. ". . . cousin said you were a rower, and I could find you every Sunday on the river."

"You've found me. You've interrupted me. Come too close, you'll swamp me."

"We need to talk."

Fallon shipped oars. "What's so important that you'd come out here to find me?"

"I'm worried about my delusional cousin. He thinks he's found something in one of my daughter's term papers."

"Really?" said Peter. "What?"

"I think you know. I think Ridley has shown you her paper."

"He's shown me some interesting stuff from Thomas Shepard, too."

"About a play?"

"Your daughter has written about it. Read her term paper."

Wedge gave his boat a touch of gas to keep it close. "Can I buy you brunch?"

"Not today. I'm rowing. Then I'm due at my brother's."

Wedge studied Fallon for a moment, and his voice lost all its clubby jocularity. "My daughter is graduating and going to law school. I don't want some failed Broadway producer distracting her . . . or some treasure-hunting antiquarian."

"I don't intend to distract anyone . . . except myself . . . maybe."

"Good." Wedge plastered a smile back onto his face. "By the way . . . I'm chairman of the Committee for the Happy Observance of Commencement. Would you be interested in serving as a marshal this year?"

Fallon almost laughed out loud. Was Wedge really trying to buy him off with a little Harvard honorific? "You mean, I get to put on a top hat and morning coat and tell everybody where to go next June?"

"It's a pleasant day . . . and a free lunch."

"We'll talk later. I have to keep moving. Don't want to tighten up." Fallon pulled at his oars and shot upstream.

Stroke. They would talk again. *Stroke.* But Fallon would let Will Wedge stew a bit. *Stroke.* And when they talked, Fallon would ask the questions, not the other way round. *Stroke.* Meanwhile, he'd do a little more thinking. *Stroke. Stroke. Stroke.*

Fallon Salvage and Restoration: an air compressor and a couple of trucks parked inside a fence on Dorchester Avenue in South Boston, an old warehouse, an overhead door opened to the afternoon sunshine, and inside, a thousand square feet of . . . stuff.

Peter Fallon did his weekday business in the Back Bay, but he had persuaded his brother that even a contractor could make money from history. So the Fallons bid on demolition jobs, rehabs, and restorations, and when they stripped an old building, they sold whatever they salvaged at the warehouse.

Business was always slow during leaf-peeping season. Just a few suburbanites scavenging around, and Peter's nephew, Bobby, waiting on them. Peter went across the floor—past the crates of old plumbing fixtures, the stacks of French doors, the collection of claw-footed tubs and pedestal sinks—to the glassed-in office at the back.

And he smelled pizza. It reminded him of his father, who used to watch the Patriots in the office, because Mom couldn't stand grown men swearing in her living room on a Sunday afternoon. Big Jim Fallon had been gone three years now, and Peter still missed him. But the smell of pizza and the sound of the game had a comforting familiarity. And now that Peter's brother, Danny, had grown a paunch and grayed around the ears, he even looked like their father.

"What's the score?" Peter asked.

"Three to nothin'," answered Danny. "Defense doin' the job. Offense doin' shit."

"And as we all know," said the gray-haired gentleman eating pizza with a knife and fork, "the best defense is a good offense."

"Hello, Orson," said Peter. "What brings you to South Boston?"

"I missed the chamber music concert at the Gardner Museum."

"He came to complain." Danny Fallon took a gulp of beer. "As always."

"I came to confer." Orson Lunt held a 15 percent stake in Fallon Antiquaria and Fallon Salvage and Restoration, and whenever he visited the warehouse, he proclaimed that the collective IQ of South Boston had just gone up by five points.

"All I know," Danny Fallon would answer, "is that the number of skinny old fags wearin' carnations and three-piece suits just doubled."

On that basis, Orson Lunt and Danny Fallon had become unlikely friends, one who clipped his white mustache twice a day, the other who never shaved on Sunday if he'd gone to mass on Saturday night; one tall and perfectly tailored, the other all neck and shoulders in a Sears work suit.

It had been twenty years since Orson Lunt had helped Peter sell the sugar urn, the only piece of the Revere tea set to survive. Then Peter had used the money to make restitution for the damage he had done trying to get it.

A few years later, after Evangeline had left him alone in Iowa, Assistant Professor Fallon's car had broken down on the edge of a cornfield. An old farmer had let him use the phone. And Peter's eye had been drawn to a shelf of books, including half a dozen volumes by Emerson and Thoreau and other Transcendentalists, all first editions, some of them signed. Peter had bought them on the spot for six hundred dollars.

Orson Lunt had brokered them for a profit of $60,000. Peter Fallon had found a new line of work. An old Iowa farmer had opened his mail one day to find more money than he had ever received at one time in his life. And Orson Lunt had decided to take a young partner.

Orson said, "I'm convincing your brother that this new contract in Sudbury will be an excellent opportunity. The Bleen-Currier-Whitney House is a treasure."

"And Sudbury is a fuckin' hour in traffic," said Danny. "You don't have to go out there. I do. Startin' a week from Monday."

"Good money," said Orson. "And a good challenge."

"Challenge, my ass," answered Danny. "Time is money. Too far. Too expensive. From now on, we stay inside Route One twenty-eight."

Peter popped a beer. "Let's talk about something closer to home: Will Wedge."

"Will Wedge"—Orson dabbed tomato sauce from his mustache—"another tenth-generation Yankee floating in a gene pool without tributaries. Loves to play Harry Harvard—"

"So do you," said Danny through a mouthful of pizza.

"I play Orson Lunt, retired antiquarian, bon vivant, and man about town."

"Give me more about Wedge," said Peter.

Orson lifted another piece of pizza from the box. "Runs the family brokerage, Wedge, Fleming, and Royce. Serves on the boards of prominent financial and cultural institutions. . . ."

"You can make it sound like the social page," said Peter.

Danny gave out with a "shit" as the Patriots fumbled.

"You know, Dan," said Peter, "that's why Mom stopped Dad from watching the games at home. It's why we're here on a Sunday afternoon."

"So let me swear."

"Yes," said Orson. "Let him swear. It passes for conversation. Now . . . Wedge isn't all social page. He has a brother, an old radical who's still living the rebel's life."

"What's his name?"

"Franklin. I once heard their mother, Harriet, say that however straight Will was, that was how far-out the brother was."

"Far-out?" said Peter.

"Come on, Peter," said Danny. "Even I know what that means. It means he's a pinko commie dope-smokin' hippie."

"Where does he live?" asked Peter.

"Officially, somewhere in Vermont. He has a teaching appointment at a college up there. But from what I hear, he just follows the revolution. One week, he's riding rafts for Greenpeace, and the next, he's in New York, picketing trade conventions, and so forth. . . ."

"Sounds more interesting than Will," said Peter.

"Not if you're in a line of work like ours," said Orson. "Now why this interest in the Wedge brothers?"

"Will's daughter wrote a paper about a Puritan preacher named Thomas Shepard."

"What are you onto? Shepard's *Confessions*? I thought the Mass. Genealogical Society owned the manuscript."

"It's what's in the *Confessions* and the diary."

And from out on the warehouse floor came the sound of shouting.

Through the office windows, Peter saw a burly guy in a Boston Bruins jacket hurrying along a row of crates with Bobby Fallon calling after him, "Hey, you!"

The hockey fan reached the front door and kept going, as if he didn't hear a thing.

Now Peter and Danny were out of the office, moving across the floor. Bobby reached the front door and shouted another "Hey, you!"

The Bruins fan pointed at himself: *Who? Me?*

"Yeah! You!" shouted Bobby. "I know you . . . Jackie Pucks."

"Jackie McShane's my name. Want me to spell it for you?" And before Bobby could say more, Jackie McShane was driving off . . . in his brown Toyota.

"What's going on?" Danny asked.

"He came in just after Uncle Peter . . . poked around, worked his way to a crate of faucet handles by the office door, picked up every one, looked 'em over, and kept peekin' in the office the whole time."

"Maybe he was interested in the football game," said Danny.

"Looked to me like he was snoopin'," said Bobby.

Peter watched the Toyota spinning away. "Do you know him?"

"He's a bum," said Danny. "Works for Hanrahan Wrecking. He hangs out at the Risin' Moon. They call him Jackie Pucks because he likes hockey. They say he breaks legs for Bingo Keegan."

"Bingo Keegan," said Orson, "South Boston's latest self-styled Robin Hood."

"Big trouble," said Danny. "Drug dealin', loan sharkin', fencin' stolen laptops—"

"Art theft, too," said Orson. "A lot of people think Keegan was behind the robbery at the Gardner Museum years ago." Orson shook his head. "Rembrandt's *The Storm on the Sea of Galilee,* gone forever."

"Keegan would be about fifty-eight now, wouldn't he?" asked Peter. "Five foot nine, gray hair, favors a scally cap and a black raincoat?"

"Have you done somethin' to piss him off?" asked Danny.

"I don't know. But I know who to ask."

* * *

"Bingo Keegan?" said Ridley Royce. "Who's he?"

"Trouble. Hanging around me since I started hanging around you. Why?"

"I wouldn't know," said Ridley.

They were having dinner at a sushi bar near Harvard Square. Ridley was drinking saki, Peter a Sapporo tall.

"I'm guessing," said Ridley, "that 'Bingo' isn't his given name."

"His mother named him James. But when he was a kid, he got caught rippin' off the bingo game at Gate of Heaven. They say the nickname irritates the hell out of him. And he's not someone you want to irritate."

"Should we order some spider rolls?"

"Don't change the subject," said Peter. "What does some local thug have to do with this? And why do you think that a play by Aeschylus is worth so much?"

"If I knew the answers, I wouldn't have called you in the first place."

"I called *you*. What's going on, Ridley?"

"I'm just putting it together myself, Peter. This Keegan guy is a new wrinkle."

Peter sat back. "All right. What have you put together? What do you know?"

Ridley sipped at his saki. "I don't think the play is *by* Aeschylus."

"Why not? Shepard said it was by Aeschylus."

"But he also talked about a 'modern' play, a play that John Harvard had owned." Ridley took another sip of saki, studied the cup for a moment, like an actor playing a scene. "Who were the 'modern' playwrights of that time, Peter? Marlowe, Ben Jonson, Shakespeare."

"But—"

"Have you ever been to Stratford-on-Avon?"

Peter took a deep breath. "Ridley, the words *Stratford-on-Avon* to a rare-book dealer are like the word *Yahweh* to an old Hebrew. Not to be trifled with."

"But you've *been* there? You've walked from Shakespeare's birthplace to the house where Katherine Rogers was born? John Harvard's mother?"

"It's right up the street. They call it Harvard House. It's a museum."

"And you've been to London? To St. Saviour's, the Southwark Cathedral, where they have the statue of Shakespeare and the chapel where John Harvard was baptized?"

"You have my attention, Ridley. Enough with the travelogue."

"Peter, the Harvards and the Shakespeares were neighbors in Stratford, and they probably did business in Southwark. The English make a big deal of it."

"But John Harvard was a Puritan," answered Peter. "And Dunster told Nicholson that no modern play came back in the trunk of books Isaac Wedge sent ahead. It's right in the diary, printed by the Colonial Society of Massachusetts."

"Go with me on this, Peter." Ridley leaned closer. "Harvard's parents weren't big Puritans, just God-fearing English folk. What if they had a play by their friend Will, a quarto, maybe, and it ended up in their son's collection? And then someone, for some reason, decided to steal it before the Puritans who ran the college destroyed it—"

"Rank speculation."

"Maybe . . . but isn't that what you're supposed to do? Speculate?"

Peter couldn't deny it. Ridley might be drinking too much saki. And he talked so fast that he could barely keep up with himself. And in the overhead light of the sushi bar, his hair plugs looked as ridiculous as tufts of grass growing out of his forehead. But he was right. Speculation was at the heart of the business.

"All right," said Peter. "Let's assume for a minute that it's a Shakespeare quarto—and not Aeschylus."

"Quartos are pretty rare, right?"

"Right," said Peter. "A folio was printed on one large piece of paper folded once to make four pages. A quarto got its name because there were four leaves, to make eight pages, then the pages were cut. The book was much smaller, from six-by-six inches up to six-by-nine. So someone could carry it around, almost like a paperback. Books like that don't last. So *rare* is the word."

"So if there's a quarto out there, it's worth . . . what?" Ridley threw back a shot of saki. "A million bucks?"

"Hold on, Ridley. You're getting ahead of yourself. Let me look a little more, ask a few more questions. Starting with this: Why are you bothering my old girlfriend?"

"I don't want to steal her from you." Ridley chuckled. "It's just that Evangeline descends from the Howells. And Katharine Nicholson, Isaac's girlfriend, married a Howell. I want to look into that gene pool."

"Under the heading of 'no stone unturned'?"

Ridley took his chopsticks out of their paper wrapping, split them, rubbed them together. "We turned over a few stones at the game, didn't we? I watched what went running. Will Wedge went running right up to your boat this morning."

"I figured you were using me yesterday. I'm not surprised."

"I'm a producer. I use everybody. And I wanted you to meet the rest of the cast."

"Including the mystery guest who followed me home?"

"He's a mystery to me, too."

Then the meal came, and they turned their attention to tekka maki and maguro and brain-steaming wasabi.

They had both parked on Mount Auburn Street. Peter made sure that no one followed them. No guys in Bruins jackets. No Bingo Keegans. He also made sure that Ridley could drive, despite the saki.

"The sushi soaked it all up," said Ridley.

"You ate enough to bait a longline."

"Speaking of which, I'm going fishing in the morning. Want to join me? Nothing more fun than chasing stripers in my Grady White."

"No, thanks. I'm on another kind of fishing expedition now."

Ridley got into the car, then rolled down the window. "Peter, I've been failing for ten years . . . at everything. If fishing's all I have to get me out of bed in the morning, I'd rather *sleep* with the fishes. Help me find that play."

Peter leaned closer to him. "This didn't start with a term paper, did it?"

"It did for me. I think it did for Will's daughter, too. But I get the feeling that there are other people after this thing, too." Ridley took an envelope from his pocket and handed it to Peter. "This is from the commonplace book of John Wedge, Isaac's son. It's some kind of quote. This is what really got me interested."

Peter looked at the quote, three lines of blank verse and beneath it, a parenthetical remark, all in a tight little scrawl. "Where did you get this?"

But Ridley was already driving off. "We'll talk tomorrow."

On Sunday night, Peter found a parking spot right away. No one followed him home. And there were no surprising e-mails waiting for him. But there was still some port to finish and enough questions in his head to keep him awake.

First, he sent Orson Lunt an e-mail:

> Come to the office in the morning. I want to pick your brain about commonplace books and Shakespeare in Puritan New England.

Then he went to a bookshelf and pulled down a volume of *Sibley's Harvard Graduates*, a series of short biographies of all Harvard men up to 1775. If he was going to start this quixotic search by investigating the Wedges, Sibley might point the way. So he turned to Isaac Wedge, member of the Class of 1642:

> Born, 1620, d. 1693. A veteran of the English Civil Wars, a minister to the Indians west of Boston. Married Rebecca Watson, daughter of Indian minister, 1648. In 1656, he became tutor in the Indian college opened in Harvard Yard. But the college failed. So he moved to Sudbury and took up farming. In the year 1674, he became one of the first alumni to give another generation to the college. . . .

Chapter Seven

1674–1682

THE WORDS were written in Ecclesiastes and were imprinted on the soul of Isaac Wedge: *To every thing there is a season, and a time to every purpose under the heaven.*

The season was summer, and the purpose was a journey from a farm on the banks of the Sudbury River to a college on the banks of the Charles.

A time to be born, and a time to die; a time to plant, and a time to pluck up that which is planted. A father and mother stood in the cool dark of their house, preparing for a parent's small death in their son's departure, while a son saddled the horses and prepared to be born into manhood. The journey would cover some twenty miles, the plucking up to be done in the morning, the planting to be completed before dark.

"I shall miss him sorely," said Rebecca Watson Wedge, her eyes steady on the square of light pouring through the front door. "Would that the Lord had seen fit to send us another child to ease this pain."

"Thank the Lord for what He give," said Isaac as he filled a sack with books. "One son be gift enough when he's a son like John."

"And those books," she asked, "be they gift enough for John?"

"A man will be known by his books," answered Isaac.

"So you say . . . Reason enough to keep no book of plays in your house."

Isaac cast his eyes at the floorboards beneath which *Love's Labours Won* was hidden in a wax-sealed lead box.

"Isaac, you promised you'd take the play to the college when you took our son."

"'Twas my hope that ministers and magistrates would have grown more liberal in their thinking by now," he answered, "but still I mistrust 'em."

"I be but a plain minister's daughter and true minister's wife—"

"You're no minister's wife anymore. Raisin' corn and cuttin' marsh hay satisfy me more than preachin'."

"Be that as it may, keepin' a play under our roof be blasphemy."

"Breakin' an oath to a friend be blasphemy, too," answered Isaac. "'Tis my duty to keep the play safe till changes in England make their way here—"

"What greater change do you need?" she asked. "The king is restored. The Anglicans are in the ascendance, the Puritans in retreat—"

"There may again be Christmas masses in London churches and new plays in London theaters," he answered, "but our colony and its college keep to harder standards."

"Do you not mean *higher* standards?" she asked.

To that he gave no answer. He had never doubted that he should have stolen the play from Eaton, who had stolen it only to sell it when the price was right. But should he not have returned it more openly? Should he not have forced the magistrates to confront their prejudice in public?

But in Massachusetts, prejudice remained powerful. And in Rebecca's correspondence with Cousin Katharine, it still echoed. Isaac could not change it, any more than the Reformation had stopped Catholic peasants from placing offerings before the tombs of saints. A play might reveal for man his vanities, his passions, and his appetites, but not in Massachusetts. So it had fallen to Isaac to protect a small shard of knowledge, to keep the play safe until such time as his Puritan brethren were ready for it.

Still, it pained him that he could not keep his word to Rebecca.

It pained him whenever he disappointed her, because, quite simply, he loved her. He loved her as he had from the moment he met her in the college library.

She had been beautiful then, slender and smiling and filled with simple faith. And she had offered him that faith and her love through all the years that he served in her father's ministry. And when the Society for the Propagation of the Gospel had asked him to teach at the Indian College in Harvard Yard, she had gone with him willingly. But the Indians had hardly gone at all. And Isaac had soon concluded that they no more wished to know the white man's God than the white man's books. So he had brought his family to this farm on the banks of the Sudbury, and here had they stayed some ten years.

Rebecca was heavier now and smiled less, but her faith was still simple and strong, and she said, "Plays be the devil's work, Isaac. There be imps in that box you've hid 'neath the floorboards."

"They're called characters, dear. Dramatis personae."

"Don't play the educated fool with me. They be *imps*. Some nights, I come awake, and I can hear 'em scuttlin' about the great room."

"Do they perch on the mantel?" he asked. "Or the table?"

"They be spectral things. As spectral as the devil himself, walkin' the dark woods, enlistin' the Indians to do his work."

Isaac did not dispute that. Puritans believed in Satan, especially in his presence among the unconverted Indians. Having preached to the Indians, Isaac saw them simply as human beings in whom ignorance rather than evil resided, little different from the benighted Papists of Padua worshiping the remains of their saint.

"Isaac," she demanded, "what will you do with the play?"

He gestured to the floorboards. "Keep it safe, where 'tis."

"And leave it for our son? Force him to wrestle with Satan after us?"

"Wrestle with Satan?" In the doorway appeared a gangling boy with a few tendrils of black hair covering the blemishes on his chin. "When do I wrestle him?"

"We all wrestle with him, John," said Isaac. "Every day. But today, you begin to gain such learning that Satan will never take the field against you."

"I hope only that I'm worthy, if he does," said John Wedge.

And those humble words, uttered with such sincerity, brought from Rebecca a cry of love and loss familiar to every son who has taken leave of his mother. She threw her arms around his neck, and both parents forgot the business of the play, for there were other matters at hand.

First, Isaac presented John with a blank book of a hundred leaves. "A commonplace book," he said, "to be filled with your favorite passages, with lines of verse that strike you as well phrased, and with your ruminations upon them."

Then Rebecca gave him a sack containing a dozen cornmeal muffins and a clay pot of blackberry preserves sealed with wax. "To nourish you in your ruminations."

Finally, Isaac loaded his old blunderbuss and placed it by the door. "You'll not need this," he said to Rebecca, "but 'twill make you feel more secure."

"Our Indians be docile, Mother," said John.

"Your mother fears 'em yet," said Isaac. " 'Satan's minions,' she calls them."

"Which they be," answered John, "the unconverted ones, leastways."

Indeed, thought Isaac, the mother had taught the son well. His faith was as simple and strong as hers.

"If Satan's minions come to the door," Isaac told her, "point the gun and fire. The shot will splatter wide. What it doesn't strike will be frightened off by the roar."

"I'll need no gun, Isaac," she said. "I'll simply pray, as I pray for our Johnny."

They left Rebecca in the yard, shielding her eyes from the August sun, and took the road along the edge of the marsh. After a quarter mile, they came to Deacon Haynes's garrison house, built to defend the settlers should ever there come an Indian attack, and Isaac offered a silent prayer that the garrison would never be needed for its purpose. Then they turned east, crossed the rough-hewn bridge over the Sudbury River, and made for Cambridge.

It was a brightening world that they went through, as by now the forests had fallen for some twenty miles in a wide semicircle around Boston. The Lord's people were an industrious lot, thought Isaac, and fruitful, too. Settlements had appeared along the roads, congregations were coming together in the Lord, and there were many opportunities for a young man who wished to preach the Word.

Isaac, however, would not commit his son to any goal beyond the gaining of knowledge. The boy could be a minister, if that was his choice, or a merchant, or a doctor educated at some European university. After Harvard, he might even choose to attend the University of Padua, though Isaac would not encourage him to follow the path of one who had gone there long ago, one rumored recently to have died in a London debtors' prison, one Nathaniel Eaton by name.

Isaac tried to push thoughts of Eaton from his mind, and yet, to look upon his son, riding solemnly at his side, was to remind him of his own emotions on a similar journey, made on the day that he first met Eaton, a journey made in company with the man after whom the colony had named the college and Isaac had named his son.

John Harvard would have been pleased to know that the college survived, though it could hardly be said to thrive. There were only five students in the class of 1678, twenty-three in all. Towns that once had sent the College Corn now spent their money on other things. Contributions promised were quite often deferred. And while students might pay in hard coin, they were as likely to offer "country pay"—grain, livestock, cords of wood. The only regular income derived from the Boston-to-Charlestown ferry revenue, a tradition at Oxford and Cambridge that produced a pittance at Harvard. And not only was the college a poor place. It was a contentious one, too, rife with disputes and intrigues among a new president, certain overseers, the tutors, and the rebellious students.

It may not have been the best place for a young man to earn his *Ars Bacheloris*, then, but in English North America, it was the only place.

Isaac and John arrived in the late afternoon. They came into the

Yard by old Peyntree House, into a scene that would never be immortalized in a book of engravings depicting the world's great seats of learning.

Though the college hall remained the largest building in the colony, its roof now sagged toward the east like a leaking sack of grain. Little remained of Eaton's orchard, and most of the fencing had been taken down, as the cows now grazed in farther fields. But chickens went scuttling and squabbling ahead of Isaac's horse, and three piglets rooted about in the grass, which was crisscrossed with dirt paths leading to outhouse, brewhouse, pigpen, henhouse, and a brick building erected in high expectation as the Indian College but now occupied by a printing press and a few students.

With the college hall collapsing under the weight of termites and rainwater leaking through the roof, the overseers had solicited contributions for a grander structure, to be built of brick on a stone foundation, roofed with slate, called Harvard Hall. Its timbered skeleton rose at the west edge of the Yard. And Isaac chose to make it the center of his son's attention, rather than the squalor surrounding it.

"See that framework, John," he said. "New wood, pegged tight to proclaim the Lord's favor. He would not allow such an edifice at a school that had no future. And He would not allow a student who had no future to attend such a school."

"But, Father"—the boy reined his horse—"I fear that my Latin and Greek are—"

"More than sufficient. I taught you myself."

"But some who study here studied first at the Boston Latin School."

Isaac looked hard at his son. "What have I always told you?"

John drew his upper teeth across his lower lip—an expression that reminded Isaac of his little boy, not of this young man. "About what, Father?"

Isaac slapped the sack hanging from his saddle. "About books?"

"That a . . . that a man will be known by his books?"

"Aye. And you've had my books to study. By them will you be known."

"But, Father, there will be others here who know much more."

"And others who know much less. As long as you keep to your tasks and read your Scripture, you'll do well. I believe that as sure as I believe in the Lord."

"Father," said the boy solemnly, "that remark approach blasphemy."

Isaac took off his hat and wiped perspiration from his forehead. It was a stark but simple truth that raising a son could make a man sweat. "You worry too much, John."

"I worry because I've heard your thoughts on such truths as predestination."

"I've seen men turn from good to evil and from evil to good. If the Lord permits men to change, He must hold hope for salvation to all."

"But the Lord has already chosen the elect. They reveal themselves by their good conduct and understanding of Scripture." John Wedge was a most argumentative boy . . . never rebellious, but always prepared to contend over issues of faith or politics.

And Isaac realized how deeply he would miss their clash of wits. He had taught the boy to argue for the things he believed, even as he had taught him to respect the authority of those who interpreted the Word. He sometimes wished that he had better taught the boy to think for himself, no matter the interpretations of others, because in their debates, Isaac always found himself defending the unorthodox idea, which was not the natural order of things.

Isaac sometimes wondered where he had found his own questioning spirit. Perhaps it had come in Italy, where he had seen the soaring beauties and monumental superstitions of Romanism. But more likely he had begun to question the wisdom of Puritanism when he studied under a man who pretended to all appropriate pieties in public but showed a face of rank brutality in private.

"Remember, son," he said, putting on his hat, "we are also taught that some who demonstrate strong faith will not be saved."

"And some who do not *will* be."

"'Tis a conundrum, then. Simply do as I've told you: treat others as you expect to be treated, act as Holy Scripture tells you to act, and live honestly. Now come along."

They dismounted before the Old College, and John said he

would rather go from there on his own. Isaac understood, but he had brought the sack of books as a gift for Samuel Sewall, tutor and keeper of the library, knowing that such a gift would stand young John in good stead. So father and son went into the hall together.

As they entered the library, a boy looked up from his reading. His hair was cut short, his complexion was reddish, as if heightened by the simple exertion of turning pages, and his features had yet to mold themselves into any form that would suggest the character beneath.

"Good afternoon," said Isaac.

The boy gave a grudging nod of the head, as if he disapproved of those who broke the silence of the library.

Then Isaac introduced his son. "And what is your name?"

"C-C-C-Cotton M-M-M-Mather." The young man had a powerful stammer.

"Son of Reverend Increase? Nephew of John Cotton?" asked Isaac.

A flicker of a smile crossed the boy's face. "The very s-s-s-same."

"And they have fostered a veritable genius." Samuel Sewall bustled in with an armful of books. "Master Mather is the youngest student ever to attend. All of—what is it, Cotton—twelve years old?"

"Eleven and a half, sir. 'Twas my father who m-m-m-matriculated at age twelve."

"A most brilliant family." Sewall put down the books. He was a heavyset young man whose lively eyes and strong nose overlay an especially small mouth, so that his face seemed perpetually at odds with itself. He whispered to Isaac, "Brilliant the boy may be, sir, but too young for college, if you ask me. The older lads have made rough sport of him already. He'd best quit his stammering, or they'll make even more."

Sensing that Mather was listening while pretending to read, Isaac said, "Well, Tutor Sewall, the son of Increase Mather may count on the friendship of the Wedges. Isn't that right, John?"

"Unh . . . yes, Father." John answered with little enthusiasm, for what sixteen-year-old would welcome a companion so young? But

Cotton's father was pastor of Boston's Second Church, and while friendship with the Mathers would be of little consequence to a Sudbury farmer, Isaac's son might someday find benefit in such a relationship.

More immediate benefit would come from a relationship to Samuel Sewall. So Isaac placed the sack of books on the table. "Now that I be done with these, Samuel, 'twould seem best that they be added to New England's font of knowledge."

"What have you brought us?" Sewall poked his nose into the sack and drew forth a volume. "*Clavis Homerica?*"

"Published at Rotterdam last year. Selections from the *Iliad* and the *Odyssey.*"

"Excellent," said Sewall. "We've only Chapman's Homer, from Master Harvard himself. We need more literature. Though I . . . I trust there be no play in that bag."

Play. A mere word, and the uttering of it was like the sound of a gun. Cotton Mather's head snapped up. John Wedge stepped toward his father, as if to protect him or seek protection. And Isaac took a step backward before regaining balance enough to say, "Why, Master Sewall, why would you suggest such a thing?"

"I've come into possession of a diary and notebook owned by the late Reverend Shepard," answered Sewall. "I've read them in preparation for writing a sketch on his piety . . . something I shall deliver before his congregation on the fortieth anniversary of his settlement."

"He was a good man," said Isaac warily.

"His writings include sermons, daily thoughts, and the confessions of those who accepted church membership in those days, including yourself, sir. It also comments on several of the confessions, including your own, sir."

By a quick shifting of his eyes from one slack-jawed freshman to another, Isaac tried without words to tell Sewall that he had said enough.

But Sewall went on talking as he picked through the books in Isaac's bag. "I thought Katharine Nicholson's confession most amusing. It accused you of seeking a play on a trip you made to England. A 'modern' play."

"I returned with a *classical* play. The *Agamemnon* by Aeschylus." Isaac went over to the wall and slipped the book from the shelf where it had resided for more than a quarter century. "Here is the very volume."

"Quite so," said Sewall. "I've read it myself."

"And does Reverend Shepard's little book also tell that truth?" asked Isaac.

"Indeed it does, sir."

"Then there be no need to comment in front of impressionable boys who—"

"I am n-n-not impressionable, sir," said Mather. "My conscience has been well formed by my f-f-father, who considers m-m-modern theater the work of Satan. As do I."

"So you say?" answered Isaac.

"So I say." And for a moment, Isaac was pinned by the gaze of a boy who seemed certain of the rectitude of his opinions, despite his stammer and a voice that had not yet changed. The words of young Mather, brilliant son of the colony's most brilliant father, were enough to convince Isaac that *Love's Labours Won* should remain where it was, at least until the attitudes of the next generation could be better discerned and shaped.

ii

No year in the life of the college was ever as difficult as John Wedge's first. In November, the students left in a revolt against the president, or perhaps the tutors, or was it the overseers? Nothing was certain, except that John Wedge walked the whole way back to Sudbury, appearing at his parents' door on a gloomy afternoon and staying until March, when the president resigned, the tutors returned, and the college reopened.

Meanwhile, the building of Harvard Hall proceeded fitfully, the pace determined by the speed with which the good people of Massachusetts fulfilled their pledges. But come June, the people of Massachusetts were using their money to defend their colony, and by August, they were fighting for its survival.

The great Indian War, feared for so long by so many, had finally come to pass. The wonder to Isaac was that it had taken over fifty years. The Indians had seen their forests fall. They had watched white men widen their ancient footpaths and cut new roads west. And they had heard too much of a strange new god with three names yet one being, a god said to be more powerful than all the spirits of sky and earth. So they rallied around a Wampanoag chief named Metacom, known to the English as King Philip, and they attacked towns along Narragansett Bay. Then they moved north and west, inciting the Nipmucks and Pocumtucks and igniting the frontier.

To meet the Indian threat, men were mustered in every town. And as he was fluent in the Algonkian language, Isaac was called upon several times to march out. Each time, he put the blunderbuss by the door and told his wife to use it without hesitation.

Her answer was always that the Lord would protect her.

Isaac believed that the Lord was most helpful to those who helped themselves. So he resolved to do his best to bring peace to the frontier. If he failed, he told his wife, the task would someday fall to their son.

That winter a dozen Massachusetts towns were put to the torch. As winter flamed into spring, John Wedge wrote to his parents from the college:

> Word arrives of attacks on Lancaster and Medfield. Cotton Mather says that his father—ever in a position to know such things—hears rumors of five hundred warriors gathered near Mount Wachusett. I fear for your safety. Should I come home? Or better yet, should you come here?

This letter reached Sudbury on a warm evening in April. Isaac and Rebecca were sitting together on chairs set out in front of the house, their eyes turned to the sunset, their ears attuned to the rising song of the spring peepers. And Isaac was thinking that once they had satisfied the senses of sight and sound, a husband of fifty-four and a wife of fifty-two might find it within themselves to satisfy other senses, as well.

But into this gentle scene came two riders on heavily lathered mounts.

"We bring a letter, sir," said one of them.

"And a request from Captain Wadsworth that you join him," said the other. "He's on the Great Path, marching to the Marlborough garrison."

"That's eight miles west." Isaac skimmed his son's letter. "From what this tells, there be five hundred Indians some twenty miles *north*west."

"From Marlborough, sir, we'll be in position to move against 'em, however they strike. I'm under orders to request that you join us," said one rider.

"It seems I should be stayin' here," answered Isaac, "to defend wife and home."

"We're to bring you with us, sir, forcible if we must," said the other rider.

Rebecca touched his arm. "Isaac, the Lord is my shepherd, and the garrison is close. I'll be safe."

So Isaac went into the house and, in an act that was by now ritual, put the blunderbuss by the door. Then he put his Bible in his breast pocket, draped powder horn and shot pouch over his shoulders, and embraced Rebecca. "If there's trouble," he told her, "don't bother with the gun. Run for the garrison. Run hard."

"And the book?" she asked. "Do I save it or leave it?"

"You would save the book for me?"

"I be but a poor minister's daughter and true minister's wife . . . who believes that the Lord give her husband wisdom. Those riders prove it."

"How so?" asked Isaac.

"You were the first man to see that Injuns can't be educated. You saw it at the college. They be a different breed, and there be no hope to live with 'em."

That was not exactly what Isaac had seen or said, but he made no protest.

"If you be right about that," she went on, "who's to say you're not right about the meanin' of blasphemy or the innocence of a play?"

" 'Tisn't blasphemy at all, I don't think."

"I've bet my immortal soul on what you think, Isaac Wedge. Otherwise, I would have cast that book into the fire on the first day you spoke of it. I'll not let some heathen savage do what I would not."

"You have a strange way of showin' your love." He kissed her and held her close. "But if the Indians attack, leave the book and the gun. Just run."

Dawn came early in April. The old earth turned again toward the sun, brightening the sky and bringing birdsong before five. For each dawn that he had seen, Isaac had thanked the Lord. And he said his prayer again that morning, crouched by a campfire in front of the Marlborough garrison house. But before the sun had risen far, he was saying prayers of a different sort and Wadsworth's column was hurrying back to the east, toward a cloud of smoke rising over Sudbury.

Isaac, one of the few on horseback, begged Wadsworth to let him ride ahead.

"The savages have made Sudbury already," said the captain. "How many there be, I know not. But if you ride alone, you'll die alone. Stay with the company, and we'll march straight for the Haynes garrison, Lord willin'."

But the Lord was not willin'. Wadsworth and his men were no more than half a mile from the garrison, marching through a defile between two forested hills named for farmers Goodman and Green, when the Indians struck.

One moment there was silence, except for the sound of horses breathing hard and men tramping heavy on the spring-soft ground. An instant later, muskets were roaring from both hills and Indians were exploding from the trees, like specters of the air taking human form, truly like minions of Satan.

The English soldiers fought their way to the top of Green's Hill and made their stand. But there were hundreds of Indians, and once they had surrounded the hilltop, Isaac knew there would be no escape until dark, if at all.

Looking down through the branches, he could see his house, or the smoke where it had been. He could also see the Haynes garrison, also shrouded in smoke, but it was the white smoke of gunpowder, which meant the men were fighting. So Isaac fought, too, in hopes that his wife was inside the garrison, loading muskets for the men. And he prayed that they could hold their position on the hill until the sun had dipped below the trees.

But about four o'clock, the Indians torched the dry brush on the side of the hill. Soon, a semicircle of living orange flame, driven by an easterly wind, was breathing in brush and exhaling heavy smoke that swallowed the top of the hill and forced the English to flee or suffocate.

Wadsworth ordered his men to fall back and fight their way to the Goodenow garrison, across a cornfield to the south. But Isaac had had enough of orders. Besides, most of the Indians were sweeping left and right, behind the flames, cutting off any retreat and filling the air with their furious cries. So he dropped to the ground and pressed his face against the earth.

The flames were coming closer, but he kept his head down and pulled his heavy cloak up over his neck. Most fitting, he thought, that Satan's minions should send hellfire itself against him. But the fire was moving fast. He felt the flames pass over his cloak. He smelled his own hair singe. He wanted to run. But he held his breath and waited until he could hear nothing—no Indian war whoops, no screams from the whites—nothing except the roar of the flames around him. And then, throwing off his smoldering cloak, he rose and ran.

But he did not retreat. He went east through the flames, out of the fire, straight toward a single Indian who stood on the smoking ground like a sentinel.

Isaac raised his musket, the Indian his war club. And Isaac realized that they saw each other in the same way—as devils limned in fire and shrouded in smoke.

The Indian mouthed the word "chepi." *Demon.* "Run, white demon. Run on. No chief will strike a demon who runs."

Could these be the eyes of King Philip himself? Could Isaac end the war with a single blow? No, because other Indians were rushing back to protect their chief. So Isaac Wedge accepted the courtesy of one demon to another, of one frightened man to another, and went stumbling down the east slope toward the greening marsh.

Soon he was hunkered in the strong-smelling mud, counting the columns of smoke, gauging the progress of the fight by the ferocity of the musket fire . . . from south of Goodman's Hill, where Wadsworth's men were being slaughtered; from east of the river, where the Sudbury settlement held out; and from the Haynes garrison, which Isaac could not reach for all the Indians around it. So he waited and prayed, and just before dark, a relief column from Boston reached the settlement. At the sound of their first volley, the Indians retreated . . . from the garrison houses and the settlements and all the other places where they had made their attack.

Only then did Isaac emerge from the mud, slip along the edge of the marsh, and take the path toward the garrison. A dozen copper bodies lay about, and the fine barn that Isaac had helped raise was now a pile of smoking coals, but the house stood strong, and Isaac could hear voices within, which filled him with hope. So he hailed them.

"Who is it?"

"Isaac. Isaac Wedge."

The door swung open, and Deacon Haynes appeared. "Come in, Isaac. Come in to where 'tis safe."

In the morning, Isaac walked to the charred pile that had been his house. He could not have expected that grief would feel so heavy. In his younger days, it had seemed a thing to be cried away in a day or two. But this weight lay on his shoulders like the yoke and pails that now lay on the ground before the house.

"She was fetching water from the river when we rang the bell," said Haynes.

"I promised that this year, we'd dig a well," answered Isaac.

"We saw Injuns comin' through the fields, heard 'em across the river, too. She dropped her yoke and began to run to us, then she was took by some contrary thought, and run back to her house. I cried that there was no time. But she went in, and that doomed her. The first Injun to the door she killed with your old blunderbuss, but . . ."

Beneath several smoking timbers, Isaac saw fluttering a few strips of unburned fabric, part of the dress that now covered the charred body of Rebecca Wedge.

Deacon Haynes took Isaac by the arm and said, "Let thy neighbors do this task. 'Twill be hard enough to tell your son."

And it was. Isaac rode all the way to Cambridge and returned with young John late in the afternoon. Along the road, the boy cried, sometimes silently, sometimes loudly enough for his father to hear. Isaac, who had not cried, who found that he could not cry, did his best to console the boy. And they prayed to strengthen each other, reciting Rebecca's favorite psalms and the Lord's Prayer.

It was a small grace of God that by the time they reached Sudbury, the remains of wife and mother had been placed in a pine box. Neither husband nor son was made to look upon her scalped head, her crushed skull, her blackened body. It was a smaller grace that the stench of charred flesh was swallowed by the stronger smell of burned wood.

There were burials in many corners of the town the next morning. Captain Wadsworth and twenty-eight of his men went into a mass grave near the Concord Road. Farmers and their wives were buried in plots behind their homes. And Rebecca Watson Wedge was returned to the earth in the church plot just east of the river.

Afterward, Isaac and his son went back to the ruins, to see what could be salvaged of axheads, knife blades, and other metal things.

"The Lord's ways are past our knowing." Isaac could think of nothing else to say.

"And yet, we must try to know," said John, "for this is a struggle with evil itself."

"'Tisn't evil to fight for your world and your god," said Isaac. "All men do it."

"Even men whose world is dark and whose god is Satan?"

Isaac made his way through the rubble to what had once been his hearth. How strange it seemed that this place, where he had warmed himself on so many black winter nights, was bathed now in bright sunshine. He stood over the only section of flooring that had not been burned, the section that had been beneath Rebecca's body. And in the middle of it, a plank had been lifted. It was the plank beneath which he had hidden the book. Had it been stolen? Burned? Its fate would be the Lord's will, thought Isaac.

Then John knelt, reached in the hole, and pulled out a box. "What's this, Father?"

So, thought Isaac, it was the Lord's will that the book be saved. " 'Tis living proof of what I have always told you, son. A man will be known by his books."

John pried the top off the box, revealing the brown leather. Then he flipped through the handwritten pages and stopped at the signature. *Will. Shakespeare.*

"Your mother came back for it," said Isaac. "Perhaps a woman will be known by her books, too."

"But this is by Shakespeare," said John. "If Mother came back for this, it was this that gave those red devils time to take her life."

"Men took her life . . . not devils." Isaac slipped the book from his son's hands. "She came back for this because she knew it to be the work of a man, not a devil."

"That's not what I've heard about this Shakespeare."

"Have you ever read a play?" asked Isaac.

"I've read Aeschylus . . . in the Greek."

"And were you moved?"

"Well . . . yes. But this—"

"There may come times in your life when the words you read or the ideas you confront do not glorify God but man . . . his vanities . . . his passions . . . his appetites . . . his dreams . . . all the things that lead us toward sin, yet all the things that make us human."

"Reverend Mather speaks strong words 'gainst theater. Cotton quotes 'em often."

"So I remember. But whilst a man may be known by his books, people are known by their love for one another. I loved John Harvard, so I promised I would protect this book. Your mother loved me, so she tried to save the book. If you love her, think hard on what she did. Then, if you ask me to destroy it, I will. If you ask me to save it, we'll find a way to return it to John Harvard's library, as I promised your mother I would do."

And that night, John Wedge read the play.

iii

On a June morning a year later, Isaac Wedge returned *Love's Labours Won* to its rightful place. He did not do it with ceremony, for he still feared the consequences. Indeed, the only person who knew was junior sophister John Wedge.

"Do you truly think that you can hide this volume in plain sight, Father, right in the new library?"

"I've thought hard on it." Isaac slipped the nondescript volume between two other books in a larger pile that was one of a score of piles arranged in neat rows on the table in the Old College library. "The new library is where it shall be safest."

A sheet of paper lay beside the pile of books. On it were listed the names of all the books in that particular pile. At the bottom of the sheet, Isaac wrote the words "*Corporei Insectii,* by Walter Shackford, gift of Isaac Wedge," and the numbers 12.8.6.

"*The Bodies of Insects*? By Walter Shackford?" said John. "That would be a work of natural philosophy, if such a book existed. Or such an author."

"So, we put it in case twelve, the natural philosophy case, eighth shelf, sixth space."

"And what if someone reads it and finds its true nature?"

"My hope is that a student seeking a work on insects will be put off by Shakespeare's scrawl. He'll put this book back and find something else to copy from."

"When a new keeper of the library is appointed, he must examine every volume."

"The new keeper must note only that a volume be in its proper place. And all the keepers have proved to be liberal-thinking young men like Sewall, the sort who'd think twice before destroying any volume." Isaac picked up the pile of books and put it into his son's hands. "Besides, my name be set down as donor. Should any find it, they will come to me before they destroy it . . . or to you. Then we will speak our piece."

"Leave me no piece to speak, Father," said John. "Speak it now."

"In a colony where the performance of plays is prohibited, would you challenge the court over the keeping of one in their college?"

"I respect the beliefs of our fathers. 'Twas faith brought us through the crisis with the Indians. And 'twill see us through the next crisis, whatever it might be."

"You've spent too much time in the presence of Cotton Mather and his father." Isaac slipped another pile of books from the table and said, "Come along."

They went down the creaking stairs, out the back door of the Old College, past the well sweep, past the pigpen and outhouses, across the Yard to Harvard Hall, now the largest and most impressive structure in all the English colonies.

How solid and yet how fantastical it was, thought Isaac—the several tones of red brick laid in several bonds, the white pilasters around the entries, the straight cornices over the first-floor windows contrasting with the arches of header-bond brick over the second, and the whole structure yearning upward in fourteen steep-sloped gables, upward toward two massive chimneys, upward toward the sky, toward God Himself—a building that expressed Isaac's belief that all learning should be a flight of fancy set solidly upon a four-square foundation.

Of course, no man who stopped before Harvard Hall would stand there for long, because the south and west sides were each adorned with a sun clock—a white square painted with red Roman numerals, a delicate wrought-iron arrow raised at the proper angle to show the sun's movement, a reminder to all who passed that time was our greatest and most fragile gift.

Samuel Sewall met the Wedges in the library. "Welcome, gentlemen. John Harvard must look down and smile."

"More than you could know," said Isaac.

Sewall took their catalog sheets and perused them quickly. "Books for case twelve. Natural philosophy . . . and a list inscribed by the man who first cataloged John Harvard's books. A good sign."

"I am most fortunate to be able to help," said Isaac.

"As are we all," answered Sewall. "Keeper Gookin honors the alumni."

The new room was twice the size of the old, with windows north and south, two fireplaces, and space for six thousand volumes, three times more than in the old library. And no chains, for though Harvard followed European customs wherever possible, the books in the library would never be chained to the shelves. The walls were painted robin's-egg blue, and above each bookcase was a white Roman numeral. The Wedges went for Section XII and shelved the books, including *Corporei Insectii*, leaf-side-out, the number six written on the page edge.

"So, 'tis done," said Isaac.

"It does not set well with me," whispered John.

Just then, there came a commotion at the door. A tall gentleman with long face and shoulder-length reddish hair stepped into the library, followed by his son, Cotton.

"'Twill not set well for either of us," whispered Isaac to his son, "should the Reverend Increase Mather decide to read *Corporei Insectii*."

Sewall went to greet them, but Increase Mather raised a finger for quiet, then surveyed the library and whispered, loudly enough for all to hear, "The Lord's gift. He is great and powerful."

"Indeed," said Sewall.

"A year ago, we could only pray that this room would come into being. Now we have vanquished the heathens whose land the Lord God of our Fathers gave us to possess and"—Mather's eye fell upon Isaac—"Master Wedge, who didst preach to the heathen and fight him, too. The news is good, is it not?"

"None better," said Isaac. "King Philip's head on a pike at Plymouth. His hand preserved in a bucket of Boston rum. The rest of him feed for Rhode Island crows—"

"And his followers as scattered as himself," said Increase Mather.

"The Lord is great and powerful," said Isaac.

"And the d-d-d-devil knows a mighty defeat," said Cotton.

"Aye," said Increase. "But the devil will not rest. We must remain ever vigilant. Wouldn't you agree, young John Wedge?"

"If we are not vigilant," answered John, "Satan may yet know the victory he sought through King Philip, for he is a relentless spirit."

"John Wedge speaks well," said Increase Mather. "He will be one to watch."

Isaac hoped that it would be so, but for his part, he would watch the Mathers.

iv

It was not the Mathers, however, who finally paid Isaac the visit he feared. It was a Harvard man, Reverend George Burroughs, Class of 1670, who came to Sudbury on a May afternoon some five years later.

Isaac was writing a proof on a blackboard. He had rebuilt his house on its old foundation stones and now kept a school in the great room. The sight of an old friend such as Burroughs brightened his prospects for a pleasant evening after a tiresome day of Euclidean geometry and Latin declensions.

So they supped together, then they sat in front of the house, drank beer that Isaac had brewed, and watched the river wind through the marsh. And Burroughs said, "I've visited the college library of late. I've read an interesting book on insects."

Isaac gagged his beer down and said, "Insects?"

Burroughs chuckled. "'Tis a fine book. Since you be listed as donor, I came to thank you in person."

Burroughs—a compact, muscular man, dark-haired, dark-browed—was the sort who looked as if he meant what he said. And Isaac knew that, in this case, looks did not deceive. So he decided to tell Burroughs the whole story, from the day he met John Harvard until he cataloged the book in the new library.

Burroughs said, "God would not have given Shakespeare such a gift had He not intended it to be used. John Harvard must have known it, just as he knew that the safest place for a book is a library, even in a colony where God's gifts are not always understood."

"Has anyone else read it that you know?"

"I saw no other names set down. But now that I'm settled in Salem, I shall visit the library from time to time. Should I see or hear anything, I'll let you know."

"Sudbury be a far piece from Salem . . . or Cambridge."

"Count on me, Isaac. I love a good story, whether from the Bible or elsewhere. But you must tell me, who else knows of this book?"

"Only my son. He serves in Jamaica as agent for his new father-in-law, John Cogswell, in the purchase of molasses for rum. He has never approved of my deceit."

"Tell him, 'tis deceit in service of a greater truth."

At that moment, in a fine house on the island of Jamaica, John Wedge was enjoying the pleasures of a new-married man, wrapped in a cool sheet and the soft, smooth legs of Mary Cogswell Wedge.

When his thrusting was done, she kissed him and said, "Perhaps this is the time."

"Do you think so?"

" 'Tis a simple calculation. A son may be yours in nine months."

"I already have a gift for him." John leapt from the bed, went to a drawer and took out a thin volume. "My college commonplace book. Only half filled. Our son shall fill the second half when he goes to Harvard."

"I shall pray on it," she said. And then, this demure young woman, just six weeks beyond her introduction to conjugal pleasure, whispered, "But 'tisn't prayer that's on my mind."

And she put out her hand and drew him onto her.

Later that evening, John Wedge opened his commonplace book to a page he had written upon six years before, just after his mother's death. A quote was there, the only quote he had entered from the only Shakespeare play that he had read:

A man be but a speck of dust, begot
By dust that breathed before, but dust that lives
Again, when dust itself hath turned to dust.

Beneath it, he wrote, "No man would say this after a night in which he had known the joy of love's labors."

Chapter Eight

═══════════

"SO," SAID Peter Fallon, "what do you know about commonplace books?"

"Nothing," answered Orson Lunt, "until I've had coffee."

"Bernice!" Peter called out the door of his office.

"Yeah, yeah. Coffee. Hold your horses." Bernice O'Boyle came in with two cups. She was in her mid-sixties, a little heavy in the thighs, a little grouchy in the morning, wearing a Talbots suit that made her look a little more stylish than her South Boston accent made her sound. She also had a license to carry . . . and did.

"Peter," she said, "I don't know what you and this old antique'd do without me."

"It's *antiquarian*," said Orson.

"Okay. *Antique* antiquarian."

Peter took a sip of the coffee. "Perfect. As always."

"Yeah, yeah," she said over her shoulder, "you're welcome."

"Do you think she has any idea of how wonderful her job is?" asked Orson in a loud voice. "Sitting out there in a display room that looks like a private library, lined with bookcases containing everything from a second edition of the *Bay Psalm Book* to the collected works of Sir Winston Churchill in full vellum to a first edition of *Catcher in the Rye* in the original dust jacket. And she still takes—"

"Yeah. Yeah. I still take *Reader's Digest* on the subway." She sat at her desk, just beyond Peter's door. "You wouldn't want me ridin' the Red Line with some ten-thousand-dollar book on my lap, would you, you silly bastard?"

Orson looked at Peter. "A dangerous precedent to hire your aunt."

"My father hired her. She used to smoke. Now she talks back. So . . . commonplace books . . . blank pages to be filled with literary quotes, meditations, musings . . ."

"In a time and place where books were scarce, if you read something you liked, you copied it into your commonplace book," said Orson. "Not many survived. Those that did aren't worth a lot because, as you say, they're mostly brain droppings. The one that's best known belonged to John Leverett, a Harvard tutor who became college president. That's at the Massachusetts Historical Society."

"Do we know if any of these commonplace books mention Shakespeare?"

"Peter, I'm brilliant, not encyclopedic." Orson went out to the display room and came back with Morison's *The Intellectual Life of Colonial New England*, 1933 edition. He flipped pages until he found what he wanted. "Morison says the only reference to Shakespeare in any commonplace book that survived is a bit from *Venus and Adonis*."

"But that's a poem," said Peter. "Not a play."

"Never a play. The Puritans took their devils seriously. They slaughtered their Indian devils. They hanged their witchy devils. They banned their playwright devils."

"*All* playwrights?"

"Not the Greeks and Romans, but . . ." Orson went out again and came back with a slipcased two-volume *Diary of Samuel Sewall*. He turned to the back of volume two. "You'll find no mention in this index of Shakespeare, Marlowe, or any Restoration playwright, even though the frontispiece shows Sewall before his congregation, making 'public repentance for his action in the witchcraft trials.' For all his tolerance and erudition, in forty-five years of diaries, Sewall never mentions a play and only one playwright."

"Who?"

"Ben Jonson. He stumbled across a folio of Jonson's plays in a tavern in Rhode Island in 1706. A tavern! Rhode Island was always more tolerant, but—"

Peter heard a knock at the outer door, then heard Bernice push away from her desk, "Yeah. Yeah. Hold your horses."

Fallon Antiquaria occupied an L-shaped space on the third floor of a Newbury Street bowfront, above an art gallery that was above a restaurant. The display room was in the long section of the L, Peter's office in the tail. And it was strictly "by appointment only."

Fallon glanced at his datebook: no appointments. Probably a delivery. So he kept his attention on Orson.

"The first mention of Shakespeare's work in a Harvard library is the 1709 Rowe edition, referenced in the catalog of 1723, and—" Orson stopped talking and looked to the doorway.

In an instant, Peter smelled Shalimar, turned, and almost fell off his chair.

Evangeline Carrington was standing there. "Hello, boys. How's books?"

"Books are great," said Peter. "How's magazines?"

"I keep writing. Now that I'm divorced, I have to."

"Books, magazines, divorces . . . You two will have a lot to talk about." Orson got up and gave Evangeline a kiss on the cheek. "Wonderful to see you again, dear."

"He's right," said Peter. "You look wonderful."

She'd been married to a plastic surgeon, but her beauty was natural. A few honest subtle crow's-feet around the eyes, subtle lines around the mouth, but nothing sagging under that strong jaw. She'd given her hair just enough frosting to cover any gray. And she'd always known how to dress: a tweed jacket over a starched white shirt with open collar, a quarter-inch gold chain at her neck, discreet gold hoops in her ears, jeans tight enough to show that she still worked out, and a nice pair of oxblood cowboy boots.

"I was expecting you tomorrow," said Peter.

"They pushed up my deadline. An article on Cape Cod guesthouses in autumn. So it's lunch with Ridley Royce today, Cape Cod with my grandmother tomorrow."

"How's your grandmother?" asked Peter. "She must be over a hundred."

"She is, and right now, I'll take the company of a female centenarian to any man I know." She sat in Orson's chair. "But if you're offering, I'll take a ride up to Royce's."

Bernice brought Evangeline a cup of coffee. "Nice to see you, darlin'."

"Bernice, you look great," said Evangeline. "Do you still have your Beretta?"

"Fits in a purse. Nice and ladylike."

"I could've used it when I found out my husband liked other women's wrinkled flesh more than mine."

"You want to shoot him, call me." Then Bernice asked Peter, "Open or closed?"

"What?"

"The door. Open or closed? Once you wipe that silly grin off your face, you two will have a lot to talk about."

"Everybody keeps saying that." Evangeline cast a smile at Fallon. "Of course, we decided about eighteen years ago that we'd run out of things to talk about."

"I'll leave the door open, then," said Bernice, "and if you want to shoot *him* . . ."

Peter grabbed his jacket and told Evangeline, "Let's go for that ride."

It was true. They did have a lot to talk about, but they started on something easy: Peter's son. Peter was a father, so he bragged. Evangeline seemed to enjoy it.

Then they moved on to their work . . . another easy topic.

Evangeline said that people were always interested in reading about interesting places. If the economy was good, they read because they were making plans and looking for pointers, and if the economy was bad, they read to fantasize.

Peter said that the trend in the antiquarian business was mostly up, good economy or bad, because rare books grew only rarer as the years went by. But it wasn't always a gentleman's business. "I'm still paying off a mistake a few years ago. I had a seller, always honest, delivered books with great provenance. Told me that he had a

Shakespeare Second Folio in red morocco. Very rare. I paid him two hundred and fifty thousand for it."

"Not in cash, I hope."

"Cashier's check. Just as bad. But I had a buyer who'd pay five hundred."

"A nice profit."

"Not as nice as I would have had if I'd put the book up for auction. But in my business, you nurture clients. If a trustworthy seller wants a cashier's check, you deliver. And you never gouge the buyer who's always there. So . . . I was making the seller happy with his check, and the buyer with a nice deal, and myself with a nice profit. Win-win-win. Except that I'd been set up. The Folio had been stolen from a private library in Illinois. By the time we figured it out, the seller had disappeared and I was a quarter million in the hole."

"So, what did you do?"

"I cried a lot. Orson, too. Even Danny cried. And Bernice, she just cussed me out. Two years ago, we saw no profits whatsoever, and a few fire-sale prices on some very rare items, just to pay the rent. . . . You know, you're the first person I've told about that outside of the office."

"I'm flattered . . . I guess."

From there, it was almost easy to move on to talk about divorce. His first, well behind him now. "And all for the best," he lied.

She showed him how well she knew him by telling him she didn't believe him.

So he said, "All right. Mine was bad. Tell me the truth about yours."

But she wouldn't say much, except that it had been messy, and she was still raw.

So he said, "Sounds like what you need is a little distraction."

And she laughed for the first time. "Peter, when some men say that, they mean, 'Maybe you should go to a chick flick and have a good cry.' When *you* say that, it means, 'I'm going on a treasure hunt. Come along, if you know how to handle dynamite.'"

"That makes me sound more interesting than most guys."

She gave him a look from the corner of her eye. He knew it well. It said: *Dream on . . . Not a chance . . . And don't even think of it . . .*

All at once. Then she said, "Ridley Royce has invited me to lunch. He's all the distraction I need right now, thanks."

"Would you be surprised to know that Ridley has started me on another treasure hunt?"

"I was afraid of that."

They drove into a fogbank around Rockport, a town famous for its granite coastline, for seaside mansions owned by stockbrokers who commuted on the 8:10 to Boston, and for Motif #1, the fisherman's shack that had been painted and photographed more times than any other scene in America.

Ridley lived in one of the mansions, which had been in his family for generations and looked as though it hadn't been painted in generations. The shingles that weren't split were paper-thin, the paint was curling from the crimson trim, the windows needed glazing. And Ridley didn't answer the door.

"Ring the bell again," said Evangeline.

"He may be ducking me," said Peter. "Probably wants to talk to you alone. He likes to play all the angles. . . . Ridley! Hey, Ridley!"

Peter's voice was swallowed up by the fog. And no answer.

Evangeline peered in a window. "I only agreed to have lunch with him because he got me tickets to *The Lion King* once when I wanted to impress my ex-husband's niece."

Peter walked over and looked in the garage window. "The car's still here. . . . Ridley! Hello, Ridley."

No answer.

Evangeline followed Peter around the side of the house. "He wanted to see my grandmother, too. He said my ancestors could have information that might have tremendous impact on world theater."

"Ridley Riddles," muttered Peter.

"I told him that the last time I let someone dig into my ancestry, it was you," she said, "and it was nothing but trouble. Sometimes Ridley strikes me as a little strange."

"And sometimes a little drunk. Hey, Ridley!"

The back lawn sloped a hundred feet down to the granite rocks and the ocean below. The lawn was mostly crabgrass, the ocean mostly covered in fog, and the house just as deserted in back as in the front. The only sounds were the gentle wash of the waves on the rocks and the drone of an outboard somewhere in the fog.

Peter reached under the back steps. "He told me he kept a key—"

"Peter." Evangeline took a few steps toward the water. "Look."

About two hundred yards out, a boat was appearing. But it did not come toward them. Instead, it disappeared again into the fog. A moment later, it reappeared, came a little closer, cut a curving line in the water, and disappeared. When it came out of the fog again, it was closer still . . . cut another curving line . . . disappeared.

"That boat's just going in circles, Peter."

"Corkscrew circles, like the helm's thrown over, but nobody's driving."

When the boat emerged again, Peter saw the brand name on the hull: *Grady White.* "I think that's Ridley's boat."

"Well, if he's drunk, he must be passed out, because he's going to corkscrew right into the rocks."

Peter saw a Zodiac tied to Ridley's mooring about twenty feet from shore. He kicked off his shoes and socks, pulled off his turtleneck and trousers, and said, "Call nine-one-one."

"Peter, that water's forty degrees. You'll freeze to death."

"Why do you think I want you to call nine-one-one?"

It was like jumping into a snowbank . . . in your shorts. If Peter had been able to focus on pain, rather than shock, he might have noticed that his testicles had retracted toward his liver, but he couldn't feel anything, so he swam as hard as he could, grabbed the side of the Zodiac, and flipped himself into the rubber boat.

The little outboard kicked over, and in a cold instant, Peter shot out to the Grady, bumped against the hull, and called Ridley again.

No answer.

He put the outboard in neutral and wrapped a line around a cleat on the port quarter, which took up enough of his attention that it wasn't until he had jumped onto the Grady that he realized there was no Ridley there, either.

The harbormaster found Ridley's body two hours later, floating out near the breakwater, about a mile offshore.

By the time he brought the body back to the wharf, Peter Fallon was dressed and waiting, along with Evangeline and a state police detective.

"Can you make the I.D. for us?" asked the detective.

The harbormaster flipped back the tarp on the deck. And there was Ridley, face as blue as his jeans, eyes open halfway, fly open all the way.

"That's him," said Peter.

"Is that exactly how you found him?" asked the detective.

"Yep," said the harbormaster, an old-timer wearing fish-stained khaki trousers and soup-stained khaki shirt. "Haven't touched a thing."

"Then it's an accident," said the detective.

"How can you tell?" asked Peter.

The harbormaster pointed to Ridley's trousers. "Fly's open. There's beer cans on the boat. Yellow dribbles on the transom."

"Wait a minute," said Peter. "How do you know it's an accident?"

"Seen it a million times," said the harbormaster. "Guy has a few beers, goes to the stern to drain his kidneys, boat lurches and he falls off, but he don't have the kill switch hooked to his belt, so the engine keeps runnin' and the boat goes drivin' off on its own."

The detective said, "Half the boating deaths in New England are middle-aged men found floatin' with their flies open."

"Does this mean you aren't looking for witnesses?" asked Peter.

"Witnesses? In pea-soup fog?" said the harbormaster.

"Witnesses to what?" The detective closed his notebook. "Accident, pure and simple."

Ridley Wedge Royce would have called it "the Full Wedge." That's the kind of send-off they gave him.

They were all there in the new Old South in the old Back Bay: Will Wedge with his porcelain wife and his English-major daughter and her halfback boyfriend; Will's mother, Harriet, stifling the kind of cough you didn't hear much anymore, now that most chain-smokers were dead; the Pacifist Physicist and Olga Basset; and plenty of theater people, too—actors and actresses, set designers and lighting technicians, a pair of New York critics, one of whom whispered to the other that he came only to make sure the no-talent son of a bitch was dead. And then there were the old girlfriends . . . enough old girlfriends, in fact, to fill a whole row.

Of course, Ridley was there, too, in a little urn that would be placed in the Royce crypt at the Mount Auburn Cemetery.

There were hymns, readings, remarks from friends. And just before the organ swelled for the recessional, one of Ridley's girlfriends delivered the best eulogy of all, in a perfect stage whisper: "I always knew he couldn't keep his fly zipped, but I didn't think it would kill him."

The service was followed by a reception at the Harvard Club on Commonwealth Avenue—five stories of conference rooms, squash courts, and guest rooms, with plenty of places for the hungry Harvard graduate to eat, from a basement snack bar to a baronial dining hall with tapestries and portraits and a massive pipe organ.

The Royce reception was held in the room at the top of the grand staircase. Since Ridley didn't really have much more family than the Wedges and a few other cousins, there was no long receiving line. Everyone just worked the buffet in the middle of the room, or took the wall space beneath the portraits of famous politicians from Harvard.

Peter, Evangeline, and Orson Lunt collected under a painting of John F. Kennedy in his academic robes.

"All the Wedges are here," whispered Peter to Orson, "except for that phantom brother. I wonder if he'll show up."

"I wouldn't count on it."

"Mr. Fallon"—Harriet Wedge approached—"it's wonderful of you and your friends to come."

Peter started to introduce the others but Harriet said, "No need. Evangeline's grandmother and I are old friends. We see each other every year in Florida. And who in Boston doesn't know Orson Lunt? A fixture at charity events and cocktail parties for fifty years."

"And I've seen you at just about every one," said Orson.

"It's a shame about poor Ridley," said Evangeline.

"A shame," said Harriet. "He was a nuisance, but he was our nuisance."

"Nuisance?" said Peter.

"Come on, Mr. Fallon. You spent time with him. You were even doing business with him. And he was about to turn you into a nuisance, too."

"I want him to stay at it." Will Wedge appeared at his mother's side and gently suggested that she get herself a plate of food.

Harriet said to Orson, "Care to squire an old woman to the finger sandwiches?"

"So long as sandwiches are the only things that require my fingers," said Orson.

"You always know the way to a woman's heart," she said.

Will Wedge gave a false little chuckle, then turned back to Peter. "Can we talk a little business?"

"I guess I'll get a few finger sandwiches, too." Evangeline excused herself.

Peter said to Wedge, "Why the change of heart?"

Wedge leaned close to Fallon. "I know what Ridley was after."

"Really?"

Wedge widened his smile, nodded to someone who complimented him on his eulogy, took a sip of white wine, and said to Fallon, "A commonplace book."

Fallon said nothing. Sometimes it was the best thing to say.

Wedge asked, "Do you know how few commonplace books there are out there?"

"Commonplace books are scarce," said Fallon.

"Would one be worth twenty-five thousand dollars if you could find it?"

"That would be the jackpot for a commonplace book."

"It's for my daughter. A primary source like that would be a wonderful addition to a senior honors thesis. Guarantee her a summa."

Like hell, thought Fallon. But he said, "The other day, out on the river, you told me you didn't want any antiquarians getting in the way of her plans."

"But if you're working for me, you're not getting in the way. You're helping."

"Helping to what?"

"To tell the story of Harvard. Isn't that why you're in this business?"

"I'm in this business for the money. Why are you in it?"

Will gestured to the walls. "I like to look at old portraits. I look into the eyes and imagine what those people saw, what they were thinking. A good portrait is like a window on the past. So are the books and documents that a man like you tracks down. Once my daughter is done with what you find, I'll give it to Harvard."

Fallon liked that, so he said, "Any particular commonplace book you have in mind?"

"John Wedge's book has come to light recently, as you know."

Peter nodded. He didn't know as much as Will Wedge assumed, but he was not giving up what little he had.

"That book offers some marvelous insights," said Will. "I think Dorothy and I would both like to know if our family left others. And if they did, where are they?"

Peter was wondering how he had missed news of the John Wedge book. He was also wondering how he would begin to look for one that had been lost hundreds of years before, like a needle in the haystack of time. But when Will Wedge offered $25,000 for commonplace books from any of his other ancestors, they had a deal.

Peter had one more question. "What do you know about a troublemaker by the name of James 'Bingo' Keegan?"

Wedge stopped, then stepped back, lowered his voice, and brought his face close to Fallon. "Bingo Keegan? You think he's—"

"You know him?" asked Peter.

Will Wedge, smoothest talker in any crowd, fumbled for something to say until he finally managed, "Everybody knows about Bingo Keegan." Then he put his smile back. "Being from South Boston, you probably knew him back when the rest of us thought Bingo Keegan was just a game they played at the parish halls."

That remark made Fallon like Wedge a bit less, but they had a deal. Twenty-five thousand for a commonplace book. And Fallon would be the first to read it.

Evangeline and Peter said good-bye in the October sunshine, in the parking lot behind the Harvard Club. They had to talk in loud voices so that they could hear each other over the roar of the Massachusetts Turnpike.

Evangeline said, "So . . . I'm off to the Cape with my grandmother, and it sounds like you're off on another treasure hunt that's just gotten more dangerous."

"You think?"

"*You* do. You think somebody killed Ridley, don't you?"

"I don't know. But I owe it to him to follow this business a little bit longer."

She got into her car and rolled down the window. "Don't think it hasn't been real, Peter. We don't see each other in years, and three hours after we do, I'm looking at a dead body. This is not a good omen, but"—she patted his arm—"stay in touch."

So he touched her hand. "Give your grandmother my best."

"She's always asking for you. Take her to lunch sometime." And she drove off.

All for the best, he thought. If they spent more time together, they'd be arguing the way they used to. But a good argument would be nice if it ended like their arguments in the old days.

Back in his office, he turned again to *Sibley's Harvard Graduates* for a little insight into the life of John Wedge:

As far as is known, he spent the first sixteen years of his life on a farm in Sudbury. His father, Isaac Wedge (H.U. 1642), had left the ministry for husbandry. . . .

The article then spoke of King Philip's War, John's career at Harvard, and his graduation in 1678, in the class made famous by Cotton Mather.

Wedge later married Mary Cogswell, with whom he had no issue. However, he was welcomed into the merchant business of Mr. Cogswell, and acquitted himself so effectively as an agent of the colony in the West Indies that when he returned, he was asked to become a member of the governor's council, which led to his appointment to the court of oyer and terminer, convened in 1692 to confront the scourge of witchcraft.

Chapter Nine

=====

1692–1694

TWO RIDERS, trailing dry summer dust, galloped hard for Salem.

Isaac Wedge saw the dust before he saw the riders. He was standing near the top of Gallows Hill, surveying all the roads that led to Salem and hoping that there might be some reprieve for his friend George Burroughs.

It was well known that Satan was relentless; he was also patient. Sixteen years he had waited after the demise of King Philip before mounting another attack on the people of Massachusetts. Many believed that Satan had begun by afflicting a handful of girls in Salem. A few, however, believed that he merely used the girls to attack the innocent people they accused of witchcraft.

If Satan were disguised in the crowd that morning, wondered Isaac, would he be happier to see the cart carrying "witches" to their death, or those distant riders who might be bringing reprieves but were as likely carrying saddlebags full of self-righteousness?

They were hanging five that day, one woman and four men. The cart was bouncing up the rutted road to the gallows, preceded by six deputies and Judge Sewall, before whom the crowd made way with all the fearful respect that such a cortege demanded.

How strange, thought Isaac, that the vision of those who founded the college was fulfilled here on this August day, where convened leaders of the colony to the second and third generation—ministers, judges, and one of the condemned, all of them educated at the School of the Prophets to guide the colony.

The girls had named George Burroughs, '70, as leader of the coven. They said he summoned his minions on Saturday nights with the blast of a horn that ordinary mortals could not hear. The witches and wizards would arrive on broomsticks from across New England; they would all alight in a Salem pasture, and there defile the Sabbath under the direction of Salem's former minister.

The girls had described Satan as a "dark little man, though not a Negro." And it was Burroughs's bad fortune that he had black hair and olive-dark skin, and despite his compact stature, he was legendary for strength that some called superhuman. It was his worse fortune, thought Isaac, that he had run afoul of the uncle of one of these girls during his ministry in Salem.

If the girls had known of Burroughs's taste for reading Shakespeare, they might have used that against him, too, and perhaps condemned Isaac as well.

But Isaac would not desert his friend. The night before, he had visited Burroughs in a dirt-floored dungeon lit by the greasy yellow light of a single lantern. Four men were imprisoned there, each absorbed in his own thoughts in his own corner.

Burroughs had spoken bitterly of Harvard-taught judges who admitted spectral evidence—visions seen only by the afflicted girls. "They had no physical evidence till the girls came in with bite marks on their arms, claimin' the devil's servant had done the bitin'. So the judges—your own smart son among 'em—made me print my teeth on a piece of wax." Burroughs had opened his mouth wide and slammed it so hard that Isaac had felt his own remaining teeth rattle.

"You are no more guilty than I," Isaac had said.

"Do not say that too loudly." Burroughs had looked around. "They have evidence 'gainst you even better than bite marks."

"Better?"

"A book on insects, given by you to the college, transformed by some dark magic into the work of a devil named Shakespeare."

Isaac had put that truth out of his mind and said, "I've been to

Boston, to prey upon the conscience of my son. He may yet bring a reprieve from the governor."

"The governor has no power here. 'Tis ministers hold sway. And your son be in thrall to one of 'em . . . that damned Cotton Mather." Then Burroughs had buried his head in his hands and sunk back into the shadows. . . .

But in the bright sun, Burroughs stood defiantly erect. Isaac offered him a gesture of encouragement, then looked toward the riders, who had reached the edge of the crowd: Judge John Wedge and Reverend Cotton Mather. And Isaac knew they brought no reprieve.

Burroughs paid them no mind, however. He was begging permission of Samuel Sewall that he be allowed to speak, and Sewall was consenting.

So the wiry little man mounted the gallows ladder, and with his hands bound behind his back, he looked out at the farmers and goodwives and girls with bite marks on their arms, and he proclaimed his innocence with a conviction so powerful that Isaac could feel it surge through the crowd.

As he was standing close to Sewall, Isaac whispered, "The people are moved."

"The people are unthinking," answered Sewall.

And now Burroughs said, " 'Tis a known fact that a witch, a wizard, or any other in thrall to Satan, cannot utter the Lord's prayer. So hear you this." And he began to speak the words: "Our Father, who art in heaven, hallowed be thy Name . . ."

And the murmuring crowd grew quiet.

"Thy kingdom come, thy will be done, on earth as it is in heaven."

The crowd drew closer.

"Give us this day our daily bread. And forgive us our debts as we forgive our debtors."

Those words, offered by a condemned man, no matter the cause of his condemnation, brought a sob from the breast of a goodwife standing near Isaac.

Suddenly, one of the afflicted girls cried out, "The black man! I see the black man whisper in Burroughs's ear." And then she swooned, which brought forth loud cries from the other girls.

Several in the crowd told them to quiet themselves, as if their antics might work in the courtroom but not in the bright sunlight of Gallows Hill.

And Burroughs thundered on, the power of his voice overwhelming the girlish cries: "Lead us not into temptation, but deliver us from evil."

"Deliver us all," said a big man in a fishmonger's apron.

"For thine is the kingdom, and the power, and the glory, for ever and ever."

An "amen" echoed through the crowd like a stone dropped into a puddle, sending out ripples that then rippled back, just as the crowd now pressed in toward the gallows.

"He is a goodly man," cried another goodwife.

"A godly man!" cried a farmer.

"Judge Samuel"—the fishmonger pushed his face close to Sewall—"are you not moved? Hear you how he prays? No wizard can pray like that!"

Sewall looked from the crowd to the sheriff to the condemned on the gallows, all of them now looking to him with new expectation. And another of the condemned cried out, "We are all innocent!"

"Innocent, indeed," whispered a man in Isaac's ear. He was tall and better dressed than most, a merchant by the name of Robert Calef, who seemed always to wear a wry smile, as if perpetually amused by human folly. "Condemned they were, by the holy ignorance of men like your son and Cotton Mather."

"You're a long way from Boston," said Isaac, keeping his eyes on the gallows.

"The story of this travesty must be told, so as not to be repeated."

Sewall nodded to the sheriff, who prodded Burroughs toward the nooses.

As Burroughs stretched his neck, the whole crowd seemed to stretch toward him. The good people of Salem, so respectful of their leaders, so willing to believe that it was evil they saw if evil it was called, gave out with a sound that was part cry of horror, part roar of anger.

Calef said, "I sense a change. Perhaps you should speak up."

"Perhaps you should," said Isaac.

"People of Salem!" A voice pierced the air, rising above the sound of hundreds of shuffling feet and cutting through the dust raised by the shuffling. It was Cotton Mather, round-faced and red-faced, standing high in his stirrups. "The devil has oft been transformed into an angel of light! Take care that he does not deceive you all this day!"

"But Reverend Burroughs recites the Lord's Prayer!" cried one of the goodwives.

"He is no reverend," answered Mather.

"He is the dark man!" cried one of the girls, gaining courage from Mather.

"He is not even ordained!" Mather added.

That, thought Isaac, was too fine a point, but Cotton Mather was a man who believed in fine points.

The fishmonger shouted, "But the Lord's Prayer—"

"Do you not see it?" Mather roared. "As he deceives you to believe he is a minister, he can deceive you with a minister's words. 'Twould be no different if he took the form of an old crone and spun wool that did not warm."

"What should we do, then?" cried another.

"See that they all receive their righteous sentence!"

Isaac had worked his way to the edge of the crowd, where Mather and John sat their horses. He made eye contact with his son, and mouthed the word "righteous?"

Judge John Wedge simply folded his hands on the pommel of his saddle and fixed his eyes on the gallows.

It was for Mather to answer, "Yes, Isaac Wedge! Righteous begun and righteous concluded."

And John Wedge said, "Sheriff, if Judge Sewall concur, do your duty."

With no further ceremony, and no words from any respectable preacher, for no respectable preacher would pray over them, the nooses were fitted and the warrants read. When the gallows dropped, there was no great shriek of bloodthirsty joy, only the sound of three necks snapped and two windpipes crushed, and five minions of Satan were left twitching in the air like puppets.

ii

The riders of righteousness did not rest in September. There were more trials and more hangings, but as the weather cooled, more learned men came to see the trials as Isaac had seen them, as persecutions instead of prosecutions.

By January, the governor had released anyone still awaiting trial for witchcraft.

Even Increase Mather saw the truth. He had returned from England with a new charter for the colony and had once more assumed his duties as pastor of the Second Church and president of the college. Coming late to the controversy, he had written, "To take away the life of anyone, merely because a Spectre or Devil in a bewitched person accuses them, will bring the Guilt of Innocent Blood on the Land."

His son had agreed, at least in principle. But Cotton Mather's pen had proved one of the most prolific resources in all of New England, and he had written a book called *Wonders of the Invisible World*, to uphold the righteousness of the trials and remind the province of Satan's universal presence.

The Mathers had their differences, then, but they remained faithful servants to the community, the college, and each other. Cotton supported the new charter, though it permitted any Protestant sect to worship in what once had been a Puritan colony. And Increase wrote of his pride in his son's book: "Nothing but my Relation to him hinders me from recommending it to the world."

John Wedge often wished that he had been as close to his father, or that his father had risen as high as Reverend Increase. How much better would be the impression that John made in Boston, had his father been minister to a respectable Middlesex congregation rather than a disillusioned preacher and failed farmer teaching grammar to the sons of bumpkins?

But some men, thought John, were destined for great service

while others were doomed by their dreams, their disappointments, and their own stubborn sense of themselves to live on the edge of God's community. John considered himself the former and his father the latter, and that was why they argued whenever they were together.

Indeed, they planned their arguments. They met in Cambridge once a month, just before the regular meeting of the Harvard Corporation. John would ride out from Boston, and Isaac would travel from his little school in Sudbury. They would dine together; they would argue until meeting time. And afterward, they would argue all the way back to John's home in Boston, and argue there until the last call of the town crier.

So they were arguing on a bright October afternoon . . . about a seventeen-year-old girl named Margaret Rule, who had fallen to fits in the Mathers' meetinghouse and had been taken home hysterically proclaiming that the devil was upon her.

"I tell you," said Isaac, "the stories of this Rule girl are nonsense."

"Father," said John, "the devil levitated her from her bed. She rose near to the ceiling. I have seen the affidavits of men who were there."

"And did they see *her* affidavits, or did her nightgown cover them?"

Father and son were crossing the greensward where the Old College once stood.

John went with the regal, slow gait of a man who knew his worth in the world, one who had married well, who had inherited his father-in-law's ships, and whose success in managing them had earned him a place on both the governor's council and the Harvard Corporation. There were thirteen Congregational ministers on the governing board, and John Wedge, so highly did President Increase Mather respect him.

Isaac moved slowly, too, but with no touch of regality. He had lived too long and seen too much, and a fall from a horse had frozen one of his hips.

Not only did their manner of motion distinguish them. The son kept his princely dark beard carefully trimmed. The father went clean-shaven but let his white hair grow to his shoulders.

John said, "Our goal in Salem was to root out true evil. We will do as much in Boston, if we must. Otherwise, we invite Satan back in."

"The trials were a disgrace," said Isaac. "Spectral evidence used against friends, neighbors, classmates—"

"Only Burroughs was charged from any college class. And half the judges on the court were educated here as well . . . Stoughton, Saltonstall, Sewall—"

"Sewall speaks of making public repentance. So should you. Burroughs was no more guilty of witchcraft than I."

"Don't say that so loud, Father. Should that remark be heard by the wrong ears—"

"Such as his?" Isaac gestured toward the courtyard between Harvard Hall and the president's house. There Cotton Mather stood in conversation with several other ministers of the corporation.

At the approach of the Wedges, Mather doffed his wide-brimmed black hat. "Our meeting may begin, now that Judge Wedge is here."

"A judge no longer, Reverend Mather," said John, responding with similar formality, though they were lifelong friends.

"You may be called on yet again," answered Mather, "should we fail to stop the devil's incursion into the body of Margaret Rule."

"Have you seen her rise to the ceiling?" asked Isaac.

Mather ignored Isaac and said to John, "I fast for her soul tomorrow. I would have you join me at her home. I hope for an audience as we pray over her and drive Satan out."

"An audience?" cried Isaac.

"We must show Satan our minions," Mather answered.

"I shall be there," said John. "And I shall make a fast for your success."

"I won't fast," said Isaac. "Old men need their victuals. But I'll be there, too."

"Come in the right spirit," said Mather, "one of vigilance. As my father says, we've claimed a corner of the world where the devil reigned without control for ages. We've claimed it from his Indians and his witches, too. We must be vigilant."

"Aye . . . vigilant," said Isaac. "I be ever vigilant."

Mather glanced at the sundial on Harvard Hall and went inside.

"Father, you must control your words," whispered John.

Isaac patted his son on the shoulder. "Go do your business. I'll go and visit my book. 'Tis a fine work of natural philosophy, but so sadly neglected that only two students have signed it out in sixteen years. One died of consumption. The other made no comment. And then there was Burroughs. Do you think the girls called him a devil because they knew he'd read the devil Shakespeare?"

"Father," said John in a low, angry voice, "I may have resigned from the court, but I have responsibilities to the colony. You should not speak to me of such things."

"Someday, I'll speak to the *world* of such things. But when simple ministers are hanged as witches, what fate would befall him who preserved the work of Shakespeare?"

Section twelve, shelf eight, space six. To Isaac's relief, *Corporei Insectii* had not been read by anyone since last he had been there. Indeed, it seemed not to have been moved. The Lord, he concluded, still approved of its presence in the college library.

And that became the topic of argument that evening in Boston.

John's wife, Mary, was racked by a cough that left her weak and feverish. So she retired early, leaving father and son to dispute the question of God's favor on a playwright whom some considered a devil but many others had come to revere.

"You've read the play," said Isaac, "and you would agree that this Shakespeare has much to say to man about men."

"'Tis why I've never cast out *Love's Labours Won*. But the law—"

"The law." Isaac Wedge laughed. "The belief that the devil can speak through playwrights is as crazy as the belief that he can raise a woman to the ceiling."

"Father," said John in all seriousness, "the devil can do anything. He is a spirit."

"We will find out tomorrow."

When the first shaft of sunlight struck his eyes, John Wedge awoke. His bed was empty, for his wife slept in another room. She did this, she said, so as not to disturb him with her coughing. She also did this, he surmised, so as not to be disturbed by a husband whose needs she could no longer fulfill.

He pulled on his breeches and threw himself onto the floor, so that his face was pressed against the smooth red nap of the Turkish carpet and his body was stretched out in the morning sun. Ordinarily, when he prayed, he retired to his study with his books and his thoughts. But on days when prayer preceded a fast, he began in prostration.

"Oh, Lord," he said aloud. "One of our neighbors is horribly arrested by evil spirits. I beg Thy help to free her. Send us Thy bright angels, to watch over us and guide us in this and all our torments and sadnesses, that we may serve Thee as Thou wish."

John had never seen his father fast or prostrate himself in prayer. These aspects of piety John had learned from Cotton Mather. And he had learned well, because God had blessed him.

John needed only to look out his window to see the Lord's bounty upon him. He could gaze across his vegetable garden and down to the Great Cove, to his ships—half a dozen his by his wife's inheritance, half a dozen his by his own intelligence. Some of them sat at the wharves, loading on the goods of New England, and some of them sailed in with the products of the wide world.

But his piety and faith had not been great enough, because the richest of the Lord's blessings—a house filled with happy noise—had not come to John Wedge. His morning sounds were always the same—the humming of the slave woman who stirred his porridge, the whisk of a broom worked by an indentured servant, and the quiet coughing of his wife. He heard no childish bickering, no motherly voice rising to calm a dispute, and for those, he would have surrendered everything else.

He went down to the dining room and kissed his wife on the forehead. She raised her face and smiled, but only briefly. She invited no further show of affection, and given her sickly appearance—eyes sunk in gray pits, lips as white as flour—it would have been unseemly of him to offer more.

"Good morning, my darling," she said. "Rosetta prepares a fine gruel."

"Save his share for me," said Isaac from the other end of the table. "He fasts."

"For the usual fulfillment?" She cast her eyes to her husband.

"He fasts for the soul of Miss Margaret Rule, that the devil may leave her." Isaac spooned a mouthful of porridge. "Possessed she is, or so they tell us."

"Most times," said Mary, "John fasts that we may give you a grandchild. A son for us, a grandson for you, another Wedge for the college."

Isaac lowered his spoon and said, "Nothing would make an old man happier, dear, save knowledge that my son walks through life with you as a companion."

For all their disputations, thought John, his father knew the right words at the right moment. The smile that brightened Mary's face was proof enough.

"You know," she said, "John even keeps his old commonplace book in his study. He would give it to his son, on the day that the boy enter Harvard."

And once more the eyes of father and son met in memory of that distant day when Isaac had first brought John from the Sudbury marshes to Cambridge.

John stepped out of the room and a moment later returned with a book. "Do you recognize this?"

Isaac took it as though it were a talisman of lost happiness. He flipped through the pages of John's tight-writ, upright, adolescent script. He read Latin quotations, passages from the Bible, and bits of conversation, including this, dated March 19, 1677:

> Cotton Mather: I h-h-h-have a new prescription to over-c-c-c-come the stammer.
> Me: By what science comes this knowledge?
> Cotton: The advice of that g-g-g-good old schoolmaster Mr. Corlet. He suggests I apply a certain d-d-d-dilated deliberation in speaking, as though I were a singer. In singing, there is no one who stammers, so by prolonging your pronunciation you will get a habit of speaking without hesitation.
> Me: I shall pray on it for you.

And interspersed with such things were passages of blank verse, including one that Isaac found familiar, dated April 30, 1676, just two weeks after the Sudbury attack:

A man be but a speck of dust, begot
By dust that breathed before, but dust that lives
Again, when dust itself hath turned to dust.

Beneath it was a parenthetical comment about the joys of love's labors.

John said, "Do you remember those days, Father?"

"I remember," said Isaac. "It please me that you remember, too, and share such memories, for they were days that showed love's labors won."

And John went on, as if he had not heard that meaning. "Today, we labor for the love of Christ, against Satan and his minions, whether they be unseen spirits or living deceivers who distract us with their work and words."

They heard Margaret Rule before they saw her. She was screaming.

She and her mother lived in a little house within the shadow of the Mathers' church, a quarter mile from the Wedge home on Hanover Street. A large crowd were peering in the doors and through the windows, for here was a grand spectacle.

"Rum!" she was screaming. "The devil bids me drink rum!"

"Aye," said a sailor at one of the windows. "The devil will do that."

"Make way," said John. And the crowd parted for the ex-judge and his father.

The sailor muttered, "Cotton Mather and John Wedge together. No wonder the devil wants her to have a dram. She'll need her strength."

"Aye," said another sailor. "I'll take one meself."

"Rum!" cried Margaret Rule again.

John and Isaac pushed through a doorway into the bedroom,

where a dozen men and women crowded around the bed in thick, stifling heat.

And there she lay, a beautiful girl in a jumble of bedclothes and wild black hair.

Sitting on the edge of the bed was Cotton Mather. "Peace, dear girl."

"Rum!" she cried, and then she began to toss her head from side to side. "Rum . . . No . . . no . . . no . . . rum . . . rum . . ."

"Dear girl," said Mather gently, "you must eat."

"But the devil . . . he forces me"—her jaw dropped and she looked about the room, then she tried to talk with her mouth seemingly locked open—"he pours brimstone down my throat. Burning brimstone! Burning!"

"I smell it," said a goodwife standing close to Isaac.

And Isaac thought, for a moment, that he smelled it, too, so convincing was this girl in her possession.

"Calm yourself," said Mather, reaching out to touch the girl's forehead.

And she closed her mouth.

"That's better." Mather was not wearing his wig or black hat, but rather a brown suit, which softened his presence considerably.

The girl smiled now and nuzzled his outstretched hand like a cat.

"See the bright angel," said Mather. "See him come to you and chase the dark man toward perdition."

"I . . . I . . ." The girl's eyes cast about the room until they fell upon John Wedge. "Who is here? Be this the white angel?"

"This is John Wedge," said Mather, "whom wicked spirits do fear."

She smiled at him. "He is most welcome, then, and most handsome . . . most . . ." Suddenly, her eyes opened wide and she gave out with a horrified shriek.

"What?" cried Mather. "What happens?"

"The devil lifts me!" she cried.

A gasp went through the room as she seemed to rise, first by her shoulders, then by her legs and feet, so that her shift fell back, revealing long, naked legs, almost to her crotch. "The devil lifts me. Help me!"

And a voice whispered in Isaac's ear, "She rises, all right, all but her arse." It was Robert Calef, the Boston merchant who was still criticizing the Mathers at every turn. "That glorious white arse that every man in the room would love to touch."

Isaac brought a finger to his lips.

But Calef kept on. "Her arse be the fulcrum for her body. She folds herself in the middle, so we get to see her parts and she gets to blame the devil for showin' them."

" 'Tis a fine arse," whispered Isaac.

" 'Tis the reason the room be so full."

Mather shot a glance in their direction, then picked up the sheet and tried to cover the girl's legs. "We must pray! Pray!"

"No!" The girl thrust her hands toward the ceiling, so her shift fell from her breasts. "I burn to hear the word *prayer*. I seethe to hear prayers. So utter no p-p-pr—" And she shrieked, then reached to John Wedge. "Please, master, lay on thy hands."

John looked at Mather, who nodded. "Lay on thy hands. It has worked before."

"Go on," said someone from the back of the room. "Give 'er a good feel."

"Quiet yourself," growled Mather.

John gently took one of the girl's legs.

She cried, "No, good sir. Not the legs. The breasts, for they be near the heart."

"Yes," said Mather. "The evil one cannot stand her to be touched near the heart. Like . . . like this." Mather pushed up the woman's shift, raised his chin, as if to say he was above reproach in what he was about to do, then firmly pressed his hand to her breast.

Immediately, her left side—stiffened arm and leg—sank back to the bed.

A cry of surprise and awe went through the room, as if it were a fine magic trick.

But her right side remained rigid, arm and leg both pointing toward the beams above her, and she cast her eyes again at John.

Cotton Mather said to John, "Quick. The evil in her weakens. Lay on thy hands."

Calef whispered in Isaac's ear, "She seduces your son. She relishes her play."

John put his hand on her right breast, and her arm and leg dropped to the bed.

"Lord be praised," said one of the goodwives.

"Lord be deceived," muttered Calef.

Isaac made no response. He was watching his son, who stood rigid at the side of the bed, his arm stretched out, his hand pressed on her breast.

"I feel the demons go," said the girl. "I feel the goodness of men."

"Look!" cried Mather. "Look there!"

"What?" answered John, eyes widening.

"Movement, under the pillow!" Mather stood up, and immediately, Margaret's left arm and leg shot toward the ceiling.

"Take my place, John, whilst I"—Mather's voice grew low—"take on the imp."

John did as he was told. He kept his left hand on her right breast and slipped his right hand onto the other, which relaxed the arm and leg. He told himself that he was acting above reproach. But her breasts were full and round and . . . he thanked God that there were so many witnesses.

Suddenly, Mather threw himself across the girl, in a flurry of flying legs, shoe buckles, and white stockings.

"What is it?" she cried from beneath him.

"An imp!" Mather drove his hands into the bedclothes. "I feel him."

"Where?" shouted John.

"Here! No, here! No . . ." Mather thrust his hands about while his muffled voice seemed to vibrate in the bedding. "Yes . . . I have him. Yes . . . no . . . no . . ." He pushed himself off of her, breathing heavy with excitement, and said, "I held it but a moment. A spirit, and yet it had substance. A living creature. It so startled me that I released my grip."

"What did it feel like?" asked John.

"A . . . a rat," said Mather. "For all the world, the imp of Satan felt like a rat."

"Then perhaps," said Robert Calef, "it was a rat."

Mather turned and glared at him. "No coffeehouse witling will turn us from our holy purpose. We are here to do the Lord's work, sir."

"But the imp?" said Calef. "If it felt like a rat, perhaps it was a rat."

"It was an imp of Satan!" He turned back to Margaret, who seemed to have settled. "And we are here to save this girl from such evil."

"You have, sir," she said groggily, and she arched her back against John's hands. "You and John Wedge . . . at least for today." And then she began to giggle.

"I now order you to leave," said Mather, "for it is her laughing time."

"That girl be taken with some female hysteria," said Isaac the next morning.

"Cotton Mather saw an imp," answered John.

"He saw a *rat*." Isaac swung an old leg over the saddle. "And I smell one."

"I'll see you in a month, Father."

"Aye," said Isaac. "But wait six weeks to see that girl again. Let her monthlies come and go at least once, then see if she improve."

John Wedge did not take his father's advice. He was back at Margaret Rule's house with the Mathers the very next day. He laid on hands, he prayed, and he soothed a young girl, all of which, he told the Mathers, felt far better than hanging her.

And he went to visit her another day when neither of the Mathers was in attendance, though the room was filled with gossiping townsfolk who had made this house a regular stop on their daily rounds.

At the sight of him, the girl cried out, "The bright angel!" Then she extended her hand and bade him sit on the edge of the bed, in the place usually occupied by Cotton Mather. As he did, her thigh pressed against his and her face broke into a smile, revealing fine, unbroken teeth.

And John had a strange thought: good teeth were the sure sign of good health.

Suddenly, the girl shrieked, and John leapt to his feet, thinking he had sat on her, or perhaps it was an imp and not her thigh pressing against him.

"The women!" she shrieked. "The women must leave!"

"Why?" asked a toothless old goodwife by the window.

"Because the dark angel is above your heads."

The goodwife ducked, as though a bird had just swept over her.

"All women leave!" Then Margaret opened her mouth and emitted an ear-piercing shriek that drove all the women and most of the men from the room.

But Robert Calef remained, at least a few moments more. He came every day to observe, comment, and scrawl notes in a small book. He stopped in the doorway and waited until Margaret had tired of shrieking, then said to John, "Be careful of the imps. They may be invisible, but they leave black droppings in the corners."

"Go and put that in your foul book," said Margaret with a sudden, cold calm.

"I believe that I will," said Calef. "And someday, I will publish your story."

Once more, Margaret became the possessed woman-child, all but levitating from the bed and shrieking for John to lay on his hands.

And so he did, in the name of the Lord, directly onto her barely covered breasts.

She arched herself into him and cried out in relief, "Ahh . . . the devil flees."

"Keep the white angel before you," he shouted.

"I cannot see him. Help me to see him." And with that, she placed her hands on his and directed them down, under the bedclothes, toward her loins.

He felt himself sinking toward her temptation. He yearned to touch her, to knead her, to caress the naked flesh under her bedclothes. But then the old sailor poked his head in the window and said, "Squeeze her good, Judge. Devil's in deep. Got to squeeze him out like the core of a boil." This brought John up straight.

"Please, good master," cried Margaret. "Massage the devil away."

Though it was meant to be a spiritual act, John Wedge was responding physically. He could not let them see his breeches bulging, not the old sailor nor Robert Calef nor the goodwives whose faces were reappearing in the window and doorway. So he left off massaging and hurried from the room, while Margaret Rule cried out for him to come back and free her from her torment.

That night, John Wedge was awakened by a torment of his own, a devil in the form of a dream, a naked spirit, a female spirit, with black hair and a dazzling smile, a spirit enticing him to embrace her, to kiss her, to press his hands against her breasts.

And when he did these things in his dream, the spirit moaned and moved against him, and the dream was so alive that even in his sleep, he could feel himself rising.

Then, his spirit lover began to cough, and the sound of the coughing woke him. And as the rising between his legs persisted, so did the coughing, for it was not a spirit that coughed but the sick woman sleeping in the next room.

For a time, John lay there and tried to will his hardness away, but it was as needful in its yearning as a soul for God. So he rose and went to the window. In the moonlight, the masts and spars of his ships looked like skeletons. But the turrets of the great triangular warehouse looked like breasts—three large, round, slate-covered breasts with flagstaff finials for nipples. How could a man look at a warehouse and see teats, unless he was going crazy or had himself been touched by Satan?

Soon he was hurrying along the moonlit street. If he met a constable, he would say that he was on the business of the colony, because he was. He was going to chase away demons. But whose?

At Margaret's house, he stopped by the window and peered inside. Though it was late, her light burned, as if the possessed did not sleep. To his surprise, she was reading the Bible. He whispered her name, and she raised her head. After a moment's start, she smiled.

"I have prayed for your visit, good master. I have prayed that you would come and pierce the evil spirit within me."

If Cotton Mather could have seen him at that moment, climbing through the window, stripping off his shirt and his breeches, slipping into her bed, pushing up her shift, John Wedge would have been cast out of church and colony, too. He might have been cast straight into hell.

But the touch of her bare legs sent a thrill through his body that made him forget everything else. He pressed against her and murmured, "We'll fight the devil together."

"Together," she gasped, "now."

And she swung a leg over him and pushed herself down upon him with a force that he had never felt in his now sickly wife. If it was glory or sin that engaged him, he did not know, but he would see it through, so he answered her strength with his own.

iii

It was a year later that Isaac Wedge heard alarming news:

"Sir, they're burning books in Harvard Yard."

"Burning books?"

"'Tis what I've heard," said the farmer who brought the story.

"What books?"

"I know not, just that Increase Mather . . . he has told his tutors to assemble the students in Harvard Yard this very night, to burn a foul book."

Isaac looked at his students, immersed in their mathematics, their phonics, their mental wanderings, and for a moment, he was a boy himself, making a promise to John Harvard.

He flipped the hourglass and told the young farmer, "Keep them in order till the sand run out. Then send 'em home."

It was a little after two o'clock on an October afternoon. If Isaac rode as hard as he could, which would not be very hard for he was an old man with a bad hip on an old horse, he would reach Cambridge just after dusk.

* * *

The Post Road flamed with the fall colors that Isaac considered one of God's most abundant gifts. But he did not think about colors as he rode, and he tried not to think about flames. He thought instead about the pain in his hip . . . and about his son.

Had John set this thing in motion? Had he finally revealed the truth about the Harvard bequest? Had he done it to curry favor with the Mathers? But to what purpose?

Any man whose wife had died in spring would not yet be himself by autumn. But whenever John spoke of his Mary's passing, he told his father, "Grief burdens me, and guilt, too . . . that I was not a good enough husband."

Isaac had assured him many times that he could not have been anything but a good husband. And yet, on quiet nights by the Sudbury marsh, the old man had let his mind take pathways he should not have followed, and they led to Margaret Rule.

Her "demons" had begun to retreat soon after John Wedge had visited her on his own, laid hands on her, and gone running from her room with a "tumescence" in his breeches, as Robert Calef had described it to Isaac. "But don't worry," Calef had said, "'tisn't your son interests me. 'Tis the Mathers."

Had his son been taken by the charms that Margaret Rule displayed for all of Boston? Had he acted upon desires that his dying wife could no longer fulfill? Was that why Mather had called him to spend a whole day in prayer shortly after Mary's death?

And if John was still burdened with guilt, might he have decided to cleanse his soul of whatever sins he could?

Isaac passed from Sudbury through the farm precinct of Watertown, then another eight miles to Watertown village, and there, his horse went lame. She was simply too old to be ridden so hard for so long, and though she was game enough to go on, she could not.

So he left her in a field, determined to go the last three miles to Cambridge on foot. The setting sun cast a long, limping shadow ahead of him, and the pain in his hip was blinding, but on he went. By the time he reached the west side of the Cambridge Common, darkness was rushing across the heavens like the evening tide across the Back Bay.

But on the other side of the Common, a bonfire had been lit.

Isaac could see it flaming in the courtyard between the president's house and Harvard Hall. So he hurried on, stumbling in holes and slipping in piles of cowflop. He ignored the old pain in his hip and the new pain blossoming in his chest, because the firelit shadows were jumping higher, and the arms of the Harvard Hall sundials seemed to be jumping, too, as if time itself had gone crazy.

Isaac realized that he must have been crazy to think he would outlive the prejudices and fears of his Massachusetts brethren. If a man would be known by his books, Isaac must proclaim himself at last. He had spent his life questioning the wisdom of those around him and seeing ignorance where others saw good sense. Reading a book had begun his rebellion. It had not been a book of philosophy or theology, but a play.

So he pushed himself through the darkness. He pushed himself toward the fire. He pushed himself across the road and came staggering into the crowd of students and townsfolk.

Increase Mather was standing close by the flames. Though he was president of the college, he seldom visited Cambridge, preferring to govern from his church in Boston. "What? Should I leave off preaching to fifteen hundred souls," he had once been heard to ask, "so that I may expound to forty or fifty children, few of them capable of edification by such exercise?" But for this night, he had come.

Isaac looked over the crowd for the tall familiar silhouette of his son, or of Cotton Mather, but he saw neither. He did not know if that should comfort him or not. He did see tutor John Leverett, however, at the same moment that Leverett saw him.

Isaac reached out to strong-armed Leverett, as much for moral support as physical. Leverett had helped run the college during the absence of the elder Mather. He had proved a liberal thinker who more than once had angered the younger Mather. And more than once, Isaac had considered revealing the truth to him. Tonight he would reveal it to all of them, if he did not pass out from the pain.

"Tutor Leverett," said Isaac, "what's happening?"

"The president shows his displeasure at a book."

"Students!" proclaimed Reverend Mather. "We come to burn the evil in this book."

Isaac tried to cry out, but the words would not come. They were strangled by an intense pain, and he staggered backward, clutching his chest.

"Master Wedge!" Leverett put his arm around Isaac's shoulders.

Meanwhile, Increase Mather raised a book high over his head. "This foul volume, which has brought so much—"

And now Isaac forced the word out. "No! No!"

The eyes of all the students turned to an old man in the shadows.

"No to what?" roared Increase Mather.

"No to burning that book."

"You would not burn a book of lies?" demanded Mather. "A besmirchment of my son, of all those who stood against the late evil, of your son, too?"

Isaac's old legs were shaking, there was a fire in his chest, and emotion was closing his throat. He tried to shout, but no words would escape him.

"The man is stricken," said Leverett.

"With ignorance," answered the president, "for his name is in this book, too."

Isaac tried to cry out that ignorance was all around and that this college should exist to drive it away. But he felt a great sinking, in his legs and in his head.

"This book is a work of lies," said Mather. "Lies are evil. Evil must be burned."

"No!" said Isaac weakly, his voice heard only by John Leverett. "That book is not evil. 'Tis truth in blank verse."

And the last sight that Isaac saw before his legs collapsed under him was the shadow of Increase Mather, hurling the book into the fire.

His last words were "Ignorance . . . ignorance."

"Massah Wedge?"

At the sound of his slave's voice, John Wedge popped up from between Margaret Rule's breasts. "Rosetta?"

"Massah Mather askin' for you, sir." The slave stood in the shadows outside the window, but she did not look into the room. "He say he have bad news."

John Wedge jumped out of bed, oblivious to his own nakedness. "Did he say what?"

"No." It was Mather himself, appearing behind the slave. "Your father is dead. Put on your breeches."

At dawn, John Wedge and Cotton Mather rode the ferry from Boston to Charlestown, on their way to retrieve Isaac's body. The sky was the gray of a dead man's cheek. The water was the gray of a headstone.

"Your father objected to the burning of a book," Mather said.

"A book?" said John. "A book in the Harvard bequest?"

Mather turned to him. "Is there a book in the bequest that should be burned?"

"No. No . . . what book, then?"

"*More Wonders of the Invisible World,*" said Mather.

"The book by Robert Calef? Just published?"

"Yes. A foul satire of my own work. Nothing but lies. Calef even claims that my father and I laid hands on Margaret Rule's bare breasts for the pleasure of it, as if we were no better Christian men than *you* turn out to be."

John Wedge studied the water and considered jumping into it.

"Be thankful Calef knew nothing of your transgressions." Mather spoke softly his hard-tempered words. "Or he would have written of those, too."

John offered no response. He simply listened to the screech of the cable pulley hauling the ferry across the narrow inlet.

"You have been taken in fornication," said Mather. "You should be punished."

"I can withstand it."

"Had you not been a judge in the court of oyer and terminer, I would expect it. But punishing you would give the witlings even more to use against us."

"Does your father intend to burn more books?" asked John Wedge.

"Worry not for the books," said Mather, "lest there be something in them to worry about. Worry for your immortal soul instead."

At the Charlestown side, they walked their horses off the ferry.

"I must consider a punishment," said Mather.

All the way down the Charlestown Road, John Wedge did as Mather suggested: he worried for his immortal soul. He worried as well for his father's. And he wondered if some truth-telling about a certain play would do both their souls some good.

But Mather, it seemed, worried less for John's soul than for the reputation of such a respected Puritan, because shortly after the little cluster of college buildings came into view, he slowed his horse and said, "You should be met with a public humiliation and fine. 'Tis the law."

"Aye."

"And Margaret Rule should be striped with a dozen lashes. But better that we ignore her, whilst you retire . . . to Sudbury perhaps, until the storm raised by Calef's book be blown over. Then, if Margaret grow big with some bastard and lay her belly to you, why . . . your distance from Boston will permit you to deny it."

John pulled on his reins. "Deny it?"

"She used us, John, as part of some grand performance to conceal her lustful desires behind the most serious of afflictions."

"You would have me deny my own seed?"

" 'Tis seed planted in hard-worked earth. Be thankful I protect you, while I inspire Mistress Rule to find other haunts." Then Mather spurred his horse and went galloping toward the college, his coattails flapping.

And in that moment, John Wedge heard the echo of his father's voice warning him that someday, if he read widely, he would read of man's passions, his vanities, his appetites, all the things that lead us toward sin. And why had his father warned him? Because there would come another day when he would meet those weaknesses in the flesh, in himself and in other men, even in a man who seemed as flawless as Cotton Mather. Best be prepared.

Chapter Ten

═══════════

ENGLISH 122. *From the Puritan Migration to the American Revolution. Professor Thomas Benedict. Tu, Th, 11 A.M. Emerson 105. An examination of literary currents flowing from Plymouth Rock to the frozen Delaware, with special emphasis on Colonial-era relationship between religious thought and political action. Readings in Bradford, Bradstreet, the Mathers, Franklin, Jefferson, Paine, etc.*

Peter Fallon slipped in at the back. He'd taken classes in Emerson 105. He remembered how bright the room was—bright sunlight flooding through the east windows, seats for 150 bright students, a stage for one brilliant professor. In Peter's case, it had been Walter Jackson Bate lecturing on the life of Samuel Johnson. Today it was Tom Benedict talking about the Mathers:

"Although Harvard's president apologized publicly to the descendants of Robert Calef in 1983, the story of book burning in Harvard Yard has the tinge of apocrypha. Most sources cite only Josiah Quincy, whose 1840 history of Harvard gives considerable space to his own anti-Mather prejudices. Quincy was president of Harvard from 1829 to 1845, a nineteenth-century Unitarian who didn't put anything past the Mathers. Neither do I."

That brought laughter skittering across the hall. Harvard students were good audiences. Laughter could clear the head during a dull lecture, and when the lecture was lively, the students wanted to sound as if they were smart enough to be in on all the jokes.

"But remember that in the 1690s, the Mathers believed the enlightenment had already happened, and they were the ones who'd been enlightened."

More laughter.

"When Calef published a book depicting the Mathers as Puritan exorcists stroking Margaret Rule's breasts for fun and spiritual profit, Cotton was furious. He said Calef had made 'the people believe a smutty thing of me.' And you didn't do that to the Mathers. So . . . they would have felt no compunction about burning Calef's book.

"He fades from the scene, but the Mathers don't. Increase spends his presidency manipulating the college charter. He tries to expand the Harvard Corporation, packing it with orthodox Congregational ministers and keeping all those Anglicans and Presbyterians out of the loop. He then helps found an institution to the south, named after Elihu Yale, that he hopes will hew more closely to the Puritan line. But the eighteenth century has arrived, and Puritan hegemony is breaking down. Consider that John Leverett, whom Cotton will deride as that 'Anglican lawyer,' is named president of the college in 1707, much to Cotton's chagrin. By then, Cotton has written *Magnalia Christi Americana*, to honor those seventeenth-century Puritans. Of which more next time."

Tom Benedict hadn't glanced at his notes or his watch, but he finished exactly at noon. He flipped the cover on his notebook, smiled, and acknowledged a round of applause that was more than perfunctory. He was good. And Peter told him so afterward.

"You do anything for twenty-five years, you get good at it," said Benedict. "Too bad about Ridley."

"They say it was an accident."

"Did he ever tell you about that 'little something from the Wedges'?"

"Only hints. That's why I'm here."

They came out of Emerson and into Harvard Yard, which was as alive with the midday class change as any high school corridor.

"Peter, I don't have much time," said Benedict.

"Just a few questions about the Wedges."

"Did you know that the Mathers and Wedges knew one another? In Cotton's diary you'll find all kinds of references. 'Had dinner with John Wedge' . . . 'Enjoyed the company of John Wedge' . . . and so on."

"Sibley writes that Isaac Wedge died in Harvard Yard on the night of 'a great bonfire.' Could that have been the night they burned the book?"

"Anything is possible . . . but that assumes that Mather burned a book."

"Why else would they have a bonfire? They didn't have football rallies."

"We may never know"—Benedict picked up his pace—"considering that those early Wedges didn't leave much more than scraps."

"Like this?" Peter took out a slip of paper. "Supposedly, it's from John Wedge's commonplace book."

Benedict stopped in front of the steps of Widener and took the slip. "Interesting. Where did you get this?"

"Ridley dug it up somewhere."

"I wonder where he got it. . . . Three lines of iambic pentameter and a parenthetical comment beneath them . . ."

"Any ideas? Plenty of blank verse back then. Marlowe, Jonson, Shakespeare . . ."

Benedict gave Peter a look usually reserved for sophomores who didn't do the reading. "John Wedge was a staunch Puritan. I don't think he'd be quoting some banned-in-Boston playwright."

"But what about the 'love's labors' remark?"

"A pleasant euphemism for the old in-and-out." Benedict studied the lines. "The passage says we're specks of dust . . . dust with immortal qualities, but still dust. A common theme. And the parenthetical, 'No man would say this after a night in which he had known the joy of love's labors.' Sounds like he set down the blank verse when he was feeling low and wrote the rest after he'd gotten laid."

"So . . . this 'speck of dust' passage . . . is it something an expert would recognize?"

"I don't, and I'm an expert." Benedict's eye drifted past Peter. "But I see someone who might. As a matter of fact, he's Dorothy Wedge's tutor. Assistant Professor O'Hill."

It was easy to pick out Bob O'Hill from the swirl of students around Sever Hall. Not because he was tall, reedy, and tweedy. There were plenty of guys around who fit that bill. And not because he had a sensitive little goatee, just a shade darker than his blond hair. He was walking out of Sever with Dorothy Wedge and two other female students.

"A pain in the ass," said Benedict. "But he's seen us, and he's coming our way with Miss Wedge, so I'll introduce you."

"Don't tell him anything," said Peter.

"My lips are sealed." Except for the introductions.

"Mr. Fallon," said Dorothy Wedge, polite as ever, "what brings you to Harvard?"

"A little research," said Fallon.

"Commonplace books?" Dorothy glanced at O'Hill. "My father hired Mr. Fallon to do some research for me . . . to help me with my honors thesis."

O'Hill, who was about six-four, smiled down at Fallon with everything but his eyes. "I hope Mr. Fallon has told your father that buying you some exotic research won't buy you a summa."

"Yes, Professor," said Dorothy. "I'll earn the summa myself."

"Of course," O'Hill continued, "there aren't many commonplace books around."

"But a rather interesting one has come to light recently," said Peter, and he offered O'Hill the three lines.

O'Hill inclined his head, glanced at it, and said, "That's the 'speck of dust' passage, isn't it?"

"You know it?" asked Peter. "Where is it from?"

"The commonplace book of John Wedge." O'Hill looked at Dorothy. "I hope your father isn't paying Mr. Fallon too much, considering that he doesn't even know that."

Fallon looked at Dorothy and smiled, but he didn't say a word. He had run across plenty of guys like this. They might be in their natural habitat in a place like Harvard Yard, but they could be found everywhere. If you asked them the wrong question, they turned it on you to make you look small. Usually they made themselves look even smaller in the process.

"I think you missed the point of the question," said Benedict to O'Hill.

"If I stay any longer"—O'Hill looked at his watch—"I'll miss my job interview."

"Pretty brusque for a member of the junior faculty," said Peter after O'Hill had headed off in one direction, Dorothy and her girlfriend in another. "Aren't they supposed to suck up to guys like you?"

"He thinks he has reason to be brusque," said Benedict. "Arrived here from a farming town in central California as an undergrad, grew into an award-winning young scholar, a good teacher, did some good work, especially in the field of seventeenth-century American diaries and commonplace books. Even did his dissertation on them. So he really knows more about them than most of us."

"But?"

"He was turned down for tenure." Benedict started walking toward the Square.

"That explains the attitude. I can almost sympathize."

"They call the Senate the most exclusive club in America, but the Harvard faculty isn't close behind. Our promotion practices are quite complicated. And almost no one who gets his graduate degree here is invited to stay. They have to go out and prove themselves at some place like—"

"Southeast Iowa State?"

"Right. Where you found out that teaching wasn't for you. It's part of the vetting process. Every profession has one. Very few spots open up in academia, especially at this level. You have to earn them."

"So, Assistant Professor O'Hill is angry but still teaching?"

"His contract expires at the end of the academic year. I've advised him to do his work enthusiastically, and I'll write glowing recommendations for him." Benedict looked at his watch. "I have to run. High table at Kirkland House."

"One more thing. O'Hill . . . did he ask to be Dorothy's tutor, or did she ask for him?"

"You know how it works, Peter. Students are generally assigned to tutorial groups as sophomores and juniors. By the time they're seniors, they find a faculty member they'd like to work with on a thesis . . . then it's by mutual agreement."

So, thought Fallon, Assistant Professor O'Hill had read the term paper that started all this. Dorothy had probably asked him the same questions she'd brought to Ridley. How much more did he know?

From his car, Peter made two phone calls.

The first was to Bernice to see if Orson had checked in with anything on the Wedge commonplace book.

"The antique antiquarian called to say he's going to the Massachusetts Historical Society to see what he can find out."

"Good. I'm going to Rockport."

"For a lobster?"

"No. I'm just following a hunch or two."

"It's like Orson always says. He does all the dirty work while you run around following hunches."

Then Peter placed a call to Evangeline Carrington's cell phone.

She answered from the deck of a Provincetown whale watcher. "We were just talking about you, Peter. I told my grandmother you were going to take her to lunch sometime."

"Tell her Monday. Wherever she wants."

There was a pause, then Evangeline said, "What are you after, Peter?"

"Lunch . . . with Katherine and her beautiful granddaughter."

"That's what Ridley said."

"That should answer your question," answered Peter.

"I feel so much better. I thought for a minute you were using her to get to me. But you're just using both of us."

The season had changed in Rockport. October's blue was leaving the water. The sky was clear, the air mild, but the sea already carried the cold monochrome of winter.

Peter rang the bell, but of course, no one answered. And from what he could tell, no one was following him. So he went around to the back, found that key beneath the steps, and let himself in.

The kitchen had been modern in the first term of Franklin Roosevelt—matchstick paneling painted green, white wooden cabinets painted a dozen times, an old sink with long legs and an oilcloth skirt. Ridley's mother had died two years before, and it looked as if the glassware on the shelf hadn't been touched since.

A little digital clock on Ridley's coffeemaker ticked from 2:15 to 2:16. Ridley's last pot was still sitting there, growing mold. He should have left something better as his last creation. Peter threw the coffee down the sink.

Then he went up to the attic and found the computer at a little desk in a dormer window overlooking the ocean.

He turned on the computer, clicked "My Documents," and several folders appeared. He clicked one called "Woody," a window opened, and a dozen document icons appeared before him with titles like "DWPaper," for Dorothy Wedge's paper, or "Shepard" for the Shepard diary. But the one that interested Peter was "Commonplace."

He clicked the icon and the document opened. *What was this?* Not a text, but the actual document, copied from Masshist.org, the website of the Massachusetts Historical Society. The subhead said "Recent Acquisitions from the Seventeenth Century."

Peter worked often at the MHS library. But one of the great advantages of the wired age was that you could sit down at a computer, hit a few keys, and summon featured documents such as this: the John Wedge commonplace book, scanned in, so that you could see the handwriting, with each page linked to a printed transcription.

Where the hell had it come from? And why hadn't Ridley told him about it? Ridley Riddles.

Forty or fifty pages of tight script, barely legible—Bible quotes, verse, comments by John Wedge, an interesting passage about Cotton Mather's conquest of his stutter, and *there:* the quote about "specks of dust," and beneath it, written in different ink and more relaxed hand, that parenthetical about love's labors.

Peter looked at the surrounding sentences. Tom Benedict's speculations had been correct. Something traumatic *had* happened just before John Wedge entered that quote.

April 30, 1676: My mother is dead not two weeks. Such things as my father bids me now read cannot soothe me, but I must read. And I will not deny that there is truth here: "Man is but a speck of dust . . ."

What was he reading? What was the source?

Peter sat there an hour, reading every line of John Wedge's commonplace book. Then there was a break of one page, and this: "To my son, Abraham: I have saved this book for you, that my firstborn may know God's promise to man through literature."

So, thought Peter. There were *two* commonplace books here. Another whole generation of brain droppings. And the MHS had only recently acquired it. From whom? For how much? He supposed he should have known, but as Orson had said, these were generally not valuable items.

For a witch-trial judge, John Wedge seemed to be a pretty humanistic guy. Or maybe he got that way when his sons were born. According to Sibley, he did not remarry for years after the death of his first wife. The implication was that he was in the throes of consuming grief that he assuaged on the frontier. He returned to Boston about 1703, resumed his shipping business, though with less success, and married Samantha Seabury, with whom he had two sons, Abraham and Benjamin. Abraham graduated from Harvard in 1723. Benjamin, two years younger, was "rusticated" and disappeared.

Rusticated. Punished. Sent for a semester to the countryside. What had he done?

It was getting late. The attic was cooling as the sun set. Peter thought about going home to his own computer to access the information from Masshist.org in comfort. But his curiosity kept him reading.

He knew that Abraham Wedge had become a minister, so he wasn't surprised to scroll through biblical quotes, attempts at religious poetry, passages from sermons by Cotton Mather, and then, surprisingly: "To be or not to be, that is the question . . ."

It was followed by this:

September 9, 1720: I have read through a volume newly arrived in the library, the complete works of William Shakespeare, published in 1709. This is the first theatrical volume

that the college has permitted, as the reputation of Shakespeare grows greater with each decade.

So . . . Shakespeare had finally gone to Harvard.

The genius of S. cannot be disputed, but to see such things
played out before us, to allow a public display of the immoral-
ities depicted here, would be a sin against a whole society. My
brother, however, has no such compunction.

The mysterious brother, Benjamin.
Peter read ahead, skimming over the various quotations, until he
came to this: "In a book of bugs, Ben finds a play and prepares to
put it on. I ask the title. He will not say. But he promises to bring
life to it in his room tomorrow night." *Book of bugs?*

With a few keystrokes, Peter logged on to the Harvard library catalog, HOLLIS, and found a volume that would give him the answer.
The Colonial Society of Massachusetts had published the Harvard
catalog of 1723. And with a little more searching, he had it before
him—a facsimile of the handwritten original, three columns, title,
author, section and shelf numbers, and the name of the donor.

And there it was.

A book about bugs. "*Corporei Insectii,* by Walter Shackford, Section
XII, Shelf 8, Space 6, given by Isaacus Wedgius." Peter Fallon, a man
who knew his books, had never heard of this volume or the author.

Had Isaac been hiding a play in a book about bugs? *But why?*

Peter kept reading. But nothing revealed itself, except that Abraham had taken to quoting Hamlet in relation to his brother's life:

Benjamin insists on performing this play. I have told him
that I should turn him in to the tutor. I should "be cruel only
to be kind."

My brother is undone. "So full of artless jealousy is guilt, /
It spills itself in fearing to be spilt." He is properly served.

My brother is rusticated to Reverend Bleen's. "Parting is
such sweet sorrow."

Reverend Bleen. *Where had he heard that name?*

Too many questions. Peter decided to e-mail the whole folder to himself.

Then he clicked the "received items": a few from himself, a few from Evangeline, and one, from Dorothy Wedge, received in the last week in September, over three weeks before Peter put in his fund-raising call:

> Dear Uncle Ridley: Thanks for taking the time to read my paper and give me any other ideas you might have. It's exciting to think there's a lost play out there. My tutor, Mr. O'Hill, has been very interested in a commonplace book that the Massachusetts Historical Society recently obtained.

Then Peter clicked the e-mail icon and, out of curiosity, checked the e-mail "sent items" box: There were several e-mails to Peter's address, to D.Wedge@fas.harvard.edu, which would be Dorothy. And one to r.ohill@fas.harvard.edu, sent the day before Ridley fell off his boat:

> Dear Professor O'Hill: Dorothy Wedge has discussed some of her speculations with me, and as a theatrical historian, in addition to a theatrical producer, I would have to say that they are very exciting. I am developing a theory that you might be interested in discussing with me sometime, either in Cambridge, or here in Rockport. Do you like to fish?

So Peter's instincts in the Yard had been good. Mr. O'Hill knew more.

What did he know about Abraham and Benjamin Wedge?

Someone was using him.

Peter Fallon figured it out on the way back to Boston. People used him all the time. That didn't bother him. But they weren't using him because of his skills as a book man. It was that line "rusticated to Reverend Bleen's" that told him.

Someone had figured out that Fallon Salvage and Restoration

had won a bid to rehab an old house in Sudbury, someone who had read this commonplace book and thought there might be something to learn at the old Bleen House.

But who? A thug from South Boston who started following Fallon as soon as he started talking to Ridley? Or the assistant professor that Ridley had invited fishing? Or Will Wedge, who couldn't make up his mind if he wanted Fallon to stop or go?

Since no one was waiting for him at home, Peter decided to drive out to Sudbury, just for a look at the property known as the Bleen House.

It was a big old Colonial set back from Route 126, with a big old barn out back. The lights were on, because the owners were still living there, as they would throughout the job. That was good, since it meant that no one could go poking around without being discovered. If there was an ancient book anywhere in that house, the Fallons would get the first crack at it.

Peter sat in the shadows at the side of the road and studied the slope of the slate roof and the slant of the light pouring out of the windows.

According to Sibley's *Harvard Graduates*, this was the last place that a young man named Benjamin Wedge had ever been seen.

Chapter Eleven

1723

"REVEREND MATHER"—Samantha Wedge curtsied before her minister—"an honor."

"I come to see your husband, ma'am . . . about the college."

"The college?" Samantha was known as a simple woman, not for want of intelligence but for a face that revealed emotions as though they had been set in italics. Her eyes opened wide, and she said, "A problem? With Abraham? With Benjamin?"

But Mather said only, "I would speak with your husband."

"'Tis Benjamin, then? Oh, Reverend, he's a good boy, but—"

Mather raised his hand. "Please, dear lady, take me to your husband."

Samantha seemed to fill with questions, but she was a dutiful wife, so she asked none of them. Instead, she admitted Mather to her home, closed the door against the noise of Hanover Street, and pointed him to the front room, where John Wedge sat reading the *Boston Courier*.

It was a small room in a house far smaller than that which John had once enjoyed. But his purse was smaller, too, his fleet of ships reduced to three by storms and bad business luck. Most houses were smaller because Boston had assumed the close-built look of a city, with long rows of joined dwellings and ever smaller lots for freestanding structures. And streets now crosshatched the old Shawmut Peninsula like a fishnet thrown over a three-humped whale.

But John Wedge did not mind his smaller house, for here he had enjoyed a love that was physical as well as spiritual. Here he had raised two strong sons. Here, as he was fond of saying, he and his wife had aged like French wine or English cheese. Samantha was fifty but looked ten years younger. John would have passed for Mather's younger brother, though he was four years older.

There was, however, no denying that John Wedge and Cotton Mather were old men—both past sixty, both gone gray, both aware that it would be sooner rather than later that they would see the fulfillment of Christ's promise.

John looked over his spectacles. "Is the reverend here because he's heard of the arrival of the *Sparrowhawk*, with a dozen pipes of Madeira?"

~~Rebecca~~ Samantha said, "Reverend Mather brings news of our boys."

" 'Tis news of the college." Mather bustled into the room.

"But a little Madeira would ease your burdens, would it not?" said John.

"So it would." Mather took his usual place in the chair to the left of the fireplace.

As Samantha went scurrying off, John regarded his friend. He held no awe for the great minister. It was one of the reasons that they had remained friends, despite Mather's inclinations to bloviate and exasperate. John knew Mather the man, as flawed as any by birth, as bowed as any by experience.

Mather's first wife and three of his children had died in the measles epidemic of 1713. His present wife was said to be as crazy as the long-forgotten Margaret Rule. His debts had brought him to ignominy, and only the help of his parishioners had saved him from the workhouse. His eldest son, Increase, had proved a wastrel and been sent to sea. And though his son Samuel had gone to the college, Mather still nurtured cold resentment toward the Harvard Corporation for passing him over fifteen years earlier, when they named John Leverett, former tutor and lawyer of liberal leanings, as president.

Nevertheless, Mather remained a man of great influence and

overwhelming industry. He had published hundreds of sermons, tracts, and books on subjects ranging from infant baptism to small-pox inoculation, which he had advocated during the epidemic that had swept Boston. And the Harvard Board of Overseers had recently turned to him to produce a report on the state of the college.

"Since you are an overseer, John"—Mather produced five sheets of paper from his pocket—"you should see my findings before they be officially submitted."

John Wedge looked at the papers. "Are you critical?"

"I see need for an investigation. From what I've discovered, and from what my Samuel saw in four years, there's notorious decay at the place."

"When I visit I see boys struggling to be men," said John, "like us long ago."

"Read." Mather gestured at the sheet.

So John read while Samantha carried in two glasses and a de-canter, poured, and peered over her husband's shoulder.

Mather sipped his Madeira. "As I said fifteen years ago, to make a lawyer who never studied divinity the president of a college of di-vines is a preposterous thing. But I may at last have reason to re-move that damned Anglican."

"I believe Leverett is Congregationalist, like us," said John.

"But were he removed, expectations of my ascendance to the presidency would be epidemical, John. You know that he's an infa-mous drone."

"Not by any account my sons have offered."

"I think," said Mather, shifting his eyes from John to Samantha, "that you should read the fourth paragraph of my report, as it per-tains to your sons."

John read aloud. "'The students, outside of their classes, read plays, novels, and empty and vicious pieces of poetry, which have a vile tendency to corrupt good manners.'"

"Oh, my," said Samantha.

"Would you not agree, John," asked Mather, "that we should be recommending proper books of theology to our sons, rather than plays?"

"My sons know nothing of plays," said Samantha.

"Oh, but they do, dear lady," said Mather. "Abraham Wedge has been seen reading from the volume of Shakespeare that Leverett allows in the library."

"Shakespeare?" said Samantha, her eyes widening.

"And Benjamin—I dread to say—has acted out scenes in chambers."

"Acted out?" John closed his hands around the paper. "Who tells you this?"

"My son saw it one night. He saw your son act out the person of Puck."

"Puck?" said John.

"A pagan spirit," said Mather, "stripped to the waist, wearing a headdress with goat's horns . . . a thing from the region of Sodom, I suspect."

John looked at Samantha, whose expression spoke for her.

"Were it up to me"—Mather stood—"there would be no Shakespeare in that library to foul the minds of our sons." He finished his drink. "Were it up to me."

"Cotton," said John, "why have you brought this to us now?"

"You should know, that you might save your son from himself before we save him for you." Mather stopped in the doorway. "There is word that Benjamin intends to act out another play from Shakespeare. He should be stopped, John, for his own good."

ii

A father could not wait when his sons were threatened, either by their own depravity or by one who believed himself ordained to sweep all depravity from the "college of divines."

So John took the ferry to Charlestown and hired a calash to take him to Cambridge. The whole way he kept his eyes on the clouds reflecting above the red horizon, and this kept his mind from his worries until he reached the college.

There were more than a hundred students, most living in the buildings that formed the open quadrangle overlooking the village. Harvard Hall and Massachusetts Hall, newest and largest, stood op-

posite each other. Stoughton Hall closed the quadrangle so completely that there was no more than five feet of space between it and
the other two. It was an arrangement of stately formality that left the
old Yard quite literally behind and completely out of sight.

But boys would be boys, no matter the environment, and ~~Isaac~~ John
could hear a rowdy song coming from one of the upstairs chambers
in Massachusetts Hall, while loud conversation echoed from rooms
all around.

There was no doubt that the college was livelier than in John's
day. Across the colony, old ideas of Calvinist predestination were
clashing with the belief that redemption was a matter of free will.
And students applied free will wherever they could. Their studies
remained strictly prescribed, but outside of class, they were in constant pursuit of new ways to vex the previous generation. They
started periodicals, convened secret societies, and formed debating
clubs, where the topics ranged from the sacred—"Is God knowable
through physical evidence?"—to the profane—"Be it fornication to
lie with one's sweetheart after contraction but before marriage?"

Abraham Wedge and several friends had started a society with
this charter:

> Whereas Vice and Folly are in their zenith and gild the
> hemisphere with meteors whose false glare is mistaken for
> stars of wisdom and virtue, and whereas Bad language and
> Drunkenness are viewed as the height of good breeding
> amongst those around us, we hereby form the Philomusarian
> Club, to meet thrice weekly for gentlemanly conversation, to-
> bacco, and beer.

That night, the Philomusarians were meeting in Abraham's
chamber. As pipe smoke floated above them, seven young men discussed the meaning of Paul's letters to the Corinthians. No conversation could have made Abraham feel closer to his friends or to the
God they sought to honor by their decorous talk, until there came
a pounding on his door.

Abraham—tall, long-legged, almost ascetic in his thinness—
leapt to the door and yanked it open, prepared to harangue some in-

terloper. Instead, he was greeted by his father's angry glare. "Sir! What brings you here?"

"Shakespeare," said John Wedge. "You've been reading Shakespeare."

"He's in the library, Father. He helps me broaden my mind, but"—Abraham glanced at his friends, then closed the door and stepped into the hall—"so does the apostle Paul."

"Good," said John. "You should read both."

"Both? Then"—Abraham's eyes widened like his mother's— "you approve?"

"I do not approve of ignorance, and not to know Shakespeare, in the modern world, is plain ignorance. So you show good sense."

"Yes, sir. Thank you, sir."

John Wedge always tried the soft discipline of a few compliments first. Those being over, he demanded, "So why have you chosen to keep *me* ignorant?"

"Ignorant?" Abraham instinctively took a step back, not that his father had ever struck him. He simply feared disappointing him.

"Do you know Puck?" asked John.

"Puck? The fairy from *A Midsummer Night's Dream?*"

"Did you know that your brother acted this fairy role?"

Abraham's silence made his answer.

And John's anger overflowed at his elder son, the dutiful one, the one who had always been conscientious, serious, religious. "Why did you not tell me of this?"

"It would upset you, Father. I hoped he would stop, but he's not the only one who acts characters in his room. Just the . . ."

"The what?"

"The leader of them."

"Have you heard that he is acting out a scene tonight?"

"He is acting out a bug, I believe," said Abraham.

"A bug? An insect?"

"That is what he told me. He said he was doing a play from a book about bugs."

* * *

A few minutes later, a door to a chamber in Massachusetts Hall burst open and Judge John Wedge stormed in, with Abraham close behind.

Sitting on a stool in the middle of the room was a young man who might have resembled John and, more strongly, Abraham, except that neither of them would ever have been seen like this— wearing a purple cape and a cone-shaped hat.

"Is this what fairies put on?" demanded John.

"No," said Benjamin, "'tis what clowns wear."

"And are you a clown, then?" John Wedge knocked the hat from his son's head, grabbed him by the collar, and shook him.

"Sir! Sir!" cried one of the other young men, who wore a hat and cloak fashioned from drapery. "Stop this."

John kept his eyes on his son. "Are you a clown to be laughed at by scoffers?"

Benjamin broke away. "I'm Costard the Clown. A character."

"*Character?* Don't speak to me of character. You have no character, to deceive me so." John turned to Abraham. "You said he'd be a bug, not a clown."

Benjamin said, "I read a play in a book of bugs, Father."

"What is this book?"

"A book of bugs," said Benjamin. "If you know nothing more, I'll say nothing more."

And there would be no further comment, because the noise had drawn Tutors Robie and Sever from their chambers. They needed only see the strange hats, the makeup, and the student feeding pages of script into the fireplace, and one of them shouted, "We have warned you about this, Benjamin Wedge."

Benjamin was ordered to appear before President Leverett the next day at two o'clock. He would be accompanied by his father, for whom he would need explanations, because his father had been entirely too furious to talk the night before.

Benjamin knew that he would hear about the family's reputation and the importance of observing the law. In response, he would tell his father that some boys were curious and some were careful, that some were smart and some were intelligent, that Abraham was intelligent but careful, but that Benjamin preferred curious and smart.

Such curiosity had led Benjamin to wonder about his grandfather. What boy would not be curious about a man who had traveled Europe, ministered to the Indians, fought them, founded a school, and died right there in the Yard? Benjamin would say that he had hoped to know his grandfather by reading the books his grandfather had left to Harvard. After all, as his father had often said, "A man will be known by his books."

In time, Benjamin had come to *Corporei Insectii* and discovered the play within. He had sat in the library and read it all and felt that Isaac Wedge was speaking directly to him, telling him that it was all right to embrace an unorthodox idea, like a play preserved under the noses of those who would have cast it into the fire. And if it was all right to preserve plays and read them, Benjamin had decided, perhaps it would be all right to perform them, too, no matter the rules of the college or the customs of the colony.

And so, late in his first year, Benjamin and a few friends had decided to act out scenes from A *Midsummer Night's Dream.*

He had chosen to portray the fairy Puck, a troublesome spirit who took joy in confounding those around him. He had dressed as Puck, or undressed, stripping to the waist and tying fake goat's horns to his head. He was beginning a scene with one of his mates, who was portraying the fairy princess Titania, when the door had burst open and the tutors had caught them.

All through their four-week summer break, Benjamin had remembered the excitement of putting on those goat's horns. He had become someone—some*thing*—else. And others had been excited simply by watching him. He knew he could not resist his feelings, despite threats of punishment. So at the beginning of his second year, he went to the library and copied out scenes to play from *Love's Labours Won.* He had resolved that if the tutors stopped him again, he would proclaim that a revered graduate had seen fit to preserve this play in darker days, and so it deserved attention.

But this August morning, he could not be certain if he had fulfilled his grandfather's wishes or violated a secret. Until he could think more on it, he should protect the book. So after morning recitations, he made his way to the library on the second floor of Harvard Hall.

He did not intend to steal the book. The suspicious eye of Jacob Jones, keeper of the library, was too sharp for that. Benjamin had another plan.

Tutor Jones said, "Here to read more plays, are we? We have only a few. But considering the fate you face, read fast."

Benjamin put on a polite demeanor and spoke polite words— "Please, sir, I would only distract myself with some reading before my punishment"—which seemed sufficient to convince Jones that Benjamin need not be watched any more closely than any other student. Moreover, Benjamin had been careful to come during library time allotted to sophomores. So Jones made a wave of the hand and turned away.

Benjamin went to section twelve, eighth shelf. He took down a book, flipped through it, and replaced it like a casual reader. Then he slipped a volume from the sixth slot and examined it; yes, this was one he would read. As he turned to go to a chair, he acted as if something else had caught his attention on the bottom shelf, so he crouched.

On a previous visit to this alcove, he had noticed that the bottom shelf was loose, held in place by no more than the weight of books upon it. Nails, after all, were expensive. If a shelf could be fitted without them, pennies could be saved.

Now his penknife was in his sleeve. Now it was dropping into his hand. And while he angled his body so that the keeper could not see what he was doing, he slipped the blade into the little space between the shelf and the base of the bookcase. There were only half a dozen books on the shelf, so he was able, with a twist of the knife, to pivot the shelf a few inches and—

"Master Wedge." It was the voice of Jacob Jones.

"Yes, sir," he said over his shoulder.

"What are you doing?" The footfalls came toward him.

What *was* he doing? He should have left the book in place. But he was committed now. With his left hand, he took *Corporei Insectii* and slipped it into the little space between the bottom shelf and the floor. There would his grandfather's secret be safe, at least until he knew how to dispense with it.

"I'll ask again. What are you doing?" Tutor Jones stood over him.

But it was done. Benjamin was standing, smiling, a copy of a Latin text in his left hand, while with his right hand, he slipped his knife back into his sleeve.

"What am I to do with you, Benjamin Wedge?" asked President Leverett.

Benjamin tried to speak, but his father spoke first. "May I ask you, sir, what punishment the tutors threatened when my son was discovered playing the fairy Puck?"

"Rustication," said Leverett, "if he played anything else."

John Wedge looked at his son.

Benjamin looked down at his hands.

The meeting was held in the president's office, in the front room of Leverett's house, where once the home of Reverend Thomas Shepard stood.

Leverett was in his sixties, and the work of governing had aged him. An unhealthy puffiness filled his face, and his lower legs appeared like sausages in white-stocking casement.

John Wedge admired Leverett's ability to balance himself between the Congregational clergy who saw the college as their seminary and those of the wider population who saw wider purposes for Harvard. Presenting himself in a fine black velvet coat and green waistcoat of grosgrain silk, out of respect to Leverett's office, John had resolved to do nothing to make Leverett's job harder. But he had also resolved to advocate for his son.

Such advocacy was difficult, however, considering the unrepentant demeanor with which his son presented himself. The boy did not even wear his academic gown.

"I am loath to rusticate anyone," Leverett said sadly, "especially a young man whose grandfather died in my arms."

"In your arms?" said Benjamin, and for a moment, he dropped his defiance.

"Yes," said the president. "He died berating ignorance. Nevertheless . . ."

"Ignorance prevails?" said Benjamin.

John said, "Quiet yourself."

" 'Tisn't ignorance," answered Leverett. " 'Tis the tutors, who bear a heavy burden, maintaining discipline amongst a hundred lively young men. I must support them. Then there's Reverend Mather, an overseer who has attended but one meeting in all my presidency, so strong is his animus against me. He's issued a report that damns students for doing no more than *reading* plays. This inspires Judge Sewall to prepare a visiting committee to look over my shoulder, to see if students are depraved or not."

"And so," said Benjamin, "I am to be sacrificed on Reverend Mather's altar?"

"Quiet yourself," snapped his father. "You were warned against this."

"You tell me that I should think for myself," said the boy, and he was a good enough actor that he could set his jaw, but he could not hide the hurt in his eyes.

"Benjamin," said Leverett, "too many saw you dressed as Puck. Too many heard the tutors promise rustication. The punishment must be carried out. Do you have anything else to say before the sentence?"

Without hesitation, Benjamin asked, "Why is it that you allow Shakespeare to be read but not played?"

"Be quiet," said the boy's father.

"No," said Leverett. " 'Tis a fair question. We live in the colony of Massachusetts. We are funded by the colony. We must fulfill the public trust. And the proscription against theatrical performance is a powerful tradition."

"You have not answered the question," said Benjamin.

"Quiet," repeated John Wedge.

"No," said Leverett. "He's young, and the young must say their say." Then the president looked at Benjamin. "The clerisy could not forever keep plays from being read. The day will come when they cannot stop them from being played, either."

"Perhaps we should usher in that day," said Benjamin.

"And perhaps we should leave it for others." Leverett put his hands on his table and lifted himself to his feet. "We have so much else to do. Don't you agree?"

"He does," said John.

Benjamin looked down at his hands again and nodded.

"Then 'tis done," said Leverett. "You'll go to Reverend Bleen's in Sudbury, where you will work for your room and board while completing the prescribed course of study under his supervision. After Christmas, you'll make a public apology during morning prayer and be readmitted as a member in good standing."

A father and son walking across the Yard: they could have been John and his own father on John's first day at Harvard, or on the day when they argued over the presence of Satan in Margaret Rule. John had enjoyed arguing with his father, and even now, he wished they could have one more go at a thorny issue. John could argue with Abraham and know that it was all part of the father-and-son debate. But with Benjamin, it was different. They did not argue because they enjoyed the challenge of testing their ideas. They argued because they *were* different.

"I shall accompany you to Sudbury," said John.

"No," said the boy. "I'll go myself." And he quickened his pace.

"That will take you a day or more on foot." John walked a bit faster.

"Why did you not stand by me?"

"But I did."

"You stood by, not *by* me. Had they tried to rusticate Abraham, you would have moved heaven and earth to keep him here, with his Philomusarian Society and his holy airs. But I wish to do things that are different."

"And so you should."

The boy stopped and looked at his father. "Then why did you not say it?"

"Because of your deceit. If you are to do things differently, do them forwardly."

The young actor allowed the shock to play across his face.

"Now then," said John, "about the book of bugs . . . *Corporei Insectii*? 'Twas your grandfather's deceit and defiance."

"You needn't worry about it. . . . 'Tis hidden, hidden better than Grandfather hid it."

"The day will come when it must be revealed," said John. "Not now, but in time."

"In time?" Benjamin could not suppress a smile. "When that time comes, I shall do it forwardly, then."

John put a hand on his son's shoulder. "I'll hold you to it, and stand with you."

And together they walked across the Yard.

iii

Two weeks later, John Wedge received a letter:

> Dear Father:
> Reverend Bleen works me as hard as he works his slave, Demetrius. Yet he expects me to expostulate daily upon Bible passages, deliver the solutions to a dozen mathematical problems, and report upon all of the readings that would have been assigned at the college. He is an unsmiling man who whips Demetrius and threatens to whip me. But I will do my best to serve my time.

John wrote back:

> I once rusticated myself, after surrendering to weakness. I likened my time in the country to our Lord's forty days in the desert. I returned a more understanding man, one who could accept weakness in himself and others. See your own rustication in the same way. By your connection to the elemental life of the farm, you learn that pride and self-conceit have no place in life. You will be better for it.

Benjamin read this letter on a straw pallet in the loft of Reverend Bleen's barn, in the thin gray light of dawn. He did not read at night because Reverend Bleen would allow no candle for reading anything but what was assigned, and no reading at all in the barn, where a flame might produce a conflagration.

So Benjamin read now, and read again, and yet again, his anger festering. How he yearned to bask in a bit of pride and self-conceit, to partake of a little of the joy he had known in reading and performing those plays that now seemed like dreams. And when anger and yearning all but overwhelmed him, he went to a corner, to the place where two beams were notched together to hold up the loft. He reached under the rough boards, into the notch, and withdrew his commonplace book from its hiding place.

Reverend Bleen had prohibited commonplace books, saying he would not "allow rusticated boys to fill pages with unholy aphorisms and commentary from scribblers who feel no fear when they write the name of God." He had also decreed that Benjamin would have ink to write no more than one letter a week to his parents, for "there was little in a boy's head worth writing."

What ignorance, thought Benjamin. And he wrote as much now, using a quill and ink also hidden in the notch. He wrote of his anger and frustration. He wrote of the chores he hated doing. He wrote of the sound of a whip, for Reverend Bleen was at that moment in the barnyard, beating his slave.

Then he wrote: *I long to read a play again. I long to play a role, for a play, well played, may take us to the far towers of Araby and show us at the self-same time the truth within our own hearts.* And he liked the rhythm of those words so much that he was taken with a small bit of inspiration, and he scrawled five lines of verse about the last play he had read, *Love's Labours Won.* Then he realized that the cock was crowing.

"Benjamin Wedge!" cried Reverend Bleen from the barnyard. "Benjamin!"

"Just a moment, Reverend."

"Not just a moment. I have told you that if you are not in the yard before the first cock crow, you'll be punished. I'm up. The nigger is up. And the cock is up. Why are you not up to join us in a morning prayer?"

"I'm up. I'm up." Benjamin went scurrying to the corner and replaced the commonplace book and hid the ink.

Then he climbed down the ladder and stood before the reverend. And in the gray light, a small slip of white paper in a pocket stood out like a lit candle in a dim room.

Reverend Bleen, of sallow complexion, as skinny as a rake and with less warmth, looked at the pocket and said, "You have been reading. What have you been reading?"

"A letter, sir."

"You have broken a rule. You are no better than my slave. Take off your shirt."

A few nights later, a message arrived at the home of John Wedge, beckoning that he come to Reverend Mather's.

There was a rumor that Mather's wife had moved out of the house, leaving him in misery. John would not be surprised, for she was utterly without constancy and had moved out more than once. So he hurried through the streets and found Mather sitting in the darkness of his library, a shadowed figure, head in his hands.

The shadow raised its head: "My father dead six months, and now this."

"Your wife again?" whispered John.

"No. My son. My poor Creasy. Dead. Gone to the bottom of the sea."

John Wedge had comforted friends before in the face of loss. But he could think of nothing to say, so he sat in the chair next to Mather and put an arm around him.

Mather turned, his eyes rheumy and bloodshot, his hair and beard a fringe of gray bristles. "Do you know that the Lord has now seen fit to take thirteen of my fifteen born children? Why? Why?"

"The Lord's ways are past knowing."

A sob burst from Mather. "Do you know what I wrote in my diary when I sent Creasy to sea? I wrote that a gracious God wonderfully made up in Samuel what I missed of comfort in his miserable brother. Why would a man write such a thing of his son? Why?"

Man's ways, thought John, were past knowing, too.

He stayed the night with Mather, praying, talking, and sitting by as his old friend cried. In the morning, Mather's wife returned. Only then did John feel he could leave.

Stepping into the sunlight, he was gripped by a powerful need to see his own sons. So he stopped at the stable and ordered that his horse be saddled. Then he went home and told his wife that he was going to see their boys. "I would tell them that I love them. It is good for the soul."

Knowing what had befallen Mather, Samantha understood.

John Wedge made first for Sudbury. He went by the Post Road, then went through the old village where the famous Indian massacre had begun. Crossing the river, he could see the Haynes garrison and, beyond, his father's fields, owned now by a man who still wrote letters complaining that he spent more time plowing up the devil's rocks than God's good earth.

He rode along the back slope of the hill where Englishmen had fought Indians a generation before. And he came at length to the farm of Reverend Samuel Bleen.

It struck him that he had never been to a farm in September that was so quiet. The acreage behind the house was planted in corn, and from what John could see, it was ready to pick.

The house was a fine one. The people of the parish had seen to the comfort of their minister. There were six-over-six windows on both floors, carved pilasters around the doorframe, a roof covered in slate, walls covered in shake. A house, thought John, built to last, with a fine barn out back.

He realized that this was not a place to sit his horse and halloo like a bumpkin. So he dismounted and went up to the door and knocked. It was a Dutch door, and the top half was opened, allowing him to peer in at the wide-board pine floors, the English paper on the walls, the mahogany furniture in the dining room.

His son, he decided, was living better here than he had at college.

"Hello! Reverend Bleen!"

A woman appeared from the back of the house. She was skinny, middle-aged, wearing a black dress and a clean white apron. "Who are you?"

"I'm Benjamin Wedge's father."

"Just a minute." The woman went away and came back with a sack, which she handed to John. "My husband said for you to take your son's things if you came. And if he don't catch up to your son, he'll be comin' to see you."

"About what?"

"Your son run off with our slave. That's stealin', which is a sin against the Sixth Commandment."

"Run off? To where?"

"If we knew, we'd have 'em both by now. Heard they run for the Connecticut. Once they reach that river, they could go anywhere, 'specially if they play master and man. And that boy of yours, he could fool a London barrister, he's so good at deceivin'. Made us think he was innocent as a flower. Then he run off."

"But why?"

The woman just shook her head. "Hard to say. Took nothin' more than a good, honest beatin'."

Chapter Twelve

PETER FALLON carried a Widener stacks pass in his wallet. It was a good deal. A hundred dollars a year for access to some 14 million volumes. If you couldn't find it in the Widener system, you couldn't find it.

But Peter didn't want a book. He was looking for Assistant Professor O'Hill. After tracking him all morning by telephone, he had him targeted.

At the circulation desk, Peter showed his pass and stepped through the turnstile into another world. His heels echoed. The smell of the books—not of dust or mildew but of paper and cloth and glue—was strong and strangely comforting. So was the embrace of the books. And the low ceilings made him feel as if he were in a maze where he could lose himself for hours and never feel lost. But he had business. He moved along narrow aisles, past a narrow elevator, to a narrow staircase.

On level four, he found O'Hill's small research office. Senior faculty and some junior faculty rated such rooms in the stacks so they wouldn't have to haul so many books around. And the door was open, an invitation to students who might come by for office hours.

O'Hill didn't seem surprised to see Peter. "I hear you've been looking for me."

"Word travels fast through the English Department."

The room was only about six by eight, with a desk, a bookcase, and an extra chair taking up most of the space. O'Hill locked his hands behind his head and put his feet up on the desk. At six-four, he just about fit the room.

"What can I do for you?" he asked.

"I wanted to ask you a little more about those commonplace books."

"I wrote my dissertation on them." O'Hill gave Fallon a little here-and-gone smile. "I'll give you the call number if you want to read it."

"What do you know about the commonplace book of John Wedge?"

O'Hill started to click his feet together. Either it was a nervous twitch, or O'Hill knew it was as annoying as hell. "A big book hunter like you, and you're asking me?"

"Commonplace books are usually not my line of work." Fallon knew the story by then. Orson had dug it up. But talking about it might get O'Hill to open up.

"The Wedge book appeared for sale in the catalog of a London bookseller called Wiley's, about six months ago. Don't you read the catalogs?"

"Not every item jumps out or stays with me." That was the truth.

"Well, the Wedge commonplace book was part of a collection of books bought in Northumberland, of all places. The books came out of an old English estate, Townsend House, and were offered as a single lot at auction. The buyer gave the commonplace book to the Massachusetts Historical Society and kept the good stuff—a signed Dickens, a first edition of *Gulliver's Travels* with uncut pages—for himself."

Peter leaned against the doorjamb, as if to seem a little more casual, maybe a little more friendly. "Probably took a tax write-off."

"Write-offs aren't something that assistant professors worry about," said O'Hill. "Anyway, the librarian at the MHS knows of my interest in these books, so he called me."

"And you contacted Dorothy?"

"It's part of my job to direct students to good sources."

"Was Dorothy your student before you knew about the commonplace book?"

O'Hill stood, as if to give Fallon the full impact of his height in the little space. "Why do I have the feeling that this is some kind of interrogation?"

"Relax," said Fallon. "I'm trying to find a commonplace book, too. And I'm hoping that those lines of iambic pentameter in John Wedge's diary might help."

" 'Man is but a speck of dust,' et cetera, et cetera?" O'Hill was here-and-gone with the smile again, and he was sitting, and his feet were back on the desk, and his heels were clicking. "I haven't got the foggiest idea where that came from or what it means."

Altogether much too cool, thought Peter. Maybe he could melt it. "One more question."

"What?"

"Do you like to fish?" Fallon watched for some flicker on O'Hill's face.

"What?"

"Fish? I hear that Ridley Royce invited you to go fishing."

And O'Hill's feet stopped tapping. "Where would you hear that?"

"Ridley and I talked a lot."

And the feet started tapping again. "I never baited a hook in my life." O'Hill looked at his watch. "I have a student coming in two minutes. I think we're done."

For now, thought Peter Fallon as he rode the elevator.

From the steps of Widener, Peter looked across the Yard. The space before him was called Tercentenary Theater, the outdoor arena formed by Widener on the south, Memorial Church on the north, Sever on the east, and University Hall on the west. In 1936, they had held the Tercentenary celebrations here, hence the name.

It could have been called Masterpiece Theater, too. There were masterpieces everywhere, and one of them was moving. She wasn't moving fast. She had just walked past University Hall and was coming toward the steps of Widener. She had one hand in the crook of her granddaughter's arm and the other wrapped around her cane. And she was older than Widener itself.

Peter Fallon bounded down the steps, and he heard her say, "There's that boy."

"Katherine! Nobody's called me a boy in a long time."

"You'll always be a boy to me, coming to my door, asking to see the papers of old Horace Taylor Pratt."

"And what fun that turned into," said Evangeline.

"Oh, be quiet, you," said Katherine, a strong voice rising from a frail body. "Peter was the best young man you ever met. It's a shame you didn't stay together."

Peter and Evangeline glanced at each other. But no regrets. That had always been the rule, whether they were married to other people or not.

"Let's go to lunch," said Peter.

"No," said Katherine. "Let's stand here for a bit and soak it up."

"You must remember a lot about Harvard Yard," said Evangeline.

"I remember when the library looked like a Gothic church with towers and arched windows—"

"Gore Hall?" asked Evangeline.

"Yes . . . yes . . . ," she said with a touch of annoyance. "Stop acting as though my memory were fading and you had to prod it along."

"Yeah," said Peter. "Sharp as a tack."

"Indeed I am." Katherine started to walk. "Now, what was I saying? Oh, yes, back in the day, I remember when there was no Widener Library . . . why, I can remember meeting Harry Elkins Widener himself on the *Titanic*. . . . The library was finished by the time I got to Radcliffe . . . of course, Radcliffe girls didn't come into the Yard much. They didn't even let us into the classrooms . . . into their daydreams maybe, but . . ."

Soon they were seated in the oak-and-crimson embrace of the Faculty Club dining room, and Katherine was still talking. "I never thought I'd live to see this . . . women as well as men. Are they all on the faculty?"

"I'm sure some of them are," said Evangeline.

"Times change," said Peter.

"What brain power . . . what brilliance. Now"—Katherine took a sip of Chablis, leveled her gaze at Fallon—"you didn't invite an old grandmother to lunch just to look at another pretty face. What are you after?"

Fallon laughed. "What do you know about Ridley Wedge Royce?"

"You mean the one who fell off the boat?" Katherine looked down at her meal, picked a bit at her salad. "I . . . I don't know . . ."

Was she wandering? Peter looked at Evangeline, who said, "Grandmother—"

Katherine's head snapped up. "I told you about questions, dear. I was just trying to sort things out. The first Wedge I knew was Victor . . . met *him* on a boat. The *Titanic*. Widener, too. That might be a little early—"

"Yes," said Peter. "Did Ridley Royce ever try to contact you . . . or anybody else?"

"No . . . why would they?"

Evangeline said, "Grandmother, as I told you, Peter hasn't grown up much in twenty years. He's still chasing treasures."

"And he finds them once in a while, from what I hear." Katherine took another sip of her wine. Her hand did not shake, though the ancient skin hung from it in pliable folds. "As for not growing up, I'd say that makes him a lucky man."

Just then, Peter's cell phone rang in his pocket. Half a dozen heads turned.

Peter excused himself and stepped outside.

It was Danny. "You wanted to know when we meet the owner of the Bleen House. Today, two-thirty. And Orson says this is one giant good news/bad news joke."

"Which do I want first?"

"The good news: this is a beautiful property. The bad news: the house was built on the foundation of its predecessor, which burned to the ground in 1754."

After lunch, Fallon drove out the Boston Post Road and turned on Route 126 for Sudbury, as he had a few nights earlier. In daylight, he noted the small graveyard where the village of Sudbury had once been. He passed the Wayland Golf Club, where you could slice drives into a marsh that once had fed Colonial cattle.

Crossing the Sudbury River, he imagined this world as it would have looked to Isaac Wedge, a place of cleared fields and few trees. Now Isaac's house and the neighboring Haynes garrison were dents in the ground grown over with trees and shrubs.

He didn't expect that too many people thought about the world the way he did. To him, the past had once been the present . . . and the future. And if you looked at it like that, not only did it keep the past alive, it made the present more comprehensible and gave contour to the future's flat horizon.

The Bleen-Currier-Whitney House was another mile up the road, just before the center of Sudbury. In the daylight, it looked smaller, less dramatic.

Danny Fallon's van was parked next to a Ford Navigator.

Danny was in the foyer, talking with a young guy in a camel-hair sport coat and slicked-back hair, who was giving orders . . . talking fast, not listening, not even looking, so he didn't notice Danny Fallon not listening right back. Danny was looking . . . at the guy's wife. She was straightening up the living room while their baby napped on the sofa.

The guy's name was Shipley, and he was going on about Internet connections, extra outlets, and how he didn't care what they ripped out, because none of it was worth saving.

Finally he took a breath, and Danny presented him with a copy of the contract. "Signed, sealed, and delivered. This lets us begin rehabilitation. We reserve the right to salvage and resell any material removed based on architectural plans, and—"

"Agreed," said Shipley. "All agreed a month ago."

"Right," said Danny, "but I like to go over things on the day the job starts. We'll be using steel lallys and steel carrying beams downstairs—"

"Just get it done fast and be clean. My wife and baby can't—" Shipley noticed Peter Fallon, looked him over, from tasseled loafers to blue blazer, and said, "I assume that this is *not* your crew."

"I'm the expert on antiques," said Peter. "Your house is one marvelous antique."

"Thanks." Shipley sounded unconvinced and unimpressed.

"I'm also the expert on competitors in the business," said Peter.

"Since our contract was signed, have you been approached by any-one who offered to buy doors or old fixtures or anything like that?"

"Are you a lawyer, too?" said Shipley. "That's a lawyer question."

"No," said Peter pleasantly. "We just like to know who the competition is."

"Well, no one has approached us," said Shipley.

"We did have a prowler a few nights ago," said his young wife, coming into the foyer. "But Rufus started barking. He's our dog. He's outside."

"You *thought* we had a prowler," said her husband.

"I put the light on and looked out. I saw someone sneaking out of the barn."

This intrigued Peter more than it did the husband. "Did you call the police?"

"We made a report, but we couldn't give them much," she said. "We moved out here because we wanted to get away from that sort of thing."

Shipley looked at his watch. Time for him to get back to business.

Peter turned to his brother. "Did you ask the Shipleys about the barn?"

"Tear it down. . . . Haul it off. . . . It's in the contract," said the husband as he hurried out and climbed into his Navigator and drove off.

"He's under a lot of pressure just now," said his wife with a wan smile.

"We all are," said Peter. "Now, if you'll excuse us . . ." He and Danny went out into the backyard.

"The guy wants a real garage," said Danny, looking up at the barn. "He has a permit for a thirty-foot addition that reaches from the house to the garage, on the footprint of the barn."

Peter looked up at the ancient structure, which still stood foursquare and solid. "Does he know how valuable old New England barns are?"

"I don't think so. But the town gave him a permit, so . . ."

Peter looked at the barn, then at the house, then at the barn again. "Orson said the house burned in 1754. Did he find anything out about the barn?"

"No. He thinks it's original."

"Take it down, piece by piece, and number the pieces," said Peter. "I think we can find a buyer. One of those New York City lawyers who buys a weekend house in Columbia County. They'll pay plenty for a picturesque barn. But be careful. There may be something hidden there that's worth more money than the barn."

"Peter, it's just rough-framed board."

Fallon went inside and looked up into the rafters. "It's post-and-beam framing."

"Yeah," said Danny. "I see it."

"You never know what you might find under some post or beam. But be fast, because if there are prowlers around here, they may be after something we're after."

It was late the next afternoon that Peter got the call from his brother. They had found an old bottle of ink under one of the beam notches. "We think there's something else stuffed in there, too. I'll let you know once we lift the beam off."

By eight o'clock, the book was in the back room at Fallon Salvage and Restoration.

Danny and his son were watching the outside doors. They hadn't seen Jackie Pucks in a few days, but now that they had the book, they were taking precautions.

Peter and Orson went into the machine shop, which also served as their workshop, and put on white gloves to protect the pages from the oil on their fingers, as well as surgical masks to protect from the blue mold growing on the binding and page tops.

"This mold will cost a bundle to clean," said Peter.

"Let's see if there's anything here worth preserving before we worry about that."

Orson clicked on a lamp, opened the book, and then took a pair of long tweezers to separate the endpaper from the first page.

The mold spores puffed in the light, then settled back onto the table.

"Make sure you change your clothes before you go back to the office," Orson reminded Peter. "One spore could ruin—"

"I know the drill," said Peter. They'd done this with old books dozens of times. He was focused on a dirty little water-stained volume that might answer the Ridley Riddles.

On the first page were the handwritten words *Ex Libris: Benjamin Wedge.*

"Quality ink," said Orson. "Didn't run or smudge."

They turned the page with the tweezers.

"Good paper, too," said Peter.

"Amazing the mice didn't get it," said Orson.

On August 20, 1722, was the entry from the Gospel of John: *In the beginning was the word. And the word was with God. And the word was God.* Followed by Benjamin's comment: *We do well to remember this. For words of all sorts can express God, not only the words that man says are God's.*

"I think," said Orson, "that we are in the presence of a rebel."

There was not another entry until the middle of September.

"A rebel," said Peter, "but not a very serious student. He didn't seem to be reading much in August."

Orson read the next quote: "'I am that merry wanderer of the night / I jest to Oberon, and make him smile.' One thing is for certain. We're in the presence of a very brave young man. That's a line from *A Midsummer Night's Dream.* A line for Puck."

"Puck the fairy?"

"The son of a witch-trial judge showed great bravery to be quoting Shakespeare," said Orson. "Especially a Shakespearean fairy."

Peter flipped ahead. "He quotes kings and lovers and clowns, too."

Orson was reading over Peter's shoulder. "He must have worn out the spine of that 1709 Shakespeare in the Harvard library."

The lines were all rendered as blank verse, carefully entered and spaced, page after page. "'All the world's a stage' . . . 'Once more into the breach, dear friends' . . . 'What a piece of work is man' . . . Shakespeare . . . Shakespeare . . . Shakespeare . . ."

Then Peter flipped to the last few entries. And there was a passage of prose, right next to September 12, 1723:

I break off writing. I have been rusticated to Reverend Bleen's. I go for the sake of my father. But I go, too, for the sake of the truth. If I carry out my sentence, I resolve to come back and commit my transgressions even more openly. My brother may study to be a minister and tell Bible stories for the betterment of man. Why may I not study to be an actor and tell stories that do the same?

On the next page was a passage expressing Benjamin's yearning for a play, for a glimpse of the far towers of Araby or an insight into the human heart. Then there was a poem. Orson read it aloud:

"In Harvard Hall, the play is kept, all hidden from the world.
'Tis written in the Bard's own hand, so every word's a pearl.
Will makes us laugh at masquerade, at love, at lies, and fun.
And when 'tis done, and all songs sung,
We cry, 'Love's Labours Won.'"

After a moment, Peter said, "Wasn't it *Love's Labours Lost?*"
"It was," whispered Orson.
After a longer moment, Peter said, "So . . . a lost play?"
"Written in the Bard's own hand."
After an even longer moment, Orson said, "Twenty million?"
Without another moment's hesitation, Peter said, "Thirty."
"If it's really a lost play."
"Maybe I should ask an expert."

Professor Tom Benedict whispered, "*Love's Labours Won.*"
It was eight-thirty the next morning. Benedict sat in his Barker Center office and sipped from the cup of Starbucks Peter had brought him.
Peter took the cover off his coffee, a small physical thing to calm himself. "I thought it was *Love's Labours Lost.*"
"Actually," said Benedict, "we think it was both."
"Both?"
"There's a book," said Benedict, "by an Englishman named Francis Meres. *Wits Treasury*, published in 1598. It compares the En-

glish poets with the Romans. Meres writes that young Will Shakespeare is as good as Plautus. Then he lists some of Shakespeare's
plays, including *Love's Labours,* both *Lost* and *Won.*"

"So you're saying that *Love's Labours Won* . . . is lost?"

"It's one of two or three plays that didn't survive to the First
Folio."

"Why?"

"Fire, flood, famine . . . maybe it was a flop. Who knows? One
thing is certain. Ridley knew that the first man in four centuries to
produce it would make a fortune."

"Produce it? How about own it?" said Peter. "There are only
seven Shakespeare signatures known to exist. If another one—just a
signature—came on the market, it would be worth two million. A
whole play could be—"

"Priceless." Benedict leaned across his desk. "Peter, if we had a
handwritten draft of a Shakespeare play, there's no end to all we
could learn . . . how he worked, how he thought, who he *was.* Why,
we could solve the authorship question once and for all."

"And the scholar who did the editing would never be forgotten."

"Neither would the man who found it."

Peter looked into his coffee cup. "I think the caffeine is getting to
us."

"Peter, we're all like Ridley. We all dream of doing one great
thing."

"There's one bad thing that bothers me. That business about the
book burning in Harvard Yard. Could the Mathers have been burning a play?"

"Look at the context of Benjamin's poem. It suggests the play was
being read in 1723. It isn't the Mathers' fire I'd be worried about.
It's the fire in 1764. Go over to the archives, look at the list of John
Harvard's books, and see which ones survived."

This was why he loved his work.

It was possible that he was onto one of the great intellectual discoveries of the age. It was also possible he was heading toward a
dead end. He didn't want that. He didn't want to find out that Ridley had been killed for nothing, which would be worse than if he

died taking a piss. And he didn't want to discover that he'd been wasting his time, because one of the things he'd learned was that time grew more precious every day.

It had been thirty years since Peter had taken this path at breakfast, lunch, and dinner—from the old Freshman Union across Quincy Street, past the flat modern ugliness of Lamont Library. And nothing seemed to have changed . . . except himself.

Then he came to the flight of stairs that led into the Yard. Those stairs had not been there thirty years before, nor had Pusey Library, so skillfully tucked below grade. Change could be imperceptible, but it was relentless.

From the top of the stairs, he looked across the Yard and wondered what the eighteenth-century Wedges would think of all this. Back in 1764, the college had been clustered over near the Square: Harvard Hall, Massachusetts, Stoughton, Holden Chapel. On this side of the Yard, there had been nothing more than fruit trees, garden plots, a brewery, pigpens, sheep commons, and, of course, a row of outhouses, where the students, in the morning, waited their turn. . . .

Chapter Thirteen

1763–1764

"HURRY UP, Wedge. Take much longer in there, I'll be shittin' in my breeches. And what will your reverend grandfather say if I come to chapel stinkin' like a dung pile?"

Caleb Wedge peered through a crack in the outhouse door. "He'll say, 'Better that thou shouldst stinketh than to come late to chapel.'"

In that the college bell rang at six in the morning, going late was an easy matter, especially if one slept too soundly. And a student who went late faced a tuppence fine. So Caleb Wedge was glad to feel his discharge at last, gladder still to be off the cold seat, pulling up his breeches, pushing open the door.

"Take some jalap, why don't you?" said the next in line. "Loosen you up."

Caleb did not stop to trade insults, because his grandfather was waiting, and the Reverend Mr. Abraham Wedge was not a man to disappoint.

Caleb hurried toward Holden Chapel, joining with those who were hurrying from Harvard Hall and Massachusetts Hall and Stoughton, too. Some were tucking shirts into breeches or buttoning waistcoats; others were flowing serenely along in the academic gowns they wore each day. Some went with a sure step; others seemed groggy and uncertain, as if blinded by the April dawn. Some, Caleb knew, believed themselves blessed by God that they studied at the School of the Prophets; others considered the college a trial to be gotten through, a set of rules to be circumvented, four years of academic imprisonment before they embraced freedom.

As for Caleb, his attendance at the college had been foreordained, his place on the college's great chain of being guaranteed.

In that he was the son of a barrister who died before making a mark, Caleb should have been ranked below the sons of royal officials and rich merchants, above the sons of country ministers and tradesmen. But his great-grandfather had been John Wedge, respected judge and mercantile investor; and his grandfather was the Reverend Mr. Abraham Wedge, heir to those investments, holder of degrees from Harvard and Emmanuel College, colleague minister of the First Church of Cambridge.

All of this guaranteed Caleb a place near the top of his class. So he marched near the head of the line in processions. And he was expected to sit near the front in chapel, which made it difficult for him that morning to slip in unnoticed.

Reverend Abraham Wedge was already in the pulpit, his Bible before him, his slender height and translucent skin conveying an air of the ethereal, as though he were preparing to elongate himself into some spirit shape and ascend to heaven. He had been delivering morning prayer more often of late, as President Holyoke surrendered to ill health and exhaustion after twenty-six years in office.

The reverend cast his eyes at the latecomers. "We shall wait a moment so that those of you who prefer the softness of your pillows to the power of the Word may compose yourselves."

Such remarks were meant to inspire fear or guilt, but most students had developed attitudes about morning chapel and skills for mockery that manifested themselves in fake coughs, scraping feet, and anonymous hooting from the back pews.

Reverend Abraham responded calmly to the noise: "Rest assured, gentlemen, that the tutors are noting your names and fines will be given out. Now, let us pray."

Caleb bowed his head and pretended to piety. He knew nothing would come of his grandfather's threats, because tutors seldom identified surreptitious troublemakers in a chapel crowded with two hundred students. He knew only that his grandfather would be in an angry mood the rest of the day, which would make things more difficult that night.

"You wish to go on an expedition?" said Reverend Abraham. "To where?"

"To Newfoundland, Grandfather. To observe the transit of Venus."

"Venus? The Roman goddess of love?"

"The *planet*, sir." Caleb fought an impulse to call his grandfather stupid; he knew that his grandfather only feigned stupidity about the ways of the world as a defense against them.

"Professor Winthrop has written a letter." Caleb placed it on Abraham's desk.

The reverend sat in his study, erect in his black suit and white collarbands, his extreme height emphasized by his extreme posture, his long face even longer in the candlelight, his white hair cropped close so that his wig would fit snugly. The wig itself sat on a head-shaped frame that cast a shadow nearly as formidable as that of the reverend himself.

"Winthrop is a man of science," he said. "But we are men of faith."

"Who better, then, to understand the differences and congruences between natural and revealed religion?" Caleb often used new words to please his grandfather; *congruence* brought a nod, so he went on. "By going to the northern latitudes, sir, to study the movement of the spheres, I shall be studying the glory of God's solar system."

"Well said," answered Abraham, "but your commitment to revealed religion seems less serious than to Winthrop's natural religion. Otherwise, you'd not have come late to chapel today."

"I'm . . . I'm sorry, sir." Caleb bowed his head.

"And you might have answered the derision of your classmates with an angry gaze instead of a bowed head. Feigned piety is worse than none at all."

Caleb knew that his best response was to keep his head bowed.

"I expect *you* to uphold the name and the faith of our family."

"Yes, Grandfather."

"'Tis what your own father would have wanted . . . and your mother."

Once, they had all lived there, in that fine house on the Watertown Road, a short walk from the Yard. But the loss of Caleb's father at sea had followed a smallpox epidemic that carried his mother away, leaving Caleb and his sister in the care of their father's widowed father. For twelve years, the children had been raised with a combination of coldness, formality, and discipline that they had come to know as Reverend Abraham's best expression of love.

"Stay the course of Calvinism," the reverend reminded him. "Beware of professors who consider their telescopes of greater import than their Bibles."

"Let him go, Grandfather."

Reverend Abraham turned to the girl appearing in the door. "Your opinion—"

"Is of no consequence. I know." Lydia Anne Wedge, all of thirteen, crossed her grandfather's study with the purposeful grace of a woman twice her age.

Caleb often wondered at the source of her self-assurance. She was an orphan and so had no mother to teach her. She was a younger child and so had a brother to taunt her. And yet, here she was, perching herself on a wing chair, her crimson dress a perfect complement to the buff and blue flame-stitched fabric, her brown hair pulled back simply, her posture as erect as her grandfather's, her attitude seemingly as unyielding.

She said, "If I were a young man seeking to broaden my horizons, I should hope that my grandfather would let me go about it."

"But you are a girl," said Abraham. "Broadening horizons is not part of your future. Deepening roots is your task. So—"

"Is that reason to deny either of us?" she asked calmly.

"I deny you nothing"—Abraham rose to his full six feet—"not even your whims . . . not even the paper and ink you beg to scribble your poems."

"Grandfather," she said, "my poems are not whimsical."

Caleb said, "May we return to the subject of me?"

"The subject is always you," said Lydia.

"A better subject than you," answered Caleb.

"It is not," she said.

"It is . . . *indeed.*" Caleb thought that sounded more mature than "It is *so.*"

But Abraham seemed to think that none of it was mature or endurable. He slammed his hands on his desk, and both children fell silent. Then he dropped back into his chair and said, "All right. All *right.* He may go."

And Lydia seized her chance. "But paper and ink, sir? Will you buy me more?"

"Only if you write more," said the old man, "and talk less."

Two weeks later, Caleb Wedge boarded the Massachusetts province sloop for the first true scientific expedition in the history of the American colonies.

Never before had he journeyed farther than fifty miles from home. Never before had he been exposed for so long to the brilliance of someone such as John Winthrop, Hollis Professor of Mathematics and Natural Philosophy, whose papers had been read before the Royal Society in London and whose reputation placed him first among America's men of science.

Everything about Winthrop was solid, thought Caleb. His face was large and square, his chest barreled, his diction dignified yet relaxed, his manner of authority quiet yet unquestionable, whether he was speaking to sailors, students, or his slave, Scipio.

Winthrop brought his four brightest mathematics students on the voyage. By day, he taught them the use of the instruments: a timepiece, two telescopes—refracting and reflecting—and an octant. By night, he held forth on mathematics, astronomy, and earthquakes, which he considered part of an intricate system of causes and effects, not "scourges in the hand of the Almighty, as some preachers would have you believe."

And for a boy of sixteen—taller than most, a bit more blemished, with a nose awaiting the maturation of the rest of his face—it was a memorable adventure.

On his return, Caleb told his grandfather that he hoped to become a man of science. He would learn the principles of fluxion, which some called calculus. Or he would buy a telescope and study the cold stars, to puzzle out the causes and effects that put them in the sky. Or he would examine animalcules through a microscope to determine why they existed and what they meant to man.

"And where does God stand in all this?" asked Abraham.

"At the heart of Creation," said Caleb, knowing that it was the best answer.

"Never forget that, no matter what thoughts Winthrop pours into you."

"There is also much to know of the human heart," said Lydia from the chair by the fireplace. "I would devote my life to knowing it. But who will pour ideas into me?"

"A husband," said Reverend Abraham, "someday."

"Why won't the fathers of Harvard College take it as their task?"

"To educate girls?" Abraham laughed out loud. "We have enough trouble educating boys. You are a most troublesome and rebellious generation."

"What generation does not say that of the next?" she asked. "Your own father exiled your brother for putting on plays in Massachusetts Hall."

"My brother exiled himself," said Abraham. "Where he went, we never learned. His performing manifested a restless spirit and an unsettled soul."

"But, sir," said Caleb, "these days, student groups put on plays."

"And are punished for breaking college rules."

"Grandfather," said Lydia, "even I have read *Macbeth* at my dame school."

"A story of witchcraft and regicide," said the old man.

"I found it exciting," she answered. "And *Romeo and Juliet* made me cry."

"Made you cry?" Abraham shook his head. "Trifles make you cry?"

"As you've told me, sir, I am a girl."

Caleb could not suppress a smile at such well-placed sarcasm.

But their grandfather did not smile. He said, "I allow you to pursue your science and your poetry, but plays are for low-class reprobates, like the debauchers who'll soon arrive for commencement. It goes without saying that neither of you are to attend any commencement event outside the college."

Caleb and Lydia did not argue, for that would surely have raised his suspicions.

ii

There was only one true holiday in Massachusetts.

It was not Christmas, which Congregationalists saw as their Puritan ancestors did: a Romanist sham linking Christ's birth to the pagan celebration of the solstice. Nor was it any other holy day, for the Puritans had believed in devoting every day to the glory of God, and Scripture decreed that only the Sabbath was specially set aside. However, the old Puritan colony was also home to Anglicans, whose ritual and calendar resembled that of the Romanists, and most royal governors were Anglican, so the Congregationalists could not prohibit holidays altogether. And there was one holiday that Anglican and Congregationalist could agree upon: the Harvard commencement.

Harvard College had existed nearly as long as the Great and General Court itself, and every class of graduates symbolized the colony's continued favor in the eyes of the Lord. From the beginning, commencement had been an occasion of ceremony and celebration, drawing those whose prayers blessed the school and whose taxes supported it. Some came for the spectacle of the academic processions. Some sought seats in the First Church so that they might witness the drama of disputations. Others hoped only to drink at a punch bowl in some student's chamber or join the feasting in the college hall.

And year by year, they came from farther and farther away, and the more that gathered, the more raucous commencement became.

And there was nothing a good minister could do.

On the third Tuesday of July 1763, Reverend Abraham Wedge climbed into the cupola atop Harvard Hall and looked out.

It was high summer. Sunlight gilded the slate rooftops of the college and the distant steeples of Boston and the green landscape all around. Brilliant white clouds floated across the sky. And columns of dust hung above every road leading to Cambridge . . . because they were coming.

They were coming down the Menotomy Road in C-spring chaises and crossing the Great Bridge from Brighton on foot. From Boston they were coming out the Charlestown Road in a parade of chariots and riders and shank's mare walkers. Along the Watertown Road they were coming from farms where every man had a good horse to carry him. On every road they were coming in heavy coaches from every province in New England. And by water they were coming, too, up the river and down, in lighters and cutters, in schooners and sloops.

And there was nothing a good minister could do, because the world was changing.

On the Cambridge Common, tents were rising. Some were grand pavilions supported by long ridgepoles, with rough-planked floors for dancing. Others were smaller, made for smaller pursuits such as pouring rum or gambling at pawpaws, or selling everything from pickled oysters to home-fashioned hats to tree-bark tonics that cured whatever disease a gullible man might think he had.

The tents were licensed by the selectmen, who marked spaces with stakes, took fees "for the betterment of the town," and left the constable and his deputies to keep order.

And there was nothing a good minister could do . . . except to warn his pewholders to remove their cushions and psalm books and prohibit his grandchildren from going anywhere near the Cambridge Common.

That same afternoon, a man who called himself Burton Bones stepped off the ferry in Charlestown. He took a bit of snuff, sneezed into his handkerchief, and tapped his walking stick impatiently while his slave wrestled with their baggage.

The slave had help, as there were three other men traveling with them, all younger, none so well dressed. Indeed, one of them seemed more concerned about the wardrobe of Burton Bones than his own. He took out a needle and thread and tried to mend a tear in the sleeve of Burton's coat . . . while Burton was wearing it.

Burton shooed him away, whispering, "Wait till we set up our tent."

Burton Bones could not deny that he was nervous. Gazing west, along the curl of the river, he could just make out the cupola of Harvard Hall, glittering in the sunlight like the tower of an ancient castle he had returned at last to storm.

Once the others had collected their belongings and piled them onto their wagon, they gathered around him. They had been with him for many years and traveled with him to many places—England, Scotland, Ireland, Jamaica, the southern colonies of America. And finally, he had persuaded them to come to New England.

Two years earlier, a troupe of London players called the American Company had put on a fine season of Shakespeare in Newport, Rhode Island. And if that colony was changing, he had told them, so must Massachusetts be changing. And in a place where there had never been theater, people would pay handsomely to see a company of English actors, even one as small as theirs. What Burton Bones had not admitted was that after Newport, the American Company had been chased out of Providence and ordered never to return. Some things were better left unsaid.

"Are we ready?" said Demetrius, who only played the slave and received pay like the others. "We ain't gettin' any younger."

"You're right," said Burton Bones, "we ain't." And with a flourish of his walking stick, he stepped into the road. He was a tall man, all arms and legs and angles, aptly named, for he was quite simply bony. But as he raised his chin and said, "Let us go amongst the holy men of Harvard," he seemed to gather weight and presence. Then he pointed his silver-buckled shoe toward Cambridge.

Any who looked closely would have seen that the shoe had a hole in it.

That evening, Caleb Wedge told his grandfather that he had been invited to a punch bowl in the room of a senior sophister but that there would be no "strong waters" in the punch. Lydia told her grandfather that she would be visiting a friend, Sally Marrett, but that they would not dare go out "with so many strangers about."

Both were lying, and while they could not be certain of their grandfather's gullibility, they were not surprised to see each other on the Cambridge Common just after dark.

Caleb and three friends were coming out of a tent where people were selling rum. Lydia and Sally were standing in front of a fruit stand, eating fresh peaches sold from a bushel basket by a Rhode Island farmer. And brother and sister both were giddy.

Fresh peaches could do that to a thirteen-year-old girl. Rum could do it to a sixteen-year-old boy. And the excitement of commencement eve could do it to anyone.

There was fiddle-and-pipe music coming from the dancing tent, loud cheers coming from a gambling tent, war whoops and shouts rising from a tent where local Indians challenged farmers to contests with bow and arrow, laughter rising everywhere, and hundreds of people hurrying from one tent to the next.

"Caleb!" Lydia called to her brother. "Do I smell rum?"

"You do." He burped. "And I taste it."

"Would you like to walk with us, girls?" asked one of the other boys.

"Where to?" asked Lydia.

"To the end of the tent row, to see the play. It starts in five minutes."

"And once the constable hears," said Caleb, "it won't *last* five minutes more."

Lydia looked at Sally and shrugged, as if to say that they had been disobedient enough already. What further harm could they do? And off they went with the boys, down the torchlit "street" that ran through the center of the tent village, a thoroughfare of straw, watermelon rinds, peach pits, and trash.

At the end was a platform in front of a wagon on which a rainbow-hued canvas had been raised as a backdrop. A handsome sign proclaimed BURTON BONES AND CO., PLAYERS OF THE MASQUE, and beneath that, more crudely lettered, TONIGHT, 7:30, THE TAMING OF THE SHREW, BY WILL. SHAKESPEARE.

An old slave was beating a drum in front of the platform while a young man wandered through the crowd, playing a flute. When the crowd had grown large enough, the young man left off playing and cried, "Good gentlefolk, a prologue to our play. Give heed to Burton Bones!" And he swept his arm toward the platform, where there was a loud bang, a flash of light, and a puff of smoke.

People jumped. Others cried out. Still others went hurrying toward the noise.

As if by magic, an actor in the robes of a Venetian gentleman stepped through the smoke, executed a bow, and proclaimed, "Your honor's players, hearing your amendment, / Are come to play a pleasant comedy; / For so your doctors hold it very meet, / Seeing too much sadness hath congeal'd your blood / And melancholy is the nurse of frenzy: / Therefore they thought it good you hear a play, / And frame your mind to mirth and merriment, / Which bars a thousand harms and lengthens life."

What a fine sentiment, thought Lydia.

From behind the curtain stepped two actors. One said, "Tranio, since for the great desire I had / To see fair Padua, nursery of arts, / I am arrived in fruitful Lombardy . . ."

Padua. Lombardy. Italy. Lydia could not imagine the beauty and romance of such places, but standing there in that field of tents, in the midst of that cow pasture, on the edge of the civilized world, she tried.

Then she noticed Selectman William Brattle go bustling away as if he had seen enough. And that, she knew, was a bad sign.

How could his grandchildren be so deceitful? How could they be so depraved? The old reverend hurried through the village, the constable's messenger at his side. With every step, he jabbed his walking stick like a rapier and asked himself again the hardest question of all: How could they be so stupid?

And how could any group of actors be so stupid as to think they could display their filth on Cambridge Common, whether at commencement or in the dead of winter?

At the edge of the Common, William Brattle was waiting with the constable and three deputies. Though educated at the college, Brattle was known as "a man of universal superficial knowledge."

He had never trained as a doctor and yet had treated the students and people of Cambridge for years. He had served no legal apprenticeship and yet had become a judge. He had never fired a shot in anger and yet had gained the rank of brigadier in the Massachusetts militia. He was prosperous, pompous, and, by virtue of his belly and rank, perfectly fit to bear the nickname "Brigadier Paunch."

"We would have chased them off," he announced to Abraham, "but there's no written law 'gainst the masque, so best we put God's law on our side."

"Trust that it is," said Reverend Abraham.

"And be warned," said Constable Henry Hull, a hard-eyed little man, "your grandchildren is standin' 'fore the stage, listenin' like 'twas one of your own fine services."

"I thank you," said the reverend, though he sensed irony in Hull's words, for no man had fallen asleep more often or snored more loudly during Wedge's services.

"We'll chase 'em off," said Hull as the group made its way onto the Common. "Better, though, if we had a written law, like what they made in Providence last year."

"Indeed," said Brattle. "Give them a stiff fine and these dress-wearing actors'll damn soon take their filth elsewhere."

"Dresses? What play is it?" asked Abraham.

"Something about a shrew," said Brattle.

"Shrews?" said the constable. "They can be nasty little beasts."

"This shrew is a woman," said Brattle.

"Oh," said the constable, "*they* can be nasty little beasts, too."

People made way as this contingent marched toward the end of the tent row and came up to the platform stage, where three actors—one in a dress and woman's wig—held the audience transfixed.

The old actor said, "Now, Signior Petruchio, how speed you with my daughter?"

"How but well, sir? how but well? / It were impossible I should speed amiss."

Having grabbed torches of their own, Constable Hull and Selectman Brattle were now pushing their way toward the front of the crowd, while Abraham looked for his grandchildren amid the shadows.

The old actor turned to the one in the dress and said, "Why, how now, daughter Katharine! in your dumps?"

"Call you me daughter?" was the response, in a high, put-on, angry voice.

The audience roared, as much at the voice as the words.

And Abraham Wedge, who believed in the power of God and the truth of John Calvin, could not believe his own eyes. For in looking at the stage, he thought he saw his own father, long dead and gone to his reward. Except that his own father would never have worn the robes of a Venetian gentleman.

Then the harsh voice of Henry Hull cried, "Burton Bones! I command you to stop, under penalty of the law."

And Burton Bones stepped out of the role of Signior Baptista, father of Kate, and shouted, "We bring joy to New England! He who stops us is an enemy of such."

Brattle shouted, "Cease and desist!"

By now, Caleb and Lydia had seen their grandfather, and both were moving to the edge of the crowd, putting distance between themselves and the reverend.

"There is no written law against the masque in Massachusetts," shouted Burton Bones, "and never has there been. So by whose authority do you stop our play?"

"By the authority of the Congregational Church!" shouted Abraham Wedge. "Planted on these shores by the grace of God, anno Domini 1630."

"And who claims this authority?" answered Burton Bones.

"Your own brother!"

A gasp went through the crowd.

The eyes of Caleb and Lydia met, each face mirroring the other's shock. Caleb mouthed the word "brother?" Lydia pointed to the stage and said, "Our great-uncle?"

Brattle, who moved with all the grace of a loose-rolling barrel, swung his whole body—shoulders, wig, belly, and torch—toward Abraham and said, "Brother?"

"Brother!" boomed the actor who called himself Burton Bones.

Then he pulled off his wig and said, "If your name be Abraham Wedge, then 'tis so. I am Benjamin Wedge, returned to Massachusetts to bring joy."

"Joy? Joy?" Abraham Wedge seemed staggered by a mingling of emotions—shock, surprise, but, above all, fury. "You do not bring joy. You bring the depravity of a man dressed as a woman, the waste of idle entertainment. The—"

"Fire!" shouted Demetrius the slave. "Fire! It's the fat one with the torch!"

"Fire? Where?" Brattle looked frantically left and right, then looked above him as the flames from his torch chewed into the canvas overhanging the little stage. "Fire!"

The actor in the dress leapt off the platform and shoved Brattle and his torch away. The other actors tore at the flaming canvas.

Some in the crowd ran for water. Some ran in panic, for nothing could spread as fast as a fire in a tent city. And some stood by, laughing and shouting as though all of it were part of the show.

Brattle cried for the constable to arrest the actor who struck him.

Burton Bones cried for water. So someone hit him in the face with a bucketful, which brought more laughter from the crowd and curses from the actors.

"Let it burn," shouted Abraham, "as punishment to you and warning to others that true joy is never brought by . . . by men in dresses!"

"Out of the way, Grandfather!" Caleb Wedge nearly knocked Abraham down, bulled through the crowd, and delivered a bucket of water to douse the flames.

"You may stay the night," said Abraham a few hours later. "I am a Christian. I would not turn out a stranger, or a brother, or one who is both."

"Thank you." Benjamin Wedge sat in the wing chair by the fireplace, sweated and sooted, and sipped a glass of port.

"Be thankful I spoke for you," said Abraham, "or the constable would have had you before the magistrate in the morning."

"It would not be the first time," said Benjamin.

Abraham stood over his brother, his shock having worn down to the anger beneath, a lifetime of anger at a brother who had fled a Sudbury farm and left a family that loved him. Abraham jabbed a finger at him and said, "But you are to leave here in the morning, you and all your players."

Benjamin looked at the children, who sat on the seraph in the middle of the room.

Lydia was taking in every word and nuance of this reunion. Caleb was holding his hand against his mouth as if to hold in all the rum he had drunk.

Benjamin said, "I was hoping to show the children the wonder of the theater."

"Precisely why you leave in the morning. If you are not on the road by daybreak, heading again for New York, where these things are permitted, I shall have you arrested."

"On what charges?" asked Benjamin.

"Assault upon a selectman, creating a nuisance inimical to good order, theft."

"I've stolen nothing."

"That slave. He's the one who ran off with you, is he not?"

"One cannot steal what is not property."

"I do not believe in slavery," said Abraham, "but I believe in the law, which requires me to tell the descendants of Reverend Bleen that their property has been returned to the province."

Benjamin looked at the two young people. "Children—"

"You have nothing to say to them"—Abraham glanced at his grandchildren—"though I do."

Lydia ignored the anger in her grandfather's voice and said, "I abhor slavery, too. And I thought the play was wonderful . . . what I saw of it."

"Good night and go to bed," said Abraham. "The both of you."

Caleb stood slowly, as if to keep the contents of his stomach from sloshing, and crossed the room to offer Benjamin his hand.

Benjamin looked the boy up and down. "You have the family height. I can see the family intelligence in your eyes. And the smell of rum shows you're a lad with some curiosity about the world."

"Thank you, sir." Caleb burped.

And Lydia spoke up. "Caleb is among the best mathematics students at the college. He went with Professor Winthrop to New-foundland and used scientific instruments."

Benjamin nodded. "A Wedge . . . a man of science. The world is changing."

"Indeed it is," grumbled Abraham.

Then Benjamin asked Lydia: "And what do you wish for?"

Lydia realized it was the first time that anyone had asked her the question. She was so surprised that for once, she was speechless.

"She is to be a wife and mother," said Abraham, "to some unfortunate soul."

"I would also be a poet," she said.

"I should like to read your work," answered Benjamin.

"Grandfather thinks my poems are whimsical and childish," she said.

"So are Shakespeare's comedies," answered Benjamin. "Till you think on them. Then they become a map of the human heart."

"See, Grandfather"—she turned to the old man—"just what I've said to you."

"And I said, 'Good *night*,' to both of you," said Abraham.

The two old men listened as the children went into the foyer and mounted the stairs. One set of footfalls went all the way up, but the heavier seemed to stop halfway, then come stumbling down again. The front door was thrown open, and a moment later, the sound of retching could be heard in the bushes.

Benjamin said to his brother, "Raising children must be a hard proposition."

"Harder than you can imagine, especially for the second time."

Benjamin said, "'Tis good to see you, Brother."

"'Tis good to see you, however you are seen. But why? Why now? Why so late?"

"I could not die without seeing this world again," answered Benjamin. "And without doing what Father once urged me—to step forward and stand in the open."

"You broke their hearts, you know. Father and Mother both."

Benjamin looked down at his hands. "Once set upon the road with a runaway slave, there was nothing else for me to do."

Abraham removed his coat and put his wig on the stand. Then he and his brother talked far into the night.

The next morning dawned bright and clear, as it always did on the day of the Harvard commencement.

In the Wedge barn, where Burton Bones and his players had spent the night, the actors packed their wagon, then downed gallons of tea and pounds of bread and jam served by the housekeeper, Mrs. Beale. Then Benjamin called for the green velvet suit he had worn into Cambridge the day before.

"No need to be puttin' on your fancies," said Demetrius. "We're leavin'."

"Not quite yet," said Benjamin.

"We's supposed to go at dawn," answered Demetrius. "And I'm nervous enough as 'tis. That constable, I think he's thinkin' to send me back to Sudbury."

"Aye," said one of the others. "And that selectman may yet press charges."

"I missed my own commencement," said Benjamin. "I'll see this one. Besides, the roads be so choked now, we'll never get out. So stay here and stay out of sight."

In the village square, the crowds were gathering for the "great and last day." The spectacle was beginning with the arrival of the governor's mounted entourage, preceded by the constable and six deputies. Waiting for them in the courtyard before Holden Chapel were portly old President Holyoke, the tutors, the Corporation, and all the candidates in their black gowns.

Benjamin Wedge had no use for the ceremony, except as a distraction that allowed him to slip unnoticed into Harvard Hall.

Inside, the college steward was directing preparations for the commencement banquet. The long tables were covered with linen. China plates clattered politely in a place where students ordinarily used pewter. And the Great Salt of 1650, the oldest piece of silver in the college inventory, sat in its place of honor before the president's chair.

A scene full of ancient tradition, thought Benjamin, all grandly symbolic and theatrical, in a province where theater was prohibited. Such a place did not deserve the fine work secreted in the library above the Great Hall.

So he took the stairs, levering himself with his walking stick, as if he were far older and weaker than he was. Once at the top, he moved quickly to the library door.

He knocked but heard neither answer nor footfall, so he slipped the handle off his cane, revealing a long, thin blade, perfect for probing locks. He bent down and—

The door was pulled open.

Benjamin stood up so quickly that he was certain he'd raise suspicion.

But the young man on the other side of the door seemed too startled. He looked Benjamin up and down and said, "The library is closed, sir."

Benjamin slipped his cane back together and bowed. "I beg your pardon, Mr.—"

"Spurgeon. Tutor Spurgeon."

"You're the keeper of the library, then?"

The young man nodded. He wore an academic gown and a harried expression, for he was clearly late to the ceremony.

"Beggin' your indulgence"—Benjamin put on his oldest voice—"I be but an ancient graduate, back to see the school. Many's the happy day I spent in the library. So—"

"That voice—"

"Sir?"

"You're the actor, the one who played Signior Baptista." Tutor Spurgeon closed and locked the door behind him and said, "You were ordered to leave Cambridge. What are you doing here?"

Benjamin looked down at his hands, his favorite gesture of contrition. "My story is true. I've just come back to see the library."

"Well . . . not today. And if your intent is to find some play to put on here—"

Just then, the meetinghouse bell began to peal.

"I am late," said Tutor Spurgeon. "So I'll thank you to be on your way."

And there was nothing Benjamin could do, except to calculate, as he went down the stairs, that it would be at least a year before

Tutor Spurgeon left his position and an old actor could walk into Harvard Hall, lift the bottom shelf in section twelve, and retrieve an ancient play. But it would only be a few minutes before Spurgeon took his place in the procession. Then an old actor might take his advantage.

Outside, the candidates in their black gowns were marching by, two abreast. President Holyoke puffed along after them, followed by the Corporation and tutors, including the harried Mr. Spurgeon, then the governor and his council. With the constable's deputies opening a path through the crowd and the clanging of the town bell providing the only rhythm, they marched in stately step to the meetinghouse, where Reverends Appleton and Wedge waited.

Benjamin was struck with a twinge of envy as the procession passed Abraham, for all the students seemed to know him and offer him some sign of respect. Benjamin had yearned all his life for such respect. If he rescued that play from the library, he might gain it, at least in those parts of the world not still mired in ignorance.

Then Constable Hull appeared beside him. "'Tis good you defied my order to leave, Wedge. The Bleens are here for the ceremony. They say you run off with their grandfather's slave years ago. Would that be the one they call Demetrius?"

"No, sir, it would not."

"Stay put till the ceremony end, so that we may have a look into this."

Benjamin knew that if he stayed, even a few moments more, it might be the difference between slavery and freedom for his old friend Demetrius. But if he left, he might never have another chance at that play. He debated no more than that. By the time the ceremony ended and the constable came knocking, he and his troupe were gone.

iii

That summer ended more quickly than the one before, as summers always did, and it ended more quickly for Abraham than for his grandchildren, which was the natural order of things.

By autumn, the furor over Benjamin Wedge had faded. The Bleens withdrew their claim to a human possession they did not wish to own. The constable, however, swore to arrest Benjamin on general principle, should ever he appear in Cambridge again. From time to time, stories were heard of his troupe, driven from yet another New England town, but as winter came on, the stories faded, too.

January brought a celebration at the opening of a new dormitory, called Hollis Hall, funded by the generous Hollis family of England.

January also brought the provincial legislators to Cambridge. The townspeople prayed that the legislators did not bring the small-pox they had left Boston to escape. But none in Boston or Cambridge would escape the storm that blew in on the twenty-fourth.

At noon, the sky was clear, the air calm, the temperature in the thir-ties. Caleb set these facts down in a meteorological diary that he kept in emulation of Professor Winthrop. At dusk, he noted that the wind had shifted to the northeast, the temperature had dropped, and clouds covered the sky.

But he paid the weather no more mind; he was expected at the home of Professor Winthrop on the corner of Spring and Wood Streets for Tuesday-night supper. The group was smaller than usual, as most students had gone home for winter recess, but there was a warm greeting from Mrs. Winthrop, a fire on the grate, a fine bottle of claret, and a succulent joint of meat. And the educated conversation began the moment the students took off their hats and the professor showed them his new brass and mahogany barometer.

"An amazing instrument," Winthrop said. "It allows us to quantify something as mysterious as the pressure of air, which enables us to predict the weather."

"What is it telling you at the moment?" asked Caleb.

"If the mercury was at 29.81 inches at noon and is now at 29.31," said the professor, "what is it telling *you?*"

"That bad weather is on the way?" answered Caleb.

"Indeed. But quantify it. What kind? How much? When?"

"Snow, coming in on a northeast wind, tonight," answered one of the others.

Winthrop nodded. "Based upon the rate at which the mercury has fallen, I would say that by the time dinner is done, it will be snowing."

And it was. Caleb and the others—overflowing with roast pork, claret, and fresh notions about the practical applications of science—stepped out into the flurries.

"It has begun." Winthrop looked up into the sky. "We'll be digging out come morning, mark my words. Good night, gentlemen."

Caleb turned up the collar of his cape and headed home. By the time he passed the house of Brigadier Brattle, his shoes were filled with snow and his feet were freezing. He hoped that his sister was still up, so the fire would be stoked, even if it meant listening to the poetry she had been writing. He also hoped that his grandfather had taken to bed, so a boy might dip into the port without hearing a lecture on temperance.

The streets were dark, except for small pools of light under the lanterns at the corners. The wind was icy, though the smell of woodsmoke promised warmth. And a lamp burned in the front window of the Wedge house, a handsome place of two full stories, dormered windows, and a white picket fence.

As Caleb opened the gate, a cold gust struck him in the back and sneaked under his cape. But it wasn't the wind that caused the hairs to stand on his neck. It was the sight of a dark figure emerging from behind a tree trunk, calling his name.

Caleb stepped quickly inside the gate and closed it. "Who's there?"

The figure lurched toward him: a tricorne dripping wet snow, an ice-crusted beard, a bony hand reaching out. "Caleb, it's me. It's Benjamin."

The house was quiet, except for the windblown rattling of the shutters. Reverend Abraham, Mrs. Beale, and Lydia were all abed. So Caleb threw a log onto the grate, poured two glasses of port, brought out a slab of ham and a wedge of Stilton.

Benjamin sat by the fire, a blanket around his shoulders, his complexion as blue-veined white as the cheese. With shaking hand, he took the port and drank it down, then he tore into a piece of ham, chewed, and swallowed.

"Why have you come back?" asked Caleb. "Constable Hull has a long memory."

Benjamin did not answer until he had finished another glass of port, sliced off a chunk of cheese, and settled back. "I came back to see you."

"Uncle," said Caleb, "what's happened? Where is your troupe?"

"Two quit." Benjamin downed another glass. "Two died."

He said that after he and his players were chased from New England, they determined to go to Quebec, where the English viceroy might enjoy a season of Shakespeare. But they were actors, not woodsmen, and they did not reckon with the northern winter. Two froze to death, Demetrius and the cart of costumes were lost in the St. Lawrence, and one refused to do anything more than take a corner in a Quebec public house and recite soliloquies for pennies.

"So I come seeking shelter for the night," said Benjamin, "and help from you."

Caleb poured Benjamin another port. "You can sleep in the loft. Grandfather will speak to the constable in the morning, and—"

"I'll be gone in the morning, God and Caleb Wedge willing."

"God, perhaps"—Caleb laughed—"but me?"

Benjamin's complexion had brightened, and he had stopped shivering as food and port coursed through him. He said, "You are a modern man, are you not?"

"I suppose."

"A student of John Winthrop?" Benjamin dropped the blanket from his shoulders. "Who preaches that you widen knowledge through research and interpretation?"

"Yes." Caleb wondered if his uncle had somehow been listening to the conversation in Winthrop's study that evening.

"Science has instruments to help us widen our knowledge." Benjamin got up and went over to the globe in the corner and gave it a spin. "But where are the instruments that help us to widen our understanding of humanity? Where are the wisdoms?"

The wind gusted so hard that the whole house shook.

"Here." Benjamin pulled a book from his coat and pressed it into

Caleb's hand. "A quarto of *Love's Labours Lost*, one of the best instruments we have . . . for the study of ourselves."

Caleb flipped the pages. "I've read it, Uncle. It's very . . . interesting."

"You must do more than read it," said Benjamin. "You must imagine it . . . played by actors in costume, on a stage made brilliant by burning limelight, with music, magical effects of sound and sight, alarums and excursions, entrances and exits. Then will you see what ignorance still prevails in this benighted province."

"But if we can read the play—"

"If a play be only read and not played," said Benjamin, " 'tis like aiming a telescope at a house across the road, when you might look at the planets instead."

"I suppose. But—"

"Were I to tell you that there was a telescope in Harvard Hall, a powerful instrument, hidden and forgotten, you'd rush to retrieve it, would you not?"

"I suppose."

"Well, there be an instrument there, a Shakespeare play, hidden long ago, by your own great-great-grandfather, hidden again by me. Will you help me to save it?"

"Save it? From whom? When?"

"From the minions of ignorance. Tonight. Under cover of a fortuitous blizzard, while most students are elsewhere, and those who remain sleep soundly in their beds."

"I . . . I don't know."

"Help him, Caleb." Lydia entered in her robe, her hair loose to her waist.

"You've been listening?" said Caleb.

"I heard voices. And I heard enough. Help him. If you don't, I will."

Benjamin said, "I ask you only to keep lookout and listen for footfalls, should Tutor Spurgeon decide to visit his library in the middle of the night."

"If he's in residence," said Caleb, "he need only get out of bed to visit. He sleeps in the adjacent chamber."

"And think," said Lydia, "of what he would do, should he find a play improperly cataloged in *his* library. He is very staunch in his beliefs."

From scholar to sneak thief in the space of two hours. A change, thought Caleb, as complete as the change in the town after two hours of blizzard. The wind had blown out every streetlamp between the Watertown Road and Harvard Yard, a foot of snow had fallen, and it was falling so fast that it filled their footprints even as they went. To one peering out into the storm, they must have appeared like spectral beings, like the witches that once haunted their ancestors.

But as he trudged along in his riding boots, his tricorne pulled down to stop the snow from stinging his cheeks, Caleb told himself that he was advancing the cause of wisdom in a world that favored ignorance as surely as it had in the days of the witch-hunts. His grandfather might not approve, but Professor Winthrop would.

No lanterns burned in Harvard Hall or Stoughton, though lights flickered here and there in Massachusetts Hall—tutors nodding over difficult passages in Plato or Deuteronomy while the storm whipped against their windows.

"Keep an eye out," said Benjamin as they scurried up to the door of Harvard Hall.

"For what?" said Caleb. "You can't see ten feet."

"All the more reason. If we're found by someone less than ten feet away, we'll have no chance." Benjamin slipped a penknife from his sleeve, and with a skill that comes only of experience, he probed the lock, picked it, and clicked open the door.

Then they were out of the storm, in the west entry of Harvard Hall, oldest and most venerable building in the college. The stairwell was to the left, the Great Hall to the right. They stood for a moment, letting their eyes accustom to the darkness, listening for footfalls. They heard none, but they both smelled smoke.

"A chimney that doesn't draw?" whispered Benjamin. "Someone has a fire going? I thought you said this entry was deserted."

"Tutor Smith is gone home," said Caleb. "And the legislators aren't here. They're boarded all about the town."

Benjamin shook his head, as if puzzled. Then he led Caleb up the stairs to the second floor, stopped again, and listened. The only sound, beyond the roaring of the wind, was the creaking of the old building itself.

The Apparatus Chamber, which held many of the college's scientific instruments and a few of its scientific curiosities—stuffed animals and the tanned hide of a Negro—was to the left. The library was to the right. And the smell of smoke was stronger.

They stepped to the library door. Benjamin leaned down, probed the lock, probed again, and put his hand on the doorknob. "Pray 'tisn't bolted."

"It shouldn't be. The legislators use it as their meeting chamber each day."

Benjamin turned the knob, the door swung open, and Caleb felt smoke sting his eyes. The room was lit by the strange, dim snowlight that came in the windows, and by the orange glow on the grate on the far side of the room.

"That chimney needs cleaning," said Benjamin. "It draws not at all."

"Or someone needs lessons in banking a fire 'fore they leave on a windy night." Caleb coughed. "Perhaps we should open a window to improve the draft."

"Perhaps you should stay by the door and listen."

So Caleb pressed his ear to the west door and watched Benjamin go straight to alcove twelve and drop to his knees, as if he had rehearsed it all a thousand times.

What Caleb could not see was the sweat on Benjamin's forehead and the shaking old hands that quickly removed all the books from the bottom shelf and piled them on the floor. The hands produced the penknife, slipped it into the corner, and levered the bottom shelf out of the bookcase frame. Nails were still expensive.

Caleb stifled a cough, and Benjamin whispered, "What is it?"

"The . . . the smoke."

"Quiet." Benjamin reached into the place where he had put the book, and the sweat on his forehead went cold. It was not there. He reached again, then again, cursing old hands. Where was the book? Forty years he had thought about this moment and . . . *there*, at the other end. Thank the Lord. His memory was not as flawless as he thought. In a few seconds, he had replaced the shelf, replaced the books on the shelf, and moved back to the door.

"Here." He pressed the book into Caleb's hands. "'Tis yours now."

"Mine?" Caleb turned it over in his hands. "What am I to do with it?"

"Whatever you think best. See that it's published. See that it's performed. Put it publicly into the collection of John Harvard. Do it tomorrow, if you wish."

"But you could do all that, Uncle."

"Fighting ignorance is a job for every generation. Fight it forwardly, as my father told me to, as I tried to when I came back to Cambridge last summer."

Caleb looked into the old man's eyes and saw something more than mischief. He saw his own complicity in a burglary rather than in the liberation of an idea. The excitement of it seemed suddenly less real than the sin.

Being a good reader of facial expressions, even in semidarkness, Benjamin sensed the boy's change of heart, so he grabbed him and pushed him into the hallway.

And Caleb noticed one of the fireplace logs flame back to life. How could that be? The fire had almost burned to ash. "Uncle . . . wait."

"We got what we came for." Benjamin closed the door and stepped quickly toward the stairwell.

Caleb stopped. "Uncle, you didn't lock the door."

"Ah, yes. We leave no trace behind. The world knows nothing until you decide to tell them." Benjamin pulled out the penknife.

But Caleb, still curious about that flame, pushed open the door.

All in an instant, he wondered why the flame was in front of the fireplace rather than inside it, he felt a rush of air around him, and he heard a roar as the fire burst from the floorboards, like a beast breaching from the sea.

"Good God!" Benjamin ran back, tearing off his cape as he went.

"Where's it coming from?" Caleb hurried after him.

"I don't know. A spark from the fireplace, maybe, smoldering in a floor beam." Benjamin swung his cape left and right as new tongues of flame burst forth. "Get help!"

Caleb threw open one of the windows and shouted, "Fire!" into the roaring snow. He may have been a student of science, but he did not consider the impact of fresh oxygen on combustion. Whatever good Benjamin did with his cape, Caleb undid.

Within a few seconds, the east side of the library was a sheet of flame.

"Get out," shouted Benjamin. "Go and get help."

"But the books . . . Tutor Spurgeon."

"Run," said Benjamin. "Fetch help. I'll get Spurgeon."

"No. You run. I'll fight the fire."

"You run faster. Go. But show the book to no one. They'll think we started this."

And the flames burst from the window frames at both sides of the building.

"It's inside the walls!" cried Benjamin. "Go, or we'll never stop it." He pushed the boy toward the west door. "Go!"

Then Benjamin ran across the library, through the east door, and across the entry. He pounded on Spurgeon's door, crying, "Fire! Fire!" Then he delivered a kick that slammed the door open. But Spurgeon was not there and his bed was made.

Meanwhile, Caleb was stumbling out the door with the book in his pocket. He screamed, "Fire! Fire!" But he could barely hear his own voice over the wind. He screamed up at Massachusetts Hall, where the lights had been burning earlier, but there was no response. So he ran into the village square and screamed into the blowing snow, "Fire!"

In the library, Benjamin Wedge was running along the shelves, pulling the books out, putting them on the tables, as if he could save them, pile by pile. But the smoke was boiling along the ceiling and filling every space not occupied by fire.

And where was the help?

He ran to the window but could see nothing through the blowing snow. So he grabbed one of the piles of books and rushed for the west door. Then he realized that trying to save five thousand books, pile by pile, was hopeless.

If he could summon help quickly, they might yet save the ancient building. So he dropped the books and ran up the stairs to the long chamber. In the middle of the room, surrounded by the empty beds of the freshmen, a bell rope hung through a hole in the ceiling, and a circular staircase led up to the cupola.

It was from here that a tutor rang the college bell for chapel twice a day, and from here that Benjamin might summon help. He grabbed the rope and pulled, but it was tied somewhere up above him. So he scrambled up the staircase just as the flames broke through the floor of the long chamber and reached upward for the roof beams.

He threw the latch and pushed up the trapdoor. Cold air and snow whipped down at him, cold fresh air and cooling snow. So he climbed up into the cupola and untied the bell rope. He wrapped it in his hands and looked out at the blowing whiteness, then down at the orange flames licking up from under the roof rafters.

Caleb Wedge had run halfway home, screaming out the warning, when the clanging of the bell struck the cold air like a hammer striking glass.

It was said that President Holyoke, lying awake in his Wadsworth House bed, ruminating on the miseries of old age and college presidency, saw an orange glow in the sky and leapt to his feet just as the bell rang out. Others heard a mysterious man running through the streets calling, "Fire!" And still others were awakened by the sight of what looked like burning snowflakes, the embers of Harvard Hall, blowing through the air.

Soon, every man in Cambridge, except for one, was rushing to fight the fire. The tradesmen went, the legislators, the tutors finally awakening in Massachusetts Hall, Reverend Wedge and Reverend Appleton, too. William Brattle came rushing with his slave. Governor Bernard came from Bradish's Tavern to help work the town fire engine. And President Holyoke lumbered through the snow in greatcoat, boots, and nightshirt.

Caleb Wedge, however, was running away with a book that he believed he had to hide, a book that made him complicit in this disaster. By going through yards, he avoided the men rushing to fight the blaze. He reached the family barn unnoticed and climbed to the hayloft. But before he hid the book, he swung open the loft door and looked up into the sky, boiling pink and orange in the snow.

"Caleb . . . Caleb." Lydia had come into the backyard and was looking up at him. "What did you do? Why did you start a fire?"

"We didn't start it."

"Then go back and help. Go now. Or people will think otherwise."

When the first firefighters arrived, the bell was still clanging, but the smoke was pouring out of the cupola as though it were a chimney. Then the flames burst up, engulfing the little tower and the shadowed figure ringing the bell.

But there was no time to worry about him, whoever he was. Volunteers dragged the engine through the snowdrifts and called for water, but the nearest pump was frozen, so a bucket brigade was organized and water passed hand over hand from the Common well to the Yard. And one set of hands belonged to Caleb Wedge.

No one slept in Cambridge that night. Those who could fought the fire. Others brought buckets of hot tea and food. Lydia Wedge wrote a poem:

> *The hero of the bell rang strong, to save*
> *The meetinghouse of thought and mem'ries deep.*
> *Townsfolk and solons both rushed forth,*
> *'Midst fiery flakes and gusts of snow,*
> *To fight the flam'd devourer, but alas! In Vain!*
> *Down rush'd precipitate, with thund'ring crash,*
> *The roof, the walls, and in one ruinous heap,*
> *The ancient dome, and all its treasures lie!*
> *And 'neath the dome, burned skull white and black,*
> *Lay the hero of the bell, unknown.*

Lydia read these words to her brother in the morning as he stood before the smoking rubble, in a world turned strangely bright, even in the gray light of the last flurries, for the grandest building in New England, as changeless as the western hills to all who lived that day, was now a black mound surrounded like a ringworm sore by a swath of mud where the heat had melted the snow and thawed the earth.

Caleb did not look at Lydia until she was done. Then he said, "Would you have me compliment your verse?"

She looked at the people standing around, some alone with their thoughts, some in small groups, and she whispered, "I want you to know, your secret lies safe with me."

Caleb shivered. He was covered in soot, soaked, and only now realizing how cold he was. "I have no secret. I ran for help. We tried to stop it."

"You stole a book from the library."

"That I am of a mind to return. 'Tis too great a burden." He patted his pocket, as he had decided that the book was safest on his own person.

"I would reconsider, Caleb."

"'Tis only a matter of doing it." Caleb looked at the men clustered near the ruins. "They're all over there, the governor, President Holyoke, Professor Winthrop—"

"*And* Grandfather . . . Do not mortify him by bringing suspicion on yourself."

Caleb was hoping he could put right what he had done. And he knew that the only way was to tell the truth. It was what his grandfather had taught him. And in that cold morning, Caleb appreciated his grandfather's advice even more. So he drew closer to the group of men in snow-covered tricornes and soaked winter capes.

President Holyoke was bemoaning all he had lost. "Five thousand volumes, the Apparatus Chamber, Professor Winthrop's instruments and discoveries—"

"My instruments can be replaced," said Winthrop, "God willing."

"God willing, aye," said Abraham Wedge.

"'Tis the loss of John Harvard's library that pains deeply," said Winthrop. "The very seedbed of our knowledge."

Hearing those words, Caleb made his decision. He would show them that a cutting from the Harvard tree had survived. He took out the book and stepped forward.

Lydia whispered, "Wait."

And it was good advice. For in Caleb's moment of hesitation, another student came up to the president from the other side, bearing a large volume. "Excuse me, sir."

Holyoke, a massive heavy old man, turned his great head to the student. "What is it that you want, on a morning like this?"

"I . . . I . . . I wish to return this book to the library. I . . . I . . . I have saved it from the fire." The student placed it into Holyoke's hand.

"Thanks be to God," said the old president as he examined it. "*Christian Warfare with the World, the Flesh, and the Devil,* one of the John Harvard books."

The student stepped back and raised his chin, as if he expected someone to pin a medal on his chest.

"Thanks be to God," said Holyoke again. He studied the book a moment longer; then, the tone of his voice dropping, he said, "How did you come by this?"

"Sir?"

"This book does not circulate."

"I . . . I know, sir," said the student. "I'm sorry, but—"

"This will require discipline."

Professor Winthrop said, "Under the circumstances, sir—"

"In times of crisis," said Abraham Wedge, "rules become ever more important."

"Indeed," said Holyoke. "Find Tutor Spurgeon. Have him go through this boy's lodgings. We'll see what else he saved for us by spiriting it illegally from our library."

And Caleb felt his sister tugging at his sleeve.

"I think we should get you home, Brother, and into some dry clothes."

"But the book?" he whispered.

"Bring it along. It will be our secret."

Chapter Fourteen

═══════

So, *Corporei Insectii* was gone. That's what the evidence told him, whether Peter Fallon went looking for answers in the archives or on the campus tour with his son.

"It was here that one of the most famous scenes in Harvard history unfolded," said the girl guiding the tour.

Someone took a picture of Harvard Hall. Someone else took a picture of the Yard. Someone even took a picture of Peter Fallon.

Why? Did he look like part of the scenery? True, he was dressed in tweed and turtleneck, like an academic. Or was it something else? Was one of Keegan's men still tailing him? But the play was gone. The story was over, and Peter had tried to put out the word to the people he thought were the players.

He had e-mailed Assistant Professor O'Hill:

I suggest that you speak to Will Wedge about the contents of the commonplace book I've unearthed. It will be a purely intellectual exercise, however, given the fate of a certain volume that Benjamin Wedge describes.

He had received a curt thank-you in reply.

He had also dispatched his brother to the Rising Moon, the bar where Bingo Keegan held court in a back booth. Danny sat at the bar and talked to a regular who had worked for the Fallons and Hanrahan Wrecking, too. Danny described the job and a book they found under a beam, a book that his brother said "was supposed to start a treasure hunt but ended one instead."

All that remained for Peter was to hand a moldy commonplace book over to Will Wedge and tell him: *Corporei Insectii* was gone, and with it, *Love's Labours Won.*

In Harvard Hall the play is kept . . . and Harvard Hall had burned.

Still, Peter couldn't be too careful, especially when he was carrying a briefcase containing a commonplace book worth $25,000.

Now the guy with the camera was lining up a shot of his wife. He was wearing a Harvard Crimson windbreaker that he might have bought in the Coop that morning. A tourist. So back to the tour.

The student guide said, "The Harvard Hall you're looking at was built in 1766 to replace the one that stood here for nearly a century . . . until the unthinkable happened."

Very dramatic. The tourists stopped taking pictures and paid attention.

"On a snowy night in 1764," she said, "the first Harvard Hall burned to the ground. With it went the largest library in America, including all four hundred books that John Harvard had left to the college . . . or so they thought."

Peter listened. Maybe this young member of Crimson Key knew something that Peter hadn't figured out yet.

"The next morning, President Holyoke was weeping over the ruins when a student came up and handed him one of John Harvard's books, *Christian Warfare with the World, the Flesh, and the Devil.* Holyoke wiped away his tears, thanked the young man effusively, then promptly expelled him for having a library book in his possession."

The story brought an explosive laugh that echoed off the ancient brick of Massachusetts and Harvard Halls. But nothing new, thought Peter.

Jimmy whispered to his father, "Is that story true?"

"Parts of it. But the student stayed anonymous. So the whole thing may be apocryphal. But the book was saved. It's in the archives. The only one."

The guide went on, "Holyoke died a few years later. His most famous remark may have been delivered on his deathbed: 'If a man wishes to be humbled and mortified, let him become president of Harvard College.'"

Then, like acolytes following the deacon, the group moved deeper into the Yard. Every day, rain or shine, the Crimson Key Society led tours for would-be students, their parents, and tourists. People came from all over the world to see Harvard Yard, as though it were another Plymouth Rock or Vatican. Peter understood. It was the beginning of things and the center of things, too, as old as the rock, and as rich, full of itself, and full of intrigue as the Vatican.

And the intrigue was right there on the top step of Widener.

Fallon saw it when the tour stopped at the bottom step, and the guide started to tell the story of Harry Elkins Widener. Peter let his eye wander up the steps: all thirty of them, with low risers and deep treads, a hundred feet across, taking up more square footage than some junior colleges. At the top were the twelve massive columns. And behind one Assistant Professor Bob O'Hill was in heated conversation with a balding potbellied guy in a gray suit. Bertram Lee, Harvard '79.

To Peter's face, Bertram Lee called himself a colleague. Behind Peter's back, he played the competitor. He sold rare books when he could beat Peter to them. The rest of the time, he sold books that weren't rare, just old.

He scoured garage sales and attics and secondhand shops all over New England. He bought books by the crate and books by the pound—forgotten novels, outdated nonfiction, old magazines—which he sold by the pound, too. But Lee moved books at his Anthology Bookshop in Boston. He moved them from people who didn't want them to people who did, if only to fill the shelves of the libraries in their big houses. And he always said that maybe, some afternoon, some bored kid in some suburb would take down a book and have his life transformed. And no man could do better than that.

So Peter liked Lee a little, even if he didn't trust him.

But what was it that had Lee so irritated? Peter told his son to stay there and listen to the story of Widener and the *Titanic*. Then he started up the stairs. But O'Hill turned abruptly and went into the library, while Lee came down, taking the steps two at a time.

"Hello, Bert," said Peter.

Lee stopped, looked at Peter, looked up at the pillars as though he might try to go up and hide behind one, then said, "What the hell are you doing here?"

"Paying homage to Harry Elkins Widener. I do it once a month."

"Really? So do I." Then Lee went past him.

"Are you also doing business with that O'Hill?"

Lee stopped. "I do business with book lovers everywhere." Then he hurried on.

Peter thought about following him, but there was that guy in the windbreaker, taking a picture of the meeting. That's what it looked like, anyway.

So Peter turned, gave him a grin, and struck a pose.

The guy didn't miss a beat. He said, "Smile for the camera. Have your boy get in it, too." He gestured to Jimmy. "Take one now and take one when you graduate."

That remark drew looks from the other parents. They all knew the odds: there were ten kids on that tour, and only one was likely to get in. Only one would hit the Harvard lottery, have the chance to be rich, famous, successful, satisfied. Only one family would get to put a Harvard sticker on the car. They all wanted it to be their kid.

But things were never as simple as they looked. And happiness was never as easy to come by. Just ask the men they'd met that day— tubercular John Harvard, humbled and mortified Edward Holyoke, hypothermic Harry Widener, and, of course, Bob O'Hill and Bertram Lee, two Harvard men, very pissed off. *Why?*

The Wedges, father and daughter, were waiting for the Fallons, father and son, in the courtyard of Lowell House.

"Thanks for coming," said Will Wedge. "This is a good way for your son to see how the students live. Do you have the book?"

Peter waved the briefcase.

"Great. Great. Excellent. Let's eat."

Lowell House was the largest undergraduate house, named for the president who started the house system in the twenties. The ten undergraduate houses each formed a self-contained community—with master, senior tutor, and students, with library, dining hall, and common rooms—modeled after a place like Emmanuel College, Cambridge, ancestor of Harvard itself.

"The house system," Will Wedge explained to Jimmy Fallon, "is what sets Harvard apart."

Dorothy said, "Your house is as important as your field of concentration."

"The freshmen live in the Yard," said Will Wedge, "and everyone else lives in these house communities. All very civilized."

Peter watched his son take in the high ceilings, the moldings, the crystal chandeliers, the black and white tiled floors, and he said, "This is a cafeteria?"

No, Peter explained. The dining halls had been intended as more than that. They were ceremonial spaces where smart people could meet and educate one another, three times a day, without food fights. To many, the dining hall experience was the heart of the Harvard experience, food notwithstanding.

Of course, Will Wedge and Peter Fallon couldn't stop talking about how much better the food was now than in the old days. The serving area off the dining hall was like a fancy buffet, with expensive cabinetry, granite countertops, salad bar, sandwich stations, grill, even soft-serve ice cream.

"We didn't get soft-serve ice cream," said Wedge as he loaded his tray.

"Dad," said Dorothy, "you make it sound like you had to sign your name on the buttery wall before they'd feed you, like our ancestors back in old Harvard Hall."

"But your ancestors never got cheeseburgers grilled to order, either," said Peter.

They took their trays to a table that overlooked the courtyard, and Will Wedge said, "Speaking of ancestors, you have news of the early Wedges, Mr. Fallon?"

Peter put his briefcase on the table and opened it. Inside was a metal box. "The commonplace book of Benjamin Wedge. In the box, wrapped in three layers of plastic, the only way that it can be safely transported until it's restored. And even then, I wouldn't bring it near any books of value."

"You mean," said Will Wedge, "I can't give it to the Harvard archives?"

"You can give it to them," said Peter, "but they might not take it. Blue mold can infect other books and make you sick."

Will Wedge considered this for a moment. "Can't Dorothy look it over?"

"If she puts on mask and gloves. We have a room in South Boston."

"A trip to South Boston," said Will to his daughter. "Exotic travel."

Peter noticed Jimmy roll his eyes, in the universal expression, *What an asshole.*

Dorothy ignored her father and asked Peter, "Is it true that the commonplace book mentions a play?"

Peter produced a piece of paper on which were written the words of the Benjamin Wedge poem.

Dorothy read it and said, "*Love's Labours Won*? In the Bard's own hand? Wow." Then she looked at her father. "Better than you ever speculated."

"Speculated?" said Peter. "What would lead you to speculate that the play mentioned by Thomas Shepard was a lost Shakespeare manuscript?"

Will Wedge swirled his ice cream. "Come on, Mr. Fallon, you must have heard rumblings in the booksellers' underground."

"The only rumblings I heard started with a term paper." Peter glanced at Dorothy.

"They actually started in my tutorial with Professor O'Hill," she said. "Once he read the John Wedge commonplace book. He gave me a few suggestions. I worked backward to Shepard's diary. But from what this poem says, it all ends here. 'In Harvard Hall the play is kept, all hidden from the world . . .'"

"Yes," said Peter. "The man who wrote that had been rusti-cated—a common form of punishment in those days. He wrote it, then he disappeared. Considering that he left his commonplace book behind, he must have left in a big hurry. I doubt that he went back to Cambridge to rescue the play in Harvard Hall."

"Which burned in 1764," said Dorothy. "Professor O'Hill will be disappointed."

"Good," said Will Wedge.

"Good?" Peter seldom felt as though he were being whipsawed, but these Wedges were doing a pretty good job of it. Did they want to find the play or not?

Will Wedge reached into his pocket and pulled out an envelope. "Twenty-five thousand dollars. It's yours, Mr. Fallon. But I'll add ten percent if you agree to say what you've just said to a man named Charles Price."

"Who's he?"

"My freshman roommate. I'm making a fund-raising call to him this afternoon."

For $2,500, Peter would be happy to spend a few hours talking to a man who collected books. He might even make a new client. And he had more to find out from Will Wedge.

So, that afternoon, he put his son on the subway back to Boston and rode with Wedge out to Weston, a rich, green suburb about ten miles from Cambridge.

"The guy we're going to see dreamed up a software program that all the insurance companies use in preparing actuarial tables," Wedge explained. "Like a license to print money. It's time Harvard got some."

"And you're the agent for the Class of 'Seventy-two?"

"Who else could do the job as well?"

"Oh, I don't know. There must be a few other Harry Harvards in the class."

"I don't like that term," said Wedge. "This isn't some rah-rah show."

Wedge drove for a time in silence, then said, "You know, in addition to my investment work at Wedge, Fleming, and Royce, I was once the chairman of the Back Bay Institute for Savings. But we were swallowed up by an outfit that runs its customer services from a telephone boiler room in South Carolina."

Peter said, "Their motto: 'Millions for advertising, not one cent for tellers.'"

"Back Bay was one of the oldest financial institutions in America, and it followed all those other great Boston institutions . . . right into the dumper. Think of Polaroid or Digital. And Jordan Marsh is now Macy's. The *Boston Globe* is nothing more than the tenant farm of the *New York Times*, for God's sake. . . ."

"But Harvard is still Harvard?" asked Peter.

"Harvard has been at the heart of this country's history since the beginning. And my family has been at the heart of Harvard. Besides, it's a special place."

"All that genius, all that money, all that self-importance."

"It's more than that. In a country that accepts mediocrity as the norm, Harvard means excellence. That's why your father wanted you to go there. It's why you want your son to go. It's why we're visiting Price. He has what they call real 'donative power.'"

"You mean, he's a soft touch?"

"Would you call John Harvard a soft touch? Anne Radcliffe? The people of Massachusetts who supported the school with a tax on grain?"

"The College Corn?" said Peter.

"Right. And later, men like Rockefeller and J. P. Morgan sent their sons and their money. Now, it's with men like us that Harvard ensures its future."

Peter resisted the impulse to say "rah-rah." Instead, he said, "Maybe men like you. I'm small potatoes."

"Small potatoes nourish, too. And it isn't just cash. Over the years, my family has given ideas, time . . . we even donated paintings in the thirties. A Copley, a Gilbert Stuart . . . major work. You can see them in a show they're putting together at the Fogg in March. Treasures from the Harvard Portrait Collection. You'll get an invitation."

Price lived in a big thirties Colonial with a nineties addition on the back and two sugar maples out front.

Wedge rang the bell and said to Fallon, "Fund-raising rule number one: 'Solicitations made in person are significantly more successful than phone calls.'"

Price opened the door himself. He was short, square, with a thick, black mustache and thicker black-rimmed glasses. He wore a sweaty sweatsuit and looked as though he had just worked out. He was a jokester, too. "I gave already at the office."

Wedge answered with one of those honking laughs.

Price led them through the foyer to the back of the house, and Peter realized where he was. This wasn't just a big addition in an overpriced suburb. It was a library, two stories high, with mahogany ladders leading to railed balconies, Palladian windows with u.v.-filtered glass, Oriental carpets, antique desks, and leather . . . lots of leather.

And it wasn't just any library. It was a Shakespeare library. There were books, busts, portraits. And right in the middle of the room, beneath a spotlight: a First Folio.

For years Peter had heard rumors of an anonymous collector living west of Boston. Anytime a book related to Shakespeare came on the market, from a first edition of Marchette Chute's *Shakespeare of London* to a quarto of *Coriolanus*, this man outbid everyone to get it. And whenever he needed an agent, he used Bertram Lee.

Peter walked over to the case and looked at the Folio, which was open to the engraving of Shakespeare. *What a face. What a book.*

"So far, the most expensive First Folio ever purchased," said Price.

"From the Berland collection?" asked Peter. "Six million?"

"A pittance," said Price. "Now, why is one of Boston's best-known antiquarians visiting me?"

"Mr. Fallon has come to dash your hopes, Charlie," said Wedge.

Price gestured to the walls around him. "My hopes are all fulfilled."

"Except for one," said Wedge. "Mr. Fallon is here to kill rumors of a certain Shakespeare play that you heard about through the booksellers' underground."

"Underground? I didn't know such a thing existed." Price looked at Fallon. "Did you?"

"There's legitimate business, and there isn't," said Peter. "You're either aboveground or you're not."

Price sat at his desk and rested his chin in his hand, looking as if he was trying to think of something funny to say.

Before he did, Wedge said to Fallon, "Tell him about *Love's Labours Won.*"

Fallon told Price what he had said at Lowell House: that if a play ever existed, it had burned up in the Harvard Hall fire of 1764.

"So," said Wedge when Peter was done, "I'm hoping the Price Foundation will release the funds currently being held for that phantom play—"

"Twenty million," said Price.

"—and put it into the project we have been discussing."

Price looked at Peter. "What do you think, Fallon? Should I spend my mad money on something else? Or should I wait? 'Written in the Bard's own hand' makes it even more attractive."

"Spend your money on whatever you want. But don't count on that play."

They chatted a while longer, but they didn't reveal to Fallon what the project was, and he didn't ask. He just ogled the books.

"Someday," Price told Fallon as he ushered them out, "my collection will rival the Folger Library. A true repository of the greatest work in the history of humanity. I had hoped to be the man who bought a copy of a lost play."

On the drive home, Wedge thanked Fallon.

"For what?"

"For setting him straight. So he can turn to a nice donation for Harvard."

"What's the project?"

"A secret. Can't tell you . . . yet. Not until commencement."

"Fair enough," said Fallon. "But how did he know about the play?"

Wedge shrugged, as if he were acting innocent or clueless. "The same way we've all known. By reading and research and speculation."

"Not the so-called booksellers' underground?"

"Well . . . that, too."

"Bingo Keegan?"

"Keegan? I wouldn't know."

"Why was it that on Sunday, you came down the river and asked me to stay out of this. And by the end of the week, with Ridley in his urn, you wanted me on your team?"

"My daughter did more research. She put the name of Bleen in the commonplace book together with the Bleen-Currier-Whitney House. We thought you might be close to it. We were right. Thanks."

Evangeline was in his office, and the first thing she asked was "Is it over or not?"

Bernice had gone home. Orson was examining a volume in the display room.

Evangeline was sitting in Peter's chair, writing an article on her laptop.

"You've made yourself right at home." He perched on the edge of his desk.

"You have an Internet connection." Evangeline typed a few more words, then e-mailed her article to her publisher. " 'Touring the Cape with a Grand Lady.' "

"Your grandmother?"

"They'll change the title." She closed the laptop. "So, is it over?"

"It would seem to be, but I get the feeling I've been used."

From the display room came a hooting laugh, followed by Orson. "Of course you were used. People like Will Wedge use everyone. It's in their upbringing."

"It's almost as if the whole story was cooked up to change the mind of a major donor."

"Another Ridley Riddle?" said Evangeline.

"Maybe . . . the real Ridley Riddle is: Who killed Ridley?" Peter described the day and laid out the characters he'd crossed: "Will Wedge, Dorothy Wedge, Bob O'Hill, Bertram Lee, and Charles Price, all on the same day. Who's the important one?"

"Bingo Keegan," said Orson.

"Yeah," said Peter. "If he killed Ridley, maybe I should stay on this."

"No," answered Orson. "Maybe you should stay off it."

Evangeline said, "I was there. I heard the detective call it an accident."

"Right," said Orson, "accidental death, manuscript burned to ash two hundred and forty years ago. Case closed. On to the next."

"Case closed," said Evangline. "So come with me to France. I leave tomorrow."

"France?"

"*Les Trois Glorioueses*, the three days of the Beaune wine auction. I'd like livelier company than a female centenarian. Separate rooms, of course."

Peter leaned across the desk. "You and me? In France? That could be fun. But I'll have to take a rain check."

"*Rain check?*" she said. "I just opened a door wider to you than any woman has since . . . since the last time I opened a door to you—"

"You're forgetting my ex-wife."

"And you want a *rain check?*"

Orson, the soul of discretion, stepped out.

Then Evangeline said to Peter, "This better be good."

"Jimmy's Harvard application is due. He wants me to read it when he's done."

She sat back. "There's not another excuse that I'd buy."

"So," he said, "how about Paris at New Year's? Or Florida in March?"

"By March," she said, "I'll be working too hard. No more articles about where to find the cleanest sheets on the Left Bank. After my grandmother saw all those women walking around Harvard the other day, she said someone should write about the Radcliffe Eight, the women who got Harvard to admit that women could be educated."

"And you're going to do it?" said Peter.

"I need something to get me out of bed in the morning, Peter."

He grinned. "*You* want something to get you *out* of bed, and I'd like to find something to—"

"Don't say another word." And she began to gather up her things.

He shrugged. "Can't blame me for trying."

She shook her head and gave him one of those looks. But then she laughed. "Like I told my grandmother, you still haven't grown up."

"You know me too well."

"I have to go back to New York." She pointed a finger at him. "But I know you well enough to know that you're still wondering. Just remember. You can't bring Ridley back, or the manuscript. So, case closed."

"Case closed. On to the next. I'll call you if it looks like fun."

Orson came in with a book. "Here's the one you wanted, Evangeline. *New England Verses,* by Lydia Wedge. A good place to start if you're interested in women who agitated for female education."

She took it and turned it over. A little volume in blue vellum.

"Very rare," said Orson, "and very little in demand. Not considered a great poet."

"But a female poet back when they were rare, too, a female poet who writes about Harvard." She flipped through the volume. "Here's 'The Bell Ringer of Harvard Hall,' about the great fire. 'Exiled by the Mob,' about the gunpowder riot."

"What was that?" asked Peter.

"The warning the British didn't heed a year before the American Revolution: 'Intolerable were the Acts decreed / in the springtime of seventy-four, / Our port was closed, our rights refused, / and troops put boots on our shore.'"

Chapter Fifteen

1774–1783

"OUR PORT was closed, our rights refused, / and troops put boots on our shore."

Lydia dipped her quill and wondered if she had chosen the best meter to capture the mood of the colony. Perhaps she should use blank verse, steady and measured. Would heroic couplets add the power of rhyme? Or should she try something more chaotic? For what was there in these chaotic days that was steady or measured? And who were the heroes? Certainly not William Brattle.

From her bedroom window, she watched him bustling through the orchard, his favored route, for if he came in by the back door, he could stop in the kitchen, ascertain the contents of pot or grate, and—if the food met his fancy—contrive for an invitation to the next meal. Small wonder, she thought, that his nickname, Brigadier Paunch, grew ever more apt as the years went by.

Lydia hurried downstairs to intercept him, because it was Wednesday, the day that she and her grandfather went to Boston, and she wanted no Brattle business keeping her from her weekly trip to the bookstores on Cornhill Street.

As there was nothing cooking in the kitchen, Brattle reached Reverend Abraham's study just ahead of her, but she thought it a good sign that her grandfather was standing and wearing his wig, for it meant that he did not intend to tarry.

Brattle was handing a letter to Reverend Abraham. "I'd not trust this to a messenger. You assure me that you can deliver it to General Gage directly?"

"Gage won't turn away a member of the Mandamus Council," said Abraham.

"Do not proclaim such membership so loudly." Lydia came into the room. "Some people do not approve of a council appointed by the royal governor rather than elected."

"Some *people*," said Abraham, "should not have thrown tea into Boston Harbor, and with it, the right to conduct a civilized government."

Reverend Abraham Wedge was in a minority among his Congregational brethren. While Anglicans believed that power descended from the king to the archbishop to the people, Congregationalists believed that the right of a minister to preach came from those to whom he preached.

Abraham agreed with the principles of his church, but he did not believe they gave his brethren the right to destroy East India Company tea. Such action, he said, would lead only to chaos. And he liked tea. He had even resigned from the First Church because he could no longer serve with Reverend Appleton, who weekly preached rebellion to students already endowed by nature with a propensity to make trouble.

For years, new taxes had been rolling in from the Atlantic, lowering over the colonies, and producing squalls of disagreement that dissipated before the breezes of conciliation. But since the December tea party, the sky had been growing steadily darker. The port of Boston had been closed. Four regiments of His Majesty's troops had arrived. The Harvard Corporation had canceled commencement for fear of riot. And a new military governor, General Thomas Gage, had discharged the elected council and put his own hand-picked mandamus council in place.

"Guard the letter," said Brattle. "It warns Gage that militia companies are now prepared to meet at one minute's notice. It also provides an accounting of what's left in the powder house on Quarry Hill."

Abraham lifted the flap on his coat pocket and put the letter inside. "I hear that the Medford selectmen have removed their powder."

"Most towns have done the same," answered Brattle. "Only the king's remains."

"Pray that it does not ignite of its own stupidity," said Lydia.

Reverend Abraham Wedge had reached the age of seventy-two with an iron will forged to an iron spine, and he insisted on driving his two-seat chaise to Boston himself.

Lydia admired the will and the spine but was uncertain of the driving, especially when Abraham saw someone he recognized and pulled the horse to a sudden stop.

And there was Caleb Wedge, walking along Spring Street, head down, lost in thought. He had often admitted to his sister that the calculations in his head were as real to him as the horse droppings in the street. So he seemed hardly to notice when the chaise lurched up and almost pitched Lydia onto the ground in front of him.

"Good morning, Tutor Wedge!" she said, levering herself back into her seat. "Are there any books you'd like from Boston?"

"I have all I need, thank you." Caleb lifted his tricorne. Unlike his grandfather, he wore no wig and tied his hair simply, though similarities were more common between them than contrasts. They reminded Lydia of two fence posts: tall, straight, skinny; one weathered, the other new-planted.

"Would you care to come along?" asked Reverend Abraham. "Show General Gage that some in the college have the interests of the colony at heart. He's seen too many Harvard men riding off to that Continental Congress in Philadelphia."

"Caleb would go to Philadelphia, too," said Lydia.

"He'd *what?*" The old man almost fell out of the chaise.

Caleb scowled at his sister, then admitted, "I've discussed it with Professor Winthrop."

"A scientific expedition?" demanded the reverend. "Or political?"

"Not political. Politics bores me," said Caleb. "*Medical*. The Pennsylvania Hospital offers a course of study for any who would become doctors."

"You don't study to be a doctor. You *apprentice*," said Abraham. "Brattle didn't study, and he doctored for years. Doctored the people of Cambridge and—"

"Killed a few, too," said Lydia.

"Times are changing, Grandfather." Caleb raised his tricorne again. "I must be off to hear recitations. If you see Miss Cowgill in Boston, give her my best."

Abraham snapped the reins and headed toward the Great Bridge. "*Study* to be a doctor," he muttered. "He may study his life away."

"I encouraged him," said Lydia. "I even observe his dissections in the barn."

"Dissections?" The chaise lurched to another stop. "In our barn? Of what?"

"Cats and dogs," said Lydia. "There's a group of students. They call themselves the Anatomical Society. They seek to learn more about the way bodies work by—"

"Cutting up cats and dogs? What can he learn from that?"

"More than he can from teaching mathematics and natural philosophy for another eight years. He's twenty-seven. Time for him to grow up and leave."

"Time for him to marry and start a family. Let him apprentice right here. Then he can still teach at the college and stay in Cambridge."

"There's a young lady in Boston who'll not marry him till she has brighter prospects than a life lived in proximity to two hundred unruly Harvard boys."

Reverend Wedge clucked at the horse, and the chaise clattered onto the Great Bridge. "So many things to agitate an old man. So many things to vex him."

The good reverend must have been vexed indeed, and agitated, too, because in Boston, somewhere between the Orange Street barn and the Province House, he lost Brattle's letter. It may have happened when he pulled out his handkerchief to mop his brow, or perhaps when he gave a penny to a beggar. But when he sat before General Gage and reached into his pocket, the letter was gone. He patted his right pocket, then his left, then he noticed Gage eyeing him quizzically, as if to ask whether the reverend suffered from some strange itch.

And he decided that the embarrassment of losing the letter would not be compounded by further fumbling. He told the general of all that Brattle had put into the letter, and he conveyed the spoken message as well as Brattle might have delivered it, had he spent all day polishing his sentences.

ii

Most mornings, Lydia was awakened by a dream . . . a dream of her husband.

Charles Townsend had come from England in 1771 to survey the forests for his family's shipbuilding business. He had soon fallen under the spell of the New England landscape and, at a dinner in Boston, under the spell of a young woman whose eyes, he had said, "glittered in the candlelight and whose wit glimmered in the conversation."

Unfortunately, Lydia's waking image was less often of their joyous courtship than of Charles Townsend's death. He had been marking trees in the New Hampshire woods—tall pines for masts, large-limbed oaks for ships' knees—when his axe glanced off a knot and struck his leg. He died a week later in the agony of lockjaw. Lydia never allowed herself to lie abed and contemplate that horror. Instead, she rose to empty her mind by emptying an inkwell in poetry.

So it was that at dawn on the first day of September, she was in the writing chair in her bedroom when she glanced over the orchard and saw thirty redcoats march up to the home of William Brattle.

* * *

That morning, Tutor Caleb Wedge heard the usual recitations in geometry, Euclid being more important to him than any rumor of soldiers in Cambridge.

Afterward, he noticed that several hundred local men had gathered on Cambridge Common, but he gave them little thought, either, because two hundred students had gathered in Harvard Hall commons, and tutors were expected to dine with students, thereby raising the level of mealtime discourse and reducing the incidence of food fights.

A puffy, red-faced tutor named Isaac Smith plunked himself down opposite Caleb and, without a word of greeting, said, "Did you see that gang of ruffians out there?"

"A political display of some sort." Caleb picked at the agglomeration of salt cod, rice, and peas before him.

"They dislike a governor with decision." Smith was a proudly unapologetic Tory.

"Decision?"

"Haven't you heard? Gage is moving to protect the king's munitions. His men woke Brattle at dawn and demanded the keys to courthouse and powder house both. They hauled the cannon out of the courthouse, then they marched to Quarry Hill and seized the gunpowder. Two hundred and seventy half barrels, now safe in Castle William."

Caleb nodded, as though he agreed or at least understood. In truth, he did not know what to think. He lamented that tea was no longer served in commons, and like his grandfather, he feared the coming of chaos. On a given day, he was as likely to agree with Tutor Smith, the Tory, as with Professor Winthrop, a firm opponent of what New Englanders now called the Intolerable Acts.

"We pray that Gage's decision is firm," he said, and he quickly finished his meal.

When he stepped into the sunshine, he saw that the men on the Common did not lack for decision, either. A mob of them were now striding past the college.

Caleb heard them cursing as they went, cursing Gage and the king and William Brattle, too. Gage and the king could worry for themselves, but Brattle was a friend, practically an uncle, so Caleb stepped into the mob and began to march along with them. Then he asked a tradesman, "Why do we speak ill of Brattle?"

"Because he wrote the letter what told Gage to seize the gunpowder. 'Twas dropped in the street and picked up by patriots."

"Aye," said a blacksmith. "'Tis to be published in the next *Boston Gazette*. Maybe they'll publish his obituary, too."

And the men around gave out with great beer-smelling guffaws.

Caleb let the mob flow past him. Then he turned and ran down the alley beside the courthouse, jumped a fence, and scrambled through Palmer's orchard. He could hear the mob surging through the village and swinging along the curve of Creek Lane, but he was well ahead of them, and in a dozen long-legged strides, he was across the Watertown Road and up Brattle's steps. He did not bother with knocking. He threw open the door and rushed into the dining room, where he found William Brattle deeply involved in a tureen of duck liver.

From her writing chair Lydia had been watching the mob move along the street while her brother took the shortcut through Palmer's orchard.

Now Reverend Abraham came into her room. "What's happening?"

As if in answer, the back door of Brattle's house swung open. Brigadier Paunch came stumbling out and scurried into his barn. Caleb came out right after, took to the orchard path, and began to heel-toe home, walking far too quickly to look casual.

"Hurry, Caleb," whispered Lydia.

The mob was now piling up in front of Brattle's house, and angry male voices were hammering the air. Then there came the sound of shattering glass—a rock flying through one of Brattle's windows, which drew a deep-throated roar from the crowd.

Unbeknownst to them, the enormous figure of William Brattle was emerging from his barn on a slender-legged mare and moving cautiously across the garden. Finally someone saw him and cried out. Brattle dug his spurs into his horse, and a hundred men went running after him.

"Ride hard, Willie," whispered Reverend Abraham.

"Walk fast, Caleb," whispered Lydia.

Then came the sound of pistol shots, small pops and loud bangs.

"Good God!" cried Abraham. "They're shooting!" And he ran from the room.

Down in the orchard, Caleb flinched at the sound, but the mob was paying him no mind. They had not even seen him approaching his own back door.

How delicate the white pistol smoke looked floating over the crowd, thought Lydia. And how frightened the lone rider looked, galloping onto the Great Bridge. It seemed as though she were seeing it all unfold in her mind's eye, as though she were reading it in a novel. Then the reality of a pistol appeared on her little writing desk.

"One for you, two for me," said Abraham. "They'll not chase me from *my* house."

When the mob could not catch Brattle, they came back and ransacked his wine cellar. The Cambridge Committee of Safety kept them from ransacking the rest of the house, but the street was soon littered with empty bottles of every shape, a fortune in French Burgundy, Madeira, and port, guzzled by a crowd growing larger all the time.

Meanwhile, Lydia had drawn the drapes of the reverend's study, so that none of the troublemakers would see an old man brandishing pistols in his window.

But Abraham's brandishing mood soon faded. As Caleb told him of the impact of the lost letter, the old man dropped his pistols, then dropped into his chair. "It was I who lost the letter. It was I who caused this. I should use my gun on myself."

"None of that," said Caleb. "We must make reasoned decisions, in case the mob turns on the members of the Mandamus Council."

"I should be punished. I should be forced to confess publicly."

"You'll do nothing of the sort," said Caleb. "Simply let this rabble dissipate."

"This rabble," said Lydia, "may not dissipate. And the best of them are no rabble."

The mob did nothing more than finish Brattle's liquor; then they straggled back to the Common, while Caleb went back to the college and climbed into the cupola of the new Harvard Hall. What he saw from there reminded him of a commencement pilgrimage, but these pilgrims came armed and called themselves minutemen.

They came from every station of life, from minister to merchant, blacksmith to barrister, and they spread rumors that flew faster than the truth could ever travel: *Gage had ordered the disarming of everyone in Boston . . . there had been fighting in Cambridge and six killed . . . the Royal Navy had fired on the city . . .*

Caleb watched their campfires flicker to life, and he waited the night through for more trouble. By morning, four thousand men had gathered, a quarter of them armed militia under the command of elected officers. But the truth had made its mark: Gage had removed only the king's powder and the Cambridge cannon. But that was reason enough to make protest. Word was passed about ten o'clock. Then the men at the north edge of the Common turned, and like a migrating herd, all four thousand began to move toward Elmwood, the riverfront manor of Lieutenant Governor Thomas Oliver.

Caleb followed, impressed and frightened by the sense of purpose that now invested these men. This was no window-breaking mob. With officers to lead them, they were orderly and disciplined and careful not to step on the flower beds as they surrounded Elmwood in a series of concentric circles.

Caleb had seen enough. Before Oliver came to his door, Caleb was hurrying back down the Watertown Road, past the handsome houses of one frightened Loyalist after another, so many houses that the road was now called Tory Row.

He was glad to see that the chaise was hitched and waiting in front of his grandfather's house. Then Lydia came to the door. "Grandfather said he'd shoot the horse if we tried to load the chaise."

Caleb found the old man sitting in the study with two pistols on his lap. It seemed that he had regained his spirit, for as soon as he saw Caleb, he picked up a pistol and said, "No one will put me out of my house."

While Lydia and Mrs. Beale rushed around collecting piles of clothes and books, Caleb tried a bit of reason. "They're making Thomas Oliver resign from the Mandamus Council, Grandfather. If you resign, you won't have to flee . . . or fight."

Lydia said, "He refuses to resign and refuses to flee."

"I'll tell them the truth." The old man rose, took his wig from its stand, and placed it on his head. "I'll admit that it was I who told Gage to seize the powder."

"Tell them that," said Caleb, "they may tar and feather you."

Abraham took a powder horn from the desk and primed a pistol.

Lydia looked at her brother and gestured to a lap blanket on the chair by the fireplace. Caleb gave her a nod, so Lydia lifted the blanket, as if to shake it out, and with a quick motion threw it over the old man's head. At the same time, Caleb pulled a tieback from one of the drapes and wrapped it around the blanket, right at his waist.

"Unhand me!" demanded Abraham. And he kept demanding and kicking and struggling all the way down the hall and out of the house, but a second tieback secured his arms, and once they had him in the chaise, another was wrapped round his ankles.

"Keep him tied up till you're on Boston Neck." Caleb helped his sister into the driver's seat. "I'll face the mob."

He watched them gallop away, then went inside and stood for a moment, wondering what to hide. *The Turkish carpets?* Too large. *The wines in the cellar?* Four pipes of Madeira and a dozen cases of port—too much to move.

But the books? Those that mattered most—a quarto of *Love's Labours Lost,* the last evidence of Burton Bones, and a far more valuable manuscript of *Love's Labours Won*—were hidden behind a panel in the library, where a brother and sister had put them on the morning after Harvard Hall burned. There was no reason to seek a safer hiding place, and no time, because there came a mighty pounding on the door.

Mrs. Beale said, "Oh, Good Lord."

Caleb tugged at his waistcoat and said, "Open the door, Mrs. Beale."

And four men from the Committee of Correspondence stepped into the foyer while four thousand more surrounded the house. The leader said, "We seek Mandamus Councillor the Reverend Mr. Abraham Wedge."

"He leaves his compliments," said Caleb, "but he has gone to Boston."

"To see Gage?" asked another one. "We know he's gone to see Gage before."

"He's gone to Boston to apprise the governor of your anger," said Caleb politely.

"When he returns"—the leader pulled out a sheet of paper— "he's to sign this."

Caleb took it. "A resignation from the Mandamus Council. I'll see that he gets it."

"If he don't sign, he'd best stay in Boston with Brigadier Paunch."

iii

"I would not sign in September or November. Why would I sign in January?"

"Because," answered Caleb. " 'Tis time for you and Lydia to go home."

"Lydia may go home anytime she wishes." Abraham bundled his scarf around his neck and pulled his hard-backed chair into the shaft of sunlight by the window. "Brattle's daughter lives in his house unmolested."

"But Brattle lives under the Crown's protection, in Castle William." Lydia measured three spoons of tea into a strainer, held it over the pot, and poured hot water from a kettle hanging in the fireplace. "Considering the looks we get in the Boston streets, we may be joining Brattle soon."

"We will stay here," said Abraham. "This is our property."

The room smelled of leather and vibrated with the tapping of small hammers striking small nails. This was the house where John Wedge had lived out his days and Reverend Abraham Wedge had grown up. The first floor was rented to a cobbler who had stored supplies in the upper rooms until the arrival of Abraham and his granddaughter.

Caleb told Lydia, "The Committee of Safety says you may go back at any time."

As Lydia filled the three cups on the little tea-stained table, she shifted her eyes to her grandfather and shook her head.

Abraham said, "I am perfectly capable of living on my own."

"Grandfather"—Lydia pressed a cup into his hand—"your legs are not strong, and neither is your memory."

"My memory is better than yours. I remember my responsibilities. So keep your Committee of Safety. I'll keep my seat on the council."

"There are others who can take care of these things," said Caleb.

"Who?" demanded the old man. "You? Your only interests are in solving mathematical problems and torturing cats."

Caleb looked at his sister. "What have you been telling him?"

The old man got up and came close to his grandson. " 'Tis time that you took a stand, Caleb Wedge, either for the government or against it."

"I take my stand, Grandfather. I teach young men."

"But *what* do you teach them? What do you stand *for*? Or do you simply lower your head and let others lead, as you did when they used to taunt me in chapel?"

"You're right, Grandfather." Caleb gulped his tea and put on his surtout. "There's nothing wrong with your memory."

Lydia followed her brother down the stairs and out into the cold afternoon.

A few inches of snow had fallen, giving Hanover Street the look of a clean country lane. A pung went by carrying firewood, but there was little other commerce in a city whose port had been closed for more than seven months.

Lydia asked, "All is in order at the house? The books are safe?"

"Behind the panel on the third shelf, third case."

"Good," she said. "Keep them there."

"What if I go to Philadelphia?"

"So long as Grandfather lives, we must keep evidence of Burton Bones hidden. Remember that after Burton disappeared, Grandfather was the moving force behind the anti-theater statutes of 1767. If it were found that we kept plays in his house, he'd become a laughingstock. And as I've told you so often since Harvard Hall burned, if you admitted how you obtained the plays, people would believe that you started the fire."

"What if I returned the manuscript secretly, as Uncle Benjamin did."

"He was a fool," said Lydia. "That book is too valuable to hide under a library case for another forty years. Better in our hands, safe from neglect."

Caleb noticed two British soldiers coming down the street, two privates from the Forty-seventh Regiment of Foot. He expected them to walk on, but they stopped, spoke politely to Lydia, and went into the house as though they lived there, which they did.

"The king considers it his right to quarter troops in our homes," said Lydia.

"He sends them where they're welcome. 'Tis a Loyalist house, after all."

"Do you think I am a Loyalist, Caleb?"

"You're here, aren't you?"

"I'm here because an old man needs me."

"Then you *are* loyal"—Caleb gripped his sister's shoulder—"in the best sense."

"In what sense are you loyal, Brother? And to whom?"

That question echoed in his mind all the rest of the winter.

Each week, he traveled to Boston to visit his sister and grandfather, and the conversation changed little, though the supply of tea finally dwindled to nothing.

After he visited them, he would go down Hanover Street, past the Government House at the head of King Street, along Orange Street, to the handsome Summer Street home of Christine Cowgill.

Theirs had been a long courtship. Caleb was not the most passionate of men, nor Christine the most insistent of women. He had approached romantic love as an equation to be solved. She had viewed her suitors as her father had viewed potential business partners. To Caleb, her quick smile, quicker wit, fleshy bosom, and rich father were balanced by her demand that he leave the employ of the college before they marry. To Christine, his intelligence and height were the best assets any man had brought to her.

One or the other might have ended this tepid romance, but Caleb admitted comfort in her presence, and Christine accepted his argument that in the long run, comfort would supersede passion.

His visits to her home, however, grew less comfortable by the week. Her father was a leading Whig merchant. But the local committeemen knew that Caleb's grandfather was a Loyalist, and they suspected him of the same tendencies. Whenever he visited, there were men watching. From the shadows, they might see Caleb and Christine steal a kiss as she greeted him at the door or said good-bye later. But they would not hear the conversation, which was as predictable as Caleb's talk with his own grandfather.

"Have you determined which side you are on?" asked Christine yet again on a windy March Sunday.

"I'm on the side that says we can talk our way out of these troubles."

"But are you Whig or Tory?" she persisted. "I want to know. My father wants to know. The Sons of Liberty who follow you around the town want to know, too."

"Which answer would better suit you?" he asked.

"I don't care. Tell me which side you're on, and I'll take that side, too," she said, "so that I may tell my father how I feel about you."

"Tell him that you love me and I love you. Tell him we'll marry when the times allow. But I can't leave the college now. Why, today, Tory students brought tea into commons, and the tutors had to put down a riot. I simply can't leave."

"I'll not marry you otherwise, no matter what your beliefs."

Nothing, thought Caleb, was simple in such times.

Lydia thought the same thing. She thought it when she tried to get food in the morning or firewood in the evening. She thought it when she walked down the street and heard the insults of Bostonians who considered her a Loyalist simply because she cared for one. She thought it when she considered the fate of the Wedge house and all its contents, should the Whig rebels succeed.

So, on a Wednesday night in early April, she went down to the ferry landing, politely answered the questions of the British soldiers as to her destination and reason for going out of the city, and then took the ferry to Charlestown. She walked the rest of the way to Cambridge, timing her arrival to the hour when her brother and certain of his students began their weekly dissection in the barn.

All was dark behind the Wedge house on Tory Row, except for the slivers of yellow light poking through the cracks in the barn wall. Caleb and the students were inside, with blankets covering the windows.

So Lydia let herself into the house, listened a moment for footfalls, then tiptoed upstairs, to the back bedroom, to make sure that Mrs. Beale was off on her weekly visit to her family. The bed was empty. But as Lydia turned to go downstairs, she heard a cart roll up behind the house. So she stepped to the window and peered down.

Though it was a moonless night, there were no lanterns on the cart. And it looked as if the horses' hooves were wrapped in burlap. Two young men, both wearing black tricornes and cloaks, jumped down.

"Just our luck to dig up a fat man," said one, going to the back of the cart.

The other went to the barn door and delivered two knocks, then one, then two. The door opened a crack and two more figures emerged.

"How long did it take you?" said the tall shadow of Tutor Wedge.

"Half an hour to Watertown. Half an hour to dig him up."

"That gives us five hours before you must take him back," said Wedge.

"You didn't tell us he'd be so fat, sir."

"Fat is good. We'll focus on the fat. Five hours to study the nature of fat."

They struggled to remove a stretcher from the back of the cart; then they disappeared into the barn and closed the door.

For a few moments, Lydia stood in total shock. They were dissecting humans, not cats. But there was little time to contemplate this.

She turned and hurried to her grandfather's study, third case, third shelf. She moved the panel and withdrew two books that she and her brother had hidden. She wrote a note and slipped it into one of the leatherbound brown volumes she had brought, and put both volumes into the empty space.

Then she slipped out by the front door, feeling strangely elated. She had taken control of the most portable piece of the Wedge legacy, *Love's Labours Lost* and *Won* in quarto and manuscript. And her brother, it seemed, had taken control of something, too, even if it was the midnight art of the resurrectionist.

iv

"*Human* dissection?" said Professor John Winthrop.

"Sir?" Caleb sat by the fire in Winthrop's study.

"Rumors reach me, Caleb. Are you leading students in secret human dissection?"

"Well . . . students have been doing dissections for some time, sir."

"Of cats and dogs." Winthrop waved his hand. "An open secret. But is there something called the Spunke Club, devoted to more elaborate experimentation?"

"Da Vinci engaged in such experimentation, sir," said Caleb defensively, "but he was forced to do it in secret because of the ignorance of his times."

"True enough." Winthrop wheezed a bit. "True enough."

"And there are many in our own times who face ignorance as great. Why, Doctor Shippen of Philadelphia had all the windows of his dissection room broken by ignorant people. Ignorance is no friend to any of us, sir. You've said that yourself."

"True enough. But are you doing it? Are you what they call a . . . resurrectionist?"

And Caleb could not dissemble further. "We do not rob the graves of gentlefolk, only suicides or criminals, and now and then, one from some potter's field."

Winthrop took off his wig and ran his hand over the gray bristles beneath it.

Caleb went on, "If we are to improve the lot of man, sir, we must study him . . . his mind and body both."

"True enough." Winthrop wheezed.

"Then you approve?"

"Only if you dissect enough lungs to determine why I feel as if I'm sucking air from a bottle this evening."

" 'Tis said that anxiety will bring on the asthma in those who are disposed, sir. As a delegate to the Provincial Congress, you must have a fair share of anxiety just now."

Winthrop coughed. "We hear Gage plans to arrest us, should we assemble again."

"And will you?"

"Of course. Otherwise, we become like a parcel of slaves on a plantation."

"Still," said Caleb, " 'tis a hard choice, between Whig mobs and British troops."

Winthrop studied Caleb for a moment, as if weighing his words or the man before him. "You are not someone who readily steps forward, are you?"

"I'm a scholar, sir. I've written papers. I've studied."

"You also have a woman who would marry, yet you wait. You understand the value of dissection, yet you do it in secret. You must take a side in the coming fight, yet you temporize. You've been stepping back, Caleb, rather than forward, since the day old Harvard Hall burned."

Caleb felt his cheeks redden.

"I watched you that day," said the old professor. "I watched you approach Holyoke, then retreat, as if you feared your fate if you spoke. I've often wondered—"

"That was many years ago, sir."

"I have a long memory."

And from upstairs came a call. "John, 'tis the latest you've sat up in weeks."

"Yes, dear." Winthrop looked at Caleb. "I have a long memory, and so does my wife. She remembers when I was young and strong, and so she waits for me to come to her bed, that we might remember together. So, I'll bid you good night."

Winthrop led Caleb to the door and opened it to the cool April night. The spring peepers had set up a loud symphony on the marsh. The buds on the trees seemed to be swelling, even in the moonlight. And the damp-earth aroma of the air promised spring.

Winthrop said, "I am not a Scripture-quoting man, Caleb."

"No, sir."

"But the Lord said, 'Be ye either hot or cold. If ye be lukewarm, I shall spit you out of my mouth.' You have much to think about. You have—"

Just then, they heard the sound of hooves thundering across the planks of the Great Bridge. Then they heard shouting, then galloping, then shouting again.

Lights burned to life in Stedman's Tavern, near the river. The rider shouted something, someone answered, the rider shouted something more, and the hooves hit the ground again.

Then Caleb saw horse and rider, galloping hard. But as they came to the corner of Wood and Spring Streets, the rider pulled at his reins, and the horseshoes sent sparks and a spray of stones scattering toward Caleb and the professor.

"Are you Winthrop?" The rider was a big man, dressed in good boots and brown coat, on a gelding that showed not a bit of lather, however hard he had been ridden.

"I am," said the professor.

"Be warned then. The Regulars are out."

"Who are you?" asked Winthrop.

"William Dawes. We're spreading word."

"Word of what?" demanded Winthrop. "Why are the Regulars out?"

"To arrest the leaders of the Provincial Congress in Lexington and seize the arms in Concord. The troops go by way of Medford, so I come this way."

"God damn them," said Winthrop. "Can we . . . can we see to your horse?"

"See to yourself, sir, for once they're done arresting the leaders, they may seize the delegates, too." Dawes spurred the horse.

Winthrop and Caleb watched him gallop off, then Winthrop

said to Caleb, "You've not much time now. Step forward or step away, but step."

All that night, Caleb lay awake listening to church bells ringing the alarm in distant villages. Twice he rose to see groups of armed men hurrying past the college. He heard doors open in Stoughton Hall, and three students went out with muskets on their shoulders. By four o'clock, some seventy men had collected on the Common, and from his window, Caleb watched them march up the Menotomy Road.

About five-thirty, he heard a rider gallop south through the village—a British courier, headed for Boston. With what news? Had they done their business in Lexington? Had they reached Concord?

And Caleb made a decision. He decided to get up. He used the chamberpot, then he wrote down his weather observations: temperature, 46° F; barometer, 29.56 inches; wind light from the west. It promised to be a beautiful day.

By midmorning, the temperature was sixty degrees. Cambridge should have been a-bustle, but nothing stirred in the street, and little stirred behind pulled shutters, because word had arrived: provincials and soldiers had clashed at Lexington, and they were now fighting around Concord.

The college was not in session, since students were allowed to go home for spring planting. But not all students were farmers. Many stayed during the recess, so Caleb Wedge spent the morning in commons, talking with the sons of barristers and merchants, trying to calm them and by his own words calm himself, though neither he nor the students believed a calming word he said.

Then, about eleven o'clock, came the sound of drums. Caleb and two students, Jeremiah Digges and Charles Sterret, hurried up to the cupola to see what was coming. And Caleb's eye was drawn immediately to movement below—a dozen mounted officers cantering back and forth in front of the college, stopping, conferring, looking about, riding ahead to reconnoiter, riding back, all as seemingly confused as hounds that had lost the scent.

"Master Wedge!" Digges pointed toward the river. "Look!"

And what Caleb saw was almost beautiful.

A long line of red etched itself across the greening marsh, rose onto the Great Bridge, and pointed up Wood Street, as if it were coming straight at them.

"My God," said Charles Sterret. "Four regiments."

"How many men is that?" asked Caleb.

"About a thousand. A relief column, I suspect, summoned at daybreak."

And now the sound of fifes trilled above the beat of the drums: "Yankee Doodle," a favorite tune when the British were in the mood to insult the people of Massachusetts.

They came on four abreast, all but filling the road. They marched with colors grimly cased. And the left-right-left lockstep of each man produced a left-right-left movement of the line itself, so that it seemed a great scarlet serpent was slithering along, its bayonets flashing like polished fangs.

"That's the Fourth Regiment of Foot in the van," said Sterret. "The King's Own."

"How do you know?" asked Caleb.

"The blue facings on their coats."

"No . . . how do you know so much about these things?"

"My father's in the Danvers militia, sir. I expect he's marching, too. That's the Forty-seventh behind the King's Own, then the Royal Welsh Fusiliers. And the King's Artillery. Two six-pounders." Sterret squinted to see the last unit. "Those lads crossin' the bridge? Royal Marines. Serious business, sir."

Caleb's stomach had been clenching and releasing all day. Now it closed like a fist.

"What's this?" Moses Richardson, the college carpenter, a skinny little piece of rawhide, poked his head through the trapdoor. "Cupola's closed. Railin's rotten."

"We won't lean on it," said Caleb.

Recognizing a tutor, Richardson changed his attitude, but slightly. "Beggin' your pardon, sir. You should read the notes I send 'round. . . . Be that music?"

Caleb reached down and drew him up into the cupola.

"Lord in Heaven," said Richardson, looking out.

The first units, led by mounted officers, were coming into the village square. The pounding of their drums and the tramping of their boots were loud enough now that Caleb could feel the vibrations in the floor of the cupola.

"That's General Lord Percy." Sterret pointed to the one in the gold-trimmed hat.

"A damn big nose on him," said Richardson.

"A damn good soldier," said Sterret. "Aide-de-camp to the king when he was nineteen. They say the king has the same kind of big nose and popped-out eyes, too."

"The king's bastard, then?" asked Digges.

"They're *all* the king's bastards," said Richardson.

Directly in front of Harvard Hall, Percy reined up and raised his hand. The fifing stopped instantly. In the time it took for the sound to travel from the front of the column to the rear, the drumming stopped, the tramping stopped, and all four regiments stopped, like a mighty mill hammer stopping in mid-motion when the brake is thrown.

After the noise, the sudden silence seemed to have a volume of its own.

"Have you reconnoitered, Colonel?" asked Percy of a mounted officer.

The curved ceiling of the cupola acted like a bowl to capture the rising sounds, so Caleb could hear every word perfectly.

"There are three roads north," said the colonel, "and forgive me, sir, but I can't tell which one we should take."

"You're joking," said Percy, entirely unamused.

"'Tisn't a morning for jokes, sir."

Percy looked at the deserted courthouse, the shuttered homes, the Harvard buildings, and he said, "Is there no one in this village who knows how to leave it?"

"Many seem to have left it already, sir," said the officer, "or hidden."

"In that," answered Percy, "they show more wisdom than their countrymen."

Up in the cupola, Moses Richardson whispered, "Damn shame my musket's in the cellar, or I could pick me off one fine kingbird right now."

"And you'd see the college burned to the ground," said Caleb.

Then Percy stood in his stirrups and shouted at Harvard Hall, "Is there anyone in this repository of provincial learning who knows the geography of his own town?"

"Say nothing," whispered Caleb. "Say nothing."

"We'll say nothing," said Sterret.

"Not you," said Caleb. "I mean the whole college."

"I ask again!" Percy's voice echoed off the buildings. "In the name of the king, who will show us the way to Lexington?"

Then Percy sat back in his saddle, folded his hands on the pommel, and waited. A horse snorted. A drummer boy dropped one of his sticks.

And Caleb whispered again, "Say nothing."

"I'll point your way." It was the voice of Isaac Smith, Loyalist tutor.

Caleb cursed him as he walked out of the hall and up to Percy's horse.

"Take the Menotomy Road, your lordship." Smith raised his walking stick and pointed northwest. "You'll cross Alewife Brook in two miles and pass the village of Menotomy a mile beyond. Then you'll be well on your way."

"Thank you, my good man," said Lord Percy.

"God save the king, sir," answered Smith.

"God save the king, indeed," growled Caleb Wedge to Isaac Smith.

The tail of Percy's column had crossed the Common, the sound of their drums was receding, and students and villagers were now pouring out of buildings all around.

"An officer of the king asked for information," said Smith defiantly. "A subject of the king could not tell a lie."

The basement door of Harvard Hall banged open and Moses Richardson came out with his musket in his hands. He went up to Smith and said, "Be gone by sundown, or I'll have you tarred and feathered."

"*You'll* have *me* tarred and feathered?" shouted Smith. "How dare you? The college carpenter does not address a tutor in that way."

"Isaac—" Caleb put a hand on Smith's arm.

"Tutor Smith!" A student in a window in Massachusetts Hall tore open a pillow, so that the feathers came fluttering down. "All we need now is the tar."

Caleb pushed Smith toward Stoughton Hall. Then he looked up at the student. "You face a fine, unless you clean up these feathers and write an apology to Tutor Smith. The rest of you get about your business."

"The business," said Moses Richardson, "ain't finin'. 'Tis fightin'."

"Not for boys who haven't signed muster sheets," said Caleb. "Those who have may follow their conscience. The rest are to return to their rooms."

Just then a rider came pounding up the road and right into the courtyard, adding to the confusion. "Hey, lads! There's men rippin' up the bridge. We need help."

They all knew him—John Hicks, a burly man with big, nail-scarred hands, another carpenter. He lived in a neat white house near the river, and if any man's life defined the arguments of those days, it was his. His older son published a Tory newspaper, the *Boston Post Boy*. His younger son, a former student of Caleb's Anatomical Club, was a doctor and a known patriot. And it was an open secret that Hicks himself had been one of the "Indians" who had dumped tea into Boston Harbor.

"By whose order are they tearing up the bridge?" said Caleb, trying to infuse calmness into his voice.

"Who cares?" said Richardson. "We'll burn it and build it again later."

Hicks said, "General Heath ordered the Watertown militia to tear it up this mornin'. But they piled the planks on the side of the road like they was plannin' a barn raisin'. The king's men laid the planks down again and marched across as pretty as you please. Now Cap'n Gardner's lads are throwin' the planks in the river."

"Gardner of Brookline?" said Caleb. "Class of 'forty-seven?"

"A good man." Hicks looked up the road toward the cloud of dust above the British column. The sound of the drums had almost faded. "Gardner's fixin' to follow 'em once he's done at the bridge. However Percy gets out to Lexington, he'll have hell to pay on the way back."

"You joinin' Gardner?" asked Richardson.

"I'm fifty," answered Hicks. "Too old for a real militia unit, but I can still fight."

"That's my thinkin', too," said Richardson.

Hicks looked at Caleb. "What about you, Tutor Wedge?"

Richardson said, "Tutor Wedge don't drill, and he don't carry a musket, and his grandfather would rather live under Gage's wing in Boston than among strong Whigs like us. So don't count on him, any more than you'd count on Tutor Smith."

Caleb saw that a dozen students were listening, so he said, "Tutor Smith is right about one thing, Richardson. A carpenter should know his place."

"I know my place." Richardson hefted his musket. "Do you know yours?"

"Excuse us, Tutor Wedge." It was Sterret and Digges.

Caleb was glad for the distraction. It was unseemly for a tutor to engage in angry discussions with the college staff, even on a day such as this. "What is it?"

"Jeremiah and I have our names on muster sheets," said Sterret. "Him for Salem, me for Danvers. We'd like to join Captain Gardner, sir, but we don't have muskets."

"Neither do our tutors," said Richardson.

Without another look at the college carpenter, Caleb said, "Come with me."

Tory Row was choked with people, carts, horses, and wagons, all fleeing for the safety of Fresh Pond and Watertown. Caleb thought of Exodus, and such terrified flight made the reality of war even more vivid than the passing of the British army.

"Caleb! Caleb Wedge!" A chaise pulled by a chestnut gelding rolled up. Mrs. Winthrop was driving. Her husband was beside her, wheezing.

"A calamity, Caleb!" she said. "Did you see them? Marching like ferocious barbarians . . . Oh, God, what a day! What a horrible day!"

Professor Winthrop leaned forward, bringing his gray face into the light. "Have you . . . have you made your decision, Caleb?"

"I have, sir," answered Caleb. "Tutor Smith stepped forward to show Harvard's loyalty. Another tutor should show Harvard's more rebellious spirit."

"True enough," said Winthrop. "True enough."

Caleb smacked the horse on the rump and the chaise kicked ahead. "Keep safe."

"Much blood must be shed this day," cried Mrs. Winthrop.

"See that yours stays in your veins," added the professor.

Caleb watched the chaise a moment, then led the two students to his grandfather's house. He armed each boy with a musket and outfitted himself with his favorite fowling piece and two pistols. "Now, then, let's show Lord Percy what Harvard really thinks."

By afternoon, the road from Concord through Lexington to Cambridge was drawn in the red of British uniforms and drying blood. The mighty serpent of morning was now a beast that, having kicked over a hive, could not escape the swarm, no matter how far or fast he fled. And the farther he went, the larger the swarm became. And the more furious the stinging, the more ferocious became the beast. In the last mile before the British recrossed Alewife Brook, there was hand-to-hand fighting. Prisoners were shot. Houses were put to the torch. Innocents were massacred.

What resembled a swarm of militia would later be called "a moving circle of fire." Units from dozens of towns had been following the British retreat, firing, then running or riding ahead, along fences, through pastures, in and out of woods, stopping and firing again before scrambling for the next stone wall or streambed.

About a mile south of Alewife Brook, at a place called Watson's Corner, Caleb Wedge waited in a blacksmith shop. He had been gripping his gun for so long that his hand was cramped. So he rested his weapon on the windowsill and flexed his fingers. Then he mopped his brow. Though he was no more than a mile and a half from the college where he had spent most of his life, he felt as if he had come to the edge of the earth to face a demon. But he had stepped forward at last.

Sterret and Digges crouched on either side of the main door. John Hicks waited at the other window. Moses Richardson knelt behind the trough outside. And across the road, shielded by a barricade of water casks, Captain Isaac Gardner and a dozen or so Brookline irregulars waited.

They could see the British column now, some half a mile north, spouting smoke and flame into the fields and farmhouses and stands of trees that flanked the Menotomy Road. Caleb and the others had agreed that when the vanguard reached the farmhouse about fifty yards north, they would volley and run.

Caleb listened to the voice in his head, telling him over and over that he could do it. He would not listen to John Hicks, who was nervously whistling "Yankee Doodle"; or to Moses Richardson, who gave out with a hooting laugh every time another explosion of musket smoke blew into the British column; or to the students, both of whom were muttering psalms while they waited.

Then Captain Gardner rose from behind his barricade. "Another few minutes, lads, 'twill be hotter than blazes along this stretch. Best wet our whistles." And he walked to a well a short distance beyond the water casks.

The bucket splashed and echoed. How comforting such a simple sound could seem, thought Caleb, on such a terrible day.

And suddenly, a volley of musket fire exploded from the trees beyond the well. Gardner was knocked backward, and a dozen Regulars appeared, as if from thin air.

As Caleb stood and aimed his musket, another volley exploded somewhere behind him, sending half a dozen balls smacking against the blacksmith shop and one right through Moses Richardson, who spouted a mist of blood from his mouth and fell dead in the road.

These moment's-notice soldiers had not reckoned with the tactics of professionals. Now, there were flanking parties behind them, on both sides of the road. And already they were finishing Gardner with their bayonets.

So the Brookline men fired a ragged volley and ran.

At the same time, the back door of the blacksmith shop burst open. Young Sterret whirled and fired, blowing an infantryman back into several others.

The explosion of the gun was so loud that it had physical force, like the blow of a hammer against the side of a head. For a moment, Caleb was stunned, but two more soldiers were forcing their way through the door. So Caleb pointed his musket and pulled the trigger. Instead of a blast, he heard the pop-click of a pan flash. Then a bayonet was thrusting straight at him.

But John Hicks fired his musket into the chest of the soldier doing the thrusting and saved Caleb's life. Then Hicks grabbed the door and slammed it shut. "Run!" he screamed at Caleb.

"No!" Caleb fumbled to pull out his pistols.

More soldiers were trying to push through the door, and from the corner of his eye, Caleb saw a flash of red at the north window, so he whirled and fired.

"Run!" Hicks pushed hard at the door. But an infantryman was forcing his way in, bayonet first, and he managed to stick Hicks in the side.

The big carpenter cried out in pain and the soldier was able to get through the opening, but Caleb grabbed the smithy's hammer and smashed it against the soldier's head, sending his helmet and its owner flying toward the furnace.

The weight of Hicks's body forced the door shut again, and again he shouted at Caleb, "Run! Run now! Save those boys."

Jeremiah Digges fired at a soldier who stopped at the window on the south side.

"See that!" cried Hicks. "We're flanked. And flanked means dead!"

The door was pushed. So Hicks roared up his strength and pushed back, despite a stain of blood widening under his rib cage. But a pistol found its way through the opening, and like the head of a snake, it turned to Hicks and went off against his belly.

Caleb fired his pistol into the face of the man holding the gun, and the door slammed shut again.

"Run!" cried Hicks as his body slid down the door toward the dirt floor. "Run!"

So Caleb shoved the two boys out the front and they ran. They had to parry bayonet thrusts, and they heard muskets scattering lead after them. But there was no marksman worse than a British Regular, and no pursuit slower than a soldier who had been marching since the middle of the night.

V

A few days later, Caleb wrote a letter to Lydia and had it smuggled into the city:

> Tell Grandfather I have taken a stand. I have thrown my lot with those who would resist the rulings of a distant government. It will pain him, but it would pain him more were I untrue to my beliefs. Tell him to remember the words of the Lord: "Be ye either hot or cold. If ye be lukewarm, I shall spit you out of my mouth."
>
> Horrible is the only word for the fighting. I will leave to your imagination the effect of a pistol ball on a man's face. Consider instead the bravery of a man who lays down his life that others may live. That was what our good neighbor John Hicks did. Badly wounded, he held off the Regulars until two students and their tutor could escape from a blacksmith shop that had become a charnel house.
>
> We retreated—nay, we ran—all the way to the Common, wherefrom we were ordered to join thousands of militia gathered at the river. But Percy, seeing what awaited him if he came through the village, avoided us by taking the Charlestown Road. This was all for the best, as the furious Regulars, who had been burning houses and fighting with vengeful fury all afternoon, must surely have put the college to the torch.
>
> After the battle, I went with John Hicks's son back to the blacksmith shop. We found a cart and loaded on the mortal remains of his father and Moses Richardson and brought them to the graveyard beside Christ Church. And what a scene of melancholy was there! As we buried them in a common grave,

the son of Richardson cried out that they did not deserve to have dirt thrown onto their faces, then he leapt into the hole and laid his father's cape on them both. My emotions, and those of other observers, were very strong, for the dirt falling upon those shrouded faces was surely the face of war.

And we are come to this—you besieged in Boston, I serving as a doctor's apprentice, and the dear old college now headquarters for an army unlike any the world has ever seen, twenty thousand men—farmers, merchants, ministers, Negro freedmen, Indians, boys of seventeen, men of forty-five—all come together under the command, I am glad to say, of Harvard men: Artemas Ward, '43 and Dr. Joseph Warren, '59.

Where this will lead, who can know? But word has reached me of a truce, whereby the Loyalists in the countryside may go into Boston while the Whigs of Boston may leave. I have written to Christine and pray that she and her family will come out.

The next morning, Lydia hurried down to Dock Square with an envelope in her apron.

Any who wished to leave were required to turn in their weapons at Faneuil Hall, so hundreds of wagons had collected there, and dozens of soldiers were shouting orders amid chaos that grew as the rumor spread: Boston Tories were begging Gage to stop the exodus and keep the Whigs in the city as insurance against the rebels burning it.

After ten minutes of searching the crowd, Lydia found the Cowgills' wagon, piled high with trunks, furniture, two children, a fretting mother, and Christine, who in truth seemed almost happy to be leaving.

"Lydia!" she shouted. "Your brother has done us proud!"

"Will you go to him?" asked Lydia.

"He's made a decision. Even if he stays in Cambridge, 'twill be a changed place."

Lydia pressed an envelope into her hands. "See that he gets this. It contains a poem called 'John Hicks and Other Heroes.' It expresses my patriotic emotions. And a letter explains why I must stay with my grandfather."

"Your grandfather needs you," said Christine. "None would say otherwise."

Lydia was loath to lose the company of the Cowgills, who had treated her more amiably than anyone else in Boston, so she walked along beside their wagon as it rolled down Orange Street in the train leaving the city.

As they approached the gates on the Neck, Lydia looked out across the Back Bay and yearned to go with them. But then the train slowed. Mrs. Cowgill wrung her hands, Mr. Cowgill clucked at the horses, and Christine talked of Caleb's courage, as if to summon her own. When they were six wagons from freedom, the gates were closed. Gage had decided that the Tories were right, and the Cowgills were trapped.

On the morning of June 16, the Provincial Congress ordered that the college library be removed to Andover. By that time the students had no need of books because the Committee of Safety had sent them all home.

Caleb thought that now would be the time to return a certain volume. He could slip the Shakespeare manuscript into a pile, or he could do it more publicly, in that he had committed to living by hard decisions. But the day was too busy for him to go looking for books, and by evening, other matters had taken his attention.

About nine o'clock, twelve hundred men were drawn up on Cambridge Common to hear Harvard's president, Reverend Samuel Langdon, deliver a prayer. Then, behind masked lanterns, the men took to the Charlestown Road. Their destination was secret, but Caleb guessed that it would be Bunker Hill.

The next morning, the people of Boston were shaken in their beds by the concussion of a naval broadside. Several seconds later, the blast rattled windows in Cambridge, and the Battle of Bunker Hill was begun.

By nightfall, a pile of limbs lay by the door of Elmwood, and a dozen wounded men lay in every room. Lieutenant Governor Oliver had long since fled, and his home was now a hospital. Caleb

Wedge, apprentice to Dr. John Warren, was in the dining room, beneath a smoky lantern, putting his study to practice.

"This one's lucky," said Warren, who had the same confidence of manner that characterized his brother, Joseph. "He's passed out." Warren looked into the patient's face. "Why . . . a classmate."

Caleb said, "Pratt, isn't it?"

"Horace Taylor Pratt, a general pain in the arse"—Warren lifted Pratt's arm—"with a specific pain in the elbow."

Such coincidences had become the norm rather than the exception.

"First," said Warren, "probe the wound. A finger is best. It allows you to feel the damage." He put his little finger into the hole in the patient's elbow. "There's jagged bone. The elbow is shattered. The arm must come off. You're going to do it."

"Me? I'm not ready."

In other rooms men could be heard screaming, crying out, whimpering.

"Tutor Wedge"—Warren was small and slender, but there was an intensity in his eyes, deepened by the emotions of that day—"my brother went on the hill today. He has not returned. I am driven near distraction. If I can do my duty, so can you."

Warren then wrapped a tourniquet around the patient's upper arm and told Caleb to take the amputation knife. "Wipe the blood off the blade, then cut to the bone, in a circular motion, while I hold the arm."

The patient rolled his head from side to side.

"He stirs," said Warren. "Be quick."

And Caleb made the cut, then grabbed the bone saw and placed it against the humerus while Warren held back the flesh and muscle of the patient's upper arm. In four swift strokes, Caleb was through and the arm came off.

Horace Taylor Pratt awoke with a scream.

"Congratulations, Tutor Wedge," said Warren, "you are now a doctor."

"Give me back my arm," said Pratt.

One hundred and twenty-seven rebels died at Bunker Hill, among them Warren's brother. But there was little time to mourn, for there were near three hundred wounded, and hundreds more falling ill every day in the great semicircle of camps around Boston.

So many men had collected so quickly that they were digging new necessaries each week, so many men that a single college chamber was now occupied by eight or ten soldiers and rough barracks were rising in the Yard and on the Common, so many men packed so closely together that a few with smallpox might bring down the whole army.

Such problems would have challenged doctors educated at Edinburgh or Padua. How much greater, then, was the challenge for men like John Warren and Caleb Wedge, self-taught medicos who spent hours discussing the sources of sickness, the movement of disease from man to man, and the defenses they might put up?

They were standing outside Elmwood on a rainy July afternoon, musing over the effects of summer humidity on camp fever, when they were distracted by a commotion on the road. Soon there appeared a pack of dogs, barking and snuffling, then a group of riders, and at their head, a tall man on a white horse, wearing a military-style coat of blue with buff facings. George Washington had arrived.

The story of the subsequent eight months of siege had as many subplots as players, but the story of Caleb's part was simple. He served, and he learned. While the college was removed to Concord, he stayed with the army to continue his apprenticeship. And by March 17, when the British and the Loyalists took to their ships and left Boston, Caleb Wedge was called doctor by all.

And Dr. Wedge, who had been inoculated against smallpox many years before, was among the first to enter the city after the British left.

He marched in with a detachment of General Greene's Rhode Islanders and was shocked to see so many majestic trees reduced to stumps for firewood, even more shocked to see how haggard and melancholy the inhabitants looked as they came out to greet their liberators.

At Summer Street, Caleb fell out of line and hurried for the Cowgill house, his heart pounding, his head filled with fearful visions of disease and starvation. But before he had taken his hand from the knocker, the door swung open and he was greeted by the happiest smile he had ever seen. "Thank the Lord," he whispered.

Christine threw herself into his arms and he pulled her against his body, and whatever hesitation he had felt, whatever calculations he had struggled with in his decisions of the heart, whatever uncertainties he might have known before he had seen men die from disease and wound, were all gone.

He turned her face to his and kissed her, his lanky body drawing warmth from hers.

When he stopped kissing her and looked into her eyes, he saw other eyes—those of her little brothers on the stairs, of her mother and father peering from the dining room. So he straightened himself, tugged on his waistcoat, and said, in the direction of the dining room, "Mr. Cowgill, I would beg the honor of your daughter's hand in marriage."

The door opened a bit wider, so that Mr. Cowgill's face appeared. His hair had been turned gray by the siege, and he had lost three teeth. "When?"

"If your daughter will have a military sawbones, I would marry her tomorrow."

"Tomorrow?" said Christine. "Why not tonight?"

There was a letter waiting for Caleb that day. It came from Lydia:

You know that I have no wish for exile, but Grandfather refuses to stay, and a man so old and broken cannot cross the Atlantic alone. The Townsend family has promised a welcome for their widowed daughter-in-law, and their manor in Northumberland will be at our disposal. But know that I am in sympathy with this cause. Someday, I shall return to taste the fruit of freedom, which I hope will be offered as willingly to my gender as to yours.

So, thought Caleb, Lydia would not be there to see him marry or march off with the Continental army, two events that occurred in short order.

On the night before the army departed for New York, he could not sleep. He lay beside his new wife and studied the shadows on the ceiling and wondered what would become of the fine house on Tory Row if he did not return. He had lived there during the siege because he had grown up there. But he did not own the house. It was still in the name of Reverend Abraham Wedge, departed Loyalist. So it would be subject to confiscation as soon as a commission was established.

Caleb considered it good news that one of the men on the commission was Professor Winthrop, who would see that Caleb's service was taken into account when the fate of the house was determined. Still, there was no guarantee that the house and everything in it might not be handed over to the state and offered for sale.

Caleb rolled closer to Christine, asleep on her stomach. He placed his hand on her bottom, which had expanded nicely after two weeks of decent food, and he contemplated how terrible it would be to leave such pleasure. And the smooth softness of her flesh was enough to inflame him. So he let his hands slide down. . . .

"Caleb," she said. "Caleb, what are you . . ."

"I perform love's labors."

And when they were done, he told her there was a book on love's labors that he wanted her to know about.

"I need no picture books to show me the ways of love," she giggled.

"'Tisn't a picture book. 'Tis an ode to love's labors."

He lit a candle and led her past the rooms of the Continental officers who had taken up residence in the house, down to the study, to the third alcove and the third shelf. Behind a panel were two books, just as he had expected.

"You must know of this, in case we have done our last love's labors together."

"Don't say that, Caleb."

"The British have left Boston, but there's much fighting yet."

He pulled out the books and opened to the title page of one: *Fanny Hill, Memoirs of a Woman of Pleasure*. And he gasped, "Good God!"

"Not a *picture* book," said Christine. "A *word* book on dirty business."

Caleb saw a note in the middle of the book. It was in Lydia's hand: "The day will come when we need not do our research in barns or hide our books behind panels or leave our women to educate themselves. That day is not yet here, and so we hide our best until then. You see to your research. I will see to our books."

"What about love's labors?" asked Christine.

Caleb thought for a moment, put the note back into the book and put the books behind the panel, then he took her hand. "Better to perform them than read about them."

vi

Dr. Caleb Wedge was proud that eight signers of the Declaration of Independence were Harvard men, and he was proud of an army that refused to quit through all the defeats and retreats of 1776. He marched with them in brutal heat and bitter cold, and it was the cold that finished him. Just after Trenton, he lost his left foot to frostbite.

By the spring of 1777, he was back in Boston, learning to walk again on a wooden foot fitted into a high boot and helping John Warren organize the Continental Massachusetts General Hospital. There they sought to understand how diseases passed from person to person, and though they felt that they had gone far toward stopping the spread of smallpox, they were still puzzled by other maladies.

They decided that the best way to understand the transmission of yellow fever would be to inhale the germ. So they cut a deck of cards, and it fell to Warren to place a glass tube over the nose and mouth of a yellow fever patient and breathe in the exhalations while Caleb set down the clinical observations. Warren remained healthy, so they concluded that summer heat and poor sanitation were the causes of the disease.

With several others, they founded the Massachusetts Medical Society and, in the new spirit of the times, initiated a series of lectures on human dissection. They no longer needed to be resurrectionists. Their subjects were the unclaimed bodies of soldiers who had died in the hospital. Their students were upperclassmen and faculty at the college and any man over twenty-one with an interest in physick.

When Caleb Wedge appeared for his first lecture and threw back a sheet, revealing the body of a man who had died from a gunshot, he heard a gasp. He looked out and said, "If we are to improve the lot of man, we must study man . . . his mind and body both." And he wished that John Winthrop had lived long enough to see him step forward and perform dissections in the bright light of day.

Students who completed the lectures received a certificate, engraved by Paul Revere with images of Hippocrates and a physician making an incision in a dead body. It attested that the student had "attended a course of Anatomical Lectures and Demonstrations, together with Physiological and surgical dissertations at the Dissecting Theater in the American Hospital, Boston; whereby he has had an opportunity of procuring an accurate knowledge in the structure of the human body."

Formal medical training had begun in New England.

On October 7, 1783, with the last battle of the Revolution a memory, Warren, Caleb, and two others went to the Cambridge Meeting House, swore themselves to be "of the Christian religion as maintained in the Protestant communion," and were inaugurated as the first professors in the Medical Institution of Harvard University.

Caleb understood the oath. The candles of ignorance guttered, but it was important to reassure the ignorant that when a medical professor dissected a body, he did it with no dark intent. This was, after all, a society that had been hanging witches less than a century before.

Caleb also understood the importance of family and friends, for without them, nothing mattered. Christine and their children, Joseph and George, sat smiling before him. And there was the Tory tutor, Isaac Smith, who had stood where he thought he should . . . and the widow of John Hicks . . . and Horace Taylor Pratt, his first patient. And there were ghosts, too. Grandfather Abraham, who died an exile . . . William Brattle, who left the siege of Boston, sailed away to Halifax, sat down to his first good meal in over a year, and ate himself to death . . . John Winthrop . . . John Hicks . . . even a forgotten old actor called Burton Bones. The one person he missed was his sister.

But soon, a ship arrived from England, carrying a trunk, a flat wooden crate, and Lydia herself.

Letters had passed between them. Lydia knew the fate of the house—confiscated by the Massachusetts Commission, bought by Samuel Cowgill, given back to his daughter. Caleb knew of Lydia's lonely exile in a manor in Northumberland, where she cared for a senile, sightless old man whose only joy came from her readings of the Bible and Shakespeare and his old commonplace book.

Caleb was in the study, preparing his first lecture on female anatomy, when there was a commotion at the front door and a cry of joy from Christine.

The supply of joy increased that night in proportion to the supplies of port, sweetmeats, cake, laughter, and tears. Everyone agreed that no one had aged a day, and all knew that it was a lie, except for the two little boys. They had already announced that Lydia was their new favorite aunt, then they went off to play with the lead soldiers she had brought for them.

It was not until the boys were bedded down that Lydia bid her brother help her to open the wooden crate. Inside was a painting, wrapped in heavy canvas.

Lydia placed the painting on the desk, supporting it with her grandfather's old wig stand, and she told them to close their eyes. Then she tore away the canvas and revealed a perfect likeness of her grandfather and herself. They were seated against a background of heavy crimson drapery and dark shadow, and light poured onto their faces. The artist was so skilled that one could feel the polished texture of the table at which they sat, taste the grapes in the bowl on the table, read the words in the book open before them.

"Grandfather wanted you to have this," she said.

"It looks like the work of Copley," said Christine, who had an eye for such things.

"Yes. Another exile. He spent time with the Townsends and decided to paint us. There is little background, because an exile has little behind him."

Caleb went closer to the painting. "And the book on the table? *Love's Labours* . . . you can read no more."

"Grandfather came to enjoy Shakespeare more and more. Aside from his old commonplace book, which I read to him because it reminded him of his youth, he enjoyed Shakespeare more than anything."

Caleb said, "Grandfather was a minister. He should be shown with a Bible."

"But he laughed most heartily when I read Shakespeare's comedies to him, and he was seldom one to laugh at all."

"He liked plays?" said Christine. "He wrote a law to ban them."

"He changed," said Lydia.

"Did you read him *Love's Labours Won?*" asked Christine.

Lydia looked at Caleb. "You revealed our secret?"

"I'm his wife," said Christine. "It is now my secret, too."

"Where is the manuscript?" asked Caleb.

"It will be accounted for," said Lydia.

"Is it in England?" asked Caleb. "It belongs to the college, you know."

"When women are educated at Harvard," said Lydia, "Harvard shall have the benefit of *Love's Labours Won*, and we all shall laugh . . . most heartily."

"But . . . but . . ."

"Caleb," said Christine, "don't sputter, or we shall laugh heartily right now."

A few days later, Lydia visited a neat white house on Water Street. The slate roof was tiered in the Dutch style. The trimwork was simple. The clapboards showed no sign of rot. It was the house of John Hicks. And while he might not have been a rich man, he had sited his house on two acres at the edge of the Charles River marsh.

Lydia knocked on the door and looked out at the yellows and reds of autumn spilling across the marsh, at a view that changed by the day and yet was changeless.

The widow Hicks, a heavy woman with drooping eyes, welcomed the author of "John Hicks and Other Heroes" as though she were royalty. For a time, before grander heroes and better poets had come along, Lydia's poem had rallied Massachusetts. "Oh, noble is the man who dies to save his fellow man . . ."

That morning, the two women drank tea and talked about John Hicks.

"Such a fine poem you wrote for him, and such a fine craftsman he was," said the widow. Then she brought Lydia into the tiny foyer to show her the turned stairwell and the pendant acorns that decorated it. "Such a fine craftsman, but never able to quiet the creaking of the third tread. 'The telltale tread' he called it." She put her weight down on the tread, which emitted a loud creak.

Then she told Lydia of the night her husband sneaked off to the Boston Tea Party. "He climbed out our bedroom window, since this was supposed to be a secret gatherin'. But when he come home in the middle of the night, he couldn't climb back in. He had to come up by the stairs, so he took off his boots and tried to sneak up. But I heard the tread creak and came thundering down on him, for why had my husband been sneaking about in the middle of the night?"

"And what did he say?"

"He just showed me his boots. They was filled with loose tea leaves, so I knew he hadn't been doin' anything but the work of the Lord and Massachusetts."

"He saved my brother's life," said Lydia. "We shall always be in his debt." Then Lydia glanced at the tallboy clock and said, "Nearly eleven. I must go."

"Can you not stay longer?" said Widow Hicks. "Gentle company is a pleasure."

"I'll come again and bring a copy of a poem I shall call 'The Telltale Tread.' And perhaps something else. But my brother is delivering a lecture on the female anatomy this morning. I hope to peer through a crack in the door of old Holden Chapel, so that I might see the first appearance of a woman in a Harvard classroom, even if it is a cadaver."

Chapter Sixteen

═══════

PETER AND Evangeline were hurrying across the Yard, side by side, though not arm-in-arm. It was one of those March evenings when the lingering light promised spring, but the air was as cold as February, and January still whistled in the wind.

They had been talking regularly on the phone, and they'd had dinner at New Year's in Manhattan. Now she had come to Cambridge for a few weeks of research on her book.

Peter was telling her that after three months, he was still mad at Harvard.

"So your kid didn't get in early," she said. "He might be accepted in April, right?"

"The odds drop."

"He's still a legacy. I hear that legacies have a five-to-one rate of acceptance, while everyone else has a nine-to-one."

"We'll see. But right now, I'm doing no more phone calls for Harvard."

"After what happened last time, I'm surprised you'd even think about it."

"Well, I still wonder what really happened to Ridley."

"Anybody bothered you since?"

"No. No Bingo Keegan. No conversations with Will Wedge. Not

even a Christmas card. Nothing until Wedge sent me the invitation to this exhibition."

The Fogg Art Museum held most of Harvard's paintings, a better collection than you could find in most medium-size cities. A banner outside proclaimed the new show: FACES FROM THE PAST. TREASURES OF THE HARVARD PORTRAIT COLLECTION.

"Nice to get a little preview," said Evangeline.

"Well, those old families thought it was nice to give Harvard their paintings," said Peter. "They got all the write-offs and their ancestors got spots on the walls. The Winthrops gave a dozen portraits, just as long as they were all enshrined in the Winthrop House library."

They went up the stairs to the second floor of the museum, turned, and there it was, the centerpiece of the show, displayed so that it could be seen even before you entered the gallery.

Peter recognized the work of John Singleton Copley at a glance. It was all there . . . the confidence with which the subjects inhabited their space, the powerful light, the sense of realism that invested every detail and gave the painting psychological reality, too. Before he knew their names, Peter knew that the old man had been tough-minded and unyielding, and the young woman had inherited those qualities, adding a skill for making herself a general pain in the ass.

"Reverend Abraham Wedge and his granddaughter, Lydia," said Evangeline.

They walked into the gallery, which was full of Harvard professors, a few students, and a lot of descendants sipping champagne and admiring their gene pool.

Looking down from the span of Harvard history were two dozen faces, and as many opinions on the meaning of education, of society, of God Himself . . . or Herself. There was the stiff, primitive portrait of William Stoughton, unrepentant judge of witches . . . the magnificent full-length Copley of John Winthrop and his telescope . . . Anne Mowlson, Lady Radcliffe . . . Dorothy Wedge Warren, one of the Radcliffe Eight, in an oval portrait from the 1830s . . . official portraits of Harvard presidents. . . .

Peter grabbed a glass of champagne and walked up to Abraham

and Lydia and the tall guy admiring them. "Evening, Will. I like the little half smile on Lydia's face."

"Why do you think she's smiling?" said Will Wedge, not even turning to Fallon.

"Maybe it's the book on the table," said Evangeline, stepping closer.

Peter inclined his head to read the title. "I'll be damned."

"It used to be a Bible," said Wedge. "All my life, it was a Bible. Now . . ."

The book looked to Peter like a quarto. It was open to the title page on which were written the words *Love's Labo* . . . before the image trailed into the fold.

Evangeline went over to a display panel just far enough away not to distract from the portrait, but close enough to draw the viewer's attention. The caption read, "Restoration Renders Surprise." Beneath it was a photograph of a conservator touching a brush to a crudely painted Bible in front of Reverend Abraham.

"They restored most of the portraits for the show," said Wedge, through clenched teeth. "Patched cracked frames, X-rayed, infilled, and cleaned. And they found the play. It seems that someone had decided that a man who sponsored the anti-theater laws of 1767 should not spend eternity reading a play. So they painted a Bible over it."

"They did that sort of thing a lot back then," said Peter.

"I wish they hadn't," said Wedge.

"So," said Evangeline, "is it *Lost* or *Won?*"

"I think we have to find out," said Will Wedge. "Charlie Price will want to know, once he sees this. He'd be here tonight but he's off on vacation. Hawaii or someplace."

A young woman came up to them, a reporter for the *Boston Globe*. She explained that she was doing an article on the show, and she was interested in visitor opinions.

Peter could have refused, but it was easier to offer some vanilla remark, the kind she wouldn't bother to use, once she talked to someone more interesting. So he said: "A restoration like this shows you just how interesting the past can be when you give it the attention it deserves. Our history is alive and kicking."

She wrote it down, asked his name, then went wandering off.

Wedge said to Evangeline, "Back to your question—*Lost* or *Won?*"

Peter said, "Do you see how, beneath the title, Copley has put in a dramatis personae, just for a little more detail? I recognize some of the names but not all of them."

"And on that basis you conclude . . . what?" asked Evangeline.

Will Wedge said, "I conclude that you quiet down. Old Prof. G. and Olga just came in. He's going to have plenty to say about this as it is."

Peter turned and shook Prof. G.'s hand. "How's the book collecting, Professor?"

"Slow and pleasant, as always." The old man looked at the painting. "My . . . my. I haven't seen this in years. Very interesting."

While the old man went over and read the article, Olga asked him, "Mr. Fallon, have you had any luck with that *Anglorum Praelia* that we asked about back in the fall?"

"I know that Orson has been looking into it," said Peter. "He's—"

"My God," said Prof. G., almost as though he couldn't keep the words from escaping. "It's . . . it's true."

"What?" asked Peter. "What's true?"

The old professor looked at Fallon and the others and gave out with a little laugh. "Who could imagine that Copley was such a jokester, putting a play in front of old Reverend Abraham."

"Oh, yes, a jokester," said Will, and he added one of those big, honking laughs of his own.

Afterward, Peter and Evangeline went to Rialto, an upscale restaurant in the Charles Hotel.

"Try the *soupe de poisson,*" he said.

"In our day," she said, "we got clam chowder at Cronin's. No *soupe de poisson.*"

Peter looked out at the white lights on the trees in front of the hotel. "No Rialto, either. And no Charles Hotel . . . God, we sound like old farts."

"Late forties is old-fartdom to most of the kids in Cambridge," she said. She was wearing a black turtleneck and a touch of red lipstick, which brought out the blond highlights in her hair. She looked to Peter like anything but an old fart.

He smiled across the table and said, "Tonight I got an infusion of youth."

"The painting?"

"If *Love's Labours Won* made it to 1780, we are back on the trail. You saw how Will Wedge was acting, how surprised that old professor seemed."

"Peter, it's more likely *Love's Labours Lost,* and when Copley painted in a dramatis personae — which he didn't intend you to read as if you were going to play one of the parts, by the way — he made up a few names."

"Considering what it would mean, and how much it would be worth, I think we should proceed as if it's *Love's Labours Won.*"

She sipped her water and looked at him.

"So," he said after her look hung there for a moment, "are you going to help?"

"I'm starting a book about the Radcliffe Eight, Peter. That nice oval portrait of Dorothy Wedge Warren, I can see that on the cover. That's my focus right now. But . . ." She took another sip of water. "But the holidays did make me feel awful old."

"The first Christmas after your divorce is a bad one," he said.

"You got that right."

The wine arrived just in time, a Jean Brocard Chablis. Peter toasted, "To keeping our youth."

"To finding it again." Evangeline sipped her wine. "Of course, Lydia Wedge was young in that painting. Now she's up in the Old Burying Ground."

Peter whistled softly. "If researching the lives of dead Wedges is going to do this to you, go back to researching villas in Tuscany or bars in Key West."

Evangeline drank a little more wine. "I can't do a lot to help you, you know."

"Just do your research," he said. "Every forty or fifty years, the Wedges drop a clue, like Hansel and Gretl dropping bread crumbs. That painting was like a whole loaf."

"After the grandfather died, Lydia came back and lived another fifty years," said Evangeline. "She left a few more bread crumbs. I'll show you one after we eat."

"Another appetite whetted," he said. "I'm feeling like I'm back in my twenties."

"So"—she opened the menu—"let's eat like we were in our twenties."

"You mean red meat?" asked Peter.

"Actually, I was a vegetarian in college."

"Maybe that's why you feel old. Have a steak."

When they were filled and satisfied and just a little drunk, they went for a walk. The wind had settled into one of those gentle snowfalls that deadens the traffic noise, even in Harvard Square.

They strolled along Brattle Street, past the century-old Brattle Theater, where the Humphrey Bogart cult had been born in the fifties. Next door, separated by a narrow alley and dwarfed by the theater, was a yellow clapboard house with white trim and black shutters, the Cambridge Center for Adult Education.

"This was William Brattle's house," said Peter. "Once, his gardens reached all the way to the river. The Brattle Theater, the Charles Hotel . . . all part of Brattle's spread. He was exiled in the Revolution, like Abraham Wedge."

"At least his house survived," she said.

"A thread in the tapestry of time. You find a lot of those around here."

A little farther along, they came to what was called Architects Corner, where Walter Gropius and José Luis Sert had left their mark. The famous Design Research building shimmered in four stories of glass and golden light.

"This was where the Wedge house was," said Peter. "What do you think Lydia would say now?"

"Maybe we should ask her." And Evangeline led Peter up Church Street.

Soon, they were slipping into the ancient burial ground beside the Unitarian Meeting House. The traffic growled in the street, but the graveyard was shadowed and dark, something from another time, with a core of silence that let them hear the snow falling, almost flake by flake, on the granite slabs and headstones.

With the little flashlight she carried in her purse, Evangeline led Peter to a far corner of the cemetery and a simple headstone: LYDIA WEDGE TOWNSEND, 1750–1842.

"I was here this afternoon. I should have my head examined for showing you this, but"—Evangeline pointed her light at the stone—"another bread crumb."

Fallon read the inscription. "Seek truth through the years, but seek it for all, / Bestow knowledge freely to those who may call / Make this your goal till a century turns, / And the Bard will applaud as humanity learns."

"'The Bard,'" she said. "When it's capitalized, it means Shakespeare, doesn't it?"

"I think Lydia is telling us to keep looking."

They came out of the Old Burying Ground, feeling younger all the time.

She slipped an arm into his. "I've rented a studio on Memorial Drive . . . for when I come up to do research."

"A studio in Cambridge, a co-op on the East Side . . . sounds like you won your divorce."

"Nobody wins a divorce. You know that. But no more divorce talk," she said.

She'd sublet a place in a big stone building across the river from Harvard Stadium. Except for an air mattress in the corner, there was not a stick of furniture, not even a lamp.

So Peter flipped on the overhead light in the little kitchen and an educated Cambridge cockroach went scuttling.

"Put that out," she said. "Come over and look at the river."

The snow was dancing in the orange streetlights and the headlight beams and in the bright lights of the athletic complex across the river.

She took off her coat and put it on the windowsill. He threw his onto the mattress. Then he came up behind her and put his hands on her shoulders.

"Promise me one thing," she said, without turning around.

Before she could say any more, he leaned forward and kissed her neck.

She took a sharp breath and inclined her head so that he could kiss a little higher, the way he used to kiss the places he knew she liked, and he liked, too.

As he kissed, he inhaled Shalimar. She had been wearing it when they first met, and it intoxicated him now as it had when they were in their twenties.

And then she turned, took his face in her hands, and kissed him.

Soon enough, their clothes were dropping onto the floor and they were falling together onto the air mattress.

"This is yours, right?" he asked.

"Yeah. I slept on it last night."

And that was all they said until they had completed a little tour of youth.

When it was over and they were returning to reality, she said, "Falling into bed was not part of the plan."

"It wasn't a bed. It was an air mattress. And . . . you wanted me to promise you something."

"Don't push me further than I want to go, Peter. I left you once because I thought you were crazy. We're not even together now, but I'll leave you again."

"Honey"—he pulled her on top of him—"we may have eaten like we were in our twenties, and played like it, but if you think I'd risk my life like I did when I thought that finding a lost tea set was the road to salvation, forget it. I'm older and wiser."

"Are you?"

"Well, maybe not. But I'm a father."

"Detective?" said Peter Fallon. "I didn't know Harvard had detectives."

It was the next morning. Peter had come into the office feeling better than he had in months. Now there was a detective outside. What could *he* want?

Bernice ushered him in. He was about five-eight, with dark eyebrows and a Robert De Niro mole on his cheek. Beneath the bomber jacket he showed the thick neck and sloping shoulders of a power lifter. He flipped his badge and introduced himself. "John Scavullo."

Peter invited him to sit. "I thought university police just sent kids back to their rooms when they drank too much and kept people from parking in the Yard."

"Uniforms do that," said Scavullo. "I'm in the criminal investigation division."

"I didn't even know they had one. There's crime at Harvard?"

Scavullo smiled. He did not look as if he laughed much. "Anytime you bring a lot people together in one place, you'll have crime, no matter how smart they are. We enforce laws and university policy on drugs, thefts, assaults, vandalism. . . ."

"Like the tradition of kids pissing behind John Harvard's statue?"

"Tradition to some, misdemeanor to others."

"Misdemeanors I can understand. But felonies?"

"There aren't a lot because we're good at what we do. But bad things happen, sometimes. And sometimes in the libraries. Book thefts, for example."

Fallon sat back and folded his arms. He saw where this was going. He decided to let Scavullo do the talking.

"Our security in the library is excellent, but over the years, we've had thefts by students who wanted books so that they could underline them instead of taking notes . . . thefts by students who wanted the best books for themselves so they would get the only A's . . . thefts by people who know that a book of engravings is worth more if it's cut up and the engravings are sold separately . . . thefts by people who erased library marks on rare volumes, so that an honest bookseller like yourself would buy it." Scavullo looked into the outer office. "You may have bought stolen books you don't even know about."

"There's no stolen property in those cases," said Peter, keeping his tone flat neutral, saving indignation for later.

"We know you're honest. And you made good on the stolen Second Folio you bought a few years back."

"At great hardship . . . so, what do you want with me?"

"You have some interesting friends."

"It's an interesting business."

Scavullo took an envelope from his inside pocket, took two photographs from the envelope, and placed them in front of Fallon. "Look at those."

First was a photo of Fallon going into Ridley's house.

"That," said Scavullo, "would be on the day you went poking through his computer. We were watching Ridley's house."

"Because you think he was murdered?"

"No. State police said it was an accident. But they also looked over his computer and found the names of people we suspect of stealing and fencing books."

"Such as?"

"Assistant Professor O'Hill, for one. And O'Hill has dealings with a bookseller named Bertram Lee." Scavullo handed Fallon a photo. "Here you are, moments after Lee and O'Hill have parted company, meeting Lee on the steps of Widener."

"Do you always have people taking the tours, in case I come by with my son?"

Scavullo said, "We weren't watching you. We were watching Lee."

"This was taken in October," said Fallon. "It's March. What took you so long?"

"We thought we'd just keep an eye on you. Study your catalogs, just to see what you've been selling."

For the second time, Fallon decided to say nothing.

Scavullo took out three more photographs. They had been taken by a telephoto lens. They showed Bertram Lee, on a city street, in heated conversation with a man in a black raincoat, scally cap, and dark glasses. In one, Lee was holding up a locket.

"These were taken this week," said Scavullo. "We don't know what's going on here, but that's Bingo Keegan, as you know. We think he's the distribution point for a lot of stolen material—art, Oriental carpets, rare books. In his world, everyone pays cash and nobody pays sales tax."

"A denizen of what some have called the booksellers' underground."

"Right," said Scavullo. "So . . . when we see him in conversation with Lee, it gets our attention, and we begin to work back."

"To me?"

"I don't know how good your computer skills are, but we looked at the deleted files recovered from Ridley Royce's computer. In one, he tells Lee that he's thinking of using an 'old friend from Eliot House' as his broker for 'the maps.' A set of maps in folio from County Roscommon in Ireland were stolen out of Widener last fall."

"And you think I sold them?"

"Ridley also lists some other things." He handed Peter a printout. It included the titles of a dozen books of engravings, including William Blake's *Songs of Innocence* and *Experience* and an Audubon portfolio.

"You know," said Peter, "the Audubon is thirty-six by thirty-six. And it contains seventy-five hand-colored copperplates of Audubon's birds. It's so heavy you couldn't smuggle it out of a library with a forklift, let alone a briefcase."

"But," said Scavullo, "if you slice the paintings out and sell them individually, they're worth more than the book. And strangely enough, we have an Audubon at the Museum of Natural History recently damaged."

"And you think Ridley did it and I did the selling?"

"I know you're clean," said Scavullo. "I'm just trying to save Harvard's treasures. And you should be wondering who is stealing these books and subtly laying the blame onto you." He took out his card. "If you think of anything, give me a call."

Peter was still trying to figure that out when his son arrived, ready for lunch and an argument. The remnants of Peter's good mood had burned off like a fog.

Jimmy had already told his father that he wasn't sure he wanted to go to Harvard, now that Harvard had turned him down once.

Peter had already imparted the best wisdom he knew: No matter what decision Harvard or Jimmy made, in a year, Jimmy would be happy with his school, as long as he was happy with himself. He knew that Jimmy didn't believe it. But it was true.

Today, despite the distractions of a police visit, Peter wanted to give the kid another pep talk: "Just think of all the giants who began their growth at Harvard, of the rebels who began their rebellion there, of the great pioneers, the great novelists, the presidents, the scoundrels. But while Widener is the greatest library in the world, it's not where they *keep* the books that counts, Jimmy. It's what's in them."

Then he showed Jimmy all the books behind all the locked cases in his office. He said that few of those books were written by people who went to Harvard.

"Maybe they didn't want to," said Jimmy.

"Some did," said Peter.

"Yeah? Who?"

Peter went to the case where he shelved his poetry and pulled down the 1842 edition of *New England Reveries,* by Lydia Wedge. "She wanted to go to Harvard, but they wouldn't let her in. She wrote her poetry anyway."

He flipped through the book. "Here's 'John Hicks and Other Heroes': 'Oh, noble is the man who dies to save his fellow man, / And noble are the men who stand on honor's noble span, / So noble was the man named Hicks, who fought that desperate day, / And stood resolved, as bullets flew, to neither fall nor sway . . .'"

"No wonder they didn't let her in," said Jimmy. "That sucks."

"It served its purpose back then." Peter flipped through the book. "Or the one about the Harvard Bicentenary."

"Don't you mean bicentennial?"

"Bicentennial . . . bicentenary"—Peter shrugged—"either way, it was an amazing accomplishment for an institution to have survived for two hundred years."

Chapter Seventeen

=====

1836–1841

ANCIENT HANDS wrote a poem that ended: "And that is where to find *Love's Labours Won*." The hands slipped the poem into an envelope made of fine rag bond paper edged in gold leaf. Though the hands belonged to a woman, they sealed the envelope with the stamp of man, "CW," Dr. Caleb Wedge. Then they slipped the envelope into a larger one, addressed to "President Josiah Quincy, Harvard College, Cambridge, Massachusetts." This was left on Dr. Wedge's desk for the next day's post.

On a cloudy September morning a few weeks later, Dr. Caleb Wedge leaned on his cane in Harvard Yard, but he did not lean heavily. He had reached the age of eighty-nine firm in the belief that a man stood straight and stepped forward, even a man with a wooden foot. So none of the seven hundred graduates gathered for the Bicentenary would see him slouch now, not on one of the greatest days in the history of the college.

It had been two centuries since the first students studied under Nathaniel Eaton; 128 years since John Leverett became president and Puritan influence began to wane; six decades since Lord Percy forced Harvard men to take a stand; a quarter century since a Unitarian minister named John Kirkland had become president and the faith of their fathers had made room for a new religion.

Unitarianism, as one of Caleb's grandchildren had phrased it, was the faith of the future. Caleb said that he was born Congregationalist and would die that way. But he could not deny that the college of his youth was running fast toward the future.

Once, a red brick quadrangle had looked out on village and Common. But old Stoughton had been torn down, so Massachusetts and Harvard Halls had become the frame for a larger and deeper picture.

The brewhouses and woodsheds were gone, the pigpens and sheep commons had been planted over with tall elms and trimmed grass. A new Stoughton had been built beyond Hollis; Holworthy Hall had closed off the north edge of the Yard. And University Hall—chapel, classrooms, four dining rooms for the four classes— had risen in brilliant white granite that drew every eye from the red brick and greenery around it.

Even the outhouses had been improved. The old row of two-holers had been replaced by a single long shed on the east side of University Hall, shielded discreetly by pines. Smart-aleck students called it "university minor."

Some still considered Harvard as no more than a boarding school for smart alecks, where the average freshman was sixteen, the average class fewer than a hundred, the average attitude of the students alternately rebellious and shirksome. But the improvements in the Yard reflected many changes—in the expansion of the faculty, in the creation of law and divinity schools, in the direction of a university that no one would ever mistake for Increase Mather's Puritan seminary on the Charles.

Then the bell began to toll and the grand marshal called to form the procession.

The sudden movement of random groups into ordered lines reminded Caleb of a military camp when drums beat the march. The band took the lead, followed by the undergraduates, among them his grandson, Theodore, '37. And falling in behind them were the governor and the officers of the university.

Then the marshal called the name of Senator Paine Wingate,

Class of 1759. For a moment, there was silence. The wind rustled the elms and all waited to see if a ninety-seven-year-old man would have the strength to appear. He did not, so the classes from 1760 to 1763 were called. There were no living graduates in any of them, but the formalities had to be observed. Then the name of Dr. Caleb Wedge, Class of 1766, echoed through Harvard Yard.

The applause began as a gentle stream and rose quickly to a cataract of cheers.

Caleb had known grand moments and frightening times within that circle of buildings, and in an instant, he remembered them all. But he knew that the other graduates were not cheering just for him. They were cheering the longevity of the college, and they were cheering themselves, for as long as such an old man moved ahead of them through time, that long would they all stay young. Still, Caleb's eyes filled with tears, and he felt a weakness in his legs that caused him to hesitate before stepping forward.

So his son George, Class of 1800, hurried over, followed by his grandsons, George Jr., '30, and Theodore—two more generations of good height and sharp features.

"Back to your places," said Caleb. "I need no arm to lean on. I don't even need a cane." As proof, he took off his tall beaver hat, put it on the tip of the cane, raised the cane above his head, and shouted, "Follow me, Harvard!"

And the applause became a joyful shout.

Across the road, beyond the portals of Massachusetts and Harvard Halls, the Wedge ladies waited in the new Unitarian Meeting House, but not in comfort.

Lydia fanned herself with her program. "Just like the fathers of Harvard to keep the women in the balcony, where it's too hot, while the men have their cheers outside."

Christine worked on her knitting. "Let them have their day."

"She's right, Grandmother," said Dorothy, a young woman of nineteen who wore a fashionable bonnet framing a slender and symmetrical face. "You and Aunt Lydia deserve to march with them. My mother, too, had the Lord not taken her."

Christine said, "Having her with us would be blessing enough."

"Yes . . . yes," said Lydia. The curse of longevity, beyond watching your own deterioration, was to outlive so many people you loved. Lydia had buried her husband and an ardent suitor who died before they could marry, and more friends and relatives than she could count. But she had lived long enough to see this day, when she would make a statement that would define her for generations to come.

Outside, the band had stopped. The undergraduates had lined up on either side of the meetinghouse door, creating a corridor of youth through which the aged graduates would ascend the stairs. And there was Caleb Wedge, appearing first in the doorway, standing straight, putting his real foot forward.

"He looks so handsome," said Christine.

"Handsome?" snorted Lydia. "He was made for tricorne and breeches, not pantaloons and cutaway and beaver hat, any more than toothless old women were made for frilly bonnets and curling-iron hair."

"We're not toothless." Christine flashed what was left of her smile. "You have six teeth and I have nine."

Young Dorothy brought a hand to her mouth to stifle a laugh. She had no interest in Harvard's latest act of self-congratulation, but she never regretted time spent with her grandmother or great-aunt, especially when they were bickering, which they did until the meetinghouse had filled with graduates.

When all the Wedge men were in their places—Caleb, George Sr., and George Jr. in the pews, young Theodore standing with the undergraduates—Christine said, "A bold Wedge lineage."

Lydia brought a hand to her ear. "Did you say 'bold' or 'bald'?"

"Wedge men aren't bald," said Christine, looking out on a sea of male pates.

"Those with Cowgill blood go bare pretty quick on top. Even young Theodore."

Dorothy said, "Theodore's inhaling every detail, to write about it."

"And there'll be details aplenty"—Lydia looked at her program—"God help us."

Three hours later, Caleb's chin sat squarely on his chest and his snoring could be heard in the balcony. Lydia had napped and awakened not once but twice during President Quincy's two-hour address. But all had been awake for the singing of the new hymn, "Fair Harvard," and all were awakened for the recessional, "Old Hundred."

Even Lydia sang. But soon enough, she was complaining again as the graduates processed back to the Yard. "All men. All men marching. All the time. All men."

"We're invited to the president's levee tonight," said Christine. "That's good enough for *this* Wedge woman."

Lydia snorted.

From the steps of the meetinghouse, they watched the men parade in a great ceremonial circle along the edge of the Common, across the road, past Holden Chapel, and back into the Yard. There, they made another circle and headed for a grand pavilion, atop which fluttered a white and crimson banner.

"What are the words on that banner?" asked Lydia.

"They're not words," said Dorothy. "They're letters. Ve . . . Ri . . . Tas. *Veritas.* The Latin word for 'truth.' "

"Did you hear that, Christine? Truth." Lydia took Dorothy's elbow. "Your granddaughter deserves something more than an invitation to a levee and lip service to truth."

The banquet lasted through eight hours and forty toasts. It was hard to believe that President Josiah Quincy and his wife might have the energy to host a levee that night. But few could remember when spirits in Harvard Yard had been so high, or when the buildings had glowed in such brilliant illumination. On such a night, who could surrender to exhaustion?

Certainly not the Wedges, who went as a family to the levee.

Lydia led them through the door of Wadsworth House, saw Quincy receiving guests in the front room, and made straight for him.

Dorothy sensed that Lydia was up to no good, so she followed, and instinctively, so did all the other Wedges, which meant they came at Quincy in a group.

He was a new kind of president, the first not to have received training as a minister. He had been a lawyer, businessman, congressman, mayor of Boston, builder of a marketplace that bore his name, and something of an autocrat, too, condescending to students and disliked by faculty. His collar was starched so stiff that he had to move his whole body to move his head, and his unruly shock of red hair defined his prickly demeanor so well that portraitist Gilbert Stuart had made it his most conspicuous feature.

"A pleasure to see you all," said Quincy, reaching for Caleb's hand.

"The pleasure is all ours, sir," said Caleb.

"Indeed," said George Sr.

"Indeed," echoed George Jr.

Quincy was standing before a table on which a package was displayed with the words "Letters from Alumni of Harvard College, written in August 1836, responding to the invitation of the Committee for the Bicentenary. To be opened by the President of Harvard College in the year 1936 and not before. Josiah Quincy, President of Harvard College, September 1836."

No one knew that Lydia had slipped an envelope of her own into the packet. Looking at the words and the wax seals, she reveled in her little secret.

Quincy said, "I would thank the Wedges for the service they've rendered the college. And I am especially grateful for the letters they have contributed." Quincy gestured to the packet. "They guarantee that your voices will be heard a century hence."

"Including the ladies?" asked Lydia. "Will their voices be heard?"

Quincy turned to the old woman. "My dear madam, your voice sings in your poetry. I would hope for you to honor us with an ode to the day just passed."

"I'll consider it." Lydia could not deny that she was flattered.

"'Twould be another fine gift from your family," said Quincy.

"We have been glad to give," said George Sr.

"Glad, indeed," said George Jr., who followed his father's lead in most things, as if to express confidence that he would one day replace his father in the most important thing, the running of the family business.

Dorothy had nicknamed her elder brother "the long-legged Napoleon."

"And we thank you for your generosity in this bicentennial year," said President Quincy. Then he raised his glass. "Ladies and gentlemen, to the Wedges."

Once the hear-hears were heard, Lydia raised her glass. "To all who will stand here a century hence, educated by the college, nurtured by her ideas and ideals. Pray that some of them"—she paused and looked around—"will be women."

There were a few more hear-hears, mostly from men who'd had too much punch or from wives who would have cheered out loud, were their husbands not scowling.

Quincy said, "My dear lady, women learn all they need to from their mothers."

"My dear Mr. President," responded Lydia, "until Mother Harvard learns to educate women, she'll get no more of my money. Once she does, however, I will enrich her with a small gift of majestic proportion."

Quincy's face reddened, from his starched collar to his hairline.

And the long-legged Napoleon saved the day by doing what he did best. He turned the talk to money. "Mr. President, we cannot be certain of what will come in a hundred years, but we can be certain that those who follow us will respect us more if we leave them a better library. Herewith, I pledge that Wedge Shipping and Textile shall donate one thousand dollars to the construction of a new library."

"Bravo," said one of the men in the crowded room, and then came a fine soft rain of applause to wash away any unpleasantness.

"And," he added, "I will urge my friends in the Boston Associates to do the same." He was referring to a loose affiliation of capitalists, many of them Harvard men, who were advancing the cause of American business, North and South, by providing the money to drive the mills and build the ships and lay the iron rails.

"Let the gentlemen of the Boston Associates spread the wealth they take from the rest of the nation," said Lydia. "We ladies will become the conscience of the nation."

"Oh, Aunt Lydia," said George Jr. "You read too much of your own poetry."

And everyone in the room laughed. Except for the poet.

ii

Lydia Wedge had not spent her life campaigning for female education. Achieving such a thing would be a Sisyphean task, the work of generations, perhaps unfinished when that packet of letters was opened in another century. Her true battle was against an enemy she believed could be beaten in her own lifetime: slavery.

Every Tuesday, Lydia directed her driver to take her down Brattle Street—the new name of the Watertown Road—across the Great Bridge, and into Boston. There, she would stop on Beacon Hill and pick up her grandniece, Dorothy. Then they would ride to the Washington Street office of the *Liberator*, the abolitionist newspaper published by William Lloyd Garrison and his Harvard friend Wendell Phillips.

In the hall that adjoined the offices, the ladies of the Boston Female Anti-Slavery Society met once a month to hear a talk from Garrison or Phillips, to discuss philosophies and strategies, and, as one husband joked, "to swap recipes." They also hired a sergeant-at-arms to discourage visits from certain Boston gentlemen.

These gentlemen were known as the Broadcloth Mob, a name they earned when they invaded a meeting in search of Garrison. They were, as Wendell Phillips said later, "not rabble, but gentlemen of property and standing from all parts of the city." Garrison had leapt out a window to escape them, but they had caught up to him and nearly lynched him. And all of it was done, according to Phillips, "in broadcloth and in broad daylight."

Why, in the city that called itself the Cradle of Liberty, was there such anger for the abolitionists?

One of the Boston Associates, who himself wore a fine broadcloth cutaway and a tall beaver hat, might offer the answer. He stepped out of a dark doorway as Lydia and Dorothy left a meeting on a September evening.

"Georgie!" cried Dorothy.

"I've been waiting for you." George Jr. was the tallest of the tall Wedges. Of the male Wedges, he had the most and the darkest hair. Of the latest Wedge generation, he had the most ambition and, thought Dorothy, the darkest designs.

She said, "Even the *short*-legged Napoleon would not wait to accost women in the shadows. He'd stand under a streetlamp instead of scaring them half to death."

"Not half to death." Lydia started walking. "I'm well beyond half dead."

"And you've lived long enough to know that the world is a complicated place," said George Jr. "You cannot solve its problems by waving a wand or a pen or a purse."

"You wave *your* purse when you think it will benefit you," said Lydia.

"You mean promising Harvard a library? I did that to benefit the family," said George Jr. "What you did last week at Quincy's levee was unforgivable."

"So you told me that night, with the Yard all aglow and the sparks coming out your ears. You can't be here to tell me again." Lydia took Dorothy's arm.

"I'm here to tell the both of you that Father is very unhappy with your participation in this abolitionism business. And so am I."

"As you've said before," answered Dorothy. "And as we've said before, we don't care."

"I'm here to make the point at the scene of the crime. Dorothy is to resign from this organization, or Father may disinherit her."

"Good evening, ladies." It was the sergeant-at-arms, Amos Warren, a polite young gentleman who wore a gray cutaway and waistcoat, plaid trousers, and a visored cap cocked at a jaunty angle. A beaver hat, easily knocked off, would not suit a man whose job was to scuffle. But Warren was no ruffian. He kept his club discreetly at his side and sometimes entertained the ladies by reciting the poems of Longfellow, under whom he had studied at Harvard. He peered at George Jr. and said, "Is this man bothering you, ladies?"

"*You* are bothering *me*, sir," said George Jr., rising to his full height, which seemed all the grander under his beaver hat. "You abolitionists are bothering all of us."

"He's here to disinherit me," said Dorothy to Mr. Warren.

"The kind of work I would expect," answered Warren, tapping his club against the palm of his hand, "from a man who disinherits twenty percent of America's humanity every time he goes to work."

"We disinherit no one," said George. "We provide the opportunity for honest labor. The Boston Associates control one-fifth of all cotton spindles in America. If they stop turning because of abolition, there will be hungry mouths to feed in New England."

"Tell Father to keep his money," said Dorothy. "I won't be muzzled."

"You can have my inheritance, dear," said Lydia.

But Dorothy kept her eyes on her brother. "You Boston Associates, you broadcloth thugs, you're a greater affront to humanity than southern cotton growers, because you're Bostonians, Harvard men, and you should know better."

George said, "I only hope that our father's threat brings you to your senses." And he walked off through a pool of yellow lamplight.

"I don't believe that Father had anything to do with this, George," Dorothy shouted after him. "You're simply afraid for the world to see Wedge women with will."

"There is nothing that I fear in any woman," he called over his shoulder, "except misbegotten ambition."

They watched him go; then Dorothy looked at Amos Warren. "Thank you, sir."

"You're welcome, Miss Wedge." And he extended his arm. "It would be an honor if I might escort you back to your carriage."

Dorothy looked at him . . . and looked at the elbow . . . and looked at him . . . and at the elbow . . . and Lydia cleared her throat loudly, just to speed this little pantomime along. So the young man offered an arm to her, too.

The old woman said, "Take me to my carriage, then walk Dorothy home."

Young Mr. Warren and young Miss Wedge looked into each other's eyes, and not for the first time, as Lydia had observed. In truth, the old woman thought that Dorothy's interest in abolition had not sprouted until she had first heard Mr. Warren recite "Evangeline." But however she came to the truth, it was good that she was arriving.

Later that night, as Lydia drifted to sleep in the house on Brattle Street, she rolled a term over in her mind: *Wedge women with will.* Rather too much alliteration, but boldly said. Perhaps she had finally found someone to whom she could pass her secret, someone who might not be there at the Tercentenary, but who would certainly be there for a long time to come and who might produce female offspring to carry the truth forward.

iii

In some families, a daughter born after two sons would bind her affections to the elder brother and engage in ceaseless rivalry with the younger. So it had been in the Wedge family when George Jr., Theodore, and Dorothy were children.

Some little girls might have been happy for a brother who liked to play with doll babies, but young Dorothy had always sensed that there was something different about Theodore. Even in her adolescence, she had noticed that he did not engage in rugged games with the boys on Boston Common but spent his afternoons reading instead. Nor did he evince any interest in the opposite sex, except as companions for conversation.

It was natural, then, that as a child Dorothy had looked up to George Jr., a masculine boy with an aggressive demeanor. It was also natural that as she grew toward adulthood, she had come to appreciate Theodore's sensitivity and enthusiasm for the life of the mind, qualities that she believed George Jr. denied in himself or lacked altogether.

Shortly after the Bicentenary, Theodore told Dorothy that he might become a writer. He even showed her the journal he had begun to keep.

She suggested that he should be the Wedge to take up the mantle of Aunt Lydia.

"I would not write poetry," he said. "Novels, perhaps . . . or sermons."

And by the end of his senior year, he had chosen sermons. He announced himself at a dinner at Grandfather Caleb's on the day before his commencement. He leaned across the roast pork, looked at his father, George Sr., and said, "I have decided to attend the Harvard Divinity School."

"Divinity?" cried George Sr. "You'd be a minister?"

"We have a tradition of ministry, Father."

"But why not assist your brother in business?" asked George Sr.

"I don't think he's made for such things," said George Jr.

Theodore, almost as tall as his brother and even more elongated of feature, had also inherited the family skill for stretching himself to seem taller, even when seated. He pulled himself up, looked around the table, and said, "Lydia calls herself the conscience of the nation. I will be the conscience of the family, which has grown in devotion to nothing but Mammon."

"Such offspring!" George Sr. turned to his own father, who was sipping his wine at the head of the table. "A daughter who tells southerners how to conduct their lives. Now a son who would tell the family."

And Caleb, who seldom laughed, chuckled softly. "Another rebellious generation. Though not so rebellious as ours, eh, Lydia?"

Lydia was slicing her pork into tiny pieces and mixing the pieces into her mashed potato so that they would be easier to swallow. She glanced up briefly from her plate and said to George Sr., "Don't forget that you have another son who is already breeding Wedge money and Cowgill wealth to produce many offspring."

"Indeed," said Caleb. "Business, politics, and religion—three children to form a three-legged stool upon which a family may sit comfortably."

"But the politics of my daughter"—George Sr. looked across the table at Dorothy—"is typically female, driven by romantic notions for a young abolitionist."

"Father!" said Dorothy. "That is not true."

"I've seen you holding hands with Amos Warren. And I know that you've kissed him when he escorts you home on Tuesday nights."

Dorothy forced herself to stay in her seat and remain calm. "I hate slavery, Father, whether I love Amos Warren or not."

"Good," said Caleb. "If my grandchildren remember nothing else, remember this: you must step forward. I encourage George Jr. in business. I tell Dorothy that if her father disinherits her for her opposition to slavery, I will disinherit her father."

"What?" said George Sr.

"Quiet, Georgie." Christine spoke for the first time, as if from a haze. "Your father is talking." Then she turned to George Jr. and said, "You be quiet, too, Joseph."

No one told her that it was not Joseph, that her younger son had died of scarlet fever at the age of twelve; all understood that her spells were coming more often of late.

Caleb simply went on with his speech. He looked at Theodore and said, "As for you, I have just one question: Unitarian or Congregational?"

"Unitarian." That was what Theodore said, and what he wrote in the journal that he offered to Dorothy, so that she might read his narrative of his commencement.

If ever I wondered, my mind was made up at the Phi Beta Kappa lecture. There Reverend Emerson, '21, minister from Concord, delivered a message of true inspiration. When he said: "The one thing in the world of value is the active soul," I felt that he spoke to me, for the active soul of which he speaks is nourished by the active mind to which I seek.

The revolution that my grandfather helped to foment in our civic life has flowed into our religious and intellectual lives, too. We accept Christ as our teacher, but we revere God as the center of the universe, so that we remain Christian and yet find our own way, one no longer darkened by the Calvinists' cold belief in predestination.

We live in a time when freedom of thought, rather than power of dogma, will lead to an understanding of our existence in this world and our passage to the next. As Emerson cried, "What would we really know the meaning of? The meal in the firkin; the milk in the pan; the ballad in the street; the news of the boat; the glance of the eye; the form and the gait of the body . . . one design unites and animates the farthest pinnacle and the lowest trench."

We must, each of us, explore the farthest pinnacle and the lowest trench. To lose myself in Emerson's lofty ideas takes me to a pinnacle. But sometimes my own feelings are worthy of the trench. And if I am to be true to myself, I must confront them:

During Class Day, when we danced and sang and rioted across the Common, there came a moment when we played snap-the-whip. It so happened that I gripped hands with my friend Henry Thoreau, and in that touch, something passed between us, a sense of knowledge, and for me, a feeling in the loins that was undeniable. As we began to run in our great circle, I quickly let go of his hand, and so went spinning away.

I do not know what Thoreau felt. I was glad that he disappeared after commencement, as I was saved from looking upon his gentle face and once more into the trench where my soul sometimes resides. But is not the body the seat of the mind? And is not the mind the soul? Do we not have a responsibility to hear the truths that our body speaks to us?

I hear the words of Emerson echo in my head. "If the single man plant himself indominably on his instincts, and there abide, the huge world will come round to him."

Theodore and Dorothy sat together as she read.

They were in their father's home on Beacon Hill, which remained their home as well, despite their father's disagreements with them. It was late afternoon. The tall case clock was ticking in the foyer, the servants were preparing the evening meal down in the kitchen, and Theodore's foot was bouncing, causing the floor to creak beneath his shoe.

"Your writing is very . . . *philosophical*," said Dorothy.

"Do you understand its meanings?"

"I believe that I do," she said, trying to find a word that would not seem judgmental. "You are . . . different."

"And?" Theodore's foot continued to bounce.

"So am I," she answered.

"You are?"

"Well . . . not *that* different. My attraction to Amos Warren—"

"The sergeant-at-arms?" Theodore leaned forward, face brightening.

"His arms are strong, but don't change the subject. And stop bouncing your foot."

Theodore sat back, placed his hands between his knees, and pulled his shoulders up tight, as if to keep his body from moving and his lips from flapping.

"I've heard of men who are drawn to members of the same gender," she said. "I've even seen images of such men on Greek urns in museums."

"What museums?" Theodore sat up again. "Where?"

Dorothy raised her finger for quiet.

Theodore slumped again and asked, "Do you think me . . . unnatural?"

"I don't know what to think," she said. "So I will dwell on things that make us *both* different, for those are the differences that make us more alike."

"You confuse me, Dorothy." Theodore's foot began to bounce again.

She put her hand on his arm. "You and I are different because we refuse to accept old ways in a new world. We hear the words of Emerson . . . or Aunt Lydia. Words that others fear."

"Do you fear my other . . . differences?"

"I shall try not to imagine how they are satisfied. I shall look at no more Greek urns. But remember, 'tis very hard for an unmarried man to find settlement as a minister."

That summer, Dorothy Wedge spent much time with Great-Aunt Lydia. Grandmother Christine had suffered a stroke and could neither speak nor, it seemed, think. This sad fact reminded Dorothy of the importance of trying to see the world through the eyes of those who had been watching it the longest.

So she never missed a meeting of the Boston Female Anti-Slavery Society and the opportunity to sit with Aunt Lydia.

One cool September night, as they left in company with Mr. Warren, Lydia said to them, "You're not getting any younger, you know."

"Now, Aunt Lydia," said Dorothy, her face reddening.

"I'm old enough to know how fast life goes by. Why have you waited this long?"

Amos said, "I do not believe that Dorothy's family would welcome an abolitionist son-in-law who makes his living writing for the *Liberator* and shooing Boston broadcloths away from the door."

Lydia thought for a moment and said, "You are young people of conscience, doing right by the world. As for certain Wedges, to hell with them."

"To hell with them," said Dorothy later, after they had walked Lydia to her carriage and were crossing the dark of the Boston Common.

"To hell with them," said Amos, and he kissed her.

They had kissed many times before, but never with such certainty of their commitment or such awareness of how easily a kiss could inflame other passions.

It was Dorothy who drew Amos by the lapels into the deserted bandstand. It was Dorothy who hiked up her skirt and petticoats, so that he could slip his hand along her thighs and upward to the place where her legs met. It was Dorothy who spread her legs wider to allow his fingers to go higher. It was Dorothy who cried out at the wondrous pleasure as his fingers slipped into her. It was Dorothy who said, "To hell with everyone . . . but us." It was Amos who unbuttoned his trousers.

The wedding took place two months later, which was good because Dorothy Wedge Warren was already a month pregnant. But no scandal arose. Her father never even knew, for she miscarried a month after that.

As Dorothy devoted time to Lydia, Theodore did to Caleb. When Grandmother Christine died that winter, he moved into the house on Brattle Street to watch over the old man and his querulous sister. And he sometimes wrote about them in his journal.

Is this the fate we face? To bicker over meaningless things, like the temperature of the soup or the number of logs on the grate? If I remain unmarried, and Dorothy should outlive Amos, perhaps we shall end our days like Caleb and Lydia, sitting at a table in the house where we grew up, going on about the unimportant, the mundane, or the mysterious, by which I mean the fate of a book that sometimes I hear them argue over. They never bring up this subject in my presence and brush it away when I enter the room. But it is a strange thing they discuss, as though they were talking of some bastard child.

That winter, Theodore grew side whiskers like Emerson's and read more of the Concord philosopher than of the works assigned to him.

In July of 1838, Theodore was thrilled to learn that Emerson would be coming to Cambridge once more to deliver a lecture at the Divinity School. He made sure that he had an invitation for himself and his grandfather.

And from Emerson's first words—"In this refulgent summer, it has been a luxury to draw the breath of life"—Theodore was overwhelmed. But this was not a speech of which most Divinity students would approve, because Ralph Waldo Emerson had returned to Cambridge not to praise organized religion, but to bury it.

From the start, Theodore sensed his grandfather stiffening with anger. Emerson admitted that he admired Christ, but "I do not see in him the love of Natural Science. I see in him no kindness for Art; I see in him nothing of Socrates . . . or of Shakespeare."

"Shakespeare?" whispered Caleb. "He wants Christ to read Shakespeare? Shakespeare should read Christ!"

And the old man grew increasingly agitated as the speech unfolded, sighing and clucking and shifting in his seat.

The Concord philosopher questioned the importance of historical faith, of Christ's divinity, of the belief that God is a personality, somewhere out in the cosmos, rather than a flame burning in the human heart. "That which shows God in me fortifies me. That which shows God out of me makes me a wart and a wen."

"I cut out many a wen in my day," whispered Caleb. "I'd do the same for him."

Emerson glanced in their direction, and Theodore told his grandfather to be quiet.

Emerson went on, rising toward this conclusion: "Let me admonish you to go alone; to refuse the good models, even those which are sacred to the imagination of men, and dare to love God without mediator or veil. Yourself a newborn bard of the Holy Ghost, cast behind you all conformity, and acquaint men at the first hand with Deity."

Afterward, Caleb Wedge said, "It is time for an old Congregationalist to die."

"He has opened my eyes," said Theodore. "I will cast conformity behind me."

And both were true to their word.

Theodore took his grandfather home to Brattle Street, then returned to the library in Harvard Hall, took a seat in the north corner, and wrote out his resignation from the Divinity School. He had planted himself firmly on his own instincts and would wait now for the world to come round. While he waited, he would write . . . a novel or essays like Emerson's *Nature*, or perhaps a history of Harvard, which he would frame as a history of thought and belief in America.

Meanwhile, Old Caleb went out to his barn and said good-bye to all the ghosts who had inhabited it, a few of whom might inhabit it still, considering the dissections he had performed there. He went through the study and remembered all the nights he had talked there with his wife, his children, and old Burton Bones. He said good-bye to the portrait of Reverend Abraham, seated as he always should have been, before a Bible rather than a play. Then he slowly climbed the stairs. And at the landing, he was greeted by a portrait of his wife in her youth.

"Christine," he said, "we shall soon embrace again."

He then went into the bedroom, slipped off his boots and trousers and wooden foot, and slipped into the bed that they had shared for sixty years. It was two o'clock in the afternoon, and the summer sun was hot and bright on the treetops outside his window. He closed his eyes and wondered if he could die.

"What is this foolishness?" Lydia marched into the bedroom two hours later with a tray of tea. "Are you sick?"

"No." Caleb's eyes popped open. "I've decided it's time. I've seen enough."

"Enough of what?"

"Enough of new ideas, I suspect." Theodore came in right after Lydia.

And Caleb sat up. "I spent the first third of my life learning that a man must step forward when the moment demands. I should know when it's time to step aside."

"Why?" asked Lydia.

Caleb looked at Theodore. "If Harvard is letting someone like Ralph Waldo Emerson lecture to our divinity students, I leave the world to the rest of you while I rejoin those who believed in a faith with form and a God with identity."

Lydia set three cups on the nightstand and filled them. "If you're going to die, have some tea first."

And the three of them spent an hour drinking tea and talking.

Then Theodore rose to leave. "Don't die, Grandfather, at least not until the cornerstone is laid for the new library."

"We are all invited," said Lydia, "because of the contribution arranged by George Jr. from the Boston Associates."

After Theodore's footfalls had receded down the stairs, Caleb said to Lydia, "'Tis time for us to deliver the book, now that our family has helped to deliver a new library."

"You've decided to take yourself out of the world, so you have no say."

"Lydia, it should be *my* decision. It was *I* who stole the book."

"And destroyed John Harvard's library in the process."

"You know that's not true."

"But it's what people will believe. I've always told you."

"Our ancestors wanted the book in the possession of the college. So did John Harvard. I won't rest until I've done my duty."

"Then don't die. Outlive me, and you can decide what to do with the book. Die first, and I'll follow Emerson's advice. I'll stand on my instincts. I'll wait for the great college to come round and educate the other half of humanity."

"In that case"—Caleb Wedge swung his legs out of the bed— "give me my foot."

iv

Over the next two years, the entries of Theodore Wedge in his journal were filled with references to the building of the library:

October 8, 1838:
    The cornerstone was laid this day, in bright sunshine. President Quincy, the Fellows, and many others were in attendance. Our father did not attend, saying that it was a day for George Jr. to receive adulation for his fund-raising. Aunt Lydia and our rejuvenated grandfather, however, would not miss the moment.
    Afterward, George Jr. received much in the way of praise. Even Dorothy and Amos Warren congratulated him.
    George Jr. said to her, "None of this would be possible without the hard work of the Boston Associates."
    "And their southern slaves," added Lydia.
    George Jr. turned to me. "These women do not understand, we build a house of granite and glass, so that men like you can build your castles in the air."
    "The airy castles of thought," I answered, "are the bastions of change."

October 20, 1839:
    The structure has risen, a gray Gothic cathedral of learning, modeled after King's College Chapel, Cambridge. Grandfather and I walk around it often, although he walks slower all the time. I have written an essay on the meaning of nature that I have sent to Emerson.

November 10, 1840:

Assistant Librarian John Sibley and I talked yesterday. He said that President Quincy has asked him to prepare a triennial report of graduates, and he needs assistance. As nothing I have written has borne financial fruit, I have decided to accept a job in the Harvard libraries, for what better place will I have to enrich myself?

April 18, 1841:

Today, there is a procession of joy in Harvard Yard, a mirror of yesterday's sad procession. Of which shall I write first?

Why, the happy. By cart, by box, by bucket and arm, the books are moving this morning from Harvard Hall, across the Yard, to our new library. President Quincy says it will be a hundred years before the library is full. I think it may be much sooner.

But yesterday, we went in sad procession from Brattle Street to the Cambridge graveyard, where we interred the great Dr. Caleb Wedge. A light went out in the world. In his dying, our grandfather raved about a book. I asked him about it, but he could not elucidate. I am left to puzzle here at my new desk in the new library.

But Emerson has responded well to my latest effort on the existence of the soul. I must now return to my writing. Dorothy has enlisted me to write articles on abolition for the *Liberator*, my first publication, much to my brother's chagrin.

V

Ancient hands wrote another poem and put it into another gilt-edged envelope. Then they wrote a set of instructions and placed them in another, simpler envelope.

Both envelopes were in Lydia's purse when she rode to Boston for the next meeting of the Anti-Slavery Society. Before she went to the offices of the *Liberator*, she went down Summer Street to the offices of Fleming and Royce, the lawyers who handled Wedge estate matters. She had the gilt-edged envelope deposited in the safe and the second envelope placed among her estate papers, with this codicil attached: "Contents to be passed to Dorothy Wedge Warren, and to her only. If Dorothy is deceased, to her daughter. Contents to be held in secret."

The inspiration for Lydia's decision was the birth of Dorothy's first child, a baby girl whom they named Lydia Diane, born in the house that Amos Warren's father had bought for them on Colonnade Row in Tremont Street.

On a warm Sunday in the fall of 1841, Lydia went to visit mother and child. They sat together looking out over Boston Common, while the carriages clattered by in the street and the babe slept in her mother's arms.

"She is so small," said Lydia, sliding her little finger into the child's hand.

"She is, you might say, 'a small gift of majestic proportion.'"

Lydia looked into Dorothy's eyes and smiled. "Indeed she is."

A coach stopped below the window. As it was a Sunday, the driver was singing the hymn "A Mighty Fortress Is Our God."

Lydia began to hum it, then she said, "It satisfies an old woman to hold such a young child, for I shall be going to God's fortress soon."

And Dorothy said, "I must know . . . is it a book, the small gift you've spoken of?"

"The small gift of majestic proportion?"

"Theodore thinks it's a book. He's always asking me what I know."

"Theodore thinks a great deal. You shall know more when I die. And this child shall know the truth when we are all dead and gone."

But three nights later, the child developed a fever, and a frightened mother sent for the doctor. When he arrived, the infant seemed to be burning from within.

"'Tis an infection of some sort," said the doctor.

"Can you do anything to comfort her?" begged Dorothy. "Hear how she cries."

"Bathe her in cool water. Use ice if you have any left. But I'm afraid that it is in God's hands . . . unless you would consent to bleed her."

"Bleed her? Bleed a baby? That's barbaric."

"It's old-fashioned, and I'm an old-fashioned doctor. Bleedin' sometimes works for generalized inflammation. But bleed her or not, trust in God."

And God saw fit to take Lydia Diane Warren the following day.

When Great-Aunt Lydia heard, she knew that she had lived too long.

Chapter Eighteen

A FEW days after the gallery opening, the *Globe* carried an article about the Harvard Portrait Collection and the restoration of a Copley painting.

Evangeline saw it first and called Peter at his condo. "Have you seen the paper this morning?"

Peter was making coffee. "What section?"

"Probably the Living section. I'm reading it online. I'm in New York."

"No wonder I couldn't get you yesterday. I thought you were going to stay in Cambridge for a few weeks."

"We could use a little cooling-off period. I'm not ready for the whole Peter Fallon experience again . . . at least not the total-immersion version."

"You mean enthusiasm becoming obsession, sweeping everyone else along?"

"It can be fun while it lasts. But it can be dangerous, too."

"I agree." Peter found the Living pages, and there was a color photo of Abraham and Lydia with their copy of *Love's Labours* . . . something. The article speculated on the reasons a Bible would have been painted over a play, and it quoted several people, including Peter Fallon.

"What do you think?" asked Evangeline.

"I think I was right. History is alive and kicking. The people in that painting are as alive as the people in the photos that Scavullo put in front of me the day before yesterday, or the people who were looking at the painting the night before that."

"So you're saying what? Total immersion?"

"I'm saying we have a few more bread crumbs here. I guess I have to follow the trail."

After a pause she said, "I'll be back Monday. Call me here if you want to talk."

"I was hoping you'd say that. I'll call you tonight, after I have dinner with Will Wedge."

Before dinner, a little row.

Inhale on the stroke. Exhale on the backstroke.

The days were getting longer, but the cold could still pierce the best Gore-Tex, especially when the ass was in direct contact with the seat of a little scull, and the sun was going down, and the temperature was, too.

Still, Peter needed to row every few days, winter or summer. Otherwise, he tended to feel sluggish and dull. And when things were heating up in the rest of his life, he needed the river even more.

So he put on the Gore-Tex, the fingerless gloves, and a Red Sox baseball cap, because spring training was under way and this was the year they were going to win the pennant. And he rowed.

Inhale on the stroke. Exhale on the backstroke.

He would start upstream from the MIT boathouse. He would pull slow and steady, pull himself into that tunnel of sensation where there was only the rhythm of movement and the air rushing by. And before long, the buildings would fade, and the four-wheeled world of headlights and taillights would fade, and his arms and shoulders would warm and loosen and seem to lengthen, and his mind would empty of all but the most elemental ideas.

Tonight, the idea came from Emerson: a man should stand on his own two feet and let the great world come round. Peter liked that.

Stroke. Stroke. Stroke.

Or maybe it was Lydia Wedge, channeling Emerson in her last published poem: "We must live like the sage of old Concord, who saw the one soul in us all, / who urged us to find the firm ground for our spirit, / And there, we were sure to stand tall."

Stroke. Stroke. Stroke.

Or maybe that was too many ideas. He put Lydia and Emerson out of his mind and concentrated on the stroke, because he was coming to the place where the river made the big fishhook turn around Soldier's Field, where the banks were dark and overgrown with brush that shielded them from view.

That's where he'd break rhythm and head back downstream.

He was making the turn in the last light when he heard the roar of an outboard.

Outboard? A noisy stinkpot in March?

Only two kinds of people ran outboards on the river in March: coaches for the college crews and mechanics test-driving tune-ups from the Watertown Yacht Club.

But there was another kind of stinkpotter out that night. The dangerous kind, in a seventeen-foot Boston Whaler that was shooting downstream, right at him.

Before he could react, it smashed into his scull broadside, just forward of the seat.

The fragile little vessel seemed to explode, and Peter Fallon was flung into the freezing black water. He popped to the surface just as the boat cut a sharp turn and came at him again.

So Peter dove again into the blackness. As he did, the propeller cut through the brim of the Red Sox cap, and the boat cut so quickly through the water that the driver couldn't turn it before slamming into the bank, bouncing off, and kicking up a splatter of mud. Then it roared into reverse, right at Peter again.

And Peter dove again. And the boat blew past again.

Chest deep in water, ankle deep in mud, Peter tried to make it to the bank, some fifteen feet away.

He made it to waist-deep then tripped on a submerged log and fell into the water.

This was it. Whoever that guy was in his black turtleneck and

black ski mask, he had Peter Fallon pinned. Right . . . where . . .
he . . . wanted . . .

The roar of the engine turned to a scream, and the boat stopped
suddenly, stuck in the mud.

The driver slammed the engine into reverse and it roared again,
backing up, back over the shattered remnants of Peter's scull. Back
into the middle of the river.

That gave Peter just enough time to scramble through the brush
and up onto the bike path that ran along the bank.

Then he heard an alarm on the boat. An intermittent whistle:
overheating. The engine had sucked a glob of mud into the cooling
intake, and now it was crying for water.

And the boat was shooting down the river with the alarm still
whistling.

Peter decided to go after him. Because of the turn that the river
took there, he might be able to intercept the boat at one of the
bridges, and if he was lucky, the boat might overheat.

So he started to run, heading for the Larz Anderson Bridge. He
was in shape to do it. He was in better shape than men ten years
younger. But he was running in his stocking feet, because the
footwear always stayed with the scull.

The boat was leaving a white wake, but now that it was approaching the Harvard boathouses, the driver smartened up
enough to put his running lights on. Otherwise, he'd attract the attention of people who might chase him just because he was driving
unsafely on their river. Whoever he was . . .

Fallon tried to stay on the grass and soft ground and ignore the
rocks and bottle caps. He whacked his toe on the bike path curb,
and he almost knocked over a pair of joggers. And by the time he
reached the bridge, the soles of his feet were like two shredded blisters. But the boat stopped briefly so that the driver could raise the
engine and clear the plug of mud.

From the bridge, Peter could jump on the boat. Just take aim
and . . .

Wait a minute. Someone had died jumping off this bridge, even
if he was a fictional character: Quentin Compson in Faulkner's *The*

Sound and the Fury. They had actually put up a plaque to mark the spot. Only at Harvard.

By the time Peter processed that, the outboard shot through the corner arch and sped downstream. But there was still one more bridge, if Peter could get to it first.

A cyclist had stopped to watch the last light of dusk reflecting off the buildings of downtown Boston. So Peter grabbed his bike, shouting, "I'll be right back."

And he pounded the bike down off the bridge, along Memorial Drive, in front of Eliot House, and Winthrop, and—yes—he was sure to get this guy at the Weeks footbridge, because he was well ahead of the boat again. He left the bike at the base of the bridge, then ran up and planted himself above the middle arch.

Was he crazy? This boat was moving. If he hit it wrong, he'd kill himself, or the guy would kill him.

No. With the boat still coming, he jumped the ten or fifteen feet straight into the water.

Then he started waving. "Hey! Hey! Over here!"

Perfect, the driver seemed to be saying. He aimed the boat at Fallon again and leaned on the throttle. But Fallon was trying to draw him off course, away from the center of the arch. Right . . . toward . . . the footing of one of the three arches.

But at the last instant, the driver saw that if he hit Fallon, he'd hit the bridge. He threw over the helm, scraped the side, missed Peter, and went shooting off downriver.

Gone.

Now what? Peter swam out of the river to face the guy who owned the bike, shouting and waving his arms.

Peter picked up the bike and ran it right at the guy. Then he ran toward the crosswalk on Memorial Drive and jumped into a cab that was stopped at the light.

About two hours later, Peter Fallon limped into the first-floor lounge of the Harvard Club.

He had showered and dressed in a gray suit complemented by a pair of black cross-trainers, which might be more comfortable on his blistered feet than just about anything else.

"Ah, Peter." Will Wedge stood and introduced the gentleman with whom he was sitting. "This is Bertram—"

Peter put out his hand. "Hello, Bert."

"My noted colleague." Lee extended his hand, though Peter wondered, was Lee surprised to see him?

Was Will Wedge? No. It was plain that Wedge had been expecting to see him.

"My noted competitor," said Peter to Lee.

Lee looked down at Peter's footwear. "The latest in fashion?"

Peter let Lee's comment pass, because Lee always commented about dress, maybe because Lee was better at dressing than he was at doing business. He favored the English country look—heavy tweed, contrasting vest, white shirt with blue crosshatching, blue regimental stripe tie, interesting brown suede shoes. He could have been on his way to an afternoon shooting party. Except that there was an unhealthy puffiness about Bertram Lee that suggested he hadn't taken a long walk in ten years.

But more important than all that, what was he doing here?

Peter ordered a glass of merlot to warm him up. He crossed his legs, which made the throbbing in his feet less intense, and he waited for one of the others to say something.

Will Wedge went first. "Bertram came by because he has something that he thought I should see."

Will picked up a gold locket and showed it to Fallon.

It was a beautiful piece of work. Finely engraved around the edges. On the back were the words "From D. to A., With All My Love, May God Keep You." Inside was a hand-painted miniature of a woman almost ethereal in her beauty.

Peter remembered one of the photographs of Lee and Keegan. In it, Lee was showing Keegan a locket just like this one.

"We think it's Dorothy Wedge Warren," said Will. "One of the Radcliffe Eight."

"One of the women who helped to start female education at Harvard," said Bertram Lee. "And one of Will's ancestors."

Peter examined the locket. "What makes you think so?"

Lee said, "I compared this with the portrait of Dorothy done in the 1830s, on display in the Portrait Collection show. This miniature could have been a study of it, or a knockoff. But the resemblance is amazing. Then I did a little research and, sure enough, Dorothy Wedge marries Amos Warren. 'D. to A.'"

"Good work, Bert," said Peter. "But so what?"

Will said, "Peter, this is something that should be in our family, or in the Harvard Portrait Collection."

Lee said, "I'm hoping that we can arrive at a sale before I put it into a catalog or offer it at auction."

Wedge looked at Fallon. "What do you think?"

"I'm no art expert," said Peter.

"Come on, Peter," said Lee sarcastically. "You're an expert in everything. Remember when they brought you in to do an appraisal on a complete set of President Eliot's Five-Foot Shelf?"

"Those were books," said Peter. "Not paintings."

In 1909, the president of Harvard, Charles William Eliot, had lent his name to a series of books, called the Harvard Classics, which would constitute no more than five feet of shelf space and would impart, to those who read them, an education as good as any that could be had anywhere, even at Harvard. This, of course, was not true, but Dr. Eliot's Five-Foot Shelf had become a fixture in American homes.

About 1985, Peter Fallon got a call from one of his clients, who asked if a set would be worth $20,000. Peter had said that they had published so many sets that they were virtually worthless, unless Shakespeare, Homer, Dickens, and all the other authors had signed them.

Bertram Lee had been the bookseller. And he had never forgiven Fallon.

"Are you saying you don't know anything about this miniature?" asked Lee.

"Not enough to comment."

Lee turned back to Will. "I'm prepared to do business at fifty thousand dollars."

"Well," said Wedge, "if Peter doesn't have a figure, and you don't want me to have it appraised, I'm not sure we can do business at all."

Lee looked at Peter. "Tell him you think this is worth fifty grand."

Peter just smiled. "Where did you get this?"

"From a motivated buyer, who came to me because he knew of my relationship with the Wedges."

"Assistant Professor Bob O'Hill?" asked Peter.

The name caused Lee to sit back a moment, furrowing his brow.

Wedge said, "What would he have to do with this?"

That gave Lee the chance to regain himself. "Yeah. He's not part of this."

"Just a wild guess," said Peter.

As if he were taking his toys and going home, Lee bundled up the locket with the marvelous miniature of Dorothy Wedge Warren and stood. "Mr. Wedge, this is solid gold, a superb likeness, an important artist. If you can't buy it, I'll find someone who will." Then he stalked off.

Will Wedge looked at Fallon and said, "Lee is bringing me material all the time. Sometimes I buy, sometimes I don't."

"A wise attitude."

On the way into the dining room, Will said, "You were quoted in the *Globe*. A lot of people saw it. Maybe it will bring a few out of the woodwork."

"Either *Love's Labours Won* is out there," said Peter, limping along, "or Lydia and Reverend Abraham were just enjoying *Love's Labours Lost*."

"What's wrong with your feet?"

"I was chasing someone who tried to kill me tonight."

Wedge turned white. "Kill you? Over what?"

"Who knows?" Peter shrugged. "My quote in the *Globe*. My suspicions about Professor O'Hill and his friend Bertram Lee."

"Are they friends?"

"I've seen them together. Maybe Lee wanted to have me killed before I told you not to buy that locket."

"I'm wondering where he got it."

"Did Dorothy have any descendants that you know of?"

"She had a son named Douglass. There's a picture of him in a scrapbook somewhere. He's wearing a uniform."

* * *

His feet were killing him, so Peter took a cab back to his office. It was late, and no one was there. He was thinking that he would have been happy to see Bernice sitting at her desk, with her purse at her feet and her Beretta in her purse. Things were getting a little too dangerous.

He called Detective Scavullo to tell him about the evening, though he decided to keep the business about the locket to himself.

"So," said Scavullo, "they spoil your good name, then they try to kill you. Maybe I'll have a couple of state police come by and take a report from you."

"Not yet," said Peter.

"Not yet? Attempted murder, and you say 'not yet'?"

"It could have been an accident," said Peter. "Maybe we should let it play out. Harvard might get more back if we do it this way."

"And what if the next attempt succeeds?"

"We won't know who it is until they try, will we?"

After a long pause, Scavullo said, "We should stay in touch."

Then Peter called Evangeline and told her what had happened.

"Like I said this morning, Peter. It can be fun. But it's dangerous."

"Maybe you'd best stay in New York, if people are trying to kill me."

"No. I have work in Boston. I'm coming back to Boston. Nobody is going to keep me from it."

"That's what I was hoping you'd say. Now . . . you've been reading about Dorothy Wedge Warren. Do you know anything about a locket she might have given to her husband?"

"Amos? Her husband's name was Amos Warren. A strong abolitionist. He was killed running guns to free-state settlers in Kansas in 1856. It was like a little prologue to the Civil War. Her son Douglass served in the war, in the Twentieth Massachusetts . . ."

After Peter hung up, he went out to the case where he kept his Civil War editions, including signed firsts of books as disparate in time as *Uncle Tom's Cabin* and *The Killer Angels*. He also had several regimental histories, including that of the Twentieth, which came to be known as the Harvard Regiment.

Chapter Nineteen

1860–1864

"A MOTHER does not show her face in Harvard Yard on the first Monday of the fall term," said Theodore. "Don't you know what the students call this day?"

"Bloody Monday?" Dorothy Wedge Warren sat in a chair opposite her brother's desk, her bonnet on her head, her hands folded on her lap.

"Bloody Monday . . . bloody foolishness. And if you're a freshman, the only thing worse than being hazed is to have your mother—"

"Douglass knows how to defend himself," said Dorothy. "His late father taught him well . . . perhaps—" She was interrupted by the sound of a drum.

Theodore went to his window. Outside, a gang of sophomores were marching behind the drum, and behind them was a cart on which a tub of water sloshed and splashed, ammunition for the water syringes they carried. And another gang, similarly armed, was appearing from somewhere on the far side of Appleton Chapel.

Theodore turned to his sister. "The annual football match between sophomores and freshmen was banned because it always ended in a fight. So now, the sophomores dare to haze the freshmen in broad daylight on the first Monday of fall."

"Boys will be boys," said Dorothy.

"Hazing should be prohibited. The oldest and richest college in America . . . the second-largest library, public or private . . . heritage that reaches to the beginnings . . ."

"You sound like our brother." Dorothy put on a deep voice, to impersonate George Jr. " 'If America must have an aristocracy, let it be borne in the bower of our own of good breeding, good learning, good faith, and hardheaded business sense.' "

"You didn't come here to berate George," said Theodore. "And you say you didn't come to protect Douglass from the sophomores. So why *are* you here?"

"Mr. Garrison asked me to sound out the sentiments of Harvard College on the candidacy of Mr. Lincoln. We may, at last, elect a president who agrees with us."

"It just so happens that"—Theodore went to his desk, piled high with books for cataloging and newspaper clippings for the Triennial Report of Graduates—"a straw vote was taken and"—he shuffled papers—"fifty percent support Lincoln."

"Certain sons of the Broadcloth Mob seem to have developed consciences, then."

"Some have, but thirty percent of our students are sons of the South, and they have their influence, even over our nephew, Heywood, who is usually seen in company with a well-dressed bully from Virginia named Hannibal Wall."

Just then, a roar came echoing off the old brick buildings, reverberated off the new-set granite blocks of Boylston Hall and the sandstone of Appleton Chapel, and rattled the windows of the library. It had begun.

"You and you," shouted the big one with the trimmed beard and stovepipe hat.

Douglass Wedge Warren pointed to himself. "Me?"

"Yes. You. Who do you think I'm pointing to?" His name was Hannibal Wall, and even when he wasn't wearing the stovepipe, they called him Tall Wall. He pointed again at Douglass, then at a skinny minister's son named Smithson. "You, too."

"What do you want us to do?" asked Douglass, who was near the height of Tall Wall, but skinnier, clean-shaved, with an adolescent face, all nose and jawbone.

"We want you to box!" Someone shoved Douglass into the middle of a circle that was forming, sophomores all, bent on punishing freshmen as they had been punished a year before.

"Box?" Douglass turned to the one who'd pushed him. "Why?"

"Because we say so," shouted a familiar voice, and Douglass saw his cousin, Heywood Wedge, shoving little Smithson into the middle of the circle.

All around the Yard, similar circles were forming, gangs of sophomores clustering around smaller gangs of freshmen, giving out beatings and soakings, knocking off hats, and cutting out those who looked compliant, because they would make the best fags.

Douglass had already resolved that he would be no one's fag, no one's errand boy, not even his cousin's.

"Come on, Douglass," shouted Heywood, "take it like a man. All in good fun."

"Yes, Douglass," said Hannibal Wall. "All in good fun!" And Wall squirted him square in the face with a water syringe while all the sophomores roared and skinny little Smithson broke and ran.

Douglass remembered what his father had always told him: "In a fight, go for the biggest bully." So he smacked the water syringe aside and knocked Hannibal Wall's hat off his head, right into the bucket of water.

"Why, you little turd!" cried Wall, and he flew at Douglass, who sidestepped him and tripped him, delivering a sharp punch to the kidneys as he went by.

The gasp of the sophomores sounded like a dozen boys gagging on their own vomit. Wall rolled over, looked at his muddy sleeves and trousers, saw his hat floating in the tub of water, and climbed to his feet, but he must have thought better of fighting, because Douglass Wedge Warren stood with fists as ready as if he were posing for the cover of *Marquess of Queensberry Rules*.

Wall looked at his mates. "Time to show these freshmen the river!"

There was another roar, and students began shouting, "To the river! The river!"

Before he knew what was happening, Douglass was lassoed from behind so that his arms were pinned, then he was blindfolded, and Hannibal Wall grabbed the rope. "Come on, fag!" And he pulled Douglass after him.

"I'm nobody's fag!" Douglass began to kick and curse.

Then he heard an angry voice hiss in his ear, his cousin Heywood's: "Good fun, Douglass. Take it as good fun, or you'll never be well thought of."

Theodore Wedge was peering out the library window. "Oh, good Lord."

Dorothy was still sitting by Theodore's desk, her hands in her lap, her bonnet on her head. Without turning around, she said, "What?"

"They're heading for the river."

"Isn't that where they always head?"

"Yes, but they're dragging your son at the front of the mob."

Dorothy jumped up so quickly that the hoop on her skirt knocked the chair onto the floor with a resounding crack.

The sophomores, maybe a hundred, had managed to corral about half the freshmen, many of them blindfolded, most of them intimidated into accepting a rite of passage that they would not forget when it came time for them to torment the next class.

But Douglass Wedge Warren always tried to live a rule his late father had left him: "Brook no insult, follow no crowd, and never allow yourself to be laid hands on." So, when Douglass could smell the river, could see through the blindfold the little chips of sunlight on the brown water, could feel the boat dock beneath his feet, and hear the splashing and shouting as other gangs of sophomores flung freshmen into the water, he resolved to resist.

But there were four who grabbed him, hands and feet, and they swung him over the water—*one*—then back, then out—*two*—and back—

Then, "Do we let this one go?"

"Some we scare. Him we punish."

Douglass kicked angrily, but on *three* he went flying through the air like a penny whirligig. He heard screaming, laughter, then a splash—himself hitting the water.

In an instant, he was struggling to his feet, the blindfold half off but the rope still tight around his arms. And as soon as he stood, Hannibal Wall placed a boot in his chest and sent him splashing backward.

"Dunk my hat, will you, Dougl*ass?*"

Douglass came up, coughing and sputtering, and Wall's foot struck him in the chest again.

"That'll teach you to strike a sophomore, Dougl*ass!*"

And all the sophomores were roaring now, and shouting, "Douglass! Douglass! Ass! Ass! Ass!"

"Stop this!" Onto the dock strode a tall man with muttonchop whiskers and a birthmark on the right side of his face: Assistant Professor Charles William Eliot, '53. "Stop this at once."

"All in good fun, sir. All in good fun," said Heywood Wedge.

Eliot looked at the student in the water. "Who bound him?"

"Sir," said Heywood, "it's all part of—"

Douglass was coughing and sputtering his way out of the water again.

Eliot ignored Heywood and glared at Hanniball Wall. "Since you're so willing to wet others, you won't mind getting wet yourself."

"But, sir . . . it's all in—"

"Yes," said Eliot, his voice dripping in sarcasm. "All in good fun. Boys will be boys. But boys will not bind other boys, hand and foot, and throw them into my river."

"Sir?" said Wall.

"Will they?" Eliot leaned toward Wall, and as far as he leaned forward was as far as Hannibal Wall leaned back. Wall's eyes shifted to Heywood, as if to ask another Yankee for help with this stern Yankee professor whose port-wine birthmark was turning an angry shade of red. Heywood shrugged, as if he had no help to offer.

And then Wall's gaze went past Heywood, past the knots of sophomores hazing freshmen along the riverbank, to a man and woman watching from the Great Bridge. And Wall's eyes narrowed, as if something had come clear to him.

Heywood glanced over his shoulder, toward the object of Hannibal's gaze, and there were Uncle Theodore and Aunt Dorothy. In an instant, Heywood was jumping into the water, to save Hannibal Wall from the ignominy of helping a freshman.

"I don't mind getting myself wet, sir," he was saying, "since it's all in good fun."

Eliot folded his arms and watched impassively as Heywood fumbled with the ropes binding Douglass.

Meanwhile, Hannibal Wall was putting on his soaking hat, bowing to Eliot, and striding away, with most of his sophomore mates around him.

"Now you've done it," Heywood growled at his cousin.

Just then, there was another splash and another roar from another group. Eliot turned to the noise. "That boy's bound hand and foot. No one is to go into the water like that, Bloody Monday or not." He stalked away, shouting, "Stop! Stop this at once."

Heywood pulled the rope off Douglass. He was not as tall, but his shoulders were wider, his mustache and chin patch made him look older, and he was, if anything, angrier. "You couldn't just take it like a man, could you?"

"I *took* it like a man," answered Douglass. "I fought back."

"I had it all settled," said Heywood. "A little scuffle with a minister's son . . . that's all the lads wanted. Then everyone would have said you were a stout fellow, ready to visit the best eating clubs and have yourself a rum go all round."

Douglass wasn't listening. He was watching Tall Wall leave. "Look at him, bowing to those people on the bridge." And Douglass recognized them. "Good God."

"Good God, indeed," said Heywood. "Your mother and Uncle Theodore, come to protect their freshman. Now, the lads'll make your life miserable. Your new name will be Mama's Boy. They may even brand you a poof."

"Poof?" said Douglass.

"It's what they call Uncle Theodore. 'The old poof in the library.' I don't want that name rubbing off on anyone else in the family."

"But . . . a poof is—"

"Yes. One of those." Heywood climbed onto the dock, took off his coat, and threw it down with a loud, wet slap. "*Pickle sniffing's* the plain term for it."

Douglass remained in the water, waist-deep, unmindful of how miserable he should have felt.

Then Eliot appeared over him again. "You like that water so well, you should join the college eight. We have a strong first boat. We're looking to fill another, Mr.—"

"Warren, sir."

"He's my cousin, sir. And he's skinny as a rail," said Heywood, flexing his shoulders as if to show his more substantial bulk.

Eliot said, "Gangling lads are what we need. Long arms for long oars."

Douglass climbed up onto the dock. "I saw you the summer before last, sir, when you beat those musclebound Irish down on the basin."

Eliot smiled for the first time. "A splendid victory, well remembered. But if you come out, know that it's fun, health, and recreation we're after." Eliot turned to Heywood. "You may come out also. Perhaps you'll both don the crimson neckerchief."

"Yes, sir," said Heywood. "Thank you, sir."

"Sir," said Douglass. "Did my mother ask you to help me? Or my uncle?"

"Your mother?" said Eliot. "I've never met the woman. And your uncle is never seen near the boathouses."

Douglass looked up at the bridge, but his mother and uncle were gone.

"So then," said Theodore as he and his sister walked back toward what was now known as Harvard Square. "Do you still think that boys will be boys?"

"As Aunt Lydia said, 'Boys will be boys, even when they grow into men.'"

"She said many things to remember," answered Theodore. "I still remember the scene she made at President Quincy's levee, though it's near twenty-five years ago."

"All in a good cause," said Dorothy.

They walked for a bit in silence, then he said casually, "Do you ever wonder what she meant by 'a small gift of majestic proportion'?"

Dorothy glanced at him from under her parasol. "Theodore, you ask me that question every six months."

"Someday, you'll tell me."

"I'm bound not to. Bound by a codicil in her will."

"Why did she tell *you?*" Theodore persisted.

"She believed that someone should know the truth."

"About a book? How many nights I listened to Lydia and Caleb argue over a book, I cannot say."

"Nor can I. 'Tis a legacy to pass, preferably to a female in the next generation."

"Female? Why female?"

"Because Harvard gives our males a legacy while, as your friend Emerson says, they deny education to one half of humanity."

"My friend Emerson." Theodore kicked at a stone. "Were he my true friend, he might by now have helped me to publish. He helped Thoreau."

"Thoreau . . . Richard Henry Dana . . . it would have been too much to hope that another great writer would emerge from the Class of 1837. Accept your fate."

Theodore stopped in the street. "You don't accept yours."

"I seek to change what I can . . . the low status of women . . . the enslavement of our sable brethren. But I accept what I cannot control . . . a daughter dead in infancy, a husband dead at thirty-three . . . a son who must grow to manhood and leave his mother . . ."

"Tell me this," said Theodore. "What was it that you intended to do when you went rushing out of the library today?"

"Save my son from those bullies."

"Then thank God for Eliot. He saved Douglass from far worse than a little dunking."

ii

In truth, it might have been better if Eliot had not intervened. Douglass might then have proved his mettle with his fists or taken such a pummeling as would have satisfied the sophomores. Instead, no statement was made, except that Douglass Wedge Warren was a mama's boy and a poof's nephew.

So, on rainy days, the sophomores jostled him, causing him to drop his books in the mud. On sunny days, they threw gravel in the window of his room. One morning, as he headed to chapel, which now convened at the civilized hour of 7:30, he was doused with buckets of water by three sophomores hiding behind three trees. And one afternoon, as he stepped into the entry of Hollis, he was struck by an odor both foul and universally familiar. As he climbed the stairs, it grew stronger. As he opened his door, he gagged.

The goodies had been through the rooms, so the beds had been made. The blankets on his roommate's bed were pulled up tight, but Douglass's bed was neatly turned down, and right in the middle of the sheet was a large brown turd.

One of the goodies, Anne Callahan, was bustling up the stairs. She carried a dustpan and broom and wore a hoop skirt that itself looked like a giant feather duster skimming dirt off every step. She stopped and peered in over Douglass's shoulder. "You must have made someone very mad, sir. Shite in the bed . . ."

The goodies came in two sizes—skinny and stringy, or as broad-beamed and big-boned as the mastodon skeleton on display in Boylston Hall. Mrs. Callahan was among the latter, with a wide face, a small mouth, and a mop of curly brown hair.

"I'm not going to take this much longer," said Douglass.

"Oh . . . take it just a little longer, sir." With her dustpan, Annie scooped up the turd and told Douglass to open the window.

"The window? I want to put it into someone else's bed."

"And get caught doin' it? Don't be silly. Just do as I say."

A moment later, the turd was flying through the air, hitting the slate roof of Holden Chapel, and rolling down into the copper gutter.

"'Tis a fine sunny day," she said. "In a hot gutter, that turd'll dry up in no time."

"What if it should rain this evening?"

"Oh, it won't rain, sir."

"How can you be certain?"

Goodie Callahan stretched her small mouth into a smile. "I been on this earth fifty-one years. The last ten of 'em, I've walked from Boston to Harvard, six mornin's a week, to save carfare. I got a nose for rain. And I tell you, Mr. Freshman Warren, a lad does himself no good stirrin' up a storm over a little shite in his bed."

"You're saying I shouldn't report this?"

"Complain and word'll get out." She took off the sheet, bundled it, hurried out to the linen closet, fetched another. "You'll be called a snitch and get more trouble."

"So what do I do?"

"Act like nothin' happened." She spread the clean sheet and re-made the bed. "That'll get *them* upset. Whoever *them* is. Mean-while, follow the rules like they was the Ten Commandments."

"The college rules? They're silly."

"The rules was meant to go by. No freshman wears a high hat or carries a cane afore Christmas. He don't smoke, even in private. He goes to chapel every mornin' and church every Sunday. And he keeps a straight face, even when he finds shite in his bed."

Douglass thanked her, pulled a nickel from his pocket, and gave it to her.

"Five cents?" she said, her eyes brightening. "You're very kind, sir."

"If not for you, I'd still be wondering what to do with that turd."

"I've done as much for other lads, but never's the time I got a penny. You're a gentleman, sir." She dropped the nickel into her apron. "Now, remember . . . let it pass. But if ever you need a bit of help with these shite-spreaders, my son is a fine, brawny hod carrier with some fine, brawny friends. His name's Daniel. Dan Callahan. I hoped he'd be a college man, but—"

"Perhaps he will be someday," said Douglass.

"Oh, no, sir. Bein' a college man ain't easy. He knows it. Me, too."

Douglass Wedge Warren determined that since he *could* be a college man, he would be the best college man possible.

He applied himself to his studies though it bothered him that most classes were devoted to the regurgitation of facts rather than their interpretation. Every student in the class was required to recite each lesson each day, and the curriculum still began with Greek, Latin, and mathematics, much as it had two centuries before, de-spite the efforts of certain professors. It all struck Douglass as medieval. But he did as he was told and sought intellectual stimulation outside of class.

He found it in the evening lectures of the Swiss naturalist Louis Agassiz, who theorized that a mile-thick sheet of ice had sculpted the landscape of New England. Some students wondered how this could be, since Genesis told of Creation in seven days, but Douglass had been raised in a Unitarian household where such stories were interpreted more liberally. So he imagined the ice and tried to think about the world in new ways.

On a rainy October afternoon, he was standing before the mastodon skeleton in Boylston Hall, trying to imagine an elephant covered in long hair crossing a field of ice in New Hampshire, when he smelled cigar smoke.

A voice behind him said, "An amazing creature, no?"

Douglass turned to look upon another amazing creature: Louis Agassiz himself, his cigar between his teeth, his eyes looking up at Douglass from beneath a great square forehead that some said was the perfect receptacle for his great brain.

"You are Douglass Wedge, no?" Agassiz took the cigar from his mouth and snubbed it out with his fingertips. "Your mother is friend to my wife."

"My mother speaks often of the girls' school that your wife runs in your attic."

"A very hot attic sometimes, a very cold attic others. Very hard work at all times, educating a houseful of girls. But my wife believes they deserve to be educated. So do I."

"So does my mother."

"Good. Now, since you are so interested in this creature, educate yourself. Write down your observations, and you may present your findings in my next lecture."

Douglass sat for three days before the skeleton, because Agassiz sent him back three times, demanding that he look more closely and find something new with each viewing. But when Douglass was done, Agassiz pronounced his work "as fine a collection of paleontological observations as any undergraduate has yet produced."

Douglass had never felt greater satisfaction. Until, that is, he was given the sixth seat in Eliot's first boat, a high honor for any freshman.

And through it all, he kept his peace over hazing and fagged for no one.

By late October, Heywood could tell him, "I've spoken for you. Even Tall Wall admits you've borne it well. I think you may see an invitation to a club table or two."

It was the goal of Harvard swells to join a club such as the Hasty Pudding or the Porcellian, for membership meant a place to gather with young men of like mind and money, to play billiards, to read the papers, and, most important, to dine. Indeed, so many had chosen the clubs for their meals that Harvard had closed its commons, leaving the unclubbed to eat in local boardinghouses.

"I would rather keep eating at Mrs. Danson's than sit with Wall," said Douglass.

"Come, Douglass, peace is the best course. On the campus and in the nation. If Lincoln wins the election, Hannibal says he'll go home to Virginia."

"Good."

"My father says it would be best if Lincoln lost. War will do nothing good for the textile industry."

"In the Warren house," said Douglass, "we hold a somewhat different opinion."

"As always," sniffed Heywood.

Such conversations were unfolding all over America that fall. This one took place in a horsecar on the way to Boston. The iron wheels crunched in the rails. The horses' hooves set up a hollow percussion on the cobblestones. And the high-pitched jingling of the trolley bell mingled with the high-spirited laughter of Harvard boys bound for Boston on a Friday night.

As one college official complained, "The passage of the horsecars to and from Boston nearly a hundred times a day has rendered it impossible to prevent our young men from being exposed to all the temptations of the city."

And temptations there were.

Sometimes Douglass went to the theater, though an obsolete college law still prohibited Harvard students from seeing plays in Boston, not because of the impact of Shakespeare as performed by Edwin Booth or his ilk, but because of the pernicious effects of melodrama upon a young man's mind.

Sometimes Douglass found a corner in the Parker House bar, where he and his chums would sip brandy that burned their gullets and puff publicly on cigars, all in contravention of the college rules. If it was a Saturday afternoon, they might spy a group of Harvard men, some aging in body but all still powerful in mind—Oliver Wendell Holmes Sr., Neptune-bearded Henry Wadsworth Longfellow, Ralph Waldo Emerson, and Louis Agassiz among them—convening for the Saturday Club, an excuse to eat, drink, and expose themselves to one another's brilliance.

Douglass usually spent Saturday nights at his mother's home and accompanied her to church in the morning. He would later return to Harvard with a note from her, stating that he had attended a church, any church, on the Sabbath. To the Unitarians who ran the college, a man's religion was his own affair, though it remained unthinkable that he should not have one.

But Douglass did not spend Sundays in Boston simply to hear a familiar minister. After services, there were always invitations—to teas, to dinners, to "at homes" in the houses of people who were like the Wedges, or liked the Wedges, or would like to know the Wedges.

As Uncle Theodore said, on Sunday afternoons, a man could go from Beacon Hill to Church Green and at every stop see faces that might have been seen on the *Mayflower* or the *Arbella*, hear voices that would have sounded familiar to John Winthrop or John Harvard himself, and meet members of every Harvard class back to the War of 1812.

They were not always like-minded people, for these were contentious times. There were deep fissures among the Republican abolitionists, the Constitutional Unionists, and the live-and-let-live Democrats. And the Boston religion, as they now called Unitarianism, was not embraced by all. There were still Congregationalists among them, and other Protestants, too, though all were united in their fear of the Catholic hordes now crowding the waterfront tenements.

They had names such as Jackson and Cabot, Appleton and Forbes,

Saltonstall, Pratt, Weld, and Wedge, and though they associated in business and leisure, they no longer called themselves the Boston Associates. Oliver Wendell Holmes Sr. had given them a better name. He called them Brahmins, after that caste of Hindu priests who passed wisdom, guidance, and good example to all the other Hindus.

They invested together in shipping lines, textile mills, and railroads. They directed hospitals, banks, and charities. They opened their ample coffers to the college. And they taught their children that from those to whom much was given, much was expected, while also hiring lawyers to devise ever more complicated trusts to protect what they would give from the very children to whom it was given. They were like a great, extended family, and they intermarried so often that the metaphor had become fact.

Douglass did not go to their Sunday gatherings, however, to begin his climb up the social ladder. He was an independent boy who dreamed of seeing the Wild West from the back of a horse before he set foot on any rung of Boston life. But there was a girl. . . .

Her name was Amelia Fleming, daughter of Joseph C. Fleming, of the law firm of Fleming and Royce. She was seventeen, a graduate of Madame Dorian's School for Young Ladies. Her gaze was frank and straightforward, her brown hair was parted in the middle and pulled back simply, and her whole aspect was one of well-read seriousness . . . until she smiled or laughed, and one followed the other as inevitably as young men were drawn to the sound of that laughter.

Of course, young men would have been attracted even if she never cracked a smile, for while she always wore dresses with high collars, modesty could not disguise the endowments that nature had bestowed upon her.

"As fine a pair of bubbies as ever I've seen," Heywood had said to Douglass after Amelia made her first appearance that fall.

And Douglass had warned him that if he said anything so coarse about her again, it would be Heywood rather than Hannibal Wall who felt the power of Warren fists.

"So, you like her bubbies, too," Heywood had responded.

"Mother," said Douglass on the Sunday before the presidential election, "you're not dressed. Are you not coming to Mrs. Bentley's?"

Dorothy sat at her desk, which overlooked Tremont Street. A carriage clattered by on the cobblestones. Autumn colors were fading on the Common.

"I have a headache, dear," said Dorothy.

"But you can still come to tea, can't you? Everyone will be there."

"Yes, dear." Dorothy returned to her writing. "Including that girl?"

"You mean . . . Amelia?"

"On a first-name basis, then, are we?" said Dorothy.

"Well . . ." Douglass knew that his mother had been watching him more closely at Sunday gatherings, watching from behind a teacup as he gravitated to Amelia's side.

"It isn't surprising," said Dorothy. "I suppose many boys know her by her first name. Uncle George says that Heywood speaks of her, too. She must be quite the thing."

Douglass gave no answer to that. In the four years since his father's death, he had tried never to argue with her, never to disappoint her, never to interrupt the uneasy calm with which she went through her days, because he knew that she had gone through many nights in an agony of grief, then despair, and at last a lonely acceptance.

She no longer cried every night, but Douglass had heard her crying more often as the time approached for him to leave for college. So he had restrained his excitement all summer, and he restrained his anger now. He left her at her writing desk, silhouetted in the bright sunlight, in a bubble of daytime serenity as transparent as it was fragile.

From childhood, he had chafed at her hovering presence. When he and other boys had engaged in rough games on the Common, he could always look toward his home and see his mother watching from the window, and always she would question him when he came in. *Was he hurt? Who was the boy who jumped on him? Should she call on the boy's mother and complain?*

And always it would be his father who reminded her that it was in the nature of boys to test themselves against one another. And it was his father who explained to him that their first child had miscarried, their second had died in infancy, and so he should expect his mother to hold her third child close.

His mother no longer sought to protect him from roughhousing boys, he realized, but from members of the opposite sex who might spirit him away forever.

He stepped into the cool November air and went a few doors down Colonnade Row, nineteen joined facades of elegance—delicate wrought-iron balconies supported by solid Doric columns, high windows, fine westerly views. And the names on the doors bespoke the Brahmin aristocracy—Lawrence, Lowell, Wedge, and Abigail Pratt Bentley, another voice in the Boston Female Anti-Slavery Society.

As proof of the premise that this was a very small world, the story was often told that Mrs. Bentley's father, Horace Taylor Pratt, had been Caleb Wedge's first amputation patient.

In the foyer, Douglass found Uncle George and Pratt's grandson, Artemus, deep in conversation about the impact of the coming war on business.

Douglass liked Uncle George. The Long-Legged Napoleon, as his mother still called him, had served as a surrogate father for Douglass, always ready to offer advice, encouragement, and a sense of continuity as the boy moved into manhood.

"Ah, Douglass." George smiled. "Heywood is upstairs in the dining room."

That was what Douglass was afraid of. He took the stairs, two at a time, excusing himself as he went, greeting Mrs. Bentley as he brushed past her, spinning around the walnut banister into the upstairs hallway, and . . . there was Amelia, sitting in a shaft of sunlight by the floor-to-ceiling windows, an absolute vision.

But Heywood was sitting next to her, talking, and she seemed to be listening.

As Douglass approached, he could see it—in her carriage, in her bearing, in her smile, even in the way that her voice trilled when she said, "Why, Douglass"—she liked him. He knew that she liked him more than she liked his cousin.

Heywood made a quick gesture with his head and eyes—*Get out of here, Douglass*—but Douglass slid a chair across the carpet and sat on the other side of Amelia.

Heywood said, "There are some tasty sweetmeats on the far end of the table, Douglass."

"But, Heywood," said Amelia, "Douglass may have an opinion."

"He's a freshman. Freshmen do as they're told, and if they have opinions, they don't offer them." Heywood's words were for her, but his frown was for Douglass.

Douglass ignored him and said to Amelia, "Opinions on what?"

"Do you think the southern students will leave if Lincoln is elected?"

"I hope not. Then who would civilize them? And if they aren't civilized, who will there be to talk their brethren out of leaving the Union?"

"Yes," said Heywood, "and Douglass has enjoyed the southern students so much. . . . What is it they call you, Douglass? 'Mama's Boy' or 'Poof'?"

That, thought Douglass, was a low blow.

But Heywood's remark had the opposite of its intended effect. Instead of diminishing Douglass in Amelia's eyes, it brought her to his defense. She turned on Heywood. "What an awful thing to say about your own cousin."

"B-b-b-ut," Heywood stuttered, "I . . . I didn't say it. The southerners said it."

"Then you shouldn't repeat it," she said.

"Especially," said Douglass, "to a member of the Female Anti-Slavery Society."

"Indeed," said Amelia. "Give me a man who makes southerners mad, rather than one who parrots their silly insults."

"B-b-b-ut," Heywood continued to stutter. "I've made them mad . . . many times. Haven't I, Douglass?"

"If you have," said Douglass, "they seem not to mind. They still let you run with them."

Amelia stood and took Douglass by the arm. "Let us try Mrs. Bentley's sweetmeats." And they left Heywood sitting in the shaft of sunlight, fuming.

That night, a note was slipped under Douglass's door. *Dear Cousin: You may have won a battle, but the war for Amelia will be long.*

But I will fight for her mind, thought Douglass, while you dream of her bubbies.

iii

A few nights later, Douglass Wedge Warren broke a rule. He smoked a cigar. Worse than that, he lit it in the room of another freshman, Robert Lincoln.

Then he hurried through the Yard to reach his dormitory before nine o'clock, when freshmen were supposed to be in their rooms. He expected that tutors would be vigilant that night. High emotions ran higher than usual, because Lincoln's father had been elected president, with what consequences, no one knew.

The trees in the Yard were mostly bare. The leaves crunched underfoot. Gaslight, that wonder of the age, glowed from hall windows and lampposts. And Douglass heard footsteps behind him. He quickened his pace and puffed up his cigar for courage. Then he saw shadows moving from tree to tree on either side of him. And from behind, he heard, "That's a violation, mister!"

It was not the voice of a tutor, so Douglass kept walking, but he clenched his fists.

"I said, 'That's a violation.'"

Douglass stopped and turned to face Hannibal Wall, whose cigar glowed orange in the gaslight. "So is that."

Wall blew smoke. "It doesn't matter to me. I'm leavin'. So are a lot of the lads."

And several more students stepped out of the shadows.

Douglass noticed flasks flashing and cigars flaring, but he could make out no other faces. He said, "Are you there, Heywood?"

"I'm here . . . with my friends," said a shadow. "We're mourning for America, and for friendship between North and South."

"And *you've* been in Bobby Lincoln's room," said Wall, "celebratin' our sorrow."

Douglass could see other figures moving here and there in the Yard. One of them might be a tutor. If he could keep talking, he might avoid a beating. So he said, "What's coming will bring sorrow for us all."

"What's coming will bring sorrow for you tonight," said Hannibal Wall, "because you still owe me a hat, and I still owe you a beating."

Douglass looked around, as the shadows closed in on him, and he decided to run. But he was surrounded. So he turned and punched Wall right in the nose.

At the same moment, he was hit from three sides.

Not only tutors were abroad in the Yard that night. Assistant Librarian Theodore Wedge patrolled whenever he feared trouble. Unruly boys sometimes liked to break windows, and the long, Gothic fenestrations of Gore Hall made a most appealing target.

That night, he made his rounds in company with another librarian, his close friend and traveling companion, Samuel Bunting. Theodore wore a tall hat and carried a brass-headed walking stick. Mr. Bunting was known for his polished boots and his colorful handkerchiefs. And naturally, they were drawn toward the sound of a scuffle.

Theodore saw shadows, heard grunts and hollow thuds as boots struck ribs and fists struck faces. Then he heard the name of Douglass Warren growled out.

"Here now," he said. "Stop this. Stop this at once."

"Stay out of it," said a shadow leaning against a tree.

"Heywood?"

"Stay out of it, Uncle." The shadow sent a strong cloud of brandy into the air.

And one of the others said, "Quiet, you old poof."

"Poof?" cried Theodore Wedge. "Poof, did you say?"

"Uncle, stay out of it," said Heywood. "You'll only make more trouble."

Theodore pushed his way into the gang of students, raising his cane over his head. "Hannibal Wall, unhand Douglass Warren this instant!"

Now, Harvard Yard was not the exclusive domain of students, scholars, and educated men such as these. Cambridge folk passed as they wished, and at that moment, a young Irish laborer was walking by with his sweetheart. He was hoping to steal a kiss in the shadows, but it would not really be stealing, for Dan Callahan loved Alice O'Hara, and she loved him.

Dan also loved his mother, a college chambermaid. A story was told around the clubs of a student who once complained about her feather dusting. The complaint had earned Anne Callahan a week's suspension. It had earned the student an anonymous Saturday-night thrashing in a Boston alley, at the end of which he was relieved of exactly $4.47, a chambermaid's weekly salary.

Not only did Dan Callahan remember slights to his mother, however. He also remembered those of whom she spoke well. So, when he heard the name "Douglass Warren" roared out above that knot of Harvard scufflers, he stopped.

"Now, Dan," said Alice, herself a chambermaid at the Fay House on Garden Street. " 'Tis a fight amongst swells and none of yours."

"No, darlin'." Dan took off his derby and handed it to her. " 'Tis a friend in trouble, even if he don't know it."

Dan was of average height, but he had the bulk of one whose life-work had been to carry bricks in a v-shaped receptacle mounted on a pole. He smoothed his mustache, then lowered his shoulder and, like a huge bowling ball, rolled straight into the scrum. Bodies and hats, cigars, flasks, and walking sticks went flying.

And that small, angry scene played like a prologue to the great conflict ahead.

When Assistant Professor Eliot and several tutors came running to put down the trouble and take as many names as they could, this much was certain:

Hannibal Wall had a bloody nose and another ruined hat.

Eliot told him to report the next day for disciplinary action.

"I need no discipline," said Hannibal Wall. "I'm withdrawing from the college. So are most of the boys from the South. So keep your discipline." And Wall stalked off.

Eliot then turned to Theodore Wedge and Mr. Bunting.

Theodore had blood on the head of his cane, a swelling under his eye, and a smile on his face. Samuel Bunting stood on the steps of University Hall, fanning himself with his red silk handkerchief, all but overcome by the excitement.

"You gentlemen should know better," said Eliot.

"We've struck a blow for freedom, sir," answered Theodore proudly. "Southern boys may withdraw from the college, but we shall not withdraw from the field."

Eliot shook his head and looked around.

A young Irish hod carrier was helping Douglass to his feet.

Douglass said, "Thank you, Mr. —?"

"Callahan. Dan Callahan. I never forget a kindness, to myself or my mother."

"Your mother?" Douglass could say no more, because Eliot was approaching.

"I'm told you were set upon," said Eliot.

"Indeed he was," said Dan Callahan. "Me and Alice seen it with our own eyes."

Eliot did not even look at the Irishman or his lady friend. He kept focused on Douglass. "There are cigar butts on the ground. Were you smoking one?"

"Well, yes, sir."

"That's a violation. The nation may be falling apart, but Harvard isn't. Report tomorrow for punishment."

One scuffler nowhere to be seen was Heywood Wedge. He had gone into the fight and simply started swinging, in the hope that no one would know whose side he was on. At the approach of the tutors, however, he had slipped around to the back of University Hall and hidden in the outhouse, where he stayed on a cold seat, his breeches at his ankles, until Eliot had finished chiding Douglass and the voices had receded.

iv

In June, on commencement day, the descendants of Dr. Caleb Wedge came together at his old home on Brattle Street. They invited family and friends for a collation, but before the ceremonies, they met privately to discuss the family business.

It was not a large group that gathered in the spring of 1861. The descendants of Caleb Wedge had not been especially fertile. His grandchildren, George Jr. and Dorothy, had produced Heywood and Douglass, respectively. Theodore, for reasons that most had by then divined, would sire no children.

Though Theodore continued to live in the house and was, in effect, the host for the day, it was the eldest of the siblings, the Long-Legged Napoleon, who took the chair at their grandfather's desk, opposite the portrait of Reverend Abraham, his Bible, and Great-Aunt Lydia, and delivered his annual invocation about aristocracy borne of good breeding, good learning, good faith, and hardheaded business sense.

He then described the impact of war on family investments: "The demand for uniforms will be of great benefit to textiles, and the need to move men and matériel will serve our railroad holdings."

"Assuming," said Heywood, "that the war lasts long enough."

"There seems little doubt of that," said Theodore.

"Then we can look forward to a positive balance sheet for 1861," said Heywood.

Dorothy glared at him. "You are your father's son. But I'd prefer not to talk about profits. We should be discussing ways to assuage the suffering of the troops."

"No," said Douglass.

And all heads turned. None could remember Douglass ever contradicting his mother in public, least of all his mother.

"No to what, Douglass," she said, her calm seemingly unruffled.

"No to the assuagement of suffering. We must *increase* the suffering of the enemy, even if it means enduring the worst hardships ourselves."

"Ourselves?" Dorothy folded her hands on her lap. She had worked hard to control her fears since Fort Sumter. "I pray you speak figuratively."

He looked straight at her and said, "I am my father's son, too. Amos Warren died fighting for free soil in Kansas. I shall fight for free soil in America. I've enlisted."

"Well done," said Theodore.

"Damn fool," said Heywood.

And Dorothy fainted dead away.

As the guests arrived after that most somber commencement, word passed that Douglass was to be commissioned second lieutenant in the Twentieth Massachusetts Infantry, already known as the Harvard Regiment, since so many of its officers had been at the college: Oliver Wendell Holmes Jr.; J. J. Lowell; Will Putnam; Norwood Hallowell; Paul Revere; Samuel Bunting's nephew Jason;

the Pratt cousins, Artemus II and Francis—twenty-two Harvard officers in all, plus half a dozen medical personnel.

When Louis Agassiz heard the news at the punch bowl, he cried out, "Oh, no. Not another bright young man."

Elizabeth Cary Agassiz told her husband to quiet himself.

"They are going into a meat grinder," said Agassiz, shaking his great head. "We shall lose so many."

As if to answer Agassiz, Amelia Fleming urged everyone in the parlor to join in a toast, "To a young hero." Then, in front of everyone, she kissed Douglass on the cheek.

Dorothy thought that she would faint again.

Douglass turned crimson with embarrassment.

Heywood sat in a corner and turned a brighter crimson with anger.

A few days later, Heywood went to the State House and spoke with Henry Lee, chief recruiting officer in Massachusetts. He asked that Lee assign him to the Harvard Regiment. "For it is time to do my duty."

Lee said, "I'll tell you what I told your cousin: You can't prove yourself until you're in the field. But you descend from a man who fought on April nineteenth and marched with Washington. That's the kind of breeding we're looking for."

In truth, it was not duty or patriotism that drove Heywood. But if Amelia wished for a young man in uniform, he would wear one.

On a Sunday in late August, a train came out of Boston to Camp Meigs in Readville, a gridiron of tents on the dusty plain between the Neponset River and the Blue Hills. The train carried the governor, his aides, and the families of many of those young Harvard officers.

Dorothy Wedge Warren and several of the other mothers had made a white silk banner. On one side was the Massachusetts coat of arms, on the other, the Latin words *Fide et constantia*, faith and constancy.

That afternoon, the regiment proudly carried the banner as they passed in review before their loved ones.

"Who could believe," said Theodore as the drums beat and the dust rose, "that in six short weeks our boys have been turned into officers."

"And who could believe," said George Jr., "that those Irish hod carriers and stevedores could learn to keep step."

"Let us hope that they fight as well as they march," said Samuel Bunting, who had come to see his nephew.

"I think they all look smashing," said Amelia, who had come out with her family.

"Pray that they smash the Rebels," said Uncle Theodore.

Dorothy glanced over her shoulder at Amelia. If there was anything good about her son's enlistment, it was that he would soon pass from the girl's orbit. In those dark days, a mother might not be able to save her son from putting on a soldier's uniform, but she would do what she could to protect him from marrying before his time.

After the parade, the young officers mingled a final time with their families in a pavilion that had been set up on the edge of the grounds. Though the sides of the great tent were open to the breeze, it was hot under the canvas, and the dust from the field puffed in.

Dorothy did not care. She had not seen her son in six weeks. But she was shocked at how hard and angular his body seemed now that his shoulders were squared by lieutenant's bars, and by how mature he seemed now that a mustache curled around the corners of his mouth.

He ran his hand over the mustache and said, "Do you like it, Mother?"

"Oh . . . I'm not the one to ask. Let some young lady answer that." Dorothy gave a little laugh that they both knew was as false as the sentiment. "Now, then—"

But his eyes were lifting from her face and scanning the crowded tent.

"She's over there, Douglass," said Dorothy sharply, "behind you. She's giving something to Heywood Wedge. Apparently, she is as drawn to his uniform as to yours."

"Mother—"

"Oh, darling, enough of other people"—Dorothy threw her arms around him and tried not to cry—"I'm so worried . . . and so proud."

"Father would have wanted me to do this, Mother."

"Yes . . . yes. And he would have wanted you to have this." From her handbag she withdrew a gold locket that she pressed into his hands and said, "I gave this to him when he went to Bleeding Kansas to fight slavery. It was all that came back of him."

Douglass took the locket with awe. " 'From D. to A.'—from you to father—'With All My Love, May God Keep You.' He will, Mother. He will."

"Open it, dear."

There were two tiny clasps. Douglass fumbled with them, so his mother slipped the locket from his hand and pressed on one. The locket opened to reveal a miniature of the young and angelic Dorothy Wedge, her hair raven black, her skin the color of porcelain.

"Mother, you were . . . you *are* beautiful."

She laughed as her eyes filled. "I *was* beautiful. Now . . . there's another compartment, a secret compartment, where you'll find a small sentiment from me."

Douglass went to open it, but his mother put a hand on his. "Not now, dear. Not here. Not ever, unless I die before you return."

"Mother, don't say that."

She put her hands on his arm. "Wear the locket. Protect the sentiment, because it shows my trust in you, which shows you my deepest love."

"I know you love me, Mother."

"And I knew Lydia loved me, but I never knew how much until she passed me a secret codicil in her will. It told of two gilt-edged envelopes and a small gift of majestic proportion. I transcribed the codicil and put it into the locket."

Douglass laughed. "Mother, isn't all this secrecy a bit silly?"

Dorothy shook her head. "I don't know what the gift is, or where. I know only that Lydia trusted me. She wanted me to pass the information to a trusted heir, preferably female. If you have a daughter, pass it on to her. Once Harvard educates women, open the locket. If that never comes to pass, you are to open the locket one month before the Tercentenary."

"Mother, I'm going off to war. What do I care about some distant tercentenary?"

"You should care because you'll be there, Douglass, an old man, like Grandfather Caleb, tottering across the Yard at the head of the procession."

Douglass slipped the locket around his neck. "I'll be in my nineties, Mother."

"But you *will* be there, Douglass." She spoke with sudden ferocity, as if to convince herself and allay her fears. Then she pulled her son close to her breast. "You will be. You must be."

Then the sound of a bugle burst through the din of conversation, and a sergeant announced that the officers had to return to their duties. A great gasp of sadness rose to the top of the pavilion and then seemed to boil back down on everyone. Mothers embraced their sons, while fathers stepped back bravely and stood stiffly.

Soon, Dorothy was swept along with the crowd, back to the carriages that would take them to the train. As she turned to wave a final time, she saw her son and Amelia embracing. Then Amelia handed Douglass a card that seemed to fill him with emotion. He brought it to his lips, as if to kiss it, then put it into his breast pocket.

Dorothy sat in the carriage and fixed her eyes on the largest of the rocky hills above them. And she told herself that her jealousy was no more than selfishness, that whatever had just passed between Douglass and Amelia was as timeless as the Blue Hills themselves. And then she began to cry.

A short distance away, Heywood was also watching Douglass and Amelia. He was still tingling from his talk with her, from her kiss on his cheek, and from the carte de visite she had given him, a beautiful photo of herself, preserved on cardboard, "so that you may carry it next to your heart," she had said.

Now Heywood was seething, because Douglass had been the last to speak with her, to feel her breasts press against him, to kiss her. Heywood resolved to write to her every week. And if Douglass wrote every week, Heywood would write every day.

Neither Heywood nor Dorothy knew that the last words Douglass had spoken to Amelia were "Wait for me." And Amelia had said that she would.

V

The morning mist burned away so that the sun beat down on bodies and broken cornstalks. Thousands were dead, and it was not yet nine o'clock.

They had fought for three hours, back and forth, north to south, in a cornfield where the Federal Twelfth Corps had been decimated and the Confederate left wing had been shattered. Then the fighting had broken off. The field had fallen silent, but for the cries and moans floating on the fetid breeze.

Now Sedgwick's Division, Federal Second Corps, was coming up from Antietam Creek on the east, crossing the blasted cornfield, making for the woods to the west. Somewhere beyond, the Confederates had pulled back. And Sedgwick's Division—fresh, rested, five thousand strong—meant to strike them.

They went by brigade front, three full brigades, each brigade stretched in a line some five hundred yards wide and two ranks deep. They went as if their generals knew the ground and were certain of their battlefield intelligence.

Lieutenant Douglass Wedge Warren marched with the Twentieth Massachusetts in the third brigade. Someday, he thought, some artist might paint their advance as a magnificent moment, paint it and put it on a calendar—banners fluttering, blue lines etching the landscape, bayonets glinting in the sun.

Why did bayonets always glint in the sun? he wondered. And why did artists never paint the blood that turned the corn furrows to red mud? Or the chunks of human flesh, splattered by artillery, squishing now under thousands of hobnailed boots? And what pigment could capture the cries of the wounded, who reached up from the corn stubble, calling for help, grabbing like ghosts at the cuffs of those who now had to step over them?

Douglass tried not to think about them. Better to think about doing his job. In every attack, he concentrated on putting each part of himself in place—speech calm, stride steady, posture erect. He was like a watchmaker putting springs and gears in alignment, in hope that the terror of the moment would hold no more power over him than the passage of time held over the watchmaker.

But so many had died . . . like Lowell and Franny Pratt at Fair Oaks. And so many had been wounded . . . some lightly, like Heywood, grazed by shrapnel at Malvern Hill, some terribly, like Oliver Wendell Holmes Jr., shot in the chest at Ball's Bluff. So many . . . and yet they kept on . . . even Holmes, recuperated and promoted and back on the line.

Neither Captain Holmes nor Lieutenant Warren flinched when the Confederate batteries on the far side of the woods opened up. There was a distant report of cannon fire, the whistle of shells arcing in over the trees, and explosions among the ranks of blue.

The veterans kept moving ahead. But the green troops faltered, a few crouched, a few even fell to the ground in fright.

Douglass heard someone behind him say, "No use duckin', lads. We're a target as big as the town of Sharpsburg. Duck and you just may duck the wrong way."

It was the voice of Dan Callahan, and it calmed Douglass to hear. Callahan had enlisted in the Twentieth because, he said, there were good officers in the Twentieth. The officers now said that there were good sergeants, too, like Callahan.

A shot exploded between the second and third brigades, sending up clods of dirt, sprays of corn, and metal fragments that flew out like shards from a broken platter. Three men in the forward brigade were struck, and the second brigade went slack in the middle.

"Dress that line!" shouted Heywood Wedge, motioning with his saber. "Dress it and keep it dressed!"

Where Douglass tried to lead by calm example, Heywood led with shouting discipline, but his men obeyed. Every officer had his own way.

And on they went, out of the cornfield, across the Hagerstown Pike, past the Dunker Church that looked like a little whitewashed cottage, and into the cool woods.

The underbrush was thin, the trees wide spaced, so the brigades kept their formation. To their left were outcroppings of rock catching the sunlight. Good shelter there, thought Douglass, but the fight would be up ahead, where the trees fell away.

And he was right. Almost as if it had been planned, the enemy engaged the first brigade just beyond the trees, in the next field, bright and green in the September sun.

Douglass watched them go into it, but there was no room for the second or third brigades to be brought forward. So they bunched up behind the first, listened to the volleys, saw the smoke rise, and watched it all as though it were a baseball match.

Douglass ordered his men to stand at ease. No use coiling yourself for a fight until it was time. His men rested the butts of their muskets on the ground and leaned on them, like satisfied hunters with full bags. One of them started to whistle. Douglass glanced at the rock outcroppings to his left and wondered what Professor Agassiz would say about their composition. Heywood Wedge broke out his pipe and struck a match.

And it was as if he had touched a fuse that caused those rocks to explode.

Douglass swore that he felt a blast of heat, so powerful was the volley.

In an instant, thousands of Confederate muskets were raking the Federal lines. White smoke billowed out of these rocks, and the air pulsated with 50-caliber balls whizzing past and striking home, splintering tree trunks and smashing skulls. Instead of flanking the Confederates, Sedgwick's Division had themselves been flanked.

Captain Holmes shouted for his men to wheel left and face the rocks. But some of them were already turning to the rear and firing at will.

Douglass shouted at one soldier to wait for orders, but the soldier reloaded and fired again, and so did several others.

Then Holmes came riding over and struck one of them with the flat of his saber. "Dammit, man. Wait for orders. You're firing into your own men."

"Bejesus, sir, but the enemy is behind us!"

An instant later, there was another explosion of fire . . . from the rear.

"By God, they *are* behind us." Holmes raised his sword, opened his mouth, and a bullet struck him in the neck.

It was the most withering fire that Douglass Warren had yet

faced. In twenty minutes, half of Sedgwick's Division was cut down in long rows, like the cornstalks they'd come through a few minutes before.

It was then that Captain Macy called for a retreat. What was left of the 350 men in the Twentieth prepared to retire to their right in columns of four, at ordinary step, with arms at the shoulder. That was what the official battle report would say. But a report could not express the bravery of those men doing their job—forming their ranks, shouldering their arms, wheeling away, piece by piece, doing it like watchmakers, and doing it all under fire.

Douglass was at the rear, standing straight, keeping calm. Heywood was at the head, waving his sword, shouting at the men to dress ranks, because discipline would get them out. Discipline would keep them alive.

And as the regimental colors moved and the line kicked forward, Douglass saw Heywood go down, face first, a bullet just below his knee. The men around him hesitated, perhaps in shock at seeing another officer writhing in pain, perhaps in thought of saving him, but Captain Macy called for them to keep moving.

As Douglass went by, Heywood called out to him.

But Captain Macy shouted, "Lieutenant Warren! Keep your company moving!"

"Yes, sir!" Douglass knew they had to keep the men in good order. But this was his cousin, so Douglass hesitated.

That was when Dan Callahan stepped out and shoved his musket into Douglass's hands. "Hold this, sir." Then he picked up Heywood and threw him over his shoulder like a hod of bricks. "We can't be leavin' officers on the field."

And out of those bloody woods they came, out of the dappled, smoke-shrouded shade, into the bloody bright sun. But they did not run. They crossed the Hagerstown Pike at the quick step and went into the cornfield, where they formed a line. A unit that held its ground could turn a whole army, and a unit that covered a retreat could save one.

Seeing the resolve of the Twentieth, the First Minnesota fell in next to them, and then came the remnants of other units. And then, like game flushed from cover, the last of the Federal stragglers came running, followed by the *yip-yip-yip* of the rebel yells.

"Stand ready!" said Douglass, reloading his big Colt as calmly as he could—removing the cylinder, dumping spent cartridges, inserting new bullets one by one.

Dan Callahan had placed Heywood at the rear and was back in line.

"Make ready, lads!" shouted Captain Macy.

Federal muskets dropped into position like gears.

Douglass snapped his pistol shut and took a deep breath.

"Give me one good volley!" shouted Macy, riding back and forth behind the men. "One good volley and fall back by company."

Yip-yip-yip! Hundreds of Rebels were pressing the attack, hundreds in homespun clothes dyed butternut gray, as gray as the tree trunks around them.

"Hold your fire, lads," said Dan Callahan to his company.

"Hold, hold!" cried Douglass.

"Hold . . . Hold!" cried Macy. "And . . . *fire!*"

Hundreds of muskets blasted into the mouth of that charge, turning the rebel yell into a great gasp, a moan, a cry of disbelieving shock.

Then Captain Macy cried, "Retreat!" and the Twentieth bugler sounded the call.

Douglass cast one look back at the field, at the hundreds of young southerners who were down, crying, dying, at all those hopes, all those years yet to live, all the love that had been spent on them, all thrown away in an instant.

And that was when one of them shot him.

He felt the bullet go through him, almost as if it were happening to someone else. It entered his chest on the right side, halfway to his belt, and almost knocked him over. He looked down at the hole and thought, for a moment, that it wasn't that bad. Then he tasted blood in his mouth. He cursed and dropped to his knees.

Just as he collapsed, Dan Callahan put a shoulder under him, another Harvard hod of bricks pouring blood down an Irishman's back.

* * *

The rest, for Douglass, was a series of bright flashes and fading images. . . .

He was on the hard floor of a farmhouse . . . there were others around him . . . a veritable Harvard club, one of them said . . . Was it Holmes, '61, bleeding from holes in both sides of his neck? Or Hallowell, '61, leaning against a wall, left arm limp? Or Artemus Pratt, '60, who sat with his boot off and blood pouring on the floor. Or Heywood Wedge, '64, tourniquet on his leg, crying in pain as Dan Callahan laid him down . . .

Somewhere men were yelling . . . guns were firing . . . sweat was dripping onto Douglass's face . . . from Dan's forehead, and it was Dan's voice . . . "Ambulance corps is here, sir. They'll get you to hospital in no time."

There were cracks in the ceiling . . . and smoke hung in layers . . . a black powder stain ran up the right side of Dan's face.

The locket . . . Yes . . . Douglass had felt it when he reached inside his tunic to feel the hole in his chest. . . . Now he pressed it into Dan's hand. "See that Miss Amelia gets it. . . . See that she knows I love her. . . ."

Dan looked at the locket. It was open to the photograph of Amelia, cut from a carte de visite and fitted into the oval space.

The ambulance drivers pushed Dan aside and glanced at Douglass; then one knelt beside Lieutenant Pratt and examined the wound in his leg.

"I'm all right," said Pratt. "Take Douglass first."

"We'll take Captain Holmes first," said the other driver.

"Take Lieutenant Warren here," said Dan. "Captain Holmes can't live. He's shot through the neck."

"But Captain Holmes is alive . . . for now. Lieutenant Warren is dead . . . forever."

vi

The Twentieth was mustered out in July of 1864, their three years served, their blood spilled, and their hearts, as Holmes would write, "touched with fire."

Of the twenty Harvard officers who had trained at Camp Meigs, five remained. To preserve the Union, the Twentieth had taken more casualties than any other Massachusetts regiment, and when it was finally over, of the two thousand regiments in the Union Army, the Twentieth would have taken more casualties than all but four.

Sergeant Dan Callahan was a hero in the Irish districts of Boston. Friends and strangers stood him to pints. His mother cooked him lamb stew on his first day home and invited the cousins. On his second day home, Alice O'Hara invited him to the kitchen of the Fay House in Cambridge, cooked him chicken pot pie, and agreed to marry him.

On his way home that night, he went through Harvard Yard. It was a place he had thought about many times during the war, but not even in his dreams had it seemed so serene, so peaceful, so unreal, as it did on that embracing summer night.

He thought to linger, but for Dan and men like him, there was no longer serenity in silence. It was in the deepest silence that they would hear most loudly the roar of muskets, the thunder of cannon, and the cries of men left dying on the field. And Dan had to hurry away from his own sense of guilt, because so many were gone while he was still breathing, with a belly full of chicken and a life full of promise.

He got himself out of the Yard as quickly as he could, out to the Square, out to where there were people and sounds and the distractions of life. He jumped onto the Boston horsecar and sat down next to a well-dressed young man who carried a cane and wore a wooden leg beneath his trousers.

"Good evening, Sergeant," said the young man.

For a moment, Dan did not recognize the man, who now sported side whiskers in addition to his mustache. "Why, Lieutenant Heywood Wedge. How are you, sir?"

"Glad to be done at the college, and"—Heywood hefted a pile of books on his lap—"preparing now for the law school. And how are you?"

"Happier than I've been in some time, sir. You know Alice O'Hara, maid to the Fay family? We're to be married, sir."

"Congratulations." Heywood offered his hand. There had been a time that he would not have touched an Irishman, but the war had changed all that. "I'm to be married, too. To Miss Amelia Fleming, of Beacon Hill."

And Dan, an honest and reliable man but a simple one in many ways, said, "You know, sir, that's a fine bit of a coincidence, for I've somethin' I promised to give her. 'Twas a promise I made on the field at Antietam."

Heywood's smile faded. "Promise?"

"To give her a locket, sir, give to me by your cousin. A message goes with it."

"What message?"

"Well, sir . . . considerin' the circumstances"—Dan looked out at the horses—"'tisn't one you'd want to hear. A message of undyin' love, you might say."

Heywood's face lost all its false friendliness. "Dan, it will do no good. For her . . . or for me . . . or for Douglass."

"But, sir, 'twas a battlefield promise, and the locket's engraved, D. to A., Douglass to Amelia."

"Miss Fleming has only recently emerged from grief," said Heywood. "To remind her of Douglass now . . . well, take it from one soldier to another. Leave it to the Lord."

"One soldier to another," repeated Dan. To men who had fought and survived together, it was a term that mattered.

Heywood leaned close. "Leave it, and I'll be even more beholden to you, Dan. I'll see to it that there's always work for a loyal member of the Twentieth. No heavy liftin' and a warm place to shit, eh?"

"A fine prospect, sir, but . . . what about Douglass's mother? Should I give the locket to her?"

"She remains insensate with grief. Never leaves the house. That locket would only remind her of her loss, and my future wife would wonder why Douglass hadn't thought of her. Then she would think ill of Douglass. We wouldn't want that, either."

"But the locket—"

"Keep it. Let it remind you of Douglass. Or better yet, melt it down and make a ring of it. Then give it to your future wife. I know Douglass would be pleased with that."

And the horsecar clip-clopped across the West Boston Bridge.

* * *

Dan considered his mother a philosophical woman, one who had learned how to make her way through a hard world with few skills but a strong back. So he told her the story of the locket, showed it to her, and asked her what he should do.

She took the locket, opened it, turned it over. "If I was a grievin' mother, I'm thinkin' I'd want to hear the story of my son's last minutes."

"So . . ."

"But I'm your mother, and I'm thinkin' that what Mr. Heywood is sayin' may be right. Life is for the livin'. And the Wedges are folks who can help you on life's ladder."

"So . . ."

"So, do as Mr. Heywood says. 'Twill be the better way. Better for the livin'. And better for the Callahans."

And that was how a certain locket came into the possession of the Callahan family.

Chapter Twenty

=====

"A LITTLE breaking and entering," said Orson Lunt. "This should be fun."

"If Evangeline is with us, it isn't breaking and entering," said Peter.

She was waiting in front of her apartment on Memorial Drive. It was the end of March, cold and windy, sunny and bright.

"This better be good," she said.

Peter pointed to a book on the seat of the car. "Take a look at that."

She read the title. "*Twentieth Massachusetts Regimental History, 1861–1865 . . .*"

"Go to the page I bookmarked." Fallon swung the car around and headed east on Memorial Drive, so that the river sparkled on their right. "Read the list of officers."

"Oliver Wendell Holmes . . . Heywood Wedge . . . Douglass Wedge Warren . . . Artemus and Francis Pratt, my own collateral ancestors."

"I was looking up Douglass," said Peter, "and I remembered the first time I went to your grandmother's attic to go through the Pratt papers, all those years ago."

"The day we met," she said. "How could I ever forget?"

"There were Civil War artifacts in that attic . . . Civil War papers."

"So?"

"So, maybe Ridley wanted to see you because he wanted to get at them."

"Peter," said Orson, "Ridley's research hadn't gone beyond seventeenth-century commonplace books. He never saw the restored Copley portrait or had his curiosity piqued by a locket. He was acting on hunches."

"Ridley wanted to see me because of my ancestry," said Evangeline.

"Before you gang up on me, remember that there were Pratts in the Twentieth Massachusetts with the Wedges. So . . . let's see if they had anything to say to one another."

"Just remember," she said, "I'm not on a treasure hunt. I'm writing a book."

"But of course you are." Orson Lunt laughed.

Searidge: home to generations of Pratts and Carringtons. The big white house always reminded Peter Fallon of a clipper ship cresting a wave. But this ship had never sailed, and the wave was the granite coast of Marblehead.

"Pity your grandmother's in Florida," said Orson. "I always enjoy her stories."

"Come back in June." Evangeline took out the key, opened the door, and punched in the alarm code on the little keypad in the foyer.

"At least she decided to join the twentieth century," said Peter.

"Alarm system, CD player, too . . . one of those little chairlifts to get her upstairs," said Orson.

"But the good stuff is still the old stuff." Evangeline led them up to the first landing, where they looked into the face of Horace Taylor Pratt, another Copley portrait. Once, the original had hung there. Now it was a large Polaroid reproduction. The original was on loan to the Boston Museum of Fine Arts.

Peter hadn't been in that attic in over twenty years, but attics don't change much. There was a new spiral staircase rising to the trapdoor and the widow's walk on the roof. The rest was a jumble, just as it had been twenty years earlier—clothes, furniture, piles of books, steamer trunks, metal boxes and filing cabinets filled with family papers, an old sword hanging from a rafter.

"Tell me again why your grandmother never let us go through this attic and conserve these things," said Orson.

"She's old," said Evangeline.

"So are all these things." Orson examined the sword.

"I'm just thankful we could persuade her to send the Copley to the museum. As for the rest of this stuff, she says it's like having family members in the house. If she wants to visit them, she can just come right up."

"She doesn't strike me as the eccentric sort," said Orson.

"She also says the longer it sits here, the more valuable it gets, like real estate."

Peter went picking through the junk.

Orson flipped open a steamer trunk and looked in.

Evangeline said, "Those are old family Bibles."

Orson lifted out the Bible on top.

"That's the one from the twentieth century. It was begun by my grandmother's father, George. He was the son of Artemus II, the one at Antietam. He died on the *Titanic*. There are three more Bibles there, from the 1600s on," said Evangeline. "Grandmother always said they were too big to keep downstairs. One Bible was enough."

"Worry about Bibles later," said Peter. "Here's what we came for." He pointed to a metal box. There was a label on it: ARTEMUS PRATT II. Peter pulled out a folder of correspondence, all yellowed pages crumbling around the edges.

Soon he and Evangeline were sitting in the dormer at the front of the attic, with several piles of ancient papers spread out around them.

"Here we go," said Peter. "Dated August twenty-first, 1861. 'Dear Father, I am proud to say the regiment is well trained, and the family is invited to see the effects of six weeks' drilling Sunday next at one o'clock. Bring everyone to see how brave we look under our banners. The Rebels will surely run at the first sight of us.'"

"Young men are so full of confidence when they go off to war," said Orson.

Then something dropped out of the packet. It was a sepia-tinted image of a young woman seated against a curtained background in some ancient photographic studio.

"A c.d.v.," said Orson.

"A what?" asked Evangeline.

"Carte de visite. A nice collectible." Peter turned over the cardboard-backed image. "To brave Lieutenant Artemus, God Bless You and Keep You, Amelia Fleming."

"That's the girl who married Heywood Wedge." Evangeline slipped the carte from Peter's hands and looked at it more closely.

"I guess she liked young Pratt, too," said Orson.

Peter read on through the letters, written once a week from Artemus Pratt to his father. They described the trip south, tenting on the Potomac, "the strange southern world of pic-a-ninny Washington," and the bloody horror of Ball's Bluff.

Then Orson said, "With a little editing, we have a publishable manuscript here."

"I might do it myself," said Evangeline.

"Well, you'll need your strength," said Orson. "And I know of a marvelous little Marblehead boîte where they make the most divine fried clams. Strictly take-out. While you two read on, I'll go get three orders for lunch."

"Make mine fried scallops," said Evangeline.

"Get some onion rings, too." Peter threw him the keys.

"What's the alarm code?" asked Orson.

"I left it off," said Evangeline.

"Fine. I won't be long."

By the time Orson drove off, they were back to reading Pratt's letters, all through the horrors of the Peninsula Campaign in the spring of 1862, all of it fascinating, but few mentions of Lieutenants Warren and Wedge, or the girl in the carte de visite.

Then Evangeline found it: " 'September eighteenth, 1862. I write from a farmhouse in Keedysville, Maryland, now a field hospital for officers of the Twentieth. I have survived a bloody day with a wound in the calf. Holmes is here, miraculously alive despite being shot through the neck. Neddy Hallowell lies incoherent from fever and infection. Heywood Wedge had his leg amputated below the knee and bears it bravely. The maggots have not yet found his stump. But poor Douglass Wedge Warren has—'"

"Did you hear that?"

Evangeline looked up from the reading. "What?"

"Someone's in the house."

"Orson?"

Peter went to the dormer and looked down. No car. Not Orson.

Evangeline went to speak but fell silent when Peter pointed to the staircase. *Footfalls.* Two sets, climbing the stairs. It sounded as if they stopped a moment in front of the portrait of Horace Pratt. Maybe they were trying to decide if they should steal it. Then they continued up.

"They're going through the house," said Evangeline.

"Room by room."

Evangeline's eyes widened at the sound of drawers being pulled and contents dumped in the room right below her.

"Make that dresser by dresser," he said.

She gestured to the staircase that led to the widow's walk. "We could hide on the roof."

"Been there. Done that," said Peter, recalling his last visit to this attic. "What happens when Orson comes back?"

"But what if these guys are armed?"

He pulled out his cell phone and handed it to her. "Call nine-one-one. But whisper." Then he tiptoed to the top of the stairs.

Before she could dial, the door from the second floor to the attic stairs opened.

"Do you think there's anything up there?" whispered one guy.

"Could be shit up there. Could be what we're lookin' for, too."

Peter looked at Evangeline and mouthed the words "lookin' for?"

Then the two young men started up the narrow staircase.

Peter put a finger to his lips, then he turned to the rafter behind him and carefully lifted the sword, scabbard and all, from the peg on which it hung.

Evangeline shook her head. What if they had a gun? But the top of one of the heads was appearing now, wearing a Boston Bruins cap.

Peter yanked at the hilt, expecting the sword to swing out of the scabbard with a resounding *thwang*. But it wouldn't budge.

And now, the guy in the Bruins cap was looking right at them.

"Oh, God," said Evangline.

"What the fuck?" The guy in the Bruins cap: Jackie Pucks.

"People!" cried the other one, a little guy with a ring in his eyebrow. "You said the people left."

"They did," cried Jackie. "Or at least their car left."

Peter knew these guys were more surprised than he was. So he pulled back the sword, scabbard and all, and held it ready to strike. "Stop right there."

"Yeah," said Evangeline, pressing the buttons on the phone. "The police are on the way." Except that she dropped the phone.

"Let's get the fuck out of here." The little guy turned and went stumbling down the stairs.

Jackie Pucks would have been right behind him, except that Evangeline bent down to grab the phone, and Jackie grabbed for it first. So Peter smashed the sword down on Jackie's wrist and sent him tumbling back.

Peter went after him.

And Evangeline called the police.

But as Peter burst out the door to the attic stairway, he was met by a fist in the belly, then another off the side of the head.

He stumbled back into the stairwell, the door was slammed shut, and a deadbolt was thrown from the other side, locking them into the attic.

By the time the police got them out, Orson had returned and Peter and Evangeline had their stories straight: They had come to the house to do some cataloging work for Evangeline's grandmother. They left the alarm off, and someone sneaked in, thinking that the house was empty. Peter persuaded Evangeline that they should not mention that he recognized one of them.

She demanded a reason, of course.

"Because somebody put those guys on our tail. And somebody

tried to run me down in the river. It's all connected to *Love's Labours*. I need to find out how. When it's time for police, I'll know who to turn to."

"I could stop this right now," she said. "Just blow the whistle."

He slipped his arm around her. She was still shaking from the fight. He held her tight and whispered, "Do you really want to do that?"

"Remember, Peter, I'm writing a book . . . about the Radcliffe Eight."

"So let's get back to reading about Dorothy's son. Maybe he was an inspiration."

While the local police dusted for fingerprints (though both intruders had been wearing gloves), Peter, Evangeline, and Orson ate their fried seafood feast, and Evangeline finished the letter from Artemus Pratt.

"'Douglass Wedge Warren died the day of the battle. I saw him put a locket into the hands of Sergeant Callahan and whisper several words to him before expiring. Whether he intended to return the locket to his mother, send it to someone else, or give it to Callahan for his brave services during the battle, I do not know.'"

"So," said Fallon. "The locket passed to someone named Callahan."

"How did Bertram Lee get it?" asked Orson.

"I don't know. But I think it's time to ask Mr. Keegan."

"Are you sure you want to do that?" asked Evangeline.

Peter Fallon and his brother, Danny, stepped out of a bright March afternoon and into the drinker's darkness. Half a dozen sets of eyes looked up from their boilermakers.

Peter hadn't been in the Rising Moon Pub in twenty years. "Just as I remembered it," he whispered to Danny. It was still the same narrow, crowded dump, with a row of booths along one wall and a few tables in the middle of the floor, and still that smell—stale beer mingled with the essence of urine-soaked disinfectant cake and well-done pastrami grease.

"Don't ask for any fuckin' French wine," said Danny out of the corner of his mouth. "Beer only. And drink from the bottle."

They sat at the bar.

"Danny Fallon," said the bartender, an ex-con called Smithy, not because Smith was his name but because of his forearms, which were the size of Peter's thighs. "Haven't seen you in a while. Come in to drink with the men?"

"Bingo?" said Danny.

"You mean 'bingo' like, 'Yeah, Smithy, I'm here to drink with the men'? Or 'Bingo' like 'Mr. Keegan'?"

Danny said, "I want to talk to Mr. Keegan."

Peter noticed a black raincoat hanging from the hook on the last booth, and just visible above the seat back was a Bruins cap and a pair of eyes. Jackie Pucks.

Peter told his brother, "Stay here."

"Be polite," said Danny.

"Yeah," said Smithy, "we got good fuckin' manners in here."

As Peter approached the back booth, Jackie stood. There was a mirror over Jackie's head, so the guy seated opposite him could see everyone who came in or out without turning around. Jackie looked down, nodded at something the guy said, then stepped over to the bar.

Peter did not say a word to the young thug. He just sat down and looked James "Bingo" Keegan in the eye.

Keegan was wearing a gray scally cap, a white dress shirt open at the collar, and a plaid vest sweater with three lottery tickets sticking out of a pocket. A cup of black coffee, a pack of Camels, and a silver cigarette lighter were spread on the table in front of him.

"So"—Keegan smiled, revealing teeth as gray as his cap—"the saints are singing your name."

"You know who I am?"

"Big Jim Fallon's kid, gone all Back Bay on us. What are you drinkin'?"

"Coffee."

"You sure? Maybe Smithy has a bottle of Olivier LaFlaive Puligny-Montrachet 'ninety-six back there. If he doesn't, I know where I could get my hands on a few cases. What's that wine go for these days, about seventy bucks a bottle?"

"Eighty. You have a wide range of interests, Mr. Keegan," said Peter. "And you pronounce your French quite well."

"*Merci.*" Keegan gestured to Smithy for another coffee, which appeared on the table in front of Fallon, in the bandaged hand of Jackie Pucks.

Fallon ignored the coffee—and the hand—and said to Keegan, "Why are you so interested in me that you know I like white Burgundies?"

"Local boy made good. That interests everyone."

"Enough to be causing me trouble since October?"

"Trouble?"

"You followed me home one night last fall."

"Me? Follow you?" Keegan's bemused expression did not change.

"Well, someone borrowed your scally cap and your raincoat, then. And someone tried to run me down in the Charles River a few days ago. And one of your boys broke into a house in Marblehead this morning."

"I heard about that."

"Word travels fast."

Keegan took a measured sip of coffee. Then he said, in the same pleasant tone, "Peter Fallon, who the fuck do you think I am, some mailman, all done with my route, killin' an afternoon in here before I go home to the wife? If somethin' happens around me that I should know about, I know about it . . . usually before it happens."

Fallon glanced toward his brother.

"Don't look for backup," said Keegan. "I'm not gonna hurt you, unless you're interferin' with somethin' that matters to me."

"I deal in rare books and documents."

"Some of the guys who work for me can't even read." Keegan slipped a cigarette from the pack, put it in his mouth, and lit it, all without taking his eyes from Fallon's face. "Rare books mean less to me than rare steaks."

"So what does interest you?"

Keegan blew smoke out the corner of his mouth. "Money."

"Money interests everyone," said Fallon. "I can see where there's money knocking over old houses in Marblehead, but running down guys on the river? Or ruining an honest bookseller's reputation?"

"I don't think anyone could ruin the reputation of a guy who once made good on a quarter-million-dollar loss." Keegan took another puff and placed the cigarette on his saucer. "The river stuff, whoever did that to a smart guy like you should be told to stop. As for a little B and E on the North Shore . . . rich old bags go south for the winter, and poor boys from the neighborhoods go north for opportunity."

"What do you think they were after when they broke in?"

"The good stuff, I guess. Don't pay to waste time stealin' DVD players when you can get Oriental rugs and oil paintings."

Fallon looked at Jackie Pucks, who was now sitting at the end of the bar, watching ESPN. "How's the wrist, there, Jackie?"

Jackie put his bandaged wrist under the bar so that no one could see it.

When Peter looked across the table again, Keegan was smiling. "I like your style, Fallon. A smart guy. Figured it all out back in the fall, or so I've heard, even if Wednesday's *Globe* says you got it all wrong. And a good father, from what I can see."

Peter didn't like that remark. Way too personal. "How would you know what kind of father I am?"

On the seat beside him, Keegan had a *Racing Form,* a *Boston Globe,* and a folder. He flipped open the folder and took out a photograph of Peter on the steps of Widener.

"We were watchin' you to see what you found out at the Bleen House, and who you gave it to. Had my boy in the Harvard windbreaker follow you on a Crimson Key tour."

"Like you said, nothing happens around here that you don't know about." Fallon stood. "Just do me one favor. Stay away from my son."

"Agreed." Keegan took another long drag on his cigarette. "But one favor for another. This business with Jackie Pucks . . . Jackie's my sister's boy, and you know how nephews can be. I'd take it as a personal favor if you kept the police out of this."

Fallon leaned his hands on the table. "If you can tell me he had nothing to do with the death of Ridley Royce, I'll say nothing about Jackie Pucks."

"That I can guarantee."

Peter started to leave, then he turned back to Keegan. "Since you know about everything that happens around here, what do you know about an old locket that just came on the market?"

Keegan blew smoke through his nose and laughed. "Rare books, lockets . . . you must think I want to run an antique shop instead of a bar. You thinkin' of sellin' yours?"

"Not this year," said Peter. "But if I ever do, I'll call you."

Keegan laughed again. "Not only are you a smart guy, you're a smartass, too."

Danny Fallon didn't say anything until they were back in the car, heading down West Broadway. "He's too dangerous to fuck with, Peter."

"Maybe, but after talking to him, I feel a little safer. He knows that I know how to find this play better than anybody else in the game. So I'm safe for a while."

"For a while, but remember Billy Gallagher. He inherited the Risin' Moon. Always wanted to own a bar. Then Keegan come along. Offered a price. Billy said no. So Keegan come back the next day and offered ten percent less. Billy said no. So Keegan come back the next day with Smithy and offered *another* ten percent *less* and said that if Billy didn't sell, he'd lose ten percent a day until *he* owed *Keegan* money. Next thing, Billy's movin' to Florida and Bingo's doin' business in the back booth. Whatever he wants, he gets. If he wants this book, he'll get that, too, whether you lead him to it or not."

"Puligny-Montrachet," said Peter.

"What?"

"He told me he knew where he could get a case of Puligny-Montrachet. He's probably got it in the basement."

"Yeah . . . along with a few fuckin' bodies."

While Peter was having coffee, Evangeline and Orson went back to the Newbury Street office and waited. And looked for distractions.

For Orson, there were three crates of books.

Evangeline held up a folder of papers. "I have some reading." She had taken the letters of Artemus Pratt II with her, because after the war, her great-great-grandfather had returned to Boston to move in the same circles as many of the women who helped found Radcliffe. Artemus might now have something to tell her about that world.

She had not read far before she came to his description of the third day at Gettysburg:

When Lee's bombardment began, the Twentieth was on Cemetery Ridge, and it was as if the heavens had opened and let hell fall out. There was nothing to do but lay down and endure it.

Then, they came on, fifteen thousand Virginians, marching out of the woods by brigade front, at parade step, marching bravely and beautifully, right into our guns—the rifled cannon firing exploding shot, then the muskets, finally the canister. At the critical moment, when the Virginians breached our lines, our regiment went in smartly, smashing into their flank.

What had begun as a scene of battlefield majesty ended as a dirty street fight, with men clubbing, punching, biting, bayoneting, and shooting at close range. By God's mercy this swirl of blood and horror ended in victory, as the southerners one by one and then in groups came to realize that there were no longer enough of them to carry the attack and threw down their arms.

Afterward, we tended the wounded and I heard someone calling my name. A Confederate lieutenant lay against the wall, a circle of red widening on his belly. He asked if I were not Pratt of Harvard. I recognized him as Hannibal Wall, '63. He asked after the others in the regiment. How fared Heywood Wedge? Wounded and mustered out, I said. Jason Bunting? Somewhere on the field, I said. And stubborn Douglass Warren? Dead, I said, and gone to his reward.

Wall said he'd known he was going against the Twentieth that day and was hoping to squash Warren's hat. He reckoned now that they could squash each other's hats in the hereafter. He then reached for his own red forage cap, which lay in the dust. I placed it in his hand, leaving him to place it on his head. His last words were, "Had we known, we might have been better friends. So many have died . . . so many."

So many, indeed. In our own unit, our dear friend Paul Revere, '62, was killed today. And young Lieutenant Bunting, '61, lost his head during the bombardment.

Thanks be to God that you do not need to mourn for me, but in the Wall house, the Revere house, and the Bunting house, there will be sadness. In Harvard Yard, the elms and old men will weep. And in Gore Hall, where Samuel Bunting and Theodore Wedge spoke so proudly of their nephews, they will weep again, as they did, I'm sure, over the death of Douglass.

Evangeline wrote down the name Samuel Bunting, for no other reason but that he was a friend of Theodore Wedge. As Peter had taught her . . . it could mean nothing. It could mean everything.

And though she did not say so to Orson and wouldn't say so to Peter, she was starting to enjoy this.

Chapter Twenty-one

=====

1872–1898

"TEN YEARS since we heard the news from Antietam," said Dorothy Wedge Warren one bright September afternoon.

"Your son had true gifts," said Louis Agassiz. "We shall never stop mourning."

Elizabeth Cary Agassiz took Dorothy's hand. "We are just glad to see you again."

"It's time to enter the world again." Dorothy and Theodore stood on the veranda of the Agassiz home after lunching with their old friends.

Theodore took out his watch and popped it open. "I'm afraid we must be off. The president doesn't like to be kept waiting."

"A frank talk with President Eliot on the matter of female education seems a good way to announce myself again," added Dorothy.

Mrs. Agassiz, a heavyset woman with a quick laugh and lively eyes, said, "Remind him, as I often do, of the success we enjoyed in our girls' school."

"And remind him that the work was exhausting." The old professor lit his cigar. "Now we leave it to Gilman at his Cambridge School for Girls."

"That's a preparatory school," said Dorothy. "Girls need college experience."

"Ah, yes . . . college experience." Professor Agassiz pointed across Quincy Street to a triangle of land called the Delta. "Once, our young men enjoyed college experiences over there, on a field that echoed with the sounds of games and competition. Now we build their monument on the very grass."

The monument was called Memorial Hall. It honored Harvard's Union dead. And though it was shrouded in scaffolding, the Gothic majesty of it had moved Dorothy to tears when she looked upon it for the first time, earlier that day.

"I would prefer the shouts of college boys to the clatter of construction," said Agassiz sadly.

"So would I," said Dorothy, and she felt herself moved to tears once more, so she made a quick good-bye and hurried down the steps.

Soon, she and Theodore were walking along Cambridge Street.

Looking up at Memorial Hall, Dorothy said, "Heywood was right."

"About what?" asked Theodore.

"In his fund-raising letter, he wrote, 'The mighty tower will surge into the sky like a column of soldiers marching to their rightful reward.' And I see it, Theodore. I see it."

"I think that losing a leg drained Heywood of his bile."

"Perhaps it was his marriage to Amelia." Dorothy dabbed her eyes. "In any event, his efforts to build Memorial Hall will stand us in good stead with President Eliot."

"Eliot is a hard nut, you know," said Theodore.

"So am I."

Theodore was not so certain of that.

After Douglass's death, Dorothy had not left her house for three years, except to attend memorial services for other young men who had fallen. It had taken her four years more to come to Cambridge for the inauguration of Charles William Eliot. And Eliot's speech had been enough to keep her away for two years more.

On that day, the stiff-spined new president, just thirty-five, had stepped before an audience in the Unitarian Meeting House and outlined his vision for a style of education that would challenge young men rather than restrain them.

"Until recently," he had intoned, "all students at this college passed through one curriculum. Every man studied the same subjects in the same proportions, without regard to his natural bent or preference—one primer, one catechism, one rod for all children."

"But the new elective system," Eliot had continued, "gives free play to natural preferences and inborn aptitudes. It relieves the professor of students compelled to an unwelcome task by substituting lessons given to small, lively classes. We will persevere in our efforts to establish, improve, and extend this new system."

And the applause had poured forth.

"You may not have felt it," Theodore had whispered to his sister, "but the academic world just moved beneath our feet."

Dorothy had felt it but had restrained her applause, hoping that if Eliot would slip the bonds from the minds of young men, he might do the same for young women.

Then Eliot had come to the matter of female education: "The world knows next to nothing about the natural mental capacities of the female sex. Only after generations of civil freedom and social equality will it be possible to obtain the data necessary for an adequate discussion of women's natural tendencies, tastes, and capabilities. . . ."

And that had been enough for Dorothy. Rising conspicuously in her black dress, she had stepped over several people in her pew and bustled out. She had stopped by the burying ground just long enough to listen for the sound of Lydia spinning in her grave. Then she had boarded a Boston horsecar, resolving not to set foot in Cambridge again until Eliot's term had ended.

But now she was back, a fact very much on her brother's mind as they came into the Yard. He said, "It's good to see you wearing colored clothes again, Dorothy. A crimson dress flatters you."

"Crimson is the Harvard color, is it not?"

"Ever since Eliot gave his rowers crimson neckerchiefs."

"Yes. I remember. Douglass wore one."

"But, Dorothy"—Theodore stopped in the shade of an elm and

looked into his sister's slender face, as heavy with lines as his own—
"why now?"

"A decade in black is enough." She spoke with the calm confidence that she had always tried to maintain, even in grief.

"You haven't shed your widow's weeds in honor of the elective system. Does this have to do with the birth of a baby girl, even if it *is* Heywood's?"

"I've made a deposit toward the child's education in the Back Bay Institute for Savings. But women should not have to wait through 'generations of civil freedom and social equality' before Eliot decides we're worth educating. Without education, we'll have neither the freedom nor the equality."

"But why now? Was there something in the envelope from Aunt Lydia? A gift you must distribute now, perhaps?"

Dorothy smiled. "'The small gift of majestic proportion'?"

"It's a book, isn't it? Caleb and Lydia argued many times over a book."

Dorothy glided on, spiritlike in the leaf-dappled September sunlight, her long dress skimming the ground, her feet moving invisibly beneath it.

"Dorothy!" Theodore strode after her. "I am assistant college librarian. I should know if there's a rare book bequeathed to the college. I've read the poem on Lydia's tombstone a hundred times. I think it's a book by Shakespeare."

"'And the Bard will applaud as humanity learns,'" said Dorothy. "*Bard* may mean Shakespeare. It may simply mean *poet*. Lydia may even have been referring to herself. She was a poet, after all."

"Not a very good one," he said.

In front of University Hall, Dorothy stopped and said, "I don't know what Lydia left us. I know only that an envelope sits in a safe in the Wedge-Fleming-Royce block in Boston. It's not to be opened unless and until Harvard educates women. There's a similar envelope in the Tercentenary packet. I have now told you more than I ever told anyone but Douglass. My appointment with the president is private. So . . . good-bye and give my best to Mr. Bunting." And she started up the stairs.

"You still haven't answered my question, Dorothy. Why now?"

At the top step, she turned. "Because you're right, Theodore. Time *is* fleeting. Thirty years since we lost Lydia, ten since we lost Douglass . . . we can't wait forever to do what's expected of us. And if we succeed, we can all find out what Lydia's gift was. I'm curious, too."

President Eliot's office was as austere as he was. It contained a desk overlooking the Yard, a bookshelf, three wooden-legged chairs . . . and on that afternoon, it also contained Dorothy's wooden-legged nephew.

"Heywood!" she said. "What a surprise."

He was standing to greet her, and doing it with only slightly more wobble than Grandfather Caleb on his wooden foot.

Eliot said, "Your note mentioned 'a small gift of majestic proportion.' Hoping that it is more generosity for Memorial Hall, I invited a member of the Committee of Seventy, one of seventy veterans who are building us the great monument."

"I've already made a contribution," said Dorothy, regaining her composure and taking a seat. "I expected a private conversation."

"Well"—Heywood puffed up his long mustaches—"if you'd prefer that I leave—"

Dorothy motioned for him to sit again. "Now that you're the father of a little girl, you should hear what I have to say."

"How may I be of service, Mrs. Warren?" Eliot folded his hands on his desk.

And with all the blunt force she could muster, Dorothy said, "Commit to educating Heywood's daughter as you would his son."

"Now, Dorothy," said Heywood, "President Eliot is too busy for this."

Dorothy looked at Eliot. "Are you, Mr. President?"

Eliot raised his chin. He wore glasses and bushy sideburns, which few people noticed until they had glanced at the birthmark that ran down the right side of his face. It began at his hairline and ended at his upper lip, and even when he was listening impassively, it seemed to give him an intimidating air of disapproval.

Heywood said, "We've been discussing Harvard's brave young men . . . and you reduce the conversation to this."

"I reduce it to its simplest terms," she said. "If our young women are educated, they may learn to avert wars. Then we won't need memorials to our young men."

"Mrs. Warren"—Eliot's voice conveyed calm authority and, as Holmes once said, all the decorum of a house with a corpse in it—"practical, not theoretical, considerations must determine the policy of the university."

"So they must," she answered. "And the enlistment of one half of humanity in the great work of the other half is a purely practical consideration, I would say."

"We do our best," said Eliot.

"You educate five hundred and sixty young men, including"—Dorothy took a small notebook from her purse and glanced at it—"by my count, seven Catholics, three Jews, and a Negro graduated in the Class of 'Seventy. But no women."

"Do not forget," said Eliot, "we offered lectures to enrich women in pursuit of the one learned profession to which they've acquired clear title: teaching."

"What teacher has time for an afternoon lecture series?" she asked. "Especially when it costs a hundred and fifty dollars, the equivalent of a Harvard tuition, yet offers no degree? Small wonder that neither Emerson intoning on the history of the intellect nor Howells expostulating on Italian literature could draw a crowd."

"The experiment proved the hypothesis, then," said Eliot. "This is not the time to be educating women at Harvard, no matter how many 'small gifts of majestic proportion' may be offered. Our principles are not for sale."

"But you *are* interested?" said Dorothy. "In the gift, I mean."

"Mr. President," explained Heywood, "Lydia Wedge Townsend offered a mythical gift to President Quincy at the Bicentenary. My father often told of how embarrassed the family was at the scene she made that night."

"Your father embarrassed too easily," said Dorothy.

Eliot stood, as if he had no time for familial bickering. "George Wedge Jr. was a good friend to the college. He did great service in raising funds for the library. He understood the true meaning of aristocracy and passed it on to his son."

Heywood gave the president an appreciative nod. Among gentlemen, certain gestures were universally understood—a slight inclination of the head, a small smile, a wordless expression of assent or approval.

Dorothy felt as if she were in a club rather than in the president's office.

Eliot went on. "We seek to build more than an aristocracy of inherited wealth or affectation of manners here."

"Ah, yes"—Dorothy recited the words that George Jr. had spoken often—"'If America must have an aristocracy, let it be born in the bower of our own good breeding, good learning, good faith, and hardheaded business sense.'"

"You remember it well," said Heywood.

"I prefer to remember what President Eliot said in his inauguration . . . that Harvard is 'intensely American in affection, intensely democratic in temper.'"

"Democratic, yes"—Eliot glanced at the clock—"but Harvard's sons must stand firmest for public honor in peace, and in war they must be first into the murderous thickets. That's the work of a true aristocracy. Your family has always understood it."

"If the sons are joined by the *daughters*," she answered, "we can do even more."

Eliot picked up his tall hat and gloves. "I'm afraid we must continue this at another time, Mrs. Warren. Unless your nephew offers you a ride back to Boston."

Heywood laughed nervously. "That means twenty or thirty minutes more with my aunt complaining in your ear, sir."

"Stimulating conversation is never complaining," said Eliot.

"In that case"—Heywood turned to Dorothy—"allow me to offer you a ride. The president and I are bound for the office of the college treasurer."

"Yes," said Eliot. "We're off to visit Harvard's money."

The Wedge carriage went by way of Harvard Street. Any who gave it a glance would have seen a burly Irish footman at the reins, then heard a female voice counterpointed by the muffled bass mutterings of two males repeating, "Yes . . . perhaps . . . hmmm . . .

yes . . . yes," until the famous Eliot birthmark flashed by, the voices receded, and the carriage clattered on.

But the woman never stopped talking, because on that day, she had felt the energy of expansion everywhere—before Memorial Hall, monument to past glory and bright future; in Eliot's office, where that future was planned; on the elm-lined avenues of Cambridge, now a town far grander than the quiet academic village of her childhood; and on the West Boston Bridge, with the city rising before her, a living, breathing brick-and-granite creature of capitalism. How, in the midst of such energy, had she remained grief-stricken and silent for so long? She owed it to those who had gone before her never to be silent again.

As they passed Massachusetts General Hospital, Heywood instructed his driver to stop first at the office of Harvard's treasurer, on State Street. Dorothy's talking had so plainly exhausted him that he couldn't get out of his own carriage fast enough.

But Eliot stepped out slowly, looked back, and doffed his hat. "Thank you, Mrs. Warren, for a marvelous monologue."

"You'll hear more," she said. "For I intend someday to bestow Lydia's gift."

"You would do us all a favor," said Heywood, "if you told us what it was."

"I shall tell you when I know, which will be when Harvard educates women."

"We all wait breathlessly," said Heywood.

"I know that you have allies," said Eliot. "Tell Mrs. Agassiz that I agree with you. Together we shall arrive at a solution. If not in the immediate future, in good time."

Dorothy no longer lived on Colonnade Row, which had fallen to the creature of capitalism. Like most who had lived there, she had moved to the Back Bay, the fashionable neighborhood built on landfill expanding over the Charles River estuary. She lived on the first block of Marlborough Street, in a four-story brownstone that some said was too large for a fifty-five-year-old widow and her domestics.

As she alighted, she took the footman's hand for support and thanked him. As she started up the walk, she heard these words: "I knew your son."

She turned and looked the Irishman up and down. "You knew Douglass? Where?"

"In the Twentieth, ma'am. I carried him from the field at Antietam."

She put a hand on his arm, more to keep her balance than as a gesture of affection. "You saw my Douglass on the day that he died?"

"Never's the man died more bravely," said Dan Callahan.

"Why, in all the years that you've driven this carriage, have you not told me?"

"Well, you been wearin' widow's weeds so long, announcin' how sad you were, I didn't think it was my place to make you sadder by talkin' about him."

"But . . . but news like this—"

"I'm sorry, ma'am."

With the same bluntness she had used on Eliot, she said, "My son was gutshot."

"Yes, ma'am. Gutshot it was."

"And a man suffers greatly with such a wound. Does he not?"

"He was a brave one, ma'am, brave on the field, brave in the hospital, too."

"Brave . . . yes." She started to walk into the house. Then she stopped and said to him, "Did he have any last words for me? Did he give you anything to bring home?"

"Nothin' . . . nothin' to send to you," answered Dan Callahan, "but he said to tell you that . . . that he loved you."

"He loved me . . . yes. Thank you." And she shook her head. "An Irishman."

"What do you mean, ma'am?"

"Who would believe that the last friendly eyes my son would see would belong to an Irishman?" And she went into the house.

Driving back to State Street, Dan Callahan felt relieved that he had finally revealed himself to Mrs. Warren, worried that Mr. Wedge might find out, and guilty that he hadn't offered her the truth about the locket. He felt angry, too, because in Boston, old prejudices died hard, even among ladies like Mrs. Warren.

She had campaigned most of her life to free the slaves, she had just spent half an hour lecturing the president of Harvard himself on the rights of women, but she still had that old Yankee blind spot: No dogs or Irish need apply.

A strange organ, the human mind, that it could hold such contradictory thoughts: it was all right to free darkies or educate flighty girls, but the thought that an Irishman could have carried your son from the battlefield was enough to give you the vapors.

Dan's mother had warned him about such things, just as she had warned him that if he did not speak to Mrs. Warren about her son right away, he should not speak at all, for doing so later would only raise her suspicions.

He had never felt compelled to speak to Amelia, for her happiness with Mr. Wedge was plain. But every mother should know if her son showed courage in his final moment. By telling Mrs. Warren that truth at least, Dan had lifted a weight from himself. It was too late to tell the truth about the locket, however, because the locket now belonged to his wife.

Dorothy Wedge Warren did not give Dan Callahan a second thought. She could not have imagined how deeply she had insulted him. The truth was that those Irish she had known, whether in service or in chance meetings between one social class and another, seemed incapable of noticing when they had been insulted.

She went into her house, dropped her hat and shawl on a chair, and called for tea. Then she went upstairs, to her writing desk, which she had placed in a bay window so that she could look east toward the Public Garden, west toward the marshlands disappearing under the landfill.

She picked up the framed photograph that she kept on the desk—her brave young lieutenant in his uniform—and she began to cry. She had cried for a time when her father died, and for a time longer when her husband died. But she had cried for her son every day for a decade, and she dreamed of him every night, of the sweet child drawing pictures at her desk while she wrote letters, of the gangly boy growing faster than clothes could be bought, of the serious young man going off to Harvard, of the serious young soldier going off to war.

ii

Dan Callahan would have preferred to live in a home of his own, no matter how humble, for he was a proud man. But the Wedges insisted that their footman live in the servants' quarters, because a man with one leg had particular need of a footman.

So Dan cared for the Wedge horses, while his wife, Alice, became the Wedge cook. The Callahan couple had one day off a week and time for mass on Sunday. They shared a warm bed in a room off the kitchen of the Wedge bowfront on Louisburg Square. They saved a few dollars each month. And they dreamed of having a son who might someday take another step up the ladder of Boston respectability, one whose son after him might climb all the way to Harvard College.

They knew that it was only a dream. But on cold nights, as they performed love's labors, the dream enhanced their pleasure. Dan would unbutton the front of his union suit and Alice would push up her nightgown. And in the intimate dark, beneath the blankets, they would dream as one, and for a few moments, there would be no reality but their dream and no sound but their movement.

On one particularly chilly Saturday night in November, their dream was so loud that they did not even hear the thumping of a wooden leg on the kitchen floor or the pounding on their bedroom door, and it was not until they were finished that they heard the voice of Heywood Wedge: "Dan, get up! Boston's on fire!"

In Cambridge, on that same chilly night, Theodore Wedge and Samuel Bunting were strolling up Quincy Street after an evening at the home of Professor Charles Eliot Norton. There, a group of students had staged a reading of Shelley's *Prometheus Unbound*.

"Marvelous, just marvelous," said Samuel. "I'd love to see such a play staged."

"They call it a closet drama for a reason. It wasn't *meant* to be staged."

"Then those boys should be doing Shakespeare. Such marvelous young actors . . ."

Theodore could think of no better place to be than in Cambridge on a cool November night, his stomach full of port, his head full of poetry.

The passions of youth—and the disappointments—had faded. He had accepted that he would never be a great writer, that his name would be carved on no buildings, that he would leave no issue. He was a librarian, a profession to be proud of, especially in a library as majestic as Harvard's. And he was, in most things, content.

He puffed his cigar and said, "Do you realize, Samuel, that our ancestors didn't allow Shakespeare in the library until 1723. Yet this evening, we've heard students read a play in a professor's own home, while in other professors' homes, they are debating things like Darwinian evolution—"

"We did *not* descend from the apes," said Samuel. "Professor Agassiz insists."

"But unlike our ancestors—ape or otherwise—we may consider the possibility without fear of hanging, imprisonment, or rustication."

"A naive man would say that we live in an enlightened world."

"At least we have Eliot to enlighten Harvard," answered Theodore. "He's changing everything. In the Law School, they now teach law by studying real cases. There's to be a course in something called organic chemistry. And that Professor Adams teaches not by lecture and rote recitation, but by having students engage in discussion, as they do in Europe. It's called a seminar, I think."

"Adams demands that we create a 'reserve shelf,'" huffed Samuel, "to keep books for his medieval history course. Before he came, no one even took medieval history seriously."

"Precisely why Eliot appointed him," answered Theodore. "Eliot is blowing gusts of fresh air in every direction."

"Hot air, if you ask me . . . or half the members of the faculty."

"Ah, yes, the faculty. Experts all in the principles of hot air."

The two gentlemen were taking Quincy Street to Massachusetts Avenue so that Samuel might catch a horsecar for Boston. Though they were close friends, Samuel still lived in his family's old town house on Church Green in Boston, while Theodore resided in the Wedge house on Brattle Street.

Certain appearances still mattered, even at enlightened Harvard.

And though it was well after eleven, President Eliot's house was also enlightened. Lamps burned all through the handsome array of gables, turrets, and great windows. And the front door was just then banging open.

"Be careful, Charles!" A woman in a dressing gown followed Eliot out the door.

"The university securities are irreplaceable." Charles Eliot jumped into the chaise under the porte cochere. "They must be saved tonight."

"Are you sure you don't want to fetch help?"

"There's none to be had." Eliot snapped the reins and the chaise kicked forward. "Most men are either abed or drunk at this hour on a Saturday night."

"We're neither!" shouted Theodore as the chaise came out the drive.

"Who is it?" Eliot pulled up on the reins.

"Bunting and Wedge," said Theodore.

"The librarians? Wedge of Brattle Street? Bunting of Church Green?"

Theodore smiled up at a face that looked ghostly blue in the gaslight. "Your memory is excellent, sir."

Eliot looked at Bunting. "And your home is on fire, sir, if reports are correct."

"My home?" Samuel Bunting gasped and brought a hand to his mouth. "On fire?"

"It began in a building on Summer Street, not far from Church Green. I'm told it's spreading," said Eliot. "I'm bound for the office of our treasurer to rescue our records."

"Oh, God," said Samuel Bunting. "Theodore, what am I to do?"

"Get in," said Eliot. "The both of you. Perhaps we can help each other."

* * *

By the time Eliot's chaise clattered over the West Boston Bridge, the hump of Beacon Hill was silhouetted against a sky radiating waves of red, pink, and purple, as if there were a great bruise expanding somewhere beyond.

"Hurry. Please hurry," said Samuel Bunting.

"I'll hurry only so fast as a single mare pulling an overloaded chaise will go," answered Eliot.

"But my house . . . the family portraits . . . my father's Orientals."

Theodore said, "I asked you to move away when everyone else did."

"There you go"—Samuel waved his handkerchief—"always criticizing."

Theodore was jammed between the grim president and the hysterical librarian, who leaned around Theodore and said to Eliot, "If the university paid us a decent wage, we wouldn't have to live in our families' old houses long after the neighborhood had sold out to merchants and banks. Even the New South congregation left."

"Then you should have left," said Eliot. "If your congregation moves, take it as a sign."

"Oh, Mr. President, but you are heartless, sir," said Bunting.

"If he were heartless," said Theodore, "he would have left us to ride the horsecars. Stop complaining and make a plan."

"A plan!" cried Bunting. "You make a plan. I can't even think."

The chaise lurched past the hospital, up the slope of Cambridge Street, amid crowds hurrying toward the flames.

"The plan," Eliot told them, "is to go through Scollay Square and down State Street to the treasurer's. Once we've rescued our securities, we'll make for Church Green."

Eliot's horse was growing more skittish, as if she could smell the smoke. Or perhaps she was spooked by the sight of ten firemen hauling a big steaming pumper up the street.

"Where are their horses?" asked Theodore.

"Distemper. It's killed most of the fire horses in the city." Eliot snapped his reins.

As they pushed through Scollay Square, the deep roar of the fire became a living groan, and Theodore swore that he could feel the heat, though they were still shielded by block upon block of five-story granite buildings, far more substantial than the wooden structures lost in the Chicago fire the year before.

No one could have imagined that such modern buildings—with their huge plate-glass windows framed in cast iron, with their square slate-covered mansard roofs framed in wood—could burn so ferociously. But the hundreds of joined structures were built on streets just wide enough for two carts to pass, and as the heat shattered the windows and as the wood in the mansards ignited, they became perfect granite chimneys.

At the intersection of State and Washington Streets, a police officer stepped in front of Eliot's chaise. The horse reared and almost turned them over.

"Here now! Here!" shouted the policeman. "You can't be goin' down Washington, 'cept on foot. A chaise with a spooked horse'll clog things for certain!"

"Do you think we're here to gawk?" demanded Eliot. "Let us pass. We're bound down State Street."

"And who might you be, up to no good on State Street?"

"I'm the president of Harvard." Eliot thrust his face forward so that the policeman could see it, and almost as if he had planned it, a column of flame jumped somewhere, illuminating the birthmark. "I'm going to retrieve the college financial records."

"Oh, yes, sir," said the policeman. "If you're goin' down State Street, good luck to you, sir, but just keep the horse away from the fire."

And on they went to Devonshire Street, where one of the few steamer companies with a healthy team came roaring past, its bell clanging, its three big horses straining, the smoke pouring from the engine stack.

Theodore could actually feel the wind from the galloping horses. Then he looked to his right and realized that it wasn't the horses that were causing the wind, but the fire, which was sucking air along the narrow streets, sucking it in like a living thing, causing—there—an explosion of flame to burst through the smoking roof of a building three blocks away.

"Oh, God!" cried Samuel. "My house! I must save my house!"

The little man leapt out of the chaise and began to run toward the fire.

Theodore jumped down and called after him, then looked back at Eliot. "Sir—"

"Go," said Eliot.

"But the university records."

"I'll save them myself." Eliot looked up at the flames jumping from roof to roof. "I have time. Your friend may not."

A few blocks away, men who had seen hell in war were seeing it again in Boston.

Heywood Wedge and Dan Callahan needed only to park on Tremont Street and step into the crowd surging down Winter, toward the flames rising beyond Washington.

Even on two good legs, Heywood would not have ventured into such a maelstrom, except that the company offices—investment, accounting, and legal—were in a magnificent new structure called the Wedge-Fleming-Royce Block, built on Summer Street, on the old Cowgill land. Shortly after Heywood and Amelia had merged families, their families had merged firms.

"Stay on my left, sir," said Dan Callahan. "That way I can keep the mob from knockin' you off your cane."

Though gas lamps on Winter Street still put out their bluish white glow, the light all around was red—shimmering in the plate-glass windows, reacting like a chemical that turned gray granite to pink, and glowing on the faces of hundreds of men pushing toward the flames.

But those men did not go like mindless creatures drawn to disaster. Most carried bags or boxes or satchels. A few pulled handcarts they hoped to fill with what might be left of their own goods or someone else's. And neither the thunderous roar of a wall collapsing into Summer Street nor a blizzard of embers exploding into the air could keep them from surging forward.

Then a unit of Veteran Guards—wearing old uniforms and forage caps, with bayonets fixed—came rushing along Washington Street, and like a sluice gate, they closed the intersection.

"We can't let you through!" shouted the captain. "The fire's comin' this way!"

"The fire's goin' *every* way," cried someone in the crowd. "Let us through!"

And a hundred voices joined in. "Let us through! . . . Stand aside! . . . Let us save what we can!"

"Now, lads," answered the captain, "let the firemen do their jobs."

"Dan," said Heywood, "we have to get through. There are papers to save."

Then they heard the clanging of a fire bell, followed by cries of "Gangway! Gangway!" And Steamer Number Twelve came rolling down Winter Street, hauled by a crew of firemen in leather helmets.

Dan whispered to Heywood, "Give the lads a hand." And they helped push the steamer past the guards and onto Summer Street.

And somehow, in the midst of this disaster, four men met.

Theodore Wedge and Samuel Bunting rushed south along Devonshire, past buildings igniting one after another like Roman candles. Then they came by the brilliant white Beebe Block, which dominated Winthrop Square on sunny days and dominated it now, with fire roaring from hundreds of windows, while firehoses sent streams of water hissing impotently against the red-hot granite walls.

Meanwhile, Heywood Wedge and Dan Callahan slipped away from the steamer crew and hurried east on Summer Street, past C. F. Hovey and Company, past Trinity Church, past Stedman and Penners, Wholesalers of Drygoods.

"They're all doomed"—Heywood looked up at the flying firebrands and the smoke seeping through the roofs—"every building from here back to Washington Street."

"Includin' yours." Dan looked ahead.

"We have to try to save the company papers," said Heywood.

So they hurried on, with carpetbags over their heads to protect them from red-hot flecks of granite and from plate-glass windows that exploded as the pressure built up behind them and sent shards of glass flying into the street.

If there was any good in this, it was that there were no families caught in their beds. This was a district for business. Most of the people who would have been living here had moved away long ago. One who had not was the man they saw as they approached the intersection of Summer and Devonshire.

They knew him. And even though the fire was roaring, the firemen shouting, and the granite walls cracking like thunder, they could hear him crying.

Samuel Bunting was on his knees in front of the y-shaped intersection where the majestic New South Church had once stood. Now, a mercantile building was there, and the flames were tearing it apart. But Samuel's eyes were fixed on an ancient bowfront on the far side of the intersection. It was the last private home in the neighborhood. It was his, and it was a four-story tower of flame.

"Theodore!" Heywood came hobbling up to them with Dan Callahan close beside. "Get him out of the street before he gets hurt."

"I don't care if I get hurt," cried Samuel.

"Don't say that." Theodore put his hands under Bunting's arms and tried to help him to his feet. "Here, here . . ."

"No." Samuel curled up like a ball on the street.

Theodore said to Dan and Heywood, "Help us."

"No!" cried Heywood. "If that old poof can't—"

"Don't call him that!" cried Theodore. "Don't call anyone that, damn you!"

"Let him stay there and cry, then," Heywood said. "You cry with him. I'm going to save the family papers."

"I don't know about that, sir." Dan was looking ahead to the W.F.R. Block, as it was called, and flames were leaping in half the windows.

Heywood said, "The office windows are still dark. The fire hasn't gotten there yet. But we must hurry."

Samuel Bunting continued to cry, "My house, my paintings, my carpets."

Heywood looked at Samuel, shook his head, and said to Dan, "Come on."

Theodore grabbed Heywood's sleeve. "You can't go into that building."

"Would Aunt Dorothy say that?" demanded Heywood. "What about family wills and secret codicils? What about that 'small gift of majestic proportions'? Its whereabouts may even be told in one of the safes."

"But a good safe is supposed to be fireproof!" cried Theodore.

And a row of windows blew out right beside them.

Samuel Bunting screamed in fright, and the others all dropped to their knees as though a Confederate battery had just opened up.

And Heywood brought his big, drooping mustache close to Theodore's face. "Tonight, nothing is fireproof."

"For certain not that wooden leg," answered Theodore. "So don't go into that building."

"Then who will?" Heywood looked down at Bunting. "This old poof?"

"I'll do it," said Dan. "I been in tighter scrapes."

Just then, the roof of Bunting's bowfront fell in with a tremendous crash that sent flames leaping into the sky and Samuel screaming toward his house.

"No!" cried Theodore, and he ran after his friend.

Dan went to follow them, but Heywood grabbed his arm. "Let him go. Let the old poof burn. Burning is all that men like that have ahead of them, anyway."

"But, sir . . ." Dan wiped the sweat from his forehead and looked hard into Heywood's eyes. "He's a human man, just like me or you."

"He can't be saved."

"I saved *you*, sir," said Dan, "when they told me you couldn't be saved."

For a moment, Heywood Wedge seemed to soften. He opened his mouth to speak, but the words were blown away with the row of windows that exploded out of the W.F.R. Block. Then Heywood pointed Dan down the street. "Now, you must save my papers."

By the time they had gone another block, the gold-leaf lettering—WEDGE, FLEMING, AND ROYCE—was beginning to bubble.

"Here." Heywood shoved a piece of paper into Dan's hands.

"This is the combination to the safe. Open it, fill the carpetbags, and get out fast."

Meanwhile, a big fireman had grabbed Samuel Bunting and pushed him back to Theodore, shouting, "Save your friend. There's nothin' we can do for his house."

Theodore wrapped both arms around Samuel and wrestled him into the middle of the street, where Samuel collapsed in tears. Then Theodore looked down the street and saw Heywood giving a slip of paper to Callahan.

The Irishman glanced at it, looked up at the burning building, took a deep breath, and ran inside.

Few Bostonians slept that night. In the tenements of the North End, on the rooftops of South Boston, and along the avenues of the Back Bay, people watched the sky to see which way the sparks might blow. But only the city's commercial heart was devoured. And just as they would never know how the fire started, they did not understand why it stopped about seven o'clock on Sunday night, with so much more yet to burn.

But it had burned enough, and Monday's dawn revealed a panorama of destruction. Almost everything from Washington Street to the waterfront, from Summer Street to Liberty Square, was gone. Here and there, a wall stood starkly, its windows framing broken columns, or mounds of smoking brick, or ash heaps of burned goods—china, cutlery, fabrics, footwear, carpet, furniture, books, hand tools, harpsichords, all the manufacture of a modern society—all of it, for sixty acres, all utterly gone.

In the brokerage houses, men calculated the chances of survival for the city's insurance companies. On the streets, they said that Boston's business district now resembled Richmond after the siege.

The fire never reached State Street and the offices of Harvard's treasurer, but the midnight ride of Charles William Eliot instantly became part of college lore.

And the efforts of Dan Callahan became part of the Wedge family lore, though the fire took him and the family papers both.

On that bright and sunny Monday afternoon, Theodore and his

sister went down Summer Street, through the devastation, toward the W.F.R. Block.

There were guard units about, keeping order, and steamers were still pumping water onto smoldering rubble, and the stink of melted metal and baked stone hung heavy in the air. But the business of cleaning up had begun.

On one side of the street, men were removing coffins from the crypt of Trinity Church. On the other, scavengers hunted for melted silver in the ruins of Shreve, Crump, and Low. And in the middle of the street, a man had set a large camera on a tripod. As Theodore and Dorothy stepped around him, he asked if they would stand in the middle of Summer Street, so as to give scale to the disaster. They kept walking.

They found Heywood with several others, including Amelia's father, the rotund Augustus Fleming, watching workers pick through a mountain of granite debris and rubble that had been the W.F.R. Block.

When Heywood saw his aunt and uncle, he stepped away from the others and came up to them. "Why are you two here? There's nothing to be done."

"Amelia told us you were trying to find your safe," said Dorothy.

"Better to find the body of the man who died opening it," said Theodore.

Heywood ignored his aunt and said to his uncle, without a trace of true sympathy, "How's your friend?"

"Mr. Bunting is at my home," said Dorothy. "Recovering."

"Good," snorted Heywood. "Keep him there. Half the city is digging out of the ruins, and poor Mr. Bunting is indisposed."

"That's very unkind," said Theodore.

"Unkind or not, I don't want him living in any property of mine."

Theodore Wedge said, "If you mean the house on Brattle Street—"

"I do," said Heywood. "Given our losses here, I may be forced to sell it."

"Sell it?" sputtered Theodore. "Where will I live?"

"You and Samuel both can live with me," said Dorothy. "This long-*mustached* Napoleon holds no deed on my house."

Heywood ignored them both, because half a dozen men had tied a rope to a large safe and were hauling it out of the rubble. He stepped closer and asked, "Is that it?"

"'Fraid so," said one of the workmen. "Looks like the combination was worked."

And sure enough, the great safe had been opened.

"My man must have gotten it open before the roof fell in," said Heywood.

"Wouldn't have made any difference," said Mr. Fleming. "I thought the safe in my office was fireproof, too, but when I opened it and reached inside, a thousand dollars in cash turned to green powder in my hands. Fire just plain baked it."

Theodore stood beside his sister and whispered, "A small gift of majestic proportion . . . will we ever know what it was that Lydia left us?"

"You and I won't. Not now. Not after this. But we are not freed from the responsibilities Lydia left us." Dorothy turned on her heel and started back up Summer Street. "Come along, Theodore. We have work to do."

iii

"It has taken me most of my life," said Theodore Wedge on a rainy March afternoon twenty-six years later, "to understand what the gift was that my aunt Lydia promised to Harvard at the Bicentenary."

The hundreds who crowded Appleton Chapel leaned a little closer. A few had heard of a "small gift of majestic proportion." Most had no idea what Theodore was talking about. But all considered it a strange way to begin a eulogy.

"The gift was my sister herself," he said, "and her commitment to the education of the gentler half of humanity, a commitment learned from Aunt Lydia.

"Today, at the midday class change, you may follow professors from their morning lectures, across the Common to Appian Way, where they lecture again to bright young women. But as my sister often said, she was only one of many who made this possible."

Theodore's vision was clouded by cataracts, so he had memorized both his speech and the places where certain people were to sit. He turned now to the ramrod-straight figure in the front pew. "She counted President Eliot a friend and a man of his word who promised female education, 'if not in the immediate future, in good time.'"

The figure nodded in polite appreciation. Eliot was now the most famous educator in America, the man who modernized Harvard, expanded its curriculum and endowment, and, with the help of brilliant professors, enhanced its reputation.

"And there are so many others." Theodore looked at them in turn. "Mr. Gilman, who suggested a school where professors could make extra money teaching female students . . . The professors themselves. Charles Eliot Norton . . . William James . . ."

He turned to a row of women. "They called you the Radcliffe Eight, the committee that came together in 1879 to provide the bedrock upon which this new college would rest. Dorothy was proud to count herself in your number." Several of the ladies nodded their thanks.

"And President Agassiz." He looked at the gray-haired woman who sat across the aisle from Eliot, a force of gravity in her own right. "When it became clear that Harvard would co-sign diplomas but would not absorb the Society for the Collegiate Instruction of Women, commonly called the Harvard Annex, the school was incorporated with the name of one of Harvard's first benefactors, Lady Mowlson, Anne Radcliffe. My sister, however, wanted to name it after the woman who has guided it since its inception. She wanted to call it Agassiz College."

Many in the pews nodded. A few applauded. Mrs. Agassiz smiled and made a small gesture of her hand, as if to deflect further compliment.

So Theodore looked toward Heywood and Amelia. Though Heywood had brilliantly managed the company's recovery, Theodore had barely spoken to him since the Great Fire. But Amelia had become a strong supporter of female education and a good friend to Dorothy, and that day, Theodore was speaking for his sister.

"Dorothy expressed great pride in the family that you raised together—a fine son and two fine daughters. She was grateful that you sent your girls without hesitation to the school now known as Radcliffe. And the nation is grateful for the service of your son. We pray that as he sails for war in Cuba, he will be safe and serve honorably. As President Eliot once said, the Harvard man must seize the highest honors in peace and lead others into the murderous thickets in war."

These last comments Theodore directed at Heywood Wedge Jr., '87, who wore the uniform of the First U.S. Volunteer Cavalry, and to the nine-year-old boy at his side. The boy, named Victor, was gazing at his father with a mixture of pride and concern, as if he could imagine both the excitement and danger a man faced when he went off to war.

"Dorothy often said that with a father like Heywood Sr. and a son as bright as little Victor, Heywood Jr. was a man well placed in time, for such a father and son demonstrate both the reliability of the past and the promise of the future."

In preparing the speech, Theodore had written the term *heroism of the past* but had crossed it out, for he had never seen anything heroic in his nephew. Now he saw Heywood's gray head nodding in approval, and he concluded that even *reliability* was too positive a term to bestow upon him.

He was glad that he was almost done. "Like the generations spread before us, like the college itself, Dorothy looked toward the future and borrowed the best of the past. And she oft paraphrased my mentor, Ralph Waldo Emerson, 'If a man—or a woman—stand on their principles, the great world will come round.'"

Theodore died not long after his sister, at the Bunting family cottage in Nahant.

He had been keeping a journal off and on for many years, and he had saved his most important entry for the very last:

I wish that in my eulogy I had made further allusion to the "small gift of majestic proportion." But I think I put it best. Besides, our knowledge of it was lost in the Great Fire, and none of us shall live to see Harvard's tercentenary. I asked Dorothy so often what the gift was that, finally, she forbade me to speak of it. And I did not, for my sister was one of the most formidable people I ever knew.

But I have my speculations, which herewith, I set down: it is a book of some sort. That much was I able to discern from conversations that unfolded between Grandfather Caleb and Great-Aunt Lydia. I believe further that Lydia's tombstone inscription suggests a work by Shakespeare. I believe that someday, it will be found, once the gilt-edge envelope in the Bicentenary packet is opened. And then will it be over.

Chapter Twenty-two

PULIGNY-MONTRACHET '96. A whole case, sitting right there in the office. He could almost taste the French white, with its layers of flavor and its fine finish.

There was no name on the case, but Peter knew where it came from, and why. Peter had said nothing about Jackie Pucks, and Jackie Pucks had not showed his face. And for a week, no one had tried to kill him on the river or anywhere else. Of course, that didn't mean there wasn't someone watching him and telling Keegan—or somebody else—about every move he was making.

And Will Wedge called him every other day to ask if he had figured out anything more beyond the Copley portrait.

He hadn't.

So, for one day, he was trying to tell himself he didn't care. He was taking a day to get back to his routine, which started with coffee and book catalogs.

Like everyone else in the rare-book business—everyone who'd survived more than five years, anyway—Peter had a list of titles that he always watched for. They might be arcane things such as *Anglorum Praelia* for Professor George Wedge Drake. Or they might be simple things that always produced a profit, like James Bond.

A first edition of *Casino Royale*, bought for a hundred dollars a few years ago, now sold for $325. No big score, but you chipped away every day, or you went hungry waiting for the big deals. And even they could be disappointing. In London, he had once stumbled across a first edition of *Tess of the D'Urbervilles* in three volumes, each volume signed by Thomas Hardy. He bought it for two thousand, held it a year, and offered it for ten in his catalog. He ended up selling it for six.

There was a pyramid in the rare-book business. At the bottom were the thousands of people who'd pay up to $15,000 for a rare book. Above them were hundreds who would spend up to a hundred and fifty thousand. And at the top was that small number who would pay anything for what they wanted, a very precise and constant group—wealthy people like Mr. Charles Price with his Shakespeare obsession.

For the really big ones, you might have to move fast, or you might have to sit patiently and wait and not watch the pot you were hoping would boil. Right now, he was waiting and wishing he could go out and dig up Lydia and ask her what she meant by "a century turns." Did she mean 1900 . . . or something else?

He sipped his coffee and imagined a wide plain, like something Salvador Dalí would have painted. Time as a place, as real as Harvard Yard. Across this plain, where decades and centuries sometimes pooled and sometimes ran together, there were old buildings and new buildings, men in tricornes and women in miniskirts, all meeting and mingling. Over there was a meetinghouse where people were listening to Reverend Thomas Shepard, and over there, someone was restoring a Copley portrait, and Lydia Wedge was writing a poem in a house on Brattle Street, and Charles William Eliot was announcing that women needed to spend a few more generations in the kitchen, while Dorothy Wedge Warren and Mrs. Agassiz were discussing a name for the new women's college. . . .

It had all happened and was all happening. Shepard's meetinghouse sat on the spot where J. Press now sold suits. Maybe the people in the meetinghouse were straining today to hear a sermon over the sound of the traffic on Mount Auburn Street. Or maybe the salesmen were puzzling over a linen waistcoat with brass buttons, hanging among the Harris tweeds. Or maybe . . .

Peter looked into his cup and wondered what Bernice was putting in the coffee.

The simple fact was that the trail had gone cold. As long as nobody was trying to kill him, and it seemed that Bingo Keegan had taken care of that, he could afford to do a day's work. After reading the catalogs, he had phone calls to make, copy to write for his own catalog, a private library to appraise in Chestnut Hill, and—

The phone rang.

It was Evangeline. "You have to come and see this."

The Massachusetts Historical Society was one of the great repositories of America's past—the papers of the Adams family, the personal correspondence of Jefferson, the table from which Lincoln delivered his Second Inaugural, the gorget that Washington wore in the French and Indian War, rare books and manuscripts, daguerreotypes and photographs, portraits, paintings—all housed in a deceptively prim-looking double bowfront on the corner of Boylston Street and the Fenway.

Peter Fallon was a fellow of the society and sometimes an adversary. More than once, he had found himself bidding against the society for some rare book or manuscript, and individual buyers were usually more willing than institutions to spend that extra money for a cache of letters from Wendell Phillips or that very fine copy of Bail's *Views of Harvard to 1860*. But Peter had also seen to it that a few of his clients had bequeathed libraries to the MHS, so he was always welcome.

He signed in and found Evangeline in the reading room overlooking the Fenway. Portraits of old Colonials looked on curiously as Evangeline transcribed notes onto her laptop.

"What's so important?" he said.

"Good morning to you, too." She gestured to the folders. "I've found the journals of Theodore Wedge, an assistant librarian at Harvard."

"I thought you were researching Dorothy Wedge Warren."

She gave him one of her looks. "Theodore was her brother."

"I know, but so what?"

"His journals have been misfiled for ninety-seven years."

"That's rich." Peter laughed. "The guy could keep thousands of volumes straight in the Harvard libraries, and he couldn't get his own writing cataloged."

"Somehow, his journals ended up in the papers of Edward Bunting, Class of 1870. Bunting was a munitions manufacturer and art collector. Had a big stake in the Watertown Arsenal. Made a fortune in government contracts. Endowed a chair in art history at Harvard. Left three boxes of family papers to the MHS in 1922. They were accessioned, cataloged, and forgotten."

"So"—Peter thumbed a few pages—"what's the Bunting-Wedge connection?"

"In the Artemus Pratt letter from Gettysburg, a Confederate named Hannibal Wall asks for Douglass Wedge and Jason Bunting. Then Artemus talks about elms and old men weeping in Harvard Yard. The old men were Theodore and Samuel Bunting."

"You know," said Peter, "for someone who insists she's doing her own book project, you keep finding ways to get into mine."

"Yours keeps getting in the way," she said.

"It's fate." He sat down across the table from her.

"We'll see about that," she said. She turned back to business. "In her letters to Theodore, Dorothy would often write, 'Say hello to Mr. Bunting,' or, 'It was a pleasure to have you and Mr. Bunting stay with us. . . .'"

"So, they were gay?"

"I found this in the back of one of Theodore's journals." She slid a letter to him. "It's from Theodore's nephew, Heywood."

Peter picked it up. "'Dear Edward—'"

"The munitions manufacturer. He and Heywood probably knew each other."

"All those old Brahmins knew each other," said Peter. "'Dear Edward, Thank you for the offer of my uncle's papers, which you have found amongst those of your own late uncle Samuel. My condolences on his death, but I have little interest in my uncle's writings, as he and I had little to do with one another. His friendship with your uncle was, as you know, a somewhat "unconventional" one.'"

"Unconventional," said Evangeline.

"Code for gay."

"Which itself is code," she said.

Peter continued reading: "'It is a relationship that I do not care to embrace, so as not to indicate approval of it, especially in the eyes of my grandson Victor. Since the death of his father in Cuba, I have become a father to him. I wish to raise him with the same strong sense of masculinity that invested his father, the sense of sacrifice my generation learned on the battlefields in our youth. Keep my uncle's papers with those of your own uncle. If they are commingled, perhaps they will reproduce.'"

"So," said Evangeline, "a wonderful chronicle of Harvard life ended up as a file in the Bunting family papers, not cataloged, never read."

"Unless you follow that trail." Peter flipped through the books. "*Look* at this stuff . . . Emerson's Divinity School speech . . . Eliot's inaugural . . . the birth of Radcliffe . . . football . . . and hello—"

"You've come to one of his speculations about the book?"

Peter read: ". . . 'the fate of a book I sometimes hear them argue over. They never bring up this subject in my presence and brush it away when I enter . . .' And nobody saw this?"

"That's where you're wrong." She flipped to a page she had marked, near the end.

Fallon began in a read-to-yourself mutter, but his voice rose quickly to "'But I have my speculations, which herewith, I set down: it is a . . .'" He flipped the page and said, "Shit." Right out loud.

So, who tore out that last page? And when?

"Someone who had access," said chief librarian James J. Fitzpatrick, Harvard '72, a skinny bachelor with an explosive laugh and an encyclopedic knowledge of . . . well . . . just about everything in the collection.

Peter had never been able to stump him. That was why it was surprising that the Theodore Wedge Papers had been buried for so long. Peter and Evangeline were sitting in Fitzpatrick's office. On the wall was the original of Burgess's *View of Harvard*, an antique engraving from 1759, another treasure.

Evangeline said, "Wouldn't it have been someone who had access to the papers and knew enough about the family to know what he was looking for?"

"Right," said Fitzpatrick. "To find the Wedge diaries, you have to access the Bunting Collection. There's the further complication that the Bunting Collection was cataloged under Edward, not Samuel."

"In short, only someone who knew about Theodore and Samuel Bunting could figure this out."

"Or someone very lucky," said Fitzpatrick. "But stories like this abound, particularly with papers that were accessioned in a more"—he searched for a word—"*gentlemanly* era. Fortunately, we have records."

"Records?" said Evangeline. "Of what people *read?* Isn't that an invasion of privacy?"

"Some librarians think so, especially these days," said Fitzpatrick. "In certain collections, your call slip is destroyed as soon as you return the book. But in other libraries, records are kept. Harvard's Houghton Library keeps call slips forever."

"Please tell me that's what you do here," said Peter.

"Please don't," said Evangeline. "Patriot Act or not."

"I'll please you both and disappoint you. All of our call slips from 1936 to about 1982 are on microfilm. Since then, we keep call slips for two years, so that if something turns up missing—"

"I don't think I like this," said Evangeline.

Fitzpatrick picked up a sheet of paper. "Do you want this information or not?"

"We'll worry about the ACLU later," said Peter. "Just give us the names."

"Only because you might help us apprehend a book vandal."

"*Apprehend?*" said Evangeline. "That makes us sound like cops."

Fitzpatrick said, "I wish the cops—and the courts—cared a little more about the theft or defacing of material like this. It's cultural vandalism."

"Agreed," said Peter. "But the Bunting Collection?"

Fitzpatrick said, "It's been requested half a dozen times, but you'll find these two names of interest: in 1969, Harriet Webster Wedge requested the file. And last September, William Wedge asked for it."

"Are you sure?" said Peter. "Will Wedge? Did you see him?"

"He's a fellow of the society, so he's around often enough."

"So you saw him. So you're sure he saw this material?" asked Peter.

"I didn't see him, but" . . . Fitzpatrick showed them the slip. Signed: *William Wedge.*

"Shouldn't we call first?" asked Evangeline.

"And miss a golden opportunity to catch Will Wedge unawares? I'm going to see him right now, and you deserve to be in on it."

She stopped in the middle of the Boylston Street sidewalk. "A lightning strike? Like we were TV reporters? Don't you ever get tired of all this?"

"Yes, a lightning strike. No, not like reporters, like intrepid historical detectives. And no, I never get tired of it."

She rolled her eyes.

"And now that you've had a taste of it again," he said, "I think you're enjoying it, too. Otherwise, you'd be back in there, reading old manuscripts."

After a moment she said, "I just wanted you to convince me." And she started walking beside him.

"Now," he muttered, "if I could just convince you to go to bed with me again."

"Stop trying to plan it. Plan what you're going to say to Wedge instead."

"All right," said Peter. "I'll do the talking and you watch his reaction."

"How about if *I* do the talking and *you* watch his reaction?"

"That works, too. Except he thinks I'm the one who knows what's going on. If we preserve the illusion, it leaves you free to use your brilliant powers of observation."

"'Brilliant powers of observation.' I like that more than 'women's intuition.'"

The offices of Wedge, Fleming, and Royce were at One Federal Street. Perfect for Will Wedge, because the downtown Harvard Club occupied the top floor.

In the reception area, the ambience was modern day money-making rather than Yankee dollars reproducing the old-fashioned way. Phones were ringing. Young women in business suits and young men in bow ties and wireless telephone headsets were hurrying here and there. Clients were sitting on sofas, reading the *Journal* or watching the stocks slide by on a television screen, courtesy of CNBC with the sound turned down.

In the corner office, Wedge's view was west, up the river, all the way to Harvard. On the wall were two portraits, his father and grandfather.

Wedge gave Peter and Evangeline his grin and good handshake, gestured for them to sit on the sofa, then settled in behind his desk. The venture capitalist in midmorning mode: gray suit jacket hanging behind the door, white shirt so starched that it crackled when he moved, crimson braces and yellow bow tie. With the grin still plastered, he said, "My instinct says you wouldn't be here unless this was very important."

"My instinct," answered Peter, "says you've been jerking me around for five months."

Wedge did not move a muscle, nor did his color rise or his voice change. He simply said, "How would that be?"

Peter put a copy of the call slip on the table in front of Will Wedge. "Did you rip the back page from a journal at the MHS on September thirtieth of last year?"

"That signature's a forgery." Wedge checked his desk calendar. "I was in Los Angeles September thirtieth."

"So who would forge your name to get a look at something? Your daughter?"

"The late Ridley, more likely, or maybe Keegan's goons. You said they were sniffing around. And I have to tell you, they frighten me."

"They frighten me, too," said Peter.

"Bingo Keegan," said Wedge, "is a name to conjure with. But someone should tell him that the play is worth exactly zero to anyone but the president and fellows of Harvard University."

"How do you figure that?" asked Peter.

"A priceless Shakespeare manuscript, part of the original John Harvard bequest, survives the Harvard Hall fire and comes onto the market in, say, 2005." Wedge stood and started pacing behind his desk, as if to take control of the conversation. "Do you really think that all the king's horses and all the king's men of Harvard will say, 'Oh well, finders keepers'? Does the expression 'Harvard lawyer' mean anything to you? They'll claim it's belonged to them since day one, and they won't rest till they get it."

"But if Keegan finds it, he won't announce it," said Fallon. "He'll sell it to some Midas who'll be happy just to own it, even if no one else knows about it. There are guys like that all over . . . Japan, London, even out in a fancy private library in Weston."

"Charles Price is completely legitimate." Wedge went back around his desk.

"He does business with a bookseller who isn't," said Fallon.

"You, however, are a bookseller who *is* legitimate," said Wedge, "so work with me, not against me. Follow this story. Find the truth."

"Why?"

Wedge sat on the edge of his desk so that he could swing his leg. "I don't know who ripped those pages out, but I simply want this thing to be over. I have important plans for this family. But until the fate of that play is known, one way or the other, my plans are up in the air."

"Have you asked your mother about it?" asked Peter. "She seems to have read the story in the Theodore Wedge journal back in 1969. Where do you think she heard of it?"

Will Wedge pointed to the portrait on the wall. "Probably from my grandfather. Victor Wedge. A great man, by all that I've heard. His grandfather was Heywood, who lost his leg at Antietam. And Heywood knew Theodore."

"Heywood *hated* Theodore," said Evangeline.

Wedge seemed surprised by that. "How do you know?"

"I read the journal," she said.

"Do you think your mother would have torn out the last page?" asked Peter.

"I don't know. I don't know who knows what," said Wedge. "All I know is, that if you can come up with proof, one way or the other, of the existence of that book by commencement week, I'll personally guarantee your son's tuition."

"My son hasn't been accepted yet," said Peter. "We won't know until next week."

"By commencement week, Peter."

"Why commencement week? You've been pointing toward that for five months, asking me to join the committee and all."

"Blame him." Will gestured to the portrait of his grandfather, a vibrant-looking man in a gray three-piece pinstriped suit, painted in the 1930s. "Victor Wedge always said, 'Of those to whom much is given, much is expected.'"

Chapter Twenty-three

═══════════

1909–1912

THE EARL of Mount Auburn. Victor Wedge relished his nickname. He could have called himself a prince, but "Earl of Mount Auburn" had a certain euphony and a bit of false modesty as well, an earl being less important than a prince. And as one of his friends had said after a night of strong punch at the Porcellian Club, they were *all* princes, all rich men's sons living rich men's lives.

If there was a center to the universe, thought Victor, it was here on Mount Auburn Street, on the Gold Coast, the stretch of apartment buildings that housed those rich men's sons, and in the clubs where they ate, conviviated, and congratulated themselves for being who they were.

Victor stood before Claverly Hall and squinted in the bright sun. Spirits had flowed rather too freely at the Porcellian the night before. Still, he had gotten home by midnight and squeezed out three pages for English 47, Professor Baker's drama workshop. He was writing a play about the Civil War, and he was certain that it would someday make him the Earl of New York, too. But not yet, for he was only a junior, and he had much to do.

There was that touchdown he planned to score against Yale. And he still hadn't kissed Barbara Abbott, though he had danced with her at half a dozen Boston cotillions that fall. And a new club was starting up called the Harvard Aeronautical Society, devoted to the newest and most scientific form of transportation.

Victor had taken to heart the advice of his grandfather, who had said that when his time at Harvard was over, Victor's first emotion should be exhaustion . . . from trying to experience too much.

Grandfather Heywood was an extraordinary man, thought Victor, a credit to his class. He had lost a leg at Antietam but had still managed to captivate the most beautiful girl in Boston. He had graduated from Harvard and Harvard Law School, fathered two daughters and a son, and, after the Great Fire, had rebuilt the Wedge family firm into one of the most powerful financial houses in Boston. Now, he was a leading figure in many walks of Boston life and a founder of the Immigration Restriction League, an organization that sought to protect America's borders and blood.

But most important, after Victor's father had died of yellow fever in Cuba, Grandfather Heywood had seen to it that Victor never lacked for knowledge of the traditions that carried the Wedges through time. Victor may have grown up without a father, but thanks to his grandfather, he knew who he was.

Just then, a Pierce-Arrow motorcar came puttering along, filled with his chums.

"Hello, Victor!" shouted Bram Haddon, a fine fellow with a marvelous laugh and a father in the steel business. "Do you like my new car?"

Victor said, "I expect a ride today!"

Victor's cousin Dickey Drake jumped out. "*After* the ceremonies, of course."

"Of course," said Victor. "Today will be historical!"

"Then come along," said Bram Haddon. "We want to get close to the platform. Though someone with a Harvard name like yours should be sitting *on* it."

"My name, among other reasons, is why they call me the Earl of Mount Auburn." As his friends hooted, Victor straightened to his full six feet, cocked his straw boater, and struck a pose. There was no denying that he had presence: features even and smooth, mustache trimmed, brown suit cut stylishly with four buttons. He could be forgiven if he thought a little too much of himself, because they all did. They were the Gold Coasters.

In the kitchen of Memorial Hall commons, sophomore Jimmy Callahan finished scraping the remnants of poached egg and chipped beef from a dish. The great hall, with its mighty oak hammer beams, oak paneling, and portraits and busts of Civil War heroes, was as baronial a space as could be found in New England. But Jimmy felt no sense of entitlement or aristocratic fellowship washing the dishes of his classmates.

He was just happy for the job. Students did not ordinarily work in the kitchens. Such labor was seen as beneath a Harvard gentleman, best left to lower classes. Indeed, the waiters in the hall were all Negroes. But Mr. Flanagan, who oversaw the dishwashers, had served in the Twentieth Massachusetts with Jimmy's grandfather, and he would "bend a rule to help out a local lad with a hard schedule." Flanagan came bustling through the steam and told Jimmy to be on his way, though the shift had not ended. "The new president might take it personal if you missed his inauguration."

Jimmy hung up his apron, threw on his tweed jacket, and stepped out into a sea of straw boaters and fashionable ladies' hats flowing into the Yard. Jimmy didn't have a hat, but he would have stood out anyway, because he was taller than most, and his delicate features were coarsened by a nose broken in a street fight. As for his clothes, *fashionable* was not the word. The cuffs of his corduroys were an inch too high, and the elbow patches on his jacket were more functional than decorative. What he had not outgrown, he had simply outlasted.

Most Americans saw Harvard as an enclave for rich men's sons, and it surely was. At the beginning, there had been no place else. Later, it had become tradition that there was no place better. And Charles William Eliot had done much to make truth of that tradition, fashioning Harvard into America's largest and richest university, with four thousand students and an endowment of $12 million.

But from the beginning, Harvard had also educated the sons of New England tradesmen and mechanics and country ministers, boys who held scholarships and small jobs and did their best to make no hardship for their parents. As Harvard's reputation grew after the Civil War, young men of modest means brought their ambition from all across America, because they had heard that at Harvard, they would meet the giants of American thought, choose from more than four hundred courses, and enjoy brighter prospects for financial aid than at any other college. Not all of them had heard, however, that financial aid might sometimes need the augmentation of a menial job.

The Gold Coasters called these boys Greasy Grinds because they worked too hard and studied too hard and put altogether too much effort into everything. The Greasy Grind might consider a grade of C to be cause for alarm; the Gold Coaster saw it as the emblem of a young gentleman far too busy imbibing college life to spend time studying.

Gold Coasters and Greasy Grinds and young men of all gradations between met in the classrooms, on the athletic fields, and in commons. But there was little reason for the grandson of Dan Callahan and the grandson of Heywood Wedge ever to meet. So it was not by their own design that they were sitting near each other that morning.

Thirteen thousand people had crowded into the Yard. The band played "Fair Harvard." And the inaugural procession advanced from Holden Quadrangle, across the Yard, to a platform at the west front of University Hall.

Leading the procession were the corporation secretary, the bursar, and the librarian, carrying in turn the college seal, the college keys, and the 1650 charter of the Harvard Corporation. Behind them came President Eliot, now seventy-five and white-whiskered, moving with a regality that proclaimed him every inch the academic patrician. Then came the column of gentlemen in silk top hats and tails, in robes and mortarboards. And finally came the new president.

A. Lawrence Lowell had Brahmin roots as deep as Eliot's, but he was shorter and stockier and, even in procession, moved like a man impatient to get on with things.

"What do you think?" Dickey Drake asked Victor as Lowell took the platform.

"That drooping mustache, that barreling gait, that puissant presence—"

"*Puissant* . . . a fine word, Victor," said Dickey.

"Yes, it is. But just *look* at him. When he puts on his pince-nez, he could be brother to the most puissant man of the decade, Teddy Roosevelt himself."

"Well, they *are* friends," said Dickey.

Jimmy Callahan overheard this conversation because he was sitting with Joe Kennedy, who had positioned himself behind Victor. Jimmy had met Kennedy on the baseball diamond, and he now counted the amiable, square-shouldered son of an East Boston tavernkeeper as a good friend.

Kennedy said to Jimmy, "Wedge is right. Lowell reminds me of Roosevelt."

Victor Wedge looked over his shoulder and offered a thin smile.

Callahan had seen that smile before, usually when some Gold Coaster dined in commons and smiled at the Greasy Grind who dared sit next to him. To Callahan, the smile said noblesse oblige, which was worse than being ignored. But Kennedy didn't seem to mind. He answered Wedge's smile with a toothy grin of his own.

As the ceremony unfolded beneath the elms, there were invocations and speeches, and in the undergraduate section, jokes and whispered sarcasms. Then the corporation secretary announced that he had a telegram from Mr. Heywood Wedge, and Victor and Dickey elbowed each other, for Heywood was grandfather to both of them.

The telegram congratulated Lowell on his inauguration and informed him that, as representative for the university, Mr. Wedge that very day had accepted the deed to the home of Katherine Rogers, mother of John Harvard, in Stratford-on-Avon.

"That's the town where Shakespeare lived," Kennedy whispered to Callahan.

And once more, Wedge glanced over his shoulder and bestowed his smile.

" 'Her house,' " read the secretary, " 'bequeathed to the university, shall henceforth be called Harvard House, a home away from home for all alumni who visit.'"

As the applause rolled across the Yard, Victor doffed his boater and bowed his head left and right to his friends, who guffawed and joshed and slapped him on the back.

Then Joe Kennedy leaned forward and offered his hand. "Congratulations, Victor. Your grandfather's done Harvard quite a service."

"Yes"—Victor's smile froze in place—"thank you, Kennedy. But in truth, my grandfather is touring in England. They asked him to receive the deed to the house because it was convenient."

Victor's coolness froze Kennedy's smile, too, so that the young men were now looking into each other's eyes, as if taking the measure of each other, of their social classes, their character, and their aspirations, all at once.

"Others did all the work," Victor went on. "One of the best things to learn in life, Kennedy, is how to take credit while others do the work."

And then, Victor turned back, whispered something in his cousin's ear that caused Dickey Drake to snicker, and did not turn around again or acknowledge Kennedy in any way for the rest of the ceremony.

All the while that Lowell was taking the oath, stepping before the audience, and delivering a speech that promised to join new academic discipline to the elective system, Jimmy Callahan could feel Joe Kennedy seething. Jimmy knew that Kennedy wasn't seething at Wedge but at himself, for giving Wedge the chance to condescend to him.

Jimmy was as indifferent to the Gold Coasters as they were to him. They had nothing that he could ever hope to afford, need, or want.

Kennedy, on the other hand, always put himself forward with clubmen like Victor Wedge. As he said, "It's the best way to guarantee that they'll remember you when it comes time to vote new members."

"That Kennedy is an upstart," said Dickey Drake.

"I've seen his type before," answered Victor as they made for lunch at the Porcellian. "Because he plays baseball and has an easy manner, he thinks he can ingratiate himself into the Porc. He's the sort of hail-fellow-well-met that a true gentleman can't stand."

"Well, he *is* in the DKE. That's the first step up the ladder."

"Anyone can make a waiting club like the DKE. Few are elected to a final club like the Porc. We even turned down Theodore Roosevelt's cousin."

"Franklin . . . I heard about that. What about T.R.'s *son?* Will he make it?"

"Kermit? He has a chance. He's a fine fellow."

"What about me? I won't be blackballed, will I?"

"Bad form to be asking about yourself, Dickey. And bad form is not what we're about. A final club becomes the center of your world at Harvard and a mark of distinction later. No bad form allowed."

"No bad form. Sorry." Dickey was shorter than Victor and looked up to his cousin in more ways than one. He took most of the same courses as Victor. His skimpy mustache was as carefully trimmed as Victor's. He used Victor's tailor and, following Victor's example, ignored the tailor's bills.

"Of course," said Victor, "it isn't bad form unless we say it is."

They stopped at a nondescript doorway on Massachusetts Avenue. Victor rang the bell, then turned to Dickey. "I'd say that your chances are excellent, as long as you don't dribble soup on your cravat or snort cider through your nose when I tell a joke at lunch."

A Negro in a white jacket opened the door. "Good afternoon, sir."

Victor handed the Negro his hat, and Dickey did the same.

"We have a delicious clam chowder this afternoon, sir," said the Negro.

"The difference between you and that Irish fraud Kennedy," Victor said to his cousin as they started up the stairs, "is that you come from fine stock."

"Fine stock . . . yes," said Dickey. "Grandfather always says that. Fine stock."

"And a fine apple pan dowdy for dessert, too," said the Negro.

ii

Jimmy Callahan kept to a routine. It was the only way for a young man of high ambition and small means to succeed at college.

He rose at five o'clock in the East Cambridge house where he lived with his parents, his grandmother, and his sister. He ate breakfast with his father, an engineer on the Boston & Maine. Then, no matter the weather, he walked down Cambridge Street, past tripledeckers and storefronts, all the way to Harvard.

At six, he would arrive at the kitchen. At nine, he would hurry for class. At noon, he ate a brown-bag lunch with friends in commons. Then there would be afternoon classes and an hour at the gymnasium, unless it was baseball season. After that, he would study until nine, then make for home and a bowl of leftover stew.

Jimmy liked the Gore Hall library. It reminded him of a medieval cathedral. And how medieval it must have felt before electricity was introduced in 1891. Until then, the library closed when the sun went down, because the fear of fire was so ingrained that neither candle nor gas mantle had ever been allowed to shed light on the books.

Jimmy was glad for electricity. He was glad to be living in the twentieth century, glad for the explosion of knowledge that had rendered this library all but obsolete, glad for the opportunities open to a young man of any background, if he was willing to work.

He reminded himself of his opportunities every night as he left the library and headed onto Massachusetts Avenue. And even there, the twentieth century was unfolding, in a trench framed with steel beams and covered at the intersections with heavy planking. When the work was completed, an electric subway would whisk riders from Cambridge to Boston in just nine minutes.

As he walked along one chilly March night, Jimmy was thinking about something the excavation had unearthed: the foundation of Peyntree House, first building at Harvard College. What would the denizens of that distant time make of the twentieth century, especially on a noisy night like this? Up ahead, a gang of students was marching through the Square, singing "Yo Ho!" Down on Plympton Street, another gang was carrying torches and singing "Ten Thousand Men of Harvard." And voices were rising from the Yard, too, and echoing up from Mount Auburn Street.

It was club selection night, when sophomores sat in their rooms and clubmen went from dorm to dorm with flasks and invitations, gathering up inductees and marching them through the streets to their new clubs. For those who heard good news, it was a memorable night. For those who expected a knock that never came, it was a night memorable only for its misery.

Jimmy Callahan expected nothing. He just walked along the subway trench, lost in thought, until he was stopped by a voice from the shadows. "Not one, Jimmy."

There was someone standing beneath the Porcellian Gate, which led into the Yard. It was Joe Kennedy, and he was looking up at the windows of the Porcellian Club as though looking up to the top of a mountain he had failed to conquer.

"Not one *what*, Joe?" asked Jimmy.

"Not one Catholic was asked to join a final club. Not one."

And Jimmy Callahan laughed.

"What's so funny?" growled Kennedy.

"That you'd expect otherwise." Jimmy gestured across the trench at the windows. Within a square of golden light, two young men were touching champagne glasses. "That's the aristocracy up there, Joe, old money screwing older money, trying to make more money."

"You're crude, Callahan, and cynical."

"I'm realistic. If you want people to respect you for who you are, go to a Jesuit college. If you want to *make* them respect you for what you *do*, come to Harvard and do it. Worry about the *merito*cracy, Joe, not"—he gestured upward—"not that."

Kennedy turned his eyes back to the windows, and Jimmy walked on.

When Victor Wedge ate breakfast at all, he ate it in Memorial Hall commons.

He liked to remind his friends that the magnificent structure had been built by men like his grandfather to honor men like his great-uncle.

So, on a Wednesday about a week after club selection night, Victor and Jimmy crossed paths. They paid little attention to each other at first. Jimmy was stopping to pour himself a cup of coffee from the urn in the corner before he left for a nine o'clock class. Victor and his friends were lounging at table because they did not have a class until ten.

"I wish you'd give us lessons, Victor," said Dickey, who seemed to be standing a little taller now that he was a member of the Porcellian. "Skirts flock to you."

"I thought you had your cap set for Barbara Abbott," said Bram Haddon.

"She's a lady," said Victor. "She defends her virtue, which pleases me—"

"But doesn't satisfy you?" Dickey had also grown bolder.

Victor shifted his eyes to his cousin and said, "Precisely," in a tone that suggested he did not appreciate Dickey's newfound attitude.

Jimmy, who was standing nearby, did not appreciate what Victor said next.

"So where do you find . . . satisfaction?" asked Bram Haddon.

Victor grinned. "Have you ever seen the East Cambridge girls who troll through the Yard for Harvard men on a Sunday afternoon?"

"The Irish girls?" asked Haddon.

"Some are Irish," said Victor. "Or have Irish parents."

Jimmy Callahan leaned over him. "Excuse me, sir, but could you pass the cream?"

Victor flashed the phony smile and slid the cream along the tabletop. Then he turned back to his friends and dropped his grin back into place. "If you snag one on a Sunday afternoon, you can have yourself a fine time. A little stroll, a ride in your motorcar, a little tip from the flask, and who knows how much satisfaction you can get before you send her back to her dreary little life?"

Jimmy Callahan calmly set down the cream, spooned two sugars, and spilled his coffee right into Victor's lap.

"Good God!" Victor jumped up. "Could you be any clumsier, man?"

"Oh, excuse me, sir," said Jimmy without a trace of apology.

"Stupid bastard." Victor grabbed Dickey's napkin and began to wipe off the coffee.

"He's not stupid," said Dickey. "He did that on purpose."

"Look at my trousers. . . . Ruined," said Victor. "This comes out of your pay."

"I'm sorry, sir," said Jimmy. And without changing tone, he added, "And you'll be sorry, too, if I ever hear you say anything bad about East Cambridge girls again."

Victor straightened up and looked Callahan in the eye. "They're all whores."

Anyone who hadn't been watching when the coffee went over was watching now, and the clatter of cups and conversation receded across the dining hall.

Jimmy stepped back and began to unbutton his jacket.

Then someone whispered in his ear, "Not here. You'll lose your job." It was Joe Kennedy.

"Yes," said Victor. "Then you might have to carry a hod for a living."

"Hemenway Gymnasium," said Kennedy. "Boxing ring. Three o'clock. Are you man enough, Wedge?"

Wedge did not hesitate. He might act the dandy, but they had all seen him on the football field. "Three o'clock."

"I'll second you," Dickey told his cousin.

"Don't back down," said Jimmy.

"Fourteen-ounce gloves. Marquess of Queensberry rules," answered Victor Wedge.

They went at it in Hemenway at three o'clock sharp. Sunlight poured through the Gothic arched window. Ropes and rings and swings, all part of Dr. Dudley Sargent's strength apparatus, hung above them. And students crowded the balcony.

Drawn by the commotion, Dr. Sargent came out of his office and looked at the two boxers and the gang of students above. "What goes on here?"

"A dispute to be settled, sir," said Kennedy.

Victor Wedge raised a glove to his forehead as a gesture of respect to Sargent. Jimmy Callahan kept his eyes on Victor, as if to concentrate his anger.

Victor was wearing trunks and a crimson T-shirt. Jimmy, who could not afford gymnasium clothes, had stripped to his union suit and trousers.

Dr. Sargent stroked his beard, looked them both up and down, and said, "Three rounds, three minutes a round. No more. How heavy are the gloves?"

"Fourteen ounces," said Kennedy.

Sargent went into his office and brought out two pairs of twenty-ounce gloves. "Use these." He pulled a watch from his pocket. "I'll keep time." Then he looked up at the balcony. "And the rest of you, outside. This is between two men, not the whole college."

A few of the students in the balcony protested, but they all did as they were told.

As Dickey tied on the big gloves, he whispered to Victor, "Sargent's on your side. Your arms are thicker. It's plain you're more powerful. He made us use heavier gloves because *you'll* be able to hold them up longer. He wants you to beat this mick."

"How do you know that?"

"Haven't you read Sargent's book? He believes that all these rings and swings and parallel bars are the way to build strong circulatory systems to purify us of all that foreign blood that's flooding into the country."

"He *wrote* that?" asked Victor.

"I think he meant the Irish micks." Dickey laughed.

In the other corner, Joe Kennedy was telling Jimmy, "On the football field, he comes straight at you. I suspect he'll come straight at you with his fists, too. He's a fullback. You're a skinny outfielder, so dodge and feint, pick your spot."

"I plan to hit him in the face," said Jimmy.

"Then what?"

"Hit him again."

And that was how it went.

The one who should have boxed was a puncher, and he hit Victor Wedge right in the nose straightaway.

The one who should have punched was a boxer, and after he recovered from Jimmy Callahan's first blow, he circled to his left, started flicking jabs. And . . .

Jimmy ducked a jab and hit him again, right in the nose with the big glove that looked like a pillow but knocked Wedge onto his rear end.

Sargent jumped in, and round one closed with a standing eight count for Wedge.

In Victor's corner, Dickey said, "You're doing fine. He's wilting. Keep—"

"Shut up."

In Jimmy's corner, Kennedy said, "You knocked him down. Now he's mad. So be ready. Box more. And watch that jab. His hands are fast."

"Right."

Jimmy went in punching again, but this round, he boxed more.

Victor boxed but punched more, and those quick hands produced jab after jab.

After two minutes, blood was dripping from Jimmy's nose, splattering on the canvas. After three minutes, both of them were tiring.

"Time!" shouted Dr. Sargent. End of round two.

Dickey whispered, "You showed him. He'll never spill coffee on you again."

Victor said, "I've shown him nothing."

Joe Kennedy said to Jimmy, "Now, go after him. He's tired."

"I'm tired, too." Jimmy took two or three deep breaths through his mouth because Kennedy had stuffed a roll of cotton up his nose.

"Well, stay on your feet, whatever you do," said Kennedy. "Close with him. Hit him in the belly a few times, then hang on. I bet fifty bucks."

"That I'd win?"

"That you'd stay on your feet."

Jimmy stayed on his feet. So did Victor. They stood for the final three minutes and pounded. The gym echoed with the sound of the gloves expelling air as they struck. Both men felt their arms start to burn, then their lungs, and both were staggering when Sargent shouted, "Time!" And both collapsed onto their stools.

Sargent stepped into the ring, looked at them both, and said, "You're a disgrace to Harvard . . . a pair of quivering jelly bowls. Where's the stamina? You're supposed to be athletes, but you're so busy with your games—hitting balls and running into people—you aren't prepared for manly combat. Games are for boys. Conditioning is for men."

Then Dickey Drake looked at Kennedy. "A draw?"

Kennedy looked at the boxers. Both nodded, so he said, "A draw."

Sargent said, "Shake hands and report to me tomorrow for conditioning."

Victor and Jimmy walked to the middle of the ring and touched gloves.

And Jimmy spoke first. "Say nothing bad about my mother or my sister or any other woman in East Cambridge, and I won't spill coffee on you."

"I suppose that's as close to an apology as I get for my trousers," said Victor. "Don't spill coffee on me, and I won't call your women . . . I won't insult your women."

"Good," answered Jimmy. "And if you ever want to meet the woman whose husband saved your grandfather at Antietam, you'll have to come to East Cambridge."

Victor had heard the story of Antietam at his grandfather's knee, the missing knee. He knew that an Irishman had carried Grandfather from the field that day and served as family footman until his death in the Great Fire. While Victor may have heard the name Callahan, he had never put the footman together with the Greasy Grind.

Now Victor was faced with a dilemma. Would he go through Sargent's exercise regimen at Hemenway and say nothing to Callahan, learn nothing from him, teach him nothing, either? Or would he do the surprising thing and accept Callahan's invitation?

Usually, Victor preferred to do the surprising thing, whether he was running a football or changing the way people thought about him. And there might be some benefit in meeting members of the Callahan family.

After all, Professor Baker urged his students to absorb experience wherever they could, because experience was the raw material from which the playwright fashioned his drama. If his play about the Civil War was going to electrify New York, or get an A from Professor Baker, Victor should take the opportunity to talk to a foot-soldier's widow.

So, on a beautiful Sunday in May, he donned a seersucker suit and straw boater, went to Boston and borrowed his grandfather's motorcar, then drove over to East Cambridge, the neighborhood that had grown up around the New England Glass Company in the 1840s. Smoke from local factories still stained the sky, and the rumbling of trains in the freight yards could be heard night and day, and the men went off to work with lunch pails in their hands and came home with dirt under their nails.

Victor could not imagine that anyone around here would ever have seen a 1910 Stevens-Duryea six-cylinder touring car parked at the curb. So he gave a boy five cents to watch over it. Then he took the bouquet of flowers he'd bought, went up the stoop of the two-family house, and knocked on the door.

As it opened, he believed that he was looking at the face of an angel.

"Yes?" Her auburn hair fell to her shoulders, her eyes had an ethereal greenish hue, and while she seemed suspicious at the sight of a stranger bearing flowers from a car worth more than any house on the block, there was curiosity beneath her suspicion and beneath that, a layer of warmth so beguiling that Victor thrust the flowers into her hand.

"I'm a friend of your brother's," he said. "Jimmy told me how beautiful you were, but I didn't believe it until now."

Emily Callahan laughed and told him that her brother was playing baseball and their parents were at the game. Then she invited him into the parlor.

The house smelled of onions and herbs and braised lamb, because someone was cooking a stew. Antimacassars covered stains on the furniture and well-placed tables covered holes in the rug. There was an upright piano in the corner and—Victor almost laughed—lace curtains on the windows.

As he took a seat, Emily's grandmother, Alice Callahan, came in from the kitchen. She was a heavy old woman wearing a gingham bib apron over her Sunday dress, a gold locket around her neck, and slippers with the insteps cut out so that there would be room for her bunions.

She seemed suspicious, too. What did a Wedge want with her? She had left their service nine months after her husband's death, when her only child was born.

Victor explained that he wanted to meet the woman whose husband had saved Heywood Wedge. "I've come just to say thank you."

And the old woman's suspicions melted.

In the next hour, Victor heard Alice Callahan's tale of Dan, son of a Harvard goody, who courted her on long walks through the Yard and marched off to war because he believed it was the right thing to do. When he came home, he proposed to her. But instead of a ring, which he couldn't afford, he gave her a gold locket with his picture in it.

"It's inscribed," she said, holding it up under her chin. " 'From D. to A.'—Dan to Alice—'With All My Love, May God Keep You.' And never's the time I've took it off."

Looking at the oval photograph of the man in his soldier's forage cap, he told her that her husband was as handsome as her story was beautiful, and her smile told him that his charm could work even on an old Irish woman with bunions.

And she kept talking . . . of the Great Fire, the birth of her son, and her return to Fay House in Cambridge. "Once the Fays gave the house over to the woman's college, I took over the food service. Served meals there for twenty-five years. And now, I have a Harvard grandson. My Dan would be so proud."

Emily asked Victor, "Do you know any young ladies at the Radcliffe College?"

"I know several, yes," he said.

"Are they smart?"

"Many, yes."

"And pretty?"

"Some, though few are as pretty as yourself." By the time he said that, he had forgotten the reason he was there—to surprise the Callahan ladies. Instead, he surprised himself by inviting them for a ride. He was thrilled that Emily accepted, only slightly disappointed when her grandmother said, "I'll get my hat."

And what a hat. It rose a foot above her head and tied under her chin, about ten years out of date, but as Alice Callahan perched in the backseat of the touring car, with her purse held securely against her chest, she looked as regal as Queen Victoria.

It pleased Victor that Emily sat in the front seat and engaged him in small talk all the way across the new Longfellow Bridge, over Beacon Hill, and around the Public Garden. Later that night, he could not remember anything that they talked about, but he could not forget his pleasure in her presence, even when he drove by the Somerset Club just as Bram Haddon, coming out with his family, called Victor's name.

"My sister?" whispered Jimmy Callahan as he passed Victor in Sever Hall the next morning.

"Your sister? What about her?" Victor had gotten control of his infatuation. A pretty Irish face was still Irish. He had been telling himself that since he woke up.

"You brought my sister flowers?"

"Actually, I was bringing them for your grandmother, who turned out to be a wonderful resource for my new play." Victor spoke loudly enough that anyone who was listening, including Bram Haddon, would understand.

Jimmy leaned closer and whispered, "My sister said you were very nice to her. That's good. But don't be too nice. That would be bad . . . for both of you."

And for the rest of the week, Victor Wedge tried not to think of Emily Callahan. He was too busy finishing his play. And there was a tea on Friday afternoon at Fay House, where he sat with Barbara Abbott.

Barbara had a more subtle beauty than Emily. Her hair was a plain brown, her eyes a trifle too close, her nose a bit too long, but when she swept her hair up from her face, the severity of the nose gave her the classical look of a Greek bust in a Boston museum. Simpler beauty faded, thought Victor, and Irish girls grew bunions on their feet. And if he could not remember his conversation with Emily in the car, perhaps it was not worth remembering. Barbara and he, on the other hand, had taken many of the same classes and came from the same class, so there were ideas to discuss, and when they ran out of ideas, there were all those people to gossip over. Besides, Barbara's father had been a classmate of Victor's father and another Porcellian.

So . . . the daughter of a Porcellian or the daughter of a man who ran an engine on the Boston & Maine? What could Victor have been thinking?

Victor's mother had remarried and lived in New York City, so Victor always said he claimed dual citizenship in the Athens and the Sparta of America. Whenever he wanted the pleasures of family without a train ride to New York, he took the trolley to Boston and walked up Beacon Hill to his grandparents' home.

If it was a Sunday morning, Victor would sit at his grandfather's dining-room table, under the gaze of Reverend Abraham and Aunt Lydia, who themselves were sitting at some English dining-room table 130 years before, and he would read the newspapers with his grandparents.

"Did you see this, Grandfather?" Victor looked up from the obituary page. "Samuel Bunting has died."

Heywood made a little snorting sound that ruffled the long white mustache drooping down around his mouth.

"There's to be a memorial service at Trinity. Should we go?"

Heywood glanced at his grandson. "I think not."

"But wasn't he a close friend of the family?"

"He was a close friend of Uncle Theodore," said Heywood. "Too close, actually."

Victor glanced at Grandmother Amelia, who was serenely tapping her teaspoon around the top of a soft-boiled egg.

Without looking up, she said, "Heywood, perhaps you should explain yourself."

After a moment, this was muttered from behind Heywood's newspaper: "They had an . . . unusual attraction."

"A bit more, dear," said Amelia.

Heywood lowered the paper and looked over his spectacles at Victor. "Have you ever heard the expression, 'the love that dare not speak its name'?"

"You mean, the . . . h.s. sort of love?" asked Victor.

"A polite obfuscation," said Heywood. "Theodore and Mr. Bunting were poofs."

"Poofs?" Victor thought a bit, then said, "Do you think they could help it?"

"Of course they could help it," said Heywood, turning back to his paper, then lowering it again. "I hope you're not sympathetic to such . . . feelings."

"Oh, no, sir," said Victor.

Amelia lifted the top off her egg.

Heywood spent another few seconds behind his paper, then he looked hard at his grandson. "Speaking of unusual attractions, Dickey Drake says that Bram Haddon saw you squiring my old footman's wife around Boston, in my Stevens-Duryea, no less."

"I gave Alice Callahan a ride, sir, though it was her granddaughter who—"

"A woman who spent time in my service does not ride in the backseat of my car."

"I'm sorry, sir."

"Appearances matter. The help is the help and doesn't ride in the backseat."

iii

Grandfather was right as always, thought Victor. The help was the help.

Besides, summer would take Victor to Bar Harbor and his stepfather's palatial cottage. Eight weeks of boat handling in the pellucid waters of Maine might clear his head of his fantasies about an Irish girl and his disappointment about a grade of C on his play, which was returned with a note from Professor Baker suggesting that he may have reached his limits as a playwright.

Barbara was headed to an art school in France, where she hoped to learn to "capture light with daubs of color, like those marvelous Impressionists."

As far as Victor knew, Jimmy Callahan was working as a stoker on the Boston & Maine, and Emily was working at the fragrance counter at Jordan Marsh.

Many letters passed between Victor and Barbara that summer. And in August, Victor sent a picture postcard of Mount Desert Isle to the Callahan family.

But the help was the help.

Victor reminded himself when he addressed the postcard to the family, rather than to Miss Emily Callahan. He was reminded again in September, in Memorial Hall, when he glimpsed Jimmy Callahan changing into his white coat.

By then, "the help" had a new meaning for Victor—an English housemaid who worked for his stepfather. During the first week in Bar Harbor, she had paid particular attention to the handsome young stepson. In the second week, as she straightened his room one morning, she mentioned that she didn't wear bloomers in the summer. It did not take Victor another week to discover that she was willing to bend over the washstand and raise her skirts, as long as he left a gratuity on the dresser when he was done.

For all his bragging over his success with East Cambridge girls, the maid with the Cockney accent was Victor's first real conquest. Of course, even if the help was the help, he knew that Emily Callahan would never have offered herself like that.

So, when he was not studying his new subject, economics, or going to football practice, or thinking about that maid, he contented himself with plotting to get a kiss from Barbara Abbott.

It happened on an October night, as he walked her home. He had scored a touchdown against Dartmouth, and many flasks had been passed, so they were both a little drunk. Halfway across the Common, she admitted to him that during the summer, she had kissed a young French artist from the village of Giverny. Without another word, he grabbed her and pulled her to him. And as if she had been waiting for his kiss, she opened her mouth against his and then . . .

She pulled away as if he had poked her with a billy club. "Victor . . . you're . . . no, we can't. Not until we're married." And she hurried across the Common to Fay House.

Married? Well, yes, he supposed. Married. It seemed likely. Someday.

Just before Christmas, Victor went to Boston to buy Barbara a bottle of Chanel scent. He went to Jordan Marsh, because Emily worked there, and the help might help him decide between Chanel No. 5 and something else.

Emily was touching a perfume bottle to her wrist and offering the scent to a woman who wrinkled her nose and went trundling off as though she had been insulted.

Victor had almost forgotten how beautiful she was. He said hello and felt a fluttering in his stomach, as if a big game were beginning.

She was cool to him at first, even pretended not to recognize him. But soon, he was taking her to lunch at Jacob Wirth's, the kind of German saloon where Barbara Abbott would be found only if she had been kidnapped.

Emily ate delicately enough—one knockwurst to his two—but she matched him draft for draft. And the longer they sat together, the more interesting Victor found her. She didn't simply sell perfume. She read. She quoted Irish poets. She loved Yeats.

She said she had taken to following Harvard football because she knew the fullback. This pleased him. She licked the mustard from her fingers. This made him laugh. And for the first time, as he listened to her description of her brother's daily routine, he saw the world through someone else's eyes. This surprised him.

"He comes home exhausted, falls into bed," she said. "Many's the night I find him asleep with a book on his chest. I've offered him a few dollars from my salary—"

"You can't be making a great deal," said Victor.

"I'm not, but he won't take what I offer. He says he's determined to be a burden to no one. So am I." Just then, the check came and she offered to pay half.

"No. This will be my Christmas present to you," said Victor. "As long as you promise to have lunch with me again after New Year's."

She smiled, as demure as Barbara Abbott.

"And wish your brother a Merry Christmas."

The Saturday night before Christmas brought the annual Wedge party.

The guests began arriving at six o'clock. Motorcars puttered up Mount Vernon Street to deliver ladies in mink and gentlemen in silk hats. The more traditional still arrived by coach-and-four, with side lanterns glowing in the cold air, as though the nineteenth century had never ended. And if the night was snowy, sleighs would deliver fine ladies and gentlemen.

But however they arrived, they left in high spirits, enveloped in carols and full of the best cheer that Heywood Wedge could provide, because after all those dark New England Decembers, the descendants of even the staunchest Puritans had come to realize that faith should inspire joy rather than hold it back.

Part of the celebration was a buffet—great hams, roasts of beef, trays of lyonnaise potatoes, tureens of creamed onions, pickled oysters, broccoli florets and . . . desserts, cakes, sweetmeats, oranges, tangerines, nuts . . .

Before the butler rang the dinner bell, Victor took Barbara by the elbow and pivoted her into the dining room, away from the people milling through the front parlor, the study, the foyer, the stairwell. The room was brilliant with candlelight and, for a moment, deserted. So he kissed her.

She giggled and kissed him back, and the kiss grew more passionate than either of them had expected.

Then she pulled away. "Victor, this is terribly naughty, kissing me in your grandfather's dining room with your trousers looking like . . . like a tent at a campsite."

Then Victor heard someone step into the dining room and discreetly clear his throat. Victor turned toward the painting on the wall and said to Barbara, "Marvelous work, don't you think?"

"What . . . oh, yes . . . Copley, isn't it?" Barbara stepped closer to the painting. "Of course, it looks to me as if someone else painted that Bible on the table."

"Someone did." Heywood Wedge stepped into the room, doing it as gracefully as a man with two good legs. "Your eye is excellent."

Barbara smiled. "Well, I have studied in France."

"What does the Bible cover?" asked Victor, angling his body so that the old man would not see his trousers, which had not fully deflated.

"A play, supposedly, and since Reverend Abraham was one of the authors of the anti-theater laws of 1767 . . ."

"That's ironic," said Victor.

"Whenever Aunt Dorothy and Uncle Theodore came, you'd find them in front of this painting, bickering over the play that is supposedly beneath that Bible."

"What was the play?" asked Victor.

"A quarto of some sort," said Heywood. "I once overheard Theodore asking her if they left it in England, in the house where they were exiled."

"Have you ever been there?" asked Victor.

"No. But perhaps you two can go exploring there someday."

Victor and Barbara shot each other nervous glances.

"Yes," Heywood chuckled. "Young people stealing kisses at our Christmas parties quite often end up married. Rather a wonderful honeymoon can be had in England. . . ."

Victor could almost feel the heat of embarrassment from Barbara.

"Yes," mused the old man, "Wales, the Lake District, Scotland . . ."

Victor stammered, "It . . . it sounds wonderful, Grandfather, but—"

"But not for a while." The old man pivoted on his cane and made for the door. "Victor has much yet to learn. All that playwriting business was fine, but economics . . . money . . . there's a future for a young man."

When Heywood had left the room to rejoin his guests, Barbara slipped her hand into Victor's. A moment later, a servant rang the dinner gong. Victor was glad to hear it, though talk of marriage had tightened his stomach considerably.

Commencement seemed to come in six weeks rather than six months. By then, Barbara Abbott was no longer speaking to him.

On a night in May, he had been enjoying billiards and cigars with his mates at the Porcellian when he heard a commotion, followed by the sound of someone rushing up the stairs, and one of the porters shouting, "S'cuse me, ma'am, s'cuse me, but you ain't supposed to be in here."

Victor looked up to see Barbara, in riding boots and jodhpurs, striding toward him, teeth clenched. "Baseball?" she growled. "You like baseball that much, do you?"

"Barbara, dear." He put out a hand to usher her out.

"They say that you've sat with the same little hussy from East Cambridge at every game this year!" And with a crack that resounded like the cue ball, her open hand struck his cheek. Then she turned and stalked out.

Victor stood for a moment, his hand to his face, then he heard Dickey Drake say, "Bad form, Victor. Bad form all round."

"Shut up," said Victor.

"We haven't had entertainment like that in here," said Bram Haddon, "since Biff Mulvehill's mother found out he was tickling burlesque cunnies at the Old Howard."

Victor stalked out to the sound of his mates' laughter, something he might court as a rule but did not welcome now.

The rumors had flown, and those who spread them assumed that even though this East Cambridge girl was the sister of Harvard's right fielder, there could be only one way that she might attract a Porcellian.

Grandfather Heywood had some intuition in all of this. And in Dickey Drake, he had a fine spy. The week before commencement, Heywood heard the latest from Dickey, the son of his eldest daughter.

"And Barbara slapped him? Just like that?" said Heywood.

"Just like that," said Dickey.

"Because he's been to the baseball games with that . . . that Irish girl?"

"I don't know if he's taking her to the games, actually, but he sits with her and cheers for her brother."

"And you saw them kissing?"

"I'm afraid so, sir. They got into your car on Mount Auburn Street, after one of the baseball games. They looked at each other and smiled and then, it was as if they couldn't wait or didn't care who saw them. They just . . . kissed."

Heywood Wedge puffed his cheeks and blew up the sides of his mustache and made a plan to separate Victor from his Irish paramour.

But before Victor heard from his grandfather, he heard from Jimmy Callahan.

Victor was going into the Porcellian for a late dinner. He was alone, though he knew that he would meet friends inside. They would distract him from his predicament and from the sense of melancholy he felt now that his college days were almost over.

He had sent Barbara a note telling her that she had a right to her anger but that there was nothing between him and the Irish girl. This was a lie, but he knew that his attraction for Emily could not last. She could never be suitable company in places where a young man with ambition hoped to go, so he shouldn't burn his bridges with someone as companionable as Barbara. Still, he could not stop seeing Emily . . . for lunch at Jacob Wirth's or long walks on Boston Common, well away from the prying eyes in the Yard.

Just before he stepped into the club, Victor heard someone calling his name.

Beneath the Porcellian Gate, he saw the shadow of Jimmy Callahan. So he stepped across the street and said hello.

A flask flashed in Jimmy's hand. "A year ago, Joe Kennedy stood here, looking up at all you swells celebrating yourselves. He was crushed that he was down here. I told him he was a fool to worry about your phony aristocracy."

"Good advice," said Victor, accepting the proffered flask. "What did he say?"

"Nothing, but I think he took the advice."

"He'll checkmate the lot of us."

"The other night, I told my sister the same thing about a phony aristocrat. Told her to put you behind her and get on with things."

Victor took another sip. "What did she say?"

"She left the room. Went off and cried. She's in love with you, Victor."

"She's a wonderful girl." Victor handed the flask back to Jimmy.

"Your grandfather doesn't think so."

"My grandfather?"

"He came to Memorial Hall yesterday. Found me in the kitchen. Promised to pay my tuition if I saw to it that you and Emily stopped seeing each other."

"Why . . . the old bastard," said Victor. "What did you tell him?"

"I told him to go and fuck himself."

Victor had to smile. He could not imagine anyone saying that to his grandfather.

Now Jimmy took a step closer to Victor. "But here I am, saying what he wanted me to say, all on my own."

"I'm listening."

"If you love her, stop, because it won't work. If you're using her, stop, because I'll kill you." And Jimmy Callahan walked off into the shadows.

The elms were dying in Harvard Yard. The leopard moth blight had attacked in 1909. Two years later, the famous Class Day Elm in front of Holden Chapel was dead, and half the trees, seemingly as permanent as Harvard itself, were gone or pruned so drastically that they looked like amputees, their hacked limbs sprouting sad leaves that gave little shade and less inspiration.

Across this sad space marched the Class of 1911 to their commencement in Sanders Theater. All the Wedges attended—Victor's mother and stepfather, his two aunts, his grandparents. As they paraded back through the Yard to a luncheon in University Hall, Grandfather Heywood hobbled along beside Victor.

"It's a proud day, Victor," he said.

"Yes." Victor walked slowly so the old man on his cane could keep pace. "Though I wish the trees were alive."

"Some change cannot be stopped. But some can."

"What do you mean?"

"The greater changes in the country. The mingling of classes, creeds, races. You know, President Lowell joined our Immigration Restriction League because he agrees."

"Yes, sir," said Victor with a touch of sarcasm. "The help is the help."

"To have order in society, there must be a chain of being," said Heywood. "On the battlefield and in the bedroom. You can't have the rabble overturning things. So we control immigration and see that we don't marry beneath us."

Victor stopped and looked at the old face, heavy, drooped, reddened by the bright sun. "I won't marry beneath me, sir. No matter who I marry . . . when I marry."

Heywood waved the rest of the family on, then said, "Your father would tell you that it's time for you to put off boyish enthusiasms and consider your future."

"I have, sir. You know that. I start in the accounting offices in September."

"That can wait." The old man smiled and took out an envelope and put it into his hand. "A steamer ticket. A year in Europe did marvels for your father. He saw the sights. Met the right people. I want you to do the same."

"Do you want me to meet people, Grandfather, or leave them behind?"

"Just go. You'll see things clearer when you come back."

iv

Victor Wedge was not so much in love with anyone that he would turn down the grand tour, but he did not leave until September, after the second Harvard-Boston Aeronautical Meet, during which he paid a hundred dollars to fly in a Blériot monoplane.

Then he took a month in France. He was in Bavaria for Oktoberfest. He reached Rome in time for a Boston Protestant to hear Christmas mass in St. Peter's. He spent January skiing in the Alps, February in Spain. And at every stop, he followed his grandfather's prescription. He saw the sights, both simple and grand, and he met the people, especially the right people, because in every European capital the Wedges had friends and business associates who saw to Victor's comfort, entertainment, and female companionship.

In late March, he arrived at last in the land of his ancestry and made the pilgrimage to Stratford-on-Avon.

After visiting Shakespeare's birthplace and the site of New Place, he walked up the street to Harvard House and signed his name in the guest book set aside for Harvard men. Then he toured the rooms, peered through the wavy old glass, ran his hand along the ancient adze-hewn beams. He had found one of the taproots of American civilization, sunk in the same sacred earth that formed Shakespeare, for in this house, Robert Harvard had courted Katherine Rogers.

Then he went north to the Lake District, where Wordsworth and his friends had found their inspiration. He climbed the Grisedale Pike. He sat at the head of Derwent Water, at the spot that Ruskin had called the most beautiful view in the world. He felt as if he were taking a grand survey course in English literature. So after Shakespeare and the Romantics, he should have gone back to London and visited some Dickensian slum.

Instead, he hiked west across the greening hills, following the ruins of Hadrian's Wall until he reached the Northumberland village of Barrasford. In the churchyard, he found a grave: REVEREND ABRAHAM WEDGE, 1702–1782, A MINISTER OF GOD, LOYAL TO HIS KING.

A mile beyond, Victor came to Townsend House, an ancient half-timbered manor presided over by Mildred Dunham, Lady Townsend, a wizened old widow with a cynical laugh, a grouchy staff, and a powerful taste for port.

That night, over a dinner of spring lamb and mint jelly, she told him stories passed down to her, of Reverend Wedge and Lydia in exile. Then, she filled her port glass for the fourth time, took him into the library, and showed him the table at which John Singleton Copley was supposed to have painted them.

"The painting hangs in my grandfather's dining room," he told her.

"Does it indeed?" Then she pulled down an ancient volume with a flaking binding. "This is the very book that was on the table before them. The granddaughter was reading *Love's Labours Lost* to the reverend while Copley did his work. She left it as payment for Townsend hospitality."

Victor opened the book and saw two signatures on the endpapers. He did not recognize the first name—Burton Bones—but beneath it was "Ex Libris Lydia Wedge Townsend." And beneath that, the inscription: "To Lord and Lady Townsend, We leave this gift, left to us by an old actor born Benjamin Wedge, as thanks for your hospitality. Your loving American daughter-in-law, Lydia."

Victor could see Lydia before him, reaching out of the past. Then he turned to the title page and saw that it was a quarto, printed in 1598. "I would like to buy this from you, if I might, Lady Mildred."

"Buy it?" The old woman seemed insulted. "I shall give it to you. If I could find the reverend's old commonplace book, which is buried somewhere in my attic, I'd give you that, too. But be satisfied with this."

The next morning, he offered to pay her again, believing that it had been the port speaking the night before, and she reiterated. "It belonged to your ancestor."

"But it's very valuable."

"I have no children. What my greedy nieces and nephews don't know won't hurt them. So take this back to America."

"And she just *gave* him a quarto of *Love's Labours Lost*. Isn't that so, Victor?"

"She gave it to me because it was inscribed by two of my collateral ancestors," said Victor. "One was a minor female poet, the other apparently an old actor."

Harry Elkins Widener looked at the other gentlemen around the table. "I scour Europe for rare books, and he comes up with a treasure worth tens of thousands just by visiting some distant relative."

"Distant in time, space, and blood." Victor wrapped his hands around his snifter. "Rather distant between the ears, too."

The other gentlemen all had a chuckle at the expense of Lady Townsend.

Outside, the stars glittered coldly, and RMS *Titanic* sliced through a calm sea at twenty-two knots.

In the first-class smoking lounge, Victor Wedge basked in the sound of sophisticated laughter, the taste of good brandy, the smell of fine cigars. This, he knew, was where he belonged, aboard the most luxurious vessel ever built, passing witticisms on topics great and small. This was why his grandfather had sent him on the tour— to remind him of his place on the great chain of being.

On boarding, Victor had gone over the passenger list and had found that the ship was like a floating Harvard Club. A good contingent of the best people, as his grandfather would have said, all of them connected by interest, income, breeding, background.

The night before, he had dined with family friends from Boston, the Pratts—George, '90, his wife, their two young sons, and their eleven-year-old daughter, Katherine. Tonight, he was socializing with the Wideners of Philadelphia, beginning with a dinner in honor of Captain Smith and finishing now with brandy and cigars.

Harry Elkins Widener stood and said to the other gentlemen, "You'll excuse Victor and me for a few moments. I must show him some of the treasures I've collected on the trip. Then we'll be back for bridge."

Taking their brandies in hand, the two young men sauntered down to B deck and Widener's luxurious stateroom.

Though he had graduated in 1907, a few months before Victor arrived, they had hit it off immediately. Widener was a fine fellow all around, Victor had concluded, and plainly handsome—hair parted in the middle and slicked to the sides, orderly features, white tie and tails. A pity, Victor thought, that so few single women were aboard, for two such dashing young men as Harry and himself could cut a wide swath.

But Harry seemed more interested in books than in women. "Look here," he said, taking a small dispatch box from the safe in his sitting room. "A first edition of *A Tale of Two Cities.* Mint condition, pages uncut, and—what's best—it's signed by Dickens."

"Marvelous. Marvelous novel, too," said Victor.

Next came a thin pamphlet. *"Heavy News of an Horrible Earthquake in the City of Scarbaria.* It's from 1542. The only one in the world. I also sent back a complete first edition of Gibbon's *Decline and Fall* and a Second Folio, which is not as valuable as the first that I bought a while back—"

"The First Folio brought a record price, didn't it?"

"The most ever for a Shakespeare. But here's the real treasure of this trip." And like a little boy pulling a favorite toy from the bottom of his chest, Widener produced a small, nondescript brown book. "The 1598 edition of the *Essaies* of Sir Francis Bacon. Extraordinarily rare. More valuable than that quarto of yours."

"Really."

"Bernard Quaritch found it. Finest antiquarian in London, Quaritch."

"I've heard of him."

"He asked me if I should like to have the book shipped home with some of my other purchases. I said, 'No. I'll take it along. If the ship sinks, the book will go with me.' Quaritch laughed and said I was going on the *Titanic,* which, of course, is—"

At that moment, the light fixture above them rattled and the brandy in the snifters sloshed back and forth. And from somewhere forward came a low but unmistakable groan, like a giant piano string plucked and vibrating against the side of the ship.

"What's that?" asked Widener.

"Good God!" Victor looked through the window, across the B deck promenade. Something was scraping along the side of the ship, something white.

Widener looked over his shoulder. "Good God!"

They rushed up the staircase to the first-class promenade deck and hurried to the stern as a mountain of ice, towering as high as the ship itself, receded into the darkness.

"Good God," said Widener again.

A dozen other gentlemen had come out of the smoking lounge, while down on the fantail, third-class passengers, mostly immigrants in rough clothes, had set up an indistinct chattering. But they were all talking about the same thing.

"A bloody big growler," said George Pratt of Boston.

"I know I called for ice"—Mr. Carter of Philadelphia looked into his tumbler—"but this is ridiculous."

"Well, she steams on," said Archie Butt of Washington. "She can't have sustained much damage."

"Indeed not," said George Widener, Harry's father. "I'm going to bed."

Someone suggested they return to the bridge table, and Victor said he'd play.

But Widener said he was going to turn in, too. "Enough excitement for one night. See you in the morning, Wedge."

"Yes. Good night." Victor was looking down at the crowd of immigrants who had come out onto the stern deck. Though it was bitterly cold, a dozen of them—Italians and Eastern Europeans and Irish—were starting a game of soccer, using a chunk of ice from the berg. It looked like more fun than four-handed bridge.

Victor was glad it was so cold, or he might have been tempted to join them. But he would be gladder still for another brandy.

As he turned to go back inside, the engines stopped.

Less than half an hour later, Victor Wedge was telling himself to act as his grandfather and his late father would have expected.

He had gone calmly to his cabin and put his topcoat on over his evening dress, then his heavy cork life jacket over his topcoat. Now as he stepped into the C deck companionway, he bumped into the Pratts, all five of them. They were hurrying along a deck that was now canted slightly forward, tilted slightly starboard, and packed with passengers, some of whom were putting on their life jackets and doing as they were told, others of whom were spending more energy complaining to the stewards about the inconvenience.

"Come with us, Victor," said George Pratt. "We'll be your family tonight."

"Thank you."

And the little girl, Katherine, slipped her hand into his. Then Victor stopped. He had not been acting as calmly as he thought.

"What is it?" asked Katherine.

"I have to go back to my room. There's a book I've forgotten."

"What book could be so important?" George Pratt called over his shoulder.

"A quarto"—Victor released Katherine's hand—"of *Love's Labours Lost.*"

"We'll see you on the boat deck then," said Pratt, "and hurry."

It took Victor just moments to retrieve the book, but it was enough time to lose the Pratts. He went along the companionway to the grand staircase and looked for them, but there were scores of families gathering under the great skylight, lining the steps, crowding the vestibule that opened onto the boat deck, and raising a din of nervous conversation.

Then a male voice—very calm, very controlled, entirely British—ordered women and children to the lifeboats, causing the din to rise suddenly in pitch and volume, like a crosscut saw working smooth wood suddenly striking a knot. It was not a sound of panic, thought Victor, but of annoyance.

Stepping out onto the boat deck, however, Victor realized that this was far more serious than a series of precautions. He was struck first by the ferocious roar of steam venting from the stacks. And in the frantic movements of crewmen uncovering lifeboats, he saw fear. Then a white rocket shot startlingly into the sky and exploded above the ship.

Victor told himself again to do what would be expected of him. He helped put ladies aboard lifeboats on the port side. He lashed deck chairs together to form a sort of gangplank, so that when the list from starboard over to port grew more pronounced and the boats swung farther out over the water, passengers could climb from the A deck windows into the boats. And he told himself that if he remained calm, he would survive.

But when he began to notice second- and third-class people pressing upward onto the boat decks, he realized that there were not enough boats for everyone. By then, the roar of the steam had stopped, and the sound of ragtime from the ship's orchestra provided strange accompaniment to the shouts of the officers, the creaking of the davits, and the cries of families separated.

Victor decided that it was time to consider his own survival—calmly, of course. No bad form allowed. So he made his way aft, away from the rising water, away from the crowd, over to the starboard side, near the stern, where the sense of panic was more controlled, and lifeboats were taking men aboard, especially men in expensive overcoats.

"Victor!" Widener was standing near a boat.

"Where are your parents?" asked Victor.

"My mother went onto one of the port boats. My father's—"

"Here." Mr. Widener stood at the rail with Mr. Thayer of Phila-delphia.

"Do you have your book?" asked Widener.

Victor slapped his pocket. "Right here."

"I have Francis Bacon," said Widener. "I wish to God I'd brought the other two."

Victor noticed three women coming along the boat deck. He said to Widener, "By the time they load those ladies, you could go and be back."

"I've been thinking to stay with the ship, Victor." Widener paused for a moment and said, "But if you can, hold the boat—"

"There'll be no holdin' anything, sir," said First Officer Mur-doch, who was in charge of the loading on the starboard side.

But Widener was already disappearing into the first-class stairwell.

"Harry! Wait!" shouted Victor.

Just then, a dozen people from third class, eight men and four women, came clamoring from somewhere, shouting in their brogues and accents and foreign tongues.

Seeing them, Murdoch shouted, "All right! Lower away."

"Let us on!" cried an Irishman. "There's room."

Victor said, "Wait for Widener."

"No more waiting," cried Murdoch, looking down the canted deck. "We're running out of time."

"Here now!" screamed another Irishman. "Take the women, any-way."

"All right," shouted Murdoch. "But only the women." And he showed them the pistol in his hand. "Women only."

Victor watched the four women climb aboard while the men, by hand gestures and eye contact, told one another that they would rush the boat. Victor put himself behind Murdoch, in a position to fight them. But they made no move.

Once the women were aboard, Murdoch looked at George Widener and Mr. Thayer, as if offering them the chance to climb aboard, but neither of them moved. They were true to their class, thought Victor, and acted like gentlemen.

So Murdoch shouted, "Lower away!" and the lifeboat dipped below the level of the boat deck.

And then, thought Victor, the third-class males did what he should have expected of them. All eight rushed the boat.

Murdoch screamed for them to stop, but they kept coming. So he fired, not into the air—it was too late for that—but right into the biggest of them. The man stopped suddenly, but none of the others did, for in that night of rising panic, the collapse of one man was nothing, and the rest leapt past Victor for the boat.

And somehow, Victor was knocked backward, so that he was flying, twisting, reaching out.

He saw the black water below him. Then he struck the gunwale of the lifeboat, heard one of his ribs crack, and struck his head against the boot sole of the one who'd jumped ahead of him. At the same moment, he heard two loud splashes thirty feet below as two immigrants missed the boat.

And he was falling, too, sliding backward as the boat swayed crazily from the impact of several bodies.

Then one of the Irishmen, safe on the lifeboat, grabbed his sleeve. "Hang on."

And an Italian grabbed the shoulder harness of his life vest.

And from somewhere above him, he heard Harry Elkins Widener's voice. "Hang on, Victor, old boy. And good luck."

"Aye, hang on," said the Irishman who had almost killed him and was now saving his life.

Victor looked up into their faces—one dark and bearded, one ghostly white with a bulbous potato nose, and he thought, what a place for the Earl of Mount Auburn.

Chapter Twenty-four

═══════

"SO . . . YOU'RE telling us that Victor Wedge went back for a book?" asked Peter Fallon.

"Yes." Katherine Pratt Carrington looked out over the Gulf of Mexico. "They say that people who survived the sinking either remembered every detail or buried it as if it never happened. All I need to do is think of a cold clear night, and it all comes back."

Florida in early April: like Massachusetts in late August. Temperature in the eighties, breeze light, cumulus clouds floating over the Gulf. A good place for a weekend getaway, especially if it meant a chance to talk to someone who had actually looked into the eyes of Victor Wedge.

Peter and Evangeline were sitting with Katherine Pratt Carrington on the little veranda of her winter home on the island of Captiva.

"You know," said Katherine, "I lost my whole family that night . . . father, mother, both brothers."

"Didn't your mother go onto a lifeboat with you?"

"Yes. But they filled the boat only halfway on the boat deck. As the ship settled, the lifeboats on the port side swung away from the hull. So they cranked the boat down to the promenade deck, A deck, and called for ladders."

"Ladders?" asked Peter.

"Once the boats were level with the promenade deck, they wanted to run ladders out the windows for gangplanks. But no one could find any. So they lashed chairs together and used boathooks to draw the boat against the ship. Three more women climbed aboard, and then two men.

"My mother pulled herself up—she was a great one for high dudgeon—and glared at the men. 'This is a boat for women and children *only!*'

"'There are no more women and children *around*,' said one of them. And you know, he was right, at least as far as the promenade deck was concerned. Some of those boats were only half full when they left. So, my mother looked at the young officer in charge of our boat and said, 'If we're letting men aboard on A deck, there are men on the boat deck who should be allowed aboard, too.' She shouted up, but it seemed that our men had gone looking for another boat, so she said to the young officer, 'Wait here.'

"'Madam,' said the officer, 'we can't wait.'

"But my mother jumped onto the deck, stuck her head back out the window, and said, 'I am a first-class passenger. I *demand* that you wait here until I fetch my husband and sons.' She had a great sense of herself, my mother did. She looked at me and said, 'I'll be right back.'

"That was the last I saw of her. The people from second and third class were finding their way up from below, the people in the boat were shouting to leave, and—"

"What about Victor Wedge?" asked Evangeline.

"I didn't see him until next morning, aboard the *Carpathia*. He was very kind to me, but what could anyone really do for me by then?" She looked off toward the Gulf.

Evangeline put her hand on Katherine's arm.

The old woman said, "You know, longevity can be a curse. I've lived over ninety years with that memory. I've outlived both my children, too."

And Evangeline's eyes filled with tears. Her mother had been one of those children, dead of breast cancer just a few years.

The old woman patted her granddaughter's hand. "One of the

lessons of longevity is to keep looking ahead. So . . . I'm glad that you two have come down here together. That bodes well for the future. I'm glad you're—"

Evangeline said, "We're in separate bedrooms, Grandmother."

"Oh, hell," said Katherine, "sleep with him. You'll be dead for a long time."

"I couldn't agree more," said Peter. "But can we get back to the story?"

"See," said Evangeline. "He wants to sleep with me to get something."

"Maybe *you're* what he wants to get," said Katherine.

"The wisdom of old age," said Peter. "But the book . . . Did Victor Wedge have it with him on the *Carpathia*?"

"I asked him. He said he had it in his pocket."

"Do you remember the title?" asked Peter.

"Yes. He even offered to let me read it to take my mind off my grief. Very nice of him, though not too effective. It was . . . Oh, I'm not sure. . . ."

"Was it printed or handwritten?" asked Peter gently.

"Oh . . . printed."

"Did it have the word *Love* in the title?"

"Yes," she said, brightening. "I remember. It was *Love's Labours Lost.*"

"Not *Won*?"

"The title of the play is *Love's Labours Lost,* Peter. I know my Shakespeare."

Peter sank back in his chair. "Then it's a quarto. *Love's Labors Lost.* It has to be."

"But what happened to it?" asked Evangeline.

"Oh," said Katherine, "I don't know. Victor and I were never close, because you know, all the men who survived without going into the water were a little suspect, especially to those of us who lost our families that night."

After dinner, Peter and Evangeline walked across the road and out onto the beach. As their eyes adjusted, the deep Gulf darkness became more than a black sky pinpricked with light. There were so many stars that the sky seemed iridescent, as alive as the plankton-blooming sea below.

"So, is it over now?" Evangeline started to walk.

"If Wedge brought back a quarto of *Love's Labours Lost*, I think we're still on the job. A quarto can be a million-dollar book these days."

"You know," she said, "I have to admit I like it."

"The chase?"

"The sense that people are watching you, wondering what you're up to, trying to beat you to the prize. The sense of purpose."

"I like it, too." He put his arm around her, and they walked together for a time in silence, the cool sand massaging their feet.

Then she said, "Did you love your wife?"

"At the beginning. Your husband?"

"I met him in Siena. I was doing an article on great views in Italy. I was climbing the campanile and bumped into him on the stairs. He'd come to deliver a paper on face-lifts in Florence. He invited me to lunch . . . and then . . ."

"Why didn't you have kids?"

"We couldn't. Nothing worked. I suggested adoption. But he said if we couldn't have kids of our own, he didn't want to tie himself down. So, it was boob jobs, then Barbardos; tummy tucks, then Tuscany; liposuctions, then—"

"Lithuania?"

"We went everywhere else. It was fun at first, but after a while, it seemed to me like we were running away. When I heard you'd had a son, I envied you."

"The only reason I'm enviable," he said.

"A good answer, even if it isn't true."

Then he stopped and kissed her.

"So, it's not over?" she said.

"The search for the Shakespeare?"

"The search for something."

"We'll know in the morning."

They woke up in the same bed and agreed that it was a good place to be.

About ten, they drove to the 'Tween Waters Inn, rented a Boston Whaler, and headed up the Intracoastal Waterway to the island of Useppa.

If there was a Bostonian's fantasy of Florida, Useppa was it. An island a mile long, maybe a quarter mile wide, a handsome old lodge put up by some railroad baron at the end of the nineteenth century, a hundred condo units clustered here and there—all painted Nantucket gray and white, with tin roofs and balconies and views of the mangrove islands to the east or the barrier islands to the west.

They tied up at the main wharf, amid cabin cruisers, cigarette boats, and a hundred-foot yacht with a uniformed captain and a crew.

Hoi polloi didn't just land at Useppa and get out for a stroll, so Fallon told the harbormaster that he had come for lunch with Mrs. Harriet Wedge.

"Good that Mrs. Wedge invited your grandmother to lunch a few times," whispered Peter to Evangeline.

"Let's hope she's there." And they started walking, because there were no cars on the island, just golf carts puttering along paths that wound through the palm fronds, along the beach, and across the open expanses of grass.

At the north end of the island, Peter and Evangeline came to a cluster of two-story units baking in the sun. Three golf carts were parked in the little cul-de-sac. Two of the condos were already closed up as the Florida summer approached and the Yankee snowbirds headed north.

They went up to the door of number sixty and rang the bell. No answer.

"I told you this was a long shot," said Evangeline.

Peter looked down the little service alley between number sixty and number fifty-nine. The air-conditioning units were running. "Someone's here." He went down the alley, and Evangeline followed him.

At the back, there were verandas overlooking a little cove, a dock, a few small boats. A big pelican was perched on a piling, on a plastic piling cap that was supposed to make it harder for pelicans to perch. The bird glanced at Peter, fluttered its wings as though it considered leaving, then went back to thinking about whatever it had been thinking about. Probably fish.

It was hot enough that one of the distant mangrove islands seemed to have water running through it—a mirage. And the heat heightened that funky smell, distinctly Floridian, of sweet earth, decaying vegetation, and . . . marijuana?

Just then, one of the air-conditioning units shut off, and Peter realized that there was another sound, somewhere above him. Someone—two someones—were having sex. He could see the naked bodies through the railings on the second-floor deck, going at it doggie-style.

Thump-bump, thump-bump. Oh, yes. Oh, God. *Thump-bump. Thump-bump.*

"Peter," whispered Evangeline, "I don't think that's Harriet Wedge up there."

Thump-bump. Harder. *Thump-bump.* Faster. *Thump-bump-thump—bump.*

And Peter called up to them, as innocently as he could, "Hel-lo?" *Thump-bump . . . bump . . . thump . . .*

"Excuse me," called Peter.

Bump . . . bump . . . The man's head popped up. "What? Who the fuck are you?"

"I'm . . . I'm sorry to bother you. I'm looking for Mrs. Wedge."

"Well, she's not here. Good-bye."

"Do you know when she'll be back?"

"No."

"Could you tell her that Peter Fallon and Evangeline Carrington were here?"

And the man said, "Fallon? The book guy?"

"Yes."

"Wait a minute." There was a rustling of bathing suits and bodies, and a middle-aged man with good Wedge height and firm Wedge features and an un-Wedge ponytail and a decidedly un-Wedge earring came down to the back sliders. "I'm Franklin."

"Will's brother?" asked Fallon.

"Yeah. The one they never talk about." He offered his hand. "I'm still marching to the barricades while my brother marches to the bank."

"It was your mother I wanted to talk to," said Peter.

"Mom's not here. She's . . . peripatetic. Gone to the Bahamas for a few."

A dark-haired woman wearing a bikini appeared from the house.

"Meet Marie," said Franklin. "She's more fun than Mom. And Marie, could you bring us some iced tea?"

Marie looked at Peter and Evangeline as if they owed her money, or a good orgasm, then she went padding away.

"Great girl." Franklin gestured for them to sit beneath an umbrella table on the deck. "She's one of my graduate students, writing a thesis on images of female subjugation in the novels of Hemingway. Such a pig, that Hemingway."

"I . . . I kind of like him," said Evangeline.

"The original male chauvinist." Franklin looked down at his suit. "Now that the Viagra is wearing off, is there something that I can help you with?"

"My business is rather personal," said Peter.

"The lost Shakespeare?" Franklin laughed, as if relishing the look of consternation that spread across Fallon's face.

"Well, yes," said Peter. "What do you know about it?"

"Can't tell." Franklin brought his fingers to his lips and laughed again, a little giddy, as if he was stoned. "If there's a manuscript out there, I'm after it, too."

"You, too?" said Fallon. "You know, your brother says that Harvard will lay claim to it."

"Harvard University. Oppressor of the people. Tool of the rulers." He winked. "You like that? Alliteration followed by assonance."

"That's why you're an English professor, baby." Marie returned with a tray of iced teas and a little Baggie of marijuana.

Franklin looked at Peter. "If I find it, I'll liberate it. But a guy like you, you're just in it for the money—"

"There's more at stake here than money," said Peter.

"There always is. That's how I've lived my life, right, Marie?"

"Principles all the way." Marie began to roll a joint. "That's you."

"Principles," said Franklin. "Something my baby brother lacks."

Evangeline said, "Hard to picture Will Wedge as anyone's baby brother."

Franklin lit the joint and inhaled. "Hard to imagine him smokin' a bone, either." He let out the smoke. "The Revolution lives, baby." Then he offered the joint to Fallon, who hesitated, then reached for it.

And Evangeline stood. "I think we'll be running along. Wouldn't want you to waste all this good dope and Viagra . . . on conversation."

Peter swung his hand to the iced tea and finished it in a gulp. Then he stood and said, "I have just one question. Did your mother ever tell you anything about this play?"

Franklin took another long toke. "You know, I can't fuckin' remember just now."

"Well, *that* was enlightening," said Peter.

"I had to get you out of there," answered Evangeline. "I saw you stoned once."

"*Once.* I smoked three joints in my whole life. If I smoked with him, I'd only be doing it to get information."

"He's a professional stoner, and you think *you're* going to get information out of *him*? Before he told you a thing, you'd be so wasted, you'd be telling him the numbers of your bank accounts."

When they were in the middle of the sound, speeding south, Evangeline said over the roar of the engine, "You know, Franklin Wedge looks like Will."

"A little."

"How long do you think he's been growing that ponytail? A year, maybe?"

"Yeah. Maybe. So what?"

"Will Wedge signed in at the Mass. Historical Society last September thirtieth. But Will was in Los Angeles."

"You think Franklin is the one who went through the Theodore Wedge Papers?"

"Could be."

They sped on for another mile or so, then Peter turned the boat and ran it onto the back shore of an uninhabited barrier island.

"Where are we going?" she asked.

"For a swim. There's a deserted beach on the other side," he said.

"I'm not wearing my suit."

"I know. Neither am I."

By Monday, Peter was back in Boston, and it was snowing. The forsythia had bloomed, and the tulips were trying, but winter was giving New England the finger one more time.

Peter was sitting a little gingerly because he was sunburned in some strange places.

"You met him?" said Orson. "The phantom Franklin?"

"He's no phantom. He's a professor of English at the University of Vermont."

"*Associate* professor. As I told you, he's mostly a professional crusader. Once disappeared for six years. Said he was off fighting for the Cause."

"What cause?"

"Come on, Peter. Don't you remember the sixties? The *Cause*."

Just then, the doorbell rang. Bernice got up to answer it, and a moment later, Jimmy was standing in the doorway.

"In or out?" said Peter.

"In," said Jimmy, never one to waste words.

Peter and Orson let out a shout. In an instant they were both at the boy's side, shaking his hand and patting him on the back.

Bernice came in carrying a tray—four glasses and a bottle of champagne that Peter kept in the office refrigerator. "Your dad's a happy man," she said. "But remember, Jimmy, Harvard means nothin' unless you're a good man, too."

"I think Jimmy knows that," said Peter, and he proposed the toast. Then Peter said, "Have you sent in your acceptance yet?"

"To tell you the truth, I'm waiting to hear from the other schools I applied to."

Peter put down his champagne glass. "Why would you do that?"

The boy shrugged. "Harvard made me wait. I'll make them wait."

Orson laughed. "As contrary as your father. I like that."

"So do I," said Peter after a moment. "But don't forget, Jimmy, Harvard stands for something."

"Yeah," hooted Bernice. "Big tuition bills."

Peter said, "A tradition of questioning conventional wisdom while swimming in a sea of it, of testing yourself against some of the smartest people in the world, of—"

"Blah, blah, blah." Bernice took her champagne and went to answer the phone.

"But what if everyone's better at being the best than you are?" asked Jimmy.

"You might be intimidated at first," said Peter. "But you'll figure out that you're just as smart as most of them, or you'll learn how to make it seem as if you are."

"So that's what makes Harvard special? Learning how to bullshit?"

"Insight already," said Orson.

Bernice called from the other room. "Will Wedge is on the phone."

"Tell him I'll call him back. I'm taking my son to lunch." Then Peter looked at the boy. "To celebrate the fact that he now has an option and can take it or not."

Evangeline had gone back to New York.

It was time for her to sit down with an editor over lunch and see about selling a nonfiction book on the history of the Radcliffe Eight. She hoped that the restaurant had soft chairs, because she was sunburned in strange places, too.

She liked to walk from her co-op to midtown, along a route that led her past several bookstores. One of her favorites was a second-floor place called Books in the Attic, on Madison Avenue. And one of her favorite corners was the New England section. She'd already come across half a dozen interesting titles for her research there, including a reprint of the poems of Lydia Wedge from the 1920s.

She said hello to Mr. Gordon, the owner with the thick glasses, the hairpiece, and the voice that sounded like a parrot with a Bronx accent. She left her bag and briefcase at the counter, and went browsing.

A quick scan of the New England shelves showed nothing new. But her eye was drawn to a red spiral binding on the bottom shelf, among the oversize books. The binding held a thin volume of fifty-four pages, eleven by fourteen inches, with heavy cardboard covers: *John Harvard's Tercentenary 1636–1936*. On the cover was a photograph of dozens of men in tall silk hats listening to President James Bryant Conant deliver a speech.

"Just got that in," said Gordon, peering down the aisle. "Bought out the attic of an old Harvard grad in Chappaqua."

"Interesting." She flipped it open.

The book had been published by the Associated Harvard Clubs to commemorate the Tercentenary. It was filled with portraits of the participants and candid shots of the celebration that unfolded in the second week of September 1936.

While Mr. Gordon told her that six people had already looked the book over and that it would probably be gone by tomorrow—a line he repeated a hundred times a day—Evangeline flipped through the pictures. How different the world must have been, she thought, and yet how familiar Harvard looked.

And there he was. The same face she had seen in the portrait in Will Wedge's office: Victor Wedge, appearing not once but twice in a two-page spread with the heading "Opening the Bicentennial Package, September 8."

There was a large photograph of the package, wrapped in string and sealed with wax. She read the words "Letters from Alumni of Harvard College in August 1836 . . ." Beneath it was a picture of the faculty meeting room where the unveiling took place.

On the opposite page were photographs showing white-haired old President Emeritus A. Lawrence Lowell and Conant bending over the package, while four gentlemen, including Victor Wedge, '11, secretary of the Alumni Association, looked on.

Wedge was handsome, with just a little gray around the ears and in the mustache. In the first photo, he was looking down at the package and the envelopes spilled across the table. In the second, President Lowell was preparing to sign something, while Victor held an envelope in his hand and looked at the camera.

Evangeline Carrington studied the man staring at her from out of the past, captured by chemicals and light almost seven decades before, and she wondered: Was he challenging her to figure him out, or inspiring her to finish his work? Whichever it was, she felt now that these people were talking to her, and she had to listen.

She bought the book for forty dollars, then took out her cell phone and called Peter's office.

But Peter was already on the trail of Victor Wedge. He'd had lunch with his son, now he was walking through the slushy snow in Harvard Yard, on his way to the Archives.

And he was talking on his cell phone with Victor's grandson. "You called me?"

"I hear you've met my brother," said Will Wedge with a big laugh.

"I wanted to meet your *mother*." Peter stepped over a puddle. "If you won't let me see her, it makes me suspicious."

"I didn't send her away. If you'd wanted, I would have set up an appointment." Wedge's voice grew colder. "I thought we were working together on this."

"Then when can I see her?"

"She's gone to England. She goes every spring. Best time of year there, April and May. She'll be back at commencement, but I'll get her number for you."

"Something's happening at commencement," said Peter. "What is it?"

"Just get me something definitive. By commencement. And congratulations on your boy's admission. I hope my letter did some good."

By the twentieth century, Harvard alumni no longer needed Mr. Sibley to memorialize them. They did it themselves in the Class Reports.

Every five years, in advance of reunions, alumni were asked to fill out forms: address, occupation, degrees, names of their spouses, birth dates of their kids, and brief narratives of their lives. These were then printed as Class Reports so that everyone could compare themselves with all those kids who had seemed so smart all those years before.

Some people would write a paragraph or two. Some wrote nothing. A few decided, on some anniversary, that it was time to define themselves for friends they hadn't seen in years. The reports were a unique literary form. When people examined their lives, especially for public consumption, they could produce narratives that might be boastful or modest, despairing or hopeful, regretful or smug, superficial or profound, flippant or serious . . . and sometimes all of the above, all at the same time.

But whether Class Reports came from 1930, 1960, or 1990, they provided fascinating pictures of the human parade. People always remembered where they were on December 7, 1941, or November 22, 1963, or September 11, 2001. And for all the differences between generations, human nature changed little.

Old Class Reports were kept on file at the Archives. Peter ordered the reports for the Class of 1911 and started with the Fifth Reunion Report from 1916.

Victor Wedge, A.B. Home Address: Louisburg Square, Boston, Mass. Occupation: Pilot, Lafayette Escadrille. Current Address: Somewhere in France.

Peter was already impressed. He read on:

Hello to all you lucky lads warm by the hearth with your sweetheart on your arm and your pipe packed with good tobacco. I am in France, repaying Europe for the pleasures I enjoyed on my postgraduate tour from Paris to an ancestral home in the wilds of Northumberland.

Was that the house where Reverend Abraham and Lydia had posed for Copley? wondered Peter. Was it the house that the commonplace book had come from? Had Victor been there?

On the return trip I enjoyed the company of Harry Widener, so you know the name of the ship on which I sailed.

Victor knew Widener. Did they talk about rare books? Was this the definitive answer that Will Wedge had been seeking for six months? Peter read on:

My survival was a result of dumb luck, good fortune, and the strong hands of two complete strangers, immigrants seeking a better life in America. As all who knew my grandfather can imagine, he and I engaged in many spirited discussions after that. He had been founder of the Immigration Restriction League, and up to the time of his death, I was attempting to change his mind.

I believe that we are Americans, but we are citizens of the world, too. That is why I joined the ambulance corps. Then I heard that Norman Prince, a fine aviating chap from '08, had gotten permission from the French to form an American flying corps. Some of you may remember that I was a member of the Aeronautical Society, so it should come as no surprise that I went running, especially when I realized that the squadron contained several stout Harvard fellows. And now we fly and fight.

Chapter Twenty-five

═══════

1918–1936

VICTOR WEDGE no longer called himself the Earl of Mount Auburn. He had earned a better title: lieutenant. And he was no longer awakened by dreams of the *Titanic*, because other terrors had crowded out that night from his mind. And he no longer relived the moment when he survived while his friend Widener was left to die.

He had questioned his actions many times afterward. Why had he suggested that Widener go back for his books? Had he hoped to take the seat that would have been Widener's? Why had he positioned himself as he did, before those men charged the boat? Did he hope to stop them, or go over with them? And once he was in the boat, why didn't he demand to get off and rejoin the other gentlemen? Because he was no different from any man. He wanted to survive, and he did.

After that, a strange sense of guilt followed him for years. But if he needed redemption, he found it in war, among men who judged him by his actions, in a world where survival was often no more than a matter of chance. He came home with a fractured spine and a Purple Heart earned in a crash landing, and the doctors said he would live the rest of his life in pain, but some pains were easier to bear than others.

On a cold November afternoon in 1918, he came into the Yard by the Quincy Street gate, and before he had passed between Emerson Hall and Sever, he saw it. Where Gore Hall had raised slender Gothic spires toward heaven, twelve massive columns and a giant staircase now dominated the Yard.

Harry Widener's mother had built a library for Harvard as a monument to her son. Some were shocked by its size and mass, but Widener Library expressed something altogether new in the way that Harvard saw itself.

President Lowell had put it best to a group of freshmen at the start of the war. "If the torch of civilization is to be carried forward, it is for the youth of America to take the place of those Europeans giving their lives. You are recruited and are now in training."

The vision was as grandiose as the library. But in a world where every new insight into human existence was met with an advance in the science of human slaughter, a library such as Widener was important not only to scholars but to society, just as John Harvard's books had been vital not only to a new college but to a colony planted on the edge of a wilderness.

At the dedication ceremony, Library Director Archibald Coolidge had borne a single volume up the steps, past the assembled faculty, and into the library. It was not the Bible but Downame's *Christian Warfare with the World, the Flesh, and the Devil,* the only John Harvard book to have survived, the last cutting from his tree of knowledge.

Six hundred and fifty thousand volumes had sprouted from it, and Victor was about to add another.

First, he had to meet someone. He hoped that he would recognize her. But when she came up to him and said hello, he had to look twice, because she had pushed her hair under her hat, wore a black coat over a dress, and seemed years older than twenty-seven.

"Emily?" He had thought often of her smile, had seen it often in his mind's eye.

"You look dashing." She touched the Purple Heart on the lapel of his uniform. "It's been years."

"Six, to be exact. At your brother's last baseball game."

"He had three hits," she said. "A week later, you left to work in your grandfather's New York office. Next thing I knew, you were writing from France."

"Now I'm home," he said. "To stay."

"I wish Jimmy was," she said.

"Let's go." He offered his arm, and together they climbed the steps of Widener.

The archivist was waiting for them in the Harry Elkins Widener Room, the magnificent repository of Widener's books, the heart of the library.

Victor glanced at the portrait of Harry looking down on his treasures. Then he placed the 1598 quarto of *Love's Labours Lost* on the table.

"Are you certain about this?" asked the archivist.

"It's in honor of Miss Callahan's brother," said Victor. "He died in the Argonne."

"He's a hero," said the archivist. "Giving a quarto in his name is an honor."

"Indeed," said Victor. "The bequest should read, 'In Memory of James Callahan, Class of 1912, May 5, 1890–September 27, 1918. He embodied the best of Harvard and performed the highest of love's labors for family and friends, for college and country.'"

That evening, they had a dinner in Jimmy Callahan's memory.

It was held in a private dining room in the Harvard Union and was organized by Jimmy's old friend, Joe Kennedy.

There were a dozen men from 1912 there, a dozen more from other classes. They talked of the war, which seemed at last to be ending; of the terrifying influenza, which had swept into Massachusetts in September and was abating after killing thousands; and of old times, which seemed happier with each passing year.

Before the meal, Kennedy and Victor made wide circles around each other as they worked the crowd. Finally, they passed close enough that they had to speak.

Kennedy raised his glass and eyed Victor's Purple Heart. "You've done the nation a great service."

"So have you." Victor eyed Kennedy's silk cravat and expensive suit.

Kennedy had already served as a state bank examiner, as president of one of the few Boston banks not controlled by men related to Victor Wedge, and as a director of the Bethlehem Steel shipyard. He said, "Building ships to defeat Germany seemed a good use of my skills."

"You know," said Victor, "one night under the Porcellian Gate, Jimmy and I talked about you. I said you'd checkmate the lot of us. I think I was right."

"Jimmy and I talked there, too," answered Kennedy. "He said the best way to checkmate you Brahmins was to outwork you. He said we'd come to Harvard to do more than join your aristocracy. He said we'd build a meritocracy."

"To meritocracy, then." Victor touched his glass to Kennedy's.

"To Jimmy," answered Kennedy.

Victor Wedge and Joseph Kennedy did not become friends that night. That would be for their sons to do. But when Kennedy offered his hand at the end of the evening, Victor accepted, because he had decided on the *Titanic* that he would accept any hand offered to him, whether it came from a gentleman in first class or an Irish immigrant in a lifeboat.

After dinner, Victor asked Emily to walk with him in the Yard. It was chilly, but they had been warmed by good spirits, good stories, and sentimental speeches.

After they had gone some distance into the shadows, he thought to take her hand, but when he brushed against her, there was no yielding of her posture, no suggestion that she would welcome his touch. So he clapped his hands behind his back and listened to his bootheels clicking on the path.

"I thought there were some lovely sentiments expressed tonight," she said. "Jimmy would have loved to be there."

"He *was* there." Victor put his arm around her.

She pulled away. "Victor . . ."

"Your brother always told me this couldn't work. But—"

"What about Barbara?"

"She married Bram Haddon while I was working in New York."

He stopped and looked into her eyes. "It's half the reason I joined the ambulance corps."

"Victor—"

"I'm not asking for more than a chance—"

"Victor, I'm engaged."

He supposed that he shouldn't have been surprised. It had been six years and they had corresponded only sporadically, but he felt his stomach shrivel at her words.

"He's in the infantry. His name is Ed O'Hill. We're moving to California after the wedding." Emily stepped back and withdrew a locket from around her neck. "My grandmother gave me this before she died. But when I took out my grandfather's picture to put in my Ed's, I found a picture of a woman. An ancestor of yours."

Somewhere in his head, Victor heard the voice of his late grandfather, reminding him that the help was the help. "Ancestor? How do you know?"

Emily fiddled with a tiny set of clasps, and a second compartment popped open. "I don't think my grandmother ever had any idea this was here." She slipped out a browned sheet of onionskin paper and gave it to Victor.

He unfolded it, and in the dim light of a gas lamp, he read:

Lydia Wedge Townsend's small gift of majestic proportion: revealed in two gilt-edged envelopes, one in the safe at Fleming and Royce, the other in the packet to be opened at the Tercentenary. If, by 1936, Harvard has not educated women, if ignorance prevails, Douglass Wedge Warren and his assigned successors are granted access to the envelope in the Fleming and Royce safe and are authorized to deny Harvard the gift.

Victor finished reading and said, "I don't understand. . . ."

Emily gestured for him to follow her . . . across the Yard, through the Johnson Gate, which now formed Harvard's portal to the world, past the Unitarian Meeting House, and into the burying ground. It was dark among the headstones. But Victor knew the resting place of Lydia Wedge Townsend, the family poet.

"I memorized the inscription," said Emily. "'Seek truth through the years, but seek it for all, / Bestow knowledge freely to those who may call / Make this your goal till a century turns, / And the Bard will applaud as humanity learns.'"

He mused on the last line. "'The Bard will applaud as humanity learns.'"

"That's Shakespeare, right?" said Emily. "*Love's Labours Lost.*"

"A small gift of majestic proportion," said Victor, "which we just gave to the Harvard rare book collection in the name of James Callahan."

"Do you think those gilt-edged envelopes give directions to Townsend House?"

"It would make sense," said Victor. "But considering all the records that were lost in the Great Fire, we won't know for certain until the Tercentenary."

Emily took his hand. "Victor, that book went to the Harvard library to honor my brother. Don't let anything diminish that gift."

"What's done is done."

"But when the Tercentenary comes around, don't forget what Jimmy always said . . . to Joe Kennedy, to me, maybe even to you. The way you fight ignorance is through meritocracy. So don't give Harvard anything it hasn't earned."

After a moment, Victor laughed. "I think Lydia would agree. And the Bard would applaud."

She looked into his eyes, and the steam from her breath mingled with his. "My brother was right about a lot. But I think he might have been wrong about us."

"Then give me a chance, Emily."

"I love my infantryman, Victor. I never knew if I loved you. It's too late to find out. Just remember Jimmy." She kissed his cheek and turned away.

He stood in the dark and watched her picking her way past the headstones. Then he folded the sheet of onionskin and put it into his wallet.

ii

The Class of 1911 Report for the tenth reunion:

Victor Wedge, A.B. Home Address: Louisburg Square, Boston. Occupation: investment banker, Wedge, Fleming, and Royce, 58 State Street, Boston, Mass. Spouse: Barbara Abbott (November 2, 1919). It has been my good fortune, after many adventures, to have married my college sweetheart. I am now learning about finance. Wedge, Fleming, and Royce is my school. And the college remains my passion. Whose heart did not swell with pride when our Crimson won the '19 Rose Bowl? After that, who would hesitate to join the Alumni Association? And after all that we have seen, who would not contribute to the college? For it is only through the expansion of knowledge that we will combat whatever lies before us. I personally have contributed a bit of knowledge to the library, a volume in memory of our classmate James Callahan. Go and read it. I hope to see as many of you as possible at the reunion.

Victor poured optimism into the report, and none of it was false. He and Barbara had reunited a year after her divorce, and the future looked promising.

But something happened a few months after his reunion that caused him to re-read that sheet of onionskin, especially the part about Harvard ignorance.

On an afternoon in the fall of 1921, he received a letter from one of Harvard's ancients, Moorfield Story, '66, a past overseer and current president of the National Association for the Advancement of Colored People. It requested Victor's signature on a petition that Harvard end Jim Crow policies in regard to the housing of Negro freshmen.

Jim Crow? At Harvard? Victor knew there had been talk about limiting the number of Jews, but what was this? He read the note included with the petition:

President Lowell has decreed mandatory residence for freshmen in the new halls he's building along the river. He sees this as a way of promoting class solidarity and identity, but not, apparently, for Negroes. A colored freshman named Knox had his room assignment withdrawn after administrators learned the color of his skin. Considering your war record and your family's association with President Lowell, your signature would carry great weight in reminding Lowell of his responsibilities.

Victor did not sign the petition. Instead, he took the subway to Cambridge.

He came up the stairs in the circular kiosk, which was like a rock in a fast-flowing stream of clanging streetcars and clattering Model Ts. The country quiet of Harvard Square was now a thing of memory. But the noise of modernity made the Yard seem even more a place of refuge from the fashion of the moment, a place out of time, perhaps because it embraced all time, at least as America marked it.

Victor walked to University Hall beneath the elms that had been replanted after the blight. He waited a polite twenty minutes and was then admitted to the office of Abbott Lawrence Lowell.

"Victor, my boy"—Lowell pumped his hand—"how's Barbara?"

"Just fine, sir. Fine."

"I can't tell you how happy the Abbotts were when you two got together."

"I was very lucky, sir."

"Yes . . . yes. Her aunts all said she married Bram Haddon 'on the rebound,' so to speak. Bram's a fine fellow, but—"

"Barbara and I are very happy, sir."

"And doing quite well, from all I hear." Even at sixty-five, his hair and walrus mustache gone gray, Lowell seemed like nothing so much as energy compacted and waiting to be released upon an unsuspecting world. "I hope you received my note of thanks for your reunion contribution. Gifts like yours—"

"I'm not here about money, sir," said Victor. "I wanted to ask you about a petition that's crossed my desk."

Lowell's face reddened. "Mr. Story doesn't understand the dilemma we face."

"I'm afraid I don't, either."

"You can't force white men, especially from the South and West, to live and eat with Negroes."

"I thought your goal was to create a sense of identity in each class, so democracy could flourish and exclusivity would be based on achievement rather than bloodline."

"A concept that should be alien to an old Porcellian like you," grunted Lowell. Though his bloodlines were as ancient as any, Lowell prided himself that he had not bothered with a final club as an undergraduate. "I've always believed that any club is useless, unless it exists to keep somebody out."

"Keeping people out is no longer of interest to me," said Victor. "I've met too many good people who were kept out, starting here at Harvard. I met them on the *Titanic,* too. Of course, on the western front, it was different. The dead exclude no one."

"Well said, Victor, and bravely done." Lowell came around the desk. "We owe the Negro the best possible education. But I'm not going to give up a plan of compulsory residence for freshmen, which is to the benefit of a vast majority of our students, simply because it conflicts with the theoretical principle of treating everyone alike."

"You once said of the Irish that we had to absorb them. You wanted them to become rich, send their sons to our colleges, share our prosperity."

"And it's happening. Look at James Byrne, the first Catholic on the Harvard Corporation. I appointed him. Look at that Joe Kennedy. It's happening, Victor, but by degrees, as it will for the Negro."

"And the Jew?"

"We have a Jewish overseer, but Jews are a different problem entirely." Lowell went back to his desk and began to shuffle papers, signaling his irritation.

"Too many Jews at Harvard?"

"Twenty-two percent of the student body. I'd say that's too many, considering the percentage of Jews in the wider population. Once we adopted the so-called New Plan for admissions and put extra weight on entrance exams, the Jews came flooding in."

"Because they did well on the exams. That's what's called meritocracy."

"Put too many Jews in one place, they all lump together. Then we can't offer them opportunities for assimilation, as we have to the Irish."

Victor saw no further point to this discussion. He stood and said, "I shall sign the NAACP petition. If another comes my way regarding Jews, I'll sign that, too."

"Just don't forget to sign your checks, or we shall be forced to raise tuition, and then it will be even harder for the Negroes and the Jews and the Irish to come here."

Victor left the Yard through the Class of 1875 Gate and was struck by the irony of the inscription. It was from Isaiah, an Old Testament prophet, a Jewish prophet: "Open ye the gates that the righteous nation which keepeth the truth may enter in."

Five years later, Victor wrote this in his Class Report:

> *Expansion is the theme for 1926. Our family has expanded with a pair of rambunctious little boys. Business expands, as my cousin Dickey Drake, '12, and I work closely in equities. Our philosophy, freely shared with all of you since it has been written up on the business page, is to pick companies with low debt, strong cash flow, steady dividends, and growth projections that are realistic rather than outlandishly optimistic. I'm proud to say that our success has allowed us to contribute to another kind of expansion—President Lowell's expansion of the college, a physical manifestation of Harvard's spiritual advance into the twentieth century.*

Victor had decided that, for all of his contradictions, Lowell served Harvard and Harvard served the nation. And if certain problems vexed Lowell and Harvard, they vexed the nation, too.

The struggles over Negro housing and Jewish quotas had simmered quietly, as they would until a new president and another war brought greater egalitarianism. But Victor's eyes had already been opened, and the best way for the gates of Harvard to remain open, so that the righteous of the nation might enter, was for alumni of conscience to remain involved.

So Victor spoke his mind, which sometimes irritated Lowell and sometimes irritated his cousin Dickey Drake.

One morning in 1928, as Victor studied the ticker, Dickey Drake stalked in and threw the *Harvard Alumni Magazine* on his desk. "Bad form, Victor. Very bad form."

"What are you talking about?"

"What you said in this month's issue." Dickey read, " 'I support President Lowell's new house system. I believe it can be both national and democratic in nature.' A lot of blather, Victor. The system we had worked just fine."

"Not if you were poor," answered Victor, "or couldn't get into a club."

"Did you know that Lowell is going to make everyone pay for meals in the houses, even if they take their meals in the clubs?"

"The clubmen can afford it," said Victor.

"Lowell is out to kill the clubs." Dickey aimed a finger at Victor. "You once told me that when your boys were old enough, you'd want them both to be Porcellians."

"I want them to be good students and good citizens. The house system will give them the chance. They'll live in the Yard as freshmen, then move into one of the houses with a few hundred students, where they'll live, eat, mingle, have their own tutors. . . ."

"Social engineering."

"I should think you'd like it, you're such an Anglophile. It's modeled on the system at Oxford and Cambridge."

"But it's all so artificial . . . bringing poor boys and rich boys together in some neo-Georgian palace by the Charles."

"Dickey, you're a snob," said Victor.

"And you're a class traitor."

In the report for 1931, Victor wrote:

Barbara and I have moved year-round to Manchester-by-the-Sea, where our family has summered for years. The town is quiet, and the train reaches Boston in an hour. I can still get to the office before the open on Wall Street, and the problems of the city can be left behind at night. The problems of Wall Street

cannot, although at Wedge, Fleming, and Royce, our philoso-
phy has protected us. I am proud to say that we began to with-
draw from the market in the spring of '29, when it became
apparent that stock prices were racing far ahead of earnings. On
the home front we are happier than ever. Our two sons grow like
weeds on the front lawn. And Barbara fills the house with her
paintings. To make room for them, we have even contributed to
the college several portraits of Harvardians in our line. Go see
them in the new Fogg Art Museum.

In the spring of his twentieth reunion year, Victor and other leaders of the reunion classes were invited on a walk with President
Lowell, a sort of fund-raising tour.

They began in the science area, north of the Yard, before the giant
rhinoceroses at the entrance to the biology laboratories, and they
came away certain of Harvard's preeminence in science. They
walked past Langdell Hall, new home of the Law School, and were
comforted that American jurisprudence was in good hands. They
admired the Fogg Art Museum but did not go in; simply knowing
that it existed assured them that good minds were caring for the cultural life of college and nation. They looked up at Memorial
Church, which honored the dead of the Great War with a tall white
spire, its delicacy a counterpoint to Widener's bulk, its elegance sug-
gestive of the neo-Georgian beauty they would find along the river.

Then they walked out of the Yard and south toward the new walls
of red brick, the chimneys and bell towers, the orderly rows of windows and slate-covered dormers—the houses, imposing themselves
on the curve of the Charles yet conforming to the ancient pattern
of Cambridge streets.

By now, Victor had slipped in beside Lowell.

"Ah, Victor. What do you think?" asked the old man.

"Hard to believe how handsome it is."

"Just two years ago, the house system was no more than a dream.
And now . . ."

Ahead of them was the largest house, named for the Lowell family, with a bell tower modeled after Independence Hall. A perfect
symbol, thought Victor, for a system meant to foster in young men

a sense of democratic idealism and responsibility. Of those to whom much had been given, it proclaimed, much was expected.

"Marvelous, sir," he said.

"We've broken up the Gold Coast now," said Lowell. "We're doing our best to give everyone a chance."

"I was a Gold Coaster," said Victor. "But I think you've done something remarkable here, even if you haven't given *everyone* a chance."

Lowell made a little grunt, then hurried ahead.

The tour ended on the Weeks footbridge, which connected the river houses and the Business School. Lowell told them to reflect on what they saw: magnificent examples of Colonial Revival architecture on both sides of the river, buildings that echoed America's idealistic beginnings and looked toward an orderly future. He reminded them that the money for the Business School had come from Wall Street giant George F. Baker and the money for the houses from Standard Oil heir Edward Harkness. And neither was a Harvard man. What's more, Harkness had gone to Yale!

And Lowell made his pitch: "If outsiders could do all this for Harvard, how much more should Harvard men like all of you be expected to do? How much . . . how much . . ."

Lowell's words faded for Victor. He was at the edge of the group now, thinking about all that Lowell had achieved, not only in remaking the body of the university but also its soul. He had been gifted with great vision.

But he had his blind spots, too. He had denied Marie Curie an honorary degree because she was a woman, or so the story went. He had approved a memorandum to house masters, telling them not to accept more Jews than "what the traffic will bear." He had sought to protect young white gentlemen from the sight of black men who did not merely serve in the dining halls but actually dined in them. Lowell, like Harvard and America itself, still had far to go in the fight against ignorance.

So in late 1935, Victor wrote:

It is impossible to believe that a quarter century has flown past. We of 1911 are fortunate to enjoy our twenty-fifth reunion in the spring and the Tercentenary in the fall. And you'll see me at both, since I am secretary of the Alumni Association.

Barbara enjoys painting and volunteering, I find relaxation in shaving strokes from my handicap. Our older boy is off to Phillips Andover, and his brother will leave next year. We are proud of them but loath to lose them to young adulthood. They both love Harvard football games, which we attend in our 1934 Ford beach wagon.

On the business front, Wedge, Fleming, and Royce has developed a series of stock-buying funds to spread risks and maintain profits for large investors and small, even during the downturn. I refuse to use the term depression. *I reserve that for my feelings when I look to Europe and the Far East. Let us hope that when we fought the War to End All Wars, we were not deceiving ourselves. Let us hope that the Harvard man in the White House perseveres and that Harvard does the same.*

There is an epitaph on the grave of one of my ancestors. "Seek truth through the years, but seek it for all." This should be carved next to "Veritas" on the Harvard seal. For if all are not inspired to seek the truth, ignorance will prevail and dark clouds will produce a deluge that drowns us all.

The night that he finished his 1936 report, he took out that thin sheet of onionskin once more, read it, and wondered what he would do when the gilt-edged envelope with all of its symbolism was finally within his grasp. And it would be. As secretary of the Alumni Association, he would be there when it finally came to light.

iii

It was the morning of September 8, 1936. Victor Wedge sat at the president's table in the faculty meeting room of University Hall.

On the walls, the portraits of Harvard presidents gazed down. In the chairs around the room sat two dozen alumni. Though the day was warm and sunshine poured through the Palladian windows of

University Hall, each gentleman wore a three-piece suit or, if he was an official of the Alumni Association, striped trousers and swallow-tailed coat.

On the president's table lay the packet of letters from 1836. It was wrapped in brown paper, bound with string, sealed in wax. President Quincy's handwriting was still easily read. Harvard's new president, an ascetic-looking young chemist named James Bryant Conant, stood over the packet, ready to break the seals.

Seated around the table with Victor were the vice president of the Alumni Association, the director of the university libraries, the chief flag marshal of the Class of '11—formidable gentlemen all—and Abbot Lawrence Lowell.

The president emeritus was turned out in a light gray suit, as though he knew it would distinguish him in a sea of dark fabric. He had entered the room with his usual quick step; he had punctuated every greeting with his characteristic nod, a gesture that some said he learned from Teddy and taught to Franklin. But for all his energy, Abbot Lawrence Lowell was ancient. What hair he had left was pure white. So was his mustache. And his eyes had all but disappeared into the puffy bags around them, as though he were a boxer pounded not by fists but by time.

And if Lowell was now ancient, Victor Wedge had to be growing old, even though he had looked better than most anyone at his twenty-fifth reunion. He was still trim and vigorous, with only a little gray at his temples and in his mustache. But the same river that swept Lowell toward the sea drew Victor, too. And that realization made him feel even closer to a woman who had ridden that river past the burning of Harvard Hall and the American Revolution and had anticipated this day in 1936. He had decided that he owed it to her to see the contents of that gilt-edged envelope before anyone else did.

"I will now open the packet," said Conant.

Gentlemen leaned forward. Victor rubbed the palms of his hands on his trousers.

The red wax seals popped, the string and paper came away, and there was . . . an inner folder. Conant carefully opened it and there were . . . letters. Some had been opened and stacked neatly. Others had remained in envelopes, also stacked neatly and tied.

Victor inclined his head and looked for an edge of gold leaf.

Conant examined the packet, lifted a few letters, thumbed the pile of envelopes.

Victor saw a flash of gold and resolved not to take his eyes off of it.

"Unfortunately, gentlemen," said Conant, "it seems as if the packet contains letters and nothing else. No newspapers, no engravings, no medallions."

"Would the president read a letter or two?" asked Lowell.

Conant looked over at Samuel Eliot Morison, a historian in owl-shaped glasses and bow tie. "Professor Morison will be inspecting them, but I'm sure he won't mind."

"I can't wait myself," said Morison.

And Victor Wedge put both hands on the table, just inches from the folder.

Conant turned over one letter and picked up another, then turned to another, until he found one to his liking. "This comes from Samuel Wragg of Charleston, South Carolina, Class of 1790. He concludes: 'May the Sons of Harvard University celebrate her centennial anniversaries to the end of time, each celebration witnessing her increasing reputation.'"

"Hear, hear," said Lowell.

"Perhaps I should read one that was kept in an envelope." Conant moved his hand to that packet and broke the string holding the envelopes together.

Victor rubbed the tips of his fingers against his thumbs. There would be a moment, very soon, when the gilt-edged envelope would be within his grasp.

Conant picked up the first envelope. "On the flap, it says, 'Not to be opened until 1936.' There are several like that, and as you can see, the wishes of the authors were respected." Conant opened the envelope and said, "Perhaps this is why: 'To the Gentlemen of the Future: Excuse me for this frank expression of feelings. But I am compelled to say that I owe nothing to the president, professors, and tutors of Harvard college from 1810 to 1814. I hope you do not say as little for the Harvard of your time.'"

This brought healthy laughter. Even in that group, most men tried to maintain a bit of cynicism about a college that took itself so seriously. And all considered it was a sign of good character to be able to laugh at themselves.

When the laughter died, Conant said, "With that, I'll hear a motion to adjourn."

So moved, seconded, approved. Then the gentlemen in the room were on their feet, milling about, clattering their coffee cups and spoons, and turning their attention to the best part of any alumni meeting—the conversation.

But at the president's table, there was still business to be done. Victor stood and gestured to a sheet of paper on the table. "Gentlemen, before Professor Morison takes the packet, we must all sign to attest to what we've witnessed."

"Ah, yes," said Conant. "Quite right."

"Yes, indeed," said the vice president of the Alumni Association.

Conant said, "And as President Lowell signs, perhaps—"

With his left hand, Victor was sliding the signing sheet across the table toward Lowell, while with his right, he was sliding the gilt-edge envelope toward himself. And Conant was saying, "Perhaps a photograph."

And . . . *flash!*

All the gentlemen around the table turned to the camera, except for Lowell, who was taking out his pen and preparing to sign.

Victor blinked away the blue spot that went floating past. He looked at the camera as another bulb was popped into place and . . . *flash!*

Victor had the envelope, and the photographer had him. But in the moment that most of the gentlemen in the room were blinded by the second flash, Victor moved the envelope to his pocket. Then all were turning to watch Lowell sign the sheet. Then . . . *flash!* Victor slid his hand to his pocket and pushed the envelope deeper.

* * *

Victor studied the letter, followed its directions, and late one evening, he became the first person in a century and a half to set eyes on the manuscript of *Love's Labours Won*. Once he had allowed his sense of awe to settle, he made his decision.

Harvard's president might co-sign the diplomas of Radcliffe graduates, but in too many ways, ignorance still prevailed. So Victor did what he thought Lydia would have wanted, what the Callahans would have appreciated, what his descendants, he hoped, would consider profound rather than clever.

He finished his work on the morning of September 17, a few hours before the meeting of the Associated Harvard Alumni.

Then he took his seat on the stage of Tercentenary Theater, the new name for the great outdoor space between Widener and the pillars of Memorial Church. He fixed his eye on the podium, on which sat the Tercentenary packet. It was the size of a briefcase. Embossed in gold on the crimson cover flap were the Harvard seal and the years 1936 and 2036. Affixed also was a handwritten note: "To be opened by the President of Harvard in the autumn of 2036 and *not before*. J. B. Conant."

President Conant described for the thousands of gathered alumni the contents of the 1836 packet, opened a few weeks earlier. Then, with appropriate ceremony, he called for the university stamp and sealed the Tercentenary packet.

Well done, thought Victor, in more ways than one.

Though none could know the contours of the world a century hence, none who attended the Tercentenary thought that the Harvard men of 2036 would be able to match the celebrations of that night. Three hundred thousand people lined the banks of the Charles to watch a barge carry the college band and a plaster statue of John Harvard up the river, while a spectacular fireworks display arched above.

And nothing entertained Victor as much as the excitement on the faces of his sons, Jimmy and Ned, sixteen and fourteen, another generation for Harvard.

The Wedges joined with hundreds of rowdy undergraduates who raised the plaster John Harvard onto their shoulders and bore him in torchlight parade from the river to the Yard, where the bronze John Harvard politely received his replica and the raucous cheers of the students.

Neddy said that it looked as though the statue were smiling.

"He is," said Victor. "And tomorrow morning, he'll be grinning from ear to ear."

But several hundred miles to the south, a hurricane was blowing off the Virginia Capes and swirling north. There was talk of canceling the climactic ceremonies, but the weather prediction for Cambridge: light showers in the morning, growing heavier by afternoon. So the show would go on.

At 9:30, bugles blew in the Old Yard, and the procession formed. The oldest living graduates, from the classes of 1860 and 1862, stepped off, followed by some ten thousand alumni behind banners representing all the living classes. They made a circuit of the Old Yard, then marched into the field of folding chairs in Tercentenary Theater, and took seats assigned by classes. Meanwhile, the band played ceremonial airs, and the skies darkened, and the wind caused pennants and banners to flutter and puff.

At the next flourish of bugles, the alumni stood like guests at a wedding, the doors of Widener swung open, and Presidents Conant and Lowell stepped out, leading one of the grandest processions of brain power ever collected anywhere on earth.

That's how Victor had described it for his boys when he left them on the steps of Widener, in a good spot to watch it all. And it was no exaggeration.

There was a professor of physics from Leipzig, of eugenics from London, of international law from Geneva, of philosophy from Peking, of physiology from Buenos Aires, of archaeology from Edinburgh, of psychology from Zurich, of art history from Paris, of chemistry from Munich, of religion from Tokyo . . . and on and on.

And the darkening of the skies, thought Victor, seemed only to intensify the colors of the academic garb—red hats and orange hoods, gold tassels, purple and green and blue satin trimmings, primary colors and pastels, too. And the darkening of the world scene seemed only to make brighter the fond hopes implicit in this gathering of the world's genius.

Victor watched them move through the assembled alumni, climb the steps of Memorial Church, and take their places in the stands that had been put up behind the podium. Victor had drawn one of the most interesting assignments of the day. He was behind the stands, by the door to Memorial Church, waiting to summon yet another president.

That was where Dickey Drake cornered him. Like Victor, Dickey was on the Alumni Committee, so he was wearing striped trousers, swallow-tailed coat, and silk hat. Still, a Secret Service man stepped from behind a column as Dickey approached.

"It's all right," said Victor to the agent.

"Yes," said Dickey. "Even if I *am* a Republican." Then he lowered his voice and said to Victor, "Where is he?"

"In the chapel." Victor gestured to the door, where another agent stood.

"Praying for forgiveness or votes?"

"No politics today, Dickey," said Victor. "What do you want?"

"You should be glad that I'm on the publications committee." Dickey pulled a pile of photos from his pocket. "These are from that meeting last week. And . . . no one else has mentioned it, but it looks to me like you're palming an envelope."

"Palming an envelope?" Victor tried to sound shocked.

"Uncle Theodore used to tell my mother about Lydia Wedge Townsend causing a scene at Quincy's levee. He said that she stood at the table where the packet was displayed and told Quincy that Harvard should educate women or they'd never get her money. I've always wondered, did she slip something into the Bicentenary packet?"

Victor decided to tell a little truth. "Yes."

"What?"

"Some nasty doggerel about the college. I don't think we should sully Lydia or Harvard by having it put about."

"How did you find out about it?"

"Dickey, I don't have time for this right now." Victor glanced through an opening in the stands and saw that all but two rows of seats on the stage had been filled by the scholars. So he turned to the agent at the chapel door and told him it was time.

Then Dickey whispered to Victor, "We're putting together a souvenir book. Just tell me which of these photos to use and I'll destroy the rest."

"Use the ones that tell the least. That would be best for the Wedge reputation."

The chapel doors opened behind them, a wheelchair rolled out, and a familiar voice said, "Is that an old Porcellian I see?"

"Yes, sir," said Victor. "Two Porcellians."

"Well, this member of the Fly Club says good morning." Franklin Roosevelt reached down and straightened his legs. Then he locked the braces beneath the trousers, and with the help of one of his agents and his military aide, he stood.

"Allow me to help you to your seat, sir." Victor offered his arm.

"Thank you, but I'll need only my cane"—Roosevelt held out his hand and an agent gave him a brass-handled cane, then he put his other hand on the arm of his military aide—"and Colonel Watson. You may direct us, Victor."

Victor glanced at Dickey, who seemed to be struck speechless by the sight of the president of the United States, in swallow-tailed coat and tall silk hat, standing on his own two feet, chin and barrel chest thrust forward, famous grin lighting his face.

Most Harvard men opposed Roosevelt's re-election. He had even lost the straw poll at Harvard in 1932. And Lowell, no lover of Roosevelt, had written to him that he might come for the Tercentenary but not bother with "the arduous demands of political speechmaking." As the fourth graduate of the college to become president, however, Roosevelt made it plain that he intended to give a speech, though not until the afternoon session. In the morning, he would provide no more than his presidential presence.

But getting that presence onto the stage without distracting from the academic procession or drawing attention to the presidential affliction proved a delicate matter. Roosevelt could not march, of course, and he refused to appear before so many in a wheelchair, so it was determined to bring him out while the attention of the spectators was still on the procession. It was Victor's task to show him to his seat and subtly shield him from view until he was settled.

"This way, sir," said Victor, putting himself on the president's right side.

"Now, Victor," said Roosevelt in that jocular tone, "you Porcellians blackballed me once. Don't be kicking my cane out from under me now."

"Don't worry, sir," said Victor. "I'm a Democrat before I'm a Porcellian."

Roosevelt threw his head back and gave a great laugh.

And out they went. By swinging his hips forward and supporting his body on the cane and Watson's arm, Roosevelt could force his paralyzed legs to give an impression of functionality. Victor could feel the force of will radiating off the man, as if he would do more than overcome the paralysis. He would deny it utterly. And such spirit, thought Victor, was what America needed at that moment.

Only a few people noticed the president when he emerged from an opening in the stands and made his way to a chair near the podium. From a distance, he and Victor looked like two more dignitaries in top hats. But as Roosevelt sat, Victor heard a murmuring among the robed scholars behind them. Then a few in the audience began to applaud. Then a wave of Harvard men was rising to greet the alumnus that so few of them had voted for.

Victor retreated behind the stands and said to Dickey, "They like him."

"They're just polite," sniffed Dickey. "He's the biggest class traitor of them all."

Just then, the skies opened up, and as the *Boston Herald* would report, "the rain fell upon the President with as much abandon as if he were a Republican."

There were many remarkable moments that morning, moments that Victor hoped his sons would always remember and that he would never forget.

He felt a chill when the university marshal said, "Ladies and gentlemen, from the Southwark Cathedral . . ." And over the loudspeakers came the sound of bells pealing on the other side of the Atlantic, bells that Harvard himself had heard.

Then, England's poet laureate, John Masefield, stepped to the podium. The canopy did little to protect him or his text from the rain, as he recited "Lines Suggested by the Tercentenary," extolling the bravery of those who had planted this college in New England: "There was a preacher in that little band, / JOHN HARVARD, son of one from Stratford town, / Who may have shaken Shakespeare's hand . . ."

And Victor thought, if they only knew.

And the rain fell harder.

So the afternoon ceremonies were moved into Sanders Theater, which held only a thousand people. Victor and Dickey were lucky enough to get seats in the balcony.

They heard a magisterial speech from A. Lawrence Lowell: "As wave after wave rolls landward from the ocean, breaks and fades away sighing down the shingle of the beach, so the generations of men follow one another, sometimes quietly, sometimes, after a storm, with noisy turbulence. But whether we think upon the monotony or the violence in human history, two things are always new—youth and the quest for knowledge. . . ."

"He may be old," said Dickey, "but he can still write."

"Youth and the quest for knowledge," said Victor. "To have the one, do the other."

Then Roosevelt stood to another ovation, though Dickey Drake sat on his hands.

"At the time of the Bicentenary," Roosevelt began, "many of the alumni were sorely troubled concerning the state of the nation. Andrew Jackson was president. On the two hundred and fiftieth anniversary of the founding of the college, alumni were again sorely troubled. Grover Cleveland was president. Now, on the three hundredth anniversary, I am president. . . ."

The laughter began slowly, then rose to a crescendo. Even Dickey chuckled.

Then Roosevelt delivered his version of Harvard history: "In the olden days, it was Increase Mather who told students that they were 'pledged to the word of no particular master,' that they should 'above all find a friend in the truth.' That became the creed of Harvard. Behind the tumult and shouting, it is still the creed of Harvard. In this day of modern witch-burning, when freedom of thought has been exiled from many lands, it is the part of Harvard and America to stand for the freedom of the human mind and to carry the torch of truth."

"Even *you* must agree on that," whispered Victor.

"He's got it wrong, as usual," said Dickey. "Increase Mather *hanged* witches."

"It was Cotton Mather who hanged them. The son of Increase."

"So the son didn't learn from the father," said Dickey. "There's a lesson in that."

"Yes. We must take care that our children develop consciences."

iv

A few weeks after the reunion, Victor sat down with Barbara to discuss that very topic — the development of their sons' consciences. He could not have anticipated where the conversation would go.

It was one of those glorious October days when it seemed that there could be no place more beautiful than New England. Husband and wife were out by the saltwater swimming pool, which filled when the tide rose, was warmed by the sun, and drained when the tide went out. The perfect Yankee filtration system, Victor called it. And out beyond the patio, the blue Atlantic shimmered.

Victor was reading the *Wall Street Journal*.

Barbara was stirring martinis. "How much did we make this week?"

"We did well. You married an equities genius, my dear."

She gave him a martini and sat in the lawn chair next to him. Then she touched her martini glass to his. "To money."

He laughed.

Then she picked up the book that had arrived in the mail that day, about the size of *Life* magazine, with a red spiral binding: *John Harvard's Tercentenary 1636–1936*.

"They must love you," she said. "There are two pictures of you at University Hall, when they opened the Bicentenary packet."

He did not look up from the *Journal*. He had already seen the pictures, but he was curious about her impression. "What am I doing?"

"Shuffling papers, it looks like."

"That's me, paper pusher of the Alumni Association." He lowered the *Journal.* "Barbara, I've been thinking about the boys—"

But she was flipping through the book. "Not a single woman."

"When Radcliffe is here for three hundred years, they can have a tercentenary."

"Where are the female scholars, the women who fought for education, the honorary degree recipients who do their work even when they have hot flashes, the—"

"Is that why you didn't go to any of the events? You were angry that there were no women honored?"

Barbara put down her drink, squinted a bit in the sun, which lit up her wrinkles and the gray hair advancing relentlessly, and said, "Victor, there's something I've been thinking about, ever since the boys went off to school."

"I've been thinking about something, too."

"Victor—"

But he kept talking. "We're worth four million dollars now, you know."

"Yes, I know, but Victor—"

"We'll never spend this money in our lifetime. I want to use some of it to establish the Wedge Charitable Trust."

"Victor, that's very nice, but—"

"The objective will be to find ways to combat ignorance and build the meritocracy."

"Victor," she said.

He did not hear the tension in her voice or see it in her face. His mind was spinning and his eyes were focused on the blue horizon. "It will be great for the boys and great for us. But we can't be sure about where the family will be in two generations, so we'll make it a trust rather than a foundation. Run it under rule of perpetuities statutes, so that twenty-one years after our sons pass away—"

"Victor!"

"Death is something we all have to face. . . . Twenty-one years later, their heirs will make final decisions about the money, all within parameters we establish." He finally looked at her. "What do you think?"

"I want a divorce."

He sat up so quickly that he knocked his glass onto the patio and it shattered. "What?"

"I sit up here all day, all alone, painting watercolors of the ocean and wishing my boys were little again."

"But . . . divorce? Have you gone crazy?"

"I *will* go crazy if I don't get one." She stood. "I want to go to the Southwest and paint like that Georgia O'Keeffe. I want to go to France and paint like the Impressionists. I want to go to Russia and paint like Miró." And she walked toward the house.

"But Barbara—"

She stopped in the doorway. "What?"

"You couldn't paint the walls of our bathroom without leaving streaks."

"Stay here tonight. By tomorrow, have your things moved into the Harvard Club."

Perhaps he shouldn't have made that bathroom remark.

Chapter Twenty-six

═══════════

By the time Peter Fallon reached the Class Report for 1941, he thought that he understood Victor Wedge, and he liked him:

The shades have darkened since last we met, in both our private life and the public scene. Some of you may have heard that Barbara and I divorced a few years back, a ghastly experience. I do not recommend it. My sons have offered solid companionship, however. Jimmy lives in Kirkland House, Ned in Lowell. At home football games, you will find the three of us dispensing good cheer at the tailgate of our '34 beach wagon, which we affectionately call the Wedge Woody.

But these days, good cheer is like thin oil floating on a deep lake of concern. At the Tercentenary, FDR saw what was coming and reminded us "to stand for the freedom of the human mind and to carry the torch of truth."

I tried to keep those words in mind when I established the Wedge Charitable Trust, which my boys and I administer. We have provided scholarship money, supported charities in Boston, and sought other ways to overcome the ignorance around us. Our gifts are not large, deriving from the interest of the trust itself, but I pray that in time, they will be looked upon as "small gifts of majestic proportion."

That term was coined by an ancestor who promised Harvard such a gift. She did not specify it, but she wished us to strive for it, as though she anticipated the words of President Lowell: "Two things are always new—youth and the quest for knowledge."

Her gift a hundred years ago was to pass to Wedge generations a spirit of the quest. I pass it to you. As we age, if we would keep our youth, we should continue the quest in our own lives.

So . . . had he found that small gift of hers? Had he sold it to establish a trust? Or had he given it to the college in 1918? This much was certain: whatever Lydia had said about her gift, Victor Wedge had given it a meaning of his own.

Peter turned to the Class Report for the thirty-fifth reunion of 1911:

*Victor Wedge died July 9, 1944. He served in Lafayette Escadrille and Ninety-fourth Pursuit Squadron during World War I. He became a principal in Wedge, Fleming, and Royce, a firm specializing in equities and investment banking. At the time of his death, he was serving in the Office of Budget and Management. He was on a flight to England when his plane crash-landed in Iceland. At Harvard, he played football and was a member of the Harvard Aeronautical Society and the Porcellian. He also served in several capacities in the Alumni Association. He leaves his two sons, James, '41, and Edward, '44.

Peter copied the seven installments of Victor Wedge's life and felt a twinge of disappointment—it could almost have been called grief. He had been looking forward to reading more, but Victor had already told him plenty.

Then he headed for Houghton Library, home to Harvard's collection of rare books and manuscripts. Not surprisingly, security was tight there.

The scholarly value of, say, Hawthorne's manuscript of *The House of the Seven Gables* was immeasurable. And the dollar value would be incalculable. Likewise the value of almost any book in the rooms housing the personal libraries of individual collectors, or any of the stacks containing contributions from men such as William Augustus White, '63, who set out to gather as much Elizabethan literature as possible, in the hope of providing an intellectual context and a cultural explanation for Shakespeare's genius.

Whenever Peter went into Houghton, he wanted to dip his finger in a font of holy water and bless himself. Instead, he did a mental genuflection before the glass case where John Harvard's only surviving book, *Christian Warfare*, was displayed, a folio-size volume open to an engraving of Satan wrapping himself around a text. Behind it were first editions of many of the other volumes that had been destroyed in the 1764 fire. Harvard had been collecting replacements for years, but it was a measure of how fragile all books were, of how susceptible to time, use, and mildew, of how miraculous it was when they survived, that some of the Harvard library might never be replaced.

In the card catalog, Peter found what he was looking for: "Shakespeare, William, *Love's Labours Lost.* 1598 quarto. Gift of Victor Wedge, given in Memory of Lieutenant James F. Callahan, November 5, 1918."

Peter filled out a call slip and was asked if the facsimile would be sufficient. Standard practice at a place like Houghton, and usually the facsimile was enough.

Peter explained that his interest wasn't in the content but in the binding and endpapers. Soon he was slipping on white cotton gloves to examine one of Shakespeare's earliest comedies, street value of about a million dollars. He didn't take long with it. The binding was the same red vellum as that on the book in the portrait. And written on the endpapers were two names: "Burton Bones," and beneath that, "Ex libris Lydia Wedge Townsend."

Then there was a note from Lydia: "We leave this gift, left to us by an old actor born Benjamin Wedge, as thanks for your hospitality. Your loving American daughter-in-law, Lydia." Then there was an inscription from Lady Townsend, signing the book over to Victor Wedge.

* * *

Peter called Will Wedge once he was outside and told him what he had discovered.

"It would seem that Benjamin Wedge, under the name of Burton Bones, came back for the book. Somehow it went to Lydia Wedge Townsend. And she brought it to England. Copley painted it on the table in front of her. Victor brought it back and gave it to Harvard in the name of a classmate."

After a long pause, Will Wedge asked, "So . . . case closed?"

"There are still plenty of questions," said Peter. "Plenty of things we'll never fill in. Like . . . how did this Benjamin Wedge become Burton Bones, and why doesn't Lydia tell us anything about him—"

"But," said Will, "on the matter of a Shakespeare manuscript . . ."

"Case closed," said Peter. But there were still plenty of questions to answer, about Ridley's death and Bingo Keegan and an attack on the Charles River.

"Can you put your opinion in writing?" asked Will Wedge. "Send it to Charles Price, and we're done."

"You still haven't told me what you and Price are engaged in."

"Negotiations are delicate, but if things work out, the Wedge Charitable Trust will invent a scholarship for Boston Latin track stars who go to Harvard. And your son will go to the top of the list."

Peter decided to deliver the news in person to Charles Price.

Two hours later, he was in an office park above Route 128, the six-lane semicircle of concrete that hemmed Boston, "America's Technology Highway." The high-tech industry had been born along 128 in the fifties, when all the local university brain factories started pumping out young engineers and scientists like molecules of smart gas. By the nineties, high tech had also made it "America's Traffic Highway."

Price Research occupied a two-tiered building with glass walls, set into a hillside above a Waltham reservoir. There was soft rock playing in the foyer, computers humming everywhere, lots of smart molecules bouncing around, all of them dressed for casual Friday, even though it was Monday.

The secretary brought Peter to the corner office and offered him a sparkling water. The only decoration was a bust of Shakespeare on a bookcase lined with programming manuals. The view was across the reservoir to the highway.

Charlie Price strolled in wearing a nylon warm-up suit. "Not bad for a computer geek from Cleveland, eh, Fallon?"

"If you were ever a computer geek," said Peter, "it was back when computers were as big as minivans."

"I used a slide rule." Price sat at his desk. "Slide rules and stationary horses."

"Stationary horses?"

"Gymnastics. My life at Harvard: math, gymnastics, politics . . . and Shakespeare."

"So, were you a Young Republican?"

"Hell, no. I was a long-haired hippie radical. A much better way to get laid." He tapped a computer key and glanced at his e-mail while he said to Fallon, "You didn't drive all the way out here to trade old college tales."

"I was wrong about that Shakespeare play. It didn't burn in Harvard Hall."

As Price scanned an e-mail, he said, "Tell me something I don't know."

"Harvard owns it."

Price looked Fallon in the eye. "Tell me more."

Peter crossed his legs. "Not until you tell me what Will Wedge is up to."

"I don't discuss private business," said Price without a trace of irritation, as if dropping his jocular tone was enough. "Now . . . either you can tell me more about this, or I'll give Bertram Lee a call."

"Sometimes I wonder why you do business with Bertram Lee when—"

"When I could do it with you? Bertram's my wife's uncle. I keep it in the family, like the Wedges with that Shakespeare manuscript."

"No," said Peter. "The Wedges gave it to Harvard in 1918."

And Price laughed out loud. "You're not talking about that quarto of *Love's Labours Lost*, are you? The one signed by Burton Bones and Lydia?"

"You know?"

"I've looked at every quarto in Houghton. I saw that one ten years ago. It is *not* what we're after here."

Peter tried to keep from showing surprise, so he just angled his chin a little bit and said, "Victor Wedge went to England, brought it back, and—"

"Yeah . . . yeah . . . Will Wedge's grandfather gave it in honor of an ancestor of—" Price caught himself.

"Who? Whose ancestor?" asked Peter.

Price sat back and picked at his mustache, as if he was considering how much to tell. Then he said, "Now I know why I do business with Bertram Lee."

"The guy's name was Callahan. Who was his descendant?" Peter persisted.

Price ignored the question. "Imagine it, Fallon, a Shakespeare manuscript and a lost play to boot. You dug up the proof: 'Written in the bard's own hand . . . we cry *Love's Labours Won.*' Benjamin Wedge wrote that. Later on, his alter ego found a copy of *Love's Labours Lost* and wrote his name in it."

"Sibley doesn't tell us anything about Benjamin's alter ego."

"Sibley did great research, but somehow, Burton Bones fell through the cracks. And Sibley didn't have the internet. Burton Bones and his troupe were chased out of every colony in New England in the 1760s. Last seen at the Harvard commencement six months before Harvard Hall burned."

Peter uncrossed his legs and crossed them again and hoped he didn't look too stupid. It never paid to look stupid. "So, you think he came back for the play?"

"I thought that before I met you. I thought that after you came and told me that the manuscript had been lost in the fire. And I think it now. I'd much rather think it's out there than not. It makes life more interesting."

"If it comes to light, Harvard will lay claim to it. You'll have to fight their lawyers, and you could lose."

Charlie Price looked around his office, looked out at the reservoir, then at the bust of Shakespeare, and said, "I never lose."

Peter stood and said, "You still haven't told me what Will Wedge is after."

"Negotiations are going nowhere, so don't worry about it."

At the door, Peter stopped. "You didn't say whose ancestor it was . . ."

And Price laughed. "You really don't know what's going on here, do you?"

Peter wasn't about to admit that. "I know that a friend of mine is dead. And someone tried to kill me a few weeks ago. And after a little conversation with a Southie thug, people *stopped* trying to kill me, at least for now."

Price shrugged. "Then you know some things that may or may not matter. Just know this. You're in a race. And the winner gets a treasure worth a lot of money."

"Tell me something I don't know."

Peter picked up Evangeline on the eight o'clock shuttle from New York and took her back to her apartment. By the time they got there, he had told her all that he had discovered about Victor at Houghton and the Harvard Archives. She told him about the Tercentenary book that she'd found in the New York store that afternoon.

"And you paid forty bucks for it?" he said.

"A bargain when you see it." Before she had her coat off, she was opening it. "There he is—Victor Wedge, palming papers while all the other guys busy themselves with signatures and conversation."

"Except for the photographer," said Peter.

"'And the Bard will applaud as the century turns,'" said Evangeline. "I think Lydia meant the Tercentenary. I think Victor thought so, too."

"Either that or he was just shuffling papers," said Peter, looking more closely.

"Bread crumbs, Peter." Then she laughed. "I'm sounding more like you, and you're sounding more like me."

"Then we're both improving."

"If Victor Wedge was just sitting at a table with a bunch of papers," she said, "I wouldn't look twice. But this happens 'as the century turns' for Harvard. Maybe he'd been following bread crumbs, too. He knew about Lydia at President Quincy's levee promising 'a small gift of majestic proportion,' the headstone, these photos."

Peter had to agree. "In his last Class Report, he wrote about that 'small gift of majestic proportion' long after he had given Harvard the quarto of *Love's Labours Lost*. He said he wanted to do what Lydia had done—pass on a spirit of the quest. He actually wrote that to 'keep our youth, we should continue the quest in our own lives.'"

"That's a little spooky," she said. "It sounds like you."

"But if you backtrack from the painting in 1780 to the fire in 1764, you arrive again at the premise we had in the fall—if there was a manuscript, it burned in the fire. Unless Burton Bones got it first."

"So, do you want to quit or not?"

"When a man tells me that I don't really know what's going on, I have to find out what's going on."

About an hour later, Peter was cooking a little dinner. He'd found two boneless chicken breasts in the freezer, some prosciutto, a little wedge of Parmesan.

"I don't eat much," said Evangeline, "but I eat well."

While Peter defrosted the chicken breasts in the microwave, he sautéed some garlic in olive oil. Then he flattened out the chicken breasts with the back of a wooden spoon, layered the prosciutto on the chicken, grated the Parmesan onto the prosciutto and sprinkled it all with rosemary and oregano, then rolled the chicken breasts and put them in the skillet and dropped a box of gemelli into boiling water.

"The most I have for a salad is some wilted spinach," she said.

"Any sesame seeds?"

"Not exactly an item you normally find in a Cambridge pied-à-terre," she said.

"Not many people around here use the term pied-à-terre, either."

"But I like buying spices in Cardullo's, so—here."

He heated more olive oil and threw in a handful of sesame seeds and the spinach.

Once the chicken was done, he threw half a can of black olives into the skillet and made a little sauce for the pasta. And they sat down with a bottle of Alsatian Riesling.

While they ate, they tried to talk their way through the events of the past six months. When they were done, she got a pile of three-by-five cards and began to write down the events. "This is the way I organize things. Let's try it here. Where does the story start?"

"Talking to Ridley. Then the football game."

She wrote down each of his sentences on a separate card. "Who did you meet at the game?"

"Harriet, the mother . . . Will Wedge . . . that old professor, George Wedge Drake, and his old lefty girlfriend— Wait a minute."

"What?"

"Drake wanted me to track down a book, something called *Anglorum Praelia*. We did a few searches, found out that it was only worth a few hundred bucks, but . . ." He went to her computer, and navigated his way to the Harvard website that contained the 1723 catalog. And there it was, one of the books in the original John Harvard library: *Anglorum Praelia*.

So he called Orson, who was having a quiet night at home "with E. L. Doctorow and a nice 'ninety-six port."

Peter asked him, "Do you remember selling a book to Professor George Drake a few years back?"

"An edition of Chapman's *Homer*. An English translation."

Peter scanned the 1723 catalog. "There it is. Chapman's *Homer*. One of the titles in John Harvard's library. Have a sip of that port to congratulate yourself, Orson. I think you've pointed me toward someone who knows more than he's telling."

"Another one?"

Fallon tried contacting Professor Drake the next day, first by phone, then by e-mail.

The e-mail prompted an answer:

Hi, Peter. Relaxing with Olga here in Barbados. If you have the *Anglorum Praelia*, I'm interested. Otherwise, we'll be back Monday. Come for lunch next Tuesday, 12:30.

Fallon wrote back: "See you for lunch." Any conversation with the old professor should take place face-to-face.

While he waited, there were books to sell, buyers to contact, a business to run, and calls to take, starting with the daily call from Will Wedge:

"How did things go with Charlie Price?"

"Oh, he's convinced," said Peter. "Convinced there's a manuscript."

"That's too bad."

"Ever since you came looking for me on the river, you've been pointing me toward commencement. It's almost here."

The voice was injected with false jocularity. "Will you be joining us on the Committee for the Happy Observance, after all?"

"Will . . ."

A long pause, then: "This June, the Wedge Charitable Trust liquidates. My grandfather set it up under rules of perpetuities, which means the trust must vest—or liquidate—twenty-one years after the death of the last interested party."

"Why didn't you tell me about this sooner?"

"I told you what I thought you needed to know. If you know more, you might tell my brother what I'm planning."

"Let me guess. It's you and your brother who get to decide how the trust liquidates, which charities and nonprofits get what, and you disagree."

Another long pause. Then Wedge said, "Commencement is June fourth. We're having our annual family trust meeting the night before. If you uncover any information between now and then, it will help determine what happens to the trust."

"Is any of the money going to individuals?"

"My grandfather knew how uncertain the world was. His descendants might need money. He constructed the trust so that the principals could take up to twenty-five percent upon liquidation. But the rest has to go to charity."

"How much is the trust worth? Millions?"

"Tens of millions."

"But not enough for . . . whatever it is you are planning with Charles Price?"

"By commencement, Peter. My brother wants to dribble this out to a hundred charities, mostly left-wing. I want to do one grand thing."

"I can't prove a negative. And I think that's what you want."

"Negative or positive, it doesn't matter to me, as long as there's proof. And I have to inform you . . ."

What was coming now? wondered Peter.

"I don't care where I get my information. You, Bertram Lee, my daughter's tutor, Mr. O'Hill. The truth is that I even bought the locket from Bertram Lee."

"How much?" asked Fallon.

"Thirty thousand. He said that if we did business on the locket, he'd come to me first when he found the 'small gift of majestic proportion.'"

"Did he use that phrase?" asked Fallon.

"Word for word," said Wedge.

"Where do you think he heard it?" asked Peter, though he had a few suspicions.

"He does his research, too."

There were five weeks left when he had lunch with Professor Drake.

Peter's first thought when he saw the professor and his girlfriend: he hoped that he looked as good at their age. Fit, bright-eyed, plus Barbados tans that said screw skin cancer and die with a healthy glow.

Peter's second thought: when he saw the photograph of Robert Oppenheimer, '26, and Harvard professor Kenneth Bainbridge on the wall, he knew that he was in for an interesting lunch. Where there weren't bookcases, there were framed certificates, awards, and photographs of some of the famous faces of science.

And above the mantel hung a portrait of Dickey Drake in a navy blue three-piece suit.

"Yes," said the old professor. "My father, partner to Victor Wedge. He guided the company into the fifties, when Victor's son Ned took over. Then came Will. Unfortunately, I am the last of the Drake line."

"Not my fault." Olga came in with a bottle of Chablis and poured three glasses.

Peter looked around at some of the photos. Prof. G. with Harvard biology professor George Wald; a group of young men in shirt-sleeves standing in front of a barracks on some barren hillside in the forties; and, yes, a nuclear explosion in a desert.

Then Peter's eye scanned the bookshelves.

Prof. G. said, "Go ahead. Look them over."

Peter got up and opened one of the cases.

There was a quarto of a play called *Roxana,* by an obscure Elizabethan playwright named Alabaster. Editions of John Calvin and Milton's *Paradise Lost.* Some were in very fine condition, covers clean, pages uncut, leather as tight as a teenager's skin. And some showed the flaws that an honest bookseller mentioned when he offered something for sale—the cracking, the flaking, the rub marks, and all the rest.

The old professor said, "You didn't really think I wanted *Anglorum Praelia* because I was a fan of obscure sixteenth-century Latin verse about the glories of England, did you?"

"You're competing here with Houghton Library."

"I am re-creating the Ur of American knowledge, John Harvard's library. Houghton has been doing the same thing, but they are bound by more scholarly requirements."

"Such as?"

"They seek the exact editions and titles, based upon the earliest catalogs. I may interpret more liberally, because it's the intellectual value of the collection that matters most. What Harvard was reading tells us who he was, what he thought, so that we may understand him better and perhaps understand ourselves in the process. It's said that a man will be known by his books. So will a society."

And Peter asked him, very casually, "What are you doing to track down the work by Shakespeare that was supposedly in the library?"

"There was no work by Shakespeare," he said, just as casual, just as false. "There was a thing called *Corporei Insectii,* however, by an author who never existed. I've hired a researcher to look into that."

"Anybody I know?"

"I think you met him in Florida," said Prof. G. "Back in September, he tracked down the papers of a Harvard librarian named Theodore Wedge, which had been filed with someone else's at the Massachusetts Historical Society."

There it was, thought Peter, information he wasn't even looking for. Franklin Wedge had been the last one to see that diary, as he suspected. Franklin knew what Theodore Wedge had written on the last page. "Where's your research assistant right now?"

Prof G. looked at Olga. She said, "Franklin's like the wind. He could be in Cambridge, interviewing potential student agitators for some labor demonstration. He could be firebombing SUVs in California. Buying land from paper manufacturers in Maine so that he can donate it to the Nature Conservancy. Who knows? The next time we can be sure to see him is just before commencement."

"The family meeting?" asked Peter. "Do you go?"

"Always. My father actually ran the meetings after Victor died. We all get a vote, though Will and Franklin get two. This year, there will be great contention over Will's grandiose schemes."

Peter almost asked what the schemes were, but he sensed that if he kept quiet these two would talk themselves right into it.

The old professor said, "As far as we know, Will hopes to give Harvard the money. Franklin, he wants to . . . to . . ."

"Save the whales," snapped Olga. "One brother loves Harvard and always has, the other distrusts it and always has."

"And I view it with the kind of ambivalence that an intelligent man always has in the presence of power," said Prof. G., "even a power as benevolent as Harvard."

"Benevolent." Olga laughed, but she wasn't amused.

Peter said, "Your books are like Harvard. They prove that knowledge is power."

"My books are like atoms, each controlling its own little corner of a leatherbound universe, each a controlled little universe of its own."

"And John Harvard was the controlling intelligence that brought them all together?"

"People are always looking for a controlling intelligence." The professor sipped his wine. "It's why Harvard has such a hold on the public imagination. Did you know that in a given year, Harvard is mentioned more times in the national news media than all other American universities combined?"

Olga waved her hand. "Harvard said *this*. . . . Harvard-educated whosis said *that*. . . ."

"But it's true," said Prof. G. "Whenever some Harvard professor, laboring deep in the bowels of a library or lab, emerges with a new theory about the human genome or the identity of Shakespeare or the positive values of taking LSD, for God's sake, the world treats it as though the whole Harvard community had a part in it, as though one big throbbing brain had excreted this idea into a great bin marked with a crimson *H*, and the rest of the world should take note."

"So . . . you're saying there's no controlling intelligence?"

The old professor looked around at his books. "These volumes inspired our ancestors at a time when science was mostly superstition and the study of faith was a science. Today, quite the opposite holds true."

"Then you're collecting Harvard's books to show how far we've come?"

"Either that or"—he glanced toward the photo of the nuclear blast—"how little we've learned."

Chapter Twenty-seven

═══════

1945–1969

GEORGE WEDGE Drake peered across the desert toward a spot on the horizon some ten miles away. A hundred-foot tower had been built there, and atop the tower had been placed a device called simply the Gadget.

George could not see the tower. But in his mind's eye, he could see the Gadget, sitting there, waiting, silent and sullen. Would it go off? Would it pop and fizzle? Or would it start a chain reaction that could not be controlled? No one knew for certain.

Thunderstorms had blown through earlier, postponing the test from 4:00 A.M. It was now 5:29:15 on the morning of July 16, 1945, and there was a remote possibility that in fifteen seconds, the world might come to an end.

Professor Kenneth Bainbridge looked at J. Robert Oppenheimer, '26, the civilian director of the project. Oppenheimer nodded, and Bainbridge pushed a button.

George Drake pulled heavy welder's goggles over his eyes, turned away from the view slit in the bunker, and put his back against the concrete wall, all as instructed. So did Oppenheimer, Bainbridge, and the others around them.

Then a voice called out, "Zero minus ten . . ."

At similar stations around the Jornada del Muerto Valley, men prepared themselves. Some may have been thinking, as George was, of all that had brought them to this moment. For many, the journey had begun at Harvard. President James Bryant Conant was chairman of the National Defense Research Committee. Chemistry professor George Kistiakowsky had worked on the detonating device. Bainbridge had helped build the Harvard cyclotron, the first atom smasher. And five brilliant Harvard undergraduates, the youngest men on the project, had been brought to Los Alamos to act as human calculators.

". . . nine, eight, seven . . ."

George had arrived at Harvard with his class in the fall of 1941.

He had tried to ignore the worries piling up around them all that autumn and had focused instead on his studies, taking the most challenging courses available in mathematics and physics. And he got all A's.

But on the night of December 8, 1941, he attended a mass meeting in Sanders Theater and heard President Conant say, "In every preceding ordeal of battle Harvard has stood in the forefront of those who toiled and sacrificed that liberty might survive. There can be no question that in the days ahead this university and its sons will bring new honors to justify the expectations of ten generations of Harvard men."

Filled with patriotic fervor and a sense of pride in his own ancestry, George walked to his parents' home on Brattle Street after the meeting.

He could not remember that they had ever looked quite so worried. Dickey Drake and Doris were not people who worried. They went to parties in the middle of the week. They went to Florida in the middle of the winter. They worshiped at Christ Church on Sundays and dined at the Harvard Club on Fridays. They enjoyed their lives. They were well-off. But what did all that matter now?

George sat with his father in the library and said that he was thinking of enlisting.

Dickey Drake was silent just long enough for George to think he was giving serious consideration to an answer that he had probably prepared beforehand, then he said, "The best thing you can do is study. Science will be one of the weapons of this war. And you're in a place where you might make a difference."

"How do you know?"

"I know Conant. He's a scientist. He's working with the government. And your skills have been noticed."

It was what George had hoped to hear. He said he didn't want to leave school anyway.

Then his father seemed to relax, as if he, too, had heard what he hoped for. He said, "So . . . have you been to any club parties yet?"

"Parties? Dad, this isn't exactly a time to be thinking about parties."

"It's never too early to be thinking about the Porcellian Club."

"Dad—"

"I was a Porcellian."

"Dad—"

"Your grandfather, too. And—"

"Dad, I don't care about final clubs."

"Don't care? You're not some kind of socialist, are you?"

George loved his father and hoped to please him, but he was not much like him. George did not play golf, though his parents were members of the Country Club. George had not had a date in his life, while his parents loved to joke about the Lothario that Dickey Drake had been. And George had worn the same tweed sport coat and black knit tie every day of the semester, though his father kept telling him to go to the Coop and buy himself a Harvard tie and a blue blazer and "some of those stylish saddle shoes, and then the girls will flock like starlings."

Saddle shoes.

No. The study of physics was enough to occupy George. That and dreams of a young woman sitting on his lap and pressing her lips to his.

So he said, "Clubs are not what they were in your day, Dad."

"Yes. Lowell took care of that. Go and study and stop thinking about enlisting."

". . . six, five, four . . ."

George Wedge Drake followed his father's advice so well that by the fall of 1943, he wasn't just studying physics. He was teaching it.

Most of the physics faculty at Harvard had gone off to work in government projects, so the teaching of it had fallen to retirees, volunteers from other departments, and, as the *Alumni Bulletin* added, "even three undergraduates and a woman." And there was much debate over which was more shocking, that an undergraduate could teach a course in physics . . . or a woman.

Though there were rumblings of change and Radcliffe students would soon be admitted to upper level courses at Harvard, the sexes did not yet mingle officially in Harvard classrooms. So George, like other instructors and professors, followed the time-honored practice of delivering his classes twice, to the men in the Yard and to the women on the west side of Cambridge Common.

George Wedge Drake liked teaching, and he thought he was good at it. So did a Radcliffe junior named Olga Bassett.

On the first day of class, George noticed her. He noticed all the girls, but Miss Bassett was wearing slacks when the others were wearing skirts, and she was five-ten, taller than her young instructor. Over the next few weeks, he noticed something new about her at each class. Her smile one day; her dark hair, worn to the shoulder, the next; her brown eyes; the flash of thigh when she wore a pleated skirt and kneesocks. And he sensed her intellectual curiosity, too, because after every class, she stopped to ask him questions about the theorems and equations he discussed.

Six weeks into the semester, he summoned his courage and asked her to dinner at Cronin's, the tavern with the grouchy waitresses and the good clam chowder.

The following month was the happiest time George had ever known, because on Tuesday nights, he could call Olga and invite her to a weekend movie, and she would accept. And sometimes, after the movie, they would sit in a booth in Cronin's, sit so close that their legs pressed together, and they would order a pitcher of beer and hamburgers, and sometimes, on the way back to Radcliffe, she would hold his hand.

When she told him that she was not going home to New York City for Thanksgiving, because her father was traveling and her mother did not celebrate holidays, he invited her to the Drake home.

George's parents acted more casual about the invitation than they may have felt, perhaps because Olga arrived with a group of George's friends, kids from California and St. Louis and other points west. And they all sat at the dining-room table with Victor Wedge and his sons and other aunts and uncles, too. So there was neither the time nor the opportunity for a father to quiz his son about a young lady from New York whose parents did not celebrate such an American holiday.

But a few days later, George received a note under his door at Eliot House: *Come home for a little chat.*

This time there was no talk of clubs. The father had absorbed the disappointment of a son so socially inept as to be uninterested in the Porcellian. This time, Dickey Drake did not even wait until his son was settled before he said, "Are you familiar with the American Communist Party?"

"I've heard of it."

"Has this Olga girl talked with you about it?"

"In passing . . . we all wonder what the world will look like once the war ends."

"Well, it won't look the way her father wants it to. He's a member of the party. Not only that, he writes articles for the *Daily Worker.*"

George Drake felt a wave of heat rise from his collar to the crown of his head.

"Someone should straighten out those people over at Radcliffe admissions." His father put a glass of port into George's hand and said, "Conant called the other day. He wants you to leave after Christmas."

"Leave? Leave Harvard?"

"He's putting you onto something top secret. You might have to defer the degree for a year or so, but it will all be taken care of."

"What is it?"

"If I knew, it wouldn't be a secret, would it? Of course, if they see you dallying with the daughter of a Communist, they'll give the job to someone else."

"Who's 'they'?"

"The FBI."

"FBI?"

"You're brilliant, George. Conant tells me you understand more about physics than half the senior faculty. And here's your chance, just as I promised two years ago. But you have to be analytical about your life, as if it were an equation."

So George went back to Eliot House and tried to be analytical. His future would be in particle physics, and particle physics would change the world. And how many men could change the world? But he was also in love. So . . . would it be physics or infatuation? The promise of future success or present happiness?

All the next week, when he saw Olga, he tried to see her as a student rather than "his girlfriend." He decided that he would tell her on Friday night, after they went to the movies. At the Harvard Square, they saw *Casablanca*. It had been out for a year and they had seen it before, but they still loved it. Noble people making noble decisions.

They left the theater arm in arm and headed back to Radcliffe, but in front of the burying ground, they stopped. He began to speak, but she kissed him instead. Then she whispered, "I think our beautiful friendship has already begun."

And he knew that he couldn't tell her that night. And he couldn't resist her. And her kiss told him that she couldn't resist him. But there were parietal rules, which meant that getting into his room in Eliot House or hers at Radcliffe could be tricky.

So he turned her toward Brattle Street, because on Friday nights, his parents were at the Harvard Club. At their front door, he stopped and looked up and down the street. He did not tell her he was looking to see if any FBI agents were watching. Then he let her into his parents' house.

In the library, he lit a fire and poured two glasses of his father's port. He wanted to tell her. Instead, he kissed her. And then his hand was on the cool smoothness of her thigh, between the kneesocks and the skirt she had so conveniently worn. Soon, clothes were askew, clasps unclasped, zippers unzipped, though nothing came off, because Dickey and Doris always came home before ten-thirty. At ten o'clock precisely—George remembered because the mantelpiece clock was chiming—he and Olga experienced the most exciting moment of their lives. At two past ten, it was over.

After that, he did not have the heart to tell her that he could no longer see her. But on the following weekend and the one after that, he manufactured excuses for staying home—too much work, a family party, a gathering of Physics Department instructors. And then she left for Christmas vacation.

On the day after New Year's, George and three other juniors boarded a train for New Mexico. On the train, he wrote her a letter, but he decided not to send it. If the train was taking him to the place he expected, there would be someone reading his mail, making sure he was not revealing anything. So he tore up the letter.

Someday she would understand. Still, he cried that night, alone in the sleeping car, as the train sped over the Appalachians and into the heartland.

"... three, two, one ..."

George held his breath. Thoughts of Olga faded. So did thoughts of Harvard.

He had given up much to be here now, but he told himself it was worth it. For eighteen months, he had operated in an environment of mental stimulation he could never have hoped for in Cambridge. Here, in what he later described as an intellectual utopia, he had exchanged ideas with the greatest physicists of the age. But in those final seconds, ideas faded, too, before the enormity of what they had done. And then there was only a single thought, a single word:

Light.

The bunker was open at the back, and even through the welder's glasses, the flash illuminated every fold and every gully on the hills to the south. It was as though the working of the universe had suddenly been accelerated, causing the sun to leap from below the eastern horizon to its noonday apex in an instant.

They had been told to expect the flash. But the light did not fade. Instead, it rose in height, in intensity, and changed from white to boiling red. George and the others could wait no longer. They had to look at it. They had to see what they had made. So they stood and turned, and in their black welder's goggles was reflected something that no one had ever seen before, the most beautiful, horrible sight in history.

Then they heard a train coming toward them—the waves of shock and sound, racing hand in hand.

George glanced at Oppenheimer, who was holding a support post in the bunker, his mouth agape, his long skinny face contorted in shock, as though he had been painted by Edvard Munch. Later, Oppenheimer said that at that moment, he was thinking of a passage from the Bhagavad Gita: "I am become death, the destroyer of worlds."

Perhaps . . . but George agreed with Professor Bainbridge, who turned to Oppenheimer a moment later and said, "Now we are all sons of bitches."

ii

"Did he really say that?" asked Ned Wedge at the family meeting the following June. "Did Bainbridge really say, 'Now we are all sons of bitches'?"

"Yes," said George. "Even the grammar was correct."

"Watch your language, Ned," said Dickey. "You may still be wearing your navy uniform, but there are ladies present, including your fiancée."

"Oh, hell," said Harriet Webster. "Don't worry about me."

George thought that Cousin Ned had gotten himself quite a prize—a fine-looking girl, a face that was all Boston bone structure, an accent all Bryn Mawr, and a serve that exploded at your feet before her racquet even followed through. And she was tall, too, which was good because Ned Wedge stood six-one, with square shoulders and a sand-colored crew cut that gave him the look of a man who knew exactly what he thought.

"It must have been something," said Harriet, "to see the bomb go off."

"Something . . . yes," said George.

"Not many have seen that sight," said Ned's elder brother Jimmy, who was shorter, quieter, and seldom seen with a woman. "Not many who've lived, anyway."

"Certainly not the poor devils in Hiroshima and Nagasaki," said Ned.

"They got what they deserved," said Dickey Drake.

"No one deserved what they got, Dad," said George. "No one."

"Well"—Dickey sat at the head of the table—"thank God it's over. It cost all of us a great deal. And now, in keeping with Victor Wedge's will, the eldest male in the family—that's me—shall preside today."

Since 1937 they had been gathering for the meeting of the Wedge Charitable Trust. All lineal descendants of Heywood and Amelia Wedge were invited to present requests, and all who were present could vote, but the sons of Victor Wedge and their children would make final determinations.

Some years, the event was well attended. Other years, just a few showed up, and the distributions were accordingly small. But it was always a pleasant reunion, a chance for the family to socialize on commencement eve over a buffet supper and to meet for business the next morning in an upstairs room in the Faculty Club.

This year, there were two dozen descendants. Heywood and Amelia had raised two daughters and a son, so the names were Drake, Royce, and Wedge, and a few offshoots of those—close relations and long-lost cousins, all sipping coffee, eating pastries, scooping eggs from the stainless-steel chafing dishes. Outside, rhododendron bloomed in the sunshine, and the crowds made their way into the Yard for the first peacetime commencement in five years.

Dickey had everyone take seats, then he began with a prayer for Victor Wedge and for all those who had lost their lives. Then he said, "As you can all see, George is wearing his academic robes. He has to get down to Eliot House to join his classmates for the procession. So we're starting early."

First order of business was a treasurer's report, delivered by Ned Wedge. He described the equities, bonds, and funds that composed the trust, and noted their performance for the year. The trust was now worth a robust $3 million.

"So," said Dickey, "let's spend some of it."

Certain contributions were automatic—five thousand dollars to the Harvard College Fund, five thousand to the American Red Cross, a thousand to the Boston Museum of Fine Arts, two hundred for the upkeep of the Old South Meeting House. The family rejected a request from a man who hoped to open a small theater in the Berkshires. And they turned down Harriet's request for a grant to a woman who wanted to teach dance in the Negro section of Boston.

"Teaching coloreds how to dance?" Dickey laughed. "That's like teaching Brahmins how to make money."

And most of the other people in the room laughed with him.

Harriet showed neither anger nor embarrassment at the rejection, which was very good form, in George's mind.

Then Ned asked, "What about political campaigns?"

"Whose?" asked Dickey.

"Jack Kennedy. He's running for Congress."

"Kennedy!" cried Dickey Drake.

"My father did business with his. He's Winthrop House and a navy man, too."

"His father doesn't need our money," said Dickey.

"But we might need his friendship someday. I think Jack Kennedy could go places." Ned had already established a reputation as a young man of hardheaded practicality and stubbornness, too. He said, "Five hundred dollars should be plenty."

But no one else spoke in support.

Then George smoothed his robes and said, "I think that we should keep politics out of our considerations."

Ned looked at his brother. "Do you agree?"

"There's too much controversy in politics," said Jimmy. "But . . . but if you think you might do some good someday in the political line, maybe it would be worth it."

And the Kennedy for Congress campaign received a five-hundred-dollar contribution from the (mostly) Republican Wedges. Dickey wondered if Joe Kennedy would laugh out loud.

* * *

That afternoon, there was a smaller meeting. It took place at the Drake table in the Eliot House courtyard. After the commencement ceremonies in Tercentenary Theater, members returned to their houses for luncheon and a degree ceremony in the company of their friends.

Before the master stepped to the podium, Dickey took out three envelopes. He gave one each to Ned, Jimmy, and his own son, George. "These envelopes contain keys to safe-deposit boxes in the Back Bay Institute for Savings. You are supposed to pass them to your descendants, who are not to access the contents until the trust liquidates."

"What's in them?" said Ned.

"'Three poems that foretell a small gift of majestic proportion.'"

Ned looked at Harriet, then said, "This sounds like a fairy tale."

"I'm just quoting Victor's will," answered Dickey. "I think your father wanted to have something for his descendants to remember him by, even after they had stopped gathering to honor the Wedge Charitable Trust."

"Any ideas of what it is?" asked Jimmy.

Dickey said, "The words come from Lydia Wedge Townsend at the Bicentenary."

"Lydia the poet?" asked Jimmy.

"The *bad* poet," said Dickey. "That's all I know."

Ned slipped his envelope into his pocket. Jimmy studied his, as if wondering what was in it. George wrote the words "small gift— majestic proportion" on his.

"That was not Victor's favorite quote, though." Dickey sipped his wine and leaned back in his chair. "The one he liked most came from old President Lowell: 'Two things are always new—youth and the quest for knowledge.'"

And it was forever true, as the seasons turned and the semesters came and went . . . as Dickey Drake took his rest in Mount Auburn Cemetery . . . as Ned and Harriet gave two sons to the Wedge line . . . as George Wedge Drake earned tenure at Harvard . . . as Ned went to Washington in 1961 . . . as Jack Kennedy, '40, faced down the Russians over missiles in Cuba and George wondered if the scientists who built the bomb were about to become the biggest sons of bitches in history . . . as the bell tolled in Memorial Church on the afternoon of November 22, 1963, and the world changed . . . as the Beatles came to America three months later and it changed again . . . as the Senate voted the Tonkin Gulf Resolution . . . as the Red Sox won the pennant but lost the '67 Series . . .

There was always someone wanting to know more, about something.

iii

George Wedge Drake had Lowell's phrase engraved and framed and kept on his desk so that students could see it when they visited him, and he could remind himself of it when he faced a student like Franklin—"don't call him Frank"—Wedge, first son of Ned and Harriet, tall, intelligent, and far more opinionated than a freshman should be.

It was an October afternoon in 1967. George had just finished a class and returned to his office in Mallinckrodt Hall. It was the fifth week of the semester, so he was talking about classical mechanics— Newtonian laws on the attraction of masses and universal gravitations. No heavy lifting for a man who had been teaching as long as he had.

Like many a Harvard professor, he saved his muscle for his research. He was working under a $2 million National Science Foundation grant for the creation of more efficient and safer nuclear power. His goal was a heavy-water reactor that would address the problem of neutron flux absorption. But the work was slow.

Science, he always told his students, required patience. But the young presence churning in the chair on the other side of the desk seemed the embodiment of *im*patience.

"So," said George, "you're having problems with Physics Ten? We can't have a Wedge failing my class."

"I'm not having any problems," said Franklin Wedge. "I just thought you should know that this building isn't going to be a good place to be in a little while."

George looked at his telephone. "Should I be calling the university police?"

With a jerk of his head, Franklin flipped his hair away from his eyes.

Ever since the Beatles came along, boys were making that motion, and George found it faintly effeminate, but not when Franklin did it. With Franklin, it was like saying, "Go ahead. I dare you."

George did not believe in taking a dare. So he said, "Stopping Dow Chemical from offering jobs to Harvard students is no way to stop a war."

"Dow Chemical makes napalm. They sell it to the military. The military drops it on Vietnam. Dow profits from murder. If you work for them, you support murder."

"It's war. Not murder. There's a difference."

"Is there?" Franklin looked at the photograph of the first nuclear explosion, on a bookshelf behind George's desk. Beneath it was a little sign: NOW WE ARE ALL SONS OF BITCHES. — KENNETH BAINBRIDGE.

George said, "I keep that picture there to remind my students that science can be our master or our servant. So can chemical companies."

Franklin scowled. He had dark brows, so he scowled well, and he had already picked up the humorless demeanor of the campus radicals. What was there to laugh about, they seemed to ask, when people were dying in Vietnam?

George Wedge Drake agreed. That was why he did not call university police. But he said, "Your father won't be happy about this."

"Maybe it will get his attention."

"That sounds like adolescent rebellion. A generation ago, boys ate live goldfish and drank too much. If the political sit-in—"

Franklin stood. "This is no prank. And even if you call the police now, you're too late. That's why I waited till now to tell you."

"Thanks." George Drake thought about going back to work, but it was not a day for work. Work required deep thought, which required an atmosphere of calm, both inward and outward. But calm had not existed at Harvard for some time.

A year earlier, Defense Secretary Robert McNamara had come

to a conference at the new Kennedy School of Government. As he left, his car was surrounded outside Quincy House by a mob from a group that called itself Students for a Democratic Society. He was the symbol of an administration that they meant to overturn and one of the architects of a war that they meant to end. McNamara, however, was not one to back down from a fight, so he stood on the roof of the car and tried to talk to the crowd, but they shouted him down.

"Imagine," Ned Wedge had told George, "there was the secretary, come to Harvard at the invitation of an assistant secretary of the treasury—me. So it's my reputation on the line. I look out, and I see kids holding signs, DOWN WITH LBJ and such, and they're shouting and chanting, and I want to shoot myself. Finally, university police hustle us into the basement of Quincy House, into the goddamn steam tunnels! We go about a mile before we pop up like a bunch of moles in Langdell Hall."

George Drake had to chuckle whenever he thought of it: the prickly secretary of defense, university police, and his know-it-all cousin, scurrying along the subterranean corridors that ran north from the river houses, under the Yard, all the way to the Law School. The tunnels carried the pipes that brought steam heat from a generating plant on River Street to all the Harvard buildings. Bare lightbulbs, wet floors, long stretches of asbestos-wrapped pipes, valves, elbows, diverters, wheels: "A real dungeon," Ned had told George. "And a dungeon is where I'll send my sons if either of them is ever involved in anything like that demonstration."

Well, George now thought, get the dungeon cell ready.

The Faculty of Arts and Sciences had voted not to punish students exercising their political rights after the McNamara incident. But the rights of "free movement" would also be upheld. So George decided that he should influence Franklin and the others before they restricted anyone's rights. He went downstairs, but he was too late.

A hallway ran from the stairwell to the door of the conference room. And two hundred students filled it. They were sitting, standing, leaning, scowling. And at the end of the hall, a balding man in a gray suit stood with his hands in his pockets and a look of utter befuddlement on his face. Mr. Dow Chemical: free movement canceled.

Deans were stepping over students, looking into faces, entering into conversations, asking politely that the crowd disperse. It was almost genteel. But no one was moving. And they didn't move for the rest of the day.

"What do I do with him?" Ned Wedge asked Prof. G. two weeks later.

"You encourage him to think for himself," said George.

"You mean, let some left-wing radical in the SDS do his thinking for him?"

"Come on, Ned"—Harriet sipped her bourbon—"it's not the end of the world. The boy is trying to develop a conscience."

"Conscience?" snapped Ned.

All around, heads pivoted from conversations or rose from reading or turned from evening drinks. George made a gesture for Ned to lower his voice.

They were in the lounge of the Harvard Faculty Club, waiting for Franklin. It was a gracious room, with polite groupings of wing chairs and seraphs, flowered drapes, Oriental carpeting, a table in the center of the room with a collection of periodicals arrayed for the reading pleasure of people who had probably written half the articles.

Ned looked around and said, "This is one of the few rooms in America where people might recognize an undersecretary of treasury and care what he thinks."

"Just lower your voice," said Harriet.

Ned whispered, "Look at Galbraith over there. He looks down on me like I was some kind of pariah, now that I work for Lyndon Johnson instead of JFK."

"He's six-seven, for God's sake," said Harriet. "He looks down on everyone. We're concerned about out our son, not the opinions of Harvard professors about you."

Ned grunted and took a sip of his scotch.

"If it matters," George joked, "this Harvard professor thinks you're a good father to come up from Washington because your son has been 'admonished' by the faculty."

"A full faculty meeting, was it?" asked Ned. "All the bright lights and great men, all hearing my son's name uttered in infamy?"

"Few students were discussed individually," said George. "Seventy-four were put on probation. Franklin and a hundred and seventy more received a slap on the wrist."

On the far side of the room, a man stood suddenly, as if gripped by an overwhelming emotion, dropped his journal on the table, and came over to the Wedges. He was short, slightly built, and wore glasses with frames of tortoiseshell and brass. He also grew his white hair to his collar and favored western-style string ties in the land of regimental stripes: George Wald, professor of biology.

"Excuse me, Professor Drake," he said. "But I wanted you to know that your eloquence in support of those students was appreciated at the faculty meeting."

"Thank you."

Then Wald turned his gaze to the Wedges. "Your son seems to have been raised to think for himself. I congratulate you both for that."

"Thank you," said Harriet. "We're proud of him."

Then Wald narrowed his focus on Ned. "Next time you see LBJ, tell him he needs his eyes checked. He can't see the forest for the trees." And with a curt nod, Wald was gone.

Ned's lips were still pulled into the smile of a man accepting a compliment about his son, but the rest of his expression had collapsed. "That old son of a bitch."

"Your administration has just been insulted by a Nobel laureate," said George, "cited for his work in the physiology of vision."

"So," cracked Harriet, "he used the right metaphor."

" 'Can't see the forest for the trees,' " said Ned. "Ha-ha. Is he with the SDS, too?"

"No. But he's concerned," said George. "How many more boys have to die?"

"They don't have to die. Just serve. Like you and I did."

George said, "I served by marrying Harvard brilliance and government money to bring the world to the brink of nuclear disaster. Now I do what I can to pull us back."

"You won a war, George," said Ned. "You saved lives. Maybe mine. And you've been taking government grants ever since."

"Governments can be dangerous, though," said George.

"Is that why someone at Los Alamos gave our secrets to the Russians?"

"There were spies there. Klaus Fuchs, the German . . . perhaps others. They decided the world would be a better place with a balance of power."

"'Useful idiots' is what Lenin called them," said Ned.

George laughed bitterly and took a sip of bourbon. "The Russians knew what we were doing all along, and all that security cost me a girl I still think about."

Ned looked at his watch, tapped his foot, finished his drink. "Where is that boy?"

But Harriet was looking at George. "Did you ever try to contact her?"

"I wrote to her a few times. But she'd moved on. All for the best, considering that the House Un-American Activities Committee got after her father in the fifties."

"Yeah," said Ned. "That would have played hell with your government grants."

"Touché," said George.

"Hello, everyone," said Franklin.

It surprised none of them that dinner did not go well.

Ned had three scotches in him by the time they sat in the dining room. This made him quicker than usual to anger, more certain than usual of his opinions.

Franklin wore a veneer of contrition that his father quickly stripped to a layer of defiance beneath.

Harriet smoked eight cigarettes and had a case of motherly fidgets, as Ned called them—verbal fidgets as she kept jumping about, looking for conversational topics that would defer the inevitable argument, tabletop fidgets as she played with the silverware, her cigarette lighter, and the food on her plate.

George just watched and hoped to play the mediator.

At one point, Harriet turned the conversation to George's hobby, rare books. This led to some speculation about an old family treasure—"a small gift of majestic proportion." George said he was working on a few theories.

Ned said he couldn't care less, because he and his brother would have to be dead twenty-one years before his sons could access the safe-deposit boxes that Victor had left them. Then Ned turned on Franklin. "My father believed that all the Wedges are in this together. So . . . when one Wedge engages in troublemaking, he's not just hurting himself. He's hurting the whole family."

"I could tell you as much, Dad," said Franklin, "when you go to Washington."

"Dammit!" Ned slammed his hand on the table. "It's not as easy as it used to be to get into this place. Just being a Wedge doesn't always cut it."

"It worked for me," said Franklin.

"I want it to work for your brother, too," said Ned. "But why should Harvard want another Wedge when the one who's here has been *admonished?*"

Franklin did not answer. Instead, he turned to his mother and said, "I've been thinking of majoring in English."

"That's wonderful, dear." Harriet put her hand on his arm.

George tried to play the mediator. "There's a long tradition of rebellion at Harvard, Ned. Harvard likes the iconoclasts and troublemakers."

"I don't," said Ned. "And that's not what Will is, anyway. He's a serious boy."

"And I'm not?" Franklin stood and pulled off his necktie. "Will is serious about girls and prep school grades. I'm serious about . . . about serious things."

And with that, Franklin Wedge stalked through the dining room, past the famous professors enjoying their *boeuf bourguignonne* and their wine, through the paneled foyer, past the concierge, who bid him a polite good night that brought no answer, through the vestibule, and into the autumn night.

* * *

Franklin was angry, and he was still hungry.

He looked at his watch: 6:50. Still time to get a meal in the Freshman Union, just across the courtyard from the Faculty Club. He jammed his necktie into his pocket and headed for a supper he might enjoy, a supper with friends.

The student handbook said, "One of the immutable laws of Harvard University is that gentlemen shall wear jackets and ties in dining halls at all times." Franklin supposed that there must have been a time when such a law had been taken seriously. But this was 1967. No one who knew the lyrics to "Sergeant Pepper's Lonely Hearts Club Band" would be caught dead in a tie, if he could help it.

So the freshmen rebelled over ties. They went to the Union wearing T-shirt, jacket, jeans . . . and a tie. Or work shirt, Bermuda shorts, windbreaker . . . and a tie. Or, the best that he had seen, bathrobe, pajamas, tuxedo shirt . . . and *black* tie.

And every day, the Union doorkeeper, a beleaguered-looking guy with receding hair and a strong Boston accent, upheld the immutable law. No one knew his name, so they called him Windsor-Knot Wally. He wore a blue blazer, a white shirt, and a crimson tie, and he watched for violators.

A few hated him, but most knew he was just a guy doing a job. If you got into the food line and weren't wearing a tie, he would produce a skinny black rayon rattail and, if you chose to put it on, you would be admitted to the wonders of mystery meat, chipped beef, and red bug juice, all consumed in a magnificent hall beneath a portrait of Theodore Roosevelt. Or you could give him an argument, and he would ask you for your bursar's card. Then he would ask you to leave.

To Franklin, it was all silly and arbitrary. There were people dying in Vietnam, and at Harvard they were worried about neckties. After the debacle in the Faculty Club, he was in no mood for anything silly or arbitrary. So he wasn't putting his tie back on.

He was almost disappointed when he did not see Wally minding the door. Dinner ran from 5:30 to 7:00, so there were just a few students trickling in, and there were loud voices in the kitchen, so Wally must have been off mediating some dispute.

Franklin showed his card, then grabbed a tray and headed for the row of serving ladies, behind their wall of stainless steel, creamed spinach, and Swedish meatballs.

"Excuse me, sir." Winsdor-Knot Wally appeared from somewhere. He was looking angry and red-faced, but seemed to be doing his best to stay polite.

"What?" said Franklin.

Wally pulled a necktie from his pocket.

"What?" demanded Franklin fiercely, though he knew exactly *what.*

Wally said in a very low voice, "I got other troubles in the kitchen tonight. I'm in no mood for any cheap shit. So put on the fuckin' tie, or get out."

"What did you say to me?" Franklin acted as insulted as he could.

And just then, there was a thunderous crash in the kitchen.

"Oh, Jesus," said Wally.

The kitchen door banged open, and Franklin got a glimpse of a dozen plates, some shattered on the floor, others spinning on their edges before they wobbled over. Out came a young man, wiry, well built, with reddish hair that he wore to his shoulders. He saw Wally and said, "Fuck you, Uncle Jack. And fuck every fuckin' cocksucker in this place."

Wow, thought Franklin.

"Walk out that door, Bingo, and you're fired," said Wally. "I can't get you another job."

"Fuck you. And don't call me Bingo. My name's Jimmy. And I ain't washin' dishes for minimum wage anymore."

"You tell him, Jimmy," said Franklin.

"Fuck you, too, asshole," said Jimmy.

And Franklin turned on Windsor-Knot Wally. "And fuck you, too, for exploitin' workers and makin' students wear neckties."

All that Windsor-Knot Wally could say was "Jesus Christ."

Franklin stalked out, too. "Hey. Hey, wait."

"What?" said Jimmy.

Franklin caught up to him. "Way to give it to the man back there."

"The man?" He laughed. "Oh, yeah."

"Can I walk with you?" asked Franklin. "If they come after

you, they should know that the students have solidarity with the workers."

"Oh, yeah? Pisser."

Franklin offered his hand and his name.

The young guy took it and said, "I'm Jimmy Keegan. And I'm never washin' another fuckin' Harvard dish or another fuckin' Harvard floor."

"I'm with you, man."

"Oh, yeah? You with me? Pisser." And they walked into the Yard. After a time, Keegan said, "So . . . you rich?"

"Not as rich as a guy who flips the bird to the world and walks out on the man."

Keegan laughed again. "Unh . . . I got an ounce of weed on me. Fifteen bucks. Want to buy?"

Franklin stopped right there, in front of Houghton Library, and looked into Keegan's eyes. "Are you a narc?"

"What?"

"They always tell us to ask that. If you're a narc, and I ask, you have to tell me the truth. Are you a narc?"

"No fuckin' way."

So Franklin dug into his pocket. He had been at Harvard for six weeks and hadn't smoked a joint yet. It was time. And from what he heard, fifteen bucks an ounce was a dollar cheaper than you could get it anywhere else.

Chapter Twenty-eight

═══

IN EARLY May, Harvard invited all high school seniors who had been accepted to come for a weekend, whether they had decided to go to Harvard or not.

It was a no-pressure sort of thing. Classes on Friday, orientation lectures, some fun on Saturday night. If you wanted to see what student life in Cambridge was all about, this was a good way to do it. Then you could make up your mind.

Peter Fallen was going to the parents' program. A nice May day, a chance to hear a few lectures. He couldn't resist.

He and Jimmy came into the Yard through the Class of 1875 Gate, the one with the inscription from Isaiah. Peter resisted a lecture on its meaning. "Open ye the gates that the righteous nation which keepeth the truth may enter in."

The leaves still had a light green tint that made them look delicate and new, but they had filled out enough that the monstrous Science Center, which now loomed over the north end of the Yard like a creature in a fifties horror movie, could not be seen.

Of course, the Yard never looked greener than in mid-May, or neater. Commencement was coming, so all the brown patches had been sprayed with grass seed in green fertilizer. And just so no one stepped on any of the new grass, miles of wire had been strung along every paved path in the Yard. As commencement week began, all the wire would be unstrung, all the wooden posts put away for another year, and in a single week, all the grass would be trampled again.

But for now, everything was green and growing, with not even a Frisbee game to take away from the scene, because no one could play on the grass.

However, springtime in Cambridge not only brought out the leaves. It also brought out the demonstrators. There was always something to protest. It might be serious, like a war or wage fight; it might be as trivial as the miles of wire that kept students from playing Frisbee in the Yard. But the weapons were always the same—slogans and signs, leaflets and chants.

That day, a group was picketing in front of the president's office in Massachusetts Hall. Their slogan, chanted and painted: "Save the 'Side! Save the 'Side! No Expansion in Riverside!"

Peter Fallon had learned in his freshman year that if he didn't want to go hunting for a trash barrel to throw away a leaflet, he should ignore all "leaflet lackeys." So he ignored the handout that someone offered him and kept walking with his son.

But the guy followed them. "You might want to read this."

"Not today."

"If not today, then soon."

Peter turned to the guy and thought he saw something familiar in the earring and ponytail. He took the leaflet, just to shut the guy up, and started walking again.

"Hey!" The guy followed them all the way to John Harvard's statue. "Hey, Mr. Book Man!"

That was it. Franklin Wedge. Peter stopped and turned again. "I didn't recognize you without your bathing suit."

Franklin came closer. "I just got into town. I'm staying a few weeks."

"Until the commencement meeting?"

"Yeah. The big one. The mother of all meetings."

"Why do you say that?"

"Read the leaflet," said Franklin, then he looked at Jimmy. "This must be your son."

Peter introduced him and said that he had been admitted for the fall. "He hasn't decided if he's going or not."

Franklin gave the boy a grin. "Remember, Harvard is many things to many people. Some think it's the portal to riches and fame. Others think it's a den of pompous self-congratulation and powermongering. And a few of us like to believe that beneath these elms, there is truth to be found, if you're prepared to demand it."

Jimmy shot a nervous glance at his father.

And Franklin burst out laughing. "The kid thinks I'm nuts, Fallon."

"So do a few other people," said Peter.

"I'll bet you're one of them. Just read the leaflet."

Peter looked at it. "'Stop Harvard expansion in the Riverside neighborhood.'"

"We've been fighting issues like that forever," said Franklin.

"Who's we?"

"The people with conscience." Franklin looked at Jimmy. "You can be both. You can be a suit who makes money like your father and a man of conscience, too."

"What's so important about the Riverside neighborhood?" asked Peter.

"That's where my brother wants to build Harvard's newest residential house—Wedge House, named for all the Wedge iconoclasts and all the Wedge phonies, too. Nothing more than self-perpetuation. He's decided that I'm not going to have any kids, and he only has one daughter, so the name dies with us."

Jimmy glanced at his watch.

Franklin kept talking. He seemed like the kind who kept talking, even when no one was listening. "I want to do something important with money."

And right there in the Yard, it was starting to come clear to Peter Fallon.

What better way to immortalize your name than to build a new undergraduate house? Harvard had planned to build an art museum on the corner of Western Ave. and Memorial Drive, overlooking the Charles, but the Riverside neighbors had resisted and Harvard had relented. Would Harvard be able to resist an undergraduate house, bought and paid for by alumni contributions, on the same spot?

Peter stepped closer to Franklin and said, "Wedge House would cost about fifty million. Does the trust have that much?"

"Hell, no."

"Will wants to find the play, then, so that he'll have all the money he needs?"

"Or some variation of that riff." Franklin glanced back at the picket line circling in front of Massachusetts Hall.

Peter sensed Franklin's impatience, so he tried to think the questions up fast. "And . . . and you're trying to get the play first?"

"I'm just trying to do what's right," said Franklin. "Harvard has too damn much power. They've bought up hundreds of acres of land on the other side of the river and they're planning what they'll do with it fifty years from now, while most neighborhood people just want to pay their rents and maybe get a little relief on their property taxes."

"Is that why you tore the last page out of Theodore Wedge's diary?"

"It was gone when I read it. Nice work figuring that out, by the way."

"Then it was your mother who did it?"

"I don't know. Ask her. She's back from England this week."

Just then, the sound of the chanting rose in volume and intensity, because a television news crew had come into the Yard.

"TV," said Franklin. "My brother will shit if he sees this on TV. He's tried to keep it quiet as long as he could, just to keep the neighbors out of it. I got the whole story out of my mother last fall. Of course, I had to get her stoned first. . . ."

Peter saw his son's eyebrows rise. So he said to Franklin, "You know, the university police won't let them film in the Yard for long."

"Then I'd better get back." Franklin Wedge clenched his fist above his head and began to chant. "Save the 'Side! Save the 'Side! Harvard out of Riverside!"

"Like I told you," said Peter to his son as they watched Franklin hurry back to the fray, "for every banker, lawyer, and businessman, Harvard makes at least one rebel."

"Yeah. Cool," said Jimmy. And he sounded as though he meant it.

Peter wasn't living with Evangeline, but they were spending more and more time together. And he was at her apartment that evening, with a bottle of Puligny-Montrachet open and a flowchart in front of them.

There was a line drawn from the quote on Lydia's headstone to a photo of Victor Wedge at the Tercentenary to a copy of the Copley portrait of Lydia and Abraham to a copy of the inscription on the First Folio of *Love's Labours Lost* that Victor Wedge had donated to Harvard. There was another line that ran from a miniature portrait of Dorothy Wedge Warren, back to a card that said "Bertram Lee meets O'Hill on Widener steps," another card that said "Bingo Keegan," and now, Peter was pinning the only leaflet he had ever saved under the name of Franklin Wedge.

"There has to be a controlling intelligence," said Evangeline.

Peter laughed. "Not according to our friend the physics professor. We are all spinning in space and time, little molecules bouncing off one another. That's what's going on here. A lot of people in the past hoped they'd have some control over something—their own lives, the lives of the people around them, the life of Harvard, and in the process, they all dropped little pieces of information."

"And Ridley picked up some of it, and Keegan picked up some of it. . . ."

"And Bertram Lee, and O'Hill, and old Prof. G. And they may have intersected, maybe not."

"Well, if you can see all that, maybe you're the controlling intelligence."

Peter clinked her glass. "Or us."

The conversation was interrupted by the electric zap of the apartment buzzer.

They looked at each other, and Evangeline shrugged.

So Peter threw a sheet over their chart and Evangeline answered the buzzer.

"This is Dorothy Wedge."

A few moments later, Will Wedge's daughter was in the apartment, sitting on the futon sofa. She accepted a glass of the wine and made a face. "Tastes sour."

"White Burgundies can be that way," said Fallon, "if you're not used to them. What can we do for you?"

The girl looked as though she hadn't slept in nights. Usually, kids her age could absorb all sorts of punishment from term-paper deadlines to drinking contests, sleep a few hours, and look beautiful again. But something more was bothering her than the simple life of the twenty-two-year-old. She said, "This afternoon, I went through the stacks to Assistant Professor O'Hill's office and heard loud voices. Someone was saying to him, 'If you can't come up with more books, you'd better find more information, because the buyer is going to decide by commencement.'"

"'The buyer'?" said Fallon. "Of what?"

She gave him a scowl, as though she were too tired for good manners. "The play, of course."

"O'Hill came to you about it, didn't he? He asked if he could be your tutor."

"Yes. But I . . . I had always liked him. And he was a very popular teacher. In one of our early tutorial sessions, he said he had been putting together a scenario and wanted me to help him on it, perhaps even write about it. That's when he directed me to the Shepard diary. But he became very angry with me when I went to Ridley Royce. He said I had gone outside of the academic community. But . . . Bob O'Hill never stays angry at me for too long."

"Bob?" The way she said that got Evangeline's attention.

The girl shot a glance at Evangeline, as if to say she had just revealed a bit too much.

"What else did this man say to O'Hill?" asked Peter.

"He said that Keegan was happy with the sale of the locket. It showed O'Hill's good faith and brought the rats into the open. . . . Mr. Fallon, my *father* bought that locket."

"Against my advice." Fallon looked at Evangeline. "It sounds as if O'Hill is the one who descends from somebody named Callahan."

Dorothy said, "He told the man that he didn't need to show any more good faith. He wanted out of this. The man told him that he was in too deep, and if he tried to back out, they'd tell Peter Fallon who it was who came after him on the river."

Peter said, "Can you describe the man who was threatening O'Hill?"

"I think O'Hill called him 'Lee.'"

"I'm curious," said Evangeline. "How did you get so close and hear so much?"

"His door was closed, and I tiptoed," she said.

"Tiptoed?" said Fallon. "Why?"

Dorothy sipped her wine and looked down at the rug. "Sometimes I like to surprise him. My thesis is done. . . . I'll be graduating soon. And Bob is so much more mature than Chad Street, and he's about to leave Harvard—"

"Leave?" said Evangeline.

"O'Hill didn't get tenure," said Peter. "I think it made him mad, so instead of lecturing about books, he started stealing them and fencing them through Bertram Lee. And whatever he's been doing, he's been getting in deeper and deeper. That's what Dorothy heard this afternoon."

"Who's 'the buyer' Lee refers to?" asked Evangeline. "Price?"

"Maybe," said Peter. "Or Lee doesn't know because he's working through a fence of his own."

"Keegan?"

"Bingo."

Evangeline considered that for a moment, then she turned to Dorothy and said, "I wouldn't go tiptoeing around Assistant Professor O'Hill for a while, no matter how you feel about him."

"Why did you come to us?" asked Peter.

"You're the only ones my father trusts in this business."

The next morning, Peter Fallon walked down Avery Street, one of those Boston side streets that always seemed to be dark, even in late May. He could always tell if Bertram Lee's Anthology Bookshop was open as soon as he came around the corner. If it was, the book bins would be out and people might be picking over the "hardcovers for a buck" collection. If it was closed, the sidewalk would be deserted.

The book bins were out. And Lee was, too.

His partner, Mr. Freitas, a dour man with a fringe of gray hair and a sallow complexion, greeted Fallon, although that might have been too strong a word. "You? What do you want?"

"Joseph Freitas, professor emeritus of English, Boston University. What a pleasant greeting," said Fallon. "Gotten your hands on any more of Dr. Eliot's Five-Foot Shelves?"

"We're busy here."

Anthology Books was not quite the "appointment only" shop that Fallon had created. The antiquarian books were in a locked room on the second floor. Downstairs was all used books, cataloged into sections, priced to sell. And there was nobody there. Boston had recently lost other used-book stores to rising rents and declining interest, but Lee and Freitas had held on. Fallon wondered for how much longer.

"I won't take any of your time. I'm here to see Lee."

"He's on a little vacation."

"Vacation? Now?"

"We had a nice sale. Beat you to a copy of *Anglorum Praelia*. Sold it to your old professor. So Bertram decided to take a week in Key West."

"Gettin' hot in Florida."

"He likes the heat."

"Then he should have stayed in Boston."

Mr. Freitas shrugged.

Half an hour later, Fallon was in Widener Library, deep in the stacks.

He took the elevator down to the study carrels at the rear.

It was silent in the stacks, except for the whoosh and thunk of distant elevators, which was like the breathing of the library itself. But O'Hill wasn't there. So Fallon had no chance of surprise.

He took out his cell phone and made a call to O'Hill's home number. Dorothy had given it to him. No answer. So he called the English department and learned that Assistant Professor O'Hill had been called out of town and would not be back until just before commencement.

So . . . what the hell.

Fallon had a pocketknife, and he had a few skills that he still remembered from the old neighborhood. He slipped the blade and popped the lock. The office was very small. The sun was pouring in.

There was a bookshelf above the desk. It contained books that might have been of some importance to O'Hill's own work, including his dissertation on seventeenth-century sermons. And whenever Peter thought about reading things like that, he was glad he wasn't an academic.

He supposed he should not have been surprised to see that among the volumes was a copy of William Blake's *Songs of Innocence* and *Songs of Experience.*

He always carried his own cotton conservator's gloves in the inner pocket of his sport coat—white, thin, delicate. He put them on and opened *Experience.*

In the place where the poem "Tyger! Tyger!" should have been, with Blake's engraving of a tiger in a forest, there was a blank space and at the binding, a neatly razored edge.

And then he noticed a copy of *Treasure Island,* by Robert Louis Stevenson. That had nothing to do with the seventeenth-century sermons that O'Hill was supposed to be writing about. But it did contain important engravings by N. C. Wyeth, and all had been razored out.

Peter realized that many of these books had been on Scavullo's list—items that Ridley Royce had offered to sell through a fence from Eliot House. O'Hill had typed the information on Ridley's computer himself, then deleted it, probably after he dumped Ridley from his boat. Framing Ridley and Fallon also seemed to be part of O'Hill's plan.

Either that or someone was framing O'Hill by planting the books. And there was a copy of *New England Reveries,* by Lydia Wedge Townsend. Fallon opened it and saw that O'Hill had put Post-it notes over half a dozen poems, "John Hicks and Other Heroes," "Standing on Firm Ground," "The Bell Ringer of Harvard Hall," and many others.

Peter copied all the notes into his own notebook, then he stepped out and locked the door behind him.

There was silence.

But someone was there.

He could sense it. Directly ahead of him was a floor-to-ceiling metal stack, with eight shelves, lined with books, running thirty feet from the east wall on his right and to the inner aisle on his left.

And someone was standing on the other side of the stack, someone big, someone male.

Fallon waited a moment, then moved a few steps to his left.

Whoever was on the other side did not move at all.

Maybe it was his imagination. Maybe the guy was just looking for a book.

So Peter took a few steps more. The guy still didn't move. So Peter stepped into the aisle.

The guy was turned away, head down, flipping pages. He had on a tweed sport coat. Whoever he was, he showed no interest in Peter Fallon.

So Peter made for the elevator, which was ten stacks away.

As soon as he started to walk along the inner aisle, the guy went to the other end of the stack, the outer aisle, and began to move along, too. Peter picked up his pace. So did the other guy.

Peter moved a little faster. Should he wait for the elevator when he got there? Or head for the staircase to avoid this guy? Or confront him, whoever he was? He knew it wasn't O'Hill. Was it one of Keegan's goons? Maybe Smithy with the big forearms?

He stopped for a moment, and the footfalls stopped at the other end of the stack. He thought about taking off his shoes, so the guy couldn't hear him. Then maybe he could sneak up and surprise this stalker.

No. If the guy wanted to corner him, they could meet at the elevator. In half a dozen strides, Peter was in front of it, pushing the button, and from somewhere below came the sound of the elevator moving in their direction.

The footfalls were coming from his right, and now footfalls were coming from his left, too.

He was cornered. Then the doors of the elevator opened. Should he step on?

It didn't matter, because there they were. One of them came up on his left. Then the other one came out of the stack, looked at Fallon, and said, "You!"

"Scavullo?"

A short while later, Fallon and Scavullo leaned against one of the pillars at Widener and looked out across the Yard.

Scavullo said, "We thought we might catch O'Hill this morning."

"English department says he left town."

"Not surprised. A copy of *Anglorum Praelia* disappeared yesterday from a locked case in the display room in Houghton."

"Locked case?"

"He used a glass cutter. Put a notebook down and pretended that he was writing something, which is the way that it looked on a security camera. Reached in and took the book. Of course, he had worked in Houghton as a graduate student, and he knew the security procedures a little too well."

Fallon laughed.

"What's so funny?" asked Scavullo.

"If he was going to steal something, he should have gone to the effort of taking something valuable. It's not even worth a thousand."

"Any idea why he went after it?"

"It's one of the books that was in John Harvard's library," said Peter. "But there's something else from Harvard's library, something lost for over three hundred years. It may have been the reason someone tried to kill me on the river, because it's worth more than anything else in Houghton . . . maybe everything in Houghton."

"That would be tough. But I'm listening."

Peter looked across the Yard, to the steps of Memorial Church, where a heavyset guy sat reading a book and watching the library. "I think that guy is part of it. In the fall, he wears a Bruins cap. Now that it's baseball season, he's wearing a Red Sox cap."

"Dangerous?"

"Maybe," said Peter. "But stupid. If we give his boss a little more rope, we might be able to track down a lot of the books that are lost. We might even connect him to Bertram Lee and O'Hill."

"Maybe O'Hill. But not Bertram Lee," said Scavullo.

"Why?"

"He turned up dead in a men's room in Key West this morning."

"Dead?"

"He liked the nose candy. He also liked the Key West boys. It seems that the mixture of cocaine and anonymous sex was too much for his bookselling heart to take."

"I'd wait for the autopsy," said Peter. "And by the way, did you ever ask this Assistant Professor O'Hill where he was on the morning that Ridley fell off his boat?"

"He said he was in a tutorial session with a student." Scavullo flipped open his notebook. "Dorothy Wedge. She's a senior. The alibi checked out."

"She may have been lying."

"A student? Lie? Let me write that down." He did, then closed the notebook again. "Now, what is this thing you're going to help me to find?"

"Just trust me. I need another week or two. By commencement."

Scavullo pointed his finger at Fallon. "You keep me posted."

"Every day," said Fallon. "I'll be glad to know I have protection, and keep jabbing your finger at me a little bit more. The guy who's watching us deserves a show."

"Should I pull out my handcuffs?"

"No. That's a bit much. The finger will do." Fallon grinned. "Now, beat it."

As soon as Scavullo left him alone on the steps of Widener, he took out his telephone and called Professor George Wedge Drake and congratulated him on the purchase of *Anglorum Praelia*.

"Thank you. I hope you don't mind that I set someone else on the trail of it, too."

"All's fair in love and war," said Fallon. "Thanks for giving me the chance. But let me give you a bit of advice."

"Yes?"

"Stop payment on the check."

"But it was a wire transfer."

"Let me guess, to a numbered account in Switzerland."

"Well, yes. Why?"

"Because the book you bought was stolen from Houghton."

Evangeline spent most of the afternoon in the archives, going through letters between Elizabeth Cary Agassiz and Dorothy Wedge Warren. She had been enjoying this kind of research, but not today. She was following a story that had gone past them, all the way to a frightened girl who was Dorothy's namesake.

So she decided to give the girl a call. She went back to her apartment, let herself in, put down her briefcase, and froze.

A man in a black raincoat and scally cap was sitting in the folding chair by the window.

"Who are you?" she blurted.

At the same instant, the door slammed behind her and she screamed. A big guy in a Red Sox baseball cap was standing behind her.

"That's my nephew Jackie Pucks," said the man. "Only now, we're callin' him Jackie Fastball. It's baseball season."

"How did you get in here?" Evangeline's knees were shaking, but she kept some swagger in her voice.

Bingo Keegan did not stand. He barely moved. "I'm a business associate of your boyfriend. I like to associate with smart guys, especially guys from the neighborhood who make good, despite a few pretensions. By the way, did you like the wine?"

"What do you want?"

"Tell him that civilians are safe in this business, and thanks to his good sense regarding a B and E in Marblehead a few weeks ago, I have been able to see to his safety up until now, even when his opinions almost cut into a nice locket sale that I had a piece of. But, honey, we're talkin' about thirty million bucks here, so I can't guarantee anything."

"Is he supposed to stop looking for the manuscript, then?"

"If I was him, I'd look even harder." Keegan stood and brushed past her.

She heard the door open, and Keegan whispered into her ear, "But I'd remember who my friends are."

* * *

"A fair warning," Peter said to her a few hours later.

"My knees are still shaking," said Evangeline.

Peter put his arm around her. "Keegan may be taking control of things. Or he may have lost control."

"You'd best be careful, Peter."

"And you'd best stay close to me."

"Better I should stay close to Bernice. She's packin' heat."

"Let's hope we don't need it."

A few days later, Peter and Evangeline drove to Manchester-by-the-Sea with Will Wedge.

Will looked as nervous and exhausted as his daughter. And he had about him an unfamiliar air of contrition. He apologized for doling out information and told them everything about his plan, most of which fell into line with what Franklin had told Peter in Harvard Yard.

"But?" said Peter. "There's always a but. You're leaving something out."

Evangeline asked, "What about Charles Price?"

"Price will give a thirty-million-dollar contribution to the building of Wedge House, if it includes the Charles Price Shakespeare Library, sitting for all the world to see, right there on the river, with the manuscript as the centerpiece."

"That's a hell of a house library," said Peter.

"To build a new residential house for Harvard will cost fifty or sixty million. The rest of the money would come out of the final liquidation of the Wedge Charitable Trust. We'll perpetuate our name for as long as Harvard is here and expand one of Harvard's greatest resources."

"Why wouldn't Price want his name on the house?"

"He cares about the manuscript. If I find it, he'll pay me for the privilege of putting it into the Price Library at Wedge House. He'll get a nice tax write-off, and Harvard will go along because they get it all, one way or the other. If the play doesn't exist, then I convince Price to make the contribution, so long as he gets his name on the library and gets to put all his Shakespeariana in there."

"And if Keegan gets it?" asked Evangeline.

"That's trouble," said Will. "It goes into the booksellers' underground. I suspect Price will be a player there, too."

"But it will be a cash sale for much less," said Fallon. "Twenty million tops, because he'll never be able to show it publicly without having to fight Harvard for it."

"Basically," Wedge explained, "we're appealing to Price's ego. He's always imagined himself as some kind of Shakespearean hero, ever since we were freshmen."

"What about Franklin?" asked Evangeline.

"My brother is the joker in any deck. We'd both like to find this thing, just to end the troubles that began back in 1969, just to exorcise the demons around the Wedge brothers. . . . and all the people we've pulled into our circle."

Chapter Twenty-nine

===

1968–1969

THE DATE was Wednesday, November 6, 1968. The class was Government 154, The American Presidency.

And this, thought Will Wedge, was why he had come to Harvard.

He took a seat two places away from the prettiest girl in Longfellow Hall, put his coat on the chair between them, and opened his notebook.

Professor Neustadt gave his students a little half smile, as if to say that he was going to enjoy the next hour, and he began: "Last night, we witnessed one of the closest popular votes in our history. But in the electoral college, Richard Nixon won, three hundred and two to Humphrey's hundred and ninety-one. I would suggest that this plurality legitimizes the election and emphasizes the importance of the electoral college. . . ."

Will took notes, but mostly he enjoyed being at the center of things. Here was a man who had been an aide to Truman, an advisor to Kennedy, and a regular on the Easterrn Airlines Harvard shuttle, which got its name when JFK started bringing professors and their former students down to work for him. And now Neustadt was lecturing to Will about things that mattered as much to the nation as they would on the exam.

Will had decided to take as many of the so-called Great Man

courses as he could in his first semester. It seemed a good way to see what Harvard had to offer and a great way to attract girls.

Like most Harvard freshmen, Will Wedge had an image of the image he projected that most girls would tell him was more fantasy than reality. He and his friends talked about "dropping the H-bomb" in conversation. Once they announced that they went to Harvard, girls were supposed to fawn. And once they announced that they were studying at the feet of, say, a Neustadt or John Kenneth Galbraith, girls were supposed to swoon.

Of course, it didn't work with Radcliffe girls, because from 1950 on, any 'Cliffie could take any class at Harvard. And it didn't work with girls from other colleges, either, because the ones who knew who Galbraith was didn't care.

Nevertheless, Will would choose a seat near a girl, take notes, and cast sidelong glances at her, while Galbraith expostulated. Will might simply have read Galbraith's book *The New Industrial State*, but in person, Galbraith delivered his opinions with a wry condescension toward just about everybody in national life, reserving special sarcasm for Nixon and Johnson, for the shapers of American policy in Vietnam, and for anyone foolish enough to suggest that the federal budget could be balanced or anyone misguided enough to try to do it.

And this, thought Will, was why he had come to Harvard.

He also took Humanities 7, Trends in Modern Drama, from Professor William Alfred, who called himself the faculty's "resident Papist." While Will picked a seat in the usual way, Alfred would arrive in Sanders Theater, his fedora pulled low, his green book bag slung over his shoulder, his three-piece suit artfully rumpled. He would sit at a table on the stage, take a text from the book bag, clip a microphone to his lapel, and speak to four hundred students as though he were chatting with one or two. When he talked about Aeschylus, he read passages in the Greek, and students who understood none of it were mesmerized. When he talked about character, he could turn a collection of words on a page into human beings as real as he was.

And this, too, thought Will, was why he had come to Harvard.

To meet his science requirement, he took Natural Sciences 10,

Introduction to Geology, also known as Rocks for Jocks. The course was supposed to be easy, though Will was pulling the first C of his life. But there were plenty of girls to sit near, and one of the teachers was an assistant professor named Stephen Jay Gould, who not only could explain what the Appalachian geosyncline was but also peppered his lectures with witticisms and sarcastic asides, quite often about organized religion.

And all of it, thought Will, was why he had come to Harvard: to hear opinions at the center of things, to hear the man who invented the term *conventional wisdom* pontificate on the wisdom of the moment, to hear the wisdom of the ages from Harvard's resident Papist, to hear an irreligious young scientist challenge any wisdom but scientific truth, and then to go back to his room and think it all through for himself, and then to think about the girls.

Will's freshman year should have been a time to enjoy a sumptuous course catalog buffet and satisfy his intellectual appetites, just as Eliot had intended, all within academic boundaries that Lowell had drawn. But this was 1968, so the joy of learning, of dropping H-bombs, of growing up, was tempered by other things.

Including Will's brother, Franklin.

After Neustadt's class, Will usually crossed paths with his brother on the Delta, in the gloomy shadow of Memorial Hall, which had seen better days before a fire destroyed its wooden clock tower. Now, thought Will, it resembled nothing so much as a man who was depressed because his hat had blown away. And the buildings weren't the only things that looked depressed the day after Nixon was elected. There were long faces everywhere.

But as Franklin came out of Sanders Theater, he had a cheerful greeting for his brother. "Nixon's the one, Willie. New president, same old bullshit."

"Yeah. Dad voted for Humphrey. You want to have lunch with me in the Union?"

"No. Lunch at Adams House. Then I'm caucusing with the WSA. After yesterday, I think the Worker-Student Alliance will be the power group in the SDS. So we need to have a response to this fucking election."

"As if the world gives a shit about your opinions."

"I might get pissed at a remark like that, but I just scored this." Franklin pulled a little Baggie from the pocket of his military fatigues. "No stems, no seeds."

Will looked around furtively, then whispered, "Where did you get that?"

"A kid from South Boston. He doesn't rip me off like the locals do. Fifteen bucks an ounce, instead of sixteen."

"Dad would kill you for that."

"Yet another reason. Come on. We'll have lunch, caucus, get stoned. It's time to loosen you up. Then we'll go to a section of Soc. Rel. one forty-eight."

"The course with no lectures, no grades, and half the section leaders are SDS undergraduates?"

"The best new course at Harvard. 'Social Change in America.' We teach ourselves . . . just the way it ought to be."

"Jesus," said Will.

"Did you know that Jesus was a communist?" said Franklin. "There's a section on that, too. Along with sections on racism, the role of women in an oppressive society, César Chávez . . . I'm taking the imperialism section."

"You mean, like the British in India."

"No, dickhead. Like the fucking United States in fucking *everywhere.*"

"But you have to get stoned before you go?"

"Shit, yeah. It's too depressing otherwise."

At least his brother showed a flash of humor once in a while. Most campus radicals never even smiled. So Will decided to have lunch with him. As for caucuses, dope, and Soc. Rel. 148, he'd pass.

They were walking through the Yard, passing directly under the gaze of John Harvard's statue. Coming toward them were two young men, one wearing a raincoat, the other a windbreaker, but beneath these, they were both wearing navy blue trousers, navy blue shirts and ties, and one of them was carrying a white officer's hat under his arm, as though he was embarrassed to put it on in Harvard Yard.

"Fucking ROTCies," whispered Franklin to his brother. "Watch this."

Will didn't want a fight, and certainly not with a pair of students who spent afternoons honing military skills as part of their naval ROTC training.

As Franklin passed, he made the sound of a pig, a loud snorting noise that caused the two young reserve officers to stop and turn. But the Wedge brothers kept walking, Will because he was too frightened to stop, Franklin because he knew enough to turn his snorting into a theatrical cough.

When they reached the Porcellian Gate, Will said to Franklin, "I think I'll pass on lunch."

"Why?"

"Because you're a jerk . . . treating those guys like fascist pigs. They're here on ROTC scholarships. It may be the only way they can come. They take a few extra courses and when they get out, they give their time to the military. Maybe we all should."

"Maybe we all *will*," said Franklin, "if somebody doesn't stand up to the military-industrial complex and stop this fucking war."

Will made a face. They were brothers. A face was all it took.

Franklin said, "Listen, you skinny prep school snot in your blazer and your loafers, this place is married to the government. Half the professors are on the take—"

"Like Uncle George?"

"At least he knows what a mistake he made in 1945, but yeah. Prof. G. . . . all those fucking scientists. All the eggheads, ridin' the Harvard shuttle twice a week, tellin' the government how to fuck up the world."

"Dad rode the shuttle for years," said Will.

"Yeah, and he helped start a war."

"He didn't work for Defense. He worked in the Treasury Department."

"You mean the *money* department, and it's all about the money. Now he can stay home and make some real dough at Wedge, Fleming, and Royce. But if we can stop the Harvard shuttle and break the grip of the government around here, we should do it."

"ROTC is a scholarship program."

"If the army doesn't have any officers, it can't go and murder

Vietnamese, so we shouldn't train officers." Then he turned on his heels and stalked off.

And that, thought Will Wedge, was Harvard 1968.

Students who had come to study met students who took Soc. Rel. 148. Students who wore coats and ties to the Union because it was an "immutable law" met students who wore jeans and military fatigues. Students taught that Thomas Jefferson was the greatest of political philosophers met students who had actually memorized passages from Mao's *Little Red Book*. Students who had never tasted beer met students who could tell the difference between Thai stick and Acapulco gold just by smelling the smoke. Students who went to football games for the football met students who went because the halftime show ended when the band played the Mickey Mouse Club March to spoof the college, the game, the government, and just about any tradition in sight.

And students who had been the shining lights of their public high schools, kids who had lived at home until they went to Cambridge, met students who had lived for years at New England prep schools, where they often developed a sense of social importance and intellectual superiority all out of proportion to any accomplishment or acquired skill, except the ability to study little and late and still pull a B.

Will Wedge had gone to Andover. So his first reaction when he met his freshman roommate had been to ask himself what had he done to warrant a public school wonk from Cleveland.

On a Sunday in late September, Will had moved into Thayer 22, then he had gone to dinner with his parents at the Wursthaus, said good-bye to them in the Square, and returned to find a small bust of Shakespeare looking at him from the windowsill.

Sitting beside it, flipping through the course catalog, had been Charlie Price. He had thick glasses, a new mustache, and a nervous laugh. His first words: "It's a fourteen-hour bus ride from Cleveland. I'm starving."

Most of his prep school friends had requested specific roommates or been put with other preppies, so, if their fathers didn't know each other, at least they were professional men. But Will's parents had suggested that a roommate from a different background could be broadening. Will had not been happy to find that Charlie's father worked at a tire plant.

But Charlie was a Shakespeare-loving, Groucho-quoting math whiz who impressed Will's friends by doing handstands on the arm of a ratty sofa. So Will had decided to cut some slack for the kid from Cleveland, even if the only club he aspired to was the chess club.

ii

Ned loved the Wedge Woody. It reminded him of better times.

Whenever he backed it out of the garage on an autumn Saturday, he would think of his parents before their divorce, packing the car with food and beer and bottles of booze, loading the blankets and banners and two old raccoon coats, gathering up the two little boys, and heading down Route 1 to Cambridge.

And whenever Ned smelled the old leather upholstery, he would remember his father, sitting motionless behind the wheel on the first football Saturday after the divorce, sitting there as the sun warmed the car and heated the interior, his hands wrapped tight around the wheel, his chin on his chest, and the tears streaming down his cheeks.

Victor Wedge had devoted himself to Harvard after his divorce, like a man who marries his mistress once the wife has left. The food and drink grew more elaborate at the Wedge Woody, the old-boy laughter louder at the Harvard Club, and the Wedge Charitable Trust supported the new wife in style. And none of it could ever do anything to erase the truth: that Barbara Abbott Wedge had left Victor and disappeared with her easel and her paints in the desert Southwest, never to be heard from again.

So, thought Ned on that bright Saturday in November of 1968, maybe times hadn't been better back then . . . just different.

But some traditions persisted. The car was packed with food and beer and bottles of booze, lap blankets were folded up, a ratty old raccoon coat was flopped in the backseat like a dead bear. And Harriet was hurrying out now, wearing wool slacks and tweed jacket, looking as good as the day he first laid eyes on her.

"The Yale game in your twenty-fifth reunion year," she said. "And it's one of the biggest in history."

"Two undefeated teams. Let's go."

"Just do me one favor. Don't drink too much."

There was an alumni spread in the field house that afternoon, but most everyone in the Class of '44 stopped at the famous Wedge Woody for a drink.

Will came with a girl he had met at a Wellesley mixer, the prettiest girl he had ever seen, at least that week, a tall, dark-haired freshman from California named Alana Juteau. He also brought half a dozen friends who had been hearing all semester about the Wedge tailgate parties, including Charlie Price.

And about fifteen minutes before game time, with the laughter loud, the drinks flowing, the hamburgers sizzling, the excitement of the biggest game in years hanging in the air, Franklin showed up, wearing fatigue jacket, denim shirt, and jeans. He brought a dark-haired girl who wore a fatigue jacket and jeans, too, and half a dozen friends of his own.

Harriet greeted them like the perfect hostess and pointed them toward the food.

"Even the SDS likes hamburgers," Will whispered to Alana.

"Look at them," Ned whispered to Harriet, "hair down to the shoulders, all dressed like they were ready for a military campaign. Boys and girls both. What frauds. And isn't the girl Jewish?"

Harriet held a plate of shrimp under his nose. "Put one of these in your mouth before you put your foot in it. And smile, because here comes Franklin."

"Hi, Mom." Franklin introduced his girlfriend, "Cheryl G. Lappen, from Radcliffe. I called her Sherry."

Ned put out his hand and gave her the Wedge grin and greeting. "Welcome to the Wedge Woody. My father bought it in 'thirty-four. We've been bringing it to games ever since."

"Wow," said the girl. "That's like a tradition . . . or something."

This remark, to which Ned and Harriet answered with polite

nods, brought giggles from Franklin's friends, who were taking to the food as if they hadn't eaten in weeks.

Alana whispered to Will, "What's so funny?"

"Nothing. They're just stoned. The munchies at midday."

"Fuckin' A," said a skinny guy with reddish hair and a pimple on his chin and a mouthful of potato chips. "Doesn't anybody around here know what a woody is?"

More snickers from the newcomers.

"And who might you be?" asked Ned. Anyone who heard the tone of his voice knew that the mood of the day was about to turn.

Franklin stepped in. "This is my friend, Jim Keegan."

Harriet said, "Well, Jim, it's nice to meet you." She shook his hand, and then tried to make some typical Harvard conversation. "What house are you in?"

Keegan grinned. "The House of the Rising Sun."

"Rising sun?" snapped Ned. "Where the hell is that?"

"In New Orl-e-unssss."

This brought another round of explosive laughter.

Will noticed people putting their drinks down, checking their tickets, finishing their hamburgers, and moving off. He did not know if Franklin's next remark was intended to distract from Keegan or make things worse:

"So tell me, Dad, what do you think of ROTC?"

And everyone within earshot held their breath.

"I think it's excellent. If you look around at some of our guests" — Ned stopped a moment, as if surprised that so many people had drifted away — "they remember that at our commencement in 'forty-four, there was a sea of officers' hats in Tercentenary Theater. Only nineteen students received regular degrees."

"The last good war," said Sherry Lappen. "That's what my father calls it."

And Prof. G. took some of the heat onto himself. "Remember what Ben Franklin said about wars."

"Yeah," said Keegan. "'Cry havoc and let slip the dogs of war!'"

"Hey," said Charlie Price to Will. "He just quoted Shakespeare. Very cool."

"Yeah," whispered Will, "for the local supplier. He's like a mascot for the Worker-Student Alliance."

Ned looked at Keegan. "Ben Franklin said, 'There's no such thing as a good war or a bad peace.' I happen to agree."

Franklin said, "Does that mean you won't mind if we drive ROTC off campus?"

"Have a shrimp." Harriet put the plate under Ned's nose.

"Better yet"—Keegan put a Budweiser in front of Ned—"have a beer."

Ned aimed a finger at Franklin. "I don't know who your wiseass friend is, but remind him that you were admonished last year over Dow Chemical. You have no right to be forcing a legitimate group like ROTC off campus, just because you and your radical friends don't like them."

"But what if the majority of students don't like them?" asked Sherry.

"Mob rule," snapped Ned.

And now Prof. G. tried again. He said, "You know, folks, the band is playing."

"I'm ready," said Will.

Franklin looked his brother up and down. "There you are, Dad. He's ready. Ready to go to the game and sing 'Ten Thousand Men of Harvard.' Give him the raccoon coat. He'll look good in it. He'll look good in a uniform, too, because Nixon isn't going to end this war, either. Fight fiercely, Harvard!" Then Franklin grabbed a plate of shrimp and stalked off, followed by all his friends.

Most people agreed that it was the greatest game ever played in Harvard Stadium. Harvard scored sixteen points in the last forty-two seconds for a tie, but the headline in the *Crimson* was, HARVARD BEATS YALE, 29–29.

Ned Wedge did not enjoy it, and neither did Harriet.

iii

It was one of the worst winters in memory. The snowbanks in the Yard were chest-high by February. So maybe it was cabin fever that made Harvard seem like a loony bin in those months. Or maybe it was spring fever. Because as the snow melted and the sky brightened in March, things seemed to get worse.

Neither the students who wanted simply to study nor the radicals who seemed never to study were able to keep up with all the leaflets and position papers, the *Crimson* editorials, the demonstrations, the outside agitators interrupting classes, or the arguments between an administration that claimed to support rational discussion and a student opposition that said there was nothing left to talk about.

Something, it was plain, had to give.

Or as Charlie Price said after reading *Julius Caesar,* "If you have tears, prepare to shed them now."

At about 11:30 at night on the Tuesday after spring break, Will was in his room. He was reading about the New Deal, History 169. He was sleepy, not absorbing much, simply underlining words, thinking about Alana Juteau . . . and then he heard loud voices that woke him like a slap.

He went to the window and stuck his head out.

University Hall was next door, and a crowd of people had gathered in front of John Harvard's statue. They were chanting, "Rotcy must go! Rotcy must go!"

In a moment, the dorm was alive with the rumble of slamming doors and pounding feet. And someone was shouting, "This is it. The SDS is going to do it."

Will Wedge stepped out of his room and into the stream of students that carried him out into the cold spring night.

Franklin Wedge was on the University Hall steps, right beside benevolent John Harvard, leading the crowd in the chant: "Rotcy must go! Rotcy must go!" while a few nervous university police blocked the doors.

Was this going to be it? The building takeover that so many had feared since fall?

Earlier, three hundred members of the SDS had gathered in Lowell Lecture Hall because the university was dragging its heels on implementing a faculty resolution to strip ROTC of credit and space at Harvard. SDS also wanted to stop university expansion in Cambridge neighborhoods.

A straw vote went against a building seizure, so did a "final" vote, and final "final" vote, which they called a "binding" vote.

Then the ones who wanted to take the building had marched out to the beat of their own chants and nailed their demands to the door of the president's house. Then they had come into the Yard. But the night must have been too cold, or the cover of dark too uninspiring, because after the first burst of noise, they just milled about, chanting and handing out leaflets.

A loony bin.

No one in Thayer Hall went to sleep early that night . . . not that they ever did. In one room, the Beatles were singing "Fool on the Hill." In another, the Chambers Brothers were singing "Time." And in one particularly retrograde room, Screamin' Jay Hawkins was screaming the famous screamer "I Put a Spell on You."

But on every floor, the usual bridge games, study breaks, and bull sessions had been replaced by one conversation, one topic: Would the WSA faction of the SDS take a building in the morning, and would the administration call the cops if they did? Will told a group of friends that he believed in one thing above all: the ability of rational people to solve their problems rationally.

But when he came back to his own room, he found Franklin standing there with Sherry Lappen and two of his other WSA friends, Jerry Royster and Theo Boss, who had a particularly unfortunate last name for a member of the Worker-Student Alliance.

Franklin said to Will, "We need your help."

Charlie, who had not cut his hair since arriving at Harvard, said, "I told them they could use the room."

"What?" said Will.

"We may need a command post," said Franklin, looking around at the phone, the first-floor windows, the doors.

Harvard students lived better than most, a fact that few of them appreciated. Will and Charlie had a bedroom and a spacious living room with a fireplace, a wall of exposed brick, and three walls painted pea soup green and lined with strips of wood, so that they could tack up pictures and posters without putting holes in the plaster.

Will had tacked a picture of John F. Kennedy above his desk. Charlie Price had put up a picture of Shakespeare in his second week. Then, about the time that his hair reached below his ears, Charlie had put up a poster of Che Guevara, the Castro lieutenant allegedly killed by the CIA in Bolivia. Che was now patron saint of the leftist students, who, as Will pointed out, would have been shot if they ever tried anything around Castro that approached what they had been doing at Harvard. The poster of Che—sometimes in black and white, sometimes in psychedelic colors that made even straight students think they were stoned—had become wallpaper in half the rooms at Harvard.

Franklin looked at Che, then turned to his brother. "We need to know you'll help."

"It's just a contingency," said Sherry Lappen.

Franklin said, "If the administration cuts the phone lines to University Hall—"

"You're going to do it, aren't you?" said Will. "Who the hell gave you the right?"

Franklin grabbed his brother and led him into the bedroom. "Listen, I'm hoping we get something positive from the administration in the morning, but if we don't—"

Will shook his head. "Dad will kill you."

"Willie, I have to do this, or I'll never be able to live with myself."

"Dad will kill me . . ."

Franklin looked into his brother's eyes. There was something fiercely ascetic about his gaze: wire-rimmed glasses that emphasized his hollowed cheeks, a scruffy beard that said he was too busy worrying about the world to shave. "I'll ask you just one question. Give me a yes or no answer. Then ask yourself what you should do. 'Is the war in Vietnam a just and moral war?' Yes or no."

"No. But—" Before he could finish, Will heard a knock on the door and the voice of Jimmy Keegan.

"I'm done here. You guys done?"

Franklin said to his brother, "I'm counting on you." Then he stepped into the living room. "Let's go."

Sherry Lappen said, "Is your brother on board with this?"

Franklin looked at Will, who said nothing.

Charlie Price chimed in. "Count on us if the shit hits the fan."

Keegan stepped closer to Will. "This member of the proletariat will be very pissed if someone should blow the whistle before tomorrow."

"You're not the proletariat," said Will. "You just sold marijuana on every floor in this dorm. You're the biggest businessman around."

"A real capitalist pig" — Keegan grinned — "that's me."

"Let's go," said Sherry Lappen.

Franklin was the last one to leave. He took his brother's hand and whispered, "This is right, Willie."

"Think hard before you do it," said Will.

"We'll take one more vote."

Will walked three circuits of the Yard that night, head down, hands shoved into his pockets. Each time that he walked past the entrance to the University Police Department, in the basement of Grays Hall, he thought about going in and telling them what he knew.

It should have been easy. Blow the whistle. Tell the cops that a faction of the SDS was planning to take over University Hall in the morning. But he couldn't.

Finally, on the third circuit of the Yard, he went out past ancient Harvard Hall and looked up at the cupola. One of his ancestors had watched the British go by from up there, then he had gone and gotten his gun and gotten into the fight.

Maybe Will should do the same thing now. But who were the British? Who were the real enemies of freedom? And was the war in Vietnam a good war? Yes or no.

So Will walked. He crossed the Square. He went past the ancient home of William Brattle, past the corner where the Wedge house had been, past the majestic old mansion where the ghosts of Longfellow and Washington communed, all the way to the Drake house, a Queen Anne Victorian with a wraparound porch and slate roof. It was two in the morning, but the lights were on. So Will climbed the steps and rang the bell.

Prof. G. opened the door as though he was not in the least surprised to have a visitor so late. He wore a fine silk robe over his pajamas. A bottle of port was open on the table in the middle of the study, and a fire was dying.

"You're up late," said Will.

"I've just purchased a copy of *Christian Warfare with the World, the Flesh, and the Devil.* Do you know what it is?" He led Will over to the table.

"Sounds heavy," said Will.

"It is. A copy of this book was the only volume saved from the Harvard Hall fire." He opened it and said, "Go ahead. Touch it. I don't handle them often, but late at night, it's a kind of guilty pleasure. Feel the words. It's like feeling the thoughts of a man who lived over four hundred years ago."

Will ran his hands over the words and felt nothing but the bumps on the paper.

"I can quantify the universe," said Prof. G., "but I can't explain it. So I'm up late, trying to see what answers the Elizabethans have. What's your excuse?"

"Do you know what happened tonight?"

"Franklin told me. He has a powerful conscience. We'd all do well with such a gift."

"He's going to take over a building," said Will. "Dad will kill him."

"Dad will also be secretly pleased that his son is taking a stand."

"I don't know if I should tell anyone or not."

"Rebellion is like a gas under pressure. The greater the pressure, the greater the explosion. This might let off a little steam and force the administration to confront the issue of the war more directly."

"So your advice would be to keep my mouth shut?"

"Think for yourself, Will. If you do, you may come to find that you agree with your brother about the war. Then everything else may fall in line."

That was the trouble with this damn place, thought Will. Nobody made anything easy, not even the scholars sitting up late puzzling over the meaning of life.

The dorm was quiet when he finally crawled into bed. He decided to see how the vote went the next day.

They voted, but it went like this:

At noon, about seventy members of the SDS stood in the sunshine on the steps of University Hall. They read their demands. Then they declared that the time for talk had ended. And with a shout of "Fight! Fight! Fight!" they invaded the hall. A few moments later, angry deans in Brooks Brothers were bouncing unceremoniously out of every door, followed by administration and staff, while an SDS banner—black field, red center, white letters—was unfurled.

In the time that it took them to do it, word spread like a stomach virus. At class change in the lecture halls, in the dining halls, in the labs and the museums, people were soon finishing what they were doing and heading for the Yard.

By 12:30, the crowd had grown into the hundreds. Someone with a bullhorn was trying to work them into a chant: "Smash Rotcy! No expansion!" And someone in Weld Hall was playing the Beatles' "Revolution" on an industrial-strength sound system that had windows rattling all around.

As Will Wedge came from a gulped-down lunch at the Union, he wondered, was this a demonstration or a festival? And what happened to the vote?

And there was Franklin, on the University Hall steps, working the bullhorn, waving his arms as "Rotcy must go!" was met with a counter chant: "Out! Out! Out!"

Finally, Franklin lowered the bullhorn, which caused the chanting to stop, then he raised it again and said, "Let's vote. How many of you oppose this takeover?"

And a roar went up from the crowd.

Franklin gave a look at Sherry Lappen, who was standing near him, then he shouted, "And how many are in favor?"

No one needed a sound meter to hear the truth: the opposition had the votes.

And someone shouted, "You just lost, so get out!"

"Get out!" shouted someone else. "Or go against your own democratic ideals."

And for a moment, Franklin seemed at a loss, so Theo Boss grabbed the bullhorn and shouted, "Be quiet, all of you. You've had your silly vote."

The crowd booed. The Beatles fan in Weld cranked up the volume.

So much for democracy among the Students for a Democratic Society.

A loony bin, thought Will Wedge.

"Hey, Will." Charlie Price sidled up, his pockets bulging with his afternoon supply of apples and bananas from the Union fruit bowl. "Let's go in."

"What? Inside?"

"Nothing's going to happen. It's been liberated, man. Power to the people."

Will hesitated, but for only a moment. He sensed that he was witnessing history. So they went in by the door on the southeast, closest to Widener Library.

In the foyer, a reporter for WHRB, Harvard's radio station, was preparing to interview a radical leader. Charlie Price went by, stopped, pulled a banana from his pocket, and offered it to the radical.

A loony bin.

Will left Charlie vending fruit to revolutionaries and went upstairs to the faculty meeting room.

Once this had been Harvard's chapel. Here hung the portraits of past presidents, here the Bicentenary packet had been opened, and here the faculty debated important issues and fought the skirmishes of academic politics, all beneath crystal chandeliers on magnificent Oriental carpets. Now a sign above the door proclaimed it "Che Guevara Hall" and the smell of cigarette smoke hung like a film over the smell of body odor.

It looked like a scene from *A Tale of Two Cities*. A hundred students were sitting on the antique tables, leaning against the priceless busts, gathering in the corners to argue their strategies, though *strategy* might have been too strong a word. It seemed as if no one knew quite what anyone should be doing, now that they were there. The loudest argument Will heard was between two members of the SDS and somebody who said he had come up from Yale to join the fight. The Yalie wanted to smoke marijuana in the "liberated" hall. The SDS wanted to have a vote on the matter.

And Franklin shouted from another group in another corner, "No dope. Not here."

"Who the fuck are you?" asked the outsider.

A good question, thought Will. But he didn't bother to stay for an answer.

He went through the doors and peered into the office of the dean of the Faculty of Arts and Sciences. Half a dozen students were standing over the file cabinets. Sherry Lappen was there, Jerry Royster, Theo Boss, and the one picking the locks on the cabinets was Keegan.

"Here we go!" Keegan popped a lock. "Faculty records. Correspondence. Everything you want."

"Far out," said Sherry. "Now we'll know who's for killing people in Vietnam."

"I wish we had some chicken blood or something," said Boss. "We could dump it all over these things."

"No," said Royster. "Better to have them and read them. They'll help."

Will had resolved to do no more than observe. But he had to speak up, "Help what?"

"Willie!" Keegan laughed. "You joinin' the cause? 'Members of the proletariat, arise! You have nothing to lose but your chains.'"

On the desk was a folder that read "Professor George Wedge Drake."

"This is private," said Will. "These are personnel files."

"The people should know what Harvard has done," said Sherry Lappen. "Your own relative helped kill hundreds of thousands of people in Japan."

"Yeah," said Keegan, "and from what I read, he has himself a house full of valuable old books."

"Oh, nobody cares about the books," said Sherry.

"No," said Royster, bundling the files and taking them back into the meeting room.

Sherry and the others bustled after him, except for Keegan, who snatched Prof. G.'s file and went back to the Xerox machine.

Will said to Keegan, "You couldn't care less about the revolution."

"Shit, no."

"So what are you looking for?"

"The cool stuff. The skeletons in the closet." He flipped the folder open. "You got all kinds of letters in here about how smart he was as an undergraduate. There's a letter from the FBI to President Conant, asking if his relationship with the daughter of a known Communist was cause for worry, back when they were sending him off to Los Alamos."

Then Keegan read a letter from Assistant Professor George Drake to the dean of the Faculty of Arts and Science in 1953. "'Dear Sir, In relation to investigations into Communists on the Harvard faculty, let me assure you that as far as my past relationships are concerned, there is nothing that anyone would interpret as disloyalty.'"

"Jesus," said Will, genuinely shocked. "He'd helped build the bomb, and Russians got the secret. Maybe they blamed him."

Keegan laughed. "Now we got commie pinko faggots all over the place." Then he put another letter under the rubber cover of the Xerox machine and pushed a button.

"What are you doing?" Will watched the copy come out.

"Go ahead," said Keegan. "Read it. Tell me what you think."

"No. I don't read other people's mail."

Keegan snatched the letter. "It's addressed to the director of the rare books collection in Houghton Library. December 1954. 'Dear Sir, Thank you for your advice in my recent purchase of the *Summa Theologica*—' You like my Latin?"

"You must be Catholic," said Will. "They teach it to you."

"Yeah, mass every Sunday. That's me." And he read on. "'By Thomas Aquinas. It represents the beginning of a pursuit that I hope will one day allow me to create a replica of the original John Harvard library. But I want to assure you that I will not interfere with Houghton's efforts in this direction, and should any book come to auction, I will defer to you in bidding. I may also know of a book that would complete the collection in a way that no other can. 'A small gift of majestic proportion' is the term that echoes in my family's history. Should I ever discover this small gift, I shall see that we share it.'"

Keegan looked at Will. "Majestic proportion. Sounds rich. Any ideas?"

Will just shook his head. "I don't know, and you shouldn't be copying it."

"Like I said, I look for skeletons, because sometimes they're wrapped around treasures." Keegan looked Will up and down, from his crew-neck sweater to his loafers. "And I've also *made* a few skeletons, too. Don't you forget that."

Will wanted to laugh in his face. But he didn't think that was a good idea. He didn't think that staying in that hall was a good idea either, so he slipped down the stairs without speaking to his brother. He didn't know what he would say, anyway.

The choices that the administration faced were few: (1) wait the demonstrators out indefinitely; (2) wait until a group of moderate students could formally condemn the takeover, then remove the demonstrators by moral force or police action; (3) clean them out as quickly as possible.

The first option was untenable. The longer the radicals stayed in the hall, the longer they would have access to sensitive material, the longer the university would be in turmoil, and the more likely that radicals heading to Cambridge from all over the country would arrive and the uprising would spin out of control. The second option was under consideration, and a meeting of moderates was scheduled for the next morning, but some in the administration believed that even a meeting of moderate students could spin out of control in that climate. So . . . the third option.

At four A.M., Will Wedge was awakened from a fitful sleep by a chest-piercing electric scream. He jumped up and grabbed for his trousers, then he realized that he had gone to bed in his clothes a few hours before. And Charlie Price was cursing and tripping over his own shoes in the dark and screaming that they had to get out, that there was a fire.

But there was no fire. The SDS had pulled the alarms throughout the Yard because the bust was coming.

Half asleep, Will stumbled onto the steps of Thayer, and it was as if his dream would not end. The alarms were still screaming everywhere, and a cold wind was whipping storms of paper and debris through the gray light, and a disembodied bullhorn-voice was echoing off the pillars of Widener.

Sleep-deprived freshmen were staggering out of every dorm. Students who had spent the night in the Yard wrapped in blankets were moving now toward the steps of University Hall like spectral figures from Cotton Mather's imagination. Journalists who had been in the Yard since the takeover began were finding vantage points. Upperclassmen from the houses were climbing over fences or through the locked gates. Even professors were arriving.

And all the while, the bullhorn kept up: "The cops are coming. Stand with us." "Don't let them take back your university." "Join us on the steps of the hall." "Sheets and pillowcases. We need sheets and pillowcases for gas masks. All who have them, bring them to the northeast door."

Will heard one of the ROTC men from Thayer saying to no one in particular, "If they hang wet sheets on the windows, they'll just make a gas chamber for themselves."

How much more surreal could it get?

Well, try big yellow school buses rumbling from somewhere north of the Yard, speeding down the driveway between Thayer and Memorial Church, pulling up in front of majestic Sever, and disgorging Massachusetts state police in baby blue uniforms, jackboots, helmets, and shields.

And as the state police formed themselves into tight phalanxes, like Romans preparing to move against the barbarian horde, local police units in darker blue uniforms appeared from corners of the Yard and moved in columns, two abreast behind shields and upraised clubs, like flanking troops.

Will shivered. And the crowd started to roar.

In the southeast foyer of University Hall, Franklin Wedge joined arms with Royster and Boss and all the others. Sherry Lappen slipped in beside him.

"You don't have to stay," he said.

"I'm not afraid," she said.

"The local pigs will clear the steps," he explained. "Then the state cops will come through the west entries and push us through the building, right out the east doors."

"I'm not afraid," she said, then kissed him.

"You'll be arrested. Maybe expelled," he warned.

And Sherry Lappen's eyes widened. "Expelled? Shit. My father would kill me."

"Here they come!" cried someone near the door.

On the steps of Widener, Professor George Wedge Drake watched in shock. He had always believed in the ability of rational people to settle problems rationally. He had never expected it to come to this.

Then a woman came up beside him with a notepad and pen in her hand. "A hell of an assignment for an old broad."

And if he wasn't shocked by the sight of the police, he was by the sight of the woman. "Olga?"

"They sent me to cover this from New York, because I'm a 'Cliffie."

"I'd say I was glad to see you, but—"

The crowd was booing, and cries of "sieg heil" and "fascist pig" were rising.

At Thayer, Charlie Price said to Will, "Come on."

"What?"

"To the steps. Come on. This is wrong. They can't do this at Harvard."

"They can. It's their college."

"It's *our* fucking college." And Charlie Price clenched his fist in Will's face. "'In peace there's nothing so becomes a man / As modest stillness and humility: / But when the blast of war blows in our ears / Then . . . then . . . something . . . something something.' It's from *Henry V*."

"To be or not to be," answered Will. "And you *won't* be if you go over there."

"Fuck it," said Charlie, and he ran over to the stairs on the northwest side of University Hall.

As the police approached, Will thought he could hear Charlie shout, "Once more into the breach, dear friends!"

From the office that looked out over John Harvard's statue, Jimmy Keegan watched the Cambridge and Somerville police wade into the students on the stairs.

By then, he had dumped a hundred dollars' worth of marijuana from his pockets and taken on two hundred dollars in petty cash that he'd rifled from desks and abandoned purses all through the building. In his jacket, he had a fine miniature portrait of Henry Wadsworth Longfellow, lifted from a wall.

"I didn't sign up for this shit," he said to Sherry Lappen, who had left the foyer and was looking out, too.

She said, "My father will kill me if I get expelled. Kill me."

"If I help you out of here, will you give me a blow job?"

"You're a lowlife."

He pushed open a window, letting in the cold air, the roaring of the crowd, and the distinct sound of nightsticks cracking bones. "Come on, anyway."

She straddled the windowsill and looked down. "It's a seven-foot drop."

"Go." With one hand, he grabbed her wrist and with the other, he pushed her, so that she half fell to the ground and crumpled on an ankle that popped when she hit.

He jumped down right after her, and she reached up to him. "Help me!"

"Sorry, babe. No b.j., no Bingo." Then he sprinted out from behind John Harvard's statue. A cop took a swing at him, but he kept going, and the cops turned to easier targets.

After running all the way over to the college pump, Keegan circled around, joined the crowd in front of Thayer, and started chanting, "Fuck the pigs! Fuck the pigs!"

And once he had everyone around him—longhairs, shorthairs, freshmen and graduate students—chanting right along, Jimmy Keegan started laughing.

Will Wedge saw Keegan, and he thought of some malevolent

Shakespearean figure churning up disorder for its own sake and taking great pleasure in the power he could wield.

Then he saw Charlie Price clubbed off the steps and dragged away, and Will started shouting, too.

Then the state police kicked forward.

Will thought of his brother, somewhere inside, and wished him luck. He might have said a prayer, but he had no time, because now that the Somerville police had cleared the steps of University Hall, they were turning on the crowd in front of Thayer.

Will slammed open the door of the dorm and dove into his room.

Meanwhile, the cops chased students up the stairs and down the halls, slamming nightsticks on the brick walls and the paneling and the metal balustrades, and shouting, "Get in your rooms and stay there!"

And Will turned to see a complete stranger, a guy in a jacket and tie, about thirty, dialing his telephone. "Who the hell are you?" asked Will.

"I'm the stringer for the *Washington Post.* I have to file a story. I'll pay for the call. They'll never believe this happened at Harvard. Never."

iv

"What a year to have your twenty-fifth reunion," said Ned Wedge on the first Thursday of June.

"Now, just keep calm," said Harriet. "Have a cup of coffee, and don't order a shot for it. It's too early. Just run the meeting, then get on to commencement."

"Yeah . . . yeah."

"And may I say, you look marvelous in top hat and tails."

"Yeah . . . yeah." Ned was one of the class marshals, a signal honor for members of the twenty-fifth reunion class, and he had announced that he'd be damned before anything, including his own son, would stop him from taking part.

There had been times in the previous two months when it

seemed that nothing would ever be the same again, at least at Harvard, and yet traditions had to be observed, because traditions mattered.

Will thought that whoever it was in Thayer who had come up with a counterslogan "Tradition Unhampered by Progress" had been onto something.

On the morning of the bust, the final chant was "On strike! Shut it down!" In the following weeks, there had been mass meetings, caucuses, guerrilla theater, position papers, leaflets . . . and committees. There were not enough letters in the alphabet for all the committees, but the one that mattered most was the Committee of Fifteen, ordained by the faculty to determine punishments for the 170 students who had been arrested, hauled off to the Cambridge District Court, and charged with criminal trespass.

Professor George Wedge Drake was on the committee, and he argued for leniency. He reminded the faculty of President Conant's words: "Harvard was founded by dissenters. Before two generations had passed, there was a general dissent from the first dissent. Heresy has long been in the air. We are proud of the freedom which has made this possible, even when we may most dislike the heresy we encounter."

It sounded good. But 102 students were admonished; 20 received suspended sentences and would be asked to withdraw if they engaged in further trouble; 16, including Franklin Wedge, were required to withdraw outright, though Franklin was told that he could apply for readmission in a year.

He told Will that it didn't matter. The world was wider than Harvard. He no longer cared about the family meeting, either, because any contributions he would want to make would be refused. So he was one of the last to arrive that morning.

It wasn't a large gathering, just the Wedges and Prof. G., who had brought his new—and old—girlfriend, Olga Bassett. Several of the cousins had submitted written requests for funding, but none had shown up, perhaps because word of Franklin's fate had spread, and the breadth of Ned's temper was well known.

Still, the trays of scrambled eggs and bacon steamed on the side of the room, and there were plates of Danish pastries, lox and bagels, a big coffee urn, a melon salad—the menu hadn't changed in thirty years. The trust, however, had grown spectacularly.

Will had come in sport coat, oxford button-down, and khaki trousers.

His father's first words to him were "Where's your tie?"

Then Franklin came in the door, and Will knew there would be trouble. Franklin was wearing sandals without socks, cutoff jeans, and a Harvard Strike T-shirt. Someone in the School of Design had created a red fist—a powerful graphic—and they had silk-screened it onto thousands of white T-shirts, along with the reasons for the strike.

Ned Wedge and Franklin had not seen each other since before the bust. Now they stood face-to-face.

They made a strange picture, thought Will, one dressed for the day like a diplomat from some Ruritanian romance, the other in the 1968 uniform of rebellion. For a moment, Will hoped there would be a few words of reconciliation.

Then, without any other comment, Ned began to read the words on the T-shirt. "'Strike for the Eight Demands. Strike because you hate cops. Strike because your roommate was clubbed. Strike to stop expansion. Strike to seize control of your life. Strike to become more human. Strike because there's no poetry in your lectures. Strike because classes are a bore. Strike for power. Strike to smash the corporation. Strike to make yourself free. Strike to abolish ROTC. Strike because they are trying to squeeze the life out of you.'"

Harriet said, "Ned . . ."

Ned smiled and took a breath. "Well, I'm glad we got that cleared up."

"That's it?" said Franklin.

"There's no poetry in your lectures," said Ned. "I'm so sorry."

Franklin said, "I can't stay. I just came by to tell you I'm headed to Canada."

"Canada?" Ned shouted.

"Oh, no," said Harriet.

"You don't need to go to Canada," said George. "Register at another college in the fall, and see what happens in the draft lottery."

"That's too easy," said Franklin. "And Wedges never take the easy way. That's what my father told me when I said I wanted to go to a small college in Vermont. He said I should be in the center of things. I should be at Harvard. He wanted me to be like you, Uncle George. Right there when the first bomb went off. But you know, even if you read all John Harvard's books, including the 'small gift of majestic proportion,' you won't ever figure out where we all went wrong."

"Because we haven't," said Ned.

"Where did you hear that?" asked Prof. G. "That business about John Harvard and the small gift?"

"I don't know. I've heard you talk about it," said Franklin. "It doesn't matter."

"No, it doesn't," said Ned, "because Uncle Jimmy here has some big gifts to give out."

"It can wait," said Jimmy.

"No, it can't," said Ned. "I'm supposed to escort one of the honorary degree recipients this morning. So I can't be late. Let's get started."

"And unless the administration lets us speak," said Franklin, "I have a commencement to disrupt."

"Do it and I'll kill you," said Ned.

"But Canada?" said Harriet. "How will you live?"

"He should have thought of that before he decided to throw his life away," said Ned.

Franklin did not answer. He was already gone.

"How's Ned doing?" asked Prof. G. the next morning.

"He got drunk at the class barbecue, stayed drunk all through the talent show. He's sleeping it off in Matthews. It's so romantic, how we all get to stay in freshman dorms during twenty-fifth reunion week." Harriet took a long drag on her cigarette.

They were sitting in the Pewter Pot Muffin House in Harvard Square. George was eating a blueberry muffin. Harriet hadn't touched her bran.

"I'm sorry I couldn't help Franklin," said Prof. G.

"I think he's glad to be going to Canada. He sees it as some kind of political exile." Harriet stubbed the cigarette out in her muffin plate. "Oh, to be young and arrogant."

"More young than arrogant," said Prof. G. gently. "Remember, 'Two things are always new—youth and the quest for knowledge.'"

"Victor's favorite quote." Harriet sipped her coffee and left a print of lipstick on the cup. "But I'm curious about the other one, about the 'small gift.' Where did Franklin pick up on John Harvard? Victor never said anything about that."

"Actually"—George took a deep breath—"Victor did."

"He did?"

"I don't know where Franklin heard about it," said George, "but Victor wrote a letter to my father in 1937. I found it after my father died in '53. He said he had filed a new will, now that his divorce was final, so there were things his executor should know. He said the Tercentenary envelope—this was the quote—'contained knowledge of Lydia's small gift of majestic proportion, the book that Grandfather Heywood had often heard Aunt Dorothy and Uncle Theodore argue over.'"

"Did he say what the book was?"

George watched the waitress refill their cups, then he said, in a low voice, "This is the quote: 'It is a book from the library of John Harvard, who wrote so wisely on his flyleaves, "A man will be known by his books."'"

"Better than being known by your brand of scotch." Harriet lit another cigarette.

"That quote started me on my little quest. At the beginning, every time I bought an edition of one of Harvard's books, I hoped that I'd find that quote written on the flyleaf. Then I'd know that I'd found a *real* John Harvard book, because there have always been rumors that more than one survived."

"Why didn't you tell me this before?"

"Victor wanted the John Harvard business kept secret until the trust liquidates."

Harriet took a long drag on her cigarette. "I wonder why."

"Because every generation tries to explain itself to the next. Victor did it in his way and Heywood in his. I'll bet Dorothy and Uncle Theodore probably did the same thing for Heywood's generation.

And we should be doing it for Franklin. But Harriet"—George reached across the table and put his hand on her arm—"we can't interfere with the plans Victor Wedge made. It would be like interfering with the working of time."

"That's rich, coming from you." Harriet lit another cigarette. "Wouldn't you love to see what's in those three safe-deposit boxes that Victor left?"

"If God is good, we'll all be dead when those boxes are opened."

"A physics professor believes in God?"

"The Elizabethans did." George shrugged. "It's either God or coincidence."

Chapter Thirty

THEY WERE sitting beside the saltwater pool. It was empty of water, a spiderweb of cracks. So they looked out at the ocean instead, warming nicely in the late-spring sun.

Harriet Webster Wedge smoked her eighth cigarette. "You know, Will, you boys were sowing dragon seeds back then."

"Not all of us," said Will.

"No. Not all of you. And not all of them sprouted." Harriet put her head back against her chair.

"Was Dad really drunk the night he died?" asked Will. "I didn't remember him drinking that much when I was a kid."

"It came later. He went to Washington because he felt that he could afford to give something back. And Jack Kennedy was a friend. He didn't start to drink heavily until after the assassination. He hated Vietnam as much as anyone, but he couldn't understand what drove your brother."

"Franklin hated that war," said Will. "And he stood up."

"He's still standing up," said Harriet, "whether you agree with him or not."

"Back to your husband," said Peter.

"The night that we got the news that Franklin had taken off for Canada—"

"How did you get it?" asked Peter.

"That Sherry Lappen girl came to the door. Came all the way up from Cambridge. We were very nice to her and asked her what we could do for her. She seemed very nervous. She had wild black hair and always wore a tight rim of mascara around her eyes. And she looked particularly wild that night."

"What did she say?"

"She said that she needed money. Ned, of course, had already had a martini or two, and he said we weren't going to give her a nickel. So Sherry looked over her shoulder very nervously. She had ridden up with someone in the car. I couldn't tell exactly who it was. She said that Franklin had left for Canada but that he owed some friends some money.

"All that Ned said was 'Canada?' And he closed the door in her face."

"Did you ever find out who was in the car?" asked Peter.

"We thought it was that Keegan. He was a drug dealer. We'd known that since the day he ruined our Yale game tailgate.

"Anyway, in the middle of the night, Ned got up and said that he was going for a swim. I just rolled over. I'd had a few myself. We found him at the bottom of the pool the next morning, naked and dead."

"That must have been terrible," said Evangeline.

"It was," said Will.

"We've always wondered," said Harriet, "if he was too drunk to notice that the tide had gone out and the sluice gate was open. Or did he jump on purpose."

"Mother," said Will, "enough."

Harriet looked at Peter. "I know what you're thinking now."

"What?"

"He had to be pretty stupid to jump twelve feet into an empty pool."

No. Peter was thinking about Keegan. Something subtle, seemingly accidental . . . a fall into an empty pool, a fall from a boat. Professional work. Cold-blooded. Somebody owed him money and wouldn't pay, so he extracted a different kind of payment. But Peter didn't mention his thoughts; instead, he asked her, "When did you look at the Theodore Wedge diary?"

"After my husband died and Franklin fled. I was looking for answers. And Prof. G. always says that each generation finds a way to explain itself to the next. So I looked to earlier Wedge generations." She lit a cigarette, took a puff, then stubbed it out. "I found Theodore's journal. And he had plenty to say about Harvard, about the Wedges, about living as an outsider but still living in society."

"Why did you tear out the last page?" asked Will.

"I wanted Franklin to read the journal, but I wanted him to hear Theodore's message rather than his speculations about the book. Of course, Franklin didn't bother to read it until last fall, after I told him what his brother was planning. Wedge House, and all. . . ."

"Thanks, Mom," said Will.

"I have tried to treat you boys equally, dear."

"Did Franklin really get you stoned before you'd tell him?" asked Peter.

"I had a bourbon. I told him to keep his funny cigarettes."

"Do you have the page?" asked Evangeline.

The old woman went into the house and came out a moment later with the very sheet. She held it in front of them and read, "'It is a book of some sort. . . . I believe further that Lydia's tombstone suggests a work by Shakespeare. I believe that someday, it will be found, once the gilt-edged envelope is opened. . . . And then it will be over.'"

"The gilt-edged envelope," said Evangeline, "in the Tercentenary packet."

Harriet looked at Peter and Evangeline. "Since you have been part of this since last fall, come to the family meeting before commencement. You should be there when we uncover the information that Victor left us in his safe-deposit boxes."

"Why not tell us now?" asked Peter.

"Because Victor specified that it be done when the Wedge Charitable Trust was officially liquidated . . . and he did a lot of good through it, so we should respect his wishes."

Will said, "I don't think Victor expected his sons to die so young.

First Dad at forty-eight, then Jimmy, out in California, drowning in the surf in his sixties. And now, twenty-one years later, here we are."

"Here we are." Harriet looked down into the concrete pool.

Since Dorothy was graduating, they had moved the meeting to the night before commencement, in the usual room in the Faculty Club.

And it was the Full Wedge, as Ridley would have said. Prof. G. and Olga Bassett got there first, because they were old and always punctual. Will Wedge and his wife and Dorothy were there. Half a dozen more distant cousins. Peter and Evangeline. Everyone had a glass of wine or a cup of coffee. And everyone waited for Franklin, who always arrived one half hour after the stated time.

He stalked in, dressed in jeans, T-shirt, and sandals, as always, shook hands all around, and said to Fallon, "You've been around us so long, you've decided to join the family?"

"I'm an observer."

Then Will Wedge turned to Prof. G. "As the senior male in direct line from Heywood Wedge, you are chairman for the day."

"Well," said the old professor, "as you all know, the trust must liquidate, so we are here to determine where the bulk of the money is going."

"The blood descendants get to take twenty-five percent for themselves," said Franklin. "We know that. What's it worth?"

"That's in the treasurer's report," said Prof. G. "We haven't had that yet. We need to read the minutes from last year."

Franklin looked around. "It's just us, George. Let's dispense with Robert's Rules of Order. Will wants to give Harvard a house. I want to give Harvard hell. It's as simple as that. It always has been."

Will looked across the table at his brother. "Maybe we can reason this through."

"Maybe," said Franklin. "For all the high ideals that Harvard preaches, it's all about power. If I hold a piece of Harvard property—one that represents hard reality in a spectacular dollar value and at the same time offers the ideal of one more Shakespearean look into the human heart—the powers of Harvard will be forced to negotiate."

"Negotiate what?" asked Harriet, lighting her fifth cigarette.

"Harvard's commitment to drop their tax-exempt status in communities where Harvard buys land and takes it off the tax rolls. That's a good start."

"You've been fighting that battle for years," said Prof. G. "Harvard makes payment in lieu of taxes and they negotiate in good faith."

"Yeah," cracked Franklin, "like the federal government negotiating in good faith with some Central American country."

Will said, "Still trying to change the world?"

"Little by little. Step by step."

"I've done more good than you. I've seen to the management of this trust, so that it's worth over thirty million now."

Peter glanced at Evangeline and rolled his eyes. She gave him a little nod, as though she knew what he was thinking: this bunch could make her Pratt relatives look like a functional family.

Peter raised a finger. "Ladies and gentlemen, whatever you want to do with the money, you still have to find the book. And there are sharks circling."

Evangeline looked at Dorothy. "A few have come very close."

"Maybe," said Franklin, "we should let them bite the expert."

Peter grinned across the table at Franklin. "I've dealt with sharks before. I may be able to predict them a little bit better than the rest of you."

"True." Prof. G. reached into his pocket and pulled out a small red envelope and put it on the table. On it were written the words "a small gift of majestic proportion." He said, "There's mine, Harriet. I've saved it since 1946. Do you have yours?"

Harriet took out two envelopes. She slid one across the table to Will, the other to Franklin.

"There are three keys to three safe-deposit boxes that Victor Wedge left behind. One was given to your father, one was given to Jimmy. I got your father's, and I was the executrix of Jimmy's estate, too. The boxes were not to be opened until today. They may point the way toward the object that Victor Wedge found in 1936."

"Perhaps you should give me the keys," Peter said. "I may have the most expertise at finding this thing."

And young Dorothy spoke up. "Why you?"

"Because it's his business," said Will Wedge, "and we've trusted him."

"Yes," said Harriet. "Although we'll hope you and Evangeline don't make the kind of mess you made when you tried to find that tea set."

"If you find this thing," said Franklin, "what's to say you won't go running off with it?"

"My word as a professional," said Peter, "and my belief that if we find what we think we're after, it should be seen by the world, which is not what your friend Keegan believes."

"My friend Keegan?" said Franklin. "I haven't seen that son of a bitch in thirty years." His face reddened and he glanced at his mother, as if they had talked before about Franklin's flight to Canada and the visit of a frightened girl to the Wedge house.

"Well, Keegan's not to be trusted," said Will.

"No shit," said Franklin. "But we both knew that back in 1969, when he Xeroxed George's personnel report in University Hall, then started buggin' me about John Harvard's small gift."

And old Prof. G. laughed out loud, as if he had just solved a difficult equation. "So *that's* how you found out."

"It's how we *all* found out," said Will.

"And now, we may find the thing itself. But remember," said Prof. G., "it's been my position all along that this book should be in the alcove in Houghton with the original copy of *Christian Warfare*."

"It should be in your own collection," said Olga. "If you find it."

"I agree with Olga," said Franklin. "Remember the golden rule. He who has the gold makes the rules. If we hold the book, Harvard has to do business with us."

Peter said, "First, you have to find it."

"Yes," said Prof. G. "Then we can reason together."

And the meeting was suspended with the agreement that they would reconvene at the alumni tent in the Yard at noon the next day, by which time Peter hoped to have figured out the location of the book. He also told them not to pass any information to anyone. He figured that they would ignore him. In fact, he expected it.

It was a short walk to the Cambridge Trust, current home of the safe-deposit boxes.

With the three envelopes, Peter and Evangeline headed for South Boston.

"I would imagine that there are phone calls being made at this very moment," said Peter. "Will Wedge is calling Charlie Price."

"Dorothy may be calling O'Hill," said Evangeline. "Unless Keegan has killed him."

"Keegan is too smart for that. He's letting this play out as far as he can before he does anything to incriminate himself."

"And wherever he can, he uses guys like Bertram Lee?"

"Lee was the middleman between a disgruntled young academic and anything-for-a-buck Bingo Keegan."

"Disgruntled because he didn't get tenure?"

"Right, and here he was, the grandnephew of a brave Harvard graduate named James Callahan, with a locket that proved an even more distant ancestor had saved the life of one of Harvard's leading scions at Antietam. At some point, probably pretty early on after his arrival at Harvard, O'Hill must have looked up his great-uncle in the card catalog, just out of curiosity, and found a reference to the quarto of *Love's Labours Lost*. O'Hill probably read the inscriptions, which no one had taken very seriously, and that got him curious. Who was Lydia? And more important, who was Burton Bones?"

"Was that before or after he started slicing pieces out of valuable Harvard books?" Evangeline asked.

"Probably before. But he would have gotten more serious about it all when he took on Dorothy Wedge as a student."

"So, who do you think brought up the story of this manuscript?"

"Hard to say. Remember Prof. G.'s description of all the atoms in their own universes. Keegan had read Prof. G.'s personnel file. Lee had done business with Prof. G. and Price."

Evangeline said, "So Keegan was probably telling Lee, from the time they first hooked up, long ago, to watch that old professor and try to figure out what this 'small gift of majestic proportion' might be."

"Then, along comes O'Hill. First, they do business on stolen manuscripts and cut plates. Then they figure out that there's a deeper connection. O'Hill probably shows Lee the locket. You know, everything has a price. And there's a piece of the story for Lee and Keegan—a guy with a locket picture of Dorothy Wedge Warren," said Peter.

"And the appearance of a commonplace book that probably came out of the attic of Townsend House and was sold last summer begins to make everything speed up," she said. "But why would they decide to sell the locket when they did?"

"I think O'Hill could smell Scavullo closing in on him, so he figured he might as well unload as much as possible while he could. He tried to kill me because he knew that I might kill that sale, which I almost did. And he pushed Ridley from the boat, because Ridley had brought a professional into the hunt."

"You don't think Keegan did that?" she asked.

"He has some dumb guys working for him. But he's not that dumb. It takes a guy who thinks he's very smart to do something that dumb and get away with it."

"And how did Lee get tied up with Keegan?"

"Bertram Lee, who dressed like the middle-aged model from the Ralph Lauren catalog, loved his cocaine. Bingo probably supplied dope and Lee supplied lots of illegal, stolen stuff of very high value, which is spread about private libraries all over the world now."

"Did Keegan kill him?" she asked.

"Maybe. Or maybe it was the drugs. Or O'Hill. He and Keegan may have decided that they don't need a middleman. If O'Hill can find the manuscript, he and Keegan can do business directly. And Charles Price will write that big cashier's check. Of course, O'Hill may disappear, and so will the manuscript."

"But you're in the way?" she said.

"I don't think that the world should be denied another work of Shakespeare, if it's out there. It's one of history's treasures."

Peter drove the BMW into the Fallon Salvage and Restoration Yard, and Danny closed and locked the gate.

Peter parked inside the warehouse, where Danny's son, Bobby, was waiting with a Savage 720 shotgun in his hand.

Peter got out of the car and said to Bobby, "What are you—goin' on a pigeon hunt or something?"

"Protection," said Danny, stepping inside and picking up his own shotgun. "If Keegan wants to come in here with his guns blazing, he'll have M-sixteens."

"So," said Peter, "don't waste your time with shotguns. Is Orson here?"

From the office came Bernice's voice. "We're both here, and I'm packin', too."

"Wonderful," said Peter. "We can have a shoot-out."

Then Evangeline got out the other side of the BMW.

And Danny Fallon grinned. He always grinned around the beautiful Yankee girl. "I heard you were around again. You haven't changed a bit."

"I'll take that as a compliment."

In the office, Peter said, "Don't be worried about Keegan. He won't do anything tonight. Tomorrow is when he'll go after this thing."

"Assuming," said Orson, "that we can figure it out for him."

Peter dropped three ancient envelopes on the table. "This is the way that we do it."

There were three poems in the envelopes. They were titled "John Hicks and Other Heroes," published in 1775; "The Telltale Tread," 1783; and "Colors Spil't Upon the Marsh," 1840.

"It looks as if O'Hill was on the right track," said Peter. "He had a book of her poems."

Then he read them aloud. First was "John Hicks": " 'Oh noble is the man who dies to save his fellow man . . .' "

The poem extolled the Cambridge patriot who sacrificed himself and in effect saved the Wedge lineage.

"The Telltale Tread" began "The story's told, of that dire night, / when tea was mixed with brine, / Of men who'd not alarm their wives and so with knotted sheets / dropped from their homes to ground below / And went upon their charge . . ."

This poem described an ancient legend—that John Hicks came home that night and couldn't climb back in the window. Fearing the noise of the telltale tread on the stairwell, he took off his boots.

The next morning, his wife accused him of wandering to some other woman's bed, although six children slept in their house. Then she went to the door where he had left his boots, found that they were filled with tea leaves, and all was forgiven.

The last poem began "I once stood here, and looking out, would see a spreading marsh / Birds of black and red of wing and mallard ducks once flew / Where now rise homes and wharves for coal / To darken history's hue . . ." And on it went, describing a world that Lydia Wedge Townsend found far less beautiful than the world she saw when first she came back to America in 1783.

"So," said Peter. "Hicks House?"

Orson went to his briefcase. "I came prepared, in case it was in a Harvard building." He pulled out a copy of Bainbridge Bunting's *Harvard: An Architectural History*. There was Hicks House, a little white Dutch Colonial that was now a library connected to the red brick mass of Kirkland House.

"Lydia admired the bravery of Mr. Hicks; she liked the story of the telltale tread," said Peter.

"And she bemoaned the way that the world changed around that house after forty or fifty years," said Orson. "She would have bemoaned it all even more if she knew that Harvard had moved the house a block from its previous spot."

Evangeline said, "That last poem might also mean that she decided to move the play, because the world was looking so different; she had to find a safer spot for it."

"It could," said Orson, "and if the house was moved and rehabbed when they turned it into the library, who knows what kind of structures they may have lost?"

"A shitload, probably," said Danny Fallon. "So you can yap about it, or go and see if it's where you think it is."

Orson flipped to the back of the Bunting book, read a few citations, including one that mentioned an extensive article from the 1932 Cambridge Historical Society *Proceedings*.

Orson said, "I know someone who might have that."

"Only you would," said Evangeline.

Orson was on the phone for about twenty minutes, then came back with this: "They moved the house in the twenties. It was originally on the site of the Indoor Athletic Building, which the kids now call the Mac—"

"Malkin Athletic Center," said Peter.

"Right," said Orson. "But here's the important quote. 'Not much of the John Hicks finish remains, due to the changes the house has suffered, but the front staircase, with its sturdily turned balusters and pendent acorns, has attracted much attention from architects. Its details are believed to be original.'"

"Now can we go?" asked Danny.

"No," said Peter. "In the morning. We'll need a couple of pinch bars, a Sawzall, hammer, and nails. And the Fallon Salvage and Restoration Truck."

"Why don't you hang out a sign?" asked Danny.

"That might not be a bad idea. Now, I have a few calls to make."

The next morning, Peter went to Weld Hall, a dormitory in the Yard.

One suite was filled with clothing racks and top hats. In one of the bedrooms, Peter put on the morning coat that he had rented, the traditional uniform of striped trousers and swallow-tailed coat worn by all members of the Committee for the Happy Observance of Commencement.

When he stepped out, Will Wedge and Charlie Price were standing there, both in the same uniform.

"What do you know?" asked Wedge.

"Plenty," said Peter.

And Price said, "We'd like to go with you."

Fallon shook his head. "If Franklin sees the two of you walking with me, he'll jump into line, too, and you'll start fighting over the damn thing. Just leave it to me. I won't go anywhere. This is the best way."

Outside, he met Evangeline, who had picked up the sun hat and red sash of a female marshal for the day.

Then they headed down Dunster Street.

The graduates were marching up the middle of the street in the bright sunshine, from Kirkland House and Eliot House, hundreds of young men and women in caps and gowns, from every state in the country and most of the countries on earth, parading that morning in the joyous harmony of shared accomplishment, in a Harvard far different from the one remembered by Peter Fallon, not to mention Victor Wedge or Heywood.

"There goes the future," said Peter.

"While we walk into the past," said Evangeline.

At they crossed the little side street known as South Street, they looked out toward JFK Street, and there was the Fallon van, parked conspicuously.

"Good," said Peter.

At the Kirkland House superintendent's office, Peter Fallon stopped in and asked an assistant superintendent if they could get into the library for just a few minutes.

"Well, we're a little busy right now." The assistant pointed out into the courtyard, where the tables were being set up for the midday "spread" and the granting of degrees.

"We lived in Kirkland House a long time ago," said Peter. "We just wanted to see the place where we . . . where we fell in love."

The guy looked them over—they were plainly people who gave the college their time—then took them across the courtyard, where dozens of caterers in white jackets were working, then into C Entry and down a long corridor to the library doors. Palladian windows looked out onto JFK Street, and Peter noticed a brown Toyota parked at a meter. *Good.*

"You know," said Peter, "if you're busy, we could let ourselves out."

Once more, the assistant looked them up and down and he agreed. "Just throw the bolt as you close the door behind you. And the only way out is past my office again."

They had chosen the right day to ask him, and they had worn the right wardrobe.

Now they were inside the ancient building. There was a librarian's desk before them, in the little area that once might have been the kitchen. They were standing in the ell of the house, which had been built after it had been moved.

There was a strong smell of old books, a little musty, strangely comforting. And there was a core of silence in the place, too. It felt like one of those little pools of time that Peter imagined when he thought about Cambridge. And he laughed.

"What's so funny?" said Evangeline.

"I'm just imagining Hicks, waking up, wondering who the hell is sneaking into his back door."

"Stay in the real world, Peter."

There was a massive center chimney separating the two rooms on the first floor. They went through the sitting room. Above the mantel was a photograph of five Harvard presidents, all sitting around a table. Among them was stiff old Josiah Quincy, who had been there when Lydia made the promise that had brought them to this.

But it was the foyer that interested them. It was eight feet across, the width determined by the chimney, and just deep enough for the front door to swing open without brushing the first tread of the staircase.

They both looked at the steps and Evangeline said, "Go ahead. It's your honors."

Peter pressed his foot on the first one. No sound. So he tried the second, then the third. Yes. A loud creak. He took his weight off it and tried again. Another loud creak.

"The telltale tread," said Evangeline.

Peter went over to the window on the north side. The Fallon van was still parked there. Peter flashed a thumbs-up to his brother. Then he unlocked the window and Danny came over and handed him a pinch bar and hammer. About as surreptitiously as a bus.

As he pushed the things through the window, he said, "Jackie Pucks is sitting in the brown Toyota."

"Do you see his boss?"

"Not here."

"Be careful."

"I'm fine."

"Hurry up," said Evangeline.

Peter jammed the pinch bar under the tread and began to hammer. A loud metallic *thwang*ing sound. About as quiet as a bus.

"Could you make a little more noise?" asked Evangeline.

"I'm trying."

And up came a tread. Then another. Then a third. Louder and louder.

And there it was. A metal dispatch box with a key left in the lock.

"We have it," said Peter in a loud voice.

"*I'll* take it." Bob O'Hill, also dressed like a commencement marshal, appeared from John Hicks's little living room. And he pressed a pistol against Fallon's head.

"I'll take it." Detective Scavullo came down the steps from the Hicks bedroom, pointed his 9-millimeter at O'Hill, and as he brought his walkie-talkie to his lips to call in the backup, O'Hill shot him in the chest. He slammed back against the wall, then forward onto Fallon, knocking the box from Fallon's hands.

O'Hill grabbed it and ran, out of John Hicks's ancient foyer, through the sitting room, past the librarian's desk in the old kitchen.

Fallon heard another gunshot as O'Hill fought his way past the officer who had been hiding off the kitchen. They had drawn him out, but now he was getting away.

Scavullo was screaming, "Man down!" into his mike. Evangeline was kneeling to help him. And Peter Fallon was racing after O'Hill.

He ran through the library, past the wounded officer, down the C-entry corridor, out into the courtyard, and there was O'Hill, walking fast toward one of the caterers, an older guy with white hair wearing a white coat. Bingo Keegan.

"Hey!" shouted Fallon. "Stop!"

At the same moment, the assistant superintendent and two university policemen appeared in the archway that led from Dunster Street. While Jackie Pucks was appearing at the gated archway—always locked—that led onto JFK Street.

Keegan tried to take the box from O'Hill, and suddenly O'Hill seemed to change his mind. He pulled the box back. Then he began to run again, sprinting up the stairs and into the Kirkland House dining hall.

Fallon didn't have a second to consider it, but here was one of the strangest tableaux that ever had been seen at Harvard. In the beautiful bright sunlight, with the tablecloths and Harvard pennants fluttering, two men in morning coats chased each other, followed by a man in a white coat, followed by the police.

Fallon leapt up the stairs and into the dining hall, worried that O'Hill might start shooting again but determined to get that box.

This had been the house where O'Hill had been a tutor, so he knew it well. He raced through the serving area, pulled open a door, knocked two or three workers aside, and rushed down the stairs.

Now, they were in the long corridor that ran from the central kitchen beneath Eliot House all the way to Leverett House.

There were people working everywhere, the subterranean world of Harvard, preparing for the commencement luncheons in all the houses. And O'Hill just ran.

He knocked people aside, sending a huge vat of salad splattering onto the floor.

"Stop!" shouted Fallon. "Stop him!"

Someone grabbed at O'Hill, but O'Hill pushed him away and kept going.

And from behind him, Fallon could hear Bingo Keegan shout, "Hey, hey, you waiters, grab those two fuckin' guys."

Keegan looked as though he belonged down there, not like the other two, so someone grabbed at Fallon, but he kept running.

They ran under the Winthrop House kitchen, then headed for Lowell House.

Then a door opened to O'Hill's left, and a custodian stepped out. As he turned to close the door, O'Hill went barreling into him. The custodian flew, his keys flew, the gun in O'Hill's hand flew, but he held on to the box, and he went through the door.

Fallon grabbed the door before it locked behind O'Hill and stepped into one of the famous steam tunnels that ran from the river to the Law School, like a great circulatory system.

Even in summer, the pipes lining the sides of the tunnels carried steam for cooking and power. And this looked like one of the main corridors, running north under Plympton Street, a straight shot all the way to the Yard. So Fallon started after O'Hill, who was twenty feet ahead with the tails of his morning coat flapping.

Then Fallon heard the sound of a gunshot behind him. Keegan was armed, and he didn't have time to fiddle with the lock, so he shot it off.

And now three men were running along this starkly lit tunnel, with one firing his pistol at the other two while somewhere in the bright sunlight above, a commencement was beginning.

O'Hill had a good lead, and he took a turn after sprinting about thirty yards.

Keegan fired at Fallon and missed.

Fallon reached the corner that O'Hill had just taken. He raced around it, and O'Hill smashed him right in the face with the box.

Fallon flew back, smacked off a big steam wheel and landed unconscious, but only for an instant.

When his head cleared, he heard a brief conversation between O'Hill and Keegan.

"The world has to see this," said O'Hill.

"Fuck the world," said Keegan. "Give me the box."

"Put down the gun."

"The cops are right behind us. Give me the fuckin' box."

Fallon could see that it was a strange kind of standoff. Keegan had a gun, but O'Hill was holding the handle of a vent valve.

"I won't let you hide this again," said O'Hill.

"Then fuck you, too," said Keegan, and he fired. The bullet went right through the box.

As O'Hill fell, he spun the release valve. A jet of steam shot into Keegan's face from somewhere, and he fell backward, screaming. Fallon saw that O'Hill was unconscious, so he grabbed the box and ran, with Keegan firing blindly after him.

A few minutes later, a family who had traveled all the way from India to see their son graduate, but who had arrived late and so had taken seats at the very back of Tercentenary Theater, on the driveway beside Weld, were shocked when the mother looked down to see a man peering up at her.

Peter Fallon lifted the manhole, which he had unlocked from below, excused himself, and stepped into the sunshine.

They were all waiting for him, as planned, in the alumni tent on the other side of Weld, in the old Yard. And they all knew by then what had gone on underground.

Evangeline threw her arms around Peter's neck and whispered in his ear.

"I'm all right," he said. "Scavullo?"

"He and the officer will be all right. He said to tell you he liked your plan to draw them out, until O'Hill started shooting."

"Well, O'Hill's half dead," he said. "Keegan half cooked."

And Franklin tapped the box that Fallon still held in his arms. "Have you looked in that?"

"Not yet. I'm glad O'Hill had a change of heart, but"—he slipped his finger into the bullet hole—"I'm not optimistic."

They put the box down on a table set up for a general alumni spread, which would follow the commencement speeches.

Peter Fallon wiped his hands on the front of the morning coat, looked at the others craning their necks—Will, Price, Franklin, Harriet, Prof. G., Danny—then he turned the key and opened the box. And it was empty.

"Oh, no," said Wedge.

"Looks like there'll be no Wedge House," said Franklin.

"Not exactly as planned," said Will. "And no club to beat over Harvard's head, either."

Then Peter took an envelope out of the box. It was dated September 17, 1936. It read:

Congratulations. You now know the truth: two things are always new: Youth and the quest for knowledge. So continue the quest until 2036. Attend the opening of the 1936 Tercentenary packet, and see the hand of Shakespeare himself, put to a play that no one has read in four centuries. Rest assured. Shakespeare will endure till then. So will Harvard. Lydia Wedge Townsend hid this manuscript because she dreamed of a better society, a City on a Hill, like those who first dreamed of a college in the cow yards. The contours of the dream have changed, as the Yard has changed. But a society will be known by its books and its dreams. So we must continue to dream. Indeed, the dream may be of greater value than its fulfillment. So let us dream for another century. And when we're done, and all songs sung, we cry, Love's Labours Won. Victor Wedge

Epilogue

PETER FALLON thought of something from Ecclesiastes: *To every thing there is a season, and a time to every purpose under the heaven.*

It was the third Sunday of September, moving day, the only day of the year when you could drive into Harvard Yard. Another father was taking his kid to college.

This was less bittersweet for Peter than for most parents. It probably meant that he would see more of his son, rather than less. More lunches, an occasional lecture, track meets.

They drove through the Johnson Gate and pulled up on the brick sidewalk in front of Hollis Hall, one of the oldest dormitories, opened in 1764, the year that Harvard Hall burned.

"Emerson and Thoreau lived here," said Peter to his son.

"Cool."

"In the Revolution, there were something like ten soldiers to the room."

"Cool."

Peter pointed to dents in the brick sidewalk. He was about to say that they were left by cannonballs that fun-loving Minutemen dropped from the windows. But he knew it wasn't true. And he was talking too much.

So he lifted out a laundry basket full of towels and bed linens and brought it upstairs to the back room on the fourth floor.

Jimmy's roommate had already arrived, a big black kid from Brooklyn named James Wilson. They were laughing about something. That was good. James Wilson gave him a firm handshake and called him Mister Fallon.

The room was typical for Hollis. It was huge, and what a view. The back windows looked out on Holden Chapel and Harvard Hall, eighteenth-century Harvard. The window by Jimmy's bed gave him a view all the way to the tower of Memorial Hall, built in the nineteenth century, magnificently restored in the late twentieth.

Peter tried to stay cool about it all. He didn't want to embarrass the kid. But how could anyone get any work done with so much to look at? But how could anyone want to do anything but work, considering how much knowledge there was in that course catalog that was splayed open on James Wilson's bed?

He envied those kids, but he didn't say so.

"Any advice, Dad?" asked Jimmy.

Peter knew his son was just looking for a way to ease Dad out. He understood. Who'd want Dad around when you had all these new people to get to know?

So Peter said, "When you're done in four years, you should feel satisfied, and mature, and well taught, but most important, you should feel tired."

"Tired?"

"Burn the candle at both ends. Never tell yourself there's no time to direct a play or sing in a choral group or play rugby. Take a course in gene-splitting if you're an English major. If you major in biology, take a course in short-story writing. Study Chinese. Learn statistics. Get drunk at least once."

The boys laughed at that.

"But remember university policy against drugs."

That said, he shook both their hands and left. On the second floor, he passed a pretty girl going into a room. Hollis was a coed dorm, as all the housing at Harvard was coed. He wondered what

Charles William Eliot or Cotton Mather would think of that, or better yet, Mrs. Agassiz.

Outside, he stopped for a moment and took it all in. The older he got, the more sacred this space felt to him. It had been here, literally, since the beginning.

He walked past the old college pump and made for John Harvard's statue.

Evangeline was waiting for him there in the gathering dusk.

"I'm starving," he said.

"Me, too." She had an envelope under her arm.

"What's in that?"

"A couple of things I found in the back of the first family Bible, the one from the 1600s. Katharine Nicholson Howell's Bible." She gave Peter the envelope. He opened it. Inside were two pieces of paper. The first that he pulled out was an ancient copy of *Quaestiones*.

"Wow," he said. "This looks like it's from the first Harvard commencement. The program of disputations. This could be worth a lot of money, Evangeline."

"Look at the other thing."

He carefully slid the *Quaestiones* back into the envelope and pulled out a small sheet of paper in exquisite condition, with not a tear or watermark. It was signed at the bottom by Charles Nicholson, June 5, 1638. "I hereby swear, as a Freeman of the Colony of Massachusetts . . ."

"My God," said Peter after he had read a bit more. "Do you know what this is?"

"No. What?"

"The Holy Grail of American antiquaria. The Oath of a Freeman. The first document printed in the New World. Printed on the first printing press, printed right here in Cambridge."

After a moment she said, "How much?"

"Evangeline," he said. "You can't put a price on something priceless."

"Try."

"Three million . . . maybe more. Do you want to sell it?"

"If you want to broker the sale." She slipped her arm into his.

After a moment, he kissed her. "I guess now I can pay that Harvard tuition. We'd better get this to someplace safe."

Arm-in-arm, they started across the Yard.

After a moment, Peter said, "Do you hear them?"

"The voices?"

"They're always loudest at dusk," he said. "The Yard echoes with them."

She looked at all the kids carrying suitcases and cartons into the dorms. "I wonder if these freshmen hear them."

"Not yet," said Peter. "But they will. They will."

And from his pedestal, John Harvard watched them go.